MESMERIZED

Also by Gayle Lynds

Masquerade
Mosaic

The Hades Factor (with Robert Ludlum)

April 27, 2001

MESMERIZED

For Mary Anne,
I loved English class.
Thank you so much for

GAYLE
LYNDS

being one of my heroines!
Warm regards,

POCKET BOOKS

New York   London   Toronto   Sydney   Singapore

This book is a work of fiction. Names, characters, places and incidents are products of the author's imagination or are used fictitiously. Any resemblance to actual events or locales or persons, living or dead, is entirely coincidental.

 POCKET BOOKS, a division of Simon & Schuster, Inc.
1230 Avenue of the Americas, New York, NY 10020

Library of Congress Cataloging-in-Publication Data

Lynds, Gayle.
    Mesmerized / Gayle Lynds.
      p. cm.
    ISBN 0-671-02407-8
    1. Heart—Transplantation—Patients—Fiction.   2. Political crimes and
offenses—Fiction.   3. Washington (D.C.)—Fiction.   4. Women lawyers—
Fiction.   I. Title.

PS3562.Y442 M47 2001
813'.54—dc21

                                                    2001021296

First Pocket Books hardcover printing May 2001

10 9 8 7 6 5 4 3 2 1

POCKET and colophon are registered trademarks of
Simon & Schuster, Inc.

Printed in the U.S.A.

For my son, Paul Stone, and his bride, Katrina Baum
for love, for youth, for the future
Happy Wedding—April 8, 2000

ACKNOWLEDGMENTS

I'm indebted to many people for sharing their expertise in the creation of *Mesmerized*.

Carolyn Campbell, Ph.D., J.D., director and senior counsel for Emerging Markets Partnership in Washington, D.C., is also an associate professor in international negotiations at George Washington National Law Center. She advised on legal aspects, plus adding her considerable knowledge of the District itself. Cheryl Arvidson, senior writer for the Freedom Forum, has covered the White House for United Press International, Cox newspapers, and the *Dallas Times Herald.* Her help in setting scenes within the District and in the White House was invaluable. Philip Shelton, author and former intelligence agent, and Gene Riehl, author and former FBI special agent, were the souls of patience in making certain the government and action aspects of the novel were within the realm of possibility. Peter Caldwell, pharmacist and owner of Caldwell Pharmacy in Santa Barbara, California, generously detailed various heart medications.

I'm very grateful to the new team at Pocket Books for their wonderful enthusiasm and high level of professionalism. From president Judith Curr to deputy publishers Karen Menders and Kara Welch, senior editor Kate Collins, publicity director Melinda Mullin and publicist Leigh Richter, and art director Paolo Pepe, I've received the best care any author could dream of. Both senior editor Lauren McKenna and assistant editor Christina Boys have stepped in to help on numerous occasions. Plus, my deepest appreciation to Ian Jackman, whose editorial magic has done so much to sharpen and strengthen this book.

My husband, novelist Dennis Lynds, was key to each stage. He is my first and last editor.

To my agent, Henry Morrison . . . my everlasting gratitude for all the myriad ways he touched *Mesmerized,* from the outline to the published book. His hours of care are duplicated by no other outside the walls of my house. And to my international agent, Danny Baror, whose influence goes around the world—thank you.

My daughter, Julia Stone, gave me the initial idea for this book, and my son, Paul Stone, detailed legal arguments for the main character. Finally, I'm also very grateful for the advice and support of Joseph Allen; Vicki Allen; Patricia Barrett; Katrina Baum; Julia Cunningham; Julia Fasick; Roberta Foreman, M.F.C.C.; Gary Gulbransen; Susan Miles Gulbransen; Frances Halpern; Fred Klein; Lumina; Deirdre Lynds; Kate Lynds; Randi Kennedy; Wendell Klossner, M.D.; Connie Martinson; Monica McCoy, D.C.; Lucy Jo Palladino, Ph.D.; Elaine Russell; Theil Shelton; Jim Stevens; and MaryEllen Strange.

Because of the tremendous need for organ donations and the lives that can be saved, please consider filling out a donor card for yourself—call (800) 355-SHARE. You can learn more about organ donations by phoning the United Network for Organ Sharing at (800) 933-0440. Part of the proceeds from this book will be donated to the cause.

Mankind's chief hope of escaping the wrath of whatever divinities were then abroad lay in some magical rite, senseless but powerful, or in some offering made at the cost of pain and grief.

—Edith Hamilton, *Mythology*

Look for things that aren't there. If we make up our minds too early, we shut ourselves off to possible answers.

—CIA intelligence trainer who wishes to remain anonymous

PROLOGUE

She was a star.

Queen of the Cosmos.

She was Beth Convey, killing machine with compassion.

She was in room 311 of Superior Court for the District of Columbia. The air was stale, stagnant in fact, but that was to be expected. Any courtroom where a high-profile trial was drawing to a close meant too many days with the doors closed, too many hours of body heat, too much anger, disgust, and sublimated violence for the air to be fresh. The overhead fluorescent lights gave off a relentless glare, and there were no windows that offered the relief of the outdoors; today was a blustery March afternoon. This third-floor room in the thirty-year-old courthouse was a claustrophobic, wood-lined sarcophagus.

Still, the packed audience gave no indication they were unhappy with, or even noticed, the conditions. They sat silent, riveted, because hundreds of millions of dollars were riding on Beth Convey's cross-examination in this headline-making divorce trial, and no one—particularly the press—wanted to miss a word.

Beth turned to the judge. "Permission to approach the witness, Your Honor." She was known for her ice-cold calm, which she felt she had probably inherited. After all, she was the daughter of Jack-the-Knife Convey, Los Angeles's top criminal defense attorney. Annoyed, she realized she was sweating.

Judge Eric Schultz was a large man with a gravelly voice and thick eyebrows. He gave her a sharp look. Beth had kept the witness on the stand all day, and there was an edge to the judge's voice as he said, "Very well. But move your questioning along, Ms. Convey."

"Yes, sir."

She marched forward, her pumps soundless on the carpeting. Behind her she could feel the worried gaze of her client, Michelle Philmalee, while before her sat the object of her cross-examination: Michelle's husband, industrialist Joel Mabbit Philmalee. A red flush showed above his starched white shirt collar, and anger flickered in his eyes.

Pretrial, his lawyers had made what they called a "sensible" settlement offer of $50 million, a fraction of the value of his privately held corporation. It was insultingly low, and Michelle had refused it. Which had forced Beth into a tactic that could easily fail: She must make Joel Philmalee's violent temper betray him in open trial, which was why she had kept him on the stand so long.

She thought she had left all this behind. Although she had begun her practice as a family-law attorney, she now specialized in international law. With her knowledge of Russian and Eastern European politics, her ability to speak a useful amount of Russian and Polish, and her hardnosed business sense, she had done so well negotiating and cutting red tape in former Communist countries on behalf of Michelle Philmalee that Michelle insisted Beth represent her in the divorce, too.

Inwardly, Beth sighed. She would have passed the divorce case on to one of the firm's other lawyers except that the managing partner had weighed in on the situation with an emphatic "absolutely not." The firm—Edwards & Bonnett—was determined to keep Michelle's business, which meant keeping her happy. If Michelle wanted Beth, she would have her, and if Beth were a really good girl and won a healthy settlement package for Michelle, her reward would be a leap onto the fast track to partnership. No fool, Beth had gone to trial.

She stopped five feet from Joel Philmalee. A strong scent of expensive cologne wafted from him as he adjusted himself and glowered. His rage was building. She repressed a smile—and felt a rush of nausea.

She inhaled, forcing the nausea away. She made her voice flat, harsh. "Isn't it true you gave the hotel chain to Mrs. Philmalee to manage in the beginning because you considered it a minor investment, and you thought she'd fail? Yes or no."

He looked straight into her eyes. "I assumed—"

She tapped her foot. "Yes or no?"

He shot a look of hatred across the courtroom to Michelle. "No!"

"Isn't it true you tried to fire her, but she convinced you to wait for the fourth-quarter report, which confirmed the success of her expansion strategy? Yes or no."

"I suppose you could say—"

"Yes or no?"

"Never! Is that good enough? No! *Never!*"

Beth knew he was lying, but she could not force him to change his testimony here. What was important was that the judge had heard her raise the questions and that she was making Joel Philmalee furious at her. To him she had become yet another pushy, insolent, aggravating female, just like his wife.

Beth had presented testimony, minutes of meetings, and financial analyses that showed Michelle had often played the deciding role in the Group's growth. Now she hoped to add a convincer without ever saying it outright: Joel was a wife-beater. There were rumors about it, and Beth knew they were true. The problem was Michelle wanted no one to learn she had been the victim of domestic violence, not even for a half billion dollars in assets. The battlefields of commerce had taught her it was far better their war over a financial agreement look like a contest between two titans of industry. In business, Michelle believed, she must never look weak.

Beth agreed, and although the strategy had made her job far harder, it was their only hope. Unlike community-property states, the District of Columbia made no assumption there would be a fifty-fifty split in divorce, which was what Michelle wanted. Instead, its laws allowed judges broad discretion.

Beth fought back another wave of nausea and plunged ahead. "Mr. Philmalee, isn't it true that your wife bought and sold, sat on boards of directors, traveled extensively to evaluate properties, and created Philmalee International completely on her own? Yes or no."

He leaned forward. "No! She did everything under *my* orders. *I'm* Philmalee Group!"

"Please confine yourself to yes or no, Mr. Philmalee." She could not seem to catch her breath. Her heart was racing again. Last week, her internist had diagnosed stress as the cause of her periodic breathlessness. He said she must slow down. Only thirty-two years old and already she had to ease back on her work? Nonsense. This trial was too important.

Joel Philmalee turned angrily to the judge. "Do I have to put up with this, Your Honor?"

Judge Schultz shook his head. "You were given ample opportunity to settle."

"But my ingrate wife wants half my goddamn company!" He shot Michelle a look of scorching rage.

Michelle tightened her lips, her face grim. She was a tiny woman, compact and fashionable in a quilted Chanel suit and red-rimmed Armani eyeglasses. She gave no evidence of the turmoil and loneliness of which Beth had caught glimpses. Michelle's isolation was something Beth understood. She and Michelle had made their work the centers of their lives. Beth had never regretted it, and from what she had observed, neither had Michelle.

Beth forged on: "The operative word for you is *our*, sir. Yours *and* Mrs. Philmalee's. '*Our* company.' The *Group*. You *both* worked—" She stifled a gasp. A dull pain gripped her chest, and sweat slid hot and sticky beneath her suit. *No*. She could not be sick now. She was so close to winning—

Joel's hands knotted. "My wife didn't do jack shit!"

The judge spoke up: "Mr. Philmalee, I've warned you about your language. Control yourself. Next time I'll hold you in contempt."

With an effort, Beth forced her voice to remain calm. "She did everything. Isn't it true that without her you'd have nothing? She gave you the money to start. You took credit for her ideas—"

"Objection, Your Honor!" thundered Joel's attorney.

"Overruled," the judge said firmly. "Continue, counselor."

Beth pressed on. "She planned tactics and told you how to implement them. Take the Wheelwright transaction. Oak Tree Plaza. Philmalee Gardens—"

"No! No! No!" Joel Philmalee jumped up. The flush that had been hovering just beneath his ears spread in a red tide across his leathery cheeks.

The judge hammered his gavel.

"Even Philmalee International—" Beth persisted, herself risking being held in contempt.

At which point Joel Philmalee had had enough. "You bitch!" He leaped over the rail straight at Beth.

Beth's heart seemed to explode in pain. It felt as if her rib cage would shatter. The pain was black and ragged and sent jolts of electricity to her brain. She tried to take a breath, to stay on her feet, to remain conscious. She had been an achiever all her life. Michelle deserved half of the Philmalee Group. Beth needed to go on fighting—

Instead, she collapsed to the carpet.

Joel Philmalee did not notice. He bolted past Beth toward his wife.

Her little face twisted in terror, Michelle whirled so quickly to escape that her glasses flew off. Screams and shouts erupted from the audience. Cursing, Joel grabbed Michelle from behind.

Just as his hands closed around her throat, a dozen journalists in the audience seemed to come alive. They cascaded down the aisle. Within seconds, two had pulled him off Michelle.

Courthouse security rushed into the room, and as order began to reassert itself and Joel Philmalee was handcuffed and forced through a side door, someone noticed Beth Convey was still lying where she had fallen.

"Did she get hurt?" the judge asked, alarmed. "Check her, Kaeli!"

The bailiff sprinted to the unconscious woman, dropped to his haunches, and felt for her pulse. Frantically, he adjusted his fingers. "Nothing, sir."

As the courtroom fell into a stunned hush, he leaned lower, his cheek an inch from her mouth, waiting for a breath. He stayed there a long time.

At last, he looked up at the judge. His eyes were large with shock. "She's dead. I'm sorry, Judge. I don't see how, but Ms. Convey's dead."

PART ONE

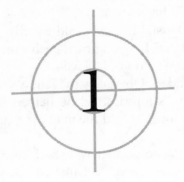

A month later, on a fine, moonlit night in April, a Washington, D.C., 911 operator took a call at 10:12: A motorcycle accident had just occurred in Rock Creek Park, apparently one man injured. The caller gave directions.

Within four minutes, paramedics and the police arrived on the scene, just as a new Lexus was pulling away. The Lexus turned sharply back onto the shoulder and screeched to a stop, its rear wheels sending gravel pinging against a metal guardrail. A distinguished-looking gentleman in an expensive business suit jumped out of the driver's seat and hurried back through the nighttime shadows to where the paramedics were bending over the fallen motorcyclist.

His face distraught, the Lexus driver's words poured out with a slight accent: "I am thankful someone called you. Can you help my friend? I did not know what to do, and I have no cellular phone, so I thought I should drive for help. I was late, yes? I was hurrying home to meet him. Then—terrible!—I saw him and the motorcycle lying beside the road." His voice rose. "He was always riding that motorcycle. I told him and told him to wear a helmet, but he never would. He was unconscious when I found him. Is he going to be all right?" He took a deep breath. His lips trembled as he watched the paramedics lift the victim onto a gurney. He looked like a diplomat or a wealthy businessman, a fact that was not lost upon the paramedics.

The lead medic said politely, "Please move out of the way, sir. He's got a serious head trauma, and we've got to get him to the hospital. You can follow us, okay? What's his name?"

"Ogust. Mikhail Ogust," the man said eagerly. "Which hospital will you take him to? He and I have known each other many years, across many continents. You would not believe—"

The paramedic nodded. Obviously the fellow was having a hard time dealing with his friend's injuries. As he helped load the unconscious victim into the ambulance, he told the man the name and address of the hospital.

At the same time, a policeman who had been measuring the skid mark on the street approached. "I'd like to ask you a few questions, sir."

The gentleman turned. "Oh. Oh, yes. Of course. Certainly."

As the ambulance sped off, beacons flashing, siren wailing, the policeman wrote down the man's name, asked him to relate what he had seen, and told him they would try to locate the Good Samaritan who had phoned in the accident. It looked as if no other vehicle had been involved.

The moment the policeman released him, the man climbed into his Lexus and drove straight to the hospital. There he discovered Mikhail Ogust had been pronounced dead on arrival. Everyone was very polite and considerate, aware Mikhail Ogust had been his dear friend.

The man bowed his head. Two tears slid down his cheeks. The nurses offered their sympathies and told him to go home, that there was nothing more he could do. He nodded, unable to speak, and trudged from the hospital.

A half-hour later he arrived at his multimillion-dollar estate in Chevy Chase, set deep in thick woods and hidden from the road. Considering the enormity of the day's events and the radical action he had been forced to take as a consequence, he should have been weary to the bone. Instead, he was exhilarated.

At the house's side entrance, the one most convenient to the garage, he tapped his code into the security system, opened the door, and strode through the kitchen and down the hall toward his den and home office. As he passed his bedroom, he caught a glimpse of himself in the long mirror of his closet.

He stopped in the doorway and appraised what he saw: A handsome older man in a dark Saville Row suit and silk tie. He moved his wrist, and his gold cufflink and Rolex watch caught the hall light and glittered. His face seemed full and prosperous, the chin lifted as if life's wealth were his due. His carriage was not haughty so much as positive, certain. He gave every appearance of solidity, a man of his time who would offer no surprises and could be utterly relied upon. It was the image he cultivated in this new world. The once-powerful official; now the successful businessman, the gentleman who might be a wealthy philanthropist, certainly a pillar of the community.

Satisfied, he continued down the corridor, allowing himself to grow taller, straighter, thinner, more athletic. To do this, he stripped away the inward pretenses of his current character. Like any accomplished actor, he had no need to stare into a mirror to see how this changed him as he knew exactly what he really looked like. More importantly, he understood who he was, despite the different appearances he presented to different audiences. This was a reality he allowed only those closest to him to witness. They were few, his true friends and associates, and always had been. Fewer every year. A man who did great things could not have friends.

He smiled to himself as he walked into his den, picked up the telephone, and dialed. As soon as his associate answered, he spoke in rapid Russian: *"Da,* it's me. The fools believed it all. Everything's fine. We can proceed."

The heart pounded against her ribs like a mighty fist. Its insistent beat drove her to swim up from the darkness. For a moment, terror shook her, and she had no idea where she was. She fought confusion, forced herself to pay attention: She could hear the *whoosh* and *click* of many machines. The air was cool, and her nose stung with the smell of antiseptic. . . .

A man's voice penetrated her grogginess: "Ms. Convey? Wake up. You're in the cardiac intensive care unit now. Do you know your name? Ms. Convey?"

Her words were a whisper. "Sure I do. But it's a secret. *Shhhhhh . . .* You have to tell me yours first."

The transplant surgeon chuckled. "Travis Jackson here. Remember? You came through the surgery with flying colors, Beth. You've got a healthy new heart. Open your eyes. What do you think about all this?"

She was aware of pain muted by morphine. She pushed away the feelings of disorientation . . . and concentrated on her chest: The cadence of her old heart—erratic and sometimes no more than a frail pulse—was gone, replaced by a beat so strong it seemed almost to thunder. Exhausted joy swept through her, and she lay motionless, smiling. *She had a new heart.*

She opened her eyes and let out a long stream of air, aware of how—

suddenly—she could breathe easily again. "Love this heart, Travis. It's got rhythm. I want to keep it forever."

"That's what I like to hear." He was in his sixties. His face was lined, and he smiled down at her through rimless eyeglasses perched on the end of a slightly hooked nose. "It's a healthy heart, a first-rate match for you. I didn't even need to give it an electric shock to get it started. And your first biopsy shows no sign of rejection."

Her head was clearing, the grogginess abating as a sober awareness of what had happened took hold.

"How can I ever thank you enough?"

"I know it seems trite, but the answer is by living a long and healthy life. That's what I care about, and that's my reward." His voice was warm. "You're young. We've caught this thing so fast the rest of your body hasn't had time to deteriorate. I expect you to have a natural life span."

"I'm so sorry about my donor's death. But I'm so very grateful, too . . ."

"I know. Of course you are."

Her smile faded as the morphine swept her back toward unconsciousness. As her eyelids closed, the surgeon studied her, feeling the awe and triumph that kept him excited about this grueling area of medicine. A month ago, Beth Convey had been barely alive, rushed in from the courthouse by paramedics, who had used a portable defibrillator to restart her heart. Because she had no history of heart problems, her internist had been sloppy; he had wrongly diagnosed stress as the cause of her shortness of breath and racing heart, when the reality was that her ventricles were diseased and she was in end-stage heart failure, probably from a viral infection she and her internist had both brushed off the previous winter as a lingering cold.

He remembered how pale she had been when he first examined her. Ghostly white, really. But that was not the worst of it. As the weeks passed, her skin turned a bilious yellow, her mind grew confused, and she had weakened to the point where she had trouble chewing food. All the result of a heart that could no longer pump adequate amounts of blood and oxygen.

But now, just hours after surgery, their conversation showed her mind was functioning again. And, too, there was the color of her skin, now a healthy peach. To outsiders, this was evidence of the so-called miracle of a heart transplant, while to him it was simply what happened when everything went right.

He smiled with relief, thinking that she seemed especially alive, vital, as she dozed in the hospital bed. She was tall—five-foot-ten—and slim. A beautiful woman with a straight nose, sculpted cheekbones, and a crown of short golden hair who, judging by the way she had looked when she had arrived, wore little makeup and downplayed her attractiveness. The doctor found that intriguing—a woman who wanted to be judged by something other than her beauty.

The cardiac ICU always smelled of disinfectant. Beth had grown so accustomed to the odor over the past three days since her surgery that she hardly noticed it. She was thinking about this because the double doors had just swung open and the odor of percolating coffee was floating in, making her salivate.

Then she flinched. A stab of fear shot through her, and she tensed. Surprised, she stared at what she told herself was simply an odd sight: Two hospital aides dressed completely in surgical green were rolling an old exercise bicycle into her state-of-the-art intensive care room. But there was something about the first aide that had startled her. Made her a little afraid. She studied him, his assured movements, the aggressive shoulders. Now she remembered him from before her surgery. His name was Dave, and he had a gentle touch. He had never been anything but kind.

Her fear made no sense. She forced herself to smile. "You've got to be kidding, Dave. An exercise bike? It's for me, isn't it?" She continued to study him, still feeling uneasy.

"Yes, ma'am. It surely is for you."

As he and the other aide locked it into place, her doctor, Travis Jackson, arrived. "Your new biopsies look good." She had convinced him to give her a report as soon as he arrived to see her. Patience was not her strong suit. "No sign of rejection or infection. Temperature, pulse, respiration are normal. Everything's on track."

"Thank God," she breathed. She eyed the bike suspiciously. "Dave says this is for me."

"Remember the bargain: You get a new heart, but in exchange you have to take excellent care of it. Come on. The bike's been disinfected. We'll help you."

She was incredulous. *"Now?* But it's only been three days. I mean—"

"I know. Everyone thinks it's going to take weeks to get strong enough to begin exercising. Maybe even months. Not true. Three days is standard operating procedure for transplants that go well, and yours has gone exceedingly well. Come on. Up with you. This is the beginning of your daily workouts."

Nervously she eased her legs over the side of the bed. The second aide put sanitized tennis shoes on her feet. She stood up, tethered by hoses and tubes and strapped up with electrodes and radios that would signal if her heart faltered. She had a long surgical wound down her chest, hidden beneath her hospital gown. Sharp pains radiated from it and then dulled, assuaged by morphine.

The doctor took one arm, and Dave was suddenly at her side to take the other. Again she flinched. She was definitely acting strangely. A cold draft shot up her naked backside. She struggled to reach behind to close her gown.

She sighed. "Oh, the indignity of it all."

"Reminds you you're alive." Dr. Jackson chuckled. "That's not too bad a payoff."

They helped her to the bicycle. Even the simple act of walking two yards was a production, but she was surprised at how strong she felt. Once she was astride the bike, Dave headed for the door. Her gaze followed him, relieved to see him go.

"Show me what you can do," the doctor said.

She pedaled slowly, and sweat broke out on her face. "Isn't this enough?" she panted. "You want me to bike up Mount Everest in my condition? Have you forgotten I almost died?"

"You did die. You're doing fine." His gaze alternated between studying her and checking his wristwatch. "Okay, stop. That's enough."

Sweating, she sat back and let her feet circle to a stop. She watched as he analyzed the effects on her heart. At last, she gave in to her nervousness and asked, "How are my readings?"

"Good. Actually, beautiful. If I were less modest, I'd congratulate myself."

"I appreciate your modesty. It becomes you."

He laughed. "My wife says something similar." His glasses caught the glare from the fluorescent lights and glinted as he wrote on his clipboard.

"I know it seems too soon to ask, but I'd like to know what I'm facing." She hesitated. It seemed to her that she had arisen from the dead like a phoenix, and it all had made her feel oddly, uncomfortably, transformed. A sense of longing for her familiar past swept over her. "When can I go back to work?"

"You miss it, don't you? Well, I don't blame you. I'd feel the same. But first we've got to make sure all your medicines are regulated, and you've got to get on an exercise-food-sleep regimen so you can regain your strength and we can fine-tune for future problems. That way, when you go back to the office, you'll be in great shape, and we won't have to worry about organ rejection, infection, or any of that sort of unpleasantness." He gave her a smile of understanding. "That means you've got to figure on at least a year for recuperation."

She was shocked. "A *year?* My firm's going to forget who I am!"

"I doubt it. From what I hear, you're something of a hotshot."

She did not contradict him, but he obviously knew little about high-stakes Washington law firms. The city was littered with the corpses of last year's young hotshots.

As he and the second aide helped her off the bicycle and back into bed, the doctor asked, "Is there anything you'd especially like now?"

She nodded. "A drink. Vodka. Stolichnaya." She hesitated. Where had that come from?

The doctor laughed. "Vodka's a little much for now. Besides, I thought you were a wine drinker."

Puzzled, she added lamely, "You're right. I guess I was just thinking we should celebrate with something stronger. I'll have fruit juice. Mango." She no longer drank hard alcohol of any kind. The last time she'd had vodka was in law school, when she had been an aficionado of it, but as the surgeon and aide left, she could taste its white-hot fire in her mouth, as fresh as if she had just downed a shot.

2

The night was black, and she was running, sweating, her feet pounding as she searched for an address. When she found the numbers on a wrought-iron mail box, she stopped and stared up a stone walk that led past a weeping willow tree to a long, ranch-style house and detached garage. Panting, she studied the house: The dark windows seemed like black holes, and the expensive property gave off an eerie air of abandonment.

Warily, she ran up the drive. As she approached the buildings, the garage door rose, and she heard the engine of a motorcycle roar to life. The great machine rolled out, riderless, and stopped, erect, bathed in moonlight. Like a Robert Rauschenberg sculpture, it waited poised in perfect balance, inviting speculation. Its chrome gleamed. Exhaust puffed out from its tailpipe in a shimmering cloud. For perhaps thirty seconds she stared, captured by the odd sight of the powerful machine, as proud as if its favorite rider were aboard.

Then with the blink of an eye, she found herself astride it. Instinctively she grabbed the handlebars, and the motorcycle tore off down the drive. As she fought to control it, a man appeared in front of her. Standing stock-still, he stared at her, then he shouted something and ran.

The motorcycle continued its headlong rush, now directed at him. She screamed. She could not stop the bike. She could not turn it. Its motor pulsing, the big motorcycle slammed into the man's back.

She screamed again. The impact hurled him up in a backward somersault toward the black sky. She could not tear her horrified gaze from

*his pain-filled face. He had a broad forehead, a snub nose, and a shock
of gray hair that flew wild. Sickened, she watched him crash head-first
onto the pavement.*

She awoke in a pool of cold sweat, shuddering, feeling guilty. The
nightmare had left her with a metallic taste in her mouth. She knew she
had killed that poor man. Where had it come from, this awful dream
that seemed so real?

She was beginning not to recognize parts of herself. The hospital
aide, Dave, still made her nervous, although he had yet to say or do
anything that could remotely be considered threatening, to her or anyone else. But then, she found herself watching many people suspiciously now, particularly men, as if she were the sole defender of a
castle under siege, or perhaps held prisoner there, awaiting torture. Her
disquiet made no sense. It was irrational, and she kept reminding herself she had nothing to fear.

There were other aberrations. Although she had always been a coffee drinker, now she yearned for cups of strong black tea and drank
several every day. She could not seem to eat enough fresh, sliced tomatoes, and she wanted them served with both salt and sugar. The dieti-
cian had laughed and asked where she had acquired such an unusual
taste. She had no answer.

One day a nurse stopped in the doorway of her room, carrying a tall
Saks Fifth Avenue shopping bag. The pewter-colored bag had the exclusive chain's name printed in white letters on the side, familiar from a
hundred shopping expeditions of her own. From her bed, she could not
see what the bag contained.

"Good morning, Ms. Convey." The nurse had a cheery face with pink
cheeks and bright blue eyes. Her manner was brusque but pleasant. "I
have something for you." The bag was clasped in her right hand, her
right shoulder lower than the other, indicating the bag's contents were
heavy.

Cold sweat drenched Beth. . . . *A city street at twilight, the pavement
wet and shiny from a recent rain. Ornate iron lamps cast wavering
pools of light, which a woman wearing a long coat, a floppy hat, and
battered tennis shoes ambled through. She, too, carried a large, bulging
shopping bag that was obviously heavy. While she blended with other
pedestrians, a man hurried behind to keep her in sight. Although
frightened, she never looked back. She turned nonchalantly into a
busy bus station.*

Before the man who followed could reach the station door, she had increased her speed and pushed into the women's restroom. Inside a stall, she swiftly took a straight pin from her hat and flushed the toilet to cover the noise as she deflated the three balloons in the shopping bag, put there to give the appearance of bulk. As she kicked off her sneakers, she removed the only other contents from the bag—a pair of new pumps. She stepped into them and, with practiced skill, yanked off her hat and long coat and stuffed them into the bag. The city's poor frequented this station, so she tucked the bag behind the stool, as if it were a donation for them.

Outside, she washed her hands and looked into the mirror. Without the hat, and now wearing the fashionable coat that had been hidden beneath the long overcoat, her makeup impeccable, her wig in place, she was a completely different woman. Except she was no woman at all. He had used this disguise many times.

Perfectly balanced on his pumps, he waited until the next woman left the restroom. Following, he asked her the time, and they entered the lobby of the teeming station as if they were two old friends, chatting about the weather, while covertly his gaze scanned all around.

Although not surprised, he was relieved when the killer's gaze settled on him, dismissed him, then resumed searching for his quarry. His cover—the woman beside him—was still talking. He said a polite good-bye and walked casually to the door and out into the safety of the night. . . .

"Ms. Convey?" The nurse was staring worriedly into her eyes. "Are you all right?"

She swallowed. Blinked. "Of course. Sure, I'm fine. Just a little daydreaming, that's all. You said you have something in your shopping bag for me." She hesitated. "It's not balloons, is it?"

The nurse straightened and laughed. "Balloons? No, no. What a silly idea. No, I heard you liked to read. We just had a donation of books, and I thought you might like to borrow one. We have all kinds." As she pulled out volumes to display, she said, "Westerns, romances, mysteries, spy thrillers. Name your poison."

Beth sighed, ran her fingers through her hair, and gave a nervous laugh. She was an idiot. A paranoid fool. "Yes, a good book to read. Give me a mystery. Just what I need. A mystery, with an ending that explains everything."

After two weeks in intensive care, she was transferred to a sunny private room. Flowers began arriving. One very large arrangement was from a very grateful Michelle Philmalee. Every time Beth looked at it, she grinned: The judge had issued his ruling, giving Michelle far more than Beth had asked—majority control of the Philmalee Group. In the end, Joel Philmalee's uncontrollable rage had cost him his case, just as she had hoped. He was out, and Michelle was now—despite a few glitches here and there—in charge of the entire, billion-dollar Philmalee Group.

It was a stunning courtroom triumph, which made Beth even more impatient to return to Edwards & Bonnett so she could collect on the managing partner's promise of an accelerated timetable to partnership.

It was not just the money she wanted, although that was important. She had heard others make the same claim and had not believed them—after all, a guaranteed $450,000 a year base salary, plus bonuses, was hard to ignore. But in this uncertain life, where one could not trust even one's own heart to keep beating, where one's mind seemed no longer under control, the firm was more than ever her anchor. There on Sixteenth Street, just four blocks from the White House, she had known who she was.

She gave her clients twenty-four-hour care whenever necessary. Instead of tennis or dates with friends, she had been known to spend a rare free weekend investigating a legal question posed by one of Edwards & Bonnett's overseas offices, for which she could not bill or receive any sort of official credit, since it was a professional courtesy. Other attorneys twisted themselves into intellectual pretzels to find reasons to avoid such requests. She, on the other hand, had enjoyed the research.

And then there were her files, which were always up to date, as if they were children whose daily routine meant security. At Edwards & Bonnett she had invested everything, including her heart-felt commitment. Which was perhaps why she had such a high success rate—she won ninety percent of her cases—and why she attracted the kind of wealthy and powerful clients who were the backbone of the firm. Considering all this, she figured it was time for payback: She had earned partnership. She wanted it. She wanted to belong.

But now she was worried. Because she would be absent a full year, Zach Housley—the managing partner—had reassigned her clients to other attorneys in the firm. It was the right thing to do, of course, since it took care of both the clients and the business.

Yet if enough of her clients decided to stay with their new lawyers, her base of power might weaken. As she mulled this, something inside her seemed to shift. She had always had an even, calm disposition, but now anger exploded through her. She shook with it. Sweat broke out on her forehead. She clenched her jaw and hugged herself, fighting back a sudden urge for violence.

It was the dark, early hours of morning, and she was carrying an old Soviet assault rifle, an AK-47. It felt comfortable in her arms, reassuring. Nearby, the sound of gunfire split the quiet night air like a long burst of thunder.

As she dove for cover, voices shouted from the shadows, and this time they were understandable. Surprised, she realized they were speaking Russian. She tamped down her fear and forced herself to listen: They were warning each other—Yuri, Mikhail, Alexei, Ivan, Anatoli—and arguing about who should make the phone call that could save them. They yelled a number over and over—703 . . . 703 . . . 703. . . . It was a Virginia area code, but she could not make out the rest of it. She pressed her palms to her ears, trying to stop the voices.

And awoke abruptly, her hands over her ears as she breathed in nervous pants. She sat upright in her hospital bed and shook her head to clear it. She began to wonder. This dream had been clear—it was about Russians speaking Russian. The names, the weapons . . . all Russian. And she was one of them. She shuddered, trying to understand whether there was some meaning she had missed.

That afternoon, Dr. Jackson arrived to discuss her home-care program. She was grateful to see him. She gazed at his reassuring, lined face with the slightly hooked nose and the glasses perched precariously on the end. And then she looked over his shoulder.

"Where's Dave?" she asked. "I thought he was going to come with you to show me some exercise charts." Dave had been the aide with the assured movements and aggressive shoulders who had spooked her soon after surgery. Since then, she had forced away her suspicions and grown to look forward to his many small acts of kindness.

The doctor sighed. "We had to let him go. I'd forgotten about the charts. I'll have someone else bring them."

"Let him go? He was fired? But why?"

"You liked him. Most everyone did, and that was part of the problem. I'm sorry, but you might as well know he was arrested this morning for stealing from patients."

"Arrested!" She was stunned, disbelieving. And yet . . . the truth was . . . in the beginning she had felt there was something not quite right about Dave, something treacherous. She should have listened to that inner knowing, but it had seemed so outlandish at the time.

The doctor had moved on. He was saying, "Whatever exercises

you choose, make sure you build up to an hour at least five times a week. You said you used to be a marathon runner. You could take up running again."

"How about karate?" She sat back and shivered. Where had that come from?

"It's a great workout. No problem."

"If I want, I can do something as strenuous as karate?" An idea was beginning to form in her mind.

"Sure, as long as you don't overdo it. Plus, of course, you've got to keep to a strict schedule of taking your meds, eating right, and getting enough sleep. You know, the routine we've been discussing. If you and your heart weren't a good match, I wouldn't be as enthusiastic about karate. But I've seen enough successes now that I think I can safely predict you're one of them. For instance, another of my patients is a triathlete. His sport can be a lot more grueling than karate. Another, who's in his sixties, is a serious jitterbugger. A third's building a house by hand. Think of all the lifting and hammering that go into that." He crossed his arms, considering. "One of my colleagues has a patient who climbed Half Dome in Yosemite ten months after her transplant. Then she went to the tops of Mount Whitney and Mount Fuji. Imagine climbing to those high altitudes and the demands on the heart and lungs even for someone with all her natural body parts."

She blinked slowly, thinking. "Tell me about my donor again."

He hesitated. "Your new heart came from a man. He was in his early forties. He was athletic and had a good, healthy heart. You know I can't reveal who he was."

"Was he Russian?"

The doctor frowned. "I gave you his age and sex, and I can tell you he died in a motorcycle accident within four hours of the District. Four hours includes flight time, of course. That's the most a heart can be kept outside a body for optimum results in transplant surgery. But I can't tell you anything more. The transplant center has ironclad rules to protect his privacy, and yours. You signed an agreement not to try to find out his identity or to locate his family."

"I'm a lawyer, an officer of the court. Of course, I'll honor any document I sign. But surely you can tell me whether he was Russian. In the scheme of things, that seems like a minor piece of information. After all, there are tens of thousands of Russians living here now."

Travis Jackson studied her. "What makes you ask if he was Russian?"

She paused. "This is hard to explain . . . but I've never thought much about Russian poetry. In fact, I don't recall memorizing any, but phrases of it began floating through my mind this week—in Russian. I've never really liked Russian food, but now sometimes I crave it. For instance, I often order sliced tomatoes with sugar and salt. One of the nurses told me that's an old Russian favorite. I've never drunk much black tea, but now I want it all the time. In some places in Russia, it's more popular than coffee." She reminded him of her request for vodka and that she had even named the kind she wanted—Stolichnaya, Russia's foremost brand. She told him about her nightmares. "In the beginning, I couldn't understand what they were saying. But now I know they're speaking Russian." She paused. "There's a song that keeps coming to me. I think it's from a Soviet movie." She sang the earthy, proletariat tune: " 'Harvest, our harvest is so good . . .' "

"Interesting." He was looking at her oddly.

"Do you know where this quotation is from?" She closed her eyes and recited: " 'If you love, love without reason. If you threaten, don't threaten in play.' "

"Never heard it before."

She sighed, frustrated, but said stubbornly, "I think it's been translated from Russian."

The doctor picked up a chair and put it close to her bed. He sat, his expression severe. "I've heard other stories from patients who claimed to have inherited tastes, ideas, even direct memories from their donors' hearts, but I've never seen a shred of scientific evidence to substantiate it."

"I'm not the only one? If there are others, then I'm not going crazy. Give me an explanation, because it makes no sense. I don't want to believe my new heart could be changing me, telling me things. This is crazy."

"You're not crazy. But you're hyped up on the miracle of your survival and all the medications you're taking. I can't impress upon you enough how very powerful the wonder drugs are that you have to take to stop infection and organ rejection. In fact, if you were to go just two days without them, you'd probably do irreversible damage to your body. On the one hand, they're life-giving, while on the other, they're industrial-strength and potentially lethal. They can impact the way you feel. The taste of food. What you remember. Your dreams . . . all your sensory perceptions. Still, you must never miss a dose. Those side effects are minor compared to losing your life."

"You mean what I've been experiencing is in my head? That because of the drugs, I'm making this up? Because if that's what you think, you're wrong. You were here when I wanted vodka."

"Right. I have no problem believing everything's happened just as you say. But that doesn't mean you 'inherited' any of it from your donor. Maybe when you were a little girl you heard some adult say vodka was good for the heart. So because of your cardiac problems, that old memory percolated up from the depths of your unconscious to remind you about vodka."

She pursed her lips. "Okay. That makes sense. But I've also had nightmares about Russians and cravings for Russian food."

"Well, you've done legal work for Russians. You've traveled extensively in Russia, and you even learned to speak the language."

"A fair amount, yes. Polish, too."

"You probably saw the movie years ago and have simply forgotten it. The Russian words you heard could've triggered the memory, and the memory could've triggered the Russian nightmares. See? One thing leads to another." He patted her hand reassuringly. "When you finally relax, as you will, and you begin to take your new heart for granted, things will quiet down. Your body's going to adjust, and all these unusual experiences will stop."

She heaved a sigh of relief. She was an attorney, trained to dispassion. For her, logic was almost religion. Her rational mind knew he was right. To think anything different was to turn her back on her past and everything she had worked so hard to achieve, including the person she had made herself.

"Thank you." She smiled. "If someone had said to me what I've said to you . . . I would've advised, 'Go immediately to a therapist. You are in desperate mental-health need.' But since I was living it, it seemed real."

"It *is* real. It's just not caused by what you think." The surgeon stood up. "Take my word for it: All of this is simply a combination of your imagination, your personal history, and the meds. Stop worrying. Your new heart isn't speaking to you. I guarantee it."

She nodded happily. He was the expert who had saved her life. She trusted him implicitly. Of course, he was right.

Freed of the machines and tubes that had monitored her, she could at last leave her room whenever she wanted, and the world seemed new and exciting. With a sense of gratitude, she visited other patients who were waiting for transplants. They were dying, just as she had been. Their fear and pain pierced her to the marrow. She sat beside their beds and asked them about their families, their hometowns, and their dreams for the future. There was a visceral bond between the dying and the saved in a transplant hospital, and each day she extended her hand across the chasm, paying back for the generosity of her donor and his family in the only way she knew.

As she grew stronger and less vulnerable, she did not discuss her odd, post-op experiences again. Whenever one of them reappeared or a new one tried to take hold, she firmly dismissed it.

In May, a month following her surgery, she signed the paperwork that allowed her to return home, where care-givers would stay with her until she could live on her own again. As the nurse left with the documents, Beth turned excitedly to gaze through the window at the spring day, at the blue sky and the grassy hospital lawn with the towering trees and the bright iris beds in bloom. The sun shone down in a warm, hazy light, and it almost seemed to her the world was beckoning her back. Her old familiar world where the future was filled with important contracts and dicey negotiations, glamorous embassy parties and business trips to St. Petersburg and Gdansk, interesting people with accents and different cultural backgrounds who needed her help as they created a new Eastern Europe.

She smiled to herself. Her colleagues at the firm called her the Ice Princess for her single-minded pursuit of success, but they did not know the joy she took from the small moments: The taste of a hot breakfast torte in Cracow after an all-night conference. The sight of autumn leaves blowing down one of Old Moscow's cobblestoned streets when just twenty-four hours earlier she had been at work in Edwards & Bonnett's futuristic glass-and-chrome Washington headquarters. She would never forget the first sight of the scarred conference table in the old Communist meeting hall in Warsaw. It had been built for apparatchik meetings but was now the birthplace of a new private company that would revolutionize the telephone system of Poland.

Suddenly a voice interrupted her reverie. "Could you give me a few minutes, Ms. Convey?"

Beth turned to look at the open doorway, where a woman stood. She was in her late forties with swept-back auburn hair touched with gray.

"My name is Stephanie Smith," she continued. "I'm working on a study for the Walters Institute for Learning. Do you know about us?"

Beth smiled and gestured at a chair. Already her world was growing more interesting. "Sorry, but I've never heard of you. Please come in."

Stephanie Smith sat beside the bed and laid a leather portfolio on her lap. "You've had a heart transplant. How are you feeling?"

"Fine, thanks." No way was she going to discuss her aches, pains, and worries. There was no point. Life was going to be much better from now on. "Tell me about your study."

"Have you ever heard of cellular memory?"

"Never."

"I'm not surprised. Few people outside the scientific community have. And within the community, it's controversial. I'm a psychoneuroimmunologist, meaning I'm a licensed psychologist who studies the relationship among the immune system, the brain, and our experiences in the world. The hospital has agreed to let me talk to patients on their last day, the assumption being you'd feel well enough to answer some questions about your experiences since your transplant."

Beth was taken aback. She asked cautiously, "What experiences do you mean?"

"Have you had any unusual incidents? Thoughts or tastes, perhaps?"

"I'm not sure I understand what you're getting at."

Dr. Smith's face remained neutral. She opened her portfolio. Beth saw files.

The woman removed one, read, and looked up. "Ah, so you're a lawyer. That explains it. A skeptical mind. Good for you."

"You have a file on me?"

"As a matter of fact, I do. I'm a scientist, also skeptical. It's a healthy approach, particularly when a research study is involved, wouldn't you agree?"

"Yes. Have you spoken to my surgeon, Travis Jackson, about me?"

"Would you like me to? Maybe you already know he finds no merit in what we're studying."

"He probably thinks it's a waste of money."

"He does. But the funding comes from outside, and it's a legitimate scientific pursuit that other doctors support. What's your opinion? Do you think it's foolish?"

For a long moment Beth was tempted to speak. There was something in her that urged her to unburden herself. Still, she believed the logic of her surgeon's explanation, and she trusted his years of transplant successes. Everything he had said made sense.

So she compromised. "Travis mentioned some patients have strange experiences after surgery, but he said they were due to the heavy medication and all the enormous life changes. What do you think?"

Dr. Smith shrugged. "That's what we're trying to find out. I'll tell you a story that may help explain why our institute is investigating these questions." She paused. "Paul Pearsall, another psychoneuroimmunologist, has worked in the field for years. He wrote a book called

The Heart's Code. He describes an eight-year-old girl who received the heart of a ten-year-old. When the child started having nightmares and screaming out that she knew who'd murdered her donor, the mother took her to a psychiatrist, and the psychiatrist called the police. They discovered her donor had indeed been murdered. The child described the time, weapon, and place, and the police used her information to develop new evidence. They arrested the murderer."

Beth was silent. She felt numb. "She saw someone killed in her nightmares." It was a statement, not a question. In her mind, she saw the motorcycle again roll out of the garage. She watched herself leap on, ram the motorcycle into the man, and kill him. She shuddered. Every time she had the nightmare, she felt as if she personally had murdered that poor stranger.

Dr. Smith continued: "Yes. Gets one's attention, doesn't it? I suppose it could be explained away as coincidence. But science doesn't like to be ignorant, and we've shamed ourselves over the centuries by taking our prejudices for facts. Five hundred years ago, the world's best minds believed the sun and all the planets revolved around the earth. Wrong. In the eighteen-hundreds, our top medical specialists were convinced it was 'utter nonsense' that tiny, invisible 'germs' could make us sick. Wrong again. And now, of course, what used to be far-fetched science fiction has become fact with the cloning of sheep. It's hard to look at those lambs and believe that there aren't more 'impossibilities' that we're on the verge of confirming."

Stephanie Smith cocked her head as if waiting for Beth to say something.

But Beth turned away to stare unseeing out her window. Hard logic was the foundation of her life. This woman was trying to use a spurious kind of reasoning to confuse her. There was no way the good, strong heart that had saved her could be tormenting her now. Inwardly she paused. She evaluated the situation. The truth was . . . it did not matter either way. A heart was neutral. Just an organ. There was no moral or intellectual base from which it operated.

Dr. Smith said quietly, "We like to tell ourselves we've come a long way from such ignorant days. But in truth, have we? If we refuse to ask questions because we think we already know the answers, what do we accomplish? What do we learn?"

Beth said nothing. She knew what she had to do. There were crackpots in every field, and some could be convincing. This woman was a crackpot. Crazy as a loon. She checked her watch. "Or another way to look at it is, why ask questions when the answers are already proved?

To pursue what's known is simply a waste of time, effort, and funding that could—and should—be put where it's critically needed. A lot of lives would be saved if you and your colleagues would devote all your time and research money to better use, like convincing people to sign organ-donor cards."

Dr. Smith gave a knowing smile and closed her portfolio. "I see." She picked up her purse, opened it, and removed a business card. "No reason to take any more of your time." She laid the white card on the bedside table. "If you'd like to learn more about cellular memory . . . about all the exciting new scientific discoveries being made that support its existence . . . if you ever have any questions at all . . . please call."

"Thank you," Beth said politely. "Good-bye."

The woman stood and left the room without another word.

A half-hour later, Beth's care-giver arrived to take her home. Excited, she had already packed her bags. As she stood, she noticed the business card on the table. She had a ten-second debate with herself, then shrugged. She grabbed the card and slid it into her purse. Then she went home to settle into the long, rigorous routine of rehabilitation.

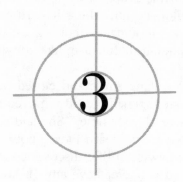

The May sun was a fireball, its rays glinting off windshields and freshly washed cars as weekday traffic roared around Washington's Beltway. It was nearly two o'clock, and people were rushing back to jobs after late lunches or off to private schools to pick up children. Or maybe, Jeffrey Hammond reflected as he sped along in his Mustang, they were, like him, going nowhere.

Every day he seemed to grow more weary of his life, and he was uncertain why. Today his nerves felt raw, on edge. In a few hours, he would meet a man to whom he had not spoken in nine years. It might be a mistake, this meeting. Yet he was the one who had asked for it: Mikhail Ogust had been dead more than a month, and he'd had no luck developing another source as useful as Ogust. He was counting on getting some help out of this meeting.

As he wove his Mustang among the lanes of traffic, he watched for a too-curious look or for a vehicle to pull out and follow. He gave every appearance of being one of the crowd, but in truth he understood things, had seen and done things, that others could never imagine. Here in Washington, he knew all too intimately, anything could happen. Anything was possible. He shook his head worriedly.

In between watching for surveillance, he read the signposts he was speeding past—Alexandria, Arlington, Langley, Bethesda, Silver Spring. Just a few years ago, they were backwaters on the palette of Greater Washington, but now each was recognized around the world in its own right. Since the fall of communism, this had become the land of global opportunity—untouchable wealth, immense power, and secrets that could topple governments, all on a scale so grand it had never before been seen. No wonder citizens from every state flocked here. No wonder so many foreigners immigrated—legally and illegally—that the INS had no hope of keeping track of all of them. Which was another reason Jeff Hammond was worried.

For an hour longer, he continued to drive, his senses alert. He'd had a feeling all day that he was under surveillance again, which was why he had taken the Beltway. Then his gaze swept to the right, and he noticed a white Ford Escort two lanes away that was about to exit at Oxon Hill. It was not the car itself that attracted his attention. It was the driver, who had grown either tired or cocky and was looking curiously across the traffic at him. No mistake about it. The idiot.

Hammond slowed and moved over a lane so he could see better. Instantly the driver made a second mistake: He averted his head. He was wearing an Akubra hat at a rakish angle to the left, blocking part of his profile but not so much that Hammond did not recognize him. He had passed the same driver miles back, somewhere near Silver Spring. He had a trained memory, so he was certain of it. Which meant the driver, who was now speeding his car off onto the exit ramp, had been tailing him until he had been replaced in a planned pattern of surveillance.

Hammond was right, but it was no consolation. He slowed his Mustang more. Watching ahead and behind, he moved the car right once again and entered the outside traffic lane. As trees and signs blurred past, he noted a blue sedan a quarter-mile behind also move right across two lanes to drive in the same lane as he. Then a pickup between him and the blue sedan accelerated and pulled into the right lane directly behind him. Meanwhile, a third car, a yellow Mazda, also moved right.

He smiled grimly as he studied the driver of the pickup, which had fallen back. He memorized the man's long face and dark eyebrows. Then at the last moment and without slowing again, Hammond turned sharply right and sped the Mustang off onto the exit ramp.

Braking, he checked his rearview mirror as both the pickup and the blue sedan followed. Counting the Ford Escort, it appeared whoever had decided he was important enough to tail had also decided on the traditional three-car surveillance team. It showed an unsettling amount of organization.

He decelerated again as he approached the cross street, where the traffic light was green. He could drive straight through the intersection and try to lose the tails somewhere on the backstreets of Oxon Hill, but he did not know the area. Concerned, he eyed the traffic light ahead and, in his rearview mirror, the two tailing vehicles.

There was little time before the light became red. He had to decide. He frowned, thinking rapidly. What he had in mind depended on his ability to time each movement carefully. It was a risk, but if it worked . . .

He felt a burst of adrenaline as the light turned from yellow to red, and he floored the accelerator, screeching into the intersection. Behind him, tires screamed on the pavement as a car that had jumped the light swerved to avoid hitting him. Sweat formed on his forehead as he pushed the Mustang forward. He checked his rearview mirror: The surveilling pickup and the blue sedan had at first accelerated but now slammed on their brakes, laying streaks of smoking rubber on the off-ramp as they skidded to stops to avoid the wall of vehicles released by the green light.

As the traffic roared past his Mustang's rear bumper, Hammond turned safely left onto the street. He smiled grimly, entertained by the pounding of his heart. Some things never changed, including his physiology. He glanced over his shoulder and saw that his two followers were trapped on the off ramp until the light changed again, which was as it should be.

Over the last week, he had shaken what had appeared to be a few isolated tails, but yesterday the surveillance had become certain and less easily lost. In one way, it was good news: Affirmation he was getting close, which excited him. But it also meant peril. He had managed to keep his work dark for years, but it appeared the principals had somehow been alerted.

Today of all days he must not be followed. He had to keep this meeting secret.

Frowning, he returned to the speeding Beltway, this time heading north. Alert for backup surveillance, he continued forty more miles until he exited again, now heading for the little town of Olney where Route 108 became a quiet, tree-bordered country lane. As the road dipped sharply between two hills, he pulled off into a wooded sink he had used before, killed his engine, and rolled down his window. A wind out of the west rustled through a stand of oak and maple trees. Somewhere in the distance a cow bell chimed, an eerie sound across the empty hills. The air smelled of mold from the creek that trickled through this low spot of land. He studied the sky and the road. When no helicopters appeared and only a tractor lumbered past, he began to believe he had finally lost his tails.

This meticulous sort of dry cleaning was ingrained in his nature, one of the reasons he had been able to lead a double life for the past ten years. Still, just in case, he stayed where he was, out of sight, another five minutes: Experienced followers knew how to estimate patience, too.

Satisfied at last, he returned to the road, made a quick U-turn, and headed south, again toward Washington. Traffic had thinned. As he continued to watch for surveillance, he exited once more and entered the parking lot of the Aspen Hills Shopping Center, where he stopped the car at the far end so he could watch the activity around the Giant Foods supermarket without attracting a lot of attention. That was where the mall's security focused, fearlessly making certain the under-aged bought no beer.

At four o'clock, as the pace of shoppers at the one-story mall seemed to reach a fevered pitch, a dusty Plymouth pulled into the empty slot next to the Mustang. The Bureau car had been described to Hammond, and when he saw FBI Special Agent Elias Kirkhart, dressed in the mandatory dark, conservative suit and pressed white shirt, sitting alone in the driver's seat, he leaned across and unlocked his passenger door.

Eli Kirkhart had once been so thin and bony that the two of them had been called Jeff and the Beanpole. But Kirkhart had filled out now, his shoulders muscular, and his face thicker, almost square. The FBI man's simple blue tie was knotted repressively tight against his throat, and his heavy brows were arched above his aviator sunglasses as he turned to study Hammond's vintage Mustang. That bulldog face with the wide cheekbones reminded Hammond of the English yeomen from whom Kirkhart had claimed to be descended, way back in the Middle Ages.

Hammond waited impatiently as his former partner scrutinized the area once more then opened his car door and, staying low, slid into the front passenger seat next to him.

"You had no problems?" Hammond asked.

"None. And you?"

"Nothing to speak of." No way would he give the FBI agent information that might scare him off from future meetings, which an organized surveillance might.

"Good." Kirkhart locked the door behind him and turned to the man who had once been his closest friend and colleague. He made no effort to smile, nor did he extend his hand. Swiftly he took in Jeff Hammond's familiar angular features and the sunglasses as dark and impenetrable as his own. But now Jeff also wore a small gold earring in his right ear, and his light-brown hair was far too long, fastened at the nape of the neck in a ponytail. "You've changed. You look like some hippie profes-sor out of the sixties. The *Post* must be desperate for help these days."

Hammond's eyes crinkled in a smile. He nodded. "Could be. On the other hand, seems to me you might do something about getting rid of that Brit accent, Eli. Three seconds on the phone, and I knew it was you. Can't disguise that upper-crust snobbery. Come on, you were born here. Chicago, as I recall. A good Midwest accent. Talk like it." He waited, remembering Kirkhart had once had a sense of humor.

The FBI man gave a low chuckle. "Hello, Jeff."

The two men shook hands, but Eli Kirkhart felt no sense of letting bygones be bygones. He kept his face friendly while he contemplated Jeff, who was tall and rangy in a herringbone sports jacket and jeans. Jeff still filled a car not only with his physique but with his personality. The difference was he now exuded something calculating and taut; he gave no evidence of being the excitable hothead Eli had known so well. There was, he decided, a secretiveness to Jeff. Something vaguely furtive that did not surprise him.

"It's been a long time, Eli." Jeff's voice sounded odd and stilted to himself. He was out of touch with his past, and now he was sitting next to a significant part of it.

"Far too long, actually. How are you?" Eli said.

"I've been better."

"Sorry to hear that. Whatever you want, it must be important, con-sidering all the hugger-mugger in the parking lot you insisted upon."

"That was to protect you more than me."

"Right." Eli gave another small smile, this time of disbelief.

Jeff ignored it. "We both know your A-rating at the Bureau would go into a nosedive if they learned you met privately with a 'disordered isolate.' "

"Ah, you heard about that then. I'd wondered."

"Of course, I heard." When they had forced him out, the Bureau's leadership had had to tar him with something other than 'disagreed with official policy,' and *disordered isolate* was the kind of psychologi-cal term that—keyboarded into his file and, therefore, soon leaked onto the Bureau grapevine—took on a kind of immortality. In his case, it was code for someone who was unreliable, not a team player, a loner—'isolate,' perhaps even a touch sociopathic—'disordered.'

He had accepted the inevitability, and necessity, of it with disgust. The Bureau was like the mafia: You either retired with honors at an ap-propriate age after appropriate service, or you were dead. Physically dead in the mafia's case; usually only metaphorically in the Bureau's, although there had been rumors that there might have been some dis-creet slippage into murder over the past twenty years.

No, the Bureau could not simply kick you out. Instead, they had to discredit you, especially among your colleagues, or someone might begin to ask details about what had happened, maybe question a supe-rior's decision, even probe into an FBI commandment or two. That, of course, would damage the monolithic discipline of the black-suited wall. Which was why, after the last of his exit interviews, his one-time friends had been too busy to have dinner or even to meet for a cup of coffee. He paused, surprised he was angry after so many years.

Eli said evenly, "The seventh floor wouldn't have approved it with-out cause. You were wrong, Jeff, you know. Way wide of the mark and off base."

Jeff said nothing, mulling over how much to believe of what Eli said. Despite spending most of his life in the United States, Eli Kirkhart had not only kept his English father's British syntax and accent, he had also retained that exaggerated civil-service sense of the infallibility of gov-ernment authority—when it was applied to others, that was. At the same time, Eli had a similarly English sense of his own, and the island nation's, overall superiority, especially in matters of war and espionage, which had often annoyed his colleagues while amusing Jeff.

"Well, maybe I was a bit wrong-headed." Jeff shrugged as if dis-missing it all. "Still, I have to admit I miss some of it. You and Aida, for instance."

For a moment as he sat there in the Mustang, he wanted to chuck it all and go have a drink with Eli. They could talk about old times, and he would find out what Eli's life was like now. Hell, Eli and Aida had been his closest friends, the three of them just weeks out of college when they had met their first day at the FBI Academy in Quantico. Competitors, sure, but also helping each other in tactics, languages, and martial arts, in which Aida had excelled. If Eli had not married Aida Devine, Jeff would have pursued her. Which might have been an excellent idea, con-sidering how rotten his own marriage had turned out.

Jeff scanned the parking lot again but saw no signs of trouble. "How is she, Eli?"

"Dead, Jeff. Pancreatic cancer. She died five years ago."

Jeff jerked around to stare at Eli. He felt as if a fist had slammed into his chest. "Dead? Eli . . . I didn't know. I'm sorry. Jesus. I'm really sorry."

Eli's face was a mask behind his sunglasses. "Thanks." He paused. "It was fast, thank God. She'd been in a lot of pain."

An awkward silence filled the Mustang. For Eli, his grief over losing Aida was still as raw as if she had died just yesterday. He missed her, and talking about her was torture for him. So he did what he always did: He pushed his thoughts from her and concentrated on his work. In this case, that meant Jeff.

As he studied Jeff, he remembered that inside the Bureau no one had been closer than they, and they had owed each other a great deal. But now, Jeff was not only *persona non grata,* he had gone to work for *The Washington Post* as a reporter and analyst, and, in that role, he had personally focused the influential newspaper's spotlight on mistakes and investigations the Bureau wanted kept hidden. True, the seventh floor had apparently given Jeff no choice but to resign, but did he have to become such a critic, and one with such a public pulpit? Jeff appeared to have turned his back on everything in which he had once believed.

Eli pointedly checked his Timex, the brand of choice of the underpaid FBI. "Well, old boy, let's talk about you. What's so vital that we had to meet like this?"

Jeff stared at Eli's broad face and reminded himself he was here to do business. "I need your help." By phoning and convincing Eli to meet and then to make it here, the location of Jeff's chosing, he had already scored two points. Long ago he had learned that people supported what they helped to create. By agreeing to both requests, Eli had already taken small psychological steps toward helping Jeff. But it might not be enough. With Eli, one never knew.

The FBI man was instantly alert. "What sort of help?"

"Don't get nervous. It's a small thing. My sources tell me you were part of the task force working on that secret KGB slush fund that was discovered last year, the huge one. They also said the investigation was closed in April."

Jeff had learned that over the past nine years the FBI had uncovered hundreds of hidden bank accounts in the United States that originated in the old Kremlin of Cold War days. Altogether, they amounted to more than a billion dollars, the result of the KGB's clandestinely sending money from Moscow to be laundered through respectable banks—particularly in Switzerland—until it was untraceable. At that point, much of the money had been deposited in U.S. front accounts with names like European Natural Resources, North Sea Excavating & Mining, and International Import Institutes. The violent purpose of these fortunes had been to fund the KGB's covert operations against Americans and their government.

Since then, new Swiss laws that required its secretive banking insti-
tutions to reveal information that had a bearing on proved criminals or
criminal acts had enabled the FBI to expose many of the secret caches.
The most recently discovered—the largest and most deeply disguised—
was the one to which Jeff referred.

"So that's it." Eli Kirkhart did not exactly smile, but he felt a surge of
excitement. Although the account had been emptied before the task
force found it, financial technicians had traced the money back to
Moscow. Somehow, Jeff had learned the investigation was closed, and
that was why he felt free to ask. But what intrigued Eli was Jeff himself—what was his real interest in the hidden stash?

To hide his eagerness, Eli gazed around the parking lot . . . and recalled that it had once been a secret KGB meeting place. He said
thoughtfully, "Rather interesting you'd choose this shopping mall for
our meeting. You knew I'd remember it was once a *yavka,* didn't you?
A bit of irony on your part, I suppose, to remind me how pervasive the
KGB was in America in its old glory days."

"Yes, and they're still here in the District," Jeff reminded him.

Eli chose to ignore that. "Since you know we closed the inquiry, you
also must know the account was a dead end. The money's safely back in
Russia. The story's over. Nothing for the *Post* there."

"I have a feeling the money might not be in Russia. I had a name—
never mind how I got it. That's part of my job, digging up information.
But the name became a corpse last month. A motorcycle accident in
Rock Creek Park. Smashed up his bike and killed himself. Now I'm
back to square one." He shook his head.

"What name might that be?"

"Mikhail Ogust."

Eli closed his eyes as if he were falling asleep. He purposely made his
voice tired and angry. "General Berianov again, Jeff?"

Jeff gazed at him steadily. "Mikhail Ogust had access to that fund.
Berianov and Yurimengri must have—"

The FBI man's eyes snapped open, and he interrupted, "We never
found the slightest hint Colonel Ogust or anyone else in this country
touched that money. I possibly should not tell you this, but because of
past favors I'll do you a good turn—we exonerated Ogust. Yes, that's
true. Exonerated him completely. Not only that, General Berianov and
Colonel Yurimengri are clean, too. Antiseptic. There's no more hint
today that any of them is hiding some cloak-and-dagger master plan
than there was when you walked off the job."

Although he pretended concern for Jeff's well-being, Eli was begin-

ning to believe Jeff's maniacal pursuit of ex-KGB general Alexei Berianov really had been a cover for other activities. He wondered what
had actually happened when Jeff resigned, and what else he had been
doing all these years besides serving as the *Post*'s expert on Russia and
Eastern Europe.

Eli had his suspicions, and that was why he had agreed to this meeting. "Take my sincere advice," he continued. "You're destroying yourself with this tiresome wild-goose chase. How many more years are you
going to waste being obsessed that Berianov is involved in some sort of
collusion to destroy America? Listen to me carefully, old friend: That
slush-fund money's back in the Kremlin now, and those three Russians
had nothing to do with it or anything else remotely disturbing. The case
is closed, Jeff. You should move on. As they say, get a life."

Jeff Hammond was motionless behind his steering wheel, his long
body tense. "You're wrong. I know they defected for a lot more than
just to save their hides from Yeltsin. I can feel it."

"Goddamn it. Let it *go!* You ruined your career, and your wife divorced you because of this obsession. What more do you want to lose?"

"Never mind what I've lost. Can you help me?"

"Help how?"

"Give me another name. Anyone who had access to the fund."

Inwardly, Eli smiled. So that was it. He kept his face empty as he increased his pose of anger. "I don't have any other names! I told you, no
one in this country—"

"What about *not* in this country?"

A name not in this country. *Yes.* Eli nodded. Jeff was implying Russia.
And once Eli gave Jeff a name, Eli would monitor and observe . . . and
with luck trace the connection back to the mole who had been under-
mining FBI missions and destroying morale for years. This could be the
first crack in the myth of invincibility that had always surrounded the
deep-penetration agent who had used the FBI as his, or her, own personal gold mine. Finding the mole was his covert assignment, entrusted
to him secretly by government forces higher up even than the FBI.

Eli let his breath out slowly. "Very well . . . we did come across one
other name: Vok."

Jeff's voice was cautious. *"Ivan* Vok? The KGB's top assassin?"

The FBI man nodded. "Yes, and he's still *in Russia.* Does that make
it clear, or are you so completely mesmerized by your obsession that
you can't think straight? Vok's in Russia. *The money's in Russia.*
Nothing's going on here. It's all *there.* Far, far away in what was once
the Soviet Union. That's the story. *C'est fini."*

Jeff shook his head. "You can't be sure the money's in Russia any more than you can be sure Vok is."

"Indeed, we can. Their government keeps close watch on dangerous men like Vok. You know that as well as I."

Jeff was quiet. "Thanks, Eli." He started the Mustang's engine. "Soon. I feel it. I'm so damn close to the bastards I can smell their stench." It was his guess that the orchestrated surveillance today had been from the ex-KGB group headed by General Berianov.

In that instant, faced with Jeff's conviction, which suddenly seemed persuasive, Eli doubted himself and his deductions. "Wait a minute. Do you have something to tell *me?*"

Jeff shook his head. "Too soon."

"If you know of any possible danger to the country, Jeff—"

"I don't."

Annoyed, beginning to worry, Eli made his voice hard: "Is this how you reporters work—all take and no give? No wonder journalists are rated for trust just above used-car salesmen."

"When I've got something to report, I'll phone you first."

"Dammit, I took a chance coming here. Tell me what you're working on that makes you think General Berianov and—"

Jeff shook his head again. "Hunches, Eli. That's all it is. Watching. Running down leads like the slush funds. That's all I've ever had. But that doesn't make the potential any less real. You and I used to solve cases on less than this, but we both know you can't take gut feelings back to the rajas at the Bureau. We always had to tie it up in a pretty ribbon, with everything proved. The one time I didn't do it, I got forced out."

If you were forced out, Eli thought. He opened the car door. "It's been good to see you, Jeff. Let's keep in touch this time, okay?" And he lied: "The past is the past."

"Sure, Eli."

Eli Kirkhart nodded good-bye and climbed into the Bureau car.

Now that dinnertime was near, the suburban mall had quieted. The sun had dropped low in the sky, making the treetops shine and sending deepening shadows across the parking area. As if they had made a silent pact, each man drove off without looking at the other again. They took different exits.

As Jeff Hammond sped back onto the Beltway, he grew increasingly suspicious of Eli. That final suggestion of warmth and friendship—*Let's keep in touch . . . The past is the past*—jibed with little Eli had said or, for that matter, with how he had acted. Despite the poker face, Eli was

distrustful and unforgiving, and he had some purpose of his own—
something else that had brought him to the meeting. Whatever it was,
it was no desire simply to help Jeff or have an innocent reunion. Jeff
frowned, thinking.

At the same time Jeff was heading in to his Washington office, Eli
Kirkhart was driving home to his empty house in Bethesda. It had been
a long, strange day, and both the high and low points had been seeing
Jeff again. In his mind, he replayed their conversation until, with sudden understanding, he knotted his fist and shook it. *Damn.*

In a flash of understanding, he came to an important conclusion:
The real reason Jeff had wanted to talk might not have been to get information to further his hopeless crusade of trying to tie the slush fund
to former General Berianov. No, not that at all. Eli had a strong hunch
Jeff had instead wanted to confirm that the FBI had closed its inquiry.
In fact, the whole point . . . Jeff's hidden motive . . . could easily have
been to make certain that every person connected to the fund was safe
from any more probes from the U.S. government. And that included
Jeff himself.

4

Her AK-47 assault rifle held chest high, she pounded down a tunnel lined with rough rock walls. Her heart was thumping with fear. At last she found a gray metal door and yanked it open. Inside was a ladder. Glancing back over her shoulder, she climbed swiftly up the long, narrow shaft and, at the top, pulled herself out into a moonless night. Breathing hard, she stared at three men who were sitting around a campfire, talking in Russian. As the firelight flickered on their faces, she recognized the two who were facing her. They were her comrades, and they greeted her: C priyézdam! *As the third turned toward her, he asked her how things were.* Kak vi pazhiváyitye? *She froze with shock: He was the man she had killed with the motorcycle.*

How could that be? Stunned, she shook her head and knew it did not matter. Nothing else mattered. She stared at him. He was alive!

As gunfire faded in the distance, she crouched with the trio, her powerful Kalashnikov rifle cradled in her arms. She did not smile. There was no need. These men did not smile. They were hard and seasoned. She was one of them.

Beth Convey awoke with a start, her pulse throbbing behind her ears. It was a new nightmare, but with the same three Russians and the same sense of danger and violence. She made herself take long, deep breaths. It had been a year since her transplant. A full year, and until yesterday the nightmares and other disturbing ideas and experiences had faded, just as her surgeon had promised. She hesitated, reevaluating. Or perhaps she had simply learned to ignore them.

But not now. This dream had been vivid, riveting. Anxiously she stared around her bedroom at the photographs of her family on the walls, at the sunlight streaming in through the windowpanes, and at the bouquet of fresh daffodils on her bureau. She took a deep breath, comforted by the familiar surroundings of her old Victorian.

Then the present flooded back and she remembered: Today was important. Crucial. She jumped out of bed and ran into the bathroom to take her morning meds and begin dressing.

Yesterday—Monday—disaster had struck. It had been her first day back at work, and managing partner Zach Housley delivered devastating news: Most of her clients had elected to stay with the attorneys to whom Zach had assigned them last year. She had expected some defections, since all the firm's lawyers were very good, but the extent of them had left her breathless. But most ravaging of all, and the least expected, was the loss of Michelle Philmalee, for whom Beth had won such a spectacular victory in the divorce trial that almost killed her.

Admittedly, Michelle's decision was "just business," but it felt like betrayal. Beth's chest contracted with worry. The anticipation of returning to work and earning quick partnership was what had kept her going through her long journey back to health.

She brushed her teeth, ran a comb through her hair, applied lipstick, and stared at herself in the mirror. Despite getting only three hours of sleep—she had spent most of last night at the office, feverishly working on ideas to win back Michelle—her skin glowed, and her blue eyes were clear and bright. She said a silent prayer of gratitude to her transplant surgeon and to her heart donor.

But her robust appearance was a sham. She fairly vibrated with stress, which made her consider whether the sudden intense pressure might have triggered the new nightmare. Plus, there was the Virginia area code, which had returned yesterday afternoon to haunt her. Fortunately, it was now only a buzz, annoying but not overwhelming.

Today was the one-year anniversary of her transplant—a time to celebrate her new life and honor the man whose strong heart beat inside her chest as if it had always been her own. Instead, she must save her career. To make matters worse, the attorney with whom Michelle had chosen to remain was one of Beth's old boyfriends, Phil Stageman. It had been a short office romance, and afterwards Beth could not figure why she had ever gotten involved with him. A case of temporary insanity, she finally concluded. Hormones overruling reason. Now she was certain of it.

She sighed, thinking about all the men she had abandoned or lost.

But then, they had always been second to her work. She vaguely recalled a vow to pursue a serious love relationship once she was well again, but now that she was fighting to regain her position in the firm, she found the idea far less compelling.

Today might be her only chance with Michelle, and she had awakened with a nightmare. But she could not think about that now. Instead, she must focus on her plan, because all her hard work had paid off: She had discovered Phil Stageman had been lax in his job of protecting Philmalee International. With that information, she knew she would win back Michelle. She trusted her intellect and her ability.

She was at the peak of her game.

Queen of the Cosmos.

She was Beth Convey, killing machine with compassion, and back in battle.

She folded her hands on the long, polished table. Her throat was dry. The meeting with Michelle and Phil was to have begun now—7:30 P.M.—but she was sitting alone in conference room B at Edwards & Bonnett. Plus, she had not received the last of the documents she needed—an important ownership list.

At 7:45, she was mildly irritated. They were fifteen minutes late, but she was hardly surprised. Disgusted, but not surprised. She knew Phil Stageman too well. It was probably one of his power plays to throw her off, and the thought suddenly infuriated her. Made her so mad she wanted to lash out with the unexpected anger that had become part of her since her surgery. For the past day and a half, her outrage had seethed. She had pushed it down. Modulated her voice. Calmed her features. Reminded herself it was simply the drugs that made her emotions rage at this humiliating comedown. Sometimes it seemed as if two people battled inside her: The former Beth—unflappable and cool. And a stranger—hotheaded and passionate. *If you love, then love without reason. If you threaten, don't threaten in play.* . . . There were those Russian phrases again. It was all so unnerving.

At 8:00 P.M., fragments of the mysterious phone number began to pulse in her ears, and Michelle and Phil had still not arrived. She knotted her hands and glared at the conference room's door. But then, as if she had willed it, it swung open.

With relief, she pushed thoughts of the annoying number away and stood, a professional smile on her face. "So good to see you, Michelle." She shook Michelle's hand and took in her former client with one practiced sweep. In her early fifties, Michelle was small and attractive, not a hair of her jet-black coiffure out of place. The chocolate-brown Armani power suit she wore, which cost at least $5,000, showed off her curves while at the same time proclaiming the kind of taste and influence that always got her what she wanted. But that was not what caught Beth's attention. One look at Michelle told Beth her former client's decision to remain with Phil Stageman had not been just business. The rumor she had heard seemed true—Michelle and Phil were having an affair: Michelle looked vibrant, almost happy, and her characteristic severity was replaced by a soft, sensual look.

Michelle said politely, "You're looking well."

"Thank you. So are you." Beth's spirits sank. If this were a love match, Michelle might never be convinced she had made the wrong choice for her attorney.

Michelle cocked her head. "She's looking like our old Beth, don't you think?"

"Beth always looks well," Phil said smoothly. He was movie-star handsome, with curly brown hair that tumbled toward his eyes. His square shoulders seemed as if they could bear the legal burdens of the world. He was also twenty years younger than Michelle. His gaze moved to Beth. "Michelle and I don't have much time, so let's hear what you have to say." His tone hinted she was at fault for starting the meeting late and that their other plans for the evening were far more important.

Beth smiled at his juvenile attempt. "Of course."

As they sat across from her, she settled back into her chair. Michelle's fast-disintegrating deal was an important cog in a U.S. government plan to remove some $12 billion worth of nuclear-weapons-grade uranium from Russia's arsenal of bombs and missile warheads as a step to make certain those death weapons never again threatened the world. Toward that end, the United States would acquire Russia's highly enriched uranium and blend it down into harmless fuel for U.S. nuclear power plants to buy and use. For that, it would pay Russia with dollars and unenriched uranium. As part of the deal, and under the watchful eye of the U.S. government, Philmalee International had been contracted by a Russian agency, Uridium, to acquire unenriched uranium to send to Russia.

Beth ran through a quick review of the facts. "But Uridium has backed out, and you need some way to convince or force Uridium to live up to its agreement. Otherwise, Philmalee will lose approximately a half-billion dollars in revenues it had counted on."

Michelle nodded grimly. "That's correct. The facts are known. So why have you brought us here?"

Beth leaned forward. "Phil has filed suit and asked the District Court for a preliminary injunction to block Uridium from backing out of its contract with Philmalee. That's the traditional legal tack—"

Sensing danger, Phil scowled. "Don't pull that damning-with-faint-praise act, Beth. The lawsuit and request for specific performance of the contract aren't just 'traditional.' They're necessary. This has to be handled in a court of equity."

"Maybe. But if it's done the way you've laid out, you're going to lose."

"Scare tactics." Phil's voice was cutting. He turned to Michelle. "We're wasting our time. Any other lawyer would've accepted your decision to move on, Michelle. It's reprehensible that she's putting you through this charade."

Beth locked eyes with Michelle. It was time to gamble. If business were still the most important part of Michelle's life, Beth had a chance. "It's in both our interests to listen to my proposal, Michelle. I've pulled off legal miracles for you in the past. Very simply, if I'm still better than anyone else, you want me. And in this case, you certainly do. I'm serious. Phil's suit is going to lose."

"Beth!" Phil objected.

But Michelle raised her small hand. "I want to hear what she has to say."

Beth smiled, but her voice was grave. "I've spent the last two days tracing the lawsuit." The difference between a good lawyer and a great lawyer was a willingness to do original work. Phil had indeed taken the classic route, while Beth had dug around in the backyards and garbage heaps of government. "This is what you don't know, Michelle: A friend at State tells me the government's going to file against you, asking your injunction be denied because Uridium has sovereign immunity as a foreign, state-operated entity"—she paused then dropped the bombshell—"and because your arrangement would interfere with national interests."

Behind her red-rimmed glasses, Michelle's eyes grew large, flat, and worried. "*National* interests?" she repeated.

Beth nodded. "It means it's the federal government against you. Someone powerful in the government wants the contract to go to your competitor, and whoever it is has the power to lay the mantle of 'national interests' on the deal. As we all know, national interests will prevail. Which means you're holding a losing hand. By the time Phil finally gets your suit to trial, it'll be too late. The uranium you were supposed to buy will have been acquired by your competitor and delivered to Uridium. No piece of the atomic pie will be left for Philmalee to make a dime from, even if you win."

Michelle paled. "That's a lot of money to lose. You have a solution?"

"Of course. Do you know the other company Uridium has lined up to acquire the uranium in your place?"

"HanTech. What about it?"

"Another of my contacts tells me HanTech is no longer owned by an American family. Instead, a group of émigré Russian investors in the United States with close ties to Minatom has acquired it. In fact, one of them is the son of Minatom's chief." Minatom was Russia's Ministry of Atomic Energy, which oversaw Uridium. Minatom was enormously powerful, almost a state within a state, and Uridium would always do what Minatom wanted.

Michelle's eyes flashed with outrage and excitement. "Then we can take charges of collusion to the press. A sweetheart deal between a Russian agency and Russians who have immigrated to this country but are still connected to Minatom. Whether they're citizens or not, it doesn't matter. At this point, it's the appearance that counts. One way or another, with good press, we can at least stop the momentum until we can find out who's behind all this national-security nonsense. But I need to know who owns HanTech *now*. Who *are* all these Russians? I need *names!*"

"I don't have the entire list yet, but I will soon."

"Excellent. Tomorrow?"

Beth blinked. Surely the list would arrive tonight. "Of course. Tomorrow."

"Ten A.M.?"

The ringing in Beth's ears was back. She forced herself to nod. "Ten A.M. here."

Phil scowled. "I warn you, Beth, if this is another of your fast and loose tricks to buy time while you hope to come up with something real, it isn't going to work."

"Thanks, Phil," she said drily. "I appreciate the warning." She looked into Michelle's eyes and said earnestly, "You can count on me, Michelle. I'll have the list. As we both know, I've invested a lot in you and the Philmalee Group, and I want only your success."

Michelle looked away guiltily and nodded. Phil jumped up and pulled out her chair so she could step gracefully from the table. She took his hand, and they walked to the door, leaning together, a couple.

Michelle stopped and gazed back. "I don't know whether I want you to be right or wrong, Beth."

Beth's head was beginning to ache. The Virginia area code had returned, gaining in intensity. "You want me to be right, or you'll lose a great deal of money."

Phil had been watching. "You'd better have the goods, or I'll report you to Zach, and Michelle will never believe you again. Right, Michelle?"

Michelle frowned. "I'm afraid that under the circumstances he's right."

Beth's smile felt plastered to her face. "Don't worry. You'll have what you need. I guarantee it."

As the pair left the conference room, Beth got to her feet. The insistent area code made her feel nauseated as she walked along the hushed hall toward her office. 703 . . . 703 . . . 703 . . . As if something—someone?—wanted her to dial it. Thank God she did not know the complete number. She groaned aloud.

In her office, she flipped on the light and checked her watch. It was time to take a round of meds. Sometimes that reduced the problem. Shaking, she pulled out her desk drawer, grabbed her pills and water bottle, and swallowed the drugs. It was already late, nearly 8:30 P.M., and the overhead fluorescent glare made her office shadowless, almost surrealistic. Michelle's schedule had been so packed, or so her secretary had claimed, that 7:30 was the only time she'd had free to meet with Beth.

Feeling steadier, she turned to her computer to check her e-mail. Maybe the information about HanTech Industries had arrived. That would cheer her up. The screen came to life, and she scrolled down the new messages. Nothing. *Damn.*

A knock sounded at her door. "Come in."

Zachariah Housley with his narrow shoulders, oversized head, and sloping paunch appeared. His pear-shaped silhouette was so famous in Washington legal circles that, when he entered a meeting, opponents had been known to duck in metaphoric respect as if he had just lobbed a fast ball at them. In one of his off-the-rack suits that bagged at the pockets, he looked like a backcountry good ole boy, one of the ploys he used to lure adversaries into legal traps so he could snap open their valises and empty their bank accounts before they sensed peril. He had been a senior partner for at least thirty years.

He came straight to the point, blunt as ever: "Phil says you claim Russians run HanTech now. That true?"

She hesitated. "Yes, Zach. Russians who may or may not be American citizens." She was furious. Phil was trying an end run. She resisted pressing her palm to her forehead. The fragments of the phone number were hounding her.

Zach eyed her. "Can you prove it?"

She filled her voice with confidence. "I expect to. Tomorrow morning."

He cleared his throat. "Interesting. That'll make some pots boil. Course, if you're wrong . . . or if you can't prove it—"

"I understand."

It would be a black mark against her at Edwards & Bonnett. In the firm's barracuda environment, the corporate memory was long and unforgiving. Too much rode on each partner and associate for the firm to dedicate time and attention to rehabilitation, especially when clients no longer clamored for that particular attorney's services. She was making an aggressive play to retrieve an important client, and if she failed because her argument was built on lies, they would avoid firing her—a heart-transplant survivor—because it would not look good in the glass house that was Washington's legal world. But she would lose her status as a senior associate and return to the level of a first-year lawyer, assigned work that would be closely overseen. Indignation churned up from her belly.

He peered at her. "How are you feeling now that you're back?"

She froze, suddenly suspicious that he was baiting her. "I'm feeling great," she said brightly. "Did you know I almost have my black belt in karate?" Describing an athletic pursuit was a male way to affirm fitness. She did not know why she had thought to say that, and she did not care. She would use anything.

He chuckled coolly. "Modern women. Whatever happened to those fine times when girls never wore trousers? They were ashamed to smoke cigarettes in public. And if there was a problem, they'd develop a case of the vapors and swoon."

She studied him, suddenly aware of what she had been denying a long time: Zach Housley did not like female attorneys. "Those days are gone," she said firmly. "We're as free to make idiots of ourselves as you."

Again online, she checked her e-mail. To hell with Zach's implied threats. Energy flowed back into her limbs as she searched. Since HanTech was privately owned, it did not have to reveal anything about its ownership. But she knew an accountant who would likely have access: Carly King, fellow graduate of the University of Virginia, now a top analyst at the behemoth Toole-Russell, Inc., and—since her days as a high school computer nerd—an accomplished cybersleuth.

When Beth learned during her investigation that Toole-Russell handled HanTech's annual audit, she phoned Carly, who—typical of her relentless curiosity—had already run a program she had written to secretly crack the encryption and discover the password to the Toole-Russell system administrator's file. With that, she had also acquired the system's internal IP—Internet Protocol—address and the blueprint for the entire computer network. That had made her "root," which meant she had access to every Toole-Russell computer file and could change, delete, and trace all data. She was the Goddess.

Still, Carly would never embezzle or defraud. Money was not her goal. What riveted her attention, made her heart palpitate, and sent her into paroxysms of joy was a challenge. Therefore, when Beth asked for her help based on the information from her contact at State, Carly grumbled, because it was tax season and her work load was heavy, but in the end she had agreed to try to find the complete list of HanTech owners.

The only question was when. With excitement Beth spotted Carly's code name. Using a server that offered such anonymous favors for a high price, the e-mail's route and the sender's name were blocked so no one at Edwards & Bonnett would be able to sniff Carly out.

Eagerly Beth scrolled past Carly's complaints about the interruption to her work. "Bingo." Thrilled, she highlighted the list and hit the PRINT button. "Hot *damn!*"

She studied the screen. Carly affirmed that not only was HanTech no longer completely owned by Earl Hansen, who had founded the trading company many years ago, but that the new majority owners had Russian names. And now, at last, Beth had the entire list. All the names were Russian-sounding except one, Caleb Bates. This Bates owned the largest share—twenty-five percent. She wondered who he was and how he fit into the picture. Since expatriate Russians had a strong tendency to keep their businesses in the family, maybe Bates was an American of Russian descent.

But that was a minor question. She paused thoughtfully. Or was it? She e-mailed back, soothing Carly's jangled nerves, and added a note asking her to check further into what this secretive group was up to with the American company. Then she erased both messages and followed them back into the protected data bank she had discovered in which the firm kept old e-mail. She erased them there, too. Now no one would ever learn Carly had been her source.

With that, she snatched up the pages from the printer, dropped them into her briefcase, and grabbed her purse and water bottle. She was going home to celebrate. She would do her *kata* ritual exercise, make herself a delicious dinner, study the list in preparation for tomorrow's meeting, and sleep well tonight.

Abruptly, the Virginia numbers thundered inside her mind: *703 . . . 703 !* Each digit was an explosion. And now there were more numbers. An entire telephone number. Was it real? She fell back into her chair. She was frightened. She had done everything to take care of herself that

she was supposed to—with the exception of the last day and a half—
but still these incomprehensible episodes had returned.

How could this be happening? She was worn down. Worn out. It
was ridiculous that this phone number could have any kind of relation
to her. As soon as she thought that, it pounded again. Her brain was
going to split open. She grabbed her ears and closed her eyes.

Instantly, the whole ten-digit number detonated again. She broke out
in a cold sweat. She could not stand it any longer. She had to know. She
could not believe—

With a growl, she snapped up the phone and dialed. Her hand was
slippery with sweat as she unconsciously dug the receiver into her ear,
dreading someone would answer. Dreading no one would.

It rang twice. A man answered in a thick Russian accent: "Yes? Who
is this?"

She repressed a gasp and thought quickly. She remembered one of
the names from her nightmares. "Mikhail. I'd like to speak to Mikhail."
Her heart thundered.

"Impossible." The voice stopped. "What is your name? Who is calling?"

"Just a friend of Mikhail's. When do you think he'll be in? I'll
ring back—"

The receiver went dead.

In the low, boxlike office in the Washington suburb of Arlington,
Ivan Vok stood motionless, still surprised, his beefy hand frozen on the
phone he had slammed down.

Who was that woman? How had she known this very private number? Only a select few knew, and Vok could personally recognize each
voice. In his sports jacket and cotton trousers, his short, hard-packed
frame was a study of controlled strength. He pursed his thick lips and
gazed across to the tall chair where his boss sat behind the big ma-
hogany desk.

"Well, Vok?" he demanded. He had dark hair, a cool, symmetrical
face, and blue-brown eyes. In his mid-fifties, he looked much younger,
with the clean-cut body of a distance swimmer. But what always struck
people about him was his compelling self-confidence. It drew them to
him, and, once they were there, he usually got what he wanted.

Vok said in Russian, "We've got a problem maybe." He repeated the
conversation.

"She asked for Mikhail?" Equally startled, he swore and answered in
Russian. "Perhaps it was a mistake. Or it was someone Mikhail knew
and you didn't learn about."

"Someone Mikhail gave this number to? No way, Alexei." From his exotic Mongolian face to his wide feet, he exuded cold disbelief.

"No, probably not." His boss sighed, annoyed more than worried. "Perhaps someone else gave her the number."

"Possibly." Vok nodded.

"We need to know. You'd better find her. Get everything you can."

"You want me to do it myself?"

He scowled. "No, I need you here. Send your best man."

Ivan Vok said without hesitation, "Nikolai Fedorov." He had trained Fedorov in the old days, back in Moscow.

His chief nodded, watching a fly balance on the edge of his desk. Just as it flew off, he reacted. He grabbed it in midair, crushed it in his fist, and let it fall dead to the floor. He smiled, pleased with himself and his incredible reflexes. "Very well. But tell him to be careful, Ivan Ivanovich. Let's find out if she's a threat before we act. We don't need unnecessary complications. If it turns out she really is a problem, we'll deal with her. But be sure. And change this phone number. We've probably had it too long anyway."

"*Ladno.*" Okay. Vok touched a button. The number from which the woman had dialed appeared on the digital pad next to the telephone. He went to work tracing it.

Jeffrey Hammond hurried out of *The Washington Post* building and into the noisy city night. The moon had risen, and the stars were out, but he paid no attention to anything but the traffic. Tall, lean, and angular, he moved quickly along the sidewalk, occasionally breaking into a trot, toward the corner. As he hurried, he pulled his long brown hair back into a ponytail and snapped a rubber band around it. Everything about him radiated impatience, and his restless gaze examined the bumper-to-bumper traffic on Fifteenth Street with more interest than that of an ordinary pedestrian.

A loud voice called out from behind: "Hey, Jeff! Don't try to run out on me. You damn well know I want to talk to you!"

It was Nate Heithoff. Swearing to himself, Hammond stopped and turned. "First thing tomorrow, Nate. I don't have time now."

"Why the big rush?"

"A hot date, okay? I'm late already." It was a lie he knew Nate would believe.

"One question. Putin's damn press attaché was insulted I didn't know what *rasputitsa* was. What—"

Hammond, who had been answering questions from fellow journalists at the *Post* all day about the forthcoming state visit, interrupted: "It's what Muscovites call spring—their 'mud season.' Sorry, Nate, but I've really got to push it. Don't like to keep a lady waiting. See you tomorrow."

"No problem." The other newsman grinned. "She must be something. Enjoy."

"Right." Hammond hailed a passing taxi, jumped in, and slammed the door.

The driver looked back. "Where to, mister?"

"Just drive ahead. Now."

Hammond watched through the rear window. Nate was still staring after him with the curiosity of all good journalists. As Hammond told the driver to turn at the next corner, he continued to check behind. When it was obvious his colleague had given up, Hammond told the driver to pull to the curb. He paid, got out, and continued cautiously on foot, stopping to gaze in store windows and watch all around.

He was edgy, jumpy, and he knew it. He saw surveillance behind every lamp post, in every darkened doorway. Over the past year there had been more and more episodes of surveillance, and he had begun to read each as a gauge of whether he was closing in or moving away from his target.

When he saw no sign of anyone's tailing him, he hurried around another corner and once more hailed a taxi. He climbed in and directed the driver back and forth, from one street to the next, around blocks, again and again until at last he told him to go to Columbia Road and Eighteenth Street. There in the heart of the multiethnic Adams Morgan district, he paid the driver and left the cab.

Sitar music and the spicy scent of incense floated into the night from one of the funky music clubs. He walked vigilantly among the potpourri of cafés, neighborhood bars, new and used bookstores, music stores, second-hand clothing shops, and nouveau boutiques. He allowed none of his wariness to show. His rugged face was a mask.

With a final glance around, Hammond entered a crowded coffee shop, ordered a double espresso at the counter, and bought a copy of the *Post*. As he gazed casually at the packed tables, he carried the espresso and newspaper back to an empty one at the very rear. He sat down there, sipped his coffee, and read. He never looked up, not even when an older man joined him at his table, uninvited.

Hammond turned his head slightly to the side, opened his newspaper wider, and from his peripheral vision studied the newcomer: Late fifties, sunken cheeks, thin gray hair combed up from the side to cover his bald spot.

Turning a page, apparently engrossed in his reading, Hammond spoke softly, in Russian, "It's been a long time."

"We always know you're there," the balding man answered in Russian. "Tonight. Ten-thirty."

"Where?"

"Meteor Express. It handles transportation—trucking, rail, air, that sort of thing." He recited an address in Arlington. "Don't be late." With that warning, the Russian left, his coffee undrunk, the gray steam curling upward like a ghost.

Hammond, who had never lowered his newspaper, finished his espresso. At last, he folded the paper, placed it neatly on the table, and strolled back out into the Washington night.

Beth's throat tightened, and she froze, her hand on the telephone. Who was the Russian who had answered? She had a moment of complete panic, and then the terror evaporated and a strange quiet came over her. There must be a real Mikhail. That was it. Probably a coincidence. Mikhail was a common Russian name. Mikhail Gorbachev, the last leader of the Soviet Union. Mikhail Glinka, the father of Russian music. There were hundreds of thousands of boys and men in Russia, and now quite a few in America, named Mikhail—"Michael."

But now a voice was attached to the phone number. There had to be a simple explanation for why she had known the number, and she intended to find out.

Because of occasional work for the current administration, Edwards & Bonnett had access to a government online reverse telephone directory, which could be used to backtrack phone numbers and addresses, including those that were unlisted. She keyboarded in her code and looked up the Virginia phone number. Alongside was listed an address in Arlington and the name of a business—Meteor Express—with a brief description. Meteor Express was an international transportation company.

She did not recognize the name, which was odd. She checked Edwards & Bonnett's database, but according to it, she had never represented Meteor Express and neither had any of the firm's other lawyers. Neither the phone number nor the address was in her personal computer address center or in her Rolodex. In the past, she had worked with several transportation companies as they tried to put together deals in former Communist countries; she had also represented Eastern Bloc businesses involved in oil development, insurance, commercial aircraft, voice and data communications, and even franchises for shops in Moscow's metro stations. Until her heart attack, she had been familiar with every international trading and transportation company in the United States, not just in Washington. But she had never heard of Meteor Express.

She collapsed back against her chair. The whole thing gave her a hollow feeling. What should she do? Her own voice answered: *You'll go home and take care of yourself right now, counselor. That's what you'll do. It's late, and you're off your schedule.*

She grabbed her briefcase, turned off the lights, and headed to the elevator, which took her down to the underground parking garage. As she drove across the lighted metropolis to the historic suburb of Georgetown, where her lavender Victorian sat off N Street, she tried to collect herself. She considered again the telephone number and who the Russian stranger might have been. As she parked her Mercedes and let herself into the house, the Virginia phone number no longer assaulted her brain, yet it left an odd void, like a tooth that had been removed while the ache remained.

She flung her briefcase onto her desk in her home office. Feeling caged, she stood at her refrigerator and ate. Then she headed down the hall and up the staircase, stripping off her business suit. She passed beautiful hand-carved wainscoting, cove ceilings, and gleaming wood floors, some of the attributes that had attracted her to this lovely old house. But tonight she was lost in thought, her gaze unseeing. In her bedroom she dressed in white cotton trousers and shirt and wondered for the hundredth time about Meteor Express.

Downstairs in her basement gym, she worked out before a wall of mirrors she'd had installed so she could refine her karate. Eager for endorphins to improve her mood, she kicked and punched. Sweat glistened on her face. Her cheeks turned rosy. Her short blond hair matted against her head. Her hands and feet slashed the air. In the mirror, she was a blond dynamo in white, without an apparent worry in the world.

She loved karate and had taken to it quickly. Always a runner, she found that her rhythmic pace had translated easily into the fluidity she needed for this new sport. After the first month, she began lifting weights, too, so her upper body would develop strength compatible with that of her legs. Karate had become her exercise of choice, and, as she had told Zach Housley, she would soon earn her black belt.

An hour later, she felt light and exhilarated, although she had found no answers. Although she had not erased the fact that it was not just any stranger who had answered the phone: The man had had a Russian accent.

She quit and climbed upstairs, feeling an eerie sense of inevitability. She could ignore this situation no longer. She had to put to rest all the intrusive thoughts and strange ideas that had begun after her surgery. She could not live as if constantly under siege. No one could, not really. Not if they wanted to get out and have a full, interesting life. Then she had an idea: Perhaps if she saw the Meteor Express building, she would recognize it. Determined, she showered, changed clothes, and found her purse. She was going to Meteor Express.

Special Agent Elias Kirkhart had barely seconds to decide whom to follow from the Adams Morgan coffeehouse—Jeff Hammond or Anatoli Yurimengri.

It had all begun earlier, when Kirkhart had gotten lucky and pulled into an empty parking space across from *The Washington Post*. From there he had waited, watching, until at last Hammond had rushed out the newspaper's front entrance. After a brief conversation with another man, Hammond hailed a taxi.

Kirkhart tailed the first taxi but not the second, losing it finally in the congestion of the downtown streets. He swore aloud in frustration. Hammond was still damn good, he had to admit that, but were Hammond's actions anything more than the automatic precautions of a trained agent? Could Hammond have spotted him? He shook his head. No, he decided. The only mistake he made was coming up with nothing again. It was the downside of intelligence work that movies and novels seldom showed—the monotony, the routine, the endless waiting that were the backbone of an operation's success.

Kirkhart drove through the District, hoping that, by some miracle, he would spot his quarry. Since he and Hammond had met in the old *yavka* shopping center a year ago, he had continued to compile information, search the Bureau's archives for blown missions and agents, and send members of his small, undercover team to make random checks on General Berianov and his close associate, Colonel Yurimengri, in case Hammond made contact. There was no news about Ivan Vok either, who was apparently still safely in Russia. An operation like this—finding the traitor who had been riddling the FBI from within for years, perhaps decades—could mean several more years of work. But the mole had to be found.

Kirkhart took the assignment personally. But then, he always did. The phenomenon of "emotional attachment" happened occasionally in the covert business, most often among field agents. Two years ago he had been warned he might have it. A Bureau shrink explained some agents had a deep need to belong and believe. Then when you added peril and privation, they could go off the deep end, supporting extreme causes and chasing unattainable goals. They said he seemed to fit that profile and he should let them help him get over it.

It had made him laugh. Because he was frustrated, the idiots wanted to diagnose him with a borderline mental disease. He wondered what they would think now, because he was ready to explode with aggravation. Where in hell had Hammond gone?

He was continuing to drive haphazardly through downtown, still swearing to himself, when a call came in on his private cell phone.

"Caligari here, Eli. That Colonel Yurimengri you sent me after is sittin' in a coffee shop in Adams Morgan with some guy. They're not talking to each other so's you can see, but it looks like a secret meet to me. I think the other party's Jeff Hammond."

As Eli Kirkhart listened to Carlos Caligari's Midwestern drawl, he remembered Jeff's complaints about his own accent with its slight tilt toward England. Jeff had always been too critical, and now perhaps that criticism had turned against the United States itself. "Indeed? I'm on my way." This was what made for success, he reminded himself with satisfaction: Preparation. Thoroughness. Persistence. Because he had sent his agents out to watch Berianov and Yurimengri tonight, he had results. Perhaps not what he had expected, but, with luck, maybe something even better.

He arrived at the coffee shop in Adams Morgan seconds before Yurimengri came out. He had just enough time to determine that the other man was really Jeff Hammond before he had to decide which one to tail. If what he suspected were true, it was more likely Hammond who would have given information to Yurimengri, not the other way around. Now he needed to know where Yurimengri would take it.

"You follow Hammond," he ordered Caligari. "I'll pick up on Yurimengri."

Yurimengri proved relatively simple to tail, which surprised Kirkhart. He had never found any KGB man easy. Either Yurimengri thought he had nothing to hide, or Kirkhart had read the situation wrong. Both possibilities worried Kirkhart, since they suggested his quarry was nothing more than what he purported to be now—an American businessman. That might mean Jeff Hammond's connection to the former Soviet official was simply his years-long obsession.

Kirkhart followed Yurimengri across the Potomac River and into an industrial area of Arlington, where he turned into a drive that ran alongside an aluminum-sided building with two large windows and a glass door in front. The sign on the building read: METEOR EXPRESS, INC. Venetian blinds covered both windows and the door, giving Kirkhart no view inside. A CLOSED sign showed on the door. He parked in the black shadow of a tree, turned off his motor, and waited. No one other than Yurimengri went near the building, and no one left.

After two hours, he decided to take what he knew back to the Hoover building where he could check out Meteor Express. As he drove away, his cell phone rang again.

It was Carlos Caligari, making a report: "Hammond went straight as birdshot back to his office."

"Still there, I presume?"

"Hasn't come out."

"Stay where you are. I'll be there shortly."

When he arrived, he sent Caligari home, and an hour later began to regret it. It was past eight o'clock, and Kirkhart had had no dinner. At nine o'clock, he walked in through the lobby entrance. The security guard at the lobby desk checked his manifest and told him Hammond had signed out. Kirkhart swore again, but not as hard this time. At least he had a lead—Meteor Express.

Moonlight shone in an unearthly silver glow over the bustling highway into Virginia that Tuesday night. Although it was late—nearly 10:30 P.M.—the perpetual rhythm of the nation's capital seemed to pulse in the streaking red and white lights of vehicles. In her green Mercedes CLK 320, Beth Convey pulled off George Washington Memorial Parkway and headed south. Driving her small but powerful sedan, she passed gaudy strip malls, neon-decorated bars, motels with dirty vacancy signs, dark banks, and fluorescent-lighted gas stations that made her think of Edward Hopper paintings.

She was resolved. Enough was enough. "So do you know where you are?" she asked her fast-beating heart. A sad and uneasy mood settled over her. She did not recall being in this part of sprawling, unincorporated Arlington, but she had an odd sense she had.

She cruised past a lumber yard and there it was: An aluminum-sided building with a painted sign attached over the front doors told her she had found Meteor Express. She paused her car on the quiet street in front, hoping for a sense she had been there before, a flash of recognition.

But all she felt was curiosity. This was the first time she had seen this place, she was sure. As she studied the building, she noticed dim light seeping out around the blinds on the door and two windows. Perhaps a cleaning crew or some ambitious executive. Anyone, it did not matter. She would talk to anyone. She had to know what, if any, connection she had to Meteor Express.

She parked, got out, and locked her car. This was a light-industrial zone, with other large, warehouse-style buildings dotting the long block. The street was shadowy, and traffic was a distant hum. The spring air smelled of diesel exhaust, like a deserted late-night truck stop in the middle of the Mojave.

A sense of foreboding fell over her, but she shrugged it away. She had to know. She dropped her keys into her shoulder bag and walked toward the building, where concrete-block planters beneath each window held struggling juniper bushes. She climbed concrete steps and searched all around for a doorbell. There was none, so she knocked on the glass door. She waited. No answer.

She impatiently tapped her foot then knocked again. Still no response. Around the Venetian blinds she could see what looked like office furniture. At last she tried the door. It was unlocked.

She pushed it open. "Hello!" She paused in the open doorway and called out again. "Is anyone here?"

Somewhere a digital clock clicked. The small, colored lights of communications equipment glowed on the shadowy desks behind the counter. She padded forward, her muscles loose, as she had been trained in karate, heading toward a glow of light at the end of the central corridor. She passed closed doors and stepped into a large back room with two more desks—these were wood, far more expensive than the metal ones in front—and more doors. Two desk lamps poured ivory funnels of light onto piles of paper where people had recently been at work.

It was strange, as if the room had been deserted at a moment's notice. A chill shot up her spine. She was just about to call out again when she heard a low, pained moan. Someone was hurt. Then she saw shoes, toes pointed up, legs spraddled. She pushed aside her nervousness and ran around the first desk to see whether she could help. Behind it lay a man in a pool of blood, a ragged red wound on his white shirt. The primeval odors of blood and sweat assaulted her in a wave of shock. Somehow, they were familiar. Carnal odors she had smelled before. When? Where?

She rushed to kneel beside him, remembering that just a year ago strangers had saved her life in the courthouse. He was in his late fifties, with cavernous cheeks and gray hair he had kept long at one side to comb up over his bald spot. She was sure she had never seen him. She was equally sure she recognized him.

She felt another chill. Maybe he was from her nightmares. Yes. She was certain. He had been one of the men sitting around the campfire. A name flashed into her mind. *Yuri.*

"Yuri?" she whispered.

When she said the name, his eyes snapped open. They were glazed and watery, intense. He grabbed her arm and squeezed. "I . . . didn't . . . know."

As blood bubbled at the corner of his mouth, she heard the faint sound of footsteps somewhere in the distance. In an instant, her trance was over. Somehow she had lulled herself into a dangerous situation. The shooter might still be here.

"I'm going to phone for help, Yuri. You need a doctor." She tried to pull away, but the man's grip tightened.

His pale eyes were compelling, demanding she pay attention. He seemed to summon energy. He forced the words out: "I didn't realize about . . . Stone Point . . . West Virginia." It was almost an apology. Seeking the understanding or the forgiveness of whoever he thought she was.

She asked, "What didn't you know?"

His hand fell away. His eyes were still open, but the light inside vanished. Flicked off as completely as an electric circuit. Some part of her mind recognized he had just died. She was motionless with horror at his death . . . and then with shock at what she had done by walking in here. How could she have been so careless? So stupid? The man had been murdered, and she could be shortly, too. Was this more insanity from all her medications . . . or from her new, dangerous heart?

She closed his eyelids, feeling a stab of regret for his death, and jumped up. But in an instant, all her questions evaporated in fear because the footsteps had returned, and this time they were distinct. The door to her right—behind the desk where the dead man lay—swung open. As she turned to leave, she glimpsed someone emerge from the shadows of the darkened doorway, pistol first. *The killer.*

Terrified, she sprinted back down the corridor the way she had come. She heard steps pounding after her. Terror clogged her chest. She could hardly breathe. She burst around the desks, tore around the counter, and hit the metal bar on the front door with all her strength. It slammed open, and she was outside, running for her car. For her life.

She could hear him thundering in pursuit. She called upon all her new muscles and put on a burst of speed. Strange sounds erupted behind her. Sounds she could not quite identify. It could be a violent scuffle, or perhaps her pursuer had stumbled and fallen.

As she neared the curb, she turned. In the silvery moonlight, she saw his profile clearly. She burned his image into her brain. *The killer.* He had a straight forehead, an aquiline nose, and a jutting chin. He wore some kind of baseball cap. She would never forget—

She dug into her purse for her keys and turned to escape to her car. But her foot landed off-balance on the street curb, and she tripped and fell. The street's asphalt seemed to slam upwards. It hit her with the velocity of a speeding car. Violent, throbbing colors assaulted her. Great sheets of blinding green, exploding red, sickening purple, and black . . . deep black . . . endless black . . .

Beth awoke with a start, drenched with sweat, trying to push a new nightmare from her mind. She threw an arm over her closed eyes. She could see it still in all its horror: The dark night, but an office this time. A Russian again, his face twisted in pain as he died there on the floor. There was a sense of danger everywhere. She remembered the sound of footsteps and the realization they could belong to the murderer. She had rushed away. And he had chased her, faster and faster. She shuddered. Why had the bad dreams not stopped, as Dr. Jackson had promised?

She sighed and rolled onto her side on the hard bed. And paused. This was not her bed. It was overly firm in the way of cheap mattresses that gave little real support, only backaches and stiff joints in the morning. Her eyes snapped open, and she sat up. Her mouth turned dry with fear. She did not recognize the room.

Two lines of sunlight from either side of the drapes sliced the shadowy gloom. There was an odor of cheap floral chemicals coming from an open door to her right—the bathroom. Where was she?

She ached everywhere. That could happen when she did not take her medicine on time—a side effect and her personal warning she needed her antirejection and anti-inflammatory drugs. Alarmed, she looked around for a clock. What time was it? How late was she with taking her pills?

She flung back the bed covers and searched the gloomy, unfamiliar room for her shoulder bag. She always kept her meds in it as well as a second set at home as a precaution. But she was not home.

Then she saw her bag: On a low table next to the window. Also on the desk stood a digital clock—8:03 A.M. She counted out medication and hurried into the bathroom. Plastic drinking glasses wrapped in more plastic stood on a ledge above the sink. She ripped off the outer protective coating with her teeth, filled the glass with water, and swallowed pills, one after the other. As she did, she caught sight of herself in the mirror.

Smudged crescents of mascara beneath her eyes made her slender face look pasty and obsessed. Her blue eyes had a dark quality, almost as if they had been bruised. A dark-red lump marked her forehead. She stared. Gingerly she touched the inflamed tissue. It hurt like hell.

Then it all came back. The dead man. The office. Her desperate running away and her fall. It had been no nightmare. She really had been running away from Meteor Express and the dead man on the floor. *Yuri.* Trying to escape from the murderer who pursued her through the building. She looked back and memorized his profile then . . . stumbled. Slammed into the pavement—

Where was she now? How had she gotten here?

She returned to the bedroom and pushed back the drape. She was on the second floor of a motel—The Biden Rest, according to the tall pole sign. Cars flew past on the street below, the ongoing symptom of a metropolis never fully at rest. The traffic was high-octane now. At a little past 8:00 A.M., the Wednesday-morning rush hour was at full throttle inside the Beltway.

She watched uneasily. Her fall while fleeing the murderer last night must have knocked her unconscious. But why had he not killed her? She breathed deeply. She must stay calm. On the edge of her consciousness she could feel a violent rage building. She would not let that control her. She had to think and analyze.

She returned to the desk and opened her shoulder bag again. Everything was inside—lipstick, compact, tissues, comb, her billfold with the credit cards and cash. Nothing had been stolen.

She looked down at herself. She was dressed in the same clothes she had worn last night—beige linen trousers, a white cotton T-shirt, and a celery-green zippered jacket. She was rumpled and messy, but whoever had brought her here had removed her Nikes, lined them up neatly beside the bed, turned down the sheets, laid her down fully dressed, and covered her. She had been neither raped nor robbed. She inhaled deeply, grateful.

Under the clear April sky, Beth marched across the motel parking lot to her Mercedes. It was a fifty-thousand-dollar vehicle with a kick-butt V-6 engine, an easy cruising speed of 120 miles an hour, and an all-leather interior that smelled as rich and inviting as a summer shower. The Mercedes was a natural target for thieves, vandals, and addicts of fine imported cars. She examined it from fender to fender, then front seat and back. Nothing had been taken. No scratch or dent indicated mistreatment. Someone had carefully parked and locked it.

Relieved but even more puzzled, she closed the door. Her stomach rumbled with hunger, but she was on a quest. She scanned the motel and parking lot. A plate-glass window looked out onto the street, and the sign over the door next to it announced OFFICE. From the cracked concrete, faded paint, and cheap accoutrements, this motel was obviously on the lower end of Washington's tourist food chain, but her room had been clean, the door lock had worked, and the insulation had been sufficiently good that she had been able to spend the night quietly in deep slumber. She headed toward the office.

Inside, behind a Formica-topped counter, sat a gray-haired woman, working at a computer. She looked up as Beth pushed through the door. She had the kind of good-natured face that was perfect for service-oriented businesses. She gave a lazy smile, showing a lot of gray-metal dental work, and dismissed Beth's crumpled, slept-in clothes with a flicker of her short eyelashes.

She said, "Can I help you, miss?"

"I hope so." How did she begin to explain? "I stayed here last night. I wonder whether you recognize me."

The woman blinked. "That depends, honey. When did you check in?"

"You don't remember me?"

"Should I?"

To the receptionist, she was just one more in an ocean of faces. Apparently nothing had distinguished her arrival, or surely this woman would recall or have been told about it.

"I got here between ten-thirty and eleven-thirty last night," Beth said. "Room two-thirty-four. Someone brought me."

"Someone?" She cocked her head to study her. "You really don't know?"

"I don't. But I'd like to. And no, I'm not on drugs, and I don't drink enough alcohol to make a crow stagger. I thought you might like it if I paid my bill."

At that, the woman smiled again in her naturally easy way. "Guess I'm curious, too. I didn't come on until eight this morning. Our night man would've registered you. You know your name at least, don't you?" She turned back to the computer and touched keys.

"Thank God, yes."

"Um-hum." As the monitor settled into a pattern, the woman leaned forward and made a little grunt of surprise. "You sure about the room number, honey?"

"Yes. Two-three-four. Whose name is it registered under?"

The woman looked up, and for the first time doubt touched her face. "No one. According to our records, no one stayed in that room last night."

Beth cruised through the streets of Arlington in her Mercedes, watching all around, wondering who knew what had really happened to her last night.

Before Beth had left the motel, the receptionist phoned the night man, who confirmed no one had checked into 234 last night. After she hung up, the woman confided the man had a drinking problem and could easily have been passed out by 10:30. Unless someone had persisted at the office doorbell, he would not have awakened.

Which made Beth realize she had seen no key in her room. But the door's lock had not been broken. Whoever deposited her there had gotten a key somehow, probably from the office, then locked the door going out and carried the key away.

There was only one place she could think to go for answers: Meteor Express. The police would surely have been there an hour or more, following the frantic call of whatever employee had discovered the dead man this morning. She needed to tell them what she had witnessed, and in return she would get information. Tense and worried, she checked her watch. She had just enough time before her meeting with Michele Philmalee at 10:00 A.M.

As she drove on, it almost seemed as if she were a stranger in her own life. It outraged her. "Heart, are you listening? If you once belonged to some creep, remember he's gone now. You're mine. If you're behind all this, stop it!"

She could not believe she was talking to her heart. Her mind searched back through time, looking for clues. Trying to make sense of the impossible. For a year she had believed her doctor. But now she had the coincidence of a Russian who had answered the phone number. Then the murdered man, who if he were not 'Yuri,' at least responded to the name.

She shook her head. It was absurd. Ridiculous. But then there was Stephanie Smith, who had visited her in the hospital a month after her surgery and who had not thought it impossible that transplant recipients might inherit some things from their donors. Maybe she had been wrong to dismiss Dr. Smith so easily.

As she turned her car onto Meteor Express's street, she sighed, remembering how sure she had been that the nightmares and intrusive thoughts would go away. She wanted badly to interview the Russian who had answered the telephone yesterday. There had to be some logical explanation for everything.

As she sped along the street, she realized she had somehow missed Meteor Express. Annoyed, she backtracked, and . . . discovered the low-lying, aluminum-sided building where Meteor Express had been last night now held a new sign: RENAE TRUCKING SERVICES. She slammed into a parking place, jumped out of her car, and hurried to it.

At the big front windows, the horizontal blinds had disappeared, and in their place hung vertical wood slats. Even the junipers had been pulled from the planters. In their places, a man in jeans and a stained American University sweatshirt was planting red geraniums. A moving van stood in the entry drive, and men were carrying desks, chairs, and lamps into the front of the building.

She pushed her way inside. "Who's in charge here?" The counter was still where she remembered, but on the other side stood new desks.

"I am." A woman walked toward her from the corridor that ran into the back where Yuri's body had lain last night. In her forties, she carried a clipboard and was dressed in jeans, a mock turtleneck, and a long canvas duster. "My name's Cass Joneson. Owner of Renae Trucking. What can I do for you?" She rotated on her heel to instruct a man placing a desk, "No, Sam. Move it more to your right. Yes. That's where I want it. We need space. That's where the copier's got to go."

Her movements were brisk and self-assured. She wore her brown hair smoothed back into an efficient bun. No makeup graced her face, which was angular and oddly thin, as if the food she ate was never in her system long enough to nourish her.

She studied Beth and her crumpled clothes. "You don't look too good. Do you need help? Or is it business? We're not quite set up, but I can answer questions and take a small order. The computers will be back online this afternoon."

It boggled the mind. For an instant Beth questioned herself. But just as quickly she erased any doubts. "I was here last night. This place was Meteor Express then. In fact, I talked to a man named Yuri. Where is he now?" *Where was his corpse?*

Cass Joneson frowned. "Don't recognize the name. We rented the building a month ago, and I've been planning the transition ever since.

Today's the day. Started moving in at five A.M. No one can afford to be out of business long. Like I said, our computers will be operating soon. If you need trucking services, this is the place."

Beth stared. Then she pushed past the woman and trotted down the corridor.

"Hey." Cass Joneson followed. "You can't go back there. That's private!"

Beth stopped on the empty spot where she had knelt over the dying Yuri. Sorrow for his savage end tightened her throat. But as she stared down and realized what she was seeing, anger and frustration replaced the sorrow. She was standing on new Armstrong flooring that looked like Spanish tiles but was really rolled-out, high-gloss linoleum. Underneath would be tar adhesive. And that tar would hide whatever traces of blood had been left by Yuri's mortal chest wound.

She looked quickly around, but of course there was no sign of a corpse. The building's transformation was too convenient. She did not believe any of it.

"Where is he?" she demanded. "Where's Yuri's body?" Rage churned her chest.

Cass Joneson glared. "What in hell are you talking about? Are you crazy? You look like you're crazy to me. Get out of here!" She moved closer to Beth. "Sam! Come back here. We've got trouble!"

White-hot fury enveloped Beth, and she made no effort to fight it. She saw the top third of a cell phone peeking out of the woman's duster pocket. It did not take an Einstein to figure out this one.

With a swift backhand *haishu* to the woman's chest, Beth pushed her to the side and snagged the telephone.

"Sam!" the woman bellowed. But fear clouded her gaze. She made no move to retrieve the phone. Beth realized the woman was afraid of her. "Hurry up!"

Feet pounded in the corridor, bearing down on them.

Beth swung to face two men. "Stop!" she ordered and spread her feet in a flexed-knee karate stance, on the alert, ready to attack or defend. "Don't anyone think of touching me. We'll let the police sort this out!"

As she punched 911, she saw the men's faces change. They had looked at her and seen something in her that worried them. Frightened them. She had never before physically frightened anyone in her life, but she had now. With a sinking feeling, she felt her heart pound excitedly against her ribs.

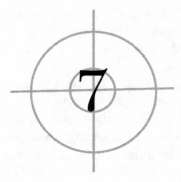

If you were a Washington attorney and wanted to report a murder, you could expect fast service. As a regular Joe or Joanna Citizen, you were likely to get decent attention, too, but there was something about the mantle of The Law—and the name of a marquee firm like Edwards & Bonnett—that conferred a guarantee of sorts. Which was why within five minutes of Beth's talking to a 911 operator, a white-and-blue squad car from the Arlington County Police Department screeched to a stop in front of what less than twelve hours before had been Meteor Express.

Before the flashing blinkers could be extinguished, two more squad cars arrived. Beth told the officers everything that had happened. They listened and questioned patiently, but after that it was all downhill.

Cass Joneson claimed she had been the one who had unlocked the door before dawn. She had found nothing but an empty building. Her employees were shocked anyone would suggest a bloody corpse had been left for them to discover. Of course, there had been no dead person on the premises, inside or out.

Beth could not say for certain even that *Yuri* was the victim's name. To humor her, one of the Arlington officers checked with headquarters. The answer was not what she wanted to hear: No Yuri Somebody with a gunshot wound to the chest had been found in the last twenty-four hours in the county, dead or alive. He asked for any other male with the same wound. Negative again.

Undeterred, Beth convinced them to check both Meteor Express's and Renae Trucking's bona fides. It turned out both companies were licensed and appeared legitimate. One of the policemen phoned Meteor, and its spokesman denied ever having been located at that address in Arlington. The lady must be mistaken.

After that, she had no more ammunition. The police filed out. Two were shaking their heads in disgust.

The last, an older officer, took Beth aside. "I'm sorry, ma'am." He was trying to remain neutral. "You know all about the elements of proof. Without any witness but yourself, we've got to have a corpse to take this investigation further." He peered closely at her, his gaze narrowing as he pointedly looked her up and down, silently reminding her of how disheveled she looked. "Are you sure you're feeling all right?"

"I'm fine. Really."

"Please don't take this wrong, ma'am, but making a false report is a crime. Also, you scared Ms. Joneson and her crew quite a bit. They felt very threatened. They've agreed not to press charges, for now. I'm sure you believe you made a legitimate report and were justified in your behavior with them, so we'll just chalk this whole episode up as a mistake. But—no disrespect—maybe you should see a doctor. Or a psychologist."

Her blood was ice. Her tongue was thick with incomprehensibility. She summoned all her strength to put on a strained smile and dismiss him without losing her temper. "I appreciate your concern, officer. In turn, you remember there's a man around here who's been shot to death. He was wearing a white shirt and dark trousers. He was pretty much bald, with a lot of gray hair on one side he combed up over the top of his head. His name may have been Yuri. Watch for him. I know what I saw."

Outraged and disgusted, she brushed past and stalked outdoors and up the street to her car. She yanked open the door, slid furiously behind the wheel—and remembered Michelle Philmalee. She looked at her watch—10:15.

Fear knocked the breath from her. *She was late for her meeting with Michelle.*

Beth raced her powerful Mercedes through Arlington and onto the bridge that would take her into the District. Her pulse thundered. Her lungs were a claustrophobic knot. She checked her watch again. Now she was a half-hour late, and by the time she reached the firm's headquarters near the White House, she would be even later. If she peeled off to her house in Georgetown to pick up her briefcase with the papers that named the Russian owners of HanTech Industries, her chance to

win back Michelle would certainly be gone, because there was no way
Michelle would wait around the firm's offices much longer. In fact, considering Phil's influence, Michelle had likely left by now.

She gripped the steering wheel, wishing for a cell phone so she could
call ahead. Her foot heavy on the accelerator, she pushed her Mercedes
on over the bridge and into downtown. What she did not need was a
speeding ticket. Still, she continued to speed. She had to get to the
meeting as quickly as possible.

She passed car after car, watching her rearview mirror for police.
She careened along Washington's streets, always on the lookout for
squad cars, pedestrians in crosswalks, and openings in the traffic. She
checked her watch again, and her stomach sank: 10:51.

How could she have allowed herself to be so distracted that she had
forgotten the time? She shook the steering wheel and swore. She was
driving recklessly, something she never did, but it seemed the only thing
to do. And she was good at it. She drove with a skill that amazed her—
darting the Mercedes between cars, slipping from lane to lane with precision, hitting the accelerator the instant a light turned green, and
rocketing ahead of pack after pack.

When she reached the kiosk to the garage under the firm's building,
she snatched the ticket and roared inside to a spot near the elevator. It
was not a real parking place, but she did not care. She clicked off the
ignition, jumped out, and impatiently rode the elevator up to the six-
teenth floor. Her hands were tight knots at her sides.

She tried to take deep breaths. She made a vigorous effort to collect
her thoughts. But how in hell was she going to apologize enough . . .
convince Michelle to give her another chance . . . put up with that
smarmy I-told-you-so grin she knew would be plastered on Phil Stageman's face . . . give up her dream of becoming a partner in Edwards &
Bonnett—

The shiny brass elevator doors began to open, and she readied herself to leap out and rush to the conference room.

"Beth?" It was Phil. His handsome, dimpled chin dropped in surprise. "Well, you're here. Very late, but here."

There were three of them talking together in the foyer of the elegant
law office, a trio in freeze-frame beneath a massive brass chandelier.
Phil was facing Beth, looking dapper in a young-Washington-lawyer
sort of way. Michelle had her back half-turned. Today she wore a
solemn black Yves St. Laurent suit, equally appropriate for Big Business or a state funeral. Deep in conversation with her was Zach Housley. He had on one of his usual suits with the baggy pockets—his

distinctive trademark that signaled the power he wielded not only in the firm but within the Beltway. In the legal profession, only the crème de la crème could afford to look like nobodies.

As soon as Phil said Beth's name, Zach and Michelle turned to stare.

"I'm sorry." Beth stepped out of the elevator.

"What happened?" Zach Housley cocked his bullet-shaped head. His imperious gaze swept over her clothes and settled narrow-eyed on her face. "You must've taken a wrong turn, Beth. The canoeing club's down on the river." He was angry. Not only was she an hour late for a meeting with a top client, she was dressed unacceptably in sporty clothes that were also wrinkled and messy. But he would never chastise a firm lawyer in front of a client—not out of any sensitivity to the lawyer, but because it would make the firm look bad. Instead, he had made a joke, and she got the point.

Beth tried to smile. "It's a long story. Entertaining, too. I'm sure you'll understand when I explain. Right now, I need to—"

Phil interrupted curtly, "Michelle, we'd better go. You have that appointment—"

Michelle waved her hand, silencing everyone. "I don't care what she looks like. I don't care that she's appallingly late. I want to know whether she's got the goods on HanTech." Her sharp gaze behind her round-rimmed glasses focused on Beth. "Do you have what you promised me?"

Beth's chest seemed to cave in. If her life last night had been normal, she would have studied the list of names and quietly planned how to present and use them to Michelle. This morning, she would have arrived hours ago, prepared and eager, and gotten quite a bit of other work done before the meeting. Instead, she had found a dying man, slept in a strange motel room for which no one was registered, and then discovered not only the corpse had vanished this morning, so had the entire company that rented the building.

Would Michelle, Zach, and Phil believe any of it? The Arlington police certainly had not. Which meant all she could do was forge ahead and rely on the exemplary work she had done for Michelle and the firm in the past: "As I said, it's a long story. Right now, what's important to you is I do have the evidence."

The corners of Michelle's small lips turned up in a smile. "Good. Where is it?"

"In my briefcase."

"Not in there?" She stared pointedly at Beth's shoulder bag, her only accessory.

"Unfortunately, no. I had to drive here directly so I'd catch you. I didn't have time to go to my house. That's where I left my briefcase last night."

"Last night?" Michelle's voice rose. "You took my list home—a list that could make the difference to me of hundreds of millions of dollars—and then you spent the night somewhere else? Let me be sure I understand clearly. You *forgot* my list?"

"I didn't forget. When I explain what happened—"

Michelle shook her head. "Of course you didn't forget. I know you far too well to believe that. You're Ms. Fix-it. Win the argument or the case no matter what. You don't make stupid mistakes like forgetting evidence." Her eyes narrowed, and she accused, "You're stalling. You don't have the list at all. Probably it doesn't even exist. Phil's right. This is just one of your ploys to buy time until you come up with something—anything—to convince me to leave him."

Beth bit back her rage. "That's not true. Remember everything I've done for you, Michelle. You know I've always played it straight. You owe me this. I'll drive home right away—"

But Michelle's voice was as sharp as the chop of an axe. *"No."* In business, you had to know when to cut your losses. "Phil, dear, you were right. I *am* running terribly late, aren't I? We'd better move along." She nodded curtly at Zach Housley, her face grave. "Good-bye, Zach. Let me reassure you: As long as Phil is willing to work closely with me, I expect to have a long and lucrative relationship with Edwards & Bonnett."

That was it: The death knell for Beth's return to the firm's partnership track. Phil had pulled ahead, the winner.

"Michelle—" Beth began.

"Don't even try." Michelle lifted her chin and stepped onto the elevator, Phil close behind. They turned toward each other, heads close, talking seriously. As the doors closed, Phil's handsome features radiated a look of utter triumph.

Beth turned slowly to face Zach. "I know this looks bad."

He glanced across to the receptionist, who was trying to appear busy. Other than her, they were alone in the foyer, which was decorated with hand-tufted sofas and chairs, oil landscapes from the late 1800s, and antique Queen Anne tables. Tasteful and expensive. A showplace, but then that was what the firm expected and demanded. After all, it had an international position to uphold. For the first time, Beth saw how nicely the fine furnishings disguised superficiality.

He lowered his voice. "It *is* bad. Very bad. Right now, I'm furious with you. This was a clear-cut situation. All you had to do was produce your data. I think you're right—Phil could be facing a political situation that might cost us Michelle's lawsuit. The 'national security' excuse is old, but it still works. But now, because of your carelessness, we don't have another way to win. Instead of saving the day, you've failed completely." His eyes were black with fury, but just as if he were trying a difficult case, he kept his tones under complete control. "However, since I'm sympathetic with what you've been through in your illness, I'll make no rash decisions. I'm going to walk into my office, close the door, and contemplate your future. I will, of course, eventually consult the partners." He indulged in a frown. She had made the firm look very bad. "Don't pursue any other Edwards & Bonnett cases or clients until I get back to you. That's an order."

His message was clear: He would not fire her, but not because he was being smart or magnanimous. As she had predicted, he would demote her and turn her into an object of pity, while making the firm look good in Washington legal circles for keeping on a poor, befuddled former star.

She did not bother to hide the steel in her voice. "I have the information at home we need to save Michelle's deal, just as I said. Yet you're ready to destroy my career. After all the impossible negotiations I've won for this firm, the fragile agreements I've held together, the clients I've attracted, the sleepless nights of research, the missed vacations . . . now you're threatening to take away my work because I've made one mistake."

Zach Housley arched back his head and peered down his nose at her. Associates were not exactly scum on the totem pole of the firm's hierarchy, but they were close. His voice was as hard as hers: "If I say the firm no longer needs your services, Ms. Convey, security will have you out the door in five seconds. Never forget you are but one among hundreds of attorneys. I will see you tomorrow. Then I will let you know whether you have a future at Edwards & Bonnett."

As he glowered, it became clear that he understood at least one thing: Her priorities had changed. This morning she had been far more interested in finding out what her bizarre experiences meant than she was in meeting with Michelle. In fact, her drive to make partner was beginning to seem beside the point. Did she really want to be a member of a firm managed by a jackass like Zach Housley?

Inside Beth, something snapped. She was disgusted, fed up. Her voice cut like an arctic wind. "You've just given me very little reason to care." Her lip curled. "What's that awful odor I smell? Ah, now I recognize it. Decayed principles. Superficiality has its price. You really must clean out your sewer lines more often."

His eyebrows shot up. "You're fired."

She let rage pour into her face and voice, and the legendary Zach Housley stepped back, intimidated. "In your dreams. I quit five minutes ago when you refused to back me with Michelle. If you had, I'd be on my way home now. And in an hour, you'd have the bullets you need to win Michelle's case. Who's the screw-up here? Who's *really* hurt the firm? Go look in a mirror, Zach. You're worse than a pompous fool and bigot. You're *incompetent.*"

His heavy-cheeked face was stunned. "I—" He was speechless.

She turned on her heel and strode back toward the elevator, her footfalls soundless in the plush carpeting, her muscles rippling.

Behind her she heard an angry, guttural sound, then the closing of the door to Zach's office suite. She felt a massive feeling of release. Of freedom. Zach had never quite adjusted to having women and minorities on the firm's letterhead. She had believed he had put his prejudices behind him if for no other reason than it was practical. In the District's competitive legal environment there was usually a leveler—results. If you won enough, you were a winner. If you lost, you were a loser. Whether you wore a skirt or trousers, whether your skin was white or black, whether your religion was Protestantism or animism. Nothing, ultimately, mattered but results.

She had always been a winner. Now Zach was trying to turn her into a loser because of another factor in District legal circles—the power to be as much of a jerk as he pleased. To hell with him.

"Beth?"

It was the soft voice of the receptionist, Joleen. She was a faded redhead with careful eyes and a brightly painted pink mouth. She leaned forward over her busy desk. One hand rested next to the day's stack of *The Washington Post,* one of the perks the firm offered its attorneys. With the other hand, she beckoned Beth.

As Beth approached, Joleen whispered, "You've quit? Good for you. But I hate to see you go. . . . "

While Joleen talked on, Beth caught sight of a photo on the *Post*'s front page. She snatched up the copy. In the picture, a man stood at some party, a cocktail in his hand. He had sunken cheeks and gray hair brushed up over the top of his bald head. Her pulse raced with excitement. She was certain: It was the dead man from last night. Quickly she read the headline and photo caption, which told her his corpse had been found in the District—miles from Arlington where she had discovered him. His name was Anatoli Yurimengri. She paused over the name, thinking about it: *Yuri*mengri.

According to the piece, Washington police were investigating his murder as a homicide committed during robbery. He was a Soviet defector who had made a fortune in the machinery-parts business in post-Cold War Russia and America. It was a fine analysis, full of detail. She noted the journalist's byline: Jeffrey Hammond.

She raised her gaze to the receptionist, who had paused. She gave her a distracted but friendly smile. "Thanks, Joleen. I've got to go." The newspaper under her arm, she strode away. When she told Zach that she quit, she'd had no idea what she was going to do next. Now she knew.

"Beth!" Joleen called after her. "You'll be at home if Mr. Housley wants to talk?"

"I'm going to see a man about a dead Russian. Tell Zach he can leave a message on my machine. Everyone knows he loves the sound of his own voice."

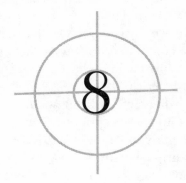

Shadowy hollows and gray, weathered barns advertising chewing tobacco appeared intermittently along the pitted asphalt road that
snaked east out of Stone Point, West Virginia. Only a few miles beyond the tiny town, the road climbed past a forest of leafy beeches and
old maples so close together they were a sieve between the sun and the
earth. Finally it dead-ended at a double-wide metal gate that was
topped with barbed wire and locked. No one was in sight, and no sign
indicated what lay beyond. But anyone with the right skills would soon
locate the hidden cameras and sensors that provided visual and electronic surveillance.

Locals knew this secluded piece of the Appalachian Mountains had
been the site of constant activity for the past three years, with hunting en-
thusiasts coming and going, often in packs. It was called Bates Hunt Club.

The mountain people figured the owner of the club's thousand timbered acres—Colonel Caleb Bates—had to be a millionaire at least. He
had completely surrounded his property with a chain-link fence topped
by concertina wire, although everyone else found the dense Appalachian foliage provided plenty of privacy. But even more unusual
was the expense. In Stone Point's two competing cafés, the villagers
gossiped about how much surveying, digging the post holes, and putting up the barrier must have set Bates back. But no one asked. In this
hardscrabble land of food stamps and spotty government assistance,
not intruding on another's business was as inbred as the poverty.

Caleb Bates was aware the town talked about him, his property, and the close-mouthed people he flew in and out of the village in his private planes. But he knew with the certainty of a man who left nothing to chance that unless he set the mountain afire or ran naked down Stone Point's main street, no one would ask, no one would bother him, no one would invade his club's privacy, and he could continue his crucial work. It was why he had chosen this rural outpost in West Virginia.

That Wednesday when Bates returned from Washington, he found a nervy energy had overtaken his people. There was a light in their eyes. Vigor infused their steps. He had announced before he left that the first big operation they had been training for, and anticipating, for so long, was just three days away—Saturday—and everyone was excited and eager.

A sense of urgency filled Bates, too, as he moved among them, advising and exhorting. With the cool, clinical detachment of long experience in such operations, he watched them fight through the scenarios he staged on the club's five-acre central plot he had named Little U.S.A. Here was where he had ordered the trees thinned out and a sixteen-building town constructed. It contained everything from a city hall and a church to two bars, a hotel, a small business district, a post office, and even apartments.

Although hollow and constructed of cinder-block, the buildings were painted the usual city hues of whites and tans. The concrete streets and sidewalks were wide, but the windows were snipers' havens. There were sewers to give invaders practice penetrating a city, and draped high above it all was camouflage netting that allowed sunlight to filter through, while to anyone who flew overhead, Little U.S.A. looked like any other part of the West Virginia forest.

The latest exercise was for his top sixteen men. Following his rules, they used only hand signals rather than radio communications, to increase their capacity to surprise. They carefully infiltrated, protecting themselves from potential snipers, and took over the city hall and post office from the home defenders.

Then suddenly a booby trap detonated inside the post office, exploding special colored paint. One of the invaders swore. Splashed with red, he was "dead." He dropped to his haunches and pounded his fist against the cement floor, disgusted he had been so careless as to be "killed" and, for this day, out of action.

As Bates observed closely, the exercise continued with episodes of live rifle and machine-gun fire to keep everyone off balance and alert. Midway, there was an attempted ambush. Finally the fifteen remaining invaders "killed off" most of the townspeople who, marked by the red paint, sat or lay among the mock buildings. Since they were supposedly dead, they were not allowed to talk, smoke, or nap. It was a reminder of failure that had worked for Bates before.

In a final triumphant sweep, the guerrilla winners rounded up the surviving defenders and barricaded them in the cinderblock shell that was one of the fake bars.

But as the sergeant who was in command of the invading squad stepped forward to announce victory, Caleb Bates spotted beyond him and the others a wiry shape slithering out a high window so small no one had ever used it to escape.

Surprised, Bates watched the youth land lightly on his feet and hug the building for cover. Bates frowned, but gave no indication he had spotted the youth. Meanwhile, since in both winners' and losers' eyes the exercise was over, the "dead" and "captured" began to converge on Bates along with the victorious attack team.

The sergeant in command of the attackers snapped a salute. "Little U.S.A. wrapped up tight, sir!" Sergeant Aaron Austin, in his mid-thirties, with buzz-cut hair and pitcher-shaped ears, had the trim waist, broad shoulders, and thick thighs of a man who knew muscles and strength mattered. Like everyone else, he was dressed in woodland camouflage.

"Good. Well done, Sergeant." Bates returned the salute. "You think we're ready?"

"I'd say so, sir," Austin nodded.

Bates looked around at the others. "At ease, patriots."

He appeared to be some sixty years old and burly in a General Patton sort of way. He had iron-gray hair that showed beneath his black beret, a low, husky voice, and brusque manner that proclaimed the assurance of a man who knew who he was, where he was going, and exactly how to get there. This, he understood, was what his troops wanted. In fact, what they needed.

There were fifty of them involved in this exercise, and they focused intently on him. His gravelly voice was measured, and it carried to the farthest ranks. "This exercise is a perfect example of what we've been talking about in urban warfare. Precision and coordination. Once you invade, you must switch to small-unit initiatives, which the sergeants will lead. Every squad must act like a guerrilla group. . . ."

As he spoke, he surreptitiously watched the agile young man—he recognized him now, it was Martin Coulson—who had slipped out the window. Armed with an automatic pistol, Coulson sped around the crowd. He was about twenty years old, with a light case of acne on his bony face. He had narrow hips and muscles that were like corded steel. A few heads turned among the defenders, while the invaders at the front of the throng were still caught up in their celebration and had not noticed.

Just as Bates began laying out the program for the next two days, Marty Coulson jumped out, raised the gun, and accurately showered paint-bullets at the invaders.

Surprised, the winners cursed and protested their outrage, while the crowd of losers erupted in cheers and laughter. Two of the invaders hurled themselves at Marty, but it was too late. All had been marked for injury or death by Marty's red blotches.

"He can't do this!" one complained loudly.

"It's too damn late to attack, Coulson." Sergeant Austin swore. "The operation's over!"

"Colonel Bates," Marty said earnestly, breathing hard. "You always say initiative counts. They missed me. I played dead, and they walked right by. Doesn't that mean for me the attack was still going on? I mean, no one calls time out in a war."

Everyone in the militia group believed Bates to be a retired U.S. Army colonel, which was close to the truth. If his followers had been real soldiers he would have applauded Coulson. The boy was right, and it was sometimes a hard lesson to learn, as he well knew from bitter experience a long way from West Virginia. But he was worried: He had already had an eye on the boy as being too clever for his own good and therefore dangerous to his plans, but he could not let the Keepers know that.

Instead, Bates nodded. "Yes, Coulson is right. He did a good job, and let it be a lesson to us all." His solemn gaze swept them, drawing them to him with his personal magnetism. They leaned toward him, eager for each word. "In battle, nothing is really finished. The dead soldier lying bloody on the ground could have enough life left to put a bullet between your eyes. The expensive wristwatch you find alongside a trail is almost certainly booby-trapped. Private Coulson has just reminded us of the basic truth of war—we're all vulnerable all the time. Your weakest moment may be just when you think you've won."

When Bates had found them four years ago, they were a rudderless, undisciplined gang of quarrelsome dissenters and government-haters, made violent by anger at a world that had failed to give them what they considered they deserved. They would lash out intermittently without plan or direction. Still, they'd had one essential ingredient—a bone-deep, generations-long, nationalism. So he joined them, impressed them with his military knowledge, and as soon as they chose him to lead, he constructed this hidden training camp.

He supplied them with the finest equipment and trained them into a small but powerful force. And in the process, he had weeded out the weak and timid, the too-smart, the too-educated, the less-committed, the loners and the whiners. Those remaining were fanatics to the core, with a single-minded obsession for all they had "lost" since the days of "true patriots" like the Minutemen, who had won the Revolution back in 1776. Never mind that the fools had never figured out that it had been General George Washington's regular army, the brief dominance of the French fleet of Admiral De Grasse, and England's concern with the far-more-urgent political situation in Europe, that won the Revolution they revered so much.

He had named them the Keepers of the Truth, and they had taken to his guidance like moths to a beguiling flame. Then he had seen his opportunity, and he summoned them, described a heroic plan, and put them through refresher training in weapons, martial arts, and loyalty to the cause. Now they were ready, and so was he.

A sense of optimism swept through him. He was a product of his past, and this was his most important war.

"One last thing," he reminded them grimly. "A single leak, and not only the mission but the Keepers could be finished. Since D-Day is just two days off, no one leaves the hunt club. Questions?"

There were none. The Keepers moved away, their faces solemn and determined, their steps brisk and purposeful. They had waited a long time for this, their chance to save their country and take their rightful places in it.

Caleb Bates's cabin, where he lived and worked when he was at the hidden training center, stood on a knoll in the forest a quarter-mile west of Little U.S.A. From the front window he could see some twenty other cabins in neat rows. Two were large, single-sex dormitories, while several others offered small bedrooms for couples. Everything was simple and utilitarian, from the garages that sheltered vehicles and supplies to the cookhouse and large dining room that doubled as a meeting hall. Bates had hired outside contractors to put up the perimeter fence, pour foundations and roads, raise walls, and create a septic system. But to keep the final purpose of the encampment secret, the Keepers themselves had finished the work.

Bates stood at his window, surveying what he had wrought. He was satisfied, even proud. Long ago, everyone had told him that motivating recruits, training them and inspiring them, was one of his greatest strengths. Perhaps he should have pursued a career in the regular military, risen to the top, leading troops into battle. But he had no regrets for the path he had chosen. He was what he was, and that was best for what he had to do now, for his great vision for the future of his country.

He was still musing over the course of his life and how it would determine the direction of the world for a long time to come, when he saw the coiled-spring body of Sergeant Austin double-timing toward him. He had given the sergeant an assignment, and from the sober expression on Austin's face, Bates already knew the results.

He stepped out onto his porch and waited. The sergeant stopped neatly before him, hardly puffing. For him to be even slightly out of breath, Bates knew he must have run a long way.

"He's gone?" Bates said.

"Yes, sir," Austin nodded. "Took a motorcycle, but didn't turn on the engine so we wouldn't hear him. He's coasting down the road toward Stone Point."

Bates showed none of his anger. "It's the girlfriend then. We suspected that, didn't we, Sergeant?" The youth, Coulson, who'd had the resourcefulness to slip out a window and escape at the end of the guerrilla exercise would also have the creativity to figure out how to have one more hot night between cheap sheets with a girl Bates was certain must be the local slut.

The sergeant was apologetic. He was a man of action, but now Bates had ordered him to be inactive. "Guess so, sir. You said not to go after him."

"You did the right thing. I'll handle it now. Go back to your regular duties, Sergeant." He watched as Austin hesitated then turned on his heel and left smartly, double-timing to the central camp.

Bates strode back inside his cabin. Checking front and back to be sure he was alone, he went to stand beside the window where he could watch the camp and see anyone heading toward him.

He pulled a cell phone from his shirt pocket. He was no computer genius, but he had people who were, and he had ordered them to find scramblers for all their phones that no one could breach. As a result, two silicon chips in this digital phone encrypted transmissions so completely they were uncrackable and scrambled so effectively no law-enforcement agency could read them. Recently, the National Security Agency had conceded the chips had effectively killed encryption controls in America, because they were made by the Japanese and could be imported everywhere, including into the United States. There was nothing the U.S. government could do.

"You're late reporting," he snapped into the mouthpiece. His voice had changed. Gone was the low, gravelly rasp of Caleb Bates. His posture grew less severely angular and rigid, became more sinuous.

In Russian, Ivan Vok apologized. "Fedorov just called, Alexei. I chewed him out good."

"We can't have such delays, Ivan Ivanovich," Alexei Berianov responded in Russian. Talking to his old KGB comrade, he felt completely himself. But then he caught his reflection in the window, and there was Caleb Bates staring back. For a split second his brain swam, and he seemed to float in a kind of numb limbo, without time, place, or identity. He shook his head angrily. He had lived much of his life in one kind of disguise or another, and this was no time to question his actions. "Have Fedorov report directly to me from now on. You have enough to do in Washington."

"Okay, Alexei." Vok described Nikolai Fedorov's report on Beth Convey, everything from her date of birth and parents to her heart transplant and job at Edwards & Bonnett. Through political contacts and their far-flung businesses and data banks, Vok and Fedorov could find out almost anything Berianov wanted.

With growing unease, Berianov listened for what he really needed. Finally he interrupted Vok: "What about last night? It makes no sense. How could she have known about Yuri?"

Vok paused uncomfortably. "Fedorov doesn't know yet. None of our people has ever seen her, and they didn't recognize her name. It's almost as if she dropped whole from the sky."

"She's an international lawyer. Maybe she worked on cases that touched us somehow. Find out."

"Of course. No problem."

Berianov paused to think. "When did Fedorov say she had the transplant?"

"A year ago to the day, Alexei."

Berianov had an odd feeling in his gut that the past thirty years had taught him to respect. His gut was telling him the date might be significant somehow. He needed to find out more. He fired off instructions to be relayed to Nikolai Fedorov.

Vok said, "Fine. Consider it handled."

Satisfied, Berianov changed the subject. "Any problems at Meteor?"

"None." Vok reported that the fake Meteor Express had been completely disappeared, and they had taken over the name of another company. It was E=Phrase, a small software designer for business services, and it would go on the sign at their new location in Reston, Virginia, in the District's new high-tech corridor. The transfer to E=Phrase had been a success, they had a new phone number, and there had been no more suspicious calls.

They had used the ruse of adopting other companies' names to protect their real purposes for the past four years in Washington's dense, changeable metropolitan area. Last night's troubles at their fake Meteor Express in Arlington were highly unusual. But even that mishap had been eliminated in the very early hours—after Yurimengri's corpse had been disposed of—by installing Renae Trucking, a legitimate company owned and operated by one of their old KGB associates.

But Berianov was already on to another nagging issue: "Now we must discuss one more thing, Ivan Ivanovich . . ." They continued talking, with Berianov giving orders as he made plans to eliminate another man, this one an American, who was on the brink of causing them serious trouble.

9

Beth parked and hurried through chrome-bright sunshine toward a boxlike, eight-story building that was the epitome of so-called modern architecture. Although it looked like a concrete-sided penitentiary, the 1970s structure housed the illustrious *Washington Post.* Here was where Beth hoped to find something useful about Anatoli Yurimengri from the journalist who had written so knowledgeably about his life.

The article had both electrified and repelled her: Not only had she been close to knowing Yurimengri's name, but once again there was the Russian connection. Perhaps other people called him Yuri. It could be a nickname. As a culture, Russians were fond of using nicknames and diminutives.

She strode quickly toward the newspaper's massive doors, feeling the pressure of lost time. She had stopped on the drive to buy a cardigan sweater to replace her dirty jacket, hoping to improve her presentation factor, and then she had stopped again at a deli for food and to take her meds. Annoyed at the interruptions, at least she had been able to study the *Post* article.

The newspaper's lobby was cool and spacious, with high ceilings. Now that she was inside, the building gave off a sense of greatness, as if important things could be expected from whatever business was conducted here.

She headed to the security man behind the desk. "Jeffrey Hammond, please."

"You have an appointment?" The man had sharp gray eyes beneath

heavy brows that drooped low. In his security uniform of blue blazer and
gray slacks, he sat smartly erect, as if he never stopped being on duty.

"No, but I'd like to see him. Tell him it's about Colonel Yurimengri."

"Your name?"

"Beth Convey." As he dialed, she reread the article's opening:

In one of the least-kept secrets of the
new century, the United States and Russia
still run espionage operations against each
other, despite the end of the cold war a
decade ago.

Last night, an apparently minor player
from those distant days was shot to death
in Washington. In its own way, his murder
signals how much the spy game between
the former arch enemies has changed, yet
remains the same.

His name was Anatoli Yurimengri, and
he was a defector.

A former colonel with the Soviet
Union's dreaded spy agency, the KGB, he
was born and raised on the windswept
taiga of Russia's bitter north, while he met
his death a half century later on a warm
spring night in a urine-spotted alley less
than three miles from the U.S. Capitol.

In the neighborhood around Orleans
Place, where police say he apparently died
from a single gunshot to the chest, brick
row houses line narrow, claustrophobic
streets, and the drug history is long and
notorious.

No one with money shops there except
for drugs. That is why the tags of cars
cruising the area are often from out of
town.

Yurimengri's expensive red Jaguar had
Virginia plates. It was found a block from
where he died. It had been stripped.

He had come a long way from poverty
and communism to die not for political
ideals but for what police are initially the-
orizing was an old-fashioned robbery.

His gold Rolex watch, credit cards, diamond wedding ring, and "gangster roll" of
cash were missing. His widow, Cheryl, a
blond former beauty queen he met locally,
told police he habitually carried those
items.

He died rich, but when he arrived in the
United States ten years ago, he was penni-
less. . . .

"Ms. Convey?"

She looked at the security man.

"Mr. Hammond says he'll be right down."

"Thanks." Brooding, she stalked across the lobby, peered unseeing out the window, and strode back to glare at the elevator, waiting. The writer had related so much detailed insight not only about Yurimengri but about the spy agencies of the old Soviet Union and the new Russia, that she figured he must be some kind of dusty researcher-type who spent his life navel-deep in piles of clippings, arcane reports, and crumbling interview transcripts. In her mind, she saw a little ink-stained man with a green eye shade, unpressed shirtsleeves rolled up above his skinny elbows, and chinos with the permanent imprint of bony knees bent from years of sitting at a desk.

What the journalist, Hammond, had written made her skin crawl. Surely she had no relationship with Yurimengri or his violent past. Silently she accused her heart, "Don't tell me you knew him or his killer!"

She continued reading:

In August 1991, Communist hard-liners tried to overthrow Mikhail Gorbachev's government and quash the opposition forming around Boris Yeltsin.

The hard-liners' coup failed utterly, and, shortly afterwards, reformers dismantled the KGB. Many long-time officers lost their jobs and were cast adrift in a world they no longer recognized. It was the beginning of today's New Russia.

Almost as if he were prescient, Colonel Yurimengri defected at the time of the fateful coup, thus avoiding job loss and perhaps execution.

Both the CIA and the FBI welcomed him with open arms. Unknown to the world at large, he had been high in the KGB's First Branch of the Second Chief Directorate, which operated counterintelligence in Moscow against the CIA.

He had heard and seen many things useful to America, and the CIA and FBI debriefed him for three weeks. Then they gave him the standard resettlement package of three weeks of classes in how to function in the United States, plus a modest living stipend.

And they cut him loose.

He chose not to disappear. Instead, he kept his real name and identity. Within a year, Wheels SovAm, the machinery-parts company he founded after his debriefing, made him a multimillionaire.

In his busy new life, he flew back and forth between Washington and Moscow, New York and St. Petersburg, Des Moines and Bratsk. He was a *biznesman,* rich in greenbacks, with a stunning new young wife.

Then last night he was killed for his American money, his British car, his South African diamond ring, and his Swiss watch. Not for his Communist ideology. Which shows how much not only the spy business but the world has changed.

Watch his funeral four days hence for who stays away. Do not expect his fellow ex-spies, many of whom remain unknown and underground, to appear.

Remarkably, they form the largest group of "retired" KGB outside Moscow.

And do not expect to see many of his acquaintances from the old days who claim to have played no part in espionage, because they are uncomfortable being associated with what happened during the no-holds-barred cold war.

Or perhaps some will stay away for a far different, more dangerous reason: They have slipped back into the spy trenches.

Intelligence operatives are more valuable than ever to Mother Russia. Even in the most remote corners of that suffering land, it is common knowledge the longer the country remains in poverty and despair, the more she yearns to be a superpower again.

And although the KGB is defunct, its violent, secret ways thrive on in its successor agency, the Federal Security Service (FSB).

So while retired Colonel Yurimengri—supposedly a reborn Capitalist and democrat—may rest in peace, we in the West have reason to wonder what is going on beneath the surface of the still waters from which he arose—the cream of the deadly KGB. . . .

"Ms. Convey?"

She whirled and tried to keep the surprise from her voice. "Mr. Hammond?"

"The same."

He had come down the stairs, not the elevator, and he walked toward her with a faint glow of sweat on his broad, handsome face. He had a ponytail and wore a gold hoop earring in his right ear. His large features were seized up in an impatient scowl. In his tight jeans and blue cotton work shirt, there was nothing small and refined about him. This was no ink-stained little man with weak, rounded shoulders. Instead, everything about him was oversized and impressive, from his aristocratic nose to his big, square shoulders and large hands and feet, which were stuffed into high-heeled, lizard-skin cowboy boots. He exuded a cocky power that seemed to knock the oxygen from her lungs.

Yet there was something else—a haunted expression around his eyes. The eyes and the impatient scowl did not match. They battled each other, as if the scowl were forced, put on, a façade he was presenting to her, and perhaps to the world. He was hiding, acting, covering something. But what was it? What was he trying to conceal?

As she regrouped, she found herself staring coldly. She recognized the emotions: She was attracted to him. In fact, very attracted. Which was the last complication she needed in her suddenly overly complicated life. Her track record with men was hardly sterling. Take Phil Stageman, for instance, male prostitute of the week. And then there was the issue of her heart. Despite Dr. Jackson's assurances, in the back of her mind lurked a certain terror. She feared the act of sex would strain her heart. If she had problems with this heart, she might never have a chance at another.

In any case, one thing was clear: Hammond did not like the looks of her. It was evident in the brusque handshake and the no-nonsense tone—"What can I do for you?" He did not say, "Make it fast," but impatience radiated from him like a neon sign. He studied her still rumpled appearance for a few seconds then dismissed that, too.

She frowned up at him. "Is there somewhere we can talk?"

"Here's good."

"I've got something private to discuss. It's about Anatoli Yurimengri."

"Right." He nodded, and his earring glinted gold in the room's artificial light. "Go ahead." He looked off over her shoulder.

She felt her urgency turn into anger. People were coming and going through the lobby. She recognized none, but he spoke names in greeting. She repressed the anger, because she needed to get his attention.

She lowered her voice: "What makes you think Yurimengri was actually killed in that alley off Orleans Place?"

It worked. His eyes narrowed. "That's what the investigating officers reported."

She leaned forward, her voice confidential. "You believe everything you're told? Since you're a journalist, I figured you'd know better."

He blinked. "Okay. I'm hooked." He took her arm and escorted her away toward the lobby entrance. "It's a nice day. We'll walk. That okay?"

"Works for me."

His stride was long. He was probably six-foot-three in his stocking feet. Maybe more. In boots, six-five and commanding. But she was athletic and not significantly shorter than he. Besides, he made all her instincts scream *compete*. So she pushed open the door and held it.

"Thanks." He passed through as casually as if he were accustomed to such favors from women. "Who are you, lady? What's this about Yurimengri's not dying in the alley?"

On the sidewalk beneath wind-rippled trees, she put on her own sunglasses and kept up with him easily. To stop the attraction from softening her brain, she focused straight ahead and decided in the end it made no difference whether he knew who she was. She wanted information, which meant she had to give a little herself.

"As I told the receptionist, my name's Beth Convey. I'm an attorney with Edwards & Bonnett." That was no longer true, but he did not need to know it. "Before I say where I think Yurimengri really died, tell me how you know so much about him. Your story read more like a treatise on the man and his times. You understand the big picture and his piece in it."

"Yurimengri was part of my beat. Obviously you're not keeping up with my series, 'Where Are They Now?' I've been digging out information and reporting about what's happened to the Soviet defectors who settled in and around the Beltway. As you probably know, we have the largest group of ex-KGB outside Moscow." His hands were shoved into his jeans pockets. "When Yurimengri was killed, I already had a lot about him. So I talked to his widow, pulled from background what seemed pertinent, and wrote the piece."

Those were more words than she had expected. "I know the series. I just didn't connect your name to it."

He shrugged. Complete disinterest. Or was that an act, too? "Your turn."

"Last night I discovered a dead man in Arlington. His body was gone this morning when I returned to report it. Then I saw the photograph of Colonel Yurimengri in the *Post*. It was the same man."

He was silent. "Assuming you're correct, you told the police?"

"Of course. But as I said, his corpse was gone. The police checked with their headquarters, but no one in the county had been reported dead or injured from a gunshot to the chest that night."

"They didn't call D.C. police?"

"I doubt it, or they would've known about your Colonel Yurimengri. So who killed him, and why? Was he really into drugs as the police think?"

"I don't know who would've wanted to murder him." He seemed to walk faster. "And I know nothing that'd rule out drugs. The toxicology report will tell us about the drugs, but it won't be available until next week." He paused. "Of course, being in the KGB meant he had enemies, and not just in the West. Kremlin politics never stopped being Byzantine and violent. What else do you know?"

She considered. "He mentioned West Virginia. That he hadn't realized something about Stone Point, West Virginia."

He nodded casually. Almost too casually. "He was *alive?*"

"Since he spoke, I think you can assume that, yes."

Hammond compressed his lips, and she suspected he was suppressing a sharp response. "What else did he say?"

"Nothing more. What do you think he meant about West Virginia?"

"In the first place, Colonel Yurimengri might not be the same guy as the one you supposedly found."

They reached the corner. "He's the same. It's not only his face. Both were shot in the chest. Don't try to convince me it was just a coincidence two identical men in two different locations inside the Beltway died from gunshot wounds to the chest on the same night. Not hardly." She glanced up as they turned back toward the *Post.*

She almost stumbled with shock. Then fear. She stared at his profile.

He moved on without her and apparently without listening to what she had said. He continued with his own thoughts: "And in the second place, it's asking a lot for me to know what some stranger meant by referring to West Virginia. That state's got enough mountain wilderness to hide all the outlaws, misfits, and politicians in the nation." He stopped and swiveled to look at her again, inadvertently giving her a second view of his profile. "Not to mention lawyers, who deserve their own special hell. Are you coming? You're the one who initiated this consultation."

As he waited, her chest tightened. It was hard to breathe. He had the straight forehead. The aquiline nose. The jutting chin. Only the long hair was different. Last night, the hair of the killer who had chased her had been short. But the profile was identical, she was sure. Although she could not explain the difference in hair, she knew that this Jeffrey Hammond—the *Post* journalist who glared not six feet ahead of her, the tall, powerful man with something hidden inside him, whom she had initially found so attractive—had to be the one who killed Colonel Yurimengri and then chased her with a gun. It was only by some miracle he had not caught and killed her last night, too.

As she forced herself to breathe normally, her terror grew into rage. She fought it, made herself think, analyze: He had met her with a coolness and gruffness she had not believed was entirely real. Maybe he had not recognized her. Or maybe he had, and he was covering it with his power tactics. When she had not identified him immediately in the *Post*'s lobby, probably he believed she had not seen his face. After all, it had been a dark night, and she had been running furiously to escape.

She must not alarm him. She had no evidence, only what she had seen. It would not be enough for the police, especially after her unfortunate encounter with them this morning.

"Let's go." Hammond's face seemed to tighten. "What are you waiting for?"

She forced herself to smile a neutral smile. "Nothing. Nice day, isn't it? Strange, but nice." As she walked toward him, she felt a sudden sense of inevitability. If she were going to die, at least now she knew the truth about who had killed Yurimengri . . . and by whose hand her own death would be.

He turned away and resumed his long-striding gait back toward the *Post*. "How did you happen to go there anyway?"

Her taut nerves jumped. How did you happen to go *there*. He was a trained newspaperman with a superb sense of detail, and he had not asked where in Arlington she had found the dying colonel. She smiled soberly. He would not make a mistake like that if he were not on edge, and unless he already knew where Colonel Yurimengri had really been killed.

She lied, "A client was interested in buying the building. He wanted me to check it out, but I was late getting out of the office, then I was late getting away from home after dinner. So when I arrived and the door was open, I walked in and found him."

"Wait a minute. Where in Arlington was this?"

Right. And if he were gullible enough to think she would believe he had forgotten to ask, she had a rusty bridge to sell him. She kept her gaze on the *Post*'s entrance, eager to reach it. She played along with his ruse and told him about Meteor Express and Renae Trucking. But then she asked, "How did *you* meet Yurimengri? From what you wrote, it almost seems as if you had some kind of personal connection with him. Were you friends?" She hesitated. "Enemies?"

He did not break stride, and she could discern nothing more than a stiff disdain as he ignored her last comment. "I already told you, he was part of my beat. I interviewed him quite a bit over the years. In case you haven't noticed, it's my job—it's every reporter's job—to make each piece as accurate as possible. I'll take your question as a compliment." Then he looked down at her.

"I see."

"If I were you, I'd forget it. You've made a report to the cops. You can't do more than that." His voice dropped, and he continued persuasively, "You know what Washington's like. Security clearances and closed-door sessions. Investigative reporters like me and freedom-of-information fanatics. Leakers, stone-wallers, and whistle-blowers. It's a culture of secrecy that breeds curiosity and hunger for revelations. But those are rotten reasons for a civilian to get involved. You can get yourself caught up in forces that chew up the innocent as well as the guilty. This whole thing about the two men who might be the same probably looks fascinating from the outside, but more than likely it's a coincidence. The police will think you're nuts if you push it. You could get yourself into a lot of trouble."

He was warning her off, giving her reason to lose interest.

She said, "You're probably right. There's nothing more I can do."

"Good thinking."

But as he was about to go in the door, and she was feeling hopeful of an escape, he stopped. His shoulders stiffened under his blue cotton shirt. As he turned back to face her, she held her breath. She was both afraid and furious. The two emotions battled within her like warring factions. Ever since the transplant, she was like this—divided, fighting herself.

"At least one man's been murdered." His voice was measured as he laced his words with meaning. "If you're right, the killer could be after you, too. You could end up dead."

There it was at last: *You could end up dead.* He was threatening her. Her chest tightened. But before the fear could take her over, anger shook her. It was this new, riveting rage that had begun with her transplant. She knotted her hands at her side.

She needed to reassure him, so she lied again: "I've got a lot more important things to do than chase a phantom." She forced a smile. "You're right. Thanks for your time." But as she left, she could feel his gaze hot and suspicious on her back. It made her skin crawl.

10

The U.S. government's far-reaching legal arm—the Department of Justice—occupied an entire city block between Constitution and Pennsylvania avenues, from Ninth to Tenth streets. It sprawled across the exact midpoint between Capitol Hill and the White House, showing its importance to both, while indicating a political distance and resistence to influence that was necessary but often elusive.

Erected in 1934, the pale stone building boasted the usual Classic Revival porticoes, the Art Deco architectural touches, and the highly principled quotations carved above the entrances. Similar public-style buildings appeared in most cities, large and small, across the country, but what appeared nowhere else this Wednesday was a critical meeting in the office of Deputy Attorney General Millicent Taurino.

A slim, diminutive woman of forty-two, Taurino was dressed in a demure knit suit with a collar low enough to display a blue butterfly tattoo just beneath her left ear. She rested her determined chin on her knuckles, elbow supported by the arm of her desk chair, and contemplated the life-sized portrait of Chief Justice John Marshall, which hung to her right on her office wall.

With her free hand, she waved flame-painted fingernails and concluded, "So you still have nothing." It was a statement, not a question.

FBI director Thomas Earle Horn, a burly, slope-shouldered, thick-necked former defensive tackle for the Buffaloes of the University of Colorado, sat in a leather armchair facing the deputy attorney general. He turned his gray slate eyes toward the third person in the office. "Bobby?"

Bobby Kelsey, assistant director of the FBI's National Security Division and, as such, overseer of the Foreign Counterintelligence Program, the FCI, bristled. "I wouldn't call Ames, Nicholson, Groat, Pitts, and Lipka over at NSA nothing. They were turncoats. Traitors. The worst of the worst, spying against their own kind. We caught them, and every damn one of them's in jail, Ms. Taurino. That's something. In fact, that's a lot."

Millicent Taurino was still contemplating the stern countenance of America's seminal chief justice as if solace for her current problem could be found through him. "Those are past successes, irrelevant now." She raised her head and spun around in her desk chair to face the two FBI officials. "The Bureau's got two hundred spy cases nationwide it's investigating. That's one heck of a lot of open files for peacetime. Worse, our conviction rate's in the toilet, a fraction of what we should be doing. Now that we've put top priority on catching foreign spies and stopping terrorist attacks, we need to see serious results."

The Cold War's passing had brought no end to espionage. As the world's last standing superpower, the United States was still the preferred target, both economically and militarily, which left it in the position of constantly having to protect itself against spies and terrorists. That was the official story. Unofficially, everyone who knew anything agreed that the spy business was addictive. Plus, equally unofficially, America intended to remain number one, which meant it must not only spy, too, but be better at it.

Taurino looked sharply across her desk at the men she had summoned. "Where's the red meat, guys? Where's the Big One you claim's in your lap somewhere? This mole who's burrowed so deep into the inner sanctum of the FBI? We've got to find and stop him!"

"These things take time," Thomas Horn announced. The FBI director's voice had a decidedly patronizing tone that was trotted out when dealing with civilian bosses. It seemed to go with the office, the wraith of J. Edgar Hoover whispering instructions in each director's ears.

"Well, now." Taurino nodded sagely. "I'd say that was quite a breathtaking observation, Mr. Director. *Time*. Consider *tempus fugit*. 'Time flies.' Let's see, how long has it been since your two predecessors started this internal investigation? Nine years? No, wait, that was when I was appointed last year, wasn't it? So a decade ago now, right? My heavens, how *time flies* when one is having so much fun." She gave Horn a withering smile. " 'It takes time.' That's the wisdom you have to give us after ten long years, Tom? I must remember to write a memo to the attorney general. He'll want to fill in the president."

"We don't appreciate sarcasm, Millicent," Tom Horn snapped.

"And we don't appreciate sloth. Are you sure you care whether we expose this deep-penetration agent of yours? Perhaps he or she is simply a convenient excuse to cover the Bureau's leaks and failures. By my count, it seems to me as if someone out there used information supplied by your traitor to sour more than forty Bureau missions. Even in the high-risk world of spying, that's too many to be coincidental. You may not be scared by that and what this Judas could do in the future, but I am!"

The FBI director jumped to his feet as if scalded. "That's all, Ms. Taurino. When you're ready to talk rationally, call us. Bobby, we're leaving!"

Kelsey stood up to join his boss.

"Sit down, *Mister* Horn!" The deputy AG stabbed a slender, red-tipped finger at the director. "You're not J. Edgar, buster. Those days are dead, and they sure as hell aren't coming back. Today the president and the AG can get a new FBI shlump for a dime, and assistant directors run a dozen for a nickel. You work for *us!* Now sit your ass back down and talk to me."

The two men exchanged angry glances then slowly sank back into their chairs, faces red but expressionless.

"Thank you, gentlemen," Taurino said, "it's so kind of you." With a final chin-jutting glare, she became all business. "Now. The Soviet Union is gone, the Cold War is over, but the losses of information continue. The KGB has supposedly been disbanded, but our missions, agents, and plans are bleeding out. Am I right?"

"I beg your pardon, Millicent," Tom Horn said, carefully making his voice conciliatory, "but when I referred to time, what I should have referred to was degree of difficulty. Three directors have grappled with this problem. A deep mole so carefully planted or turned, and so carefully used, as to go undetected for God knows how long is a counterintelligence nightmare."

"*Ten years,* Tom? How many of your people have even been in the Bureau ten years?"

"Most of our senior personnel, from top to bottom. The vast majority of agents stay in all the way to retirement. But who says all the leaks have been one person, Millicent? Maybe there have been a series of moles or traitors, each passing the torch to another when he or she leaves the Bureau."

"Was the KGB that good? Is its successor, whatever it's called? I can never keep those Russian names and acronyms straight."

Bobby Kelsey interjected, "The acronym is FSB. They're that good, all right. Almost as good as us. But there's another problem: We can't be certain our mole is Russian. Our other allies are skilled at this game, too. Maybe the leaks to the Kremlin are cover for other espionage we haven't been able to pin down yet."

The FBI director pursed his lips. "As I said, Millicent, this is hardly an easy task."

"All right," the deputy AG agreed, "it's hard. I've stipulated to that. So what are you doing today to make it easier?"

"All the usual internal measures," the FBI director said stubbornly. "Rechecking backgrounds, activities out of the office, changes in habits, attitudes, or financial circumstances. We stay on top of new connections and unusual trips. We follow up on information leaked to American agents abroad, and then we track who had access to the information. We check all leads, and then we try to connect all these bits of data in such a way that they lead to a culprit. I'd rather not go into any more specific detail, but I will say I'm confident we're getting close."

"What gives you more confidence than I have?" Taurino challenged.

"We had a break recently. It indicated that whoever passed on some newly developed data had to be a reasonably senior official, or someone who works closely with a senior official."

"What break? What data?"

Tom Horn scowled, "No, Millicent. I won't compromise an ongoing operation."

"*Compromise?*" The deputy attorney general's jaw grew so tight the jawbone stood out like a tied-off vein. "You have difficulty with authority, don't you, Tom?" Her dark brown eyes were like bullets. "Do you seriously want me to tell the attorney general and the president that you consider them security risks who could compromise your operation?"

Horn ground his teeth, but there was little he could do or say except to look at Kelsey. "Bobby, you explain it."

Bobby Kelsey nodded and said gravely, "One of my people turned an ex-KGB agent in the community of former Soviet defectors. He proved to be extremely useful. Recently, he tipped us to another buried KGB slush fund, a mammoth one that had originated back in the old Soviet days. But before we got to it, it was emptied, and the money transferred to Moscow. That looks like the work of our mole." He steepled his hands and touched them to his lips. "Interestingly, outside the FCI, no one in the Bureau below assistant director knew about that fund."

Millicent Taurino let that sink in. "So . . . you're saying it's one of your top people. How many does that narrow it down to?"

"More than you might think," Tom Horn admitted. "All current assistant directors and above have been with us more than ten consecutive years. And from what we can tell at this point, all the special agents who work closely with them—they could have passed along the information either deliberately or inadvertently—are long-time veterans, too. Besides, if I may say so, in my opinion all the people in the Bureau who could've leaked the information are above reproach."

" 'Above reproach' is what any deep-cover mole wants to appear to be, isn't it?" Taurino observed icily. "So you're really no farther along at all."

The director met her hard gaze. "No, but we'll find him."

"Or her," Bobby Kelsey said.

"Will you?" Millicent Taurino said. "I sincerely hope so. I really do." She shook her head worriedly.

Alone in her office, Millicent Taurino picked up her phone and touched a button. "They're gone. You can come in now." She sat back, pinched her chin thoughtfully, and gazed again at the portrait of John Marshall in his robes. He was her talisman, her silent mentor, and she had carried his picture with her to every job since she entered government. "Well, Johnny," she said to the painting, "are they fools, knaves, or alarmists? Is there a mole at all? You had your share of deviousness, didn't you, so how about some words of wisdom here?"

She waited as if she really expected the painting to speak. Then she broke the silence with a laugh, and almost simultaneously the door to her private entrance opened. The two men who came in were a study in contrasts. Assistant Attorney General Donald Chen, head of Justice's criminal division, was a short, portly man with black hair parted neatly on the side and a full, round face. He looked like Buddha in a gray chalk-stripe suit. Behind him, hidden by Chen's considerable girth, came a slender man no taller than Chen, with a head of wispy gray hair, a pasty, indoors face, rimless eyeglasses, and a thin, merciless mouth. His pale blue eyes were intelligent and ruthless.

Deputy AG Taurino rose from behind her desk and waved the second man to the chair closest to her. Assistant AG Chen stepped aside to let him pass. Neither Chen nor Taurino sat until the slender man did.

"What did Horn have to say?" Cabot Lowell, national security adviser to the president, asked. Once a congressman, then director of the Central Intelligence Agency, and just three years ago the secretary of Defense, Lowell had a light mild voice that Millicent Taurino sensed was never raised in anger or in joy. Still, it was compelling and intense.

"They essentially have nothing new in their internal investigation," she reported. "Which means they still have nothing."

The national security adviser allowed his pale gaze to settle on Donald Chen. "I hope you have more than nothing for our investigation, Mr. Chen. Nothing is such a useless entity."

"I don't know what the hell I have," Assistant AG Donald Chen growled in such pure everyday American that it was a shock coming from the mouth of a Buddha. The anomaly was not lost on Cabot Lowell, who smiled. Chen continued: "Except that Eli Kirkhart called me all hot under the collar, and I figured we'd better hear it from the horse's mouth, you know?"

"You figured well. Let's have our personal mole hunter in."

Taurino leaned toward her intercom. "Abby? Send in Special Agent Kirkhart."

When despite all the years of internal investigation by the FBI, no mole was found but information continued to leak from inside the Bureau, the national security adviser and the attorney general had grown alarmed. The president had not wanted to bring in the CIA, so Cabot Lowell had suggested a top-secret Justice department investigation. No one in the Bureau would be informed, because everyone within the Bureau was suspect.

Still, Cabot Lowell was convinced that the investigator who would have the best chance of success must be a Bureau insider. To find the right person, Lowell had studied the personnel records of every FBI employee. Elias Kirkhart had emerged as the most sound candidate: He was a maverick, a loner, an outsider. His wife had died a few years ago, and he was completely immersed in his work. He had neither friends, outside activities, nor family living in the area. And his British background gave him a sense of professional superiority over his fellow American agents and the attitude—held by English intelligence since Elizabeth I and Sir Francis Walsingham—that no one except the monarch was above suspicion. His only loyalty was to the security of "the realm."

As Lowell had expected, Eli Kirkhart had jumped at the opportunity. Finding a highly placed mole within the Bureau was not only a challenge but a duty.

"Sit down, Special Agent Kirkhart," deputy AG Taurino said.

Wearing the FBI uniform as usual—conservatively cut dark suit, white shirt, blue-and-gray regimental tie knotted tightly, shined black shoes, and the faint bulge of his 10mm Smith & Wesson under his jacket—Kirkhart walked toward another of Millicent Taurino's leather armchairs. His square, bulldog face showed no expression as he sat. Taurino cocked her head, studying him.

Cabot Lowell sighed. "I believe we can dispense with the dark glasses, Mr. Kirkhart. An affectation introduced by slovenly, half-trained pilots during World War Two and regrettably still with us."

Eli took off his aviator sunglasses, folded them, put them into their case, and returned the case to his inside jacket pocket. He did not apologize. He was working to save the nation, and he was not going to be intimidated by a mere national security adviser. Millicent Taurino, still studying him, repressed a smile.

"Thank you." Lowell inclined his head an inch. "Now, what do you have?"

Eli returned the curt nod. "Last night I discovered a man I've been watching for more than a year meeting surreptitiously with a former KGB colonel, Anatoli Yurimengri. After they dispersed, I followed Yurimengri, while one of my agents tailed my man. Yurimengri drove across the river to an international transport company in Arlington—Meteor Express. My original quarry went back to his office at *The Washington Post*. Meteor Express was closed, so I waited then returned to the Hoover building to check out Meteor Express. Interestingly, so far it looks legitimate, no KGB, FSB, or Russian connection, but its headquarters is in Maryland."

"Get to the point, Eli," Donald Chen snapped.

Kirkhart barely glanced at the assistant AG. "This morning I learned that Yurimengri had been murdered later in the night, and the crime had not happened in Arlington. Still, the coincidence was a bit much, so I drove back out there. Meteor Express was gone—lock, stock, and barrel." He snapped his fingers. "Disappeared. Instead, a new company had moved in overnight. That certainly got my attention, so I called the Meteor Express phone number. I found they were still in business and claimed they had never been located in Arlington."

"A front," Millicent Taurino confirmed.

"Indeed," Kirkhart agreed. "Which gave the murder of our former Soviet spy a new aspect, as did his meeting with my original quarry. The company that's taken over the building—Renae Trucking—also appears legitimate, by the way. The owner says she got a call in the middle of the night telling her the place was hers if she could move in right away. She wanted it, called everyone she knew to help her make such a fast move, and the rest, unfortunately, is history."

"Who is this quarry, and why have you been observing him for more than a year?" Cabot Lowell wanted to know.

"His name's Jeffrey Hammond. In the early nineties, he was one of the Bureau's top agents, specializing in Soviet affairs and a valuable member of the joint CIA-FBI team that debriefed KGB defectors." Kirkhart paused, and for a moment there was emotion in his voice, but it was so fleeting that only Millicent Taurino heard it: "We were partners . . . until he resigned under fire for continuing to investigate three of the defectors after they'd been cleared to stay in the country. Or that was the tale."

Millicent Taurino sat up. "You don't believe it?"

"Certainly not. I doubt he resigned at all. Rather, I believe he went undercover, hiding behind a current employment situation that legitimizes his staying in touch with the Soviet defectors and émigrés. His undercover status is probably so deep he reports only to somebody at the lofty top of the Bureau, maybe to the director himself. That would give him an almost free hand to snoop inside the Bureau, collect information, and pass it on to the Kremlin."

"You think he's our mole," Cabot Lowell decided.

Eli Kirkhart nodded. "I've suspected it for a year. Look at the whole picture: The Bureau's investigated all of its own people and found nothing. But did they ever investigate anyone who *isn't* in the Bureau? If I'm right, only the director and his top people know Hammond is still on the roster. On top of that, Hammond's a respected reporter for the *Post,* deals with Russians most days, and as a journalist has access to the Bureau. No one thinks twice if he's seen in the building. All year long, whenever I've tried to tail him, he's usually lost me. That tells me either he knows I'm after him, which I doubt, or he's automatically taking precautions because he wants no one to know what he's doing at any time, or whom he's doing it with. I think it's automatic."

Taurino nodded thoughtfully. "He's secretive and has access. Anything more?"

"Yes. He fits the profile for what the Bureau's psychologists call the John Walker syndrome or the Aldrich Ames syndrome." Walker was the navy warrant officer who became a very successful Soviet spy in the 1980s, partly to prove how clever he was, while Ames, arrested in the early 1990s, was considered the perpetrator of the worst spy scandal since the Rosenbergs stole the secret of the atom bomb during World War II. Ames, too, wanted to prove he was smarter than his colleagues. "Jeffrey Hammond's cocky. He has an in-your-face attitude, is divorced, and has few friends and no hobbies. According to our profiling, that sort of isolation breeds betrayal. Which is the reason the Bureau looks for agents to hire who make friends easily and keep them, or have some other anchor, like religion. As if to dot the *i*'s and cross the *t*'s, when the Bureau released Hammond, they labeled him a 'disordered isolate.' "

Donald Chen objected, "That's still all theoretical and circumstantial."

"And it fits the profile for *you,*" Millicent Taurino said, eying Kirkhart.

Kirkhart inclined his head. "Yes, to a certain extent." He allowed himself a rare smile. "But I have no need to prove how smart I am. I think there's a general consensus that I'm terribly bright or I wouldn't be here."

Surprised that he had a sense of humor, the two Justice officials and the national security adviser raised their eyebrows.

Kirkhart wiped the smile from his face. "There's one more thing. . . . Jeffrey Hammond is well off. Most turncoat spies do it less for psychological reasons than for money. You'll note my assets are meager. However, Hammond has an embarrassment of riches. He's got a major portfolio of investments plus a wad of cash in the bank that tells me he's got another, larger source of income besides his *Post* and Bureau salaries."

"That could be damning," Cabot Lowell agreed.

"There's more. In the Bureau, I've been checking the lost information not accounted for by all those we've caught recently, and most of it had to have leaked from the highest levels in the Bureau, but never from any one division in particular. That'd appear to indicate a mole with wide-ranging access to many divisions—such as a high-level undercover agent. Second, when he was tailed back to his office at the *Post* last night, Hammond later skipped out a back entrance. That gave him the time and opportunity to murder Colonel Yurimengri, whom I'd seen him meet earlier."

The three officials looked from one to the other. Then Cabot Lowell nodded. "All right, it's far from real evidence, but it's certainly food for thought. Keep observing this Hammond. I'll put some of my NSA people on the director and the other brass. Good work, Special Agent Kirkhart."

"Keep in daily touch with me, Eli," Assistant AG Chen ordered sternly, aware of Kirkhart's penchant for cavalierly going it alone.

Kirkhart nodded and left, his back straight and military. As she watched her outer door close, Millicent Taurino glanced at the two men. "Someone who's there at the Bureau, yet not there."

Cabot Lowell mused, "Clever, if true. Most clever."

Donald Chen said, "Let's hope our mole-hunter's right. Our betrayer's been laughing at us a hell of a lot too long. Every time I think of the harm he's done, I worry about what in the Lord's name he's up to now. The damage he could still do . . . it's almost unthinkable."

Jeff Hammond was grim as he entered the *Post*'s cluttered newsroom, where desks and cubicles spread like islands in a vast gray sea. Telephones rang, voices rose and fell, and the air was ripe with the odors of stale coffee and fresh newsprint. Repressed excitement had been percolating through the mammoth newsroom for hours, as reporters nailed down scheduling information and interviews for the state visit of Vladimir V. Putin, Russia's struggling president.

Since the days of Boris Yeltsin, Russia's economic woes had continued to spiral downward, its nuclear arms had fallen into ever more dangerous disrepair, and upstart tycoons had increased their stranglehold on the country, despite the efforts of Yeltsin's successor—the reformist Putin—to reverse the trend. Not only in Moscow but in the country's far-flung districts, nearly ninety all together, local moguls had swallowed up vast assets from the dead Soviet Union for fractions of their actual worth. Thus far they had successfully repelled Putin's tax collectors, his efforts to redistribute power, and his demand that the magnates support the authority of the Kremlin and help rebuild the country.

Unwilling to breach Russia's shaky sovereignty, the seventeen other nations of the industrialized world had waited, worried some unexpected event might tip the unstable country into an act of despair that could involve those crumbling—but still deadly—nuclear weapons.

Just two years before, Vladimir Putin had been a colorless, unsmiling unknown when he had been appointed prime minister, Yeltsin's fifth in just seventeen months. After so much turnover, no one expected the new man to last either. In fact, pundits agreed he was too inexperienced at politics, personally too naïve and unseasoned, to survive. Plus, he lacked the kind of connections necessary to make any kind of significant change in the baroque Kremlin environment.

On paper, the experts appeared to be smart. After all, trained as a lawyer, Putin had turned his back on civilian life to join the notorious KGB shortly after graduation. He soon became a spy in one of the world's most steamy, most competitive espionage hotbeds—East Germany. Only when the Berlin Wall collapsed did he resign from the KGB and return to his hometown, St. Petersburg, to become deputy mayor. Then when his boss, the mayor, lost reelection, Putin fell back on what he knew best: The Federal Security Service, the FSB—the KGB's prime successor agency—but now as its head. So relieved was he to be back where he knew how to excel, he was alleged to have strode into the imposing red-and-yellow building that housed the central Moscow headquarters—a place most people entered with fear and trembling—and announced, "I'm home at last."

But once elevated to prime minister, the decorated spy fooled everyone. He hard-lined on the Chechen war and became the most popular politician in Russia. The next year, he easily won election to the presidency, succeeding Boris Yeltsin.

News of President Putin's arrival tomorrow appeared throughout today's *Post,* making Hammond's analysis of Colonel Yurimengri's life and death particularly timely. To Hammond's way of thinking, everything was perspective.

Which brought up the issue of Beth Convey. When the call had come that she was in the lobby and wanted to speak to him, he prepared himself for whatever unpleasant course he would have to take. There was a point in their conversation when he sensed she recognized him, which could be a fatal mistake. It was too bad, too. He liked the looks of her—all that fresh blondness, and the dark brows, and the long legs. He liked the way she moved—warm and liquid. He also liked the beartrap mind. Sometimes she seemed delicate, and then within seconds she was a damn Valkyrie, all action and sex appeal. And then there was her voice, low and throaty. A bedroom voice, his grandmother used to call it.

He slumped into the chair at his desk, closed his eyes, and shook his head to clear it. He had already collected information about her—Elizabeth ("Beth") Convey, J.D.—her parents and childhood, where she worked, a client list, her publications, the heart-transplant episode, the names of her various doctors, her home address, even her unlisted phone number. If you knew where to look and the databases to tap, and if you had contacts in key places, you could usually find what you wanted. For reporters and a few less savory professions, resourcefulness was at the top of the job description. Hammond was good at his job, and so far he had fooled everybody. No one at the *Post* guessed the truth about him.

He stared at the half-dozen new Post-it notes that hung from his computer screen and lamp shade, all asking for more information and opinions that would help prepare his fellow reporters for the coming event:

"Okay, Hammond, what's so important about Murmansk?" He scribbled, *It's the biggest year-round, ice-free port in the Russian Arctic. That's where the navy has mothballed most of its nuclear fleet, which is rotting faster than anyone wants to admit.*

"So what is Ekstra? I read it's one of Putin's favorite drinks." *A domestic brand of vodka, sometimes affectionately called tank fuel, which tells you how strong it is.*

Hammond worked through the other notes, quickly addressing questions about the Duma, toasting customs, folk dances, and Leningrad State University, from which Putin had graduated in civil law. They were important to his colleagues and the paper, which made them important to him. But as he worked, pleasant scenes came back to him—a late summer afternoon as chestnut trees ripened along the Kiev esplanade . . . the broad Moscow River . . . the soaring spire of Spassky Gate, where Napoleon had dismounted to walk his horse into the Kremlin to show respect.

He shook his head to clear away those nostalgic images. Was he going soft? Losing the drive that had set him on this course? Thinking too much of the past, and, maybe, an empty future?

Angry with himself, he picked up his telephone and dialed. She would never know it, but Beth Convey had given him what he needed—Stone Point, West Virginia—and he was not going to quit now.

The afternoon sun shone sharp and bright where Beth sat alert in her Mercedes. Then she saw Jeff Hammond's profile again, this time driving up out of the *Post*'s parking garage in a vintage 1960s Mustang convertible with the top down. He paused the sports car at the exit to the bustling street.

She sat up straighter. Now she saw how he had hidden his long hair. She should have guessed it: As he must have last night, his ponytail was tucked up into a Baltimore Orioles baseball cap, creating the exact profile she had glimpsed in the dark outside Meteor Express. Even as she fought to repress another wave of fear, she felt an odd surge of excitement, almost exultation. It was the thrill of danger, and she knew instantly that before her transplant she never would have felt such a reaction, certainly never would have been sitting in her car right now, waiting for a killer.

Today she had threatened the employees at Renae Trucking, told off her boss at the law firm, quit a job she had been convinced she loved, and with cavalier pique made impossible her longtime dream—partnership in Edwards & Bonnett. And she felt unhappy about none of it. In fact, she was relieved and eager, as if a tremendous weight had been lifted from her aching shoulders. As if she could do anything she had to now.

Emotions washed through her—fear, eagerness, confusion, doubt, enthusiasm. She understood none of it. The truth was . . . she no longer understood herself. She was adrift, and she did not know even at this moment what she was going to feel or think or do next.

From where she sat parked between two cars down the block, she studied Hammond's rugged face as he eyed the street for an opening in the traffic. His features were grave, his jaw set, and his eyes masked by a pair of wraparound sunglasses. Over his blue work shirt he wore a herringbone tweed jacket, which gave him a hip, professorial air. Why would he have killed Yurimengri? For a moment she worried she might have played some unknowing role in his murder. She hoped not. Still, by dialing the phone number that had harried her throughout the year, she had stumbled onto the murder of an émigré whose name she had been very close to guessing. In fact, a man from her nightmares.

With an abrupt burst of speed, Hammond drove his Mustang into the street and entered traffic. She watched him pull away, knowing she now had to decide. Should she follow, or should she go home and try to put her life back together the way it was before? It would be smart to go home. Far safer, too. She remembered the implied threat in Hammond's "advice:" *If you're right, the killer could go after you, too. You could end up dead.*

She shook her head. She could not quit, because she could not forget. Whoever she had been before her death in the courthouse and rebirth in the transplant center was gone. She was a different person with a different emotional makeup, and—apparently—"memories" she neither recalled nor understood.

Suddenly it was no longer a hard decision, and whether it was risky seemed irrelevant. With a steady hand, she flicked on her ignition and drove off, following Jeff Hammond at a distance through the congestion that crossed the Potomac and funneled toward what was now called Ronald Reagan airport, but to locals would be forever enshrined as "National," its name for more than a half century. With its soaring domes and glass-and-steel walls, the airport was a favorite of congressmen, government officials, and lobbyists because of its closeness—just fifteen minutes across the river—to Capitol Hill.

Although she had never tailed anyone, she followed Hammond back into a private section of the sprawling airport with only a few mistakes and one heart-stopping moment when she lost sight of his convertible. When he parked outside a fence and pushed through a mesh gate, she cruised past, her gaze averted.

Oddly, she felt comfortable with these new tasks. But when she looked back at the tarmac, she had a shock: Hammond was gone. Vanished. She gazed frantically around. Mentally she shook her head. No. He must have entered the small building that stood next to a series of hangars.

She was right, because he was out again, trotting across the tarmac with the muscular ease of a halfback in his herringbone jacket and jeans. As jet engines screamed in the distance, she parked, rolled down her window, and watched. A soft spring breeze cooled her hot-cheeked face. And then she jumped out of her car. He was climbing into a single-engine plane. It was a Cessna, according to the designation on the outside, and the propellers were rotating.

She ran across the road, in through the mesh gate, and looked around for help as he taxied the Cessna away toward a runway. The plane had obviously been waiting for him, ready to fly. Either he or someone else had phoned ahead. She spotted a battered rectangular sign on the small building out of which he had run: OFFICE.

She stood motionless, frustrated, thinking quickly. She wanted to know where Hammond had gone, but she had no clout to make an employee reveal that sort of privileged information. In the past, she would have made phone calls, reaching contacts until she found someone who knew someone who had the power. But there was no time for that. She had entered a brand-new world where the rules were different, if indeed there were rules, and she had to adjust. She repressed another shiver of fear and then the same shock of excited pleasure. The strange, cool confidence she had sometimes felt in her nightmares kicked in, followed by her brain. An idea occurred to her. She took a deep breath. With luck, it might work.

She pushed open the door and walked rapidly inside, as if on a vital mission. There were three desks, but only one was occupied. Computers stood on each, surrounded by papers. An ivy plant sat in a corner, brown and dying. Various plaques and awards hung from the rough wood walls, honoring the small private air service whose headquarters this was.

She reached into her big shoulder bag and hurried toward the only employee, who was sitting behind the desk closest to the door. She infused her voice with urgency. "I have legal papers from the newspaper for Mr. Hammond. Has he gone?"

"In that Cessna out there." The man at the desk was about forty, with thinning, rat-brown hair. Dressed in jeans and a T-shirt, he leaned back and shot an appraising look at her breasts, her waist, and her thighs. He was unmoved by her show of urgency.

She ignored him. "Can you call him back?"

"Nope." His gaze did another sweep of her.

"Okay, then tell me where he's going. I'll have to fax the papers ahead."

"No can do. The boss won't let us give out that kind of information."

She made her voice hard and cold, "Then I'll deal with your boss."

He laughed and shook his head. "He's out of town. Sorry."

He was the kind of irritating person who, given small authority, enjoyed being diffifcult.

"Really?" She raised an eyebrow. "I'm from the *Post*'s legal department. These papers are important."

"Hey, that's your problem, lady. My hands are tied."

"Too bad." She made a show of pushing a sheaf of papers back into her bag. "Tell me . . . how did Mr. Hammond pay you?"

He seemed puzzled by the question. "Credit card, what else?"

"Naturally. He'll use the receipt for reimbursement from the *Post.*"

He did not know where she was going, and that worried him. "Yeah, I guess."

She nodded. "We usually do pay that way. The paper does a lot of business with your boss, but I expect our publisher will be so mad that I'll have to recommend we go elsewhere in the future. I'm sure you can explain to your boss why he lost us, and then he'll back you all the way."

His smile vanished. "Hey, you wouldn't do that."

"Try me."

He glared and ran his hand through his thin hair. Sullenly he reached into a rack of folders on his desk and threw one in front of her.

She opened it. The flight plan was on top. For a moment, her eyes glazed. She should have guessed: Jeff Hammond was going to Stone Point in West Virginia, the same town that had been on Yurimengri's dying lips.

Earlier that day, fired up after his meeting with National Security Adviser Cabot Lowell and the deputy attorney general, Eli Kirkhart had reclaimed his parking space across from *The Washington Post*. From that vantage, the mole hunter had spotted Jeff Hammond walking out of the main entrance in the company of a tall, stunning blond. What had made him come to attention was neither her beauty nor her height, it was that he had never before seen her with Hammond.

Kirkhart grabbed his Leica camera and snapped a series of shots as the pair walked along the sidewalk. He tried to read their lips, but between the pedestrians and the heavy traffic, which included many tall trucks, it was hopeless. From their expressions, the conversation looked like no lovers' tête-à-tête. Eventually they returned to the building, where Hammond pushed back inside, and she walked on to a handsome Mercedes, parked nearby. She unlocked the expensive car, climbed in, and drove off.

Kirkhart had to make the same decision he had last night, and this time decided to stay with Hammond. He had the license number of the Mercedes and snapshots of the woman, so he could find her later. He moved his car, preparing to begin a long, tedious wait. He was settling in, when the Mercedes—the blond at the wheel—appeared from the other direction and slid into a parking space three cars ahead of him.

Her surreptitious return had removed the tediousness of Eli's surveillance, and when Hammond's car emerged from the depths of the garage, and the blond drove off after him, Kirkhart gave them a good head start and followed.

Now he watched as the woman exited the charter company's office and hurried back to the Mercedes. He picked up his phone and relayed the Mercedes's license number and a description of the woman to his team with instructions to find out who and what she was. Satisfied that he might be on to something useful, he marched into the office to find out where Jeff Hammond was going this time.

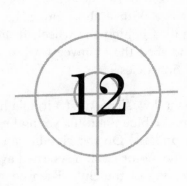

12

Afternoon had sent a sleepy warmth across Colonel Caleb Bates's vast timbered hunt club in West Virginia, but it had not slowed the Keepers. Sweat-faced, they worked doggedly, cleaning and checking arms, practicing martial arts, and fighting in the exercises Bates designed to keep them focused.

As activity infused the camp, Colonel Bates returned to his cabin, went directly to his locked gun case, and chose a 9mm SIG Sauer. He balanced it in his hand, savoring its compact, efficient design, then he snapped in a full clip and slid the pistol into the leather holster under his armpit. His tension relaxed a fraction. For him, there was nothing quite so comforting as being armed, especially with a fine weapon like the SIG Sauer. It would do the job in more ways than one.

He put on his tan bush jacket, which concealed the pistol nicely, and went to stand in front of his mirror. As he looked at his burly face and meaty frame, the product of expert makeup and padding, he had the odd sensation once again that he was losing whoever he might have been.

With an act of will, he shook off his unease and concentrated on his plan. He had three problems, any one of which could destroy the operation on Saturday, just three days away. This worried him, but not overly much. One of the prime reasons he had beaten and outlived most of his enemies was his uncanny ability to foresee problems. And, as always, he had a plan.

He slid a small leather pouch into his hip pocket and buttoned the flap for security. He looked out his window. His Humvee had arrived and was parked in front. With a short smile, he strode out into the mountain air and climbed behind the wheel, feeling reenergized, just like his old self. As he sped the Humvee toward the gate, he was already considering contingencies.

Marty Coulson was in love. The West Virginia hardwood forest was greener, the mountain sky bluer, and his young heart so full it seemed near bursting with happiness. On the Honda motorcycle he had temporarily swiped from the motor pool, he coasted away until he was certain he was out of hearing of the club. Then he stopped the big bike near a stand of hemlock, jumped the starter, and roared the rest of the way down the wooded mountainside into Stone Point.

He was wearing jeans, a short-sleeved sweatshirt, and a motorcycle helmet. When he hit the brake in front of Lila's house on the south edge of town, the wheels spun clouds of dust up from the unpaved road. He pulled off his helmet, tucked it under his arm, and ran up to her front porch.

She slammed open the screen door. "You made it! Oh, Marty. How did you get away?"

She was in his arms, and he was kissing every bit of skin he could find. He loved the peppermint toothpaste on her breath and the cologne he could smell rising up from between her small breasts. She had long auburn hair that was as straight and silky as meadow grass.

He slid his fingers through it, crooning her name. "Lila, Lila, Lila." He pulled her into the house, and the screen door banged behind them. "Are they gone?"

"Sure. They're at work. I didn't think you'd come, Marty. I thought you said Colonel Bates wasn't going to let anyone leave. But I waited and waited. I just knew if anyone could sneak out, it'd be you. Oh, Marty. I took a shower and made myself pretty for you. Do you think I'm pretty?"

"The prettiest girl ever." He dropped his helmet and maneuvered her toward her bedroom, his legs pressed against hers. "Not just the prettiest girl I've ever seen, but the prettiest one was ever born. That's you, Lila."

"Why do you work for that man Bates? What do you do up there on the mountain all day long? I don't see why I can't visit."

Marty stopped maneuvering her toward the bed. He stroked her hair and looked into her lilac eyes. She had eyes that were old already, but they had nice thick fringes and he liked the color. "I don't work *for* the colonel. I work *with* him. Don't say anything bad about him, Lila. I can't stand that. He's going to straighten out the world, and then you'll be glad for all the sacrifices we're making. We'll be a real nation again. We'll stop giving away our jobs and our money and everything we know. Everything that's precious. America's for Americans. It's the only right thing, the way God intended. You're just going to have to trust me and not say or think anything mean about him again. Promise?"

When she nodded solemnly, he laughed with delight. He kissed her long and deep, and now it was her turn to pull him toward the bed.

In another life, the man who called himself Colonel Caleb Bates had helped to lead the most elite, most dangerous force in the world. So when it came time to locate a dirty little shack on the edge of a nothing town, he could have driven directly to it. But that would not accomplish his goal. Instead, he pulled the Humvee off into the forest, covered it with brush, and melted through the trees, heading south on foot, until he spotted the motorcycle the boy had taken from the club. It was parked directly in front of the shack. A dead giveaway. He sighed. People—especially young people—were so predictable.

Resisting the pressure to close the chase, he surveyed the dirt street with its border of reedy trees and junk-strewn yards. At last the few people who were outdoors went into their houses. When the street was empty, he trotted out from cover and sped across to the shack. He did not like the looks of the porch. It was old and would surely squeak. He reconnoitered around the structure, peering in windows, until he came to an open one where he heard voices.

"Do it again." It was the laughter of a young woman. "Kiss *all* my toes. I put sexy pink polish on them just for you."

Bates took out his SIG Sauer and screwed on the silencer.

"Hey, what about me?" It was Marty Coulson's voice. "How about *my* toes? Don't you think I should get the full treatment, too?"

Carefully Bates raised up and peered in the open window. It was a girl's bedroom. The boy and girl were naked on the bed, partially covered in cheap floral sheets. There was a used condom knotted on the floor. The girl rose to her knees, and the sheet fell from her breasts. She grabbed the boy's foot and playfully opened her mouth wide over his toes—

And saw Bates at the window. She screamed. The boy jumped up and looked wildly around for what was wrong.

Bates fired. He put the first bullet through the boy's heart because he was the more dangerous of the two. Immediately he fired a second through the girl's forehead at midpoint. The silenced gun made *pop-pop* sounds. Blood sprayed the bedroom, fell onto the sheets in scarlet pools. The boy and girl were propelled back, the power of the 9mm bullets sending their bodies half off the bed.

It was all over in three seconds. Bates slid the gun back into its holster and wiped the back of his hand across his upper lip, erasing the sweat that had formed as soon as the girl had screamed. He observed the street and other shanties but saw no one.

He had one final piece of business. He took a small, flat, airtight metal box from his pocket, opened it, and removed a specially treated surgical glove. He slipped it carefully onto his left hand and gripped the windowsill, sliding the gloved fingers back as if he suddenly had to balance himself. The fingerprints would be smudged and look real, the oils would be fresh, and there would be enough of one or more of the prints to be readable—and traceable.

Earlier this afternoon he had received a phone call reporting their contact at the airport had said Jeffrey Hammond was on his way to Stone Point. That was when Bates had demanded the glove. The fingerprints laid onto it belonged to Hammond's left hand, collected during a meeting at a Washington bar some time ago and saved for this sort of contingency. Preparedness was one of the pillars of Bates's success, and the investigative reporter and onetime FBI special agent was getting annoyingly close. It was time to put an end to his pursuit.

Bates looked around once more. Whistling tunelessly, he trotted back across the street and disappeared into the forest.

Bates did not think of himself as a murderer. He had never loved the act, as he knew true assassins often did. He killed only by necessity. Still, he was exhilarated. This afternoon's work was a job well done. Since the young man, Marty Coulson, had shown too much enterprise, and Bates needed followers without the initiative or ambition to lead, Marty had to be eliminated anyway. At the same time, Bates also solved the problem of Jeff Hammond.

Now he was about to handle his third task. He needed to bind the Keepers to him as closely as if they were his own blood and tissue, and he would use the murders of Marty and the girl to do it. The symmetry of it all pleased him so much that he chuckled.

He reached camp just as the sun was setting in a radiant orange glow across the forested shoulders of the mountain. As the night grew gray and shadowy, moist with the scent of decaying leaves, he summoned the Keepers for a meeting in the mess hall. He scanned their well-scrubbed faces as they filed in. They were cleaned up and ready for dinner. From the cookhouse, the mouth-watering aromas of roast beef, rich gravy, and cherry pie wafted over the grounds.

Inside the hall, the sergeant made general announcements. Bates strode over to wait behind him. Eager to hear what his leader had to say, the sergeant sped through his presentation, and Bates took center stage, as erect and sturdy as a mighty buckeye tree. All conversation and movement stopped. He had their attention, but he wanted more.

"I have a tragedy to relate." His gravelly voice was solemn. The big room seemed to stiffen, readying itself. "As some of you may know, I've just returned from a mission to Stone Point to bring back one of our young patriots, Martin Coulson. Marty had a girlfriend down there in town, and he succumbed to temptation. He didn't follow orders to stay in camp—"

There was a groan from the audience, and Bates knew it was likely from Marty's mother. "He wasn't stopped by the police, was he?" There was an edge of horror in the woman's voice. "Tell me what's happened to my Marty?"

"I'm sorry, Mother. Prepare yourself." Bates's voice was appropriately grave. "The boy's dead."

The Keepers were family people, and the death of the popular young man hit hard. Women gasped. Men's jaws stiffened. Marty's mother buried her face on her husband's shoulder and sobbed, while his eyes glazed, trying to absorb the shock and show no emotion.

Bates nodded sympathetically. Now it was time to raise the affective bar a notch. He said harshly, "Marty is the Keepers' first casualty. But he didn't kill himself, and it was no accident. He was *murdered!*"

Just as he expected, the room erupted.

"Who did it?" one man demanded. "I'll kill the bastard!"

"Where's the son of a bitch?" another bellowed, shaking his fist. "Let me get my hands on him!"

"Tell us who did it, Colonel!" shouted a third.

Bates raised his hands, palms down, to quiet them. The iron discipline he had instilled, their unquestioned loyalty to him, and their fanatical dedication to their cause, made them quiet instantly.

"I'll tell you who did it, not so you can take revenge now, but so you'll remember later how much this nation needs us and our cause." He paused to let them hang on his next words. "Fellow Keepers, our young comrade was assassinated by an *FBI man!*"

While that was not strictly true, Bates knew they would all read it that way when the newspapers reported the arrest of the former FBI agent. With deep satisfaction, he watched their frustrated torment, the rage and hatred on their faces. Deep in their hearts, he knew they were thinking about who the "real" enemies of their country were.

Bates nodded. "Yes, fellow patriots. We know who the enemy is and what we have to do! Right?"

"Right!" they said in unison.

"And we aren't alone in our quest. Think of our brothers and sisters in the Montana Freemen who faced off the government jackals. Remember the bombings in Washington state and the bank robberies in the Midwest. And most of all, don't forget the righteous destruction of the Oklahoma City federal building. We patriots have a tradition not just of sacrifice and survival, but of *victory*. Right?"

"Right!" they shouted.

Bates raised his voice, filling it with urgency. "But since it was the FBI that assassinated Marty, that means the government must be closing in on us, too. To avenge Marty, we've got to get out of West Virginia fast so we can put the last pieces of our operation together safely. We've got an appointment with a great and glorious future on Saturday. Marty wants us to be there. *He wants us to win.* We'll do this for Marty! Is that right?"

"Right!" they roared. *"For Marty!"*

From a painful low of grief and outrage, Bates had taken them on a straight ride up to the Olympian heights of honor. There was no greater force than controlled lightning, and that was what they were in his hands. They were his, their aspirations were his, and now he owned them more than ever.

He poured urgency into his voice: "The helicopters are on their way. Pack your personals. The quartermaster will assign you which supplies to oversee. Let's move!"

With him in the lead, they double-timed as a group out onto the grounds and dispersed. They were frighteningly efficient, elite troops now, like the paratroopers with whom he had trained so long ago. Within an hour, they had struck camp. A half-hour later, some were boarding helicopters while others drove trucks, cars, and motorcycles out the secret back entrance. The noise of engines reverberated through the forest night.

As usual, Bates was the last to leave. Alone in his cabin, he became again, briefly, Alexei Berianov. He called his Maryland headquarters and spoke to Ivan Vok in Russian: "Hammond came too close to finding us this time. He could talk, or others could follow his path. Alexei Berianov needs to disappear. Send him to visit our people in Moscow, a trip home. Berianov will have an unfortunate heart attack. Death from natural causes, eh? It will eliminate the risk that anyone might see Berianov in Caleb Bates."

"I'll arrange it right now, Alexei."

"Good." Berianov clicked off and composed himself.

As Caleb Bates, he stepped out into the chilly night, sweeping his gaze over the deserted, moonlit camp as he hurried toward the last helicopter. Ghostly wisps of fog rose from the warm grounds. Around him he saw nothing but empty husks of buildings. There were no dropped mementoes, no trash, no scraps of paper with incriminating information, nothing at all to tell anyone who might arrive that those who had lived and trained here were on a life-or-death mission of targeted destruction.

With a sense of eager anticipation, he climbed aboard the noisy chopper, turned to the pilot, and jerked his thumb upward. The pilot nodded, acknowledging the signal, and the great bird shuddered and rose like a demon into the black night. For Caleb Bates—and for Alexei Berianov—there was no turning back.

A heart was just a two-stroke pump, a simple piece of human machinery. Yet this new heart—this fist-sized chunk of living tissue that thumped so vibrantly inside her chest—seemed to have turned Beth's life upside down and inside out and left her floundering not only in events she did not understand but in a sense of herself, of who she was, of a person she no longer recognized.

Jeff Hammond was on his way to West Virginia, so Beth went home, her mouth dry with worry. As the afternoon wore on, she paced her Georgetown house from top to bottom. She had always believed that life was straightforward. For her, there had been few curves. She had grown up in the golden shadow of her parents in Los Angeles. For them, the city was more than a hometown or an address: It was both playground and battleground for their glitz, glamour, and stratospheric careers.

Her father—the dramatic, compelling emperor of L.A. courtrooms—had made his name synonymous with impossible defense cases. When a potential client, usually a guilty murderer, asked what the fee would be for Jack-the-Knife Convey to beat the system, her father would study a list of the person's assets and point to the bottom line. "I think your life's worth at least this, don't you? And if you don't, then I don't have much to defend, do I?" For him, that kind of outrageous logic meant coined gold.

Her mother, on the other hand, was the high-powered, pantyhose empress of L.A. real estate. Janet Reese Convey had been on the inside of many of the Southwest's hottest projects—convention centers, vast housing tracts, shockingly large shopping malls. As a youngster, Janet first saw the value of property when her grandfather's side yard produced an oil gusher. All of a sudden, a small bungalow surrounded by bougainvillea, tomatoes, and fruit trees—and one ugly oil rig—was transformed into a world of unexpected possibility. Money flowed from the ground, and her extended family was suddenly able to afford cars, vacations, educations, and businesses. The excitement of that time, the remarkable transformation from poverty to affluence, left an indelible impression on her.

When Beth was born to the union of Jack and Janet, their only child, it was not with a silver spoon in her mouth. It was with an entire set of sterling. She had everything—the latest toys, the best nannies, the right schools, and the children of the West Coast elite for her playmates. As she grew older and turned into a leggy, blond beauty, there were also the hottest parties in Beverly Hills and Brentwood and out on the coast in Newport or on Linda Isle. The fast cars. The coutour clothing, or the hippest rags from Melrose. The hair styles created by Adamo Lentini. And of course, there were boyfriends. Gorgeous boyfriends with the bodies of surfers and the tanned good looks that only leisure and unlimited allowances could buy.

But when she turned eighteen, her life changed completely. Remembering it all, she felt a chill, but instantly she shrugged it off. That was when she ended her playgirl lifestyle and grew serious. Just as her mother had discovered the allure of the land and her father had found being a courthouse warrior endlessly seductive, Beth uncovered the power of the mind. She wanted to think, analyze, lose herself in ideas. She dismissed emotion and sat for hours, staring out across the sprawling Los Angeles basin, contemplating history, politics, fashion, even mechanics. She took language and drawing lessons. Everything fascinated her.

But now that she was thirty-three years old, she was confused beyond anything she had ever experienced. The fact that she no longer recognized herself had shaken her. If you do not know who you are, how can you know anything?

For hours that day she paced her Victorian and looked unseeing at the plush furniture and the expensive artwork, all bought with the spoils of her well-trained legal brain. She had been wrong, she now realized: Despite the occasional detour, her life was not built on the rational mind as she had always believed. Instead, she had done what was easy.

It had been easy to follow her myriad interests, financed by the trust fund her parents had established for her. Eventually that had led her into law, where it had been easy for her to work hard and succeed. After all, that was what her family did, what she had been trained to do.

She had never had a significant doubt about any of it, only a hunger to move ahead, to be as good as they had been, and then to be not only better but the best. She'd had a lot to accomplish, to compensate for. But now she was no longer the same. She doubted everything, and she had no idea where to go . . . what to do . . . who she would be next.

Beth made herself stick to her routine of exercise and shower. She examined the bump on her forehead, which had grown smaller. She wished her problems would vanish as easily as this physical injury. Restless, she dressed again. What she should do, she knew, was start phoning contacts to let them know she was looking for another job. Considering how many times she had been approached by other District firms before her surgery, she figured she would land somewhere interesting. Still, as hard as she tried, she could work up no enthusiasm to begin the process.

Instead, she wanted to discover how it was that she had recognized Anatoli Yurimengri. How she had known at least part of his name. Why she was having nightmares. Why were the nightmares about Russians, soldiers, and violence? *Why?*

Which made her think about her surgeon, Travis Jackson. She phoned his office, and, of course, he was with a patient.

"May I give the doctor your name?" the receptionist asked with little interest.

"I'm Beth Convey, one of his transplant patients."

The indifference vanished. "Hold on, Ms. Convey."

The woman had forgotten to put her on hold, and so Beth heard the sounds of a busy office—coughs, laughter, the turning of pages, annoyed voices asking how much longer the doctor would be. She was about to hang up, not wanting to interrupt a desperate person in need, when Travis Jackson's anxious voice sounded in her ear.

"Beth? What's wrong? Are you all right? Tell me—"

"I'm fine, Travis. Nothing's wrong." Then she caught herself. "No, that's not true. I'm *not* fine. At least mentally. I'm a long way from it."

She could hear him expel a relieved breath. Her heart was not failing, and this was no medical emergency. "Well, then, exactly what's the problem?"

"Strange things are still happening to me. Frightening things. The worst of it is, I'm not acting like my old self. I don't feel like myself."

She heard a sigh. In her mind, she could see him again just as he so often had been last year, sitting beside her hospital bed, his face grave but interested, the rimless glasses perched on the end of his nose, as they discussed her condition. His presence had been comforting.

He said, "Tell me the whole story."

Without names or locations, she described the events since she called the mysterious Arlington number.

His voice was startled, even shocked. "You've told this to the police?"

"Not all of it. I reported the murder, but they thought I was a mad-woman or maybe trying to pull a fast one of some kind."

"That's ridiculous."

"People are dead. I've been chased and threatened. I still have the nightmares and thoughts, feelings and ideas that I never had before. I'm acting in ways I never did. I don't recognize myself. I'm not even sure I like myself."

"Calm down. Please." An undertone of impatience intruded on his usually soothing voice. "If everything you've told me really happened, all I can—"

"If?" She was incredulous. "You don't believe me?"

"Beth, listen." Now the impatience bordered on annoyance. "Yes, I think it's all probably occurred one way or another. But it isn't your heart that's leading you on and reshaping you. I promise you that. It's the trauma, the medicine, the nervousness, your eagerness to return to work, and then the disaster of finding your client base stolen. It's prob-ably a hundred different things, and all of them are impacting your per-ceptions and memory. There's no doubt these apparent changes are straight out of your past and that you've simply forgotten what the con-nections are. Your heart is *not* speaking to you. Can't be. It's impossi-ble. Ridiculous. There's absolutely *no* concrete evidence or scientific basis for such a macabre notion. I've already told you that."

He was dismissing her. Her voice was short: "It's a year, Travis, and it hasn't stopped. In fact, it's gotten worse. The terrible things that've happened since yesterday aren't connected to anything in my life before the transplant. I promise *you* that."

There was silence. She was beginning to think he had walked away.

When he spoke again, his tone was brisk. "I want you to take a seda-tive, get a good night's sleep. You've worked yourself into a state. That's obvious. I'll have Tina make an appointment for you tomorrow.

I'm booked up, but we'll squeeze you in somehow. I'm going to bring in a colleague to meet with you. You'll like her. She owes me a favor, and I think the two of you will work well together."

"Who's this colleague?"

"Patricia Fall."

"I've heard the name. She's a psychiatrist?"

"Yes. Very prominent. Solid credentials. Perhaps it's time we faced the possibility that more is going on with you and your emotional state than either of us realized. . . ."

"I don't think so." Engulfed with sudden rage, she slammed the receiver down and glared at it. "In fact, I'm now convinced *you* need the shrink, Travis, because you refuse to listen to reality. You're *wrong!* This is all happening. You're wrong, and it's *real!*"

Shaking with outrage, she stood motionless beside the telephone. All she wanted to do was smash things. She wanted to punch her fist into the wall, break windows, destroy furniture. *How dare he.* Breathing hard, she worked to quiet herself. And slowly her anger turned into despair. The house seemed terribly empty, where once she had found the long silences a relief. Was there no answer at all? Was she helpless?

She had always known the difference between what was real and what was imagined. It was the kind of thing you figured out by the time you were five years old. Of course, you could pretend to deny it. Sometime around age four she had created an imaginary friend she called Linda. Her nanny would set up tea parties for the two of them in the gazebo, and when no one was looking, Beth would drink Linda's tea, too, and then tell the nanny how much Linda had enjoyed it.

At the same time, the boy who lived on the estate next to theirs claimed he flew regularly to the moon on his rocket ship. His stories were wild and exciting, and he would fight anyone who accused him of lying. But about the time her interests switched from Linda to books and movies, he moved on to soccer and computer games. They admitted to each other that Linda and the rocket ship had never existed. Bonded by the truth, they left that part of their childhoods behind.

Now she felt like a preschooler, shaken in her belief that she could decipher the difference between real and imagined. She sighed, raised her arms above her head, and stretched. She needed to give her brain a rest, to forget this mess for a time. She went into her office to find something to occupy her. There on her desk was her briefcase, and she remembered the printout of the secret list of HanTech owners, which was still inside. She had forgotten not only the list but Michelle Philmalee.

Michelle's loyalty had turned out to have the staying power of a gnat, and Beth pitied her shortsightedness when it came to men. Some abused women were victims in most aspects of their lives, while others were like Michelle—highly functional, but with a dangerous blind spot when it came to men and love affairs. She hoped Michelle would figure that out someday.

In the meantime, Michelle really needed the HanTech data to save her endangered uranium deal, and the truth was, Beth liked Michelle. All clients came with a few wrinkles and dents, and Michelle was no different. Besides, there was no point in punishing Michelle; Beth had been stupid enough to date that weasel Phil Stageman, too.

Relieved to be doing something useful, Beth copied the list of owners on her Xerox machine, wrote Michelle's name on a manila envelope, and slid the copy inside. She considered a moment, then jotted a note, wishing her all the best. Considering that Michelle was now hooked up with Phil, she was going to need all the good wishes she could get. Then she drove through the twilight to Michelle's house and left the envelope in her mailbox.

At home again, she set herself up in her living room. It was large and airy, with tall windows that looked out onto the dark residential street. There was a faint odor of lemon polish. Her television was hidden in an antique armoire. Beth sat in her favorite wing-back chair, propped her feet up on her marble-topped coffee table, and surfed channels. But the situation comedies bored her, the dramas paled next to her own new life, and the news depressed her.

She switched off the TV and phoned two longtime friends in Washington. They talked about inconsequential things, and momentarily she felt relieved by the normality of it all.

Cheered, she took her medicines and made herself a healthy dinner. She did another round of exercises and showered again. When her hair was dry, she threw on her bathrobe and returned to her office once more in the hopes that this time the businesslike atmosphere would give some order, some direction, to the swirl in her mind. That was when she saw the red light blinking on her answering machine.

She stared at it, not certain she wanted to know who had phoned while she was in the shower or what the message was. Maybe it was Travis Jackson calling back to apologize, to say it was entirely possible her heart was sending her messages. She looked at her watch. It was past eight o'clock. It could also be Jeff Hammond. She swallowed hard. No, surely he was still in West Virginia.

She girded herself and punched the NEW MESSAGES button.

The snotty voice of Zach Housley's personal secretary announced: "Mr. Housley has asked me to inform you that security's packed up the private things in your former office. The boxes will be delivered to your house tomorrow. COD, of course. I stayed late to expedite this. As a courtesy, Mr. Housley wanted me to warn you to be there to pay the shippers. And if I may add, Ms. Convey, we're all terribly disappointed in you." She hung up.

Beth froze. She stared at the silent machine. Courtesy? That snotty . . . No, that message was from no one but Zach. The woman would never have dared unless Zach Housley had told her to or shown her by example that Beth was fair game. It had all the Housley trademarks—mean, arrogant, a touch vicious.

All at once, her knees turned to water. Overwhelmed, she reached for her desk, for the wall, for anything to hold on to. It was pure reflex, and her hand clutching the edge of her bookcase was the only thing that kept her upright. She tried to take a deep breath, but tears burst from her eyes. Sobbing, she groped through the suddenly alien office for her chair.

She was never going to make partner. She did not even have a job, much less a career. The horrible nightmares pounded her night after night, and she had no idea why. It was as if her whole life had not simply changed but mutated. The telephone number in her head had led her to the murder of a man from her nightmares. The killer—Jeffrey Hammond—had threatened her. She had awakened in a strange motel room with no idea how she had gotten there. How? Why? To save her from Hammond? To hide her, keep her out of the way? She understood none of it, and certainly none of it could ever have happened to the Beth Convey she once knew.

Just as abruptly, the anger she had felt while talking to Travis Jackson returned. No, she *was* Beth Convey. They were *not* going to defeat her. *Nothing was going to destroy her.* Her tears slowed, and she wiped her eyes with her fingers. Who had done this to her? Who were these strangers in her nightmares, at least one of whom had turned out to be real? Were they all real? And who was Hammond? Why had he killed that KGB defector, Yurimengri?

She grabbed Kleenex from the box on her desk, blew her nose, and marched into her living room. At her home bar, which she kept well stocked for guests, she poured herself a vodka on the rocks and drank half of it in a gulp. The all-but-tasteless liquor burned her throat. *Damn.* What was she doing? She should not drink vodka like that, and the taste reminded her again of how different she was. Her career was

gone, and she seemed not to care. . . . She would be on massive medication probably the rest of her life . . . a restricted life, and perhaps a
shorter life span. Was that her future? If Jeff Hammond or someone
else did not murder her first?

Exhaustion overtook her. The glass fell to the carpet, spilling vodka
and ice. From the recesses of her weary mind, a voice reassured her—
don't worry, vodka doesn't stain. She wanted to laugh, but her lungs
would not respond. Trembling, she made her way into the foyer and
used the handrail to drag herself upstairs. She forced herself to go
through her usual nighttime routine.

She fell into bed, put out the light, and weakly rolled up in a fetal position on her side, staring out her second-floor window. She studied the
stars and listened for night sounds. A shiver ran along her spine, but
only the familiar noises of the city and the low moan of the wind
reached her ears. She told herself she was Beth Convey. Killing machine
with compassion. Queen of the Cosmos. Star of the Universe. All she
needed was sleep.

Halfway down the block, Nikolai Fedorov sat slumped and apparently drowsy in his Chevrolet van. He and the vehicle were facing away
from Convey's house to lessen the chance she would notice, not that he
expected trouble. She was a civilian. An amateur.

He kept watch in his sideview mirror. He saw her lights go out until
only the bedroom was illuminated. When that finally went dark, too, he
used his scrambled cell phone to call Alexei Berianov. Fedorov was
startled by the voice that answered.

"Report."

The booming tones sounded nothing like the former KGB general.
Plus, Fedorov could hear the rhythmic chop of a helicopter's noisy ro-
tors. Cautiously, Fedorov said, *"Shto vi dúmayitye ab étam?"* What do
you think? "It looks to me like she's in for the night."

The general's voice dropped almost to a whisper. "Stay where you
are. She and her house must be watched at all times. We have to know
who goes in, who comes out. Whom she sees, what she does. Everything." The connection went dead.

14

The three men stamped out the campfire. The leader, a handsome man resplendent in a general's uniform, urgently waved them forward into the dark night.

With the two other men, Beth followed at a fast clip, her AK-47 ready in both hands, her eyes alert for signs of the enemy. With a shudder, she realized she was running between dead men. Pacing her on one side was the nameless man she had killed on the motorcycle, while on the other was Yuri. Yuri was furious. He was pointing at their leader, angry with him, while yelling to her, but no sound came from his throat. She strained to hear, to understand Yuri's warning. . . .

Her eyes jerked open. She'd had a new nightmare. Oh, Lord, when would it end?

She heaved a sigh and moved her gaze around her bedroom, orienting herself. Morning sunlight played across her ceiling, and the scent of newly cut grass drifted into her room through her open window. Below in the neighbor's yard, a lawn mower growled.

As she listened, she realized she had awakened from this bad dream with a sense of inevitability that was strangely reassuring: She was beginning to believe the nightmares were not going to go away, which meant she might as well quit trying to explain them by the ordinary terms with which she had always dealt with life.

She flung back the covers. It was a new day, Thursday, and her clock read 10:25. She had slept ten solid hours, and she felt good. She jammed her arms into her robe, took her pills, ran down to the kitchen, and started her morning coffee. Despite Travis Jackson's opinion, she would look into the outlandish, ridiculous, unthinkable, irrational idea that her heart was communicating with her. She must talk to that psychologist who had visited her in the hospital. The truth was, all year she had been curious to hear what the woman had to say.

Beth was digging hungrily into her eggs when the phone rang. She stared at the one on the kitchen wall. Who could be calling? Not the firm. She had no firm anymore. For a moment, the fear and despair of last night threatened, but she pushed the emotions away. She picked up her plate and carried it into her office, waiting for the answering machine to pick up.

It was Michelle Philmalee, and her voice was excited: "Beth, darling! You angel. And I was so nasty to you. Stop it, Phil! No! I don't care. That was Phil, Beth. He's sorry for doubting you, too. Say you're sorry, Phil."

There was a pause.

Michelle snarled, "Dammit, Phil! She's proved us both wrong. I was just as much a turd as you were. *Apologize!* That's what grown-ups do."

In the background, a door slammed hard.

Michelle sighed. "Well, Lady Queen, the male child just jumped ship. I had to fire him. Guess he doesn't get the difference between waving a dick and being one. And he was so attractive. Such nice shoulders and other accessories. Oh, well. If I beg, will you take me back?"

Beth found herself smiling. Michelle was shameless. But this morning Michelle seemed much less important than she had yesterday. Edwards & Bonnett was a worry from the past. Whatever her future held, Michelle was no longer material.

"Please, Beth. You know I was the only one who *wanted* to believe you. I'm afraid I let the old hormones cloud my judgment and listened to bad advice from Phil and Zach. Talk about sharks. Which makes me wonder . . . how could you have worked for Zach Housley so long? Do you know he personally told your clients they should be realistic because you wouldn't live long? He told me, and I assume the others, too, that I'd be smart to stick to the great attorney he was carefully selecting for me. No wonder you were deserted, and it was personal with Zach, my dear, I assure you. He's just a short-peckered weasel who doesn't like assertive women, and he jumped at the chance to get rid of one of the firm's most dangerous. You were one of the few they'd hired who was going places, and he didn't like the way that rattled his bigoted chain."

Beth stopped eating, her fork midway to her mouth, as black rage shook her. So that was what had happened. How could she have missed the degree of Zach's sexism in all the years she had worked at Edwards & Bonnett? And then she knew: She had never believed any form of prejudice could stop her. All she had to do was win negotiations and suits, protect her clients, take care of all their legal needs, produce, produce, produce. How naïve she had been. That much was not Zach's fault. It was hers.

Michelle laughed. "But you showed him who the winner was, darling. Indeed. What a good girl you are. Remember, as an attorney, I always liked you more. So will you take me back? The Philmalee Group needs you. *I* need you. With that, I'll say good-bye. I've humiliated myself enough for one conversation. Oh, and if there's anything I can do to repay you other than keeping current with your enormous legal bills, and I'm sure the one for the HanTech ownership list will be a lollapalooza, please let me know. I mean it. Anything. I figure I owe you. I await word. I do hope it will be that you've forgiven me."

As the call ended, Beth chuckled. It had been days since she had found anything amusing to laugh about. Michelle had that effect, and that was just one of the reasons Beth liked her. But then, at the thought of the casually cruel way "important" people like Zach could toy with her life and career, she felt herself grow angry again. Damn it, she *was* Beth Convey, killer lawyer. *She was good*. She could take care of herself. Never again would she rely on, or need, people like Phil Stageman or Zach Housley. They were not going to beat her, and neither was a pack of violent strangers, or her new heart. She would find out what was going on, and she would make a new and better life for herself.

She set down her plate of eggs and toast and rummaged in her office until she found the business card for the scientist who had visited her in the hospital—Stephanie Smith, Ph.D., psychoneuroimmunologist. Dr. Smith's office was in Alexandria, but her home was right here in Georgetown. She dialed Smith's office.

The day had progressed to dusk, and the rising moon cast long gray shadows across Beth Convey's street. Halfway down the block from her Victorian, Nikolai Fedorov slept soundly in the back of his Chevrolet van until the soft pulse of an alarm awoke him. Attached to ultrasophisticated surveillance sensors, the alarm went off in response to movement around Convey's house.

Fedorov scrambled forward into the driver's seat in time to see her— dressed in black, her blond hair glowing platinum in the twilight—walk toward her garage. By the time the garage door slid up and Convey had backed her Mercedes out into the street, Fedorov's engine was running, too, and he followed as she drove away into the darkening night.

Ashen clouds drifted across the black sky as Beth arrived at Stephanie Smith's white board-and-batten cottage near Georgetown Presbyterian Church. A gnarled wisteria vine framed the roof line, and large, deep-purple blossoms cascaded around the door. In the yellow porch light the flowers seemed almost ominous as Beth stepped past and rang the doorbell.

That morning when Beth had phoned Stephanie Smith's office to make an appointment, the answering machine had announced the doctor would be out all day, seeing appointments, but the caller could leave a message. Since Dr. Smith's house was nearby in Georgetown, Beth decided to wait until evening to try to talk with her in person. So she spent the day mostly at home, unpacking the boxes that had arrived from Edwards & Bonnett and integrating the files and supplies into her office. In the afternoon, she took advantage of the fine spring day to go for a run around the Ellipse. It all made her feel almost normal, and she managed to ignore the few strange thoughts and words that tried to worm their way into her consciousness.

And now she hoped to find some answers. One of the advantages of Georgetown's relatively small size was addresses were easy to find. But as Beth stood in the porch's gloom and listened to footsteps approach from inside, all her good feelings vanished. An unknown past seemed to hover over her.

Dr. Smith opened the door. She frowned. "Yes?"

In the hospital, Dr. Smith's long hair had been pulled back in a severe French twist. Tonight, her business day finished, it lay in a tumble on her shoulders. At her temples, the hair was silver-gray, showing her age, which was somewhere in her late forties. But with her round face, soft cheeks, and long, loose hair, she looked like a schoolgirl in her blue sweatshirt, matching sweatpants, and bare feet.

Beth introduced herself and reminded her of their first meeting. "We're neighbors," she added lamely. "Please call me Beth."

The doctor's brow knitted in puzzlement. Then she grinned and went straight to the point. "I remember. You're a lawyer. I imagine you're here because you're wondering whether you're being logical about cellular memory or simply prejudiced against it. I find my prejudice sometimes masquerades as logic. It's something to watch out for. Come in. We'll talk. Call me Stephanie."

"And I thought *I* was direct."

Stephanie smiled as she led her into the kitchen and put water on to boil. "Have a seat. Since you're here, may I deduce you've been having some of the posttransplant experiences I was asking about?"

Beth sighed. "Apparently so."

Red gingham curtains hung at the large kitchen window, and classic blue-and-white delft tiles crowned the counters. The bungalow had been built sometime in the 1950s, and the kitchen with its white cabinets and straight lines still had that *Ozzie and Harriet* air. But then, so did Stephanie. Despite being an obvious career woman—Beth remembered she had looked and acted the complete professional in the hospital—there was something about Stephanie Smith that said wholesome homebody, too.

"But you're still not convinced," Stephanie said.

As the rich aroma of drip coffee filled the room, Beth admitted ruefully, "I don't want to believe any of it. A heart with a brain? A heart that talks? There's some dead guy trying to communicate with me through his heart, which is now inside me? This is beyond insane. It's stupid."

Stephanie poured two mugs and brought them to the table. "Milk? Sugar?"

"Skim milk. No sugar." With her new taste for black tea, it had been a while since she'd had coffee. Under the circumstances, coffee seemed appealing.

Stephanie pulled milk from the refrigerator, sugar from a sideboard, and sat. "It'd help if you'd tell me what's happened since your transplant."

Beth was silent. Now that she was here, all her lawyerly caution had returned. "You're a shrink. I'm relying on that, because what I'm about to say can go no further than your kitchen."

"All right. Consider it a professional courtesy."

Beth warned, "Not even for that study of yours for the Walters Institute."

Stephanie frowned. "That's asking a lot. Tell you what I'll do—I won't use anything without your permission."

"In writing."

"Agreed. In writing. You drive a hard bargain."

Beth snorted. "This was nothing."

She caught Stephanie studying her and saw immediately in her eyes she understood. Recognition passed between them—two strong women in what was still a man's world, working in professions dominated by men, who loved their work and excelled despite the odds, and yet knew it was not enough for them to achieve the recognition, money, and respect men at their level could expect automatically.

It was not a *Brady Bunch* moment. More like a *Courage under Fire* one.

Beth raised her mug in salute. "At least we're not bored."

Stephanie chuckled and raised her mug, too. "Amen."

Beth began by recounting the nightmares, new food tastes, Russian poetry, explosive temper, odd pieces of information that seemed to come from nowhere, how quickly she had succeeded at karate, and her new ability to drive well at outrageous speeds. Then she backtracked and described the phone number that had led her to Meteor Express and the dead defector, Anatoli Yurimengri, and then to the man who had murdered him—Jeff Hammond.

By the time she finished describing the mysterious house and address, the two women were on their second cups of coffee, and Stephanie was leaning back, arms crossed, a thoughtful expression on her face.

At last she said, "Beth, forgive me. I don't mean to intrude . . . but from what you've said, I believe you're afraid you've got the heart of a killer, and that, if there's anything to cellular memory, you've 'inherited' violent traits from him."

It sounded ridiculous, like some rug-chewing idea from a bad science-fiction novel or a B-grade horror movie. She wanted to deny it. She wanted to pretend nothing had happened. She wanted to slip between the floorboards of Stephanie's kitchen and disappear like a fugitive with her dreadful secret. But something inside her demanded to be understood, too.

She pursed her lips, then admitted, "Yes. I'm concerned. I'd like to take a vacuum cleaner to my brain and suck out everything that's happened since my surgery so I can start fresh."

"Oh, yes. The old suck-the-brain-clean cure."

"You don't seem shocked. What's happened to me? What does it all mean?"

"I don't know whether your donor had a relationship with Colonel Yurimengri or why this Jeff Hammond killed him, but I can address cellular memory. We'll do it the easy way and start with the brain, because a lot of that's already common knowledge." She paused. "The brain's remarkably complex. In fact, it's got more cellular connections than the Milky Way has stars. It analyzes, remembers, and decides by using the electrochemical energy that links its synapses—the little gaps between brain cells. This process has been proved beyond a doubt. In fact, scientists have recorded images of synapses firing—or what we call thinking."

Beth nodded. "I remember an article about that in *Scientific American*. But what about the heart?" She took a deep breath and asked the million-dollar question: "I can't believe a heart thinks like a brain. Are you telling me this new heart of mine has cognitive powers, and it's sending me messages from my donor? If you are, you're going to have to do a hell of a lot more explaining to convince me."

The scientist smiled. "I'll see what I can do."

15

The kitchen was quiet, the only sound the electric clock on the wall ticking, as Stephanie Smith paused to consider. At last she said, "The short answer is yes . . . and no." She held up a hand as Beth started to protest. "Give me a chance to explain. At this point, those of us studying cellular memory have evidence that indicates the heart can indeed think, but in a far less brazen, ego-driven way than the brain. You probably know about Albert Einstein's breakthrough—that energy and matter are interchangeable."

"$E = MC^2$."

Stephanie nodded. "Right. Remember, the brain needs electrochemical energy so it can think. Well, as it turns out, the heart has even more juice than the brain—in fact, *five thousand times* more electromagnetic power. We're now beginning to believe energy is interchangeable not only with matter but with information. If so, this electric power could account for how the heart can think and communicate." She paused. "On top of that, there's a lot of hardwiring between the brain and the heart—superconduits of energy and thought, if you will. It's recently been proved that not only the brain but the heart, too, has neurotransmitters."

"You mean the same kind of 'neurotransmitters' that are so important to the functioning of the brain?"

"Exactly. Most people realize there are simple neurological connections between all hearts and their brains. But now we know the link is far more sophisticated—more like a superhighway than a country road. In other words, scientists have established that neurochemical and electrochemical communication goes on all the time between hearts and brains."

"So the heart and brain have similarities I never learned about in school," Beth said, thinking.

"That's because science is breaking new ground in this area all the time." Stephanie leaned forward, her elbows on the table, her coffee mug cradled between her palms. Her face glowed with intensity. No matter that she lived and breathed this branch of science and speculation each day—she still found it fascinating. "We've known for seventy years all cells sense, learn, and recall. Every single one of them. For instance, cells in the immune system remember, find, and try to eliminate anything that doesn't belong to the body. And don't forget DNA—a nucleic acid in the center of our cells. It remembers genetic data that determine our appearance, our predispositions to certain diseases and personality traits, and even how long we might live."

"All right. That's a form of memory. But it's not like what we're really talking about in the case of organ transplants."

Stephanie nodded. "Right, but it applies. Maybe you read about this experiment, too: Back in 1993, scientists at the Army Intelligence and Security Command scraped white blood cells from inside the mouth of a volunteer. They centrifuged the cells, put them in a test tube, and stuck a lie—or emotion—detector into the tube. Then they showed a TV program with a lot of violence to the fellow who had donated the cheek cells. As he watched, the lie-detector probe read extreme excitation in the cells in the test tube, even though the man was in a different room down the hall. Scientists repeated the experiment several times, eventually separating the donor and the cells by fifty miles. Still, the cells showed the same results—responding as the man himself did right at the moment it was happening, for a full two days."

"That's amazing. Wow. Okay, you've convinced me cells can remain emotionally connected to us even when they're physically apart. But what's that got to do with me and my new heart?"

"Candace Pert, the former chief of brain chemistry at the National Institute of Mental Health, puts it all together nicely—the electrical power and connections, the neurotransmitters, the cellular memory. She explains that since the cells in the heart are loaded with molecules containing memory, some of those memories could easily accompany a heart when it joined a new brain and body. She claims that to assume the brain thinks independently of the body and the heart, that the heart is just an ignorant pump, and that cells can't remember doesn't jibe with the latest scientific knowledge."

Beth found herself smiling. It was preposterous, and yet . . . "So you're telling me I wanted beluga caviar because my heart remembered liking it?"

"It's a possibility. Yours is no isolated experience. Hundreds of transplant recipients across the nation corroborate what happened to you with their own stories. It doesn't occur with everyone, but there's enough anecdotal evidence that we've had to pay attention. Fortunately, since several of us are now studying the phenomenon, it's more legitimate for other scientists in a variety of fields to discuss it, too. And that means more transplant recipients feel comfortable coming forward with what they used to think of as shameful secrets that surely proved they were liars or lunatics. A few, like a woman named Claire Sylvia, have written books about what it's like to receive not only someone else's organs but also some of their memories. In that way, they've increased national awareness. I can give you a list of some of these papers and books, in case you want to look at them. But in the end, what occurred to you is your experience alone. You get to be the judge of its accuracy and what it means."

So she was right back where she had started. Or was she? Stephanie had not given her the straightforward, black-is-black and white-is-white answer for which she had hoped. But at least there were new discoveries that helped account for her experiences. And, too, she was not alone. Other transplant recipients had also experienced unsettling events. But she was caught in a vise—she wanted to believe her perceptions were real, but if she had the heart of a killer—

Beth rubbed her forehead. "Is it logic? Or is it prejudice? I've reached the point where I have to believe it's at least possible whoever's heart beats inside me has passed on some of who he was." She hesitated. "If it's true, then my donor was Russian or closely associated with Russians, he was good at karate, knew how to use weapons, was short-tempered, and liked fast cars. It's like putting a jigsaw puzzle together from unmarked pieces."

Stephanie nodded sympathetically. "A couple of final thoughts. Marcel Proust said something like this: The real journey of discovery isn't in seeking new lands but in seeing with new eyes." She drained her cup and set it down. "If it's true your donor was a murderer, that was him. Not you. As you sort through everything, as time passes, you can make conscious choices about what you want to keep and what you want to discard not only from your life but from his. As the years go by, transplant recipients report that the 'memories' fade. And keep in mind that just because the bad dreams seem to be connected to the other events you're experiencing, that doesn't mean they're the literal truth about what happened to him. After all, they're nightmares, just something that happens in your mind while you're asleep."

Beth nodded. Now she desperately wanted to know who he had been. If not his name, then at least his background. But she had signed an agreement not to search for his identity or to contact his family. As she thought that, she remembered the file she had glimpsed in Stephanie's portfolio at the transplant center.

Beth's voice rose, incredulous, angry. "You know who he was!"

Stephanie blanched. "What makes you think that?"

"First, you're always direct, but this time you answered my question with a question—*what makes you think that?* Second, you had a file on me when you stopped by my hospital room. I saw it. This is vital, Stephanie. *Crucial.* You know Colonel Yurimengri was murdered. We don't want anyone else to get killed, including me. I need to stop Jeff Hammond. It might make up in some small way for whatever horrible acts my donor committed. *You've got to tell me who he was.*"

Stephanie took a deep breath. Worry deepened the fine lines on her round, pleasant face. She stood up, carried her mug to the kitchen sink, and rinsed it. She returned to the table and picked up Beth's.

Beth looked up and held her with her furious gaze. "I can get a court order to find out. I've got enough so-called coincidences now to convince some judge." It was not true, but maybe Stephanie would believe it. "If you tell me, we'll save time. One way or another, I'm going to find out."

Stephanie pursed her lips. "I know you will." She took Beth's mug to the sink, rinsed it, set it carefully in the draining rack next to her own mug, and turned back to face her. "I don't remember his name anymore, or who exactly he was. A lot of time's passed. Many interviews over the dam in the past year. In any case, we're not allowed to keep donor identification in our files. It's too confidential." Reluctantly she added, "I'm afraid your best bet is to get that court order after all."

Beth ignored her frustration. "Look, neither of us wants any more corpses. If I'm in a similar position to that little eight-year-old girl you told me about—the one who had the heart of a murdered ten-year-old and helped track down the killer—then I may have critical information, even though it's just in my nightmares. I can't waste any more time. Surely you don't want to either. The hospital's organ-transplant office has the name of my donor on file."

Stephanie said flatly, "None of the coordinators will give it to you."

"Maybe not to me." Beth stood and smiled knowingly. "But they'll give it to you. Is there still a coordinator there on twenty-four duty?"

"Yes."

"Come on, Stephanie. How are you going to feel if you turn me down now and someone else gets killed?"

Stephanie's face fell. "Not especially happy. Guilty would be a good word."

"Right. We both have a responsibility to act."

Stephanie sighed and closed her eyes. They stood there in the kitchen unspeaking.

Finally Beth said quietly, "You know it's the right thing to do, Stephanie. Sometimes we have to bend rules for a higher good."

The woman nodded mutely.

"Your car or mine?"

Stephanie sighed and opened her eyes. "You're right. We'll take mine."

As Stephanie went into her bedroom to change out of her sweats, Beth waited, jubilant and relieved. After twelve long months of unanswered questions . . . bizarre, inexplicable experiences . . . terrifying nightmares . . . she was going to find out whether these so-called memories could have belonged to her donor. For good or bad, she had to know.

Out in the April night, in the moist, dank shadow of a flowering tulip tree, Nikolai Fedorov collapsed his equipment and fitted it back into his black tool box. He was nodding, preparing to repeat word-for-word what he had just heard. The big kitchen window with its narrow frame of red gingham curtains had been perfect. As the two women had talked, Fedorov had bounced a small, invisible laser beam onto the glass, the vibration from the conversation had made his reflected laser beam modulate, and he had used his demodulator to extract the audio from the beam.

He had heard everything they said.

Inside the kitchen, the light went out. The backyard with its white plastic lawn furniture and budding camellia bushes abruptly shifted from a bath of warm light to the moonlit glow of night. By feel, Fedorov checked the equipment in his box. He knew exactly where everything belonged. He tested the bands that secured each piece in place.

Satisfied, he soundlessly closed the top and, low to the ground, hurried out to the street and into the front seat of his stolen Chevrolet van. He moved as if there were no bones in his body, as if he were a shadow.

He was highly trained, efficient, and with his medium build and almost colorless features, he took great pride in being able to blend—no, disappear—anywhere.

He had a few minutes while Smith changed clothes, so he crawled into the van's windowless back where he could not be seen. He used his scrambled cell phone to call Alexei Berianov, who, by the roar of helicopter blades, was still aloft.

"Yes?"

Fedorov told him, "I have a report, sir."

"Yes, very well."

Fedorov repeated the two women's conversation, and when he finished, there was a long pause. For a moment, Fedorov was nervous. What had happened? Then the noisy *chop-chop* of the blades slowed. He waited patiently.

As soon as the helicopter landed at his Pennsylvania farm, Alexei Berianov jumped out and, crouching, moved quickly toward his Humvee, his cell phone in hand. He considered Fedorov's information. The investigation of Beth Convey's background had turned up one particularly disturbing fact: According to the medical records of her heart-transplant surgeon, Convey had complained of nightmares and changes in tastes and habits that had led her to wonder whether she was receiving information from her donor's heart. From a Russian donor. To Berianov, it was complete hogwash. But what mattered was what Convey thought.

Now it appeared she was inclined to believe it. As he drove off alone in the Humvee, he told Federov in Russian, "She'll find out who her donor was. We can't have that. It will encourage her to keep digging. She'll ask more questions and involve more people. She's an attorney with connections. She won't stop. It's not her nature."

"*Da,* you're right. What do you want me to do?"

Berianov's hand tightened on the cell phone, and then it relaxed. He could trust Fedorov. Fedorov was not as good as Ivan Vok, but he had been trained by Ivan and others in the old days and was still among the best.

He decided, "With Convey and Smith, there's too much potential for trouble. It must look like an accident. We want no possibility, no matter how remote, that something could be traced to us." As he pulled to a stop beside his mansion, one of his people trotted toward the Humvee to open the door for him. "Purge Beth Convey. Purge both women." Caleb Bates broke the connection.

*   *   *

Stephanie drove them through Georgetown toward the Fourteenth Street Bridge and the highway that would take them to the medical center in Virginia where Beth had regained her life. They continued to talk about transplants, the heart, cutting-edge discoveries in biophysiology, and the future of organ transplantation—human, animal, and artificial. It was almost midnight by the time they crossed the bridge and turned south onto the Jefferson Davis highway. The sky was black satin, and the lights of the vibrant metropolis rose in a pink glow.

They had been talking about the usual post-surgical course of treatment for organ recipients when Stephanie asked, "How are your biopsies?"

As all transplant recipients must, Beth underwent regular biopsies of her heart to assess rejection. A pathologist would examine a sample under a microscope and score it from zero to ten. It took little to rate "rejection"—anything above a four.

Beth smiled. "I've been lucky. I usually come in low. But then, that's sort of typical for my year. I've been healthier than I ever recall. A few months ago, I got a cold, but it was gone in three days, just the way it's supposed to. In the past, my colds would linger, sometimes for a month or more, and then I'd end up with a secondary infection. Plus, of course, the regular exercise makes me feel all-around better, too. I sleep like a log. Even my eyelashes are longer and thicker."

"That's the prednisone." Stephanie chuckled. "You're a walking advertisement for organ transplants. It'd be great if everyone sailed through as healthy as you."

"I know, and believe me, I'm grateful."

Traffic was scattered, with few cars out at this hour on a week night. As she stared at the dark highway with the stars sparkling overhead, she was acutely aware how fortunate she was to be here . . . to be alive. In her continuing volunteer work at the hospital, she had seen too many people die waiting for a transplant, and a few die because their transplants somehow failed. Despite being a highly successful recipient, she was still vulnerable to rejection, failure, and a host of other medical problems, too. But she seldom thought about it. Being grateful was far more important.

Stephanie said, "Have you ever held a human heart in your hands?"

"No." Beth asked curiously, "Have you?"

Stephanie's voice filled with reverence: "Yes. I swear you can feel the life force in it, even when it's not connected to a body. A sound heart is beautiful—pink and smooth. Luscious. I once held one for a few seconds. There's a quiver and a kick to it, but also a serenity. Imagine . . .

take a heart from one chest, pack it in ice for transport, put it in a strange new chest a couple of hours later, and ninety percent of the time it won't even need an electric shock to get back to work. How can any of us doubt a heart has intelligence?"

"I never looked at it that way."

They rode in silence, each with her own thoughts, on the quiet highway. Beth let her head fall back against the headrest. Her eyes relaxed into tired slits, and she played with Russian names. Was one her donor's?

"Beth . . . did you feel anytime today you were being followed?" Stephanie sounded worried.

With a jerk, Beth sat up and peered back over her shoulder. "No, I didn't. In fact, I tailed Hammond, not the other way around. Is it that van behind us?" The headlights were high off the ground. As they had rounded a curve, she had been able to get a clear side view of it—a big, glossy black vehicle. Panic tightened her chest. Could Hammond be back from West Virginia?

"I thought I was imagining it, so I drove very fast, but it kept up." Stephanie's mouth trembled. "Then I switched to the right lane and slowed down, and it fell behind in the same lane. But now as you can see I'm really pushing it, doing eighty miles an hour, and it's keeping up easily."

"Go faster," Beth commanded. Her hands clenched. She wanted to reach for the steering wheel to drive. Feeling helpless, she stared back tensely as Stephanie floored the gas pedal of her old car.

The little Ford Escort jumped ahead, and it seemed they were leaving the big Chevy behind. But then like a bolt of black lightning the van caught up. Their sedan was hurtling down the highway at a hundred miles an hour, and the van was right on its tail.

"I can't get away from him." Stephanie's voice rose, frantic with fear. "Who is he? It can't be me he's after. It's got to be *you!* He's going to catch up . . . shoot us. Or force us off the road. He's big enough. He'll make a move soon. What are we going to do!"

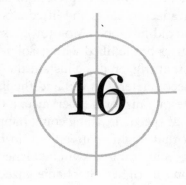

16

Tension was electric in Stephanie's old car as it rushed south on the dark highway. Beth stared back through the rearview window at the big van. It had been built to ride high, and it was so close that its headlights shone down menacingly, filling the little Ford with blinding light.

Conditions were bad: The traffic was sporadic, which meant there were times when the van's driver could act without witnesses, and the night itself would hide myriad clues. The van was so black as to be nearly invisible. And this stretch of highway had steep drop-offs to the left and right—an additional danger they did not need. The pursuit could not be an accident. Beth had to be the target, and Jeff Hammond must be in the van. But how had Hammond found her?

As she stared, the guardrails flew past in a metallic streak. A moment of disorienting fear raced through her, instantly replaced by anger.

"We've got to get off the highway," she ordered.

Stephanie's voice shook. "There hasn't been an exit in miles." She clutched the steering wheel in a death's grip, but she still had enough control to keep the car from swinging from lane to lane. At this speed, one small driving mistake could be fatal.

Behind them, in the van, Nikolai Fedorov watched the Ford. By the way it had sped up and slowed down, it was obvious the woman realized she was being followed. The driver—Stephanie Smith—was off balance. He could see it in the way the car no longer moved smoothly. This was what he had wanted. He needed her to be unnerved.

The geography, the steep declines off to both sides, the lack of traffic, everything was perfect. With cool precision, he reached down into another of his black tradecraft cases and lifted a bottle from its protective padding. It was an old-fashioned Molotov cocktail, but with a modern innovation—the glass bottle filled with gasoline was stoppered with a safe electronic fuse that triggered the instant the glass shattered.

He checked the speedometer. His van and the little Ford were going 104 miles an hour. Despite his long experience, a film of sweat formed on his upper lip. At that speed, anything could happen. Anything lethal. Certainly an accident that might shatter the thin bottle and incinerate him. He pressed the accelerator and switched lanes.

"He's coming up on our right." Stephanie gazed wildly around as if searching for escape.

"I see him." Beth felt an odd calmness. "Hold steady." They were trapped. The van had already showed it had a lot of horsepower. There was no way they could outrun it. "I think he's pulling alongside . . . he wants to force us off the highway. At this speed, the drop could make the car roll and kill us. We've got to fool him. Are you listening, Stephanie?"

"There aren't any other cars on the road right now." Stephanie's breath came in terrified pants. She was a researcher and a scientist. She had neither the skills, the psychological makeup, nor the natural talent to cope with what was happening.

"I know. But we're not completely helpless."

Stephanie said gamely, "I'm listening. I'll try . . . but Beth, I . . . I . . . I—"

Beth clutched her shoulder, trying to infuse her with confidence. She desperately wanted to drive. "I'll make it simple. When I say 'ready,' hit the brakes. Let our car drop back fast, then pull over to the right lane behind him. I know you can do it. Got it?"

Stephanie licked her lips and nodded. "He's almost at our bumper now."

Beth nodded. "Almost ready."

But in her panic, all Stephanie heard was *ready*. She slammed the brakes.

Shocked, Beth crashed forward, straining against her seat belt. Pain shot through her chest. Instantly, the car spun out of control, tossing them back and forth inside like popcorn. Pain made bright lights flash in Beth's brain.

At the same time, Fedorov was watching with his window rolled down, ready to throw the Molotov cocktail. The abrupt spin of the Ford surprised him. He swore in Russian and hit his own brakes. But he had accelerated to such a terrific speed to pass the Ford that he had only a few seconds before it would drop back out of his range. This was where training counted. He immediately analyzed, understood, and acted.

He heaved the glass bottle out his window at the spinning car. It shattered against the driver's door. A sheet of brilliant red flames erupted.

As Fedorov sped away, the out-of-control Ford burst through the guardrail, trailing sparks and streaks of fire. He laughed hard and long. To the police, it would look as if the Ford's driver had been going far too fast. She had lost control, and her gas tank had exploded as the car shot off the side of the highway. Driver and passenger both dead. Tragic. What would it take to convince people to drive safely?

But as the Ford rushed into darkness, Beth was still alert, her faculties at work. Fire had engulfed Stephanie's side of the car. Stephanie's head rolled from side to side. She was unconscious.

The heat was ferocious, but the speed of the Ford's angular descent momentarily stopped the blaze from spreading. They had to get out before the car was consumed, but the accelerating G force pinned Beth to the seat. She summoned all her strength to force her hand over to unlock Stephanie's seatbelt.

She had only seconds. "Stephanie!" It felt as if everything were moving in slow motion. She gripped Stephanie's arm. "Wake up!" The hot air scorched her throat. She gasped. "Stephanie, you've got to wake up!"

But Stephanie's eyes remained closed. Her face poured sweat and was bright red, as if from a sunburn. Beth knew it was no sunburn. The white-hot fire that had raged next to Stephanie had begun to sear her skin. As the car hurtled onward, Beth struggled to pull Stephanie from the conflagration, but all she could manage was inches.

There was no more time. Heartsick, struggling to breathe, she unsnapped her own seatbelt. As the wheels crashed at the bottom of the culvert, the car spun another 180 degrees, and Beth's door burst open. The force hurled her out into the cool night. She landed hard on grass about twenty feet from the fireball. And was up and limping back toward the Ford. The car was an inferno. She could not get close.

"Stephanie!" she screamed. She raised her fists above her head and screamed again.

There was no answer. As the fire boiled and spat, she hobbled in a big circle, searching for Stephanie. But there was no break in the blistering flames and heat, and no sign Stephanie had escaped. Beth moaned and sank to her knees. The extreme temperatures had probably welded Stephanie's door closed, and that was why she had not been thrown to safety, too.

Beth burst into tears. Metal snapped and groaned. Sparks shot up like pretty fireworks against the cavernous sky. Weeping, she said a silent prayer that Stephanie had not regained consciousness.

Then with a sickening jolt of horror, she saw Stephanie, a black shade in the center of the blazing flames. Almost immediately the figure was gone, consumed in a shroud of red. Horror wracked Beth as the fire continued to howl. And guilt hit her: She had survived, but Stephanie had not. The stink of burning rubber and oil poisoned the air.

In her mind, she saw Stephanie again—the long hair a cloud on her shoulders, the quiet eyes, the soft face. Her compassionate smile. Beth sobbed. First Colonel Yurimengri, now Stephanie. Both murdered. And Beth was somehow responsible. But why? What had she done to cause all this? Whom had her donor killed?

She wrapped her arms around herself. Sirens sounded in the distance, and she knew she could stay no longer. Stephanie was dead, but Beth was the intended victim. Tears streaming down her face, she forced herself to her feet and moved through the thick brush toward the embankment.

With each heavy step, her anger grew. No longer was it an undirected rage, easily triggered and just as easily repressed. Now there was some kind of deep, anguished power behind it. She was going to find Jeff Hammond and . . .

She stopped herself. Shuddered. It was the first time her rage had carried her to a sudden desire to murder. A cold, hard voice inside her demanded death. It would feel so good to kill him, to watch him die, the voice insisted. She tried to shrug it off, to make the desire go away, but it hung on, as attached as her skin.

Stiff and sore, she climbed the bank, the heat from the fire still licking at her back. She still had no answers, and she had only one clue left: Find out whether the house she had seen in her nightmares really existed. That was where the garage, the riderless motorcycle, and the man she had killed had been. She had to figure out how to get to the address—she had seen it on the mailbox.

Because her purse had burned up in the car, she had no car keys, cash, credit cards, or meds. She could do nothing without money and transportation. And without her meds she would die anyway. Somehow she had to get back to her house where she had all three, where she fervently hoped no more killers would be waiting. With luck, she thought bitterly, Jeffrey Hammond should believe she was dead now.

Still quietly crying, she crouched at the top of the steep slope and looked back once more at the raging fire in the base of the culvert between the north and south branches of the highway. She wiped her arm across her eyes. On the other side, two cars had stopped, and people were getting out to stare at the fire. None of the cars was a black van. Still, she could take no chances. She breathed deeply and turned away, willing her tears to stop. She had work to do, and she could not indulge her grief any longer.

Her heart pounding, she ran along the highway until there was a break in the traffic. Then she rushed across and began walking. Vehicles flew past at the usual high speeds, kicking up sand that stung her hands and face. Years ago, when she had been in college, she had hitch-hiked—a stupid practice maybe, but she had been bold and had never had a problem.

As sirens screamed to a stop across the lanes of traffic behind her, she stuck out her thumb and hoped. She could change her mind and go back to talk to the officers. If she had any real evidence to pass on, she would go back. But what little she knew would be of no use, and if she talked to them, her survival would be reported in newspapers and on TV and radio, and right away Hammond would know she had lived.

Fury stuck like a rock in her throat. She never thought she could hate anyone so much. Yet a small voice spoke from the back of her mind: Even if he had flown back or sent another killer, how had he known where she was?

When a big six-wheeler truck pulled off onto the shoulder twenty yards ahead, she approached it warily. The driver's side window rolled down, and a woman in her sixties, with gray hair braided in long pig-tails, leaned out.

She looked at Beth curiously and smiled. "Want a lift?"

"Thanks. You bet I do."

An hour later, Beth arrived back in Georgetown, her head filled with the road stories of a lonely female trucker glad for safe companionship. It was a lucky break for Beth, and she hoped that it was a harbinger of more. She pulled her cardigan close and hurried along Wisconsin Avenue, where the trucker had dropped her off, and turned the corner. She passed Georgetown Presbyterian, heading for Stephanie's bungalow, where she had left her car.

Nervously she watched everywhere. The moon glowed low in the sky, and the street was deserted. She looked in the shadows for signs of danger as she approached Stephanie's house. Even simple night sounds made her jump. Each bush was a potential assassin. From a distance, she studied her Mercedes, which was waiting where she had left it at the curb. She let fifteen minutes pass.

She approached carefully. She reached under the left front fender, found her spare car key in its magnetic holder, and hopped into the car. Her heart was pounding. The motor turned over instantly, and she sped the car away. Scrutinizing all around, she waited with dread for someone to pull away from the curb and follow along the empty street. No one did.

She parked four houses away from her Victorian. The house was dark, as it should be, and there were no signs it had been broken into. She rolled down her window. The sweet scent of dogwood was in the air. Katydids and crickets sang. She grimaced, trying to reconcile the tranquility of it all with what had happened to poor Stephanie.

Finally she drove into her driveway, parked, and got out. By the time she found the key she always kept hidden under the geranium pot by the back door, her hands were shaking with nervous relief. She let herself into the house and hurried through it, turning on lights. Upstairs in her bedroom, she grabbed her shoulder bag from last summer, and from a cabinet in her bathroom she unloaded her backup meds into it.

Then she went down to her office and pulled out the thousand dollars in cash she kept locked in her bottom desk drawer. She would report the loss of her driver's license and credit cards when she had time. As she turned to go, she noticed the red message light on her answering machine was blinking. Suddenly she was exhausted, weary to the bone. Events overwhelmed her in a rush, especially Stephanie's death. She shook her head. It was a symptom of modern times: A blinking light on an answering machine could inflict dread.

She punched the LISTEN button. Three messages had come in that afternoon, all from fellow associates at Edwards & Bonnett, saying they were sorry she had quit or been let go. One hinted he would not mind some gossip about exactly what had happened, but the other two sounded genuinely unhappy she had left the firm.

There was a fourth message. She sat down, surprised, as she heard the voice of her old friend Carly King, the analyst at Toole-Russell who had relayed the information about HanTech's new owners.

"Well, girlfriend, when I'm this tired, I keep wondering why I love numbers. Tax season's definitely too exciting." Carly chuckled, but her voice was weary. "So I finally had time to dig some more into what the new owners were doing with HanTech, like you asked." Her voice grew sober. "I don't like the looks of this. They're not just brokering the sale of unenriched uranium. Somehow they've gotten their corporate claws into weapons-grade uranium, too. They're buying it up from Third World countries like Iraq and Libya that the Russian government sold it to in the nineties when they were trying to raise money."

She hesitated then continued worriedly, "HanTech's returning the weapon's-grade uranium to Russia. What does that mean? Maybe it's good news, since the Russians are supposedly our allies. But I wonder. Should I report it to someone in the State department? Or maybe to Commerce? Think about it and give me a call. I need advice." There was a long, worried pause, and then she disconnected.

Stunned, Beth played the message a second time. Weapons-grade uranium was a closely controlled, necessary ingredient for nuclear armaments. What was an American company doing mixed up in it? It was illegal, dangerous, and frightening. And why was Russia selling its weapons-grade uranium to America while at the same time taking it back from Third World nations?

She hit the ERASE button and leaned back, considering what to tell Carly. But first, she had other work to do. She grabbed her shoulder bag and, turning off lights, hurried outside. Again in her car, she drove north on Wisconsin Avenue toward Chevy Chase. With luck, toward the house that had appeared again and again in her nightmares. Other than the Virginia phone number, its address was the only traceable piece of information the bad dreams had ever produced.

She turned right on Nebraska Avenue, passed the rolling hills of Fort Reno Park, and then made a left onto Connecticut Avenue, finally entering Chevy Chase, one of Washington's most elite areas, where multimillion-dollar houses in a variety of styles sat on large wooded lots with swimming pools, pagodas, and manicured grounds.

She turned corners. Her heart pounded. She slowed the car to stare. Shocked, she studied the black mailbox on an iron post at the street's edge and, on top of the box, the raised wrought-iron numbers. Just as it all looked in her nightmare.

She shook her head to clear it. She gazed around. The house must be at the end of the driveway, which disappeared up into the woods. She hesitated, shrugged defiantly, and cruised ahead up the drive. She was trespassing. If someone challenged her, she would apologize. If someone tried to shoot her, she would speed away. To hell with all of them.

As soon as she entered a clearing, she hit the brakes. Before her spread a surreal sight. Again it was just like in her nightmares: The thick, clipped lawn. The tall weeping willow beside the walk. And the big ranch-style house with a sloping roof, long front porch, and win-

dows black as tarry pitch. Nervous and disbelieving, for a macabre moment she half-expected the garage door to rise and a riderless motorcycle to roll out, motor growling.

She counted to ten. Then to twenty. But the door remained firmly
closed. Just as she recalled, the house, garage, and yard were deserted
and somehow threatening. Still, she would not leave. She had to find
out more. So she drove up and circled, parking so her car faced back
down toward the road, in case she needed to make a quick getaway.
She waited behind the wheel, watching for danger and studying the
house. She felt drawn to it, as if it guaranteed answers . . . or perhaps
something else.

A wave of uneasiness swept over her. She looked down at her hands,
saw they were clenched in her lap. They wanted to kill her tormenter.
She grabbed her shoulder bag, quietly opened the car's door, and
slipped out into the shadows.

17

That night in West Virginia, Jeff Hammond was tired and apprehensive as he made his way down the sidewalk of the rustic little town called Stone Point. A long time ago—nearly ten years now—he had turned his back on an accelerating career and risked everything for a hunch that had seemed so right, so accurate, so prescient that to do otherwise was to betray who he was and everything he believed. Now, after all this time, he was close to confirming his suspicions. Still, ever since he landed yesterday in this remote mountain town, he had hit one dead end after another.

He shook his head with frustration as he gazed around Main Street with its cracked sidewalks and cruising pickups illuminated in the weak light of dusty street lamps. It was the kind of poor West Virginia hamlet that had survived at first despite its isolation and lackluster appeal to outside commercial interests, and later because of them. Timber, coal, and railroads had kept it going, if barely, for two hundred years, until the booming economy of the 1990s had given hunters, fishers, and hikers the disposable income to discover the surrounding Appalachian paradise. And they'd spread the word. Now parts of Stone Point boasted fresh paint. Two new motels, one of which he had stayed in last night, sat on the outskirts. And residents had started a petition to fill potholes.

Hammond had learned all this yesterday and today. He was thinking about it as he pushed open the door to the town's second bar. The first had been a bust, which was also true of the gas station, the stores, the city hall, and the small library he had visited. He might be many things, but at the top of the list was tenacious. He had gotten one turndown after another but kept going. One way or another, he would find Alexei Berianov and uncover whatever he was plotting.

He cleared his mind. Set aside his emotions. And stepped indoors. Above the bar, neon beer signs showcased garish waterfalls and flying pheasants. From the jukebox, Johnny Cash's well-worn voice sang a melancholy song of train wrecks and lost love. The pungent odor of decades of cigarette smoke and lager made the air almost tactile. At the scarred bar, a man in jeans and a hooded sweatshirt leaned over a long-neck Budweiser, while at the small tables sat a handful of men and women, companionable, with beer bottles and shots of liquor. Not a glass of wine was in sight.

As Hammond walked toward him, the barman glanced up, gave a quick but professional appraisal, then returned his attention to the room. He had a ruddy face in need of a shave and a nose thick and bent from some long-ago fight.

"So who did it?" the barkeep asked in general. "What scumbag killed Lila?" He vigorously scrubbed a glass and set it on the shelf behind him.

"What I want to know," said the man in the hooded sweatshirt, "is who was that kid who was screwin' her that got killed, too. 'Marty' somebody. Maybe he had somethin' to do with it. Any of you heard of 'im?"

One of the women volunteered, "I was told his last name was Coulson. Martin Coulson. I'll bet he was from Bates's Hunt Club. He had one gosh-danged big bike sitting in front of Lila's place. That was a Bates Club bike, I swear. Nobody else round here'd have a bike like that."

"Think of her parents," said the woman at the next table. "Those poor people. Makes you want to cry yourself empty." Her voice broke.

Hammond leaned an elbow on the bar, watching and listening. Everywhere he had stopped, people were talking about the tragic deaths of the young lovers. Murder was uncommon here, but when it happened, it was almost always a crime of passion or revenge. The town could not figure out this one.

He was curious, hoping there might be a connection between the murders and whatever Anatoli Yurimengri claimed he had not known about Stone Point. All he had been able to find out was that Lila had been the youngest of five children, living at home. The family had no serious conflicts with anyone in town. Lila had no past boyfriends known to be jealous. She had been a clerk at the local convenience store, and she had been well liked.

Her young man—Marty Coulson—had apparently been part of a sports group led by a man named Caleb Bates, who had bought a lot of prime acreage among the slopes above Stone Point. His sporting club was one of a dozen new ones, members only, that drew hunters from all over the country and had been instrumental in reviving the area's economy. In fact, Bates's photo had been on the front page of the local weekly, with an article extolling the virtues of the backwoods life.

Hammond had studied the picture: Bates was beefy, dressed in a hunting vest, cradling a Winchester in his thick arms. Hammond had not recognized him.

From the details he had been able to pick up about the murders—single shots to both victims, no loud sounds of firing, gunshots so powerful they had knocked both young people half off the bed—he figured it had to have been someone who had known exactly how these things were done. But then, with the town's new growth, violent crimes of all kinds had been sure to increase here, too. After all, most of the villagers owned firearms of one sort or another. The police department—all three officers—were investigating.

The barman focused on Hammond. He and Hammond were the same height, but he carried extra weight around his middle that would never be confused with muscle. Despite his florid face and broken nose, there was a dignity about him that Hammond liked.

The bartender asked, "What can I get you, mister?"

"A Bud. And an answer, I hope."

Hammond pulled out a color photo from his herringbone jacket and slid it across the bar. It was of a white man of medium build with a slender, Northern European face. He was handsome in a tuxedo, confidently holding a half-full martini glass.

Hammond said, "Ever see him?"

The room was quiet as the two big men exchanged a look, and the barkeep picked up the picture. It was dinnertime in the valley, but as anywhere, there were some who did not want to or could not go home. So they drank among their fellows, girding themselves against the long night or perhaps more loneliness than they cared to admit. Bars like this were hotbeds of gossip. That was why Hammond had allowed himself some optimism as he entered.

"Nope. Doesn't ring a bell. What about you, Clyde?" The bartender handed the photo to the man in the hooded sweatshirt, who looked at it, shook his head, and passed it to the man at the table closest to him.

Hammond frowned as the photo went around the tavern, each viewer indicating no knowledge.

The last one said, "Looks kinda familiar. Can't tell you why."

"Take your time," Hammond encouraged.

The man studied the photo longer. "Nope, guess not." He handed it to Hammond. "Must remind me of someone I can't recall."

"Anyone in Stone Point?"

This time the man gave a decisive shake of his head. "Not a prayer."

"So who is he?" the barman asked. "He's wearing a tuxedo, and he's at some fancy party. Don't think a guy like that'd be living here, do you, boys?"

They laughed, the tragedy of the murdered lovers forgotten for the moment. They studied Hammond, appraising his long hair, gold earring, herringbone jacket, and jeans. But their stares were more curious than unfriendly. Take away the jacket and the earring, and he could easily fit in—an outdoors type who marched to his own drumbeat, similar to others here in the forested backcountry where individualism and eccentrics were part of the rough landscape as much as the big trees and wild vegetation.

"He's Russian. Name's Alexei Berianov," Hammond rumbled. "I was hoping to interview him for my newspaper."

"A Russian?" one of the men asked, surprised. "Whoa. No way. Here?"

"Hey, I wouldn't mind meeting a Russian," said another. "Now Russia . . . that's pretty far away. A hell of a lot farther than New York. That'd be something, meeting someone from Russia. I wouldn't mind that. What newspaper you write for?"

"The Washington Post."

"Up there in Washington, Dee Cee?" said the man in the hooded sweatshirt.

"Yes, sir." Hammond repressed a smile. "So have any of you ever seen any Russians around?"

In that they were quickly unanimous. They shook their heads.

"No way," the bartender confirmed.

"I heard Russians talk in movies," said another. "Can't miss that accent. Sort of deep and growly. Nobody I ever met sounded like no Russian to me. Guess I know just about everybody lives here."

"That so?" Disappointed, Hammond gazed around the room, hoping someone would disagree, but no one did.

One of the women had focused on the man who had said he would not mind meeting Russians. "You like that idea, don't you, Kenny," she kidded. "*Russia.* Guess you should save up your pennies and go there. If you even know where it is."

"Ah, come on, Alma. Don't you try to give me a hard time. Hell, you get lost goin' home. Three beers, and you think you're flyin' all the way to Wheeling. . . ."

As the customers broke into good-natured laughter and kidding, Hammond tucked the photo back inside his jacket, paid for his beer, and left. Outside, pickups and old cars cruised past. He was frustrated and disappointed. When Beth Convey had related Yurimengri's dying words, he had been sure he would find a connection to Berianov in Stone Point, a connection to some deadly activity the once-powerful general had managed to keep hidden all these years. But Berianov had had an unmistakable Russian accent, something no one in Stone Point would have missed.

Hammond jammed his hands into his jeans pockets, hunched his shoulders, and walked toward the drugstore, which was still alight. He was not quitting. Not now. He had invested too many years. What kind of idiot did that make him? But as soon as he asked the question, he answered with a shake of his head. He was no idiot. He was right. Someone in this benighted town would recognize Berianov's photo. . . .

Then it happened. Hammond saw a shadow on the sidewalk that seemed wrong. Most of his adult life, he had automatically checked his path—car windows rolled up or down, building doors opened or closed, the way people walked and where they looked, reflections on all kinds of glass, and shadows. He had been trained to do it, and he had learned quickly it was prudent. Almost anyone else would have missed the bulge in the shadow ahead. It was cast by the wall on the alley's left and extended out across the sidewalk. It should have been a straight line.

Either a person was hiding there, or the wall had a serious structural problem. He doubted it was structural. Hardly turning his head, he surveyed all around. Traffic was light. Four teenagers on the sidewalk were strolling and laughing, heading in his direction. As he tried to peer into the alley, which was fifteen feet ahead, Hammond's breath caught in his chest and a small, excited hum started inside his brain. He had never needed risk, but a part of him missed it. Although this was definitely low-level, it could be interesting.

He watched carefully, ready to move, as the teenagers passed the alley. But whoever was in there was not sufficiently tempted, perhaps because the young people's pockets would not make for much of a robber's haul. Besides, there were four of them to deal with.

He slowed to let them get safely past him. They were ambling with arms entwined, two young couples out looking for fun. The girls' laughter rang like clear bells. One boy stared into the eyes of his girl, and she lifted her lips toward him. Not only spring but sex was in the air.

Hammond smiled and stopped to adjust his baseball cap. He leaned back against the timbered wall of a hardware store and wiped an arm across his forehead, buying time. When at last the lively little group passed and were out of range, he again scanned the sidewalks and street. For the moment, the only movement was their retreating backs. It was time.

Using the store's wall for cover, he padded toward the alley. His motions grew liquid and smooth. An old power he had not felt in a long time seemed to take him over. His heartbeat slowed. His senses had that razored edge he recalled. With one huge fist, he reached inside the alley, grabbed cloth, and yanked.

The voice attached to the clothing he grabbed was outraged. "Jesus Christ, Hammond!"

"Shit. Steve Thoma. What in hell are you doing here?"

The two men stood motionless at the alley's mouth, Hammond's hand knotted on Thoma's lapels, their angry faces inches apart. Thoma was smaller than Hammond, with wavy hair, a stubborn jaw, and eyes that shot fury. He was dressed in the usual simple, dark suit with white shirt. But just as Thoma started to reach behind and under his jacket, Hammond slammed him back out of sight into the alley with one hand, while the other expertly yanked a 10mm Smith & Wesson from the holster at Steve Thoma's back.

"That's gonna cost you," Thoma snarled.

"Sorry, I'm allergic to guns being pulled on me. Guess you're slowing down."

"Like hell I am. I gave you a break." Thoma glowered.

Hammond stuffed the Smith 10 into his waistband. "Classy toy. So you're armed. Correct that: *Were* armed. What'd you expect to find here—some assassin?"

"You said that, I didn't." Thoma's wavy hair was tousled, and his pudgy face was swollen in anger at being outfoxed. "The question is what did *you* come here to find?"

Hammond's lower lip thinned. His exit from the FBI one step ahead of being discharged had left a lot of hard feelings against him among the other agents. "Not you bushwhacking me, that's for sure. It wouldn't have anything to do with a certain dead KGB defector named Yurimengri, would it, Thoma?"

Thoma curled his lip and checked out Hammond up and down. "Christ. You look like a bum. You need a haircut. And why are you wearing an earring? You always were a weird son of a bitch. Now it shows. God knows why the Bureau ever hired you in the first place."

"It's good to see you, too, Thoma. Only it won't get you out of answering my question. Why now? The Bureau hasn't shown any interest in me in years."

"Fuck you, Hammond." As the agent spoke, his expression changed. The anger and chagrin faded into a sly visage of . . . what?

And then Hammond knew. It was in his bones, like an old disease. Still holding onto Thoma's lapels, he twisted. The footfalls had been quiet as a cat's steps. The four men and women in their dark suits and white shirts seemed to appear from nowhere, their pistols trained on him. Somehow, Thoma had summoned them.

Inwardly Hammond swore at himself. "You had a silent alarm." It was not a question. Hammond knew it had to be true.

Thoma gave a cocky grin and popped open a seam in his belt to display a nickel-sized medallion. "It's attached to my holster. As soon as I—or you—took my gun, it was activated. All of us have them. Fortunately, I'm the one got lucky with finding you."

"Yeah. I can see that."

"Give Thoma back his weapon, Hammond. We're taking you in." It was Chuck Graham, another of Hammond's former colleagues. He was a slender man with a narrow, lined face. About ten years older than Hammond, he was in his mid-forties. Everything about him was spit-and-polish, from the knife-blade crease of his trousers to his freshly pressed, button-down shirt and smoothly shaved cheeks.

Hammond had always respected Graham, even though he had not been crazy about his by-the-book style. "Taking me in for what?" He pulled the Smith out of his waistband.

Immediately the four armed agents tightened their ring around him, their weapons aimed at his heart. So much professional firepower . . . it gave him one of those nasty moments when he knew he could get himself killed.

"Sorry." He put an innocent smile on his face and carefully rotated the gun so it was butt first. He handed it to Thoma.

Graham, who seemed to be the agent in charge, relaxed a fraction. "We want you for the murders of Lila Kennedy and Martin Coulson." The lines on his thin face deepened with disappointment. "Why'd you do that, Hammond? Hell. A couple of kids. I thought more of you than that."

"Are you nuts? I didn't kill those kids. Why would I? I never set foot in Stone Point until yesterday."

"What time yesterday did you fly in?"

They must have already checked, since they knew he had arrived by air. "Around three o'clock."

The veteran agent nodded knowingly. "The kids were shot sometime between three and five last night. And the local cops have evidence you did it. Compelling evidence. We're taking you back to Washington. Check him out, Thoma."

Despite the pudginess of Thoma's face, his grip was muscular. He grabbed Hammond's shoulders and shoved him hard against the alley wall. Thoma was like many men in service to his country, more in love with his small portion of power than was healthy. Thoma patted him down more rigorously than necessary, but Hammond had expected that. He would deal with Thoma later.

Hammond said, "If it's a local matter, local cops should arrest me. It's their jurisdiction."

"Wrong," Thoma said with satisfaction. "This is a national-security issue. The Bureau's in charge, not a bunch of hayseeds." He stood back. "He's clean. No weapon. He must've dumped it somewhere."

"Where is it?" Graham's lined face was cold and unmoving.

"I told you," Hammond growled, "I didn't kill them. Why would I? Think about it. It makes no damn sense."

"Not to us maybe," Graham said. "But to you obviously. I don't know what happened back then, Hammond, but something did. You fought with everyone before you left and pissed everyone off. Then you went to work for that Commie-rag *Post.* Now look at you. Hair long enough to braid, and a gold earring, too. You look like some kind of queer. You're a freak, Hammond. Let's go."

They re-formed themselves around Hammond, pincers in a battle already won. As they moved him onto the street, they focused their pistols on him with the concentration of robots. Hammond got the message: No way were they going to let him escape.

Hammond demanded, "What does Bobby say about this?" Bobby Kelsey had been his boss and was part of the Bureau's top management.

Thoma chortled. "Something about Icarus flying too close to the sun."

It was a typical Bobby Kelsey response, but it also told Hammond more: It was a message, and Bobby was in charge of this operation.

Hammond nodded neutrally. "Sounds like Bobby."

Thoma growled, "Yeah, Bobby's not your number-one fan. Guess you just have a talent for making enemies. Get in, asshole."

Although the Bureau had changed and modernized, some things were hard to erase. The long history of unshakable loyalty, of taking care of one another no matter the cost, of being pit bulls in an eternal battle against a danger-filled world where violence lurked around the next building, had forged an esprit de corps that tolerated little aberration. And Hammond had been very aberrant.

They stopped at a midnight-blue Lincoln Continental parked in the dark midpoint between two street lamps. Thoma shoved Hammond's head down, and Hammond crawled into the backseat.

Hammond looked up at Graham. "Come on, I'm entitled to know what's going on. What kind of 'compelling evidence' do the locals think they have?"

Graham frowned. "I've told you enough. National security, remember?"

"Where are you taking me?"

"No more questions. You know the drill."

After that, the agents were silent. It was to be the pattern for the night, an attempt at psychological intimidation. The problem for them—and they knew it—was he recognized their tricks. He'd had the same training and advanced through the same ranks. He had important work to do, and they could not stop him. They would know that soon enough.

As the night grew colder and the shadows of the Appalachians seemed to loom claustrophobically, Special Agent Eli Kirkhart watched his colleagues put Jeff Hammond into their car. He recognized the dogged, not-too-bright Thoma and the veteran Graham. They were all nervous, their pistols ready for trouble.

A flash of his badge at the air-service office yesterday had got him Hammond's destination: Stone Point, West Virginia. The deputy attorney general's budget for expenses was a lot better than the Bureau's, so he booked a plane and pilot and followed Hammond. It had been dusk when he landed, and the next morning he spotted Hammond in the parking lot—they were staying at the same motel.

After that, Eli kept his distance. In a rented car and on foot, he followed Hammond, talking to everyone he talked to. Now, far up the dark street in his rented car, he watched Graham and Thoma climb into the backseat with Hammond, while the other three agents took the front. When the Lincoln drove off, Kirkhart pulled out into the dark night, following.

18

A rising wind rustled the woods surrounding the house in Chevy Chase. When a small animal suddenly scurried through the undergrowth in front of her, Beth flinched. She continued to walk around and study the estate, and the place seemed increasingly familiar.

She followed the front porch and stepped onto a stone walk that trailed around the house's left side and into the back where a koi pond, lush hibiscus, and tropical vegetation in large earthenware pots gave the patio a sense of the exotic. She looked in all the windows and saw no sign anyone was there. Moonlight revealed the perfectly made beds to be flat, unoccupied. The furnishings were attractive and traditional. She peered into the garage. There was no motorcycle or any other vehicle parked there.

Emboldened, she tried the house's back door. It was locked. She checked the side and front doors and windows. Everything was locked. She noted the alarm system. It was monitored by the same company that took care of hers, which was not unusual, since it was the area's largest, well established even before Jackie Kennedy had hired it to help protect her privacy after Jack was assassinated.

She paused on the walk between the garage and house, where the wind skittered flower petals across her athletic shoes. She needed to get inside. That was when she had an idea. For her twelfth birthday, her mother had given her a fully loaded toolbox, the beginning of her love affair with everything from tack hammers to jackhammers. As it turned out, it was one of the attributes that made her competitive as an adult.

She had no fear of cars or computers, and when she had to talk oil, pipes, or circuits on a large or small scale with international clients or other attorneys, she was pleasantly at home.

She returned to her car, opened the trunk, where she carried a full set of tools, and took out wire-cutters and a flashlight.

She had learned this trick when her own system had gone haywire shortly after she had moved in. Her boyfriend at the time had inadvertently tripped the alarm by not punching in the primary code fast enough. But neither he nor she had memorized the instructions about what to do when that happened. When she could not find the information sheet, and the alarm continued its maddening shriek, she had simply rammed the wire-cutters up behind the box and snipped. It was against the rules, of course, but it worked. The man monitoring the alarms at the security company office had been prepared to alert the police, but when the alarm stopped, he took the lazy way and chalked it up to a case of the homeowner's finally getting the key code right. It happened often enough at the company to be routine, and the cops were rarely notified.

She hesitated, weighing an arrest for breaking and entering against everything else that had occurred in the last thirty hours. Stephanie's grisly murder—and nearly her own—made the choice simple. She returned to the kitchen door and used the wire-cutters to smash a pane. The alarm screeched, splintering the night.

She had no time to lose. She reached inside, unlocked the door, and, even though she was sore from the car crash, sprinted past kitchen cabinets to the small alarm box on the wall. It looked just like hers at home—white with a numerical keypad. But there was a problem: It was so close to the wall it could have been glued on, unlike hers, which gaped against old, crooked plaster. Somehow she had to get the wire-cutters to the wires, which would be routed through a hole in the plasterboard behind the alarm. Fast.

As the nerve-wracking alarm continued, she jammed the wire-cutters up into the sheet rock. Plaster dust exploded, but she was not far enough in yet. As the handle bit into her palm, she rammed the wire-cutters into the wall again and again until at last she felt the opening. She clipped the wires.

And there was silence. The quiet was so profound her ears rang with it. With luck, just as it had happened before, the security person monitoring alarms at headquarters would shrug the incident off, and the cops would never know about the tripped alarm. If not, she was in trouble. But she was getting used to that.

She turned on her flashlight and trained its funnel around the striking modern kitchen with its upscale appliances. She hurried through the rest of the house—living room, dining room with wrought-iron chandelier, office, recreation room with a handsome English billiards table, master suite, two other suites, and five baths. The house was dusted, vacuumed, and polished. She backtracked and looked more thoroughly. No trash lingered in the waste baskets, and no perishables waited in the refrigerator.

Even more important, there were no mementos to reveal the life of the person who lived here. No family photos, awards, collections, or books sitting out on end tables with markers to indicate where the reader would resume his or her literary journey. She did find a man's wardrobe in one of the closets in the master suite. He had a medium build and conservative tastes. In the medicine cabinet were toothbrush, aspirin, and shaving equipment. That was as intimate as it got.

It seemed to her the owner had moved on . . . or had never really lived here, which would be a strange extravagance. Then she had another thought: Maybe he had died, and the family had taken away his personal possessions.

She returned to the office, which was dominated by bookcases and heavy leather furniture. It was dark and masculine, with a strong hint of cigar smoke. She looked around for the cigar case and spotted it on a side table beside a leather armchair. It was carved and darkly handsome, expensive. She opened it. Inside were fine Cuban Cohiba cigars, treasured by connoisseurs, and the case was full to the top with them. She picked it up, balanced it in her hands, thinking.

The quiet ticking of the electric clock on the mantel caught her attention, and she listened again for other sounds: The wind had strengthened, and the pittosporum bushes squeaked against the den's windows. The noise made her shiver—like fingernails on a chalkboard. There were no traffic noises. The street was far enough away and the house so well insulated she might as well be in the middle of nowhere.

Reassured, she put down the cigar box and went to the desk, where she sat in the tall executive chair behind it, flicked on the gooseneck lamp, and searched. The top right-hand drawer held nothing interesting—just the usual pencils, pens, and pads of note paper. But the second drawer looked significant. Here were unopened bills, and all were addressed to . . . Alexei Berianov. She stared. Riveted.

She knew the name. *Alexei Berianov.* It was one of those that had tumbled through her mind after her surgery. Who was he? She hesitated. Could he have been her donor? Was that why this house felt so deserted—Berianov, its owner, had died last year, his family had donated his heart for transplant, and they had taken away his things?

She ripped open the envelopes and found recent bills—all for utilities for this house. In the next drawer were files of earlier bills, preserved for, or by, the mysterious Berianov. But the rest of the drawers held nothing interesting, just more of the usual desk accoutrements such as a stapler, paper clips, and unused file folders. There were no credit cards, no checkbooks, not even a business card, and no personal correspondence. She studied the room. There was no computer.

Her gaze returned to the cigar box. What was it about that? She crossed the room again and this time sat in the leather chair. She opened the box again, studied the neat rows of cigars. She had an odd feeling about it. . . . Impulsively she dumped out the cigars and studied the interior base. One side of the wood was slightly darker than the other, perhaps from use. She pried and prodded, and the base suddenly popped up, revealing a small stash of papers.

She stared. On top was an invoice from a fencing company in Stone Point, West Virginia. *Stone Point*. That was the place Colonel Yurimengri had told her about and where Jeff Hammond had gone. Then she saw the name on the bill. It was not for Alexei Berianov. It was for . . . Caleb Bates.

She sat back, remembering. That was the name of one of the new owners of HanTech Industries. It was peculiar that the name would be here in the house of Alexei Berianov, when so many of HanTech's new owners were Russian. Or was it? If this Bates were associated with Russians in business, why not in other ways? She thought about the weapons-grade uranium HanTech was buying up.

She stared at the bill a moment longer then set it aside. Beneath it were two more invoices, one for poured concrete and the other for electrical lines, again for the Stone Point property and addressed to Caleb Bates. She paused, mulling, then set them aside as well. Next was a yellowed newspaper advertisement for a dairy farm for sale near Gettysburg, Pennsylvania. She studied it. Someone had circled the photograph of the farm's colonial mansion.

She set it aside, too, and picked up the last clipping. It was a news story about a man who had died last year. Her hands trembled. She stared at the mug shot. And stared longer. Here was the stranger she had killed in her nightmares and who had later appeared around the campfire. The same broad forehead, the short snub nose, the shock of gray hair combed straight back. Killed over and over. The motorcycle had roared out of the garage. She had jumped on and deliberately crashed it into him. *This* man. In her mind, she saw his look of awful pain and surprise. Watched him arc up high into the air and smash head-first onto the drive.

She read the name: Mikhail Ogust. She stifled a gasp. It was another of the names from her nightmares. She stood up and paced around the room, feeling like a trapped animal. Her heart thundered. How could she have seen that face in her dreams, the face of another real man who had died? She continued to walk, rubbing her hands together as if struck by a chill. It was too much to deal with. Too many coincidences, or too much evidence her heart had indeed been "talking" to her all along.

After a time, pacing and resisting her own thoughts, she felt calmer. Of course, she would have to deal with it. She had to know. That was why she had taken the risk to be here—to learn as much as she could. She reminded herself all information was neutral. It was what you did with it that made it good or bad.

Steeling herself, she returned to the desk. She sat, picked up the clipping, and read:

> Soviet defector Mikhail Ogust, 41, who lived near Dupont Circle, died early yesterday following a motorcycle accident in Rock Creek Park.
>
> According to police who were called to the scene, it appeared he had struck an abutment, which threw him off his motorcycle. He landed on his head. Doctors report he died of brain injuries. No safety helmet was found, and he had no other serious wounds.
>
> Ogust defected in 1991 and was highly thought of in local Russian philanthropic circles. A karate instructor and sports car enthusiast, he made a fortune exporting athletic equipment to Russia while importing such delicacies as caviar.
>
> In the years before he defected, his work was rumored to be clandestine and violent. He was an influential KGB colonel in Moscow. . . .

Trembling, she checked the date on the clipping and collapsed into the desk chair. She stared at the window, where the wind pummeled the bush against the glass. She should have been exhausted, ready to keel over and sleep, but instead she was in turmoil. All she could do was think. . . .

Ogust was a man, forty-one years old, and Travis Jackson had said her donor was male and in his early forties.

Ogust had died in "a traffic accident" just a few hours before her transplant surgery.

With head injuries only, his heart would have been unharmed, and it would have been a short distance from the transplant center where she lay dying.

Plus, he was Russian, a karate expert, and he liked sports cars, which could mean he was a very good, fast driver. She remembered the other elements in her dreams—the Russian-made AK-47s, the atmosphere of constant danger, and her amazing sense of confidence and skill when violence threatened. She recalled Dave, the hospital aide who had made her jumpy and suspicious—he had turned out to be a thief. Ogust had been KGB, trained in ways that would account for everything.

She nodded to herself, trying to absorb it. After all this time, after so much confusion and worry . . . after all the bizarre experiences . . . yes, Mikhail Ogust was a perfect fit. He must be her donor—yet he was the one she killed in her nightmares. She recalled Stephanie's warning: Dreams were not direct information. They gave clues—bits and pieces—but no one could trust them for the whole picture. If they were cellular memory, her job was to make sense of the parts.

The story about Ogust explained a lot, but it left out more. It presented the skin of the man, not the flesh. Not who he really was, not what he thought about, or where his passions lay. Was he short-tempered, as she thought? Was he aggressive? She hesitated: Was he a killer?

She wanted to know more. She especially wanted to know why his heart had led her to find Colonel Yurimengri's body, and then why it had sent her here. The three must have known each other—Colonel Ogust, Colonel Yurimengri, and Alexei Berianov.

Her heart donor, Mikhail Ogust, was dead. Colonel Yurimengri had died in her presence. So where was Berianov, the one who paid the bills for this house? Dead, too? A chill sped up her spine. She snatched up the clipping, looking for the byline. She was not surprised: Jeffrey Hammond again. She scanned the rest of the story, hunting for names. But neither Yurimengri nor Berianov was mentioned.

As she folded the clipping and put it into her bag, she scanned the room, wondering where else to search. She knelt at the low bookcase between the two windows and systematically opened each leather-covered volume, turned it upside down, and shook it for papers or photographs. As she worked, she wondered whether Hammond had written an article about Berianov, too. Then she had a disturbing idea: In the past, journalist credentials had been a traditional source of cover for spies and double agents of all countries. Maybe the reason reporter Hammond knew so much about Soviet defectors was that he had spied for the KGB against the United States during the Cold War. Maybe he was still a spy.

She shivered and moved to a credenza. She opened drawers, but all were empty. Just as she was tapping the base, looking for a false bottom, she had an uneasy feeling. The hairs on the back of her neck seemed to stand on end. She looked back over her shoulder at the brightly lit office. And froze.

"Who are you?" Her pulse raced. "What do you want?"

The figure moved toward her with the slow, stalking gait of a panther. He was dressed in black, skin-tight turtleneck and pants. A black ski mask covered his face, showing only icy blue eyes. He wore black athletic shoes and socks. A holstered pistol and other equipment were attached to a black web belt at his waist.

He said nothing, and she knew immediately it was ridiculous of her to have made an attempt. His unblinking eyes seemed to be trying to hold her with his gaze—hypnotize her as predatory animals sometimes did when they closed in for the kill.

Sweat gathered on her face and in her armpits. Why was his pistol still holstered? A wave of anger hit her. She was tired of the bullshit. Tired of being a target. Tired of being afraid. Tired of trying to understand the incomprehensible.

"Obviously you're not here for ice cream." She jumped up. "If it's me you want, I'll make it easy."

Without speaking, he continued to close in. Her tension growing, she kept her hips and upper body straight, her knees slightly bent. He was her height, of medium build, and moved with the kind of smooth precision that announced intense physical training. She had no idea what he planned, and she was not going to wait to find out. She hesitated just long enough for him to get in range. Then she took two quick steps forward, raised her right leg to chest height, and drove the ball of her foot into his chest in a *mae-keage* front snap kick.

He fell back, surprise in his cold eyes. But she was even more surprised. She was tall and strong, and from experience she knew the power of her kicks could knock an opponent flat. But he was still very much on his feet. Immediately she spun and crashed her foot back at him again, aiming for his chin this time.

She never connected. He parried and slammed a fist into her ribs. As her bones vibrated with the sudden pain, she had her answer: He was a master. His punches, kicks, and strikes rained on her so rapidly that her attempts to stop him were as ineffective as a mosquito's wings against a screen door. In less than a minute, she was flat on her back, gasping for air. She could not move. Pain pulsed everywhere.

Still he did not pull his gun. He dragged her to a chair and propped her up on it. She swallowed, trying to force oxygen into her aching lungs so she could go on fighting. He took nylon cord from a waist pouch and swiftly tied her to the chair. He worked methodically, not a sound escaping his lips. As she struggled to breathe, she watched, desperate for some way to stop him.

He seemed to have thought of everything. He was not identifiable by sight, sound, or odor, and she was completely helpless. But as he knotted the last cord, she noticed the black glove on his right hand had slipped. There was a bulge under the long sleeve of his knit top that looked as if it were a watch. But in the gap between the glove and the sleeve was a little white scar on the top of his wrist. She tried not to stare.

He dropped a cloth over her eyes and roughly tied it behind her head. He gave it an extra twist as if in warning, and then she heard the sounds of a search begin. She listened as he quietly took apart Berianov's office. He must have spent an hour on what she considered an essentially empty room. But for what? And why had he not harmed her? Was he some kind of psychotic killer who liked to play with his victims first? A sadist who planned to torture her before he killed her?

Repressing her fear, she listened until she heard him pad out. Left in empty silence, she waited, straining to hear anything that would tell her where he was and what he was doing. Frantically she went to work to free herself from the tight bonds. As she struggled, she began to hear distant noises. He was searching elsewhere. Pain shot through her limbs, but still she worked as he took apart the living room, the dining room, all the rooms. She dreaded the moment when she would hear him stop. What would he do to her when he found whatever he was looking for?

She had to escape. She battled fatigue and desperation. Her fingers pulled at the strong nylon cords, but it was as if she were slogging through Jell-O. She grew more sluggish. She was weary, exhausted. Time passed. Still, she made herself work on.

PART TWO

19

In the high-powered Lincoln Continental, Jeffrey Hammond dozed as the hours ticked past midnight and on toward morning. Outside the windows, the scenery segued from forested mountain crests to wide, fertile valleys and at last to Virginia's sweeping Tidal Plain.

When early morning light at last brightened the sky to the east, Hammond sat up, fully awake. The Bureau car was gliding down a quiet side street in northwest Washington. The atmosphere was tense. It had been a long drive, and each time they stopped for food, fuel, or a bathroom break, the agents went on high alert, determined to make certain Hammond did not pull some trick and escape. Fifteen minutes before, the lead agent, Chuck Graham, had used his cell phone to call ahead and warn they would arrive shortly, which made Hammond believe they were taking him to a safe house, since they had passed downtown, where the Hoover building was located.

Now as they entered the neighborhood known as Adams Morgan, the luxury car was a pressure cooker of grim faces and tight jaws, while outside, the world continued serenely on, unaware anything out of the ordinary was cruising past this Friday morning. It was so early that the young executives, artists, and nonconformists here were only beginning to stir, stepping out in bathrobes to pick up newspapers in a variety of languages. Trendy and countercultural, Adams Morgan was renowned for colorful wall murals, a global atlas of restaurants, the flowing garb of distant lands, and fine old homes that had once housed the nation's elite. Mostly residential, its busy diversity was an ideal place in which to hide an FBI safe house.

As he watched it all, Hammond remembered being like the agents in the car, so concentrated on the assignment that he missed the real world happening out there under the trees and behind the shuttered windows. Strange to lose touch with that, since protecting it was ostensibly the whole point of the job.

The Lincoln rolled past picturesque brick townhouses built sometime in the early twentieth century. In front of the third one, a woman in a wild tiger-striped wrap, her hair piled high in a bun, tucked a newspaper under her arm. She sipped from a large coffee mug and turned back toward the house. Oddly attractive, easy in her eccentricity, she sang to herself as she ran up the steps and in through the door.

"Which place is it?" Hammond calculated Graham's fifteen-minute warning had expired, and by the way the driver was craning his neck, this had to be the block. Hammond knew the driver would not park on the street. Too exposed. He would have a more secure method to get the prisoner indoors.

Chuck Graham cracked a thin smile. He indicated the woman who had disappeared into the three-story townhouse. "Hers. She's the caretaker." Despite the long night, his trousers still had their knife-edge, his white shirt was unwrinkled, and the lines on his face had deepened only slightly with weariness.

Hammond nodded. In this bohemian area, she fit right in, and no one would suspect she was an FBI officer. He had never seen her or the safe house, but that was no surprise. By now, a lot of who and what he had known had changed. In counterespionage and antiterrorism, habit and routine could be fatal.

As he had suspected, the driver took the Lincoln around the corner and down a treeless alley that ran behind the townhouses. Their rear porches extended out toward the alley, which was framed on both sides by tall fences and occasional trash cans, waiting to be picked up. It was impossible to see into the yards, affording privacy to everyone, which made the safe house's particular need of it less conspicuous. Graham slid from his suit jacket what looked like a silver case for business cards. Inside was a small stack of the white cards, but when Graham pressed a piece of decorative filigree beneath, a garage door began to rise ahead.

The driver swung the Lincoln past two trash cans and into the garage's dark opening, pausing the car as the door closed behind. Abruptly the tension relaxed. Thoma and one of the men in the front seat loosened their ties. The female agent let out a long sigh. They had brought their quarry in safely. They appeared to expect no more trouble from him, which meant the house and grounds were loaded with every conceivable security measure, and probably a few exclusive to the Bureau. This time, he might be trapped.

Agent Thoma climbed out of the car, his 10mm Smith & Wesson in hand. He motioned it toward Hammond. "Out."

Hammond got out. As Graham strode ahead through the dank old garage, the other agents fell in behind Hammond, pistols raised. They followed Graham into an ultramodern passageway whose left wall was of dusky, reflecting glass. Through the glass, the backyard of spring tulips, irises, and a flowering pear tree was clearly visible, as well as the tall wood fence that walled the alley. But anyone in the yard or anyone foolish enough to trespass by climbing over the fence would find seeing through the opaque glass impossible, making the walk from the garage to the house a safe journey. Hammond did not like the look of any of it.

Graham halted at the townhouse's back door, where an electronic badge reader was attached to the red brick wall. He did not bother with the doorknob, which would be locked. Instead, as Hammond and the agents waited, he slipped what looked like an ordinary Virginia driver's license into the slot. The screen on the front of the electronic reader glowed to green life.

Hammond said neutrally, "State-of-the-art?"

Graham glanced up over his shoulder at Hammond. "Damn right. Security's so tight the president couldn't get in without advance approval."

As if to prove the point, a voice from the electronic scanner announced, "Hello, Charles S. Graham." The advanced software made the greeting smooth and lifelike, not the usual disembodied speech. Also unlike most such machines, this one did not try to sound like some nice woman. Instead, the voice was authoritarian and male. It ordered: "Place your right hand on the screen."

The white outline of a hand appeared on the green monitor. Hammond recognized this high-security check from his days with the Bureau. The ID card Graham had put into the scanner would be a souped-up version of a credit card with an implanted chip that could contain everything from Graham's physical description to his Social Security number, home address, blood type, clearance level, and reason for being here. God knew what else it could do now.

As Hammond examined the brick exterior wall, the door, the window, and the molding, Graham noticed. "Keep looking, pal. You'll never be able to spot all the new gizmos we have. We've got enough funding these days that the R&D boys and girls are blissful."

"Bomb-resistant glass." Hammond nodded toward the window next to the door. He gazed pointedly at the nickel-sized holes above the door. "Video and motion sensors."

"Child's play." Graham laid his right hand inside the white hairlines on the green screen, and the lines shrank to fit his hand precisely.

Although Hammond had not been in a safe house in some time, through various sources he had kept abreast of many of the improvements since his day. The scanner would make certain Graham's print verified what his ID card claimed. Since it had not returned Graham's card, he figured that if Graham did not match, the machine would permanently swallow the card and all hell would break loose. Hammond saw the telltale, slightly mismatching squares on the brick that told him automatic weapons—which would shoot an intruder, or escapee, into hamburger—were embedded behind small trap doors in the side of the townhouse. Needle-nose cameras were probably hidden somewhere near as well. Hammond shook off a feeling he was at a turkey shoot, and he was the turkey.

"Thank you, Mr. Graham," the scanner decided. "You may remove your hand." The phony driver's license popped out, and Graham took it in one neat motion and slid it into his suit jacket. "You are cleared to enter with Mr. Hammond," the machine continued. "The other agents may return to the Hoover building."

There was a quiet sound of whooshing air, and the big door inched open. It looked like wood, but Hammond recognized that it acted like special bank-vault steel, so heavy it needed a pneumatic lift to open and close.

"Take off," Graham told his cohorts. "Good job all around." He stepped away from the entry and commanded, "Inside, Hammond."

Hammond gave one last look behind and moved indoors.

Thoma could not stand it. His voice boomed out: "Hammond, I'll be watching. You used to be just a disgrace. Now you're a murderer. You make us all look bad."

Hammond frowned and turned. "Give it a rest. I didn't shoot them any more than you did. You don't know what you're talking about."

Thoma's heavy face quivered with some deep rage that had percolated there as long as Hammond had known him. But at the Bureau, Thoma had found sanctuary, a place where his fury and discontent could pass as patriotism and love of country. In his own way, to his own kind, he was useful. But now that he had found Hammond again and believed him not only a troublemaker and a quitter but also a murderer, Thoma could be dangerous.

Hammond continued to stare, reminded of how powerful belief, even mistaken belief, could be. And Thoma was not alone. The others glared angrily, too, their eyes accusatory: Hammond had not only shamed them, he was a traitor to the shield. Whatever evidence the locals at Stone Point had uncovered, it had convinced them. It gave Hammond an unsettled feeling, as if the ground had just shaken in warning.

"Move," Graham ordered again, his gun steady on Hammond.

As they advanced into the back hall of the restored townhouse, the door closed silently behind with another soft *whoosh* of compressed air. Hammond surveyed the wood-paneled corridor, which was lined with wall sconces and period prints. He noted the recessed cameras and the spots where weapons were likely hidden. As Graham had promised, the electronic surveillance and protection were dense. Plus, agents were probably stationed throughout. He was trapped, a prisoner not only of the Bureau but of his conscience. He needed to escape, but he would not kill these people.

Worried that the sign he needed to lead him to safety would not be waiting, he continued walking and observing. From its parquet floors to its Chinese side chairs, the old townhouse still had a feeling of genteel hominess. From the look of it, Hammond figured it had been specially prepared to keep safe the most important of the frightened, monied, and on the run, who had been swept into the Bureau's bosom to reveal secrets that could topple global cartels, terrorist groups, and foreigners bent on stealing American technology.

Then from a doorway ahead, a man stepped into the hallway. Hammond stared. "Ty? What in hell are you doing here?"

In his seventies, Senator Tyrone ("Ty") Crocker had the patrician face and bearing of WASP New England at its most wealthy and best educated. "Hello, Jeff. It *has* been a long time. I was just about to have a cup of Earl Grey." He had thick white hair, a high forehead, and a small sardonic smile. "My granddaughter tells me some *Star Trek* captain drinks Earl Grey, too. A strange connection to an entertainment phenomenon I don't understand. I suppose I never will. But at least it puts me current. I'd hoped you'd join me."

He wore linen trousers the color of buttercream, a brown knit golfing shirt buttoned tidily at the neck, and tasseled loafers. Probably on his way for an early round of golf at the exclusive Congressional Country Club, where the initiation fee was $50,000 and he could compare chip shots with the vice president and other top political and business leaders. He was the senior senator from Connecticut.

Hammond quickly adjusted. "Thanks. It's always good to see you,

Ty." But it wasn't good. Ty Crocker's being here probably meant more bad news.

The senator shifted his attention. "You, too, Special Agent Graham. Perhaps you'd enjoy a hot cup of tea after your long night's journey?"

"Yes, sir. Thank you, Senator." Everything about Graham's usually controlled manner exuded pleasure. His hand on his pistol even trembled a little to be in the presence of such a towering legend.

Ty Crocker had been a diplomat and now, for the past twenty years, a highly respected senator. All along he had been a vocal champion of the nation's espionage community, and for the past six years, he had headed the powerful Senate Intelligence Committee. Like Barry Goldwater before him, he was a no-nonsense conservative renowned for his integrity.

Hammond and Graham followed the old man into a parlor adorned with pale flocked wallpaper and period furniture. Three windows faced out onto the street, but filmy curtains shielded the room from prying eyes. Hammond's assumption that agents would be stationed in the house was confirmed: One was standing with arms crossed in the corner, next to a hanging fern. The agent stared neutrally back, watching Hammond's every move.

Senator Crocker followed Hammond's line of sight and told the man, "You can leave, son. Stand guard outside the door if it'll make you feel better. I appreciate your concern, but Jeff and I are old friends. You're not going to murder me over tea, are you, Jeff?"

"No, sir. Especially not if it's good tea."

The senator chuckled. "Have a seat. Wherever you think best, Mr. Graham." He paced across an oriental rug to a small writing desk that stood in front of the windows.

Graham indicated the wing-back chair next to the brick fireplace. Hammond, on his good behavior, sat, his face expressionless, as Graham settled onto the chair between Hammond and the door, creating a hazard for Hammond if he had any ideas about making a run for it. As usual, Hammond studied the room. Inwardly he gave a brief, cold smile. He would not make his move yet. There was information he needed first. But soon . . . very soon, he would have to.

Senator Crocker returned to the desk and pressed a button. In response, a bell tinkled somewhere in the back of the house. "Tea will be here shortly. Don't want to keep you gentlemen waiting." His hand rested flat on the desktop; his feet in the tasseled loafers were planted firmly on the carpet. His white hair shone in the diffused light from the windows behind him. He was contemplating Hammond from across the room as if he wished it were across a continent. A very large continent.

Faced with that gloomy, probing gaze, Hammond felt a twinge of guilt. Suddenly his favorite herringbone sports jacket was worn and tacky. His hair was too long. The gold earring was definitely over the top. And he had murdered the couple in Stone Point.

But there were reasons for everything, so he tried, "You're looking good, Ty. Sorry we couldn't be meeting under better circumstances. I assume the Bureau sent you because of your work with the intelligence committee—"

The senator waved a dismissive hand. "Give me a break, Jeff. You've been up to no good. Your father wouldn't have approved. Your mother's probably rotating in her grave. I was fond of them." His morose eyes hardened. "Can't say I feel the same about you right now."

"I understand," Hammond said truthfully. "But you're dead wrong on this. I didn't kill those kids."

"Bullshit. For the good of the Bureau, you've got to be square with me. What in hell are you up to? If there's a shred of a reason . . . something private you're working on? Maybe those kids were into illegal weapons or some kind of sick cult thing. Give me some help here. I want to understand what the situation is, if not with them, then in your mind. If there are extenuating circumstances, perhaps they'll provide a way out of this. Better yet, it'd be good if you've been investigating a national-security news angle that led you into this mess and you can turn it over."

"I had nothing to do with them or anything in this unfortunate situation. You've got nothing to defend."

Senator Crocker shook his head sadly. Studying Hammond, he continued, "National security's the ruse Bobby Kelsey used to get control of you before we lost you to the local police. With your security background, Kelsey was rightfully concerned that they not learn any secrets from the past that you might inadvertently reveal. But we've still got to deal with the charges somehow. It'd help if they were involved with terrorists or smuggling. As I recall, you write about that for the newspaper." He paused. "But if you just simply murdered that young man and woman in cold blood, then there's nothing I can or will do to help, and neither will Bobby or the Bureau."

Hammond shook his head sadly. "So you believe it, too. You've known me all my life, and you think I could do such a thing? I had no reason to shoot them." He hesitated. He had to know: "Just what in hell is the evidence that's got everybody convinced?"

The senator turned to Chuck Graham. "You didn't tell him?"

"I was under orders to wait."

The senator pursed his lips. He walked to the chair between Hammond and Graham and sat. He leaned forward, his bare forearms resting on his light-colored trousers. He delivered the bad news. "Jeff, they've got two fingerprints from the windowsill where the killer shot. Your fingerprints. Clear as a bell."

"That's crap!" Hammond said angrily. "How could that be? It's impossible!"

The senator sighed. "There's no other rational explanation for your prints to be at the murder scene, except that you killed them . . . or know who did."

"There has to be, because I wasn't there and I didn't do it. Hell, I don't even know where that girl lived!"

"The police picked up the prints, wired them to the Bureau for identification, and they were yours. No question about it. The DNA results will be in next week from the skin oils. We both know they'll match." The senator sat back and shook his snowy head. "You're not doing yourself any good denying it. The parents of the dead boy showed up at the Hoover building yesterday to make statements, too. They were pretty broken up, but they managed to say he'd been in and out of trouble since he was a juvenile, which we'd already discovered. They also said he'd been worried recently about some tall man who'd been threatening him. Somebody who used to be FBI and now worked for *The Washington Post*. This man wanted him to lie about drug use for a story he was working on. The boy's juvenile trouble all had to do with drugs."

"Let me guess," Hammond said, disgusted. "Some guy named Hammond."

"Right. How do you explain that away?"

"The parents are lying. Or the boy was. It's obviously some kind of setup. I can't explain it any more than that."

"Then how did your prints get there?" The senator's eyes glinted with disappointed anger.

As a knock sounded on the door, Hammond said, "If it made sense to me, I'd tell you. I don't write drug stories. Not my beat. Check on it. And I didn't kill those kids. All I know is I've been doing my job at the *Post*, minding my own business, and all of a sudden I'm on my way to the electric chair for two murders I didn't commit. Or does West Virginia hang or use lethal injection? I don't know. It's absurd. Preposterous!"

"It's not preposterous," the senator corrected. "It's evidence." The knock sounded on the door again. "Come in, Joyce."

The door to the hallway opened, and the woman with the wild hair pulled up into a messy bun swayed into the room, carrying a silver tray on which sat an ornate tea service. Her tiger-striped wrap was gone, replaced by an Indian-print blouse, pantaloons, and sandals. Just the right touch for colorful Adams Morgan.

Chuck Graham frowned. "Joyce, this is Jeff Hammond, our 'guest' for a few days. Don't fall for any of his tricks. He used to be one of the best. Consider him dangerous."

"So I hear." She glanced curiously at Hammond and deposited the tray on the round coffee table. "Tea's ready. I'd pour, but I've got work to do. Can you manage?"

Senator Crocker was already leaning over to pick up the tea strainer. "Be happy to handle this."

Hammond watched. His stomach was sour, and he had a disquieting feeling the world had gone haywire. He had learned everything he could here. It was time to try to escape despite his fear there was no way to get safely from the house.

Still, he said innocently, "I need to use the bathroom, Joyce. Would you kindly point me in the right direction?"

"Very funny," Graham grumbled. "I'll take you."

Hammond marched out into the paneled hall, Graham close behind. As the door guard slipped his hand into his jacket to find his weapon, Hammond turned left, heading back in the direction from which they had entered.

"That's it," Graham directed. "Last door on the left."

Hammond opened it and quickly scrutinized the interior for the sign he desperately hoped was waiting for him. There was nothing. Hiding his worry, he said, "Thanks. Are you coming in, too? You'll notice there's no window, but I suppose there's always the possibility I could escape by dematerializing."

Graham's gaze narrowed. He studied Hammond, then looked around inside the small guest bath. He even checked the toilet tank for a hidden weapon. "Guess you're not going anywhere, but don't lock the door. You've got five minutes."

As soon as the door closed, Hammond examined the walls for a mark of some kind. Anxiously, he checked the wood floor. The plaster ceiling. It had probably been difficult, maybe impossible, to create an escape route here. But his orders had been to find the nearest bathroom if he should be captured by the Bureau. In his secret line of work, there were few backup plans. He hoped like hell this one at least was in place.

His head was beginning to pound. Then he saw it: Chalk on the wood panel behind the toilet bowl, where the plumbing was. It was unobtrusive, the brown color almost invisible against the old walnut paneling. His chest contracted with excitement. He quickly wiped away the chalk, took out a dime, and turned the screw at the bottom of the panel. He flushed the toilet. They should think he was doing what he was supposed to be doing in here.

Two more screws, and the panel swung free, hinged at the top. Working quickly, he slid back away from the toilet and pulled up a piece of the wood floor. It had been cut recently, and the removal of it and the panel made an opening that was just large enough for him. A musky odor of soil and cobwebs drifted up. Here was an escape route under the house that would avoid the Fort Knox surveillance and armaments. He worked for a damn smart man. But he had to hurry. Graham was already suspicious.

The agent's voice thundered outside the door. "Hammond! Your five minutes are up." Graham had given him one break. There would be no other. "Come out of there!"

"Hey, I'll be out. One more lousy minute." Sweat beaded up on his face. Silently, he lowered his feet into the hole, eased past the plumbing, braced, and reached back up. With one hand he held up the panel, and with the other he shoved the piece of flooring back where it belonged. Then he let the panel swing quietly back into place, and he dropped down to the ground.

20

Hammond landed on his haunches in the dirt. The house had only a half-basement, and he had dropped into what was the remaining crawl space, with a ceiling so low he could not stand erect. To his right was a concrete block wall, but to his left was a gift: About a foot away lay a flashlight. His boss was not only smart, he was thoughtful.

The roar above his head, muffled through the floor of the bathroom, was still volcanic. Graham's voice bellowed: *"Hammond! Goddammit, the bastard's gone. Keller! Joyce! Ray! Get back here! Everyone, he's busted out!"*

He had to move. And fast. But where? As dirt and sawdust rained lightly onto his head from the floorboards above, he lit the flashlight and directed it through the dusty mist at the exposed beams. That's when he saw a white chalk mark, spectral on a support post ahead, and another, fainter, on a post in the darkness beyond. The odors of mold and spiders made his nose itch, and he fought off a need to sneeze as he swiftly duck-walked, following the trail of white marks beneath wood beams where telephone, television, and security cables were tacked, heading toward what he thought must be the rear of the townhouse.

Above him, feet pounded in the bathroom, searching for him and how he had gotten out. Overhead in what might be the hallway, other footsteps thundered. His pursuers were fanning out. He broke into a sweat. His quadriceps burned. He pinched his nose to stop the infernal itching and hurried past more plumbing and piles of dirt. There were no spiderwebs interfering with his journey, which told him this was a recently checked route.

He aimed the flashlight up. There was dirt overhead now, where a hole large enough for a man to squeeze through had been dug. Something wooden was sitting on top of it, and there was another white-chalk checkmark on the wood. He reached up and tested. The wood panel was heavy, but it moved. He slid it aside a few inches, allowing in fresh air. There was a heavy object sitting on top of it. As he carefully shoved the cover farther aside, metal clanked. He nodded to himself. It had to be a metal trash can. When they had arrived, he had seen the cans sitting in the alley on a strip of lawn beside the garage, waiting for pickup.

Behind him, where the house stood, footfalls still boomed and echoed across the raised-wood foundation. They were hunting for him, and it was only a matter of time until they found his route or they spilled out of the townhouse to search.

He shoved the can aside, jumped up, and pulled himself out of the hole into the fresh air. Birds sang, and in the distance he could hear traffic. He gazed around at the quiet alley with its high fences and the occasional parked car.

He glanced back and saw the garage door to the safe house was rising. Black wingtip shoes came into view. They were polished to a high military sheen. Probably Graham. His pulse throbbing, Hammond rammed the can back over the hole, glanced left and right along the alley, and dashed to the right, the shortest way to the street.

"Hammond! Stop!" Graham's shout shattered the quiet morning air. Rage was in every syllable.

But Hammond kept running. Behind him, he heard a quiet *pop*. Concrete spat up in tiny chunks next to his right foot. Graham had screwed on a silencer and was shooting. But silencers were notorious for ruining aim, particularly when firing from a distance. It gave Hammond a chance.

Sweat poured off his face. He had been a tailback at Harvard, a runner whose speed was far beyond that of most men his size. He sprinted. *Pop. Pop. Pop.* The bullets rammed into the last fence as Hammond rounded it, tore out into the street, and dashed between the line of parked cars and traffic. Horns honked. He had to disappear before Graham caught sight of him again.

Breathing hard, he glanced back over his shoulder. And with relief saw it was there: A black Cadillac with darkened windows. It purred up to him, the back door swung open, and Hammond jumped into the dim interior. Cigarette smoke wafted from the front seat and stung his nostrils.

Hammond fell into the couchlike rear seat behind his boss. "What in hell's going on, Bobby?"

Bobby Kelsey swung the Caddy into traffic and glanced up at Hammond in the rearview mirror. Kelsey was the assistant director of the FBI's National Security Division, the nation's top agency for uncovering and stopping foreign spies and terrorists, and as such he also oversaw the FCI—the Foreign Counterintelligence Program. He and Hammond were the car's only occupants, but that was to be expected. Only three people were privy to the highly secret fact that Hammond was actually still on the job and working directly under Kelsey—Hammond, Kelsey, and the FBI director himself, Thomas Horn.

As the Caddy accelerated, blending in with other vehicles on the busy street, Kelsey said, "After all these years, you still surprise me, Jeff. The first thing I expected to hear was 'thank you.' I went to a hell of a lot of trouble setting up that escape route. Crawling around under a house isn't my speciality." He stared up into his rearview mirror again. "You look like the devil." His hand moved the cigarette languidly to his mouth, and he took in Hammond with an unhurried, analytical gaze as he smoked. He had graying red hair combed back from his forehead and a short, upturned Irish nose.

Hammond touched his stinging cheek and gazed at his fingers. Blood. Probably from one of the last three bullets that had hit the fence and sprayed out slivers of wood. He had not felt the little needle-like wounds at the time.

"Yeah. Well, all in the line of duty." He took out a handkerchief and mopped his face. "How come you let them take me to an armed camp like that safe house? Wasn't there some other way to handle this?"

Kelsey's voice was hard. "Look, Jeff, I played the national-security card. Be grateful. But that's all I had time for. Once the lab ID'd you, I couldn't interfere more without raising questions." He sped the car away around a corner. "You do owe me an explanation. Did you kill that couple in Stone Point?"

"Come on, Bobby. It's bullshit. You know that." Hammond repeated the events of the last two days, everything from Colonel Yurimengri's death to meeting Beth Convey and his search in Stone Point for General Berianov. "You've got to call off the hunt for me. How am I supposed to do my job with the Bureau in hot pursuit? I've got to find Berianov!"

For Hammond, Alexei Berianov had always been the key. It all began back in 1991 as the dying Soviet Union was breathing its last, and the trickle of defecting spies fleeing the political carnage increased to a flood. Many were the best of the KGB, ranging from in-the-know bureaucrats to star operatives who had trained in the highly secret Soviet tradecraft camps.

In the beginning, the West was thrilled to be harvesting this golden espionage crop. Just four years earlier, even two years earlier, the United States would have done anything, gone anywhere, risked more than was sensible to get any one of these prime sources.

But by the time September 1991 rolled around, each new defector was costing the U.S. government at least $1 million to debrief and resettle, and many were merely repeating what others had already revealed, a waste of time and money. There was also the question of how much of this information the West really needed now that the Cold War was over. And finally, there was the dirty secret no one wanted to acknowledge: The debriefers were tired and bored. They were not interrogating the newcomers as thoroughly as they had those who had arrived in earlier waves. There just did not seem much point to it any longer, and they were eagerly looking around for more interesting assignments or, better yet, a long vacation.

All these reasons contributed to the joint FBI-CIA team leaders' decision to release Berianov, Yurimengri, and Ogust after only three weeks. Hammond had objected. When he was ignored, he filed a formal protest and request that they be held for further interrogation.

Everything about the three men's escape from Moscow reeked, as far as Hammond was concerned. They had left the chaotic city together the month before, in August, during the hard-liners' failed coup from which New Russia eventually arose. Not only were Berianov, Yurimengri, and Ogust among the highest-placed intelligence officials America had ever taken in, they had also accomplished their escapes at an extraordinarily convenient moment to themselves. At first this detail had merely intrigued Hammond, but the more he questioned them, the more he was convinced their emigration was *too* convenient. They were holding back. Something else was going on, something they had planned, something dangerous to the United States.

But Alexei Berianov had been the next-to-last leader of the KGB's feared Department Eight special forces, and because of his special knowledge he had been able to offer his debriefers a sweetener to make certain he and his comrades were released from interrogation early. He promised tantalizing details of a longtime double agent in the CIA, a clandestine turncoat responsible for mammoth leaks to the old Soviet

Union and for the tragic executions of many dedicated spies who had worked for the United States. Not since Benedict Arnold had America had such a treasonous spy hidden in its bosom, Berianov promised.

Neither the CIA nor the FBI could resist. So Berianov divulged the man's name, a list of secret drops, the numbers of a Swiss bank account, and details of an ultrasecret mission against Saddam Hussein that no one in the room knew a thing about. That was the beginning of the end for CIA agent Aldrich ("Rick") Ames, who had a drinking problem, a spendthrift wife, and a bank account far too large for his income. Excited because so much was explained if Rick Ames really was a traitor, the FBI soon verified enough—including the operation against Hussein—to know the case had merit. At which point, with their gratitude, they released the three KGB defectors.

Furious and worried, Hammond had gone up the chain of command, loudly explaining and complaining. Colleagues had told him to quit rocking the Bureau's boat. What did it matter? The Cold War was over. Frustrated and disgusted, he had resigned in protest, with hard feelings felt by all.

Or so it appeared. In fact, Bobby Kelsey had listened well to Hammond and agreed. He secretly arranged Hammond's resignation in order to hide a new assignment—to go undercover to keep tabs on all Soviet defectors who had remained in the area, while trying to get information about the mole who had riddled and weakened the Bureau. Over the years since, Hammond had uncovered essential evidence on various Americans who were spying for other countries—among them Harold Nicholson and Douglas Groat of the CIA, Earl Edwin Pitts of the FBI, and Robert Lipka of NSA—but he had never found anything directly related to the alleged Bureau mole or about his original suspects—Berianov, Yurimengri, and Ogust.

For the past month, Hammond had been trying to locate Berianov, ostensibly to interview him for his newspaper series. But the former general seemed to have dropped off the face of the planet. Hammond had left messages on his phone machine, but there had been no reply. No other émigré admitted having seen him lately. And Hammond had checked Berianov's house a dozen times but found it deserted.

Berianov, Yurimengri, and Ogust had remained close since their defection. They drank together, dined together, and helped each other in business. Hammond had lived and breathed the pasts and new lives of the three men. He knew them inside and out, or so he told himself. The other defectors and émigrés were interesting, but most had not only assimilated into the United States, they had shown few of the signs that would cause Hammond to suspect they were anything but relieved to be living here. Daily they worked hard and struggled to pay their bills. Many had already become citizens.

Not so Berianov, Yurimengri, and Ogust. From the beginning, they spent money far above their government resettlement stipends. Their businesses were not only well capitalized but instantly successful. They maintained ties to the KGB's successor agency, the FSB, in Moscow. And there were rumors . . . the kind of elusive smokescreens that could mean the fires of long-ago patriotism were banked but not out.

So Hammond had shadowed them for all these years, losing them at times, only to locate them again. Then, just last year, he had discovered the missing millions from the KGB slush fund and Mikhail Ogust's connection to it, and had gone after him. Ogust had agreed to talk, but before they could meet, Ogust was dead. At which point, Hammond had contacted his old friend Eli Kirkhart and wormed the name of Ivan Vok out of him in connection with the fund. Using Vok's name, he eventually got to Yurimengri, but now Yurimengri was dead, too. Which left only Alexei Berianov, whom Hammond had considered the brains of the trio from the start.

Hammond wanted Berianov with all the obsessive desire of a thwarted lover. He hungered for him not only for reasons of national security, but also because in Berianov he hoped to confirm that he had not wasted the last ten years of his life. So when Beth Convey revealed to him that Colonel Yurimengri's dying words were of Stone Point, West Virginia, of course he flew there immediately.

"Did you find out anything about Berianov in Stone Point?" Bobby Kelsey asked.

"Nothing." Hammond shook his head angrily. "But my gut tells me he's down there, and he's up to something we're not going to like. Something big. Before I got there, I checked my sources in Moscow. They told me they hadn't seen him. Have you heard anything?"

Kelsey was driving south on Eighteenth Street, a bustling corridor of wall-to-wall restaurants. "You're not going to like this, Jeff. So I'll give it to you straight—we've got confirmation that Berianov's dead."

"*Dead?* How? Where? When? Incredible! All three are now dead?"

"Word in Moscow is natural causes. They discovered Berianov's body just a couple of hours ago. He'd sneaked into the city a few weeks back on something hush-hush to do with his business interests. Didn't call any of his old pals at the Kremlin or any of his ex-wives. Then he had a heart attack that killed him. Died in a hotel bed. Too much food, vodka, and bimbos. He was closing some big deal with one of the new oligarchs that he didn't want to get out just yet, and they were partying him until he dropped to make sure they got all the American green-backs they could. It was a lethal combination for Berianov."

It took Hammond's breath away. "First Ogust. Then Yurimengri. Now Berianov." He thought hard then shook his head. "Ogust was killed in a traffic accident, and Yurimengri was shot dead. Maybe Beri-anov didn't die of natural causes." At least he knew now why Beri-anov's house had been deserted.

"Could be. You can look into it later if you want. Right now, I've a much bigger problem. Huge. And you're going to help me with it. We just had a message from a man calling himself Perez. He claims some kind of anti-American terrorist action is about to happen. It came through one of our street contacts."

Hammond tore his focus from Berianov. "And?"

"The contact disappeared. This was two days ago. Wednesday. We haven't been able to find him."

"Swell. What kind of terrorism? What's the target?"

Kelsey's lips thinned. "We don't know. Could be anything. The Capi-tol. The Supreme Court. The Mint. Maybe it'll be in some other part of the country, like the Oklahoma City bombing. But it doesn't look that way to us. The Bureau thinks it's going to be in Washington. The con-tact has been reliable in the past, and we have to take him seriously. Perez's message said the action was imminent."

They rode in silence until Hammond finally said, "It could still in-volve Berianov."

"Why? He's hardly the only one who could be conspiring against us."

"True. But I flew to Stone Point to inquire about Berianov, no one else. Instantly someone goes to a hell of a lot of trouble to take me out of action. Someone who might know I've been keeping tabs on the KGB defectors all these years. As soon as I started asking a lot of ques-tions about Berianov, it could've seemed to them I was getting warm."

"Okay, maybe it's a Russian. Maybe Berianov had a second-in-command in place to take over if anything happened to him."

Hammond nodded thoughtfully. "Could be someone from Moscow. Somebody with a long memory and a huge grudge."

"Possibly. Or maybe there's no relation at all between those events. We want you to stay in the area in case it goes down here. You've got the contacts, dig around. Find out what's going to happen. Unfortu-nately, this could make the World Trade Center bombing look like a teen prank." Kelsey's freckled face was worried. His hand dropped out of sight, and he handed a brown paper bag back over the seat. "For you. Just in case. The serial numbers are burned off."

Hammond opened the sack and slid out a Beretta pistol in a canvas shoulder holster. It was the model 92C, compact and easy to conceal, but with a powerful 9mm Parabellum cartridge. He hefted it, felt the balance. A good, reliable weapon. "I'll check my other sources among the émigrés." He took off his herringbone jacket and fastened the canvas straps across his back and under his arms, where his jacket would hide them. He settled the holster into his left armpit.

Kelsey agreed. "That's what we need. If you find something, let's have a signal to bring you in."

As he shrugged back into his jacket, Hammond remembered Kelsey's remark about Icarus. "How about: 'The sky is coming down in flames.' "

"Good enough. I'll pass the word to our street agents to keep an eye out for an anonymous undercover man who might be coming in. Behave yourself, Hammond. I'll do what I can to shift the heat off you, but if you get into any more trouble with the police now, I won't be able to do anything, considering what they've got on you." Kelsey stopped the car at an intersection. "I don't have to tell you this, because you already know, but let's both be clear: Once I bring you in, you'll never be able to do this kind of undercover work again. Too many people will know. When you come in, you're finished with the game. Good luck."

Bobby Kelsey did not turn around. He was surveying the traffic and pedestrians.

"Right." Hammond stepped out of the Cadillac.

A part of him still thought Stone Point was the place to start. After all, he had been framed in that little burg. He must have been getting close to something, and he was convinced that the something had to do with Berianov or someone Berianov knew. But he had already said enough to his boss. Instead, he gazed casually around at the early-morning coffee seekers hurrying to their jobs, then quickly blended into the sidewalk crowd and walked away.

From his rented car parked across the busy morning street in Adams Morgan, Eli Kirkhart had heard the shots and muffled shouts from behind the row of brick townhouses. He had started his engine, shoved the transmission into gear, and plunged into the traffic toward the closest corner.

He had managed to follow Graham, his team, and Jeff Hammond from Stone Point, and he had seen the big Lincoln turn into the alley and enter what had to be a Bureau safe house. At that point, as he had settled back in his rented car to watch who went in and came out, he had put in a quick call to his team for someone to cover the other end of the alley. No one had arrived by the time the shots exploded.

At the corner, he had skidded around just in time to watch Jeff Hammond tear out of the alley into the street and sprint alongside traffic. Brakes slammed. Horns honked. Caught behind a cursing driver in a stalled Buick, Kirkhart could only join the swearing and watch Hammond dive into the back seat of a waiting black Cadillac with tinted windows. Instantly, the Caddy had accelerated and vanished into the heavy traffic before Kirkhart could get a license-plate number.

Still swearing, Kirkhart was trying to force a lane through the traffic to follow when Chuck Graham raced from the alley, his weapon out, his eyes searching frantically everywhere. Kirkhart told himself Graham *should* be frantic. Neither the director nor Kelsey liked to lose a prisoner. The veteran agent would be lucky not to be demoted to anything worse than a desk job in Sandpoint, Idaho.

A sudden break in the congestion allowed Kirkhart to reach the next corner and make another skidding left. Traffic was lighter on the side street, and he accelerated to the next corner, turned left again, and right once more into the other end of the alley. He saw Graham running back toward the safe house and drove to meet him.

He leaned out of the car window. "Did I see Jeff Hammond running out of this alley, Graham?"

Chuck Graham hurried to him. "Kirkhart? What the hell are you doing here?"

"Coming to scope out the safe house for a prisoner," Kirkhart lied glibly. Graham would never check. "What about it? Was that Hammond?"

Graham nodded angrily. "Yeah. We had to pick him up for killing a couple of kids down in West Virginia."

"West Virginia? What was he doing there? Why'd he kill some kids?"

"Not a clue. He's working for the *Post* these days. Maybe some big story went bad." Graham shook his head. "We'll get the bastard back."

"He escaped?"

Graham was reluctant to discuss what had happened, but Kirkhart, in a smooth guise of helping out, explained, "I knew Jeff pretty well at one time." With persistence, he finally got the story of the escape from the bathroom and under the house to the hidden exit. Kirkhart could barely contain his interest. Still, he gave Graham a puzzled frown. "I don't understand. How did he know there was a way out of that bathroom? How did he know there was an escape route at all?"

"Yeah." Graham nodded miserably. His career was crashing and burning. "How?"

"Someone must've told him," Kirkhart decided. "The route had to be marked with some prearranged signal."

Graham grasped at the straw. "The mole? You think the mole set up Hammond's escape route? It makes sense. A hell of a lot of sense. Hammond's *working with the mole!*"

"It's logical," Kirkhart agreed. But he did not believe it. A mole as deep, highly placed, and successful as the one he was searching for would never have jeopardized his position with such a risk. No, he—or she—would have sacrificed Hammond in a heartbeat. His guess was that he was right—Jeff Hammond was still in the Bureau *and* working undercover. Which meant it was Hammond's Bureau handler who had somehow arranged the escape. And that brought him even closer to his second theory—that Jeff Hammond, himself, was the long-sought mole.

21

As the Friday-morning sun climbed above the quiet fields and wooded slopes in the countryside south of Gettysburg National Military Park, Alexei Berianov stood alone on the outdoor gallery of Caleb Bates's white, colonial mansion. Dressed in the gentlemanly tan slacks and open-neck shirt of an off-duty Bates, he admired the sweep of the rolling panorama while making certain he was alone on his second-floor gallery.

In a completely altered, vicious nasal voice—neither Berianov's nor Bates's—he demanded into his cell phone, "Where are the damn invitations, huh?"

His property spread among the hills southwest of the famous battlefield, and, like his place in West Virginia, it was surrounded by high-security fences topped by concertina wire. But unlike in West Virginia, his Pennsylvania grounds sported a cow barn, a prize dairy herd, bales of hay, the scent of freshly scythed grass, and Keepers with sunburned faces who looked and acted like regular farm hands, because that was what they used to be. Since the early hours of Wednesday, all of the Keepers had quietly filtered in here, but during daylight they were securely hidden. Nowhere was there a sign of the farm's real purpose nor of its principal activity over the past several weeks.

"They were due in my hands by *today,* you drunk bastard!" Berianov roared.

"It's not as easy as you think," the nervous voice on the other end of the line whined. This was White House aide Evans Olsen. Olsen knew

Bates/Berianov only by the code name Yakel. With Berianov's ability at disguise and at hiding his tracks, Olsen would never know his true identity. "Look, there are all these steps. To get the invitations, I have to talk to the chief of staff, and he's been so busy preparing for the state visit. I mean, Putin arrives today. . . ."

"Bullshit!" Berianov despised Olsen for his martini hangovers and sloth. The greed he understood. "You don't need his permission. You think I don't know you've got the authority? You trying to make me mad, huh?" When Ivan Vok reported the invitations had not been delivered, Berianov quickly located Olsen hiding out at home after another night lost to alcohol. This was the kind of day Olsen liked to call in sick anyway, since the White House would be busier than usual as it prepared for the Russian state visit. That would require a level of energy and commitment Olsen no longer could muster.

"Hey, I got you the complete schedule. Count your blessings." Olsen's voice turned snotty, showing fragments of the promising young man who had once been a Fulbright scholar. "I'll get the invitations as soon as humanly possible. The White House has protocols. I have to account for everything, you know."

"Don't try to throw attitude at me, you lousy little creep. Get off your butt and get me those invitations. *Today*, you hear!"

"Now, see here!"

Berianov's nasal voice cut like a razor. "You know what's going to happen if I make an anonymous call to the Justice department?" He had ordered $100,000 deposited in Olsen's name in a Mexico City bank. "You used to have a decent IQ. Use what's left to figure it out: You're a drunk with a long record of calling in sick. The wealthy branch of your family's disowned you. You've been in deep debt for years, but now all of a sudden you're flush with greenbacks." With satisfaction he heard heavy, worried breathing on the other end of the line. "If Justice finds the Mexico account, you'll not only be out of a job, you'll be under investigation, and they won't find just a few White House invitations missing, will they?"

Berianov could almost hear the fear at the other end, and Olsen's pathetic collapse. "I . . . I'll have them tomorrow morning for sure."

Berianov ground his teeth in frustration. The entire plan depended on those invitations. He had to have them. The problem was that Olsen could not be shamed into action. Only abject fear motivated him, but when Olsen had too much to drink, which was nearly every day, he would temporarily forget his fear, forget what could happen to him. It made him damned hard to manipulate. Still, he was vital.

Berianov growled, "Tomorrow morning at seven A.M. If I don't have them, I contact the White House. That's it. End of story. End of you. I'm not messing with you anymore, boy. Seven A.M. tomorrow, or kiss your cushy ass good-bye."

Berianov hung up, cutting off the aide's complaining protest. Damn Olsen. If Olsen were sufficiently afraid he would lose his soft life, he would come through even now. But in case he failed again, they were going to have to employ a more risky backup plan.

Swearing to himself, Berianov slid his cell phone into his pocket and strode into the house through one of the tall French doors that lined the second-story gallery of the colonial manse. At each step his padded body and face became more and more Colonel Caleb Bates, staunch American patriot. When he entered what once had been a library but now was a conference room, the transformation was complete.

The walls of the former library boasted historic Currier & Ives prints and bookcases loaded with leather-bound volumes by American authors. The Stars and Stripes hung from a sturdy wood flagpole in the center of the wall opposite the glass door. A spotlight was trained on it from overhead. Next to it stood a Bible stand with the King James version open to the Twenty-Third Psalm: *The Lord is my Shepherd. I shall not want. . . .* An adjoining wall held a built-in, wide-screen television, its modernity a contrast to the classic furnishings

But at the moment the activity in the room was focused at the oblong conference table, where Bates's three leading militiamen stood, leaning over maps and plans for Washington, D.C., the White House, and surrounding areas.

"Colonel, sir!" Sergeant Austin came to attention as soon as he spotted Bates.

Beside him, the two others straightened, but remained focused on what they had been doing. To the sergeant's immediate right was Max Bitsche, a soft-looking man with permanently hunched shoulders and a dour expression that reflected an obsession for detail. He was in charge of supplies and transportation. On the sergeant's other side stood Otis Odet, a computer wizard who had given up a high-paying job in Silicon Valley to return to his family's historic roots in the movement. He oversaw all communications. Odet broke the nerd stereotype with his California beach-boy physique, broad face, and thick-fingered hands that seemed more appropriate for a surfboard than a keyboard.

Bates demanded, "Where are we, men?"

Until the glitch with Olsen arose, Bates's morning had been nothing but gratifying. First there had been the news that Marty Coulson's parents had done such a credible job yesterday at the Hoover building of backing up the fabricated story of Jeff Hammond's threats to their son that they had convinced the FBI that Hammond was the killer. Then came Fedorov's excellent report of the fiery deaths of the meddling Beth Convey and the psychologist Stephanie Smith.

"The Commie president's plane is on time, due to arrive at thirteen-hundred hours at Andrews, and our traitorous President Stevens will meet it." It was Sergeant Austin with his buzz-cut hair, big ears, and massive muscles. No longer in their camos, he and the two other men were dressed in sports shirts and pleated slacks similar to Bates's. "Our man at the airport will let us know if there are any changes."

"Very good. What else?"

"The tape is loaded, sir."

"Let's have it." Bates turned toward the big-screen television.

The sergeant punched buttons on the remote control. The four men remained standing as they watched, an indication of their seriousness of purpose and that they could not, would not, relax before the successful completion of their mission. The operation was upon them, just a day away. As Bates considered the approaching event, a sense of renewed urgency swept aside his brief nostalgia and good feelings about last night's accomplishments.

He focused on the TV screen, clinically analyzing detail after detail of the Rose Garden, lawns, shrubbery, walkways, windows, pillars, and the placement of podiums and Secret Service agents and rooftop snipers as Yasser Arafat, Tony Blair, and a host of other heads of state, and foreign and domestic dignitaries paraded across the screen in official White House news conferences and staged tête-à-têtes recorded for television over the past year and taped on Bates's orders. Everyone watched intently until it was finished.

Bates nodded. "Notice how the number of snipers on the roof has increased. Play it again."

After three more run-throughs, Bates ordered the composite film shown later in the morning to all the Keepers, each of whom had assignments for tomorrow. It was a harmless exercise, not useful to most, but it kept them focused on their outrage over the "selling of America," feeling fanatical, and very much part of the team.

"Any problems?" he demanded.

"No, Colonel." The muscular sergeant was in charge of the actual operation. He had hand-picked three men to go with him. "My people are more than ready to go. We've rehearsed a variety of possible scenarios, and they know the terrain inside out. They're beyond ready, sir. They *need* to get into action."

Bates inclined his head. "Mr. Bitsche?"

Max Bitsche hunched his shoulders. "Supplies are in excellent order. Everyone's received their kits. The vans are painted. We've distributed cash for emergencies. Additional supplies are planted in our various depots. I've got everything except the four White House invitations." He pursed his lips and added irritably, "I don't like waiting so long. What if the guy doesn't deliver? Who is he, anyway, that he's got such an intimate connection with this decadent government?" Bitsche's gaze flitted angrily around the conference room as if seeking an answer. "He can't be one of us. We need to get those invitations right away before something goes wrong. They're critical."

"Mr. Bitsche," Bates's voice was soft, almost caressing, but layered in it was such incipient violence that Bitsche froze mid-sentence and lowered his gaze in fear. It was a reaction Alexei Berianov had elicited many times in the ranks of the KGB, back in the days when it had been worthy of his respect.

Bitsche swallowed, and his round, soft body seemed to disintegrate around the edges. "Sorry, sir. I know you're handling it. I hope you'll forgive—"

But Bates had made his point. Never relax discipline. Never let them forget who was in charge. But avoid, as his own mentors had taught him, pushing beyond a point once it had been made, because beyond that had to be the threat of real, tangible punishment. Fear of the unknown—in this case, fear of what Bates would do—was the ultimate weapon.

He pointedly shifted his attention to Otis Odet. "Communications?"

"Yes, Colonel." Odet's beach-boy good looks had puckered and tightened during the exchange. He fiddled with the pen in his shirt pocket as he reported briskly, "All the vans and personnel have radios. I've assigned cell phones, too, to strategic staff so we'll have alternate lines of communication. It's all scrambled so no hot dog with a reader can listen in. Everything's been checked out and is in prime working condition, but, just in case, I've got repair people stationed at the supply depots. And finally, I've installed tracking devices with computer chips in everyone's belt buckles. Our roving van is now fully equipped to coordinate with Sergeant Austin."

Bates's expression was unchanged, but inside he was smiling. With the exception of Olsen, everything was going right. And a failure by Olsen, while making it damn difficult, still could be overcome. Now it was time to improve the mood in the room, and by doing so to reaffirm and solidify his control. For a leader, psychological dominance was paramount. "Well done. I mean that. We're on the verge of saving our country. And it's all due to President Stevens." He snorted with derision. "We should thank him for crossing the line, men."

"We'll put a stop to him," the sergeant said promptly. Military all the way, despite the contradiction of his fanatical antigovernment stance, Austin had been unfazed by Bates's flexing of power. In fact, he seemed to bristle with new energy because of it. He added the Keepers' rallying cry: "We've got to take back America for Americans!"

Bates let his face thicken with outrage and disgust. "How dare the president invite Putin into the White House? Putin can claim he's reformed all he wants, but once a Communist, always a Communist!"

Otis Odet instantly chimed in, "That's the God's truth. A Russki president sleeping in Lincoln's bedroom? It's a travesty. It's an insult to everything this country believes in and stands for. It's like putting Satan on Jesus's cross. Stevens is—"

Until now, the chastised Max Bitsche had been silent and subdued, but this was a subject close to his heart, close to all the Keepers' hearts. And as Bates had expected, he rejoined the team with an enthusiastic outburst: "Stevens wants to make America disappear into the Global Plantation! He's worse than everyone he followed. They tore down what was left of our trade protection and gave foreigners huge pieces of our economy—"

Sergeant Austin interrupted, his grim face flushed with fury, "He's making our military pussy-weak by assigning more and more of it to serve under foreign leaders! NATO. The UN. Next it'll be France. Or England. Or even Germany calling the shots for Uncle Sam's armed forces! Why—"

They all spoke at once, voicing their outrage at the new president, but Odet's voice surged highest, fueled with hate and righteous anger: "And don't forget all the wetbacks crossing our borders and stealing our jobs, and how every day President Stevens sells our American bases and personnel to foreigners to train their soldiers on our very own soil."

The sergeant jabbed a finger and roared, "The Luftwaffe at Holloman and McGregor! I thought we beat the Germans in World War II, but now they're taking us over. They've won!" With the Pentagon's permission, Germany had established a Tactical Air Center at Holloman Air Force Base in New Mexico with hundreds of pilots and support personnel to fly and service European-made Tornado jet fighter-bombers and German F-4 Phantom fighters, and now the government had leased part of the McGregor Range at Fort Bliss, outside El Paso, Texas, to the Germans for aerial refueling exercises and combat tactics.

"There's not going to be any place in this country safe for its citizens!"

"Foreigners run us abroad. Foreigners run us here—"

"—steal our expertise, and then use it to whip our asses."

"Next thing you know, they'll be putting us real Americans on reservations and issue us blankets and tin plates to eat off!"

Behind the mask of Caleb Bates, Alexei Berianov listened with a mixture of amusement and solid satisfaction. Their skewed logic made him want to laugh, but their fanatical sense of violence toward the government they perceived as their enemy was what he was depending on. It was Yuri Andropov, the powerful and intellectual KGB leader when Berianov was just starting out, who had told him that it seemed as if no bad idea ever died. There was always someone who could turn it for his own purposes.

Inwardly, Alexei Berianov exulted. There are moments when all the objectives for which one has worked fuse in perfection. This was one of those moments. Equipment, people, and plans were aligned. Nothing stood in his way. Like Napoleon, Berianov had once been legendary for boldly pitting small elite forces against larger ones and winning spectacular victories. Excitement surged through him as he surveyed the aroused faces and knotted hands of his three chief lieutenants. They would fight to the death for Caleb Bates, and they would take their men with them.

As he was savoring all this, and the three were running out of patriotic steam, his cell phone vibrated against his chest. He told his disciples heartily, "In just over a day, it'll all be over, and everyone in America is going to have a lot to celebrate, thanks to us. Carry on, men."

"Yes, sir." Sergeant Austin's eyes were alight with the glorious future as he marched toward the door that opened into the upstairs foyer.

"Thank you, sir." Otis Odet followed, his back ramrod straight, despite his lack of military background.

"Colonel?" Max Bitsche hesitated. "I was out of line, and I just want to apologize again."

Bates clapped Bitsche on the back. "It was in the zeal of the moment. You're a valued member of the movement. We need you and respect everything you've done for America. In the scheme of things, one slip isn't so bad." As the phone vibrated once more, he finished in a cooler voice that reasserted his authority: "I'm sure it'll never happen again."

"Never," Bitsche vowed.

As the door closed, the room suddenly seemed warmer and friendlier in its emptiness. Berianov pulled out his cell phone and allowed himself the brief luxury of letting his mind drift back in time, and he was once again walking the cobbled paths of Gorky Park. His chest swelled with happiness as he savored the sound of the wind in the linden trees and watched their rustling leaves catch the sunlight and glisten like silver paper against Moscow's iridescent blue sky. His Moscow. His Soviet Union.

He remembered the old men sitting beneath the trees' swaying branches with their glasses of tea and chess games. As a child, he had roller-skated beneath those same trees and stopped to eat cubes of sugar passed out by sweet-faced *babushkas* as they related mythic folktales that filled a young boy's head with the kinds of dreams on which greatness was built. Dreams that could never be forgotten and must never be betrayed.

Shaking out of his reverie, Berianov settled into the armchair at the head of the long, polished conference table and spoke into his cell phone. "Yes?"

It was Nikolai Fedorov, and instantly Berianov knew something was wrong. His chest tightened as he listened to the bad news: Not only had Beth Convey survived the fiery car crash, but Jeff Hammond had escaped the FBI.

Fedorov said, "The Virginia patrol found only one corpse in the car, but they're not reporting it yet. If Stephanie Smith had survived, she would've stayed at the scene. Only the Convey woman would've run." He hid his mortification well. Still, he had worked with Berianov too long to think he could fool him. A complete professional, haughty, Fedorov was galled not only because he had missed his quarry, but because he had reported success prematurely.

Berianov kept his voice under control. "Where's Convey now?"

"I wish I knew. I've looked everywhere we could expect her to appear. Vok's people are watching for her."

"*Sukin syn!*" Berianov cursed. "And Jeff Hammond?"

"I don't know that either, sir."

Berianov felt a sudden stab of apprehension, even doubt. Grimly he brushed it aside. He refused to fail, but as long as Hammond was free they would never be really safe. Especially not now. The threat that Hammond posed had to be ended. "Perhaps they won't harm us, perhaps they will. We can't take the chance. Find them both, Nikolai Mikhailovich, and kill them. At this late date, we can afford no more mistakes. Everything is riding on tomorrow. Everything. You understand? *Everything.*"

If Fedorov failed again, he would send in Ivan Vok. The burly Mongol was still the deadliest assassin the KGB had ever produced. He had learned his lethal trade during the height of the Cold War under teachers who had never been matched. He was the master who had taught Fedorov. Vok did not have Fedorov's finesse, but he had something more—he never missed his mark. Nothing stopped the short, square man with the high-planed face. He loved to kill too much.

22

Beth Convey awoke slowly. In the darkness of her jumbled mind, she was unsure where she was or what had happened. She ached everywhere . . . and with a jolt of fear remembered: Some man dressed from head to foot in black had overpowered her and tied her up. He had been swift, strong, and efficient, a karate master, and she had expected him to murder her. Her chest tightened, and she opened her eyes. Maybe he was still in the house, searching.

Her blindfold was gone. That was strange. She blinked in the sunlight. It was morning. Friday morning, she reminded herself. From the east, sunshine filtered in through the pittosporum bushes outside the tall windows and made lacy patterns across the chaos of pulled-out drawers, scattered papers, and overturned furniture in the large office. The black-clothed stranger had left nothing untouched. But what had he been looking for? And had he found it?

Apprehensive, she listened. The house was silent. Emptiness had a sound of its own, an absence like a vacuum, and this house sounded and felt empty. But why had he left her alive and unharmed? Even taken off her blindfold?

She started to struggle against her ropes, but there was no struggle. The ropes gave with her first movement. She pulled with both arms and legs. All the ropes were loose. As much as she had tried last night, she had been unable to free herself. She had fallen asleep—or perhaps passed out—working on them.

The stranger again. He had needed to get her out of the way while he pawed through the house. Then, inexplicably, he made it possible for her to leave when she awoke. It gave her chills.

She was sure it had not been Hammond. Hammond had brown eyes, and the karate expert's were chilly blue. Some inner voice—her heart?—assured her he was a trained killer. It was in his predatory movements, in the cold precision of his karate, and in all the ways he had made certain she would not be able to identify him. Which ensured she would never forget his arctic eyes or the scar on his right wrist. She shivered. She had just had another brush with death. But as soon as she thought that, she saw in her mind the image of poor Stephanie trapped and dying in her car's inferno.

A surge of grief changed almost instantly into rage. She flung the ropes across the room and instantly had another thought. Maybe the intruder was the one who had saved her from Hammond on Wednesday night and then driven her to the motel for safekeeping. It seemed possible. But it also made her wonder even more who—and what—he was, and what he wanted. And would he remain "friendly"?

She stood up and stretched, her achiness easing. She gathered herself and moved across the office to stare into a mirror between two wall sconces. Her blue eyes looked haunted; her cheeks were hollow. Her dark brows seemed lifeless against pasty skin. Her short blond hair stuck out like straw. She pushed it back behind her ears. The only good thing was the ugly bruise on her forehead was smaller and paler. She smoothed down her bangs. That helped, but she needed food, rest, medicine. And answers.

As she turned away, she spotted her bag—dumped out behind her chair. Her pill bottles had been lined up on the floor like toy soldiers. She dropped to her knees and examined everything. With relief, she saw nothing was missing. But whoever had inspected her bag had also established she was on heavy-duty medication. Shaking her head, she put everything back except the clipping about Mikhail Ogust.

Then she looked for the rest of the papers that had been hidden in the cigar box. They were on the floor, too. She checked them for the fencing bill from Stone Point and for the advertisement for the Pennsylvania dairy farm. When she found neither, she searched the room, but they were gone. Perhaps more was missing, too.

Interesting . . . the man in black was after what she was after. Fortunately, she was accustomed to digesting and remembering huge briefs and arguments. She concentrated and was soon able to recall the text of both clippings. She tucked her bag under her arm and hurried to the kitchen, where she could take her pills with water. From there, she would phone the pharmacy and order a new backup set. As she strode past rooms, she saw the intruder had capsized them, too, in his search.

In the kitchen, she glanced again at her donor's photo. It sent shivers through her, but also a yearning. His handsome, Slavic features made her think of a quotation by Nikolai Gogol, the romantic Russian writer. Maybe she had read it in her Russian studies classes . . . or perhaps she had inherited it as part of her cellular memories. It seemed perfect as she considered Mikhail Ogust—

On with the journey! Russia! Russia! When I see you, my eyes are lit up with supernatural power. Oh, what a glittering, wondrous infinity of space. . . . What a strange, alluring, enthralling, wonderful world!

*   *   *

Jeff Hammond was tired and alarmed. He had spotted two men watching the *Post,* and by the lack of smoothness to their surveillance, they could not be from the Bureau. Of course, they might not be waiting for him, but he was taking no chances. He disappeared around the corner, hailed a taxi, and directed it to the residential area behind Capitol Hill, where he stopped the driver two blocks from his condo.

His herringbone jacket flapping behind, he ran up an alley. He had slept off and on during the car ride last night, but he was tired. By an act of will he kept himself going and alert. Not only had he been trained to work long, exhausting hours, he was also driven. At the alley's mouth, he stopped.

The woman sitting on a bus bench caught his attention first. She made the mistake of letting two buses go past, which was no indication in itself, but her complete lack of interest in reading the destinations of each was suspicious. Plus her gaze was constantly moving. She missed nothing. Her partner was across the street and two doors away. He was sweeping the sidewalk with a long-handled broom, just another neighbor taking care of business. But he swept the same patch twice, and he and the woman exchanged just enough glances to confirm Hammond's suspicions.

They, too, were something other than FBI. Anyone from the Bureau would be better trained. Evidently Bobby Kelsey had managed to cool the Bureau's ardor for him. So who was this pair? They could be local police, alerted by West Virginia's finest, he decided. Or they could be people associated with whoever had taken over Berianov's mission. They could also be someone else . . . but who? Both his home and his office were being surveilled, which constituted a warning he took seriously.

Since Berianov was dead, he had agreed to look into this mysterious terrorist plot that might ignite at any moment. But now he could not get to his notes, his computer, or his phone at the *Post* or at home. He gave his condo one longing look, turned, and trotted away down the alley, mulling the situation.

Hammond liked to think of himself as simple—simple of heart, simple in his goals. But the truth was that ever since he had gone underground for Bobby Kelsey, he had found himself living a life that had eventually made him question everything he had ever believed about himself.

The first casualty had been his marriage, which ended in divorce. Then his friends at the Bureau cut him off, and he never really made any close ones at the newspaper. His parents had died disappointed in him for having walked away from an honorable career in the service of his country. The money he inherited seemed meaningless. A series of girlfriends convinced him there was no way he could ever make a commitment to marriage again. And, perhaps worst of all, he had a sister living near Yosemite with her family, and he had neither seen nor spoken to her in five years, and it was his fault.

In the end, when he could tell no one what he was really doing, the lies in his life became his life, and he was left with a sham existence he kept running faster and faster to legitimatize. His one solace was that he had been able to feed Bobby Kelsey vital information that had revealed double agents within the government. That was satisfying. And in the beginning, he thought that would be enough.

Now despite Kelsey's new assignment to expose some unknown impending terrorist act, Hammond was still hooked on Berianov, Yurimengri, and Ogust. All three were dead, but Hammond was dissatisfied. Of course, he would do what Kelsey wanted. He would cajole, threaten, and mine his sources for information. But at the same time, he was not going to give up on the three defectors. He could not. To stop chasing them or their inheritors would be to turn his back on what had propelled him to go undercover in the first place, which had made him end up with this life that was no life.

He hailed another taxi and directed it to two businesses run by expatriate Russians—a restaurant and a mobile phone company. He took his contacts aside at each, good men who were assets to their communities and to America, but neither had heard anything that hinted at a terrorist plot. Then as he was just about to leave the phone company, one of the employees switched the channel of the TV on the wall to local news. With a shock, he saw his photo appear with a phone number under it.

He had taken off his sunglasses, and his face was fully exposed. The employee stared at the TV and then at Hammond.

His throat tight with anger, Hammond slapped on his sunglasses, ran into the street, and stopped a taxi. Kelsey's damage control could extend only so far. The West Virginia police intended to find and arrest him, and now the entire District knew it. He was very publicly a wanted man. Which explained the stakeouts at his condo and office. Probably local police or the West Virginia cops.

In the cab, he gave the driver Beth Convey's address in Georgetown. The police would not be there, and it was time to find out why she had really gone to meet Yurimengri. After all, it was his dying words that had sent Hammond to West Virginia.

At Berianov's house, Beth found her car untouched, sitting exactly where she had parked it in the driveway. After seeing the shambles the intruder had made of the house, the car's pristine condition was another surprise. She unlocked the door, started the engine, and drove away through Chevy Chase's bustling morning traffic. As she passed large residences set back on sloping green lawns, she watched for the big black Chevy van that had pursued Stephanie and her last night.

Then she had an encouraging thought. Maybe the police had found the black van. Maybe they had arrested Jeff Hammond. She turned on her favorite all-talk radio station and listened to the news at the top of the hour. The announcer was reporting the imminent arrival of the Russian president, at the personal invitation of President James Emmet Stevens. Stevens had made the gesture one of his first steps in fulfilling his campaign promise of global involvement. He was enthusiastic about the visit, saying he hoped to convince Vladimir Putin to join fully the democratic camp—"to bring an old Communist in from the cold," as he jovially put it.

The radio announcer changed subjects to report two murders in Southeast Washington, a new Medicare bill before the house, and—she straightened up, alert—a blazing, one-car crash in Virginia. The police had not yet released the names of those who had died. She had hoped someone had reported the black van, too, and that the driver had been apprehended. But the sound bite ended without the mention of another vehicle.

She wiped tears from her eyes so she could see to drive. Hearing the bare facts in the announcer's dispassionate voice had touched a well of grief as she thought about Stephanie Smith. She pressed her lips together, willing the tears to stop. Since the police had not released who or even how many had died in the fire, Hammond would still believe she was out of the way. Which meant she could go home and regroup.

Then she heard his name on the news: ". . . wanted for the murders of a teenager and her boyfriend in Stone Point, West Virginia. Hammond is white, six-foot-three, about two hundred twenty pounds, with long brown hair. According to reliable sources, he was fired from the FBI ten years ago. Shortly afterwards, he went to work as a reporter for *The Washington Post*. Anyone with information about his whereabouts is asked to . . ."

Beth's breathing grew shallow. Just yesterday she had walked down the sidewalk with Hammond, talking blithely, until she had recognized him. Now she knew she had been right. He killed Yurimengri, and he killed two young people in that little town in West Virginia. Maybe he finally realized she had seen him at Yurimengri's death scene, and, as she suspected, it had been him in the black van last night. She found herself clenching her teeth, at first fighting rage, then allowing it to rise and sweep through her. The bastard.

In Georgetown, Nikolai Fedorov slumped unobtrusively behind the driver's wheel in another stolen vehicle, this one a Ford station wagon, near Beth Convey's house. He had abandoned the black van in the vast parking lot of the Pentagon mall. Now with this dirty yellow Ford wagon, bearing Maryland plates from yet another vehicle, Convey had no way to identify him. Ivan Vok had also stationed people outside her law office, her last boyfriend's condominium, and two residences of colleagues from work, but knowing what they did about Convey, Fedorov believed home was where she would go if she thought she were safe.

Ivan Vok had assigned people to watch Jeff Hammond's regular haunts, too. He had faxed photos of both Convey and the newsman to all their people. Vok had warned everyone they must be careful of Hammond, since he was another professional. Fedorov was not certain why the *Post* man had to be eliminated, but he looked forward to it in much the same way he imagined an American businessman enjoyed toppling a foreign competitor.

Tiredly he took a small pillbox from his shirt pocket and opened it. He had nodded off several times in the past hour. As he tossed a caffeine tablet into his mouth, he glanced down at the floor of the passenger side where his black tradecraft cases sat, and then at his lap where his PSG1 sniper rifle lay—long, beautiful, and powerful. It was by the German manufacturer Heckler & Koch. He prized its adjustability, its big 6X42 telescope with illuminated graticule, and its outstanding accuracy. With it, he could shoot an impressive fifty rounds of match ammunition inside an 80mm circle at three hundred meters. Assessing it all now was an automatic response on his part: Having his tools close at hand was his only safety net.

Today he was dressed in an ordinary sports jacket and trousers. As the bitter taste of the caffeine tablet soaked into his mouth, he glanced into his rearview mirror. Still no sign of Convey. He was restless, on edge. He knew from the tone of Berianov's voice that this was his last chance. If he failed again . . . Berianov might send Ivan Vok to kill him. He tried to repress his fear, but he was terrified of the brutal man. Even if Berianov did not send Vok, Fedorov knew his punishment would be severe.

He fought off a sense of desperation. He'd had enough of waiting in the car. The residential street had quieted, so he slid his cell phone into his jacket pocket, picked up his H&K sniper rifle, and slipped from the car, across the sidewalk, and into a stand of trees near which he had deliberately parked. The trees were in an open area between two large properties, perfect for his purposes. He melted in among the foliage until he was about six feet from the sidewalk. From here he could clearly see Convey's Victorian. He studied it through the rifle's telescope.

He leaned back against a tree, a bush shielding him from the sidewalk. Birds twittered and called. Some small animal skittered through dry leaves. Sunbeams danced in golden shafts down through the trees. He registered the information, then discarded it. He was a man with a mission, a man whose fascination with killing had given his life purpose, and he looked forward to watching his high-velocity bullet bring the annoying Beth Convey down.

Jeff Hammond had developed many healthy habits over the years. At the top of the list was discretion, which he planned to put into full force from now on. As usual, he'd had the taxi driver drop him off two blocks from his destination—Beth Convey's house. It was mid-morning, and the April sun beat down with enthusiasm, glancing off east-facing windowpanes along the street and sending long, cool shadows from the other side.

He chose the sidewalk that had been made safer by its shadows. As he walked past stately homes with filigreed front porches and pointed roofs, he slapped on his baseball cap and tucked his ponytail up inside. He removed his gold earring, which had showed prominently in the newscast photo. There was nothing he could do about his size or face right now, although wearing the sunglasses helped. And he did have the 9mm Beretta tucked under his arm. All in all, he felt mildly optimistic.

He passed a lawn where a young cherry tree was in flower, its roots encircled in red brick. Georgetown had a distinct ambience to it, a blend of history and affluence. But right now, as his sharp gaze scoured for surveillance, it seemed ripe with incipient danger. There were a handful of cars parked on the street, but none was occupied. He could see no signs the block was being watched. He heaved a sigh of relief as he noted ahead a lavender Victorian—a three-story, rococo grande dame—and he knew from the way the house numbers were running that it had to be Convey's place.

He almost shook his head. Who would have believed such an uptight lawyer would have a purple house? It almost made him like her. And then, too, being particularly fond of legs, he had to admit she had fine ones, plus a few other traits he found attractive. But a purple house . . . he would have to think about that for a while.

He was wondering why she had made up that cock-and-bull story about a client being interested in buying the Meteor Express building, when he noticed her green Mercedes round the corner and turn onto the street, heading toward her house.

Again he scrutinized everywhere for danger. As he passed a stand of trees, she pulled into her driveway. He saw her blond head emerge, then that knock-out face. She was obviously exhausted and looked as if she could have been in a fight. Somehow he liked that about her, too.

Her furious voice carried down the block and across the street to Hammond's ears. "Phil! What are you doing here? Go away! This isn't your weekend pad anymore, I have nothing to say to you, and I'm not remotely interested in anything you could possibly say!"

Hammond stopped to watch, surprised. *Weekend pad?* They'd been lovers? The man must have been waiting behind her house. He was tall and well-built, charging out with his shoulders as if he owned not only Convey but the world, or at least thought he ought to. By his expensive, tailored suit, Hammond figured he was another lawyer or some professional who placed a lot of importance on his monetary aspirations. The man's expression was grim, but his face was handsome, if you liked the pretty-boy type. Hammond strained to hear his voice.

It was low and furious. "You've gone too far this time, Beth. You should've given that list of names directly to me. There are ethics involved here. *I'm* her lawyer. You know damn well all her legal business goes through me first. I'm going to haul you up before the bar. You've gotten too damn sleazy!"

What Hammond really disliked was the fellow's irritating air of familiarity. Hammond was just about to trot over to see whether he could assist her when his peripheral vision caught movement in the trees beside him. Birds had been singing, but now the little woods was quiet. The movement had been slight, and it came from behind him. A shaft of sunlight had glinted off what could have been metal somewhere in the foliage. But the reflection was high off the ground, not from the duff, where you would expect to find a lost mirror or a discarded metallic candy wrapper. In fact, it was shoulder height.

Alarms went off in his head. He swiveled just as a sniper's rifle homed in on Convey. His throat tightened, and in an instant he analyzed the situation. Whoever the man was, he was good. He had waited patiently and silently, and he had picked a perfect location for an ambush. It was his misfortune Hammond had been alert for trouble and that he had chosen this side of the street, too, so he could use the morning shadows for cover.

As the sniper's finger began to squeeze, Hammond slammed through the trees and hurled himself at the man's midsection. Rifle fire sang out. The assassin had gotten off a round at Beth Convey.

23

Hammond connected with force. The sniper grunted in pain, and they landed together hard on the duff under the trees, Hammond on top. Hammond's sunglasses flew from his face. Twigs and rocks jabbed his knees, but he hardly noticed as the man, who had kept his rifle high, swung it toward his head. Hammond dodged, and the blow smashed his shoulder. Pain exploded behind his eyes.

Fedorov gasped for breath. He was furious. Because of Hammond's attack, he had lost his clear shot at Beth Convey, and now he had no idea whether his bullet had hit her. He had planned to pick off Convey then Hammond, two for the price of one, as the Americans said. It had given him an excited thrill to see Hammond prowl down the street, a target so perfect it almost made you believe in God.

Killing both Hammond and Convey would restore his reputation. With an enraged growl, Fedorov swung the rifle again.

Hammond ducked, grabbed it, and straddled the man's hips, pinning him with his thighs and weight. "Who are you?" he demanded.

But the assassin still had an iron grip on the weapon. His chin was tucked deep, the veins in his neck bulged as he fought to control the rifle. Sweat beaded out on his forehead. He had an undistinguished face, clean-shaved, with regular features and neutral hair. A hired gun, trained to blend and vanish. Then Hammond recognized him—the man who had chased Convey the night Yurimengri had been killed. It galvanized him. He needed to hear the man's voice. Did he have an accent? A *Russian* accent?

"Dammit! Who are you? Who sent you to kill Beth Convey?" Fear tightened his chest. She could not be dead. Surely he had stopped the killer in time.

But the sniper was silent. With a sudden wrench, he tore the rifle from Hammond's right hand and bucked it up toward the right side of Hammond's head. The butt grazed Hammond's ear. Blood spurted out. But again Hammond caught the weapon. Using his left hand as a pivot, he slapped his right firmly onto the barrel. His lips peeled back with the effort of trying to dominate the rifle as it trembled between them.

"You bastard," Hammond snarled. "Why did you want Convey?"

Their eyes locked. The man had a dead gaze. Those eyes were so empty they could be black holes, sucking life from everywhere around. As sweat streaked down his face, Hammond glared into the dead eyes and figured this asshole was not going to quit, and although Hammond might be stronger, he was not strong enough to make a conclusive win the way things were.

Still, Hammond assured him. "You've lost. You might as well tell me who—"

That was when the man opened his mouth, laughed, and out came perfect American English: "No, Hammond, *you* can't win. Give it up. Some forces you can't control. Deep in that thick skull of yours, you know it. . . ."

Hammond did not like the message or the lack of accent, but he liked that the man was talking. It was not much of a distraction, but it would do. He dropped his right hand from the rifle and smashed it toward the sniper's jaw. But the man was good. He craned his head to the side, and Hammond's fist only grazed his neck. Hammond was ready.

Before the man's head could swivel back, Hammond released the rifle and pressed his left arm down against his throat, trapping him. At the same time, Hammond used his right hand to compress the man's carotid artery. That kind of pressure-point attack could cause great pain, unconsciousness, or kill outright.

The man struggled. He jettisoned his rifle. But Hammond continued to hold him down. By the time the assassin's eyes rolled up into unconsciousness, Hammond was breathing hard, his chest heaving. Rage consumed him. It burned and turned his entrails into a furnace. He stared down at his arm and hand. They were steady, and the big square fingers continued to press into the killer's yielding flesh. Hands that were a force almost beyond himself. He wanted to keep squeezing. Crushing. Harder. He wanted to, and his hand wanted to—

Kill him. *Kill him.* Before he could kill Convey or anyone else. But just then he became aware of his thundering heart and heavy breathing. He realized he was feeling what it used to be like—his focus so complete, so intent, so enraged, so righteous he was almost self-hypnotized. He did not like that. It was dangerous to not be yourself, and he never wanted to play that losing game again. This was no clear-cut case where he had to kill.

As the rise and fall of police sirens screamed in the distance, he released the unconscious assassin and sighed a sigh so deep it shook him. He lifted his head and listened. The sirens might not be heading here. Most people in this tony neighborhood would be at their jobs or out somewhere like a beauty establishment or doing charity work in the District. But he could take no chance someone had called the police about that single rifle shot.

Probably not more than three minutes had passed since he had attacked the sniper. He grabbed the man's rifle and leaped to his feet, ignoring the pain in his shoulder. A throbbing ache radiated from where the rifle had rammed it. He had no time to search the guy. He had to get to Convey. God, he hoped she was alive. And if she were, she might need medical help. He tore out from the trees and across the street, looking everywhere for her.

As the sound of the sirens increased, Beth started to rise above her car's hood to look across the street. She thought the shot had come from a patch of trees there.

Phil Stageman grabbed her arm and yanked her back. "Get down!" His curly brown hair had tumbled into his eyes. His square jaw was clenched in fear. He had one hand clamped to her arm, while the other held her far shoulder in an iron lock. "They could still be out there. You'll get us *killed!*"

She tried to be patient. "We've waited long enough. We can't pitch a tent here. Besides, you heard the sirens. The police are on the way."

"They're not here yet." His voice was close to her ear, husky with terror. "You're tall. You make a good target. They'll shoot you, then they'll come after me."

She snorted. It would almost be worth it. "Personally, I think your getting shot's an interesting idea. The medical insurance through Edwards & Bonnett, by the way, is great. The best. I know firsthand. And if you're lucky, you'll need a year to recover. Think of it as an unplanned vacation." She pushed free and started to rise again to check the street. "Do you have anything you'd like replaced? I recommend transplants. In your case, for morals."

He was not listening. "I told you not to expose yourself!" He yanked so hard it felt as if her arm would leave its socket.

She fell next to him again. But that did it. She hurt everywhere anyway. One more throbbing, aching place was not what her body needed right now. She pushed herself back up onto her haunches and faced him.

"You coward." Using her legs and hips for power, she rammed her fists one after the other in three consecutive *dan-zuki* punches straight into his belly.

His eyebrows shot up. She had been so fast, he'd had no time to defend himself. He was athletic, and his stomach was muscular from hours at the firm's gym, but she had surprised him, and she was strong.

He doubled over. "Beth," he gasped, his face contorted. "How could you?"

A male baritone sounded above her head. "Nice job. He looks like a real headache to me. How'd you ever get involved with a guy like this? Despite some obvious talents, Convey, you clearly don't know how to choose boyfriends."

A relieved smile on his face, Hammond stared down at Beth. She was unharmed. A bullet hole in the front fender of her car told him the sniper had missed, although only by a foot. And despite her fatigue, he decided that, at least for him, she was even more beautiful close up than from a distance. From the mussed hair to the softly pointed chin, he was caught by the dramatic qualities of her features beneath the sunglasses. The prominent cheekbones. The small ears with the hair tucked behind. He had a feeling she was not impressed by her own beauty. Probably did not fit her idea of what a tough lady lawyer should look like.

But as quickly as he thought all this, he saw her expression make a hemispheric shift. No longer surprised, she was horrified, the fear turning her already pale face ashen, the color of dead bones.

"You—" She jumped up, clutched her shoulder bag to her side, and ran.

"Beth! Don't—" Phil Stageman craned his neck.

Hammond was already gone, hurtling after her. "Convey! Wait!" As he ran, he could still hear the sound of her sexy, throaty voice hanging in the air: *"You—"*.

The sirens grew louder as he chased her past lawn chairs, jonquil beds, and a white gazebo. She was fast on the sidewalk, almost a blur in her jeans, black turtleneck, and black cardigan.

He was faster, gaining on her. "Convey! I just saved your life, dammit!"

Beth was replaying in her head the terrible deaths of Stephanie Smith and Colonel Yurimengri. She refused to meet the same fate. As her legs pumped, she recalled she had been strangely unfazed when the black van had pursued Stephanie and her on the interstate. And she was strangely collected now, even as the killer was chasing her. There was a new steel to her, a new hardness. Whatever it was, the thought flashed to her: Why in hell was she running away?

Instantly all the rage of the past few days overtook her. She was back again in that volcanic stew of blinding anger that made her want to kill Jeff Hammond.

The sirens were still screaming. From their intensity, police cars would arrive any minute. At the same time, she and Hammond were approaching the end of the block, where a huge lilac bush stood on one side, the intersection on the other. By the sound of his hammering feet, Hammond was closing in on her. As she had that thought, she felt an odd sense of déjà vu, realizing she could consciously translate sounds into distance. *Heart . . . is it you I have to thank for that information?* Somewhere inside herself, she knew exactly where Hammond was—six feet behind her—and exactly what to do. She clamped her purse to her side, stopped, and planted her left foot firmly on the ground. Instantly she looked around her shoulder and slammed her right foot back in an arc from the outside inward in a *ushiro-kekomi* kick straight to his solar plexus.

She connected with a satisfying *thunk* and spun on her heel to face him. He staggered back. His rugged features crunched with astonishment. She had the advantage of a surprise attack and of wearing athletic shoes, not the high-heeled, lizard-skin cowboy boots he had on his big feet. Plus, unlike him, she was thin and flexible, with very fast reflexes. Despite his attempt to dodge, her foot had landed where she had aimed it on his outsized body, and she had not lost her balance, a fault she had spent months overcoming.

As Hammond grunted, she slammed down a *shuto-uchi* sword-hand strike onto his wrist, knocking the rifle away. Immediately she kicked it out of reach, stepped back, raised her bent leg to her chest, and snapped out her foot in a *mae-keage* straight toward his chin.

But Hammond had recovered. She was good, he had to give her that. In fact, he had been so unprepared for her skill that he had let her dominate the fight. She had made him temporarily lose the rifle, but that was the last round she was going to win. As her eyes blazed and her Nike came at his face, he stepped back, caught the foot in midair, and using his superior height and strength, he yanked.

She landed flat on her back on the thick lawn beside the lilac bush. Her blond hair flew out around her head, her sunglasses spun away, and disgust spread across her perspiring face.

In a smooth motion, beautiful in its economy, he pulled out his Beretta, leaned down, and pointed it at her nose. "Ms. Convey, you are a real pain in the butt. You seem to think I'm going to murder you. You're flattering yourself. I wouldn't waste the bullet. With luck, someday you'll be disbarred, and that'll give me all the satisfaction I crave. But right now, I do have a few questions."

He thought about glancing back to check out the sirens screaming toward her house, but there was a large bush of some kind in the way. Besides, he had better not take the chance. He did not like the look on Convey's face—the mixture of fury and calculation. He had begun to believe there was no way he could predict her next move. Better to keep a close eye on her.

A very close eye, and a gun in her face. The last thing he needed was for the police to spot him. "Get up. Carefully. Walk away around the corner. I'll be right behind."

She started to sit up, her eyes shooting white-hot flames.

He warned, "Don't get creative."

She glared pointedly at the Beretta. "The way it looks to me, you're threatening to shoot me dead. Otherwise, why should I do what you say?"

"Because not only do I have the gun, I also saved your ass, that's why. *Twice,* as I told you. Pretend I'm a Good Samaritan. Be polite. Didn't anyone teach you manners?"

Pain. More pain. She was breathing hard. She inhaled, willing it to stop. As she stared up into his broad face, she found something in it that all of a sudden appealed to her again. What was it about him? Everything she knew . . . all her background . . . everything she had witnessed and deduced told her to avoid him as if he were a rabid dog. But here he was, saying he had *saved* her?

He was the enemy. A killer. *Remember that, heart.* "I'm getting up," she warned. "If you're planning to shoot, now's a good time. The police are just down the block. I'll be dead, but at least I'll die knowing you'll be caught."

"Ah, yes. I used to think revenge was sweet, too." He gave a brief smile. But the sirens' yelps had ratcheted up yet again, so the police cars must have turned onto Convey's street, just as she had said. With a sense of worried urgency, he grabbed up his sunglasses and slapped them on. Then he picked up the sniper's rifle and ordered, "No more talk. Move."

24

As the sirens continued to sound, Beth rose carefully to her feet, her throat tight, her gaze fixed on Hammond's intense face. With conscious effort, she repressed her fear and concentrated on her anger. Hammond kept the pistol on her as she curled upward from the grass, holding it a steady two inches from her nose. He glared, radiating threat. She held his stare, willing him to look away first.

The seconds stretched, and she fought back a sense of crude intimacy. Still their gazes remained locked. His lashes were long, black, and ragged. He blinked slowly. His dusky eyes seemed somehow like deep tunnels, as if important messages were cached inside. Messages she was certain she would dislike.

Still, he did not alter his gaze. "Quit stalling. Get back on the sidewalk and move!"

"And you complain about *my* manners?" She broke eye contact and turned. She had lost something by averting her eyes first, but she needed out. She was finished with him. Just making the choice was victory.

But in life, so much was relative. As she stepped reluctantly back to the sidewalk, she gazed past the side of the tall bush. For about six seconds she had a clear view: There were two squad cars, their red-and-blue beacons flashing, as uniformed policemen advanced cautiously to meet Phil, who frantically beckoned them. At the same time, a man in a muted sports coat and trousers emerged from the little woods across the street where she had thought the shot had originated. With a sinking feeling, she watched him slide his hand inside his jacket and peer casually—too casually—at the officers as he hopped into a dilapidated yellow station wagon.

She had planned to yell for the police. To risk Hammond's shooting her in the back so she could run to them. But what she saw now made her rethink the situation. Who was the man who had been in the trees? Some inner knowing—her heart again?—told her he must have a gun concealed under his jacket. Did that mean Hammond was telling the truth, that there had been a sniper, and Hammond had attacked him and diverted his aim?

"I said move it, Convey. Hurry it up!" Jeff Hammond pushed the pistol's barrel into her spine.

"Okay. All right, I'm going." She walked around the corner and beyond the view of the police. No, Hammond was no friend. Not with a gun in her back.

"Just pretend we're taking a stroll." His breath was in her ear, his voice low and husky.

"Yeah. Sure."

She continued forward, the heat of Hammond's body only inches behind. Millimeters. So close that, if they were machines, electricity would arc from her to him and back again. But even as she was fighting off the unnerving sensation of his being so near, she was still picturing in her mind the other man and ticking off the evidence against him: Concealed weapon, too-casual gaze, disheveled appearance, as if he had just been in a fight. Plus he was near the spot from which she was sure the bullet had been fired.

Hammond claimed he had saved her. Twice. Was one of those times just now?

She wanted to believe none of it. All the earlier evidence pointed directly to Hammond. That he had been the one hunting her, trying to kill her. She had been convinced he was truly dangerous, and unmasking and stopping him had driven many of her decisions since Wednesday.

"Faster," Hammond snapped.

The leafy, residential street along which they walked was less quiet than hers, feeding traffic onto busy Wisconsin Avenue. Vehicles moved smartly along. Ahead, children's toys were scattered across a broad lawn. A UPS deliveryman stepped out of his brown van and ran a package toward the front door of a brick Federalist house.

As the UPS man glanced at Beth, he waved. He recognized her.

"Be nice," Hammond said in a tight voice. "Say hello."

Beth saw it instantly as another opportunity for help, but what could the UPS man do? He had no gun. She could not risk endangering him.

She forced a smile and called, "Hi, Adam!"

As the man waved in response, Hammond rumbled, "Good girl."

"Don't call me girl."

"Good woman."

"Better. Since you've kidnaped me, I assume you have a plan. Personally, I could use a cup of coffee right now. We could stop at the Coffee Beanery. It's close. Or if you're interested in dessert as well, I'd suggest Dean & Deluca. But now that I think about it, we couldn't go there. Somebody might recognize you. After all, you're a wanted man—"

That was when the first shot rang out. It blistered past so close it made her eyes burn. With a sudden shudder, she was flat on the ground again, Hammond on top. As she felt his body crush her, she freed her head enough to lift it and look. The yellow station wagon had skidded to a stop on the street near them, and the disheveled stranger—gun in hand—was jumping up to stand braced with his feet in the driver's doorway.

He must have fired through the open passenger window, before his aim was true, the same inner voice advised her. He was too anxious. Desperation had ruined his focus. Meanwhile, Adam, the UPS man, fell to the ground, arms crossed protectively over his head. Traffic slowed as drivers and passengers craned to look, but as soon as they saw the weapon, their vehicles sped away.

By the time their attacker had leaned across the station wagon's roof to assure his aim, Jeff Hammond had leaped to his feet, lifted the rifle sight to his eye, and scoped in on the shooter. Beth looked frantically around for a gun and spotted Hammond's pistol. He had left it on the sidewalk beside them so he could use the rifle. As she grabbed the gun, both men squeezed their triggers. Their shots thundered.

The attacker spun off the car's roof and disappeared, leaving a pink, bloody cloud. She glanced at Hammond and saw the expression on his broad face was coldly intense, with the kind of deep-rooted concentration that alone was enough to terrify most people. Add his large size and obvious capabilities, and it sent a shock wave through her. No wonder she had feared him. No wonder she had thought him capable of killing. He *was* capable.

Already he was running for the station wagon. "Stay there!" he shouted back.

An eerie composure fell over her. Cradling the pistol, she rose in a crouch. She was not afraid now. The gun in her hands, the waning shock of it all . . . left her with a breathless kind of excitement. Her blood seemed to course more easily. Her mind had great clarity.

She wondered whether the police had heard the shots. If not, surely someone would call 911. She still wanted the police to arrest Hammond. She wanted to take no chances with him. Just a few minutes ago she had been convinced he was the killer of Colonel Yurimengri and probably Stephanie Smith. Now she was no longer sure. It made no sense he would defend her against this shooter, unless . . . she shook her head. She had no answer. Let the police sort it out.

Caught in her strange state of calm, she hurried in a crouch toward the front of the station wagon while Hammond closed in on the car's rear. He was a graceful, intent figure in his herringbone jacket and jeans. There was no sign of the shooter. As the sounds of traffic continued, she dropped low, peering under the car for feet.

And suddenly the gunman was upon her. She had expected to see him lying flat, dead or dying, on the pavement on the other side of the car. Instead he had been at the hood, hunkered down, his butt on his heels, as Hammond rounded the car's rear.

Then he sprang up and raced around the front fender, pistol aimed at her. One arm hung motionless at his side, the shoulder covered with blood. His bland face had vanished in a grotesque mask that erased any question about his motives. He was a killer. He enjoyed it. His eyes glowed with it. His lips were drawn back in a kind of ecstasy. His finger was on the trigger, and she was his target.

It was one of those instances when you do not think. You cannot. Whoever you are, whatever you have fashioned of yourself, takes over. She did not question her heart or whether it had intelligence. Or who she was or had ever been. Or even who she was becoming.

As his gun found its mark, she stayed in her crouch and pulled her pistol's trigger. And pulled it again and again. She had no idea how many times. It was an explosion of fear and relief, and it shook her. She wanted to kill this evil man because he was going to kill her, and she was happy she could do it. It made perfect sense as she squeezed the trigger. And squeezed it. And with each squeeze felt safer and better and healthier—and that she would have a future if she just kept . . . *squeezing.*

As the sound of her gunfire assaulted her brain, she watched amazed as the man flew back from the power of the 9mm bullets and landed hard against a tree. Blood burst from his chest.

Hammond was back at her side. "Jesus Christ, Convey! I wanted him alive!"

He yanked open the front door on the passenger side of the old station wagon, threw her inside, and tore around to jump in behind the wheel. As he raced the wagon away, she stared out the window at the dead man and then, as if in a dream, lifted her gaze and saw Adam Hoogensen, the UPS man who made regular deliveries on her street. Their eyes connected, and she saw the horror in his. She had killed a man. Not her heart. *She*. Just as in her nightmare. And he had seen her do it.

She averted her gaze. Neither she nor Hammond saw the squat, burly man with the Mongol face run to the dead man as if he were trying to help and give him medical attention. No one in the gathering crowd saw Ivan Vok take the dead man's cell phone and pistol and slip them into his own pocket. Nor did they see Vok slide a wallet into the pocket of the victim's ripped and bloody jacket.

Beth sank back against the car seat. Her eyelids closed involuntarily, and she began to shake. She was cold, freezing. Colder than she had ever been. As the station wagon moved with the traffic, revulsion hit her. What had she done?

"I knew the man I killed," she whispered. "I recognized his face." She looked at Hammond as if he could help.

Hammond drove on steadily. "How?"

"I saw him in my nightmares. I don't know his name, but I saw his face."

"Nightmares? What are you talking about?"

She shook her head and closed her eyes again. She retreated inside. Could not think her usual analytical thoughts. Had to feel.

"You idiot." His voice was soft now. "Why do you think I didn't shoot to kill? He could've told us who he was. Who he worked for. Why he wanted you."

She said nothing. The shaking decreased to shudders.

"Do you have any idea what you're involved in?"

She heard his voice as if he were far away. She was grieving. There was so much to regret. She had lost her heart. It had been sick, but it was hers. Her very own. Now a new, demanding one beat in her chest. She had seen two people die. She had killed a third. She did not know who she was. Something familiar and basic was gone about herself. She was new. A new person. What do you do when you are new, and you kill someone?

He was talking in that same quiet voice. ". . . things you don't know about me. I can't go into it all. There isn't time, and anyway you don't need to hear all that nonsense. But you seem to be stuck on the idea I'm dangerous. Well, I'm not. At least not to you. Last Wednesday I met secretly with Anatoli Yurimengri because he said he had important information for me. I was supposed to meet him again at Meteor Express that night, but when I arrived, you were running out the front door, being chased by a man with a silenced gun. I had to make a quick decision. Whether to help you or go inside to find Yurimengri. I decided to help you."

Beth roused herself. She turned to look at him. "Help me?"

"Yes. Help you." He glanced at her and looked away. "Just as you stumbled and fell, I tackled the man who was chasing you. Then all of a sudden there were more men, all armed. By then, I had the first guy's pistol, and I used it to hold them off while I hauled you away. I didn't know what you had to do with Meteor, and I didn't have time to wait for you to wake up and tell me. So I took you to a motel where I have an arrangement with the owner." He hesitated. The owner was one of his former girlfriends, but Convey had no need to know that. "By the time I got back to Meteor, the place was empty. No sign of Yurimengri. I drove your car to the motel, walked back to pick up mine, and drove to my office at the *Post,* hoping Yurimengri had phoned. Instead, the night editor gave me the bad news his corpse had been found downtown."

He checked her response. Her eyes were blinking slowly. She looked miserable and stunned, not so surprising since she had just shot and killed a man.

He frowned. "Did you follow what I said? Are you okay, Convey?" He was beginning to worry. She was obviously shocked. "Look, what you did was self-defense. Considering you're not trained, you did remarkably well to have stopped him and survived."

Her eyes narrowed. "You expect me to believe that fairy tale? I would've made up something a lot more credible. It's not just Colonel Yurimengri's murder you have to explain. You think I don't know about those two kids you killed in West Virginia?"

"I was framed. Obviously, someone wants very badly to get me out of the way."

"Framed? Oh, please. The next thing you're going to tell me is there's a real Santa Claus."

His jaw muscles hardened. "I can't explain more than that. I don't know who did it. Or how. You'll have to believe me."

"Right. Back to Santa Claus again."

He turned the station wagon east on M Street, heading toward Foggy

Bottom. There was more than a hint of anger in his voice: "I also saved you from the sniper today." He described how he had spotted the metallic flash in the woods, and how he had brought down the lurking shooter. "But I suppose that's not enough to convince you either."

She studied the three black boxes on the floor, the long rifle in her lap that he had dropped there as he rushed to get behind the wheel, and the pistol that lay beside it. The same pistol she had fired at the man.

She asked, "What was his name? The man I killed?"

"Sorry. Don't know. You're the one who remembered him." His voice became sarcastic. "From your dreams. And you think *my* story sounds like a fairy tale?"

Beth lapsed into a silence again.

Hammond felt instant remorse. He was beginning to sense something far out of the ordinary was occurring. It was not just that she had killed someone and that it had sent her into a tailspin. After a killing, most police departments put the shooting officer on leave, not only to investigate the incident, but to give the officer time to digest what had happened and recover emotionally. Killing was antihuman, despite what some primitive peoples believed, and the healthy spirit rebelled against it, no matter how necessary. But with Convey, there was more.

He said, "I *can* tell you one thing, though. The man you shot was there the night Yurimengri was killed. That guy was the one chasing you. If it's any comfort, if you hadn't gotten him today, he'd have killed you, possibly me, and gone on to continue killing if I hadn't been able to stop him either."

"You said he could have told us who he worked for. He was a professional? That's why you wanted to capture him?"

"It seemed like an idea."

They had left Georgetown and were now driving in the section of the District called Foggy Bottom, where the crown prince of government— the Department of State—arose stark as a large, white shoe box from what once had been an unlivable swamp. Hammond pulled the station wagon to the curb near the Watergate complex, turned off the ignition, grabbed the Beretta from beside her before she could object, and slid it into the holster under his jacket.

"Stay here," he ordered and opened the car door. He had no idea whether she would, but he doubted he was going to learn anything from her anyway.

She bit back an angry retort. Let him think she would wait in the car. Let him believe she was a sucker who believed everything he said. She nodded mutely, afraid her voice would betray her.

He was peering at her. His blunt features seemed to contract in concentration. She gazed levelly back, never quite meeting his eyes. A whiff of testosterone seemed to come at her, testing. She ignored it.

He got out of the car, glanced all around, then headed into the vast Watergate complex, made famous by the bungled burglary of Democratic headquarters back in the days of President Richard M. Nixon. The temporary home of travelers as well as the permanent residence of some of the city's elite and notorious—everyone from Bob and Liddy Dole to, at one time, Monica Lewinsky—it was a rabbit warren of luxury shops, apartments, and hotel rooms.

As Jeff disappeared down the concrete stairs that led to the lower level, Beth opened her car door and stepped out onto the sidewalk.

Hammond strode through the sunken courtyard, past Mail Boxes Etc., a grocery store, a deli, and up another flight of stairs. He watched all around, moving only his eyes. He kept expecting to be recognized. Kept waiting to have someone shout his name and scream for the police. Wondered when the next killer would arrive, for there would be another one. Professionals like today's sniper always had employers determined to achieve their ends.

He left the Watergate complex on the south side just above the Potomac, trotted across the street, and slowed to a casual stroll as he climbed the wide drive toward the Kennedy Center for the Performing Arts. Tall and imposing, the building was a commanding presence above the Potomac. He glanced up as if he were a tourist admiring it . . . and stopped. He leaned over to pull up his cowboy boots and adjust his jean's leg. There were two of them again—a man and a woman, though not the same pair who had staked out his condo. They stood in the shade of a tree, reading sightseeing brochures, but they made none of the little chitchat or showed the impatient frowns of those who had been kept waiting too long. By the way they watched the building and scanned the drive, they had a motive different from simply meeting late family members or friends.

Hammond's uncle was director of the Kennedy Center. He hoped to convince him to loan them a car and let them stay at his weekend bungalow on Chesapeake Bay.

As he watched the watchers, he wondered whether he could be wrong. Maybe the pair was innocent; maybe he had grown too jaded. After all, he had managed to walk through the whole Watergate complex without being noticed. The baseball cap had helped, but even greater was the contribution of human nature: People were preoccupied with themselves and their problems, not on the alert for a mad killer they had seen for perhaps thirty seconds on a TV screen. He was a sound bite now. At least, he was until word spread and the news reports reached a tipping point where his face and name were on too many worried Washingtonians' minds.

The couple split up. The woman moved toward the entrance to the center, while the man folded his brochures and stuck them into the hip pocket of his shorts. Both wore knee-length shorts with light windbreaker jackets zipped halfway up. A breeze gusted along the drive. Yes, he could see the faint outline of a holster beneath the nylon jacket. The man was strolling in his direction.

Hammond turned and retreated down the drive. There was no point in forcing a confrontation, in case they were police. And now he was even more concerned. Where could he take Convey that was safe? He returned across the parkway. It was obvious his contacts and usual places were being watched.

He moved quickly past a patio filled with tables where couples sat drinking coffee, eating scones and croissants, and chatting companionably in the mild April air. It was Friday, and they were winding down for the weekend.

As he pushed through the Watergate's glass doors, he had a peculiar feeling. He looked around. Adrenaline surged through him. Two men were close on his heels, and one was the male "tourist" from the Kennedy Center. These two were a pair now, the woman off somewhere else. Grimness settled over him. The good thing was that his instincts had been right. That was the bad thing, too.

He hurried across the lobby, out another door, and down a corridor that led to still another outside door. He exited again, and they were still behind him, now with their hands inside their jackets. His breathing began to speed up. He passed people. He wanted no one to get hurt. He had to keep his pursuers away from Convey.

He ran halfway down another flight of stairs, and suddenly one of the men appeared ahead, standing at the foot of the landing. He glanced back and felt a wave of panic. The other man was behind and above him. He reached for his pistol, but they had pulled theirs. He was caught. Trapped between their weapons.

"Halt, Hammond. You go no farther. Take hand from jacket. Be slow. Be nice. Maybe you live." A Russian accent, at last.

25

"I'm certain now. Jeffrey Hammond's got to be our mole."

The hulking architectural monstrosity that was the J. Edgar Hoover Building dominated the view from Assistant Attorney General Donald Chen's office. On Pennsylvania Avenue, the FBI headquarters rose seven stories in what looked like bullet-riddled concrete, while at the rear, toward E Street, it loomed even larger and more unfortunately— an eleven-story Quasimodo, the misshapen hunchback of Washington.

Today, Assistant AG Chen was dressed debonairly in a charcoal Brooks Brothers suit elegantly tailored to his short, portly frame. His black hair had its usual immaculate side part, but his round, Buddha face was unsmiling. He glared through his window at the FBI building as if he could see the mole lurking inside, a dangerous artifact of the grotesque building and of the even more dangerous and grotesque Cold War.

"How certain are you, Eli?" Chen asked.

Eli Kirkhart assured him, "Shall we say one mere step from absolute proof?" His bulldog face was as severe as Chen's. He seemed today more muscular in his dark-blue, single-button suit as he leaned back in the comfortable armchair reserved for guests in Chen's office. He felt triumphant and expansive, an unusual indulgence for him, particularly the English side of him, as he added, "It won't be long. Days, at the most."

"I don't know, Eli. Sounds like you're still missing a damn big step to me."

Kirkhart shrugged. "Have a bit of faith in me, and withhold judgment until you've heard my entire tale."

"Go ahead then. Let's hear it."

"While I was following him on Wednesday, Hammond took a bunk to a village named Stone Point in the godforsaken mountains of West Virginia. When I arrived, he was doing his usual routine of asking around for Alexei Berianov, so he could grill him for that series he's writing. Then suddenly he was arrested by the Bureau for the double murder of two local juveniles. I couldn't very well reveal myself at that point, since they would've asked what on earth I was doing in the ridiculous hamlet myself, eh? So I followed them as they drove Hammond back through the night to D.C. to a state-of-the-art safe house in Adams Morgan that I knew nothing about. The safe house surprised me. I'm usually kept in the loop about them."

Chen folded his hands across his ample stomach. "Why weren't you this time?"

"Under the circumstances, I can't very well ask without revealing myself. I suspect the safe house is either extremely new, or—my thought is—it's very high level and known only to the director and perhaps a few other officials. In other words, known probably only to Hammond's secret bosses in the Bureau."

Chen rotated in his chair. He considered the view out his other window, this one overlooking the corner of Ninth and Pennsylvania and the Navy Memorial, where the summer concerts would soon begin. "I don't see how that proves he's undercover—"

"He escaped."

"Escaped?" Chen turned back sharply to stare. "Hammond? From a safe house?"

"Slick as a weasel. Out and gone." Kirkhart detailed the exact method and route.

"Holy hell. How did he know there was an escape route under the house?"

"Yes," Kirkhart nodded. "Indeed. My question precisely. There's only one logical conclusion: He must've been told what to look for before he got there—some secret mark or other visual sign. We both know pre-arranged signals are standard with any police or government agency that's running someone undercover. Plus, Graham told me the underground route appeared to be recently set out, and that there was even a new flashlight down there with Hammond's prints. *Only* Hammond's prints, although he'd had no access to a flashlight. That tells me the flashlight must've been conveniently waiting. Too conveniently. Someone with the power to get into that safe house had to have secretly arranged the whole thing. Yes, Hammond's definitely undercover, and he's still operating for the Bureau."

Chen chewed a lip as he contemplated all the implications. "True, unless Hammond's working *for* the mole, and the mole made the escape arrangements for him."

"Impossible." Eli was emphatic. "No deep mole would ever take such a large risk that he could be discovered. For a deep-cover mole, everyone's expendable. Everyone *has* to be expendable, or he wouldn't be able to work long or even survive. Friends, wives, children. If the mole were someone else, then Hammond would be swinging in the wind right now."

"What about this business of Hammond's killing the young couple? Did he do it?"

"I can't be certain, but I wouldn't be at all surprised if that weren't arranged, too. Someone else was probably the killer, but Hammond's handler in the Bureau saw the perfect opportunity to make it appear he'd done it. I've learned there's some evidence the deaths may have occurred earlier than was reported, which means someone created time to get Hammond into Stone Point so he could be blamed for the murders."

"Why in God's name would the Bureau want to do anything like that?"

"Maybe they had some critical assignment in mind for Hammond in a prison somewhere. It's a natural—make Hammond out to be a mean, nasty killer and escape artist, and then assign him as the cellmate of some convict who has information they haven't been able to get. At that point, they sit back and wait for Hammond to worm his way into the fellow's confidence."

"It's been done successfully before," Chen agreed soberly. Then considered further. "Okay, so we think Hammond's still working for the Bureau. But ten years—and under the stewardship of three different directors—that's a hell of a long time to be undercover. Sounds fishy to me. A crazy setup at best." He shook his head and concluded reluctantly, "I'm still not convinced Hammond's the mole."

Kirkhart took a notebook from the jacket pocket of his suit. "Before I went to Stone Point, I spotted Hammond with a woman outside the *Post* building. They talked on the street. Serious talk, I'd say. When he went back inside, she drove off but then circled back and staked out the building in her car. When Hammond drove out of the garage, she tailed him. Naturally, I was curious."

"Of course. Go on."

"I got her license plate number and had my team identify her." He flipped open his notebook. "The name's Elizabeth—'Beth'—Convey, and she's a high-level lawyer with Edwards & Bonnett. I did some digging around. Last year, she won a billion-dollar divorce settlement for a wealthy businesswoman named Michelle Philmalee. In it, Mrs. Philmalee was awarded control of the Philmalee Group. Now it seems a company in the Group—Philmalee International—has a contract worth nearly five-hundred million dollars to broker the sale of unenriched uranium that will go to Russia. But the Russian agency, Uridium, backed out of the deal with Philmalee. So Philmalee's filed suit to force Uridium to live up to its contract. But another company—"

"HanTech," Chen interrupted, nodding. "That's the other company. Very interesting. That deal's part of a government project to remove nuclear-weapons-grade uranium from Russia's arsenal. We blend the highly enriched uranium into harmless fuel for nuclear power plants, and in exchange we give Russia cash and unenriched uranium. Uridium's run by their Ministry of Atomic Energy."

"Minatom." Kirkhart whistled. "And Uridium. Aha . . . a mole would be damned interested in keeping close tabs of our side in a deal like that. No way would our government tell any Russian agency or official everything when we're trying to manipulate their country's nuclear capabilities. For both economic and military reasons, they'd love to get their hooks into what we're holding back."

"Exactly." Chen stood up. "And you say this Beth Convey is a lawyer for Philmalee, and that she was talking to Hammond and tailing him?"

"That's what I saw."

"She's suspicious of him. Or she's worried in some other way about him. Maybe you've got something important after all." Chen headed for his door. "Let's go."

"Where?"

"Taurino's office."

Under the stern gaze of Chief Justice John Marshall, Millicent Taurino leaned against her stand-up reading desk, scowling over a dense and wildly overwritten analysis of a case pending before the Supreme Court. It had been prepared for the attorney general but farmed out to her on the pretext that he had to make a critical appearance before the Ninth Circuit in San Francisco instead. The truth was, the attorney general found lengthy analyses tedious.

The deputy AG's fingernails were a dark purple today, her business suit a pale mauve, her red ponytail tied low on the nape of her neck, and her expression verging on suicidal when Donald Chen burst into her office leading Special Agent Eli Kirkhart.

"Boss lady, I think Eli's uncovered a bombshell this time."

For once Millicent Taurino was grateful for her subordinate's disregard of the niceties of protocol, although she was not about to let him know that. Despite her thankfulness for the reprieve from the boring analysis, she had to attempt to instill a stronger sense of the dignity due her office. Besides, she had her hard-nosed, razor-tongued image to uphold.

So she said, "Tell me, Donald, what don't you understand about knocking on a closed door? Is it the position of your knuckles? The correct amount of force to be applied? Or perhaps a fear of injury to you or the door?"

Chen grinned. "Sorry, Millicent. I guess I just get carried away by my eagerness to serve you."

Taurino laughed. So much for her famed despotism. "Sit down, Donald. You too, Kirkhart. Now, what's this bombshell? I take it something further has developed concerning our elusive mole?"

"You bet," Chen enthused. "Tell her, Eli. All of it. Chapter and verse."

Kirkhart recited the entire story—spotting Beth Convey with Hammond, following him to Stone Point, seeing him arrested by Chuck Graham and his FBI team, and then escaping from the safe house.

Taurino understood immediately. She rubbed thoughtfully at the butterfly tattoo on her neck. "So he had a signal in case he fell afoul of agents who couldn't know he was actually still in the Bureau but undercover. Good deductive work, Special Agent Kirkhart. However, none of what you've said proves he's our ubiquitous mole."

"Maybe not, Millicent," Chen said. "Tell her about Minatom, Eli."

"Minatom?" Taurino came alert at the name of this important Russian agency.

"Yes, ma'am," Eli confirmed. He explained about Beth Convey, Philmalee International, Uridium, HanTech, and the meeting he observed between Jeff Hammond and the Convey woman.

The deputy attorney general returned slowly to her desk. "This Convey is an attorney here?"

"With a blue-chip firm. Edwards & Bonnett. Zach Housley's piranhas."

But Taurino had stopped listening to Chen, lost in her own thoughts. She sat behind her desk as if on auto pilot, hardly aware of the chair, the desk, the office, anything at all. Her voice was measured as she spoke, heavy with a tentative concern. "We've been monitoring that project, of course, since it's vital to our interests to reduce the nuclear threat to this country. But in the last few days, NSA has uncovered two situations that are disturbing. Very disturbing, as a matter of fact." She stopped, as if reconsidering what she was about to reveal.

"What situations?" Eli Kirkhart asked bluntly. "Could the mole be involved?"

"That's what I'm wondering." Taurino turned her face to look at the agent, still pondering. Finally, she let out a slow breath and gazed up at the exacting visage of John Marshall. "First, it looks possible that HanTech—on orders from Uridium—may be doing a lot more than brokering a sale of unenriched uranium. It appears they're buying up weapons-grade uranium from Third World countries like Iraq and Libya, to whom the Kremlin sold it in the nineties when it was, as usual, desperate for money. NSA has evidence Philmalee International's rival, HanTech, is shipping that weapons-grade uranium *back* to Russia."

Chen swore. "That's totally illegal! Not to mention dangerous as hell. Why would one of our own companies do such a thing? And why would Russia sell weapons-grade uranium to us to lower its stockpiles, then turn around and buy it up from Third World nations?"

"Yes," Millicent Taurino agreed. "Why?"

Kirkhart said, "Is it possible one group of Russians is doing one thing, and another group the opposite? Perhaps the left hand hasn't a clue what the right is doing."

Taurino nodded. "Could be."

Chen asked, "What's the second situation, Millicent?"

"Philmalee International just filed an affidavit today alleging HanTech is now owned by a group of former Soviet nationals, émigrés and defectors to this country."

The silence in the office was like a vacuum after a massive explosion. None of the three spoke. Finally, it was Eli Kirkhart who said, "Our mole could certainly have been useful in that entire deal. Perhaps he passed insider information to Uridium or Minatom that facilitated the takeover and switch to HanTech."

"I'm thinking along those lines, too," Taurino agreed. "Mr. Kirkhart, find this Hammond, wherever he is, and don't let him out of your sight. Report everything he does. You understand?"

"Absolutely."

Donald Chen suggested, "We'd better have NSA check out Stone

Point, too. We need to know whether Hammond went there for some reason we haven't discovered, and whether he did kill those kids. Who they were—and what, if anything, they were part of that would attract the interest of a mole."

Millicent Taurino nodded and reached for her phone. "Abby? Get me Cabot Lowell at the Pentagon."

26

It felt to Beth as if it had been a long time since she could distinguish right from wrong easily. But the truth was, she still had been confident about it until Tuesday—just three days ago—when she called Meteor Express, heard the Russian accent, and threw herself ignorantly upon a journey that with each step shredded more of the fabric of her carefully thought-out life. And now she faced another stop sign on that journey: Jeffrey Hammond. Was he telling the truth?

As she stood on the sidewalk beside the battered station wagon, her hand on the door handle, her body angled to turn away, in her mind she was already running to look for the nearest phone booth to call for help . . . while something else inside her shouted *no.*

She missed the comfort of an effortless decision. But she was also beginning to realize she had too little information to decide anything anyway. She stared a moment longer at the station wagon, trying to make up her mind. That was when her gaze settled on the black boxes on the floor of the passenger side. She frowned, climbed back into the vehicle, locked the door, and popped up the lid of the black case nearest the steering wheel.

What she saw surprised her: On top was a makeup tray containing a variety of foundations, eyebrow pencils, mascaras, creme sticks, creme liners, puffs, brushes, and sponges. A small compact contained two sets of contact lenses—one blue, the other green. Beginning to understand, she lifted the tray. Beneath were eyeglasses with uncorrected lenses, latex gloves, liquid latex, a wig, hair whitener, and the kind of skin-colored putty that actors used to reshape noses. There was also an empty bottle of thin glass wrapped in Styrofoam packing. Assuming this box was the killer's, it was obvious he had been a devotee of disguises and, by the range of possibilities, adept.

Nodding to herself, she opened the next box, which was long and narrow. It contained layers of foam rubber in which cavities had been carved. By their shapes, the holes were made to hold rifle parts, which made sense. It was intelligent to transport a sniping weapon broken down, protected, and out of sight. She picked up the rifle Hammond had been carrying. It looked as if it should fit into the hollows if it were disassembled. How interesting, she thought with a thin smile—this wasn't Hammond's car, and these weren't his black cases.

She closed the lid and opened the last box, which was rectangular and high. Inside, the graphic display brought back all the death and pain of the last two days: Here were more tools of the killer's bloody trade—three extremely sharp throwing knives with different blade lengths, clips of ammunition, vials of chemicals, a hypodermic plunger and needles, and other small items.

There was also a notepad with words scribbled on the top sheet in the Cyrillic alphabet. Among the words were numbers. Her pulse raced as she stared at the numbers of her house address. Then she saw Stephanie Smith's as well. The dead man knew not only where she lived . . . but where Stephanie had, too. How—and why—had he known Stephanie's address? No one could have known she had visited Stephanie last night . . . unless someone had followed her. Someone like the man she had just shot.

Uneasy and yet oddly relieved, she continued to explore the case until she found what looked like an electronic detonating cap and fuse. She studied it. Somehow it was important. If she could only figure out how and why. . . . She recalled the thin glass bottle in the first case and found it again. The cap fit perfectly, and she noticed a strange color to the glass. She studied it closely and saw the glass was filled with tiny metallic filaments that all ended in a kind of metal collar in the neck, exactly where the detonating cap and fuse fitted. It was a circuit. When the glass broke, an electronic signal would be sent to the cap, which would detonate.

When she was twelve years old, her father had taken her to a shooting range for the first time. Despite returning alone for months to practice, she had never become a good marksman. Still, it had kindled an interest in firearms and munitions that had paid off many years later in several legal cases. Combined with her undergraduate degree in world history, she knew one of the cheapest, most reliable, and easiest-to-make weapons of the Russian revolution—and in most wars since—was the Molotov cocktail. It was still a popular guerrilla weapon around the world.

The glass bottle . . . the detonating cap . . . plus gasoline siphoned from a car's tank was, in fact, a sophisticated Molotov cocktail. It could create an inferno that would turn a vehicle into a scorching cauldron, if the thrower's aim were good. Certainly it would set a little Ford like Stephanie's afire.

She nodded soberly to herself. The driver of this car had all the grisly accessories of a paid assassin. Of a man who could have planned and executed Stephanie's death. Plus he owned a sniper case, and whoever had fired at her from the woods across the street would logically have used a rifle not a pistol, since a rifle was more accurate at a long distance.

But assassins made good money. Why would he drive an old heap, unless he had stolen it to hide his identity. Which could explain the mysterious black van from last night. Probably stolen, too, and maybe by the owner of these three black boxes. If the man she killed was the one who had killed Yurimengri and had been stalking her all along, then Hammond might be telling the truth about her and about his being framed in West Virginia, too.

She closed both cases, thinking. She studied the traffic and the scattering of pedestrians strolling along the sun-dappled sidewalk. A flush crept up her throat as she mulled the situation. If she ran away, she would have no real way to find out what this was all about and why, and she might never be safe.

Yet, she was still unconvinced Hammond was innocent. Could she risk giving him the benefit of the doubt? Risk her life on her judgment in something unlike anything she had ever faced, a situation for which she had neither training nor experience?

She inhaled deeply, and her gaze settled again on the black boxes. As she thought about their contents, she knew her answer: Yes, she should give Hammond a chance, at least for a while. She glanced at her watch, suddenly worried. Where was he? He had been gone too long.

In the Watergate's cool, shadowed stairwell where Jeff Hammond's hand was reaching into his jacket for his pistol, the Russian's orders seemed to hang in the air: *"Halt, Hammond. . . . Take hand from jacket. . . ."* Unmoving, Hammond stared up at him, recognizing at once the long face and dark eyebrows of the man in the pickup who had been following him on the Beltway last year. But the information had little relevance now, because Hammond was the man in the middle, trapped between an armed man at the top of the cement steps and another at the bottom. The only advantage he had was gravity.

As traffic sounded out of sight on the street above, a single pedestrian walked past on the sidewalk and glanced casually down. Then hesitated and did a double take. In a panic, he ran just as Hammond pretended to follow orders. Displaying an innocent smile, he withdrew his hand from his jacket. "Sorry."

For a split second he saw the pair relax. That was when he tore down the steps. The one at the top recovered first and fired. *Pop!* The silenced shot exploded concrete chips beside Hammond's right leg. But before the man above could fire again, Jeff had slammed into the man at the bottom, regained his footing, and yanked the man around, making him a shield.

Unable to fire because he might hit his partner, the man at the top conceded, *"Ladno, zalupa."* Okay, dickhead. He ran down the steps, his gun trying to home in on Hammond.

At the same time, Beth Convey appeared at the top of the stairwell. For an instant, time seemed to freeze. Hammond was riveted by the cold face, the shadowed cheekbones, the furious eyes, all outlined by the tousled white-blond hair. His gaze connected with hers, and he had an abrupt sense something crucial about her had changed.

She stared back and decided she had been very wrong. Here he was in danger again, just as she had been. Defending himself, just as she'd had to do. Some inner voice demanded she throw aside her lawyerly caution. That she quit being so suspicious of everyone's motives. That she give up the idea she had to know and understand everything completely. That hard facts were always the answer. Still, she knew she believed him. From the beginning, she had sensed a core of integrity in him that she admired. Even more, that she had always wanted to trust him.

She plunged down the steps. The descending attacker must have heard her, because he turned and looked up. She took him by surprise, kicked his gun away and stiff-armed a karate punch to his head.

All this happened in seconds, but the man Hammond had turned into his shield took advantage of Hammond's inattention and slammed his arms up, broke his hold, and whirled around. Hammond reacted instantly. He rammed his fist into the man's ribs just as another silenced shot went *pop*. The man's eyes flashed open in astonishment, and he fell back against the metal railing, flipped over it, and landed hard on his face, unconscious.

A woman shouted from above, "Stop, Mr. Hammond. You, too, Ms. Convey. Now!" No Russian accent this time.

Higher up on the steps, Beth feinted as the second assailant rushed her again. Above them, Hammond saw the female "tourist" from the Kennedy Center, the one who had disappeared into the building when her male partner followed Hammond. She aimed her Walther coolly and steadily at Hammond and Beth Convey as she trotted down the steps.

Hammond grabbed for his Beretta, but the woman's pistol spat a silenced bullet whining past his ear. "Drop it!" she commanded. "Stop, Convey. I'll shoot."

She was only two steps above Convey. Hammond saw apprehension pucker Beth Convey's face. But it was gone instantly, and she smashed her foot into the second man's jaw, sending him sprawling against the gray concrete steps and into the legs of the woman. The woman fell.

Beth ripped away her Walther and turned the gun on her. In that instant, a powerful urge swept over her to shoot again. To kill. In the few seconds she hesitated, she was back again beside the station wagon, emptying Hammond's pistol into the sniper. She had lost control. She knew she'd had to fire, that he would have killed her if she had not. But she had gone too far: She had committed not a rational but a savage act by emptying her gun into him and enjoying the fact that she did it. That she could kill him. The strange new part of her that warred with the old liked violence, found volcanic release in it, and in that moment when life became death, it felt truly vital. Like a gnawing hunger, it demanded she kill again. Now.

She fought back a shudder as she resisted the voice. Whether it was from her new heart or some primitive part of her she had never explored no longer mattered. Nothing mattered right now but who she really was. And she was no killer. She refused to be. *This is it, heart. I'm not going to murder to satisfy you. You're going to have to learn to live with me, not the other way around.*

But as she gazed at the woman at her feet, who was staring up at the gun, Beth felt doubtful. It was a promise easy to make, but could she keep it? The problem was, she had to eliminate the danger posed by the woman, who was likely another killer.

Sweat streamed down the woman's cheeks, and a vein throbbed in her forehead. Her heavy-browed face was angry and . . . afraid. She had seen something in Beth that frightened her, just as the people at Renae Trucking had.

As the faint sound of a siren appeared in the distance, urgency filled

Beth. She had to decide—now. "You'll die. But it won't be by me." Beth kicked her in the jaw just hard enough. The woman's head snapped back, and she went limp, unconscious. Beth turned.

Hammond, who was frisking the man at the bottom of the steps, glanced up at her with compassion in his dark eyes. "You could've shot her. You wanted to."

His sympathy surprised her. "True. But now you can have all of them for questioning."

"That's thoughtful of you." He liked the way she had handled herself, and whatever inner demon had gripped her seemed gone, at least for the time being. She was a strange woman, much more complex than he was comfortable with. "So you decided not to jump ship. I figured you'd be gone by the time I got back, seeing as how you think I'm such a blood-fevered murderer."

"You aren't? Oh. Well, I'm glad you explained that."

"Right." He shot her a curious glance and moved on to go through the pockets of the others.

"You'll have to check out what I found in the station wagon in those black boxes," she continued. "Very interesting. A lot better than this haul." She was examining the pocket contents he had left on the steps. There were no driver's licenses, passports, credit cards, nothing to identify the downed attackers.

"We'll take the woman," he decided. "She's lightest. When she wakes up—"

That was when another silenced shot whined over their heads. He jerked with tension, and with one thick arm he knocked Convey over and dropped flat. He pointed his gun down toward the bottom landing, but there was no one in sight.

"Hey," she complained. She had landed in a fetal position and was lodged at the side of the staircase, all curves and strain. It renewed her aches and pains, and for a stunned second she felt paralyzed.

He glanced at her. Her face was furious. Worry swept through him as he studied the landing, waiting for the next shot. The unconscious woman moaned. The man at the foot of the steps twitched. The three could wake up any time. In the background, sirens were yelping closer. He grabbed the pistol of the man lying closest to them, which gave him two weapons. The other pistol, the one belonging to the attacker who was crumpled at the bottom of the stairs, was still down there, near his slack hand. The man twitched again, slowly regaining consciousness.

"We've got to get out of here," Hammond told her. "Dammit—"

"I know. You wanted the woman so we could ask questions."

He liked the sound of *we*. He spoke quickly, "Professionals on stake-outs like this tend to work in pairs. We have three here. Number four was out there somewhere. I managed to forget that point. And now he thinks he's nailed us. I'll hold him off." He threw keys at her. "Get the car. We'll have to forget about taking the woman with us."

She caught the key ring in midair. It stung her palm. She almost told him to get the damn car himself. Then she shrugged. "Be right back."

He nodded as he focused below, waiting for a weapon, a hand, anything to show. He heard her leave, small shoe-sounds on the cement steps. She had a light tread. But the man below must have heard, too. He rolled across in a blur, and two shots rang out—high, aimed not at him but at Convey.

Hammond shot back, missed. But at least he had stopped the man from firing more. When he glanced over his shoulder, Convey was gone, and there was no blood on the steps.

Just then another bullet sang past his ear. The unconscious man at the bottom of the steps had awakened. Fury torqued his grizzled face, and he held his gun in a shaking hand. A loaded gun in an unsteady hand could still be lethal, and there were now two men firing at Hammond. The woman and last man could wake up any second, too. These were not good odds.

As the man below squeezed off another bullet, Hammond ducked back. Convey must be in the car by now and on her way to pick him up—if she were coming at all. One way or the other, it was time to get out of there. He rose on one knee, returned rapid fire to pin them down, and bolted up the steps. As he reached the top, shots exploded furiously behind him, and he dove for the safety of the sidewalk. He rolled, came up on his feet running, and saw with relief that the station wagon was heading toward him.

Convey slowed as she reached him. He yanked open the door and jumped in as more shots exploded and pedestrians scrambled, screaming on the sidewalk. She stomped the accelerator, and the station wagon leaped ahead, nearly running down two panicked walkers, then skidded around a corner and straightened to roar onward.

She glanced at him. "Thought I wouldn't come, didn't you?"

He pushed himself up into a sitting position beside her. "It crossed my mind."

"You need to trust more." She bit back a smile.

Hammond grinned, relieved. "No kidding." He paused. "Something odd . . . I know the local Russian community well, but I've run into only one of those four, back when he was tailing me last spring. So where have they been? Who's been hiding them?"

The station wagon was filled with tension as she drove them south. Not wanting to attract any more attention, she stayed exactly at the speed limit. She scrutinized the street and sidewalks, waiting for someone to spot the rusty station wagon or Hammond's face. He wore his baseball cap low, but still he was recognizable to anyone who looked closely.

They talked. It was as if a wall had suddenly collapsed, and their words spilled on top of one another's.

"I told you about me," he said. "Now what about you? What were you doing at Meteor Express?"

"It's a long story."

"Begin at the beginning. I want to know everything."

She glanced sideways at him. "You may not believe this. I'm not certain I do. And, of course, I could be completely wrong. . . ." She described her death at the courthouse, her heart transplant, and all the apparent "cellular memories" that followed. "Do you recognize these lines: 'If you love, then love without reason. If you threaten, don't threaten in play?' "

He thought. "They're familiar. But I can't place them."

"Considering your background, I was hoping you'd know." She sighed. "My doctor said it was all nonsense."

"You don't believe it was caused by the medication and lifestyle changes?"

"Not anymore." She described dialing the phone number and the Russian voice at what turned out to be Meteor Express. "Do you know who could've answered?"

"Not offhand. That's why you went there that night?"

"Yes. I told you about finding Colonel Yurimengri." She turned the station wagon west onto Roosevelt bridge, heading into Virginia. The Friday afternoon traffic was moderate, not yet the high-tide time for Washington residents to flood out to Virginia's woodsy retreats or for tourists to jam into the capital for a weekend of plays, concerts, sightseeing, and cherry blossoms in radiant bloom.

He nodded, but his eyes never stopped moving as he watched for trouble. "You must've been surprised to find out his name really was Yurimengri. I'll go you one better: His friends called him Yuri." Beneath them, the Potomac River spread wide and metallic green, shining in the sunlight. A yacht sailed out from under the bridge, heading north, its white sails unfurled. In the cars and trucks near them, no one indicated any particular interest.

"Terrific. That just adds to my slide into believing the impossible— that I've inherited memories from my donor." She hesitated. "I can't believe I just said that."

It sounded like complete nonsense to him. "Seems pretty incredible."

"Agreed. But then lately we've changed our opinions about a lot of things we thought were true. Take genes, which we used to believe were static. Now we know they jump around. We used to think the ground was solid. Nope. It drifts in slow motion, and continents collide and divide. Species we'd listed as extinct are showing up in the oddest places. Remember when scientists pooh-poohed the idea viruses caused ulcers or heart disease? I used to think if I couldn't see it, taste it, or touch it, it didn't exist. Well, God got even with me. I'm learning a lot of lessons here."

He smiled. "I'd say you've had to rethink a few things."

"Oh, yes. One of the main reasons I exist is to learn humility."

"And have you?"

"Big time. Never again will I say never."

He glanced at her profile. She was watching the bridge traffic as she drove. Her face was tense, her eyes vigilant. Beneath it all was intelligence, a driving force that kept asking questions while remaining restless with the answers. Suddenly she turned and smiled at him. It was as if winter had turned into spring. She was beautiful. And he saw something new in her—a childlike curiosity and sense of amusement at herself that was enchanting.

"You're looking at me," she accused.

"I'm waiting for you to go on. So what happened after you reported Colonel Yurimengri's murder to the Virginia police?"

She told him about returning to the law firm too late for her meeting with Michelle Philmalee.

"Back up," he said. "Who's she?"

"Michelle was the client I was representing in the courthouse when I had the heart attack. Then while I had to stay home for a year to recover, the firm's managing partner assigned another attorney to represent her. That was Phil Stageman, the man you saw at my house. They fell in love. . . . "

"That guy who acted like he owned you was the boyfriend of both of you?"

"Sequentially. You have a problem with that?"

He chuckled. "No. But I'll bet you did. Michelle, too."

"It's a common mistake women make, confusing good looks and brains with other human characteristics. Men never make that mistake. Their big one is assuming legs and breasts are the foundation for a lasting relationship."

"Touché."

She started to smile. Instead her throat tightened. "There's a police car behind us."

Hammond dipped his head and looked back under the bill of his Orioles cap. "He's staring at us."

"Great." They were approaching the end of the bridge, where there were several routes from which to choose. "I've got an idea." Since they were in one of the middle lanes, the police would not know for certain which route she would take. Around them traffic was slowing in response to the sight of the police. "He's still with us. What's he waiting for? Why doesn't he turn on his beacons?"

Hammond was worried. "Ask, and ye shall receive. He's just flicked them on."

Pressure built in the station wagon as the police car closed in, its lights flashing. Around them, other drivers stared. Hammond's rugged face was taut. Beth felt herself start to squirm, and then her cool composure returned. It was almost as if she were going into court again with a losing case. Or stuck at a negotiating table with the worst of the lawless, domineering oligarchs. She knew how to do this, she told herself. She could get them out of this.

27

As the police car's siren screamed, Beth swung the station wagon to the right at the last minute between a pickup and a sedan, cutting so close she could feel their drafts pull at the wagon. Then before the police car could follow, she swerved the wagon off the bridge and took the exit onto Route 50 toward the Iwo Jima war memorial. She pulled in between two pickups and dropped her speed. With luck, the police car had hurtled onward toward Route 66.

Hammond was holding on to his door handle. She glanced at him once, saw his face had paled. He growled, "Mario Andretti . . . meet Beth Convey." He looked back. "He's still there, but he's a good quarter-mile behind."

Grimly she angled the wagon off into Rosslyn's busy streets, rushed ahead through intersections, until at last she rounded a corner, and another, and spun back onto Route 50, again heading west, away from downtown Washington.

Hammond stretched his arm across the seat top and turned again, staring back soberly. "The cop's gone. God knows where he is, but you can bet he's alerted the Virginia police. Where did you learn to drive like that?"

"I'm not sure. Maybe I've always known."

He took a deep breath. "We've got to get rid of this station wagon. Every policeman from Richmond to Baltimore's going to be looking for us."

"We could rent or borrow one."

"Can't borrow. Not a good plan." He described the people who had
been watching his condo, the *Post,* and the Kennedy Center, where his
uncle worked. "My guess is our friends and usual acquaintances are all
being watched. We don't want to put them in danger. And renting is
asking for trouble, too. We'd have to use a credit card. That's too easy
to trace, not only by law enforcement but by anyone with the connections that the people we're up against seem to have."

She was silent. Uneasiness swept through her. "I knew they were
killers. But I had no idea they had such organization."

"Get used to it," he said roughly. "We're not going to be safe anywhere. If we live to see daybreak, we'll have accomplished something."
Mentally he ran through his short list of friends and relatives, trying to
find one he thought might be safe. He considered his fellow reporters
at the *Post,* but the few he was close to would be watched. As for his
former girlfriends, no way. And of course, unless he wanted to give up,
the FBI and Bobby Kelsey were out. The more he weighed how few op-
tions he had, the more disturbed he was. This was payback for the isolation of all the years of his undercover life.

As they continued west on Route 50, she told him about quitting the
law firm, returning home to sort out her life, and her decision to visit
Stephanie Smith for information about cellular memory.

When she reached the part where Stephanie's car went out of control and burst into flames, her voice broke. "Sorry."

"Must have been awful for you. It's amazing you survived."

She nodded silently.

"One thing you've got to understand, Beth. May I call you Beth?
Convey seems a little ridiculous now, although you may prefer *Ms.* Convey. What do you think?"

She was taken aback. He was so formal. "Beth's fine."

"Good. Call me Jeff. Now that we've got that out of the way, let me
give you a tip. I told you that you didn't know what you'd gotten into,
and the truth is I don't know, either. Whoever's behind all this seems to
be a lot better than the usual incompetents who break the law. You
were damn lucky to get out alive. You can't feel responsible for Dr.
Smith's death. The killers are responsible."

"I tell myself that."

It was his turn to nod. The space between knowing intellectually and
convincing your emotions could seem insurmountable. So he simply
said, "Go on."

She recounted her return home and her decision to try to find the
address from her nightmares.

"And did you?"

"Yes, unfortunately. Or fortunately, depending on your view." She told him about breaking into Alexei Berianov's house in Chevy Chase, searching his office, discovering his utility bills, and finding newspaper and magazine clippings.

"A bill from a company in *Stone Point?*" Jeff was excited. With one big hand he grabbed her shoulder bag from the backseat. "I want to read what you found."

"Wish you could, but the bill and clipping are gone." She described the stranger who had attacked and tied her up. "When I awoke, he'd loosened my ropes, and I was able to get free easily. But apparently he took the clipping and bill with him."

"Odd. Tell me about them."

As they sped past the Seven Corners shopping mall with its big Home Depot and Best Buy stores, she described the bill from the tile company in Stone Point. "It was addressed to someone named Caleb Bates."

"Bates owns a big piece of property above Stone Point. Runs a hunt club there." His broad face was intent, a study of fissures and planes. "Describe the ad."

"It was publicizing a dairy farm for sale near Gettysburg. There was a photo of a lovely old colonial-style mansion." She repeated the address.

He thought about everything he had heard about Caleb Bates's hunt club, about the extensive fencing that had caused locals to speculate about Bates's wealth, and about the hunters who had visited the club over the past three years. He had heard they were close-mouthed and kept to themselves. But that could describe the locals, too.

That was when a fundamental question occurred to him: If it were a hunt club, why the fencing? Bates and his fellow sportsmen would surely have wanted game that could roam freely, unless they had something to hide, like exotic animals being kept for special shoots. But he doubted that. If exotic game was being kept so close to town, someone would have known, and he would have heard the gossip.

No, there had to be some other reason for the fencing. And now, because the clipping was found in Berianov's house, there was a connection between Bates and Berianov. That alone was important.

He decided, "I need to go there."

"Where? West Virginia? Are you crazy? You're wanted for murder in West Virginia."

"No. To Pennsylvania. It's our best lead."

"Makes sense."

He watched her as she slowed the station wagon to pass through historic Falls Church, notorious for its speed traps. Some kind of new emotion swept over him. He had seen her for the first time only two days ago, and he really wanted to get to know her better. He liked her brain, her looks, her determination. In fact, he liked her so much he was willing to overlook her being a lawyer. He was glad he had saved her, and he was glad they were now riding side by side in this ramshackle car, surveying for trouble. Although he could do without the trouble.

But he refused to put her at risk again. It was too distracting. Too hard on him. "Do you have someplace you can stay while I check out the dairy farm? Someplace safe, where no one would think to look?"

She frowned. "What are you talking about? No way are you going to do anything or go anywhere without me. I've gone through hell to get this far. I'm the one who told you about the clippings. If you think it's worth going to Pennsylvania because of them, I'm going, too. Remember, I'm the one in the driver's seat. Where I come from in California, we call that wheel control."

He was not amused. His voice was harsh. "It's a lunatic idea. You're not trained. You could get yourself killed. And me, too."

That shook her. She could not be responsible for any more deaths. But at the same time, there was no way she would back out. She had to see it through, for Colonel Yurimengri, Stephanie Smith, and her donor, Mikhail Ogust.

But also for herself. "I can't go back." Her gaze was locked on the highway ahead. "Take care of yourself. Don't worry about me. I won't ask for help, and don't you volunteer it. If I don't have what it takes to be your partner, so be it."

"Wonderful. Just wonderful. That makes everything okay. I'll let you go down like roadkill." He waited for her to say something, but she did not even bother to look at him. She meant it. He shook his head in disgust. Like hell he was going to let her die.

She turned on the radio. The announcer had just finished sports scores and was giving a preview of the coming top-of-the-news stories. The big piece was no surprise—the Russian president was expected to touch down shortly at Andrews Air Force Base. The White House was issuing bulletins keeping the press up to date about President Stevens's activities, his plans, and his agenda with Vladimir Putin.

Jeff shrugged and reached down to open one of the black boxes at his feet. He whistled when he saw it held makeup and disguise materials. "This could be useful."

As the newscast finally began, he broke down the sniper rifle and fitted it into the second box. When the announcer repeated the news story about his being sought for the West Virginia murders, he winced but said nothing. Then he opened the third box, the one that held weapons and their accessories.

"This guy was serious. Makes me a tad unhappy thinking about his replacement. Might be someone even better. And you can bet there'll be a replacement."

"Thanks. That cheers me enormously." She looked worriedly around. The traffic was growing heavier.

He closed the weapons box. "Have you checked the one in back?"

"Not yet. Why should I have all the fun?"

He gave a small smile. "Very thoughtful of you."

She gazed across at him, and they exchanged a quick look. She rolled up her eyes and shook her head. As she concentrated on the road again, Jeff reached into the rear, where the sniper had laid down the back seat, creating a flatbed. As he dragged the box toward him, the news loop on the radio finished.

She said with relief, "At least they don't have anything about me yet."

He opened the box and peeled back layers of foam rubber. He whistled again. "Listening devices. Tracking devices. A demodulator. It's like a Saks Fifth Avenue of crime and eavesdropping equipment in here."

"Yes, the fellow liked his tools." She gazed suspiciously at the traffic. They were approaching Tyson's Corner with its modern skyline of shops and offices set among the rolling woodland landscape of northern Virginia. She pulled into a parking lot.

He looked up and scowled. "Why are we stopping?"

"I'm going to get us a different car."

"*Where* are you getting us another car?" And then he saw handsome brass lettering—THE PHILMALEE GROUP—on the side of a twenty-story, glass-and-brick building. He said, "Michelle Philmalee? You're going to ask her? I don't think so." He glared at Beth as she drove into the parking lot.

"She said last night she owed me big, and I'm going to take her up on it." Beth parked the station wagon under overhanging branches in a distant corner of the lot. "It wasn't on the news that I killed a man, so she doesn't know the police are looking for me. No one—the police, the killers—will think to find me through her. And there's even less reason to connect you two to each other. We have to take advantage of the situation while we can. She'll loan me a car in a heartbeat."

"I'd rather steal one. You're opening us up to being stopped or caught."

"Where else are we going to get a car?"

"Thievery makes sense to me."

"Nonsense. It's broad daylight. Everyone watches for car thieves. I can just see you hot-wiring one and some alarm going off. Which is probably why you haven't suggested it before. Or we can keep the station wagon, but it stands out like a bruised thumb. We managed to escape the first cop who found us, but we might not be so lucky next time. Michelle's our best bet. The company keeps a raft of cars here."

"I don't like your going in alone."

"Don't worry. Phil won't be here. I'll be safe."

"That's not what's worrying me. You can handle Phil."

She unlocked her door. "Then what's your problem?"

He sighed. The answer was her. *She* was his problem. But he just said, "Are you going to sit here all day? Get going."

She smiled into his big face. "I'll miss you, too." She headed toward the Philmalee Group headquarters.

Michelle Philmalee's company had projects all over the United States and in Eastern Europe, and she stayed informed about every one. As she sat there at her desk trying to work through the stacks of papers, she thought about the past. She had risen from small-town schoolteacher to head a Forbes 500 company, and she had the scars and trophies to prove it. She liked to say she savored both. But despite all the victories, and the skyrocketing success of the Group since she had taken control of it after the divorce, she sat there in her haute couture suit and polished red fingernails and felt an ache in her throat that would not go away.

She had taken an antihistamine at bedtime and another this morning. She had gargled a dozen times. She had even seen her internist this morning, but he had pronounced her throat fine. Still, it hurt like hell. A tear seeped from the corner of her eye.

She hurried from her desk into her private bath. Her office suite was opulent, from the hand-knotted Aubusson rug to the American Impressionist originals on the wall, and she had a bathroom just as elegant. It was lined with beveled mirrors, trimmed with ebony, and decorated with alabaster statues in recessed nooks.

She snatched up a tissue, leaned over the sink's gold fixtures, and stared into the mirror at her slender face with its hidden lines and wrinkles. She dabbed the tear with a tissue. She was getting old. She saw it beneath the Chanel makeup. Worse, she was alone. Her ex-husband, that bastard Joel, had been no good, but he was at least a warm body. Her psychiatrist at the time had suggested, however, that to remain in a marriage in which the warm body could be counted upon to beat her regularly might be flawed thinking.

Still, there were payoffs. Her two sons, for instance. She loved them. And it was because of Joel that she had learned to wear makeup and dress well. Makeup could not hide swelling, but it was very good for bruises. And expensive clothing was a fine way to distract clients and competitors from the sadness in one's eyes.

In the end, the reason she had divorced the abusive SOB was because he had tried to cut her out of the business she had damn well built. Then she had rebounded and gotten involved with Phil Stageman, whose idea of a good time was counting her money. It had been amusing to sleep with a man who was young enough to be her son, and he had paid off in other ways, too. She had enjoyed the envy of her female acquaintances and employees. Still, no amount of distracting muscle and fancy manners could hide his greed.

A more intelligent and sensitive man would have seen she was connected to her business more than she was to him. But then, she was afraid a more intelligent and sensitive man would not have been interested in her. Phil Stageman was a handsome fool. Which, in the end, made her a fool, too, at least when it came to men, and she could no longer hide the fact from herself.

She smiled wearily. She was alone again, and lonely. Pressing her fingers to her throat, she tried to stop the ache as she returned to her desk. She made herself work until her secretary buzzed to announce that Zach Housley from Edwards & Bonnett was on the line. She debated whether to talk with him. He had badly mishandled the Beth Convey affair by underestimating Beth. She and Beth had the same focused, hard-headed approach to business. That was why Beth usually won, and in the rare case in which she lost, she walked away slowly, still looking over her shoulder for a way to salvage victory.

Michelle had expected Beth to phone by now. It was not like her. She was Beth's ticket to partnership at Edwards & Bonnett, and she had been anticipating some pleasure in Beth's excitement.

She sighed and punched the lighted button on her phone console. "Hello, Zach. Tilaina says you have something important to say about Beth." Maybe Beth had already told Zach she would resume representing Michelle.

But that was not it. Not it at all. Michelle listened in surprise as Zach said, "The police were just here." His deep voice was breathless with shock and excitement.

"And?" she prompted. The ache in her throat worsened.

He talked for five minutes. Murdered an unarmed tourist in George-town. Conflicting stories from witnesses. Escaped in the company of a man sought for a double murder in West Virginia. The police want her. On and on . . . Michelle not wanting to believe a word of it, not a word.

28

The afternoon sun radiated with an unaccustomed spring heat as Beth stepped away from the row of shade trees where she had parked the station wagon in the Philmalee parking lot. Clasping her shoulder bag close, she hurried toward the glass-and-brick headquarters with its striking modern architecture. A few executives entered and left through the big glass doors, all dressed impeccably. None did more than glance at her.

She pushed in through the front door and nodded at the security guard. He watched as she headed past the life-size oil painting of Michelle and went straight to the receptionist, who sat behind a granite barricade at a glass-block desk. The building had good security and a staff that had been trained to protect its executives from the annoyances of nonbusiness life.

"Ms. Convey?" The receptionist was not certain she recognized Beth without her standard business suit.

"The same. I'd like to see Mrs. Philmalee."

She was not on the appointment list, so the receptionist called upstairs. The answer came immediately to send her up, that Mrs. Philmalee was waiting. The receptionist handed Beth a badge, which she snapped onto her black cardigan. Too polite to stare at Beth's messy appearance, the woman ducked her head, trying to hide her disapproval.

Concerned for a moment that she had been followed, Beth surveyed the lobby. But there was nothing unusual amid the stark modern furniture and floor sculpture. She entered the elevator, which lifted her silently to the twentieth floor, and stepped out into an atrium foyer full of plants. Floor-to-ceiling windows looked out onto Virginia's undulating green hills. The air smelled of moss and flowers, scents that at another time would have seemed fresh and inviting, but not today. Today they cloyed and seemed oppressive.

And Michelle Philmalee was striding impatiently toward her from the corridor, her hands extended. "Beth, my dear. How glad I am to see you." Her black hair was smoothed back under a narrow black velvet headband. In a navy Yves St. Laurent suit and Gucci stiletto heels, she was put together impeccably. With a sweep of her shrewd gaze, she took in that Beth was not, but she gave no indication of it. "Come back into my office. We have much to talk about."

"I can't stay—"

"Of course you can, dear. In fact, I insist." The smile on Michelle's face stiffened. "Come along now."

Michelle's office was quiet and had the air of an art gallery with its original Impressionist paintings and sleek designer furniture. There was a fireplace in the corner, with love seats on either side. A cymbidium orchid stood on the coffee table between the love seats. When Michelle gestured to the closest one, Beth sat and put her bag at her feet.

Michelle settled on the other end and crossed her ankles. She stared hard at Beth.

"What is it?" Beth felt as if she were under a microscope.

"I'm trying to decide whether you look like a killer. I must say, dear, you have the appearance today of something wild and dangerous. Certainly an ape man would be tempted to drag you home to his cave. If I sniff your fingers, will I smell gunpowder?"

"Oh, no," Beth breathed. "How did you—?"

"What if I told you the police were on their way?" Michelle's black eyes were hard as agates.

Beth jumped up. "Then I'd have to leave."

"I don't think so. My security would stop you. They're very well trained, you know. I spent a fortune making sure they were. I learned that sort of thing from Joel. Would you like a cup of coffee?"

Beth studied her, nodded to herself, and settled back onto the sofa. "You have no intention of calling anyone, at least for a while. And the police don't know I'm here. You're curious, aren't you? You want to know what's going on more than you're afraid of me. You're a bitch, Michelle."

Michelle winked and rang a bell that was sitting next to the orchid.

"I think coffee's in order. I told Tilaina to brew a fresh pot. French roast. Something a little stronger than I usually drink. As for being afraid"—she chuckled—"don't forget I was married to Joel Philmalee for thirty years. If he didn't scare me—and, yes, I know I should've left him decades ago—I really doubt you would. Do you have a pistol in that big purse of yours?"

Beth rolled her eyes up. "Michelle, you need a life."

As a tap sounded on the door, Michelle said sweetly, "I have a life. I'm just not particularly fond of it right now." She turned to the door. "Bring the coffee in, Tilaina."

They said nothing as Michelle's secretary carried in a heavy sterling tray with a matching coffee service. She was a large woman in a serviceable serge suit and Hush Puppies, no competition for the dainty fashion plate that her boss was, which was, no doubt, one of the reasons Michelle had hired her.

"I'll pour. Thank you, Tilaina." Michelle's hands were folded neatly in her lap. As soon as Tilaina murmured her thanks and turned toward the door, Michelle poured coffee into two Haviland cups.

"There's no way I can stay," Beth insisted. "But I promise to fill you in when things settle down. Right now I need to borrow one of your cars."

"Cream? Sugar?"

"Michelle!"

"Oh, very well." Michelle left the steaming cups on the coffee table. "I'll settle for a look at your pistol."

Beth glared. She made no move for her purse.

"You have one, don't you?" For the first time, Michelle looked uncertain. "Did you really murder that poor tourist?"

Beth thought quickly. "It wasn't on the news, so someone must've called you. My office? Was it Zach? He knows you fired Phil, and then Phil was waiting for me at my house. . . . It was self-defense, Michelle. The man was no tourist. He was a professional assassin. He'd already taken several shots at me. If I hadn't fired, he would've killed me."

Michelle leaned forward. "But so many bullets. I understand he looked like Swiss cheese. By the way, Zach's congratulating himself for discharging you. He doesn't approve of keeping on attorneys after all-points bulletins have been issued against them."

"That knuckle-dragger didn't discharge me, I quit!"

"I know, dear. I was filled in on all the fireworks by Joleen. She does like to gossip, doesn't she?" She picked up her cup and sipped coffee. "Besides, I know you'd never murder anyone."

Suddenly weary, Beth closed her eyes. The whole horrible scene flashed through her mind. The killer running out from behind the station wagon . . . his gun aimed at her . . . her squeezing, squeezing the trigger . . . and then his flying back like a broken doll, blood pouring from wounds. She inhaled. She had to stop dwelling on it. She had gone too far, but on the other hand, if she had not fired she would surely be dead herself.

She opened her eyes and scowled. "I don't have time for this. Make up your mind, Michelle. If you don't believe I could murder someone in cold blood, are you going to loan me a car or not?"

Michelle cocked her manicured head, considering. She understood self-interest. It had fueled all her life. If she helped Beth, she could be arrested for aiding and abetting a fugitive. Maybe for being an accessory after the fact. From her days as a high school teacher, she remembered what Publilius Syrus, the Latin writer, had said: *He who helps the guilty shares the crime.* She was not sure, but whatever the charges would be, they would be bad for business, far worse than if it were public knowledge that she had been a battered wife. At her high-powered social and business levels, some things simply were not aired. She could see the headline on the cover of *BusinessWeek* or *Forbes* now: MAGNATE CAUGHT AIDING KILLER'S ESCAPE.

But she had always liked Beth, and she had felt guilty for hiding her relationship with Phil from her, and then acting like such a shit when Beth told them she had forgotten the evidence about HanTech at home. Beth had proved her wrong, not only because she really had had the list of owners, but because she had been big enough to hand it over, even though she had every reason not to.

Michelle felt odd. Something solemn and good seemed to blow through her. Unconsciously she raised her hand to her throat, feeling for the pain that had lodged there when she told Phil he would have to agree to bringing Beth back as her primary attorney or leave, and he had left. It was still there, aching.

She folded her hands in her lap. "My staff obviously knows you're in the building. That could be a problem. But Zach phoned not long ago, so I think I can safely pretend I received his call after you'd left. Too late to inform anyone, so why bother. But I don't think it's wise to give you a company car. They have so little speed, and besides it would mark you because of the logo on the doors."

Beth, who had been sitting stiff and angry, relaxed a fraction. Still wary, she asked, "You have another idea?"

"Of course, my dear. Ideas are my specialty." She stood and walked to her desk. "Take mine. It's a nice Ferrari. Excellent power and traction. But you have to promise—if you get out of this mess, you'll take me back. You'll represent me again. Will you promise?"

Beth stared. "I don't know, Michelle. I honestly don't know what I'm going to do. I might quit practicing altogether."

"You can't! I need you! Besides, it's not in your nature. You'd be bored silly. Remember, you *like* the law."

"Thanks. Let's leave it this way . . . if I return to it, you'll be my first client."

Michelle frowned and handed her keys across the desk. "I'd hoped for more of a commitment. Oh, well. In any case, you have to tell me what's really happened to you when this is over. Everything. I can't stand not knowing. But I can wait until your arrest is less imminent." She dialed her phone and spoke into it. "Dwight, bring up my Ferrari and leave it by my private entrance." As she set the phone back in its cradle, she smiled conspiratorially. "So where are you going—Madagascar? San Martin? Maybe Costa Rica? I hear they won't extradite anyone."

"Nothing so romantic or remote. And I can't tell you. That's for both our protection." As Beth met her in the middle of the room, gloom swept through her. Yes, there was the issue of survival. *If you get out of this mess . . .* "I'll be happy to fill you in over a couple of glasses of wine eventually. My treat."

"I'd like that." She was staring at Beth. "You're shaking. What's wrong, dear? Are you really that afraid?"

It hit her like a lightning bolt. "It's nothing. I'll eat and take my meds and the shaking will stop."

Michelle hesitated. "Well, that's not so bad. Come along. What's the advantage of owning a company if you can't have all the comforts?" She marched toward a door across the room. "Come here, dear. Food. This will be less dangerous than stopping at some horrible little fast-food joint."

Beth joined her at the doorway. "You're right." Inside was a gleaming kitchenette.

"Tilaina keeps my refrigerator stocked." There were bottles of Perrier, two French champagnes, fruit, pâté, crackers, and green apples. "Not particularly well-balanced, but perhaps it will do."

"Yes, thanks. It's great." Beth smiled as Michelle packed food into her shoulder bag. "No champagne. This isn't exactly a bubbly moment."

Michelle chuckled as Beth closed the bag, and they walked together back into her office and toward the door.

"How can I thank you, Michelle?"

The older woman reached for her throat again. The strange pain was gone. "Thank me? You may not believe this, but I really am sorry for what I did to you. I owe you a great deal. Just come back alive." Her small face spread in a wide smile. "We have a great deal of business to do together."

29

On his verandah in Pennsylvania, Caleb Bates stood up and strode away from the table, his spartan lunch finished. Cows grazed on the green hillsides behind his mansion and to his left, a farmhand touched up the paint on one of the white posts that framed the entry gates. With the verdant pastures and big, sturdy trees, it was a quiet bucolic scene to anyone from the outside. Still, as he headed into the colonial mansion, Bates felt his blood pulse with excitement. The Keepers were on the move at last toward their rendezvous with history, and there was much left to be done.

Fully outfitted, their assignments memorized, the fanatics had been trickling out of the farm all morning in pickups and on foot. Some caught the bus a mile down the road. Others rode bicycles. It was one thing to arrive en masse, hidden by the night, in a rural area. But daylight hid few secrets, particularly in a metropolis. Eventually all would reach their next-to-last stop singly and in small groups—one of two supply depots just outside downtown Washington, where they would have slipped quietly into place by midnight.

As he wandered through the mansion's rooms, he felt an acute tension between KGB general Alexei Berianov and whatever he had become as American nationalist colonel Caleb Bates. It was unsettling, as if neither of the two men was quite the same as he had been. Even more, as if he, Alexei Berianov, had somehow been corrupted. Bates was the kind of man Berianov had spent his lifetime trying to defang and then destroy. And yet. . . . He shook his head angrily. Bates was essential to his plan. But soon it would be over, and Bates could vanish into the same ether from which he had been created. Berianov was impatient for tomorrow. Eager for the world to—

His cell phone vibrated against his padded chest. He resisted the impulse to pull it out immediately. Instead, he headed upstairs, nodding to one of the Keepers who passed through the foyer on her way to the kitchen. In his second-floor office, where he was alone, he answered the phone. "Yes?"

It was Ivan Vok. Unlike Berianov and Fedorov, the burly killer had never lost his accent when he spoke English, perhaps because for him it was a third language, after his native Kazakh and Russian.

Vok rumbled unhappily, "Is not good news, Alexei."

Berianov answered in Russian. "Fedorov didn't get her?" Beth Convey was turning into a far bigger problem than he had ever imagined.

Vok switched to Russian: "The first thing I saw was Jeff Hammond and Beth Convey walking around the corner from her house, and Fedorov arriving in a station wagon nearby. There was a gun fight with goddamn witnesses, and I was too far away to stop her from shooting or to kill her myself. By the time I was close enough, it was all over." He sighed heavily. "I grabbed Fedorov's gun and shoved fake tourist papers and a billfold into his pocket. What else was I to do, Alexei? It's a good thing I always carry those drops when I'm on a job."

As he listened to Vok describe how he had decided to check on Fedorov's success and instead had witnessed his death at Beth Convey's hands, a vise seemed to grip Berianov's chest. "The witnesses will tell the police she killed him, but from what you say a lot of people could have seen him shoot first. They'll fill in the cops on that, too."

"Yes. It's lousy. Then as soon as I left there, I sent out word to all of our other people to find them, okay? Finally one of them called to say Hammond and Convey were trapped at the Watergate." Vok muttered something in Kazakh. "But they got away there, too. Today, everyone's an amateur!"

Berianov shook his head, worried. But perhaps it was not all bad. "At least the police will be looking for her now, too. That increases the pressure. She'll make a mistake. She doesn't know how to run, and that will help us locate her."

"She's got help now." Vok made a disgusted sound. "She went off with that Hammond *styervo.*"

The vise on Berianov's chest tightened. "Tell me."

Berianov had been standing beside his desk, his fist balled as he leaned on it. He straightened and moved to the French doors that opened to the outdoor gallery. He made himself look out onto his pastoral farm. His head throbbed with anger, but he fought down any sense of weakening. The future demanded he succeed, that they all succeed. He noted four Keepers leaving for their assignments, dressed in ordinary street clothes. That was what this aggravating exercise was all about. *Tomorrow.*

He said, "Tell our people there'll be an award for the one who finds them. I'll make up a story so the Keepers will look for them, too. If you can, I want you to finish Hammond and this Convey person yourself. I don't care how you do it, Ivan Ivanovich. Don't worry any longer about making it look nice or like an accident. Just kill them. Quickly."

He heard a rare note of pleasure in Ivan Vok's gruff voice. "I planted a tracking device in the station wagon, Alexei. That's how I found Fedorov. Convey and Hammond are in the same station wagon now." He chuckled. "Don't worry."

In a large, airy living room in southern Maryland, the smile disappeared from Ivan Vok's face as he pressed the OFF button on his cell phone and made a series of calls to his people. He did not pace or wave his arms as he gave orders. He was at General Berianov's secret headquarters, a luxury apartment building with patrolling security guards and a view of Maryland that included portions of the District itself.

Burly and heavily muscled, Vok headed for the glossy wood table that doubled as a desk. His blood was coursing excitedly, while his mind worked. He had a real *job* again. He was a quiet man who seldom spoke unless asked a direct question. Some believed that was because he was stupid and had nothing to say, but the opposite was true. Vok was intelligent, cunning, and so tight-lipped he had been the most trusted of all the KGB's assassins, until the tragic end of all he had valued. Until his beloved KGB was eviscerated, to be reborn as the Federal Security Service, the FSB.

He came by his lethal talents naturally. His mother was Kazakh, descended from warrior Turks conquered by Genghis Khan and his clan, while his father was a European Russian. Vok inherited his mother's Mongol features but his father's bloody ways. There was a saying in Kazakh: "If you are friends with a Russian, take care to have an ax with you."

His parents' union was tumultuous, born on the bruising infinity of the Central Asian steppe where the land stretched as flat as a tabletop. Vok grew up near a city the Russians renamed Tselinograd, but which local Kazakhs still ominously called Aqmola—"white tomb." That was where his father coolly killed his mother in their domed yurt, while their dinner of bread, sour cream, sausage, and *koumiss*—fermented mare's milk—lay waiting on the low table. She had been desperate to stay on this wind-swept plain she claimed fed her soul, while he had announced they were leaving.

Ivan had been fond of his mother, but not that fond. For him, her death meant liberation. His father moved him and his younger brothers to Moscow, where the older Vok had been offered promotion by the KGB in recognition of his deadly gifts. Ten years later, young Vok, who had committed several felonies as a teenager but was never caught, followed into service. He had his father's technical expertise and his mother's passion. He quickly distinguished himself with a series of cold-blooded successes.

Honored, medaled, and respected, he was soon promoted so high that his father worked under him until his death. Then in 1991, Vok's world collapsed. The coup to topple Gorbachev and return the Soviet Union to its former honor failed.

After that, he and many of his comrades were fired. The FSB retained mostly those who had been on the lowest rungs and therefore were less rooted in the past and more pliable. Unemployed, Vok continued to live in Moscow on a small pension that often went unpaid, growing more frustrated. He knew he was going to have to join the self-serving "democrats" who were ruining his country, or he would end up at the bottom of the pig trough as some rich oligarch's bodyguard. Russia had become a dishonorable place. Even now, the pain of it ate at him like acid.

Then Alexei Berianov gave him a second chance by inviting him to work secretly in the United States, and he went eagerly. He quickly adapted to American transportation, food, and culture. After all, he had spent most of his adult life traveling the world on assignment. He had often been in the United States.

There were a hundred ways to kill, and he knew each one intimately. Enjoyed each one. That was a language everyone understood. Now his blood was up. Every nerve felt alive. He sat with his notepad, a squat, massive figure with a Mongol face, and made phone calls.

As soon as he finished, he strode into the biggest of the three bedrooms, which had been converted into a technical lab to create counterfeit people—everything from false identities to disguises, including complete face masks. Once in the old Cold War days, when two of his killers had been required to go into South Africa under cover, his artist had created masks so believable that the two white assassins had been transformed into black revolutionaries who sat and chatted so convincingly with an American diplomat in a purring U.S. Embassy limousine in Johannesburg that he had personally escorted them into the secure building, where they completed their mission. Hollywood had nothing over Kremlin techniques.

Vok entered the walk-in closet and flipped on the overhead light. Under protective plastic hung two rows of authentic costumes in a variety of sizes—soldiers' and policemen's uniforms, priests' habits, coveralls for drivers of delivery trucks, pricey business suits, party dresses, and an array of casual clothes suitable for tourists in all seasons.

He would not disappoint Alexei Berianov. Moreover, he would not disappoint himself. He had set his people in motion. Beth Convey and Jeff Hammond would be found soon, and they would never know who had killed them. In his mind, they were already dead.

30

In Tyson's Corner, Virginia, Beth and Jeff loaded the sniper's black cases into the Ferrari, and Jeff took the wheel. As he drove onto the Beltway heading north, she passed him slices of green apple and crackers topped with soft brie cheese. She ate, too, and took her meds with long gulps of Michelle's Perrier.

It was mid-afternoon, and white clouds hung low in the sky, blocking the spring sun. The fast red sports car sliced along the shadowed highway, slowing as the Friday afternoon traffic grew more thick. They had seen several patrol cars, but none had shown interest in them or their new vehicle. They were almost beginning to feel safe.

"This car's a beauty," Jeff decided. "Handles like a dream."

"If the circumstances were better, I'd look forward to driving it, too."

He smiled and nodded while she studied him—the straight forehead, the dark brown hair tucked up under his cap. His nose was aquiline, faintly curved, in perfect balance with his solid jaw. He had strong features—dense eyebrows, heavy black lashes, big ears, and a generous mouth with a lot of nice white teeth. He might not be cover-boy material, but he was someone you definitely would enjoy looking at first thing in the morning. Ruggedly handsome, she decided.

"A question for you," she said. "You don't act like any journalist I ever met. Come on, Jeff, level with me. You're a good reporter, but you're also something else. You tell me you saved me twice, and I believe you. But ordinary reporters aren't trained to go around saving people who are being shot at. When you charged after the killer in the station wagon, you were aggressive, not some novice just off the newsprint farm. And yes, I know you used to be with the FBI. But according to the news, that was a long time ago. Amazing you've kept your skills so well-honed. It all makes me wonder . . . are you still with them?"

His expression remained unchanged. "You have a hell of an imagination, Convey. And you're exaggerating my skills. I got mad, and I got lucky."

"Nonsense. I saw you. And don't forget one major point. You've got a Beretta. That's not something regular people—even investigative journalists—carry concealed in a shoulder holster. It's a serious weapon with serious purposes. You're still with the FBI, aren't you, Jeff?"

He frowned. Then he sighed. "Just one more reason to hate lawyers. I suppose I'd end up telling you anyway, since your life's on the line as well." He paused. It was difficult for him, after so many years of secrecy. "I was on the team that debriefed many of the defectors, and that's how I ended up going undercover."

He described the influx of Soviets seeking asylum in the United States in exchange for information, and how at first the CIA and the FBI had welcomed them. Then with the stream of bodies and the repetitive information and the expense of it all, both agencies began to see little reason to continue to take them in.

"So you knew Ogust, Berianov, and Yurimengri a lot better than you let on."

"In some ways, yes. Berianov came out of the KGB's Department Eight, a highly secret group trained to do special-forces work, like assassinations of senior political and military figures. Then he was promoted to the top of the First Chief Directorate, the FCD, which handled foreign intelligence. It was the KGB's most elite agency, the one operatives aspired to join. Yurimengri and Ogust were colonels with the FCD, while Berianov ended up a full general, the top of that grisly totem pole. Yurimengri held posts in Africa and around the Mediterranean before he returned to Moscow. Ogust was a field agent for a while, too, then worked in the FCD's commercial affairs section, creating and running front organizations to cover and help finance overseas espionage."

Excited, she fished in her purse and pulled out the clipping about Mikhail Ogust. "Ogust has to be my heart donor. But all I really know is what's in the story you wrote. I signed papers before the surgery promising not to try to find out about him or his family, and they signed similar papers guaranteeing my privacy. But that doesn't mean I haven't wondered. So many things have happened that might be explained if I knew more. What kind of man was he? Where did he come from? What did he like and dislike?"

She stared down at the Slavic face in the newspaper photograph, and an odd déjà vu rushed through her. *Heart, are you paying attention? This is for you.*

Jeff nodded, understanding. "He was something of a wunderkind. Very young to rise so fast, but that was partly because he lacked something Russians usually extol as a national virtue—patience."

He had lived in his mind with these three men for nearly a decade, had heard their stories from their own mouths, had studied the classified dossiers on them, and then had added details and anecdotes from those who knew them. He had burned everything deep into his brain until he felt a visceral connection to the three. The mind was nothing without imagination, and much of what made a good intelligence agent—and a good journalist—was the ability to transcend dry statistics and facts.

She said, "Almost as soon as I awoke from surgery I felt impatient and restless, even when I was still drugged. The restlessness has never gone away."

"Sounds like Ogust. Of the three, I liked him most, although I never trusted any of them. He was enormously charming, something of a con man. But he also had a short fuse. I once saw him turn purple and ram a parking ticket into a meter maid's pocket. Petty and stupid. Of course, he ended up in jail. After the Bureau got him out, he controlled himself better. He was not only physical, but smart as hell, too. Highly educated. He came from Leningrad—"

"St. Petersburg."

"Right. The capital of the tsars and the cradle of communism. That's where the Soviet system was born, and he grew up with an intense sense of history, which his parents encouraged. They were academics and full members of the Communist party. Of course, he was an atheist, but he still talked about the Russian soul, sometimes even to explain why he had done something or why the KGB leadership made a certain decision. You have to understand that Russians speak of their souls as if they were as visible as their feet, which is probably one reason religion has made such a widespread comeback there. It never really left."

"What did he eat? What were his hobbies?"

"He never gave up his love of Russian food. He and his wife, Tatiana, often ate out at local Russian restaurants. I heard she was homesick a lot, which is probably true, since she moved back after he died. As for hobbies, he didn't really have any. You saw in the story that he was a karate master. That was a holdover from when he'd been an operative. Also, he could drive anything. Give him a tractor or a Maserati, and he was at home. But he'd like the Maserati a lot more because he enjoyed speed."

She was still studying her donor's photo, the short nose, the broad forehead, the shock of gray hair. There seemed to be a glint in his eyes, as if he had seen enough of the world to be amused. But his face was hard. Too hard.

"It all fits," she decided. "Everything. The food, the strong personality, the quick temper, the driving. Even the Russian poetry makes sense, considering his intellectual background." She sang him the song that had come to her in the hospital: " 'Harvest, our harvest is so good. . . .'"

"I haven't heard that in years."

"You know it?"

"From a 1950s Soviet movie, *The Kuban Cossacks.* I told you I was something of an expert on the culture."

"Wow. I thought it might be movie music, but I swear I've never seen the movie." She sat back and smiled. Then her heart seemed to skip a painful beat: "Was he a killer?"

"Could be," he said honestly. "He never admitted to any murders when we interrogated him, but I'm sure every defector had parts of his life he tried to hide. Most people do, no matter how straight-arrow they think they've been. A life's like an attic. The sun illuminates large patches. But it's got dark corners, too. Very dark. We all have them, some darker than others."

She had a sense he was talking about himself as much as about Mikhail Ogust, but she did not press. "So we still don't know how much violence he was involved in."

"Oh, I think we can safely say it was part of his work life. It'd have to have been, considering his profession, particularly when he was in the field. What we don't know is whether he was a killer." He glanced at her, his face kind. "We may never know. But you can live with that, can't you? After all, even if you did inherit cellular memories, one organ isn't going to change your basic personality and erase your own history. You're still you, but maybe with a few different wrinkles and edges."

She liked that. Maybe she was still fundamentally herself.

He sped the car off the Beltway and onto Interstate 270. Gettysburg was almost due north of Washington. The weekend traffic was growing dense, but that was to be expected on a Friday afternoon. Still, if it remained this slow, they faced several hours of travel.

He said, "General Berianov shared some traits with Ogust—"

"Did Berianov go back to Russia, too?" she interrupted. "His house seemed deserted. Almost as if whoever lived there had moved out. It had so little personality, you'd expect a FOR SALE sign in the front yard."

"I've never been inside, so I can't say. But we just had word he's dead. Died in Moscow sometime within the last day." He had almost revealed that his FBI boss, Bobby Kelsey, had told him, but it was not a good idea she know about Bobby.

"Murdered?" she asked.

"Cardiac arrest. Why? Do you have some reason to think he was murdered?"

"Well, Colonel Yurimengri was shot to death, and Mikhail Ogust died violently, too. What was Berianov doing in Russia?"

"On business. A very successful *biznesman*. All three made a lot of money founding companies that traded between Russia and the United States. Perfect examples of the opportunities capitalism provides."

"You don't sound as if you really believe that." She slid the clipping back into her bag. It was time to begin putting Ogust out of her life. She had probably learned as much as she would ever know, and back on the steps of the Watergate when she held a gun on the woman who wanted to kill her, she decided she was not going to turn into a murderer. She was going to tame this fierce new heart.

He admitted, "The speed of their success has always made me goosey. Almost as if it were here already, waiting for them to put their names on it. Hard to explain, unless they had access to a lot of old KGB money. And I think they did. There were a lot of hidden KGB slush funds in the U.S. during the Cold War era, and a lot were never used— they just sat in some bank. We found many of the accounts, and quite a few were empty. That's how I started on the trail of the three. Following the money."

She nodded. "It makes sense. I've seen so-called overnight successes that seem incredible, until you dig deeper and find all kinds of help. For the most part, overnight success all alone in a garage is a myth. Tell me about General Berianov. Was he from St. Petersburg, too?"

"No, Moscow. A Muscovite through and through. He was the leader of the three, and not just because his rank was higher. He had the personality to dominate even Ogust. Both Yurimengri and Ogust looked up to him, and I'd sometimes catch him giving them warning looks that told me they were close to saying something he didn't want known."

"What did you do?"

"Kept at it. Backtracking, asking the same question in different ways. You're a lawyer. You know the drill."

She gave a faint smile. "True."

"Once Berianov told me, 'You Americans will never really know us. We have an old saying in our country: To understand a Russian, you must *be* a Russian.' He liked to slice cucumbers lengthwise, quarter a tomato, sprinkle salt everywhere, and wash it all down with vodka. But he seemed never to get drunk or have a hangover. His parents were working-class. What launched him was a scholarship to Moscow University, where he studied international relations and earned a law degree. He had a brilliant mind and a chameleon's core. Perhaps that's why people were attracted to him. Yurimengri was just the opposite. Yurimengri was a dour, stolid bureaucrat who came from Irkutsk, a bitterly cold place on the Asian plain. He had a good education, and he was utterly reliable. I think that's why Berianov latched on to him. As for why Ogust was part of the team, I've always wondered about that. Maybe it was because Ogust reminded Berianov of himself when he was younger. There was fifteen years' difference in their ages."

She pursed her lips. "So that's the trio. Berianov, the wily fox. Ogust, the young Turk. And Yurimengri, the bureaucrat. Strange they became so closely connected."

He watched her stretch her long body in the small sports car. She had a feline grace—long, slender curves and an unobtrusive athletic strength. Her blue eyes were hooded, heavy with weariness. He felt tired himself. He had dozed during the long drive from West Virginia to Washington, interrupted by the various stops for gas, food, the john, but it had been inadequate. Still, he could go a long time without sleep. But with her heart transplant, he doubted she should . . . or could.

He said, "Tell me again about the nightmares you had. Maybe there's something in them we missed."

She repeated the motorcycle incident, the voices shouting Russian names—names that included Mikhail Ogust's, Alexei Berianov's, and Anatoli Yurimengri's—the campfire where they were waiting for her, the mysterious door, the sense of oppression and danger, and finally the motorcycle incident in which she killed Ogust.

"It makes no sense," she finished. "Why would I dream about killing my heart donor? At first I thought it meant he had to be a murderer, because I had his heart and I had no idea who the man I was hitting and killing was. But now I know Ogust was the one who was killed in real life."

"Killed? He was killed? Why would you say it that way?"

"He was killed in a motorcycle accident. What's so strange about the way I said it?"

He was excited. His broad face was electric. "It was your word choice. You've made it make sense in a new way. Maybe he didn't die in an 'accident.' " He smacked the steering wheel. "I should've seen this before. It's rare for a motorcyclist to die in a traffic incident that involves no other vehicle, unless there are bad weather conditions like an icy road, or the motorcyclist was high on something. As soon as I heard the police report, I drove right over. There was bright moonlight. The streets were dry. It was a fine April night. Later, the toxicology reports found his system clean, so no drugs or alcohol were to blame. And there were no witnesses. But guess who *was* at the scene . . . said he'd just happened by on his way home to Chevy Chase and seen the capsized motorcycle?"

"Berianov lives in Chevy Chase."

"The same. The police said he was driving away in his Lexus to get help, but when he saw them, he stopped, jumped out, and ran back to tell them his old friend was lying beside the road and would they please radio for help right away. Berianov could've been afraid the police had copied down his license plate number and that's why he went back."

"It said in your news story that Ogust died instantly of brain injuries."

Jeff nodded and pounded the steering wheel again. "What an idiot I've been. It explains so much. Berianov would've been able to tell quickly that Ogust was dead and beyond help. There was no reason for him to race off to get an ambulance. And your dream held the clue—in your nightmare it happened at Berianov's house. There must've been some kind of falling out between the two. I'll bet anything Berianov killed Ogust, probably at his house. He probably had Yuri killed, too, and sent that same killer after us. Damn. I'll bet Berianov's not dead! It's got to be a trick. I was getting too close. He's the one who framed me in Stone Point, and he's not only alive, he must be close to finishing whatever this is all about!"

In Pennsylvania, Caleb Bates sat at his desk in deep concentration, a glass with two fingers of sour mash whiskey by his hand. He studied the latest printout of names and arrival times of the Keepers at the depots outside Washington. No Keeper had been later than a half-hour, which had been figured into the timetable to account for unavoidable traffic delays. He smiled with satisfaction, picked up the glass, and went into his private bathroom where he dumped the whiskey into the toilet. Berianov hated the bourbon whiskey, but Bates, like his patriots, favored it. Fortunately, no one was around, so Berianov did not have to choke it down.

As he returned to his desk, his cell phone vibrated. "Yes?"

It was his financial front in Moscow, Georgi Malko, whose thin voice announced in educated Russian, "The sale has gone through for the publishing company, Alexei. You said you wanted to know when it was final." Included in the package was Russia's best and most influential daily, *Tomorrow,* a behemoth with a prized reputation for integrity. It was a must-read for the country's elite. Malko chuckled, a rarity for such a reserved man, and continued, "As it turns out, I was able to close for Boris Berezovski's shares in ORT today, too." ORT was the most popular national TV network, the only one that reached every village in Russia's vast territory. "Both purchases are just in time for your events in Washington, eh, Alexei?"

"Congratulations. Fine work. Two big closings in one day."

"Yes," Malko agreed. "Quite a victory. How goes everything on your end?"

Berianov did not like the familiarity in the man's tones. Soon Georgi Malko and all the other thieves and larcenists would learn their places. "We're on schedule," he said noncommitally. "What about *True or False*? We must have that, too." It was an independent weekly tabloid, Russia's largest circulation national paper, devoured by ordinary readers, who found its blend of news, sex, and gossip gripping. Through front companies, and with Malko as his point man, Berianov now owned outright or had majority control in daily newspapers from Moscow to Vladivostock, as well as a dozen national magazines. *True or False* would be the capstone to the mass communications empire he was creating, and with it he would control most of the nation's media.

"I'm working on it. Perhaps tonight I'll close that one, too."

"Make sure you do. I want to have all the headlines in Russia by tomorrow."

"*We* want to have headlines, Alexei. Don't forget we're partners."

Professor Malko's voice was cheerful on the surface, but Berianov heard something else in it—a warning that Malko would not take a complete backseat. Until a few years ago, Professor Georgi Malko had been New Russia's *über*-oligarch. From an ordinary proletarian background as a college math teacher, he had been at the forefront of the financial hijacking of Russia, when state assets were privatized in the early 1990s. By 1995, he was a billionaire several times over and owned so many companies and had become so powerful that he and six other new titans of industry, who also seemed to have come out of nowhere, controlled half the nation's economy. Fellow Russians began to call the new elites oligarchs, from the Greek-derived *oligarchy*, meaning the rule of the few.

Then in 1998, largely as a result of the oligarchs' looting, the bottom fell out of the ruble, Moscow defaulted on its huge international loans, and Boris Yeltsin's presidency teetered. In the end, the moguls had come close to liquidating Russia, which prompted, at last, the government's first serious challenge to their power.

Berianov thought them despicable. When he heard others liken them to America's nineteenth-century robber barons, he laughed at the stupidity. For as bad as the robber barons had been, at least they had built actual wealth—railroads, steel mills, auto plants—and from their immense profits had given back by founding schools, libraries, museums, and hospitals. Not so in Russia. Not only had the *nouveaux richeniks* plundered natural resources, they had sent their capital abroad to numbered bank accounts, from where it would never replant a forest, never make safe a rotting nuclear submarine, and certainly never feed an old *babushka.*

Then the magnates' fortunes began to change. When Boris Yeltsin vacated the presidency, they lost their easy entree to insider deals, largely because his successor, Vladimir Putin, had ordered the FSB to collect *kompromat*—information—on them when he took charge of the intelligence agency in the late 1990s. By the time Putin succeeded Yeltsin, his spies had assembled meters-high stacks of files that chronicled everything from illegal money laundering to extortion, from strong-arm tactics to teary confessions by subordinates. With that, Putin had gone to work on the oligarchs.

Still, Berianov believed the world was wrong about Putin: He was no true reformer. He recalled the lieutenant colonel from the old KGB days as not just another talented apparatchik; he was smart, ambitious, and ruthless, far more so than Yeltsin had ever been. Which made it no surprise the youthful Putin appeared to be succeeding where the doddering Yeltsin had failed. Knowing Putin, Berianov was certain Russia's recovered assets were being skimmed, and significant wealth was disappearing into Putin's, his family's, and his courtiers' pockets, just as it had with Yeltsin. And as long as Putin remained in power, he remained in control and could continue to take as much as he liked. *Lies, it was nothing but lies to hoodwink the people.* All of which made Berianov furious. He could hoodwink, too, and for now, he needed Malko.

Smiling coldly, he lied into the cell phone: "How could I forget your contribution, Georgi? It's enormous. We're a team, you and I. Each valuable in our own way. You'll always have my ear, and, as we agreed, Gazprom will be your first reward." Not only did Gazprom control a third of the planet's known reserves of natural gas, it also accounted for nine percent of Russia's gross domestic product. A state within a state, Gazprom owned farms, canneries, a slaughterhouse, seaside resorts, an airline, media properties, and massive holdings in real estate. The corporation was Georgi Malko's ticket back up to the economic stratosphere, but Berianov never intended for him to have it. There were other, more permanent ways to deal with vultures like Malko, which Berianov would see to once he had no more need of him.

"Excellent, Alexei." Malko was back in good humor, which was just what Berianov wanted. "It's good we both recall not only our duties but our rewards. Let me know as soon as the mission tomorrow is complete. Good-bye, old friend."

As he hung up, Berianov ignored the final insult—the familiarity of Malko's use of "old friend." His focus was more immediate: The "event" was on schedule. Because of Yeltsin, the oligarchs, and now President Putin, Berianov had been able to convince disgruntled former allies and contacts to join him. He had drawn upon vodka-enhanced memories and a seething patriotism that ached for the past. Even the military and special forces, as well as Minatom—with the help of his secret sources inside the U.S. government—were doing their part. Intrigue had long been the way in his country, and he had learned it well. Now he used it.

When it was half-past noon in Gettysburg, it was 8:30 P.M. in Moscow. On this cold, clear night, old snow rimmed gutters and sidewalks in glittering brown mounds. A film of ice kept trying to form on the street's bare cobblestones, but a parade of Mercedeses, Cadillacs, and Jaguars, many with escort cars and flashing blue lights, chewed up Mother Nature's frosty plans.

Interrupted occasionally by modest Trabants and Nivas, the luxury cars formed a slowly moving line in the slush outside the opulent Russian Roulette nightclub, just blocks from the Kremlin. Under the nightclub's snow-peaked awning, armed security men watched carefully and murmured into walkie-talkies as the vehicles disgorged men in Italian overcoats and women in diamonds, long furs, and Versace gowns.

As Georgi Malko's limousine driver hit his horn and forced his way into the front of the line, other drivers slammed their brakes and angrily leaned on their own horns. Malko's driver touched the intercom button. "Sorry for the disturbance, sir."

"Of course." Malko's mind was on the vital meeting that awaited him in the nightclub as he returned his cell phone to his pocket. He had one last deal to finalize for Alexei Berianov, and he intended to do it tonight. Not only was the success of Saturday's operation in Washington paramount, so was the aftermath in Moscow.

The commotion outside his limo was quieting as one of his bodyguards jumped out from the front passenger seat and opened the back door. Another bodyguard instantly followed from the front seat, while the lead security man climbed out of the back and moved swiftly around the limo to stand with the others to block open a pathway. Without a glance at the waiting cars or at the staring guests and other security men, Malko emerged into the chilly night, raised his face, and sniffed the air.

"It's going to be even warmer tomorrow night, Valentin," he assured his security chief. "A good night for a revolution, eh? I can smell victory. It's in the air."

Without waiting for a response, Malko stepped under the awning and headed for the double front doors to his nightclub. He heard the whispers: *Georgi Malko is here. That's Georgi Malko. He owns this joint. Richer than the Romanovs, or at least he used to be. They say what he's got left is stashed in New York. Switzerland. The Bahamas. Anywhere he hopes Putin can't find it. Georgi Malko!* Their gazes were hot with curiosity and envy, and he repressed a snort of disgust.

He was a bulky, small ox of a man, bundled in a mink-lined cashmere overcoat. He glanced into the glass beside the club's door and saw his unruly dark eyebrows and dark eyes, black pits in a pasty face notable for its long jowls. He was ordinary-looking, with a thin voice and awkward movements. He was also largely without charm, which he knew, so he had been forced to reach the pinnacle of Russian commerce using only his brains and his willingness to be unscrupulous. But then, the world was not a nice place. Anyone who missed that was an idiot and deserved to live the rough life under a bridge. He scowled as he marched into the narrow foyer, where the odors of alcohol, cigarette smoke, and steaming bodies instantly assaulted him.

His chief of security, Valentin Wurtchev, followed, his head swiveling as he checked the busy street for danger. There had been two serious attempts on his boss's life in the past six years, and in each case one of the body men had been killed. Valentin did not intend to join them. As for "victory" in some revolution being something Professor Malko could smell "in the air," he was unsure what his devious chief was talking about, although he had a few ideas. But that was business as usual, too.

"Good evening, Professor Malko." It was the girl behind the iron-grated counter who checked coats. Behind her, a sentry with a Kalashnikov rifle stood, its weight balanced professionally in his arms. Malko noted a pegboard on which pistols hung, weapons checked by the guests. It was a rule that amused him: In the Russian Roulette nightclub, no one could carry.

Malko nodded to her. He did not remember her name. "Good crowd tonight?"

"Yes, sir. They're jumping, sir. It's terrific to see you. It's been a long time since you last visited us." The music was loud and pulsing. She knew not to ask for his coat.

Malko nodded again and, stripping off his gloves, marched into the ballroom. Champagne was flowing at $100 a glass. Buffet tables groaned with every Russian delicacy imaginable, buckets of black and red caviar, and platters of hot meats, fresh lobsters, and pâtés. Under Winter Palace–style chandeliers, youthful bodies gyrated to live music while old friends greeted each other with both-hands-on-the-face kisses. Malko unbuttoned his overcoat and walked on through, stopping occasionally to speak with admirers and ambitious lackeys.

He found all the noise and senseless confusion annoying. Still, he smiled, for he was really, at last, back at the center of things, where these bad-boy men in their tinted glasses and slutty women with their rouged cheekbones thought he would never again be. His life had begun to fall apart last year when Putin had taken away his position as minister of the interior, since government officers and members of the parliament were immune from criminal prosecution.

No sooner was the ink dry on the dismissal letter than Putin ordered him arrested for bribery and extortion. It had taken Malko a week to make the charges go away, and he sat in prison the whole time. To buy himself out, he'd had to sign over Nova Nickel, among the world's biggest nickel producers and the largest producer of palladium; and it had been only the first of Putin's assaults. Since Putin was still successfully stealing his assets, Malko had no illusions he would stop.

Ahead of him now, Valentin plowed through the throngs, opened a brocade-covered door, and stood in the doorway, his body protecting Malko, as he inspected the interior of the next room. At last he stepped back, propped open the door with one large hand, and announced, "Mr. Dudash is waiting, sir. He has two men with him."

Professor Malko recalled briefly with sardonic pleasure the cracked-plaster classrooms in Moscow University where he had taught algebra, calculus, and statistics for nearly fifteen years. Then he increased the size of the smile on his lips and strode into the richly appointed party room he had reserved for this meeting. As the door closed, quiet descended, a relief. The room was decorated with the usual silk-brocaded walls, beveled mirrors, grand chandelier, and complete bar in the corner. To Malko, it all seemed to smell of money.

At the richly appointed table, Oleg Dudash sat glowering, arms crossed over his chest. Two guards stood behind him, one on either side, their arms also crossed. Dudash had a flat nose, a suspicious look in his eyes, and thick hair that he brushed straight back. Just weeks after the 1991 revolution, he had started *True or False* with a rickety mimeograph machine and one fellow reporter—his wife. Their racy, pumped-up coverage of events, mixed with down-and-dirty columns about society, gangland hits, and the new sex trade, had quickly found a vast audience hungering for long-forbidden topics. Within a year, the weekly had become a daily, had increased its pages tenfold, and was the most read paper in the country.

"This is a hell of a place to meet," Oleg Dudash complained. "How can you stand the pandemonium? I'm not twenty years old anymore, and neither are you."

"Aren't you?" Malko sounded disappointed. "I thought you'd enjoy a night of play after we conclude our business. It might bring back good memories of the old days, when we were all broke and just starting out. The club is yours for the night, Oleg. I give it to you. Drink all you like. Enjoy the girls until you're wrung dry. Everything's on me."

"We're not doing any business. I told you that. I'm not selling the paper."

"I remember the old days well," Malko went on, his thin voice somehow gaining depth, as if he were struck by nostalgia. "Don't you? We had some fine times then, eh?"

The publisher started to say something but changed his mind. His suspicious eyes narrowed.

"We both recall a lot, I'm sure," Malko continued as he pushed his overcoat back over his shoulders, and Valentin slid it down and off. Dudash's security team started to reach for their arms, wary so much movement meant guns were about to be pulled. "Call them off, Oleg," the professor told him. "There'll be no bloodshed here tonight unless you start it. In fact, with all the pretty young girls in the club, I'm sure your boys could find something far more entertaining to do than hang around listening to two middle-aged men reminisce. Valentin will leave, too. Then it will be just we two. Cigars, Valentin."

Professor Malko angled a chair away from the table, sat, and leaned back. He did not miss the flicker of discomfort in the newspaperman's eyes with his mention of the past.

Oleg Dudash and his two sentries watched Valentin drape his master's overcoat over his left arm and slide his right hand carefully into his suit jacket pocket so as not to excite distrust. Just as carefully he removed two cigars and handed them to his boss.

Professor Malko aimed a genuine smile at Dudash. "These cigars are a rare find, old friend. Packed and rolled a century ago in a plantation somewhere in Tennessee. I understand the tobacco is so mellow and rich a man could live a week off the fragrance. I paid ten thousand dollars for a box of twelve. In honor of the occasion, I've decided to share the first of the lot with you."

"I'm not your 'old friend,' Georgi. We knew each other, that's all." He stared at the cigars. "You must've bought them when you had that kind of money to waste."

Malko blinked, refused to frown. He knew Dudash was needling him. "As a matter of fact, they arrived just last week." He smiled apologetically. "I still have a few rubles. Did you worry that I meant not to pay for your newspaper?"

Dudash did not send his men away, but he took the cigar and allowed Malko to light it for him. Both men smoked. Finally Dudash asked, "Just where *is* all this money you're offering coming from?"

"Another country. You needn't know which. I'll have the funds deposited in any bank, anywhere you like. Of course, we will need a token amount to pass between us here in Moscow, for the sake of appearances and to satisfy the government. Really, Oleg, this is an excellent deal for you. You can walk away extraordinarily rich."

Dudash smoked. "I'm rich enough already."

"Perhaps. Still, we should speak privately. There's an issue here, a delicate issue . . . *Ellie.*" It had taken Malko's people three weeks to ferret out the information he had needed to find her.

Oleg Dudash's face tightened, and the hand holding the cigar stopped, motionless in the air on its way to his mouth. "Perhaps you're right."

He dismissed his men, and Malko sent Valentin out to the nightclub, too. As the door closed, sealing them in, Oleg Dudash leaned forward. His face was earnest, and it seemed as if he were suddenly a dozen years younger than his forty-five.

"You're the one who's cornered, you son of a bitch," Dudash said quietly. "You can't run for the presidency against Putin because your reputation's made you unelectable. And you can't assemble a power base any other way as long as Putin's president. So someone else has got to be backing you. It's time to give it up for the good of the country, Georgi. You and the other cutthroat financiers. One of you has got to be selfless, admit what you've done in raping our nation. Inspire others to turn over their assets and help save Russia. You can show the way. Be a hero. Take this advice from someone who knew you back when you were just stealing Party funds—"

"Ah, Oleg. Always the idealist. First it was communism. Now I suppose you consider yourself a democrat. Don't be an idiot. The system changes, not the people."

"Up to a point, you're right. Yes, our land and resources have always been in the hands of a greedy aristocracy, even after the revolution. After communism, of course, everything belonged to no one, and so everything was up for grabs. But this epidemic of corruption we're seeing isn't some passing phase, and it's certainly not democracy. At least not yet. It's our long-standing framework for doing business. This shameful bedrock of a criminal society we call Russia." He glared. "But that doesn't make it right. In fact, it makes it even more wrong. We should've learned something along the way. So the answer's no. Absolutely not. You can't use my paper. I won't sell it to you."

"You should think about it more," Malko advised. "Consider what so much money will mean to you and Marina. I have a little time. An hour, perhaps."

The publisher shook his head angrily. "I won't help you back up to the top, Georgi. I won't help any of you bloodsuckers. *True or False* has some dross in it, but it also reports the truth. That's what makes it popular with the people. *The truth.* I don't want to sell, and I don't have to sell. It's time someone said no and changed the framework so we can build a decent nation. If my paper keeps telling the truth, then I'm contributing in that direction, and I won't let you or anyone else take it away or stop me."

Georgi Malko had let his gaze drop as Dudash ranted. No point in antagonizing him any farther. Now he looked up. "And Ellie? What about Ellie? I've found her, you know. She and her mother are living in a shack outside the city." He set his cigar in a crystal ashtray, got up, and walked to the bar with its glistening rows of glasses and bottles. "I think we need a drink. As I recall, you used to prefer cognac when we could get it."

Dudash hesitated. Pain filled his face. "Ellie. I'd wondered. After all these years. . . . If Marina finds out, it'll destroy our marriage."

"Cognac it is," the professor said cheerfully as he poured into a gold-rimmed snifter. Then he poured vodka for himself and carried both glasses back to the table. "Incidently, Ellie has no idea about any of this. A very attractive young lady of fifteen. Looks a lot like you. Her mother recognized me instantly, which I took as a compliment. Not a very handsome woman, even in those days. Just why did you fuck her, Oleg? Not beautiful. Dumb as a samovar. That was rotten judgment."

Dudash's flat nose seemed to thicken with anger. "You bastard." He lifted the snifter and drank. He glared. He smoked. "What I don't understand is you. You surround yourself with people of talent and ambition, then you use and betray them. Over and over you do that. You fall out with everyone you deal with, and now it looks to me as if Putin himself is well on his way to pulling your eyeteeth. So why are you trying to stay in the game? Take my advice: Consolidate your assets while you're still rich and no one's murdered you. Go retire to some high-security estate in Majorca or a villa in the south of France."

Malko shook his head. "Ah, Oleg, you really don't understand. An entrepreneur has no real friends or enemies. We have only interests. The point is to win. One must always win and be seen to win. It's not a question of how rich I am, or have been, or will be. No, I must destroy or be destroyed. That's what winning is all about." Malko held up his vodka glass, which was empty. "Drink up your cognac, old friend. Drink deeply and believe that the only reason to live is to win. Without winning, no one likes you. Not the president of your country. Not the lowliest whore. Not even your neighbor's dog. Your heart feels cold. Your bed is cold. The blue sky is gray, and the very air you breathe is poisoned. I am an entrepreneur. Therefore I must win."

Dudash studied him. He seemed to make a decision. He said wearily, "Tell anyone you like about Ellie. I love my wife, and she loves me. I'm going to take the chance that she'll forgive me. Ellie happened because of a mistake a long time ago when I was wild and stupid. I think people are made of better stuff—my wife included—than you do. When I see a gray sky, I can imagine it blue. Winning is a game, a sport, that's all. It's not a person. Not life itself." He finished his drink and set the snifter firmly on the table. He leaned forward, and his chin jutted. Words exploded out of his mouth: "Damn you, Georgi! *You can't have my paper.* I won't sell it to you, you understand? And you can't blackmail it out of me! I want Ellie's address. I'll take care of her. I'll tell my wife everything. And *you can go straight to hell!*"

Professor Malko shrugged. "You're making a mistake." He felt a moment of empathy with the idealistic Dudash. Then he brushed it away. Besides, so much had occurred since his youth when he, too, might have been a dreamer that he was no longer sure what he had thought or felt back then.

"A mistake?" Dudash growled. "Why? What will you do, kill me? It won't do you a damn bit of good if you do. My wife won't sell you the paper either. She and I are alike. We believe the same." The publisher stood up and shouldered into his coat. He swayed.

Malko was instantly on his feet. "That was a large cognac, Oleg. Here, let me help you." He took the man's arm. There was still a chance he could change Dudash's mind.

Dudash pushed him away. "Pig. Capitalist pig. What's Ellie's address?"

Malko stepped back, palms raised in front of him. "If that's the way you want it." He described where the teenager and mother lived.

Dudash moved away, grabbing the back of a chair to steady himself. "Bastard," he muttered again as he dragged open the door.

The noise rolled in, and Malko remained standing where he was and smoked as he watched Dudash wait for the busy nightclub to disgorge his pair of security men. Malko was enjoying his cigar. Within three minutes, Dudash's two bodyguards had arrived, and the three of them left. Malko gave a long, slow smile.

Valentin's voice brought him from his reverie. "They're gone, sir. Did you close the deal?"

"He wants to hold on to the property."

"We had expected as much, hadn't we, sir?"

"Indeed, Valentin." He shrugged and laid the cigar butt in the ashtray. When he got home, he would light another. The dozen cigars had been worth every ruble. "I'll go into the club now and shake hands, buy drinks. I expect I'll be there several hours. Certainly past midnight. After all, I have something to celebrate." He patted his jacket pocket, which contained a bill of sale for *True or False,* Oleg Dudash's signature a perfect forgery. "I'll have to tell a lot of people how proud and excited I am about the purchase from my old friend. Which means, of course, that now you must put your arrangements in motion. All of them must die in the crash—his men as well as Oleg Dudash."

"I understand, sir. He might have told them that he wouldn't sell to you."

"Exactly. Poor SOBs. What a heartless boss he is, eh, Valentin?"

But Valentin was already leaving, eager to make his phone calls.

32

The traffic was thick, and the Ferrari was snared in it, traveling at an excruciatingly slow pace. Jeff moved his gaze away from studying the ebb and flow to check on Beth, who had fallen asleep, her cheek against the headrest. Her legs were curled up under her in the bucket seat. In her jeans and black turtleneck, her corn-silk hair brushing her cheek, she seemed all coiled femaleness.

He was fascinated by the smooth, porcelain skin. Each dark hair in her eyebrows seemed individual and distinct. Her eyelashes cast shadows onto her cheeks. Her pink lips were slightly parted. Occasionally she sighed. He liked the sound, as if it came from a far-away place of promises. He forced his attention back to the traffic. She was too damn distracting. He did not want these thoughts. He was uncomfortable that he liked her.

When she awoke, she stretched like a cat who had been dozing in the sun. Her back arched, her shoulders pushed up to her ears, and she rotated on her hips to extend her legs. Those legs seemed long enough to reach to China.

"China?" she murmured. "What about China?"

"I was talking to myself. Do that sometimes. A bad habit from living alone."

She collapsed back against the seat and pivoted her head to look at him. "Any trouble?"

"Two cop cars looking for speeders. Quiet so far."

She nodded.

He decided that she looked vulnerable and strong at the same time. He remembered something Nietzsche had said: "Two things are wanted by a true man, danger and play. Therefore, he seeks woman as the most dangerous toy." He had thought that might be true of him, the way he met, loved, and discarded women after his divorce. But before then, he had wanted a committed relationship. He was the marrying kind, or so he had believed. But after he had gone undercover, everything had changed. Divorce. Isolation. A wilderness of falsehoods. And finally questioning whether that choice had ever been what he really wanted. Whether he had been a blithering fool to shed his once-fine world for a belief that almost no one else shared.

"Why do you hate lawyers?" she asked. There was that throaty voice he found irresistible.

He grinned. "What do you call a thousand lawyers at the bottom of a lake?"

She gave a little shake of her head. " 'A good start.' That's old, Jeff. I expected better of you."

"Okay. Here's another. . . . Two lawyers walking through the woods spot a vicious-looking bear. The first lawyer opens his briefcase, pulls out sneakers, and puts them on. The second lawyer says, 'You're crazy. You'll never outrun that bear.' The first lawyer gives a big smile. 'I don't have to. I only have to outrun you.' "

She gave him a small smile. "We're practical. I admit that."

"So why don't lawyers go to the beach?"

"Dogs and cats keep trying to bury them." Beth's eyes twinkled. "Lawyers know all the jokes. We have to, so we can tell them on ourselves. But you haven't answered my question. You seem to hate us more than most people do. What did we do to you?"

"Married me," he said promptly. "My wife was a lawyer."

"You're married?"

"Sorry. My mistake. I'll rephrase that: My ex-wife *is* a lawyer."

"Ah, so you're divorced."

"Yes, and happily. Although it made me miserable at the time. But looking back, I can see we weren't suited. When I left the Bureau, she left me. I wasn't who she thought I was . . . or somesuch excuse. She remarried and moved to Minneapolis."

"And?"

"No 'and.' That's it. No children, not that I didn't want them." He glanced at her amused face. "So you think I have as lousy a taste in women as you have in men." He chuckled. "Well, you may have a point."

"Where did you grow up?"

"That's not very interesting either." He shrugged. "Oh, well, now I know something else about you—you're a glutton for boredom."

"I'd hardly call you boring."

"Your problem. Okay, standard childhood. Father in government service. OSS during World War Two, then the CIA when it was formed. He was one of the eggheads, doing analysis. A desk jockey with piles of secret papers posing riddles for him to make sense out of. He was twenty years older than my mother. She was your traditional housewife, except she was wild about Labrador retrievers. She raised them to show. My sister and I grew up on the small Virginia farm my dad bought my mother. It had all the great stuff—a vegetable garden, an old tire swing, and a duck pond ruled over by black swans." He smiled, remembering.

"Where are they now?"

His hands tightened on the steering wheel. "My parents? Dead, seven years ago. Dad had a blood disease. Four months after he passed away, a semi crushed Mom's car on the Beltway."

"How terrible! For all of you. I'm so sorry."

He nodded. "Yeah, it was pretty bad. He'd been sick a year, and Mom just couldn't go on without him. Too many tough changes for her to handle." He hesitated, remembering one of those changes had been their disappointment in him, that he had left the FBI for, in their opinion, the less-honorable profession of journalism. "You could see it in her face. From the police account, my guess is she wasn't paying attention to the traffic. It was probably sheer luck it hadn't happened sooner."

"And your sister?"

"Lives in the Sierras with her family. Haven't talked to her in a while." Again the sense of disappointment in himself. Their father's death had been bad enough, but his sister had blamed him for their mother's. In outrage and hurt, he had lashed back.

They rode in silence. She asked, "So where did you go to school?"

He told her about Harvard and his degree in government, about the master's in area studies at the University of London, where he had focused on the Eastern Bloc and the Soviet Union, and then about how it all had seemed to jell for him when he joined the Bureau. As he talked about his dreams, his love for the United States, for serving it, she had an eerie sense about herself, as if her own life had somehow been lacking.

Finally he said, "I'm tired of me. What about you? You're the one who's interesting."

"I am? Well, you should know. You're the one who dug up my background, Mr. Reporter-man."

He chuckled. "Golden California child. What was that like?"

She smiled neutrally. "A lot of sun. Travels. Disneyland. Great summers on the beach."

"That's all?"

"Pretty much, yes."

"What a liar. Let's see . . . daughter of one of the most ruthless criminal defense attorneys in Los Angeles, and one of the most hard-nosed developers. Some daddy and mommy. Must've been a warm and cozy atmosphere."

She refused to let him goad her. "It had its moments."

He frowned. "You don't want to talk about it." It was a statement.

"Clever fellow. I think we have enough on our minds to think about, don't you?"

He took his gaze from the traffic and studied her. She was staring out her side window, supposedly watching the scenery. Her face was stone.

He said, "It's your parents, isn't it?"

She seemed to stiffen.

He said quietly, "He killed her. The papers said it was an accident, and that he was so distraught that, a couple of days later, he shot and killed himself. Was it an abusive relationship? Is that another reason you don't like to talk about it?" He glanced at her again.

"You're thorough, I'll give you that. But it was a long time ago. I survived."

"Just survived?"

She blinked slowly, thinking. She sighed and nodded to herself. "All right, I'll tell you. It's not terribly exciting or mysterious. My parents didn't have an abusive relationship at all. In fact, they were deeply in love the whole time they were married. Jack-the-Knife and Queen Janet, a glittering couple who seemed straight out of central casting. When they weren't working, they were always together. I was the third wheel."

"Nannies raised you."

"Yes, and they were very good nannies, the best money could buy. Dad did teach me to shoot, and he'd take me to his office occasionally as I got older, and then into court. I loved to watch him in action. Mom made certain I had everything a girl or boy could need, including plenty of dolls, a toolbox, skateboard lessons, and a new bicycle every year. It really was an accident that she died." She paused and pressed her lips together, grief in her eyes. "They'd been out to a party . . . they both drank a lot. Mom said it was all the pressure they were under all the time. Dad was driving that night. When they got home, Mom got out of the car and walked behind it to go into the house. Dad was so drunk that he threw the gear shift into reverse and hit the gas pedal. He ran into her and crushed her against the brick wall that ran alongside the drive. She lived only a few minutes." She folded her hands in her lap and bowed her head.

"It must've been horrible. I'm sorry, Beth. Really. I shouldn't have made you talk about it."

She shrugged and looked up as she wiped shaky fingers across her eyes. "The first I knew something was wrong was when I heard the horrible sound of a howl. It was him. I heard him even though I was sound asleep in my bedroom on the other side of the house. He'd come unhinged, a madman with grief and guilt. Of course, the police arrived. They tested him, and he had triple the legal amount of alcohol in his bloodstream. He was blind drunk. They were planning to charge him with manslaughter. Instead, he committed suicide. He couldn't live . . . without her."

"How old were you?"

"Eighteen. Everything changed for me after that. *I* changed. I didn't like the frivolous way I'd been living, so I quit running around to parties all the time, started studying, and decided to make something of myself."

"Make them proud."

She nodded mutely.

He thought about her and how difficult it must have been for her to lose her parents in such a violent way when she was still just a teenager. He, at least, had been fully grown when his had died.

"They'd both be very proud of you." He hesitated and cast her a tentative grin. "Despite my low opinion of lawyers, I'd say you're probably a pretty good one." He paused again, watching her face for a sign he was going too far. "Maybe even decent. Dare I say . . . honest? Well, perhaps that's too extreme. An *honest lawyer* . . . isn't there some law against that?"

She gave a low chuckle. "Lawyers make the laws, so I'm sure you're wrong." She took a tissue from her purse and blew her nose loudly. "But I've heard that 'honest lawyer' is an oxymoron." She looked at him and smiled. "Sort of like 'objective newsman.' "

He chuckled. "Touché again."

"Thanks, Jeff. We've both had bad times. You do know how to cheer a woman up though."

She settled in beside him, and they resumed their careful watch of the congested highway. As they fled north, the road seemed an obstacle course of danger. She tried to shake off tension. Time passed slowly as they approached the Catoctin Mountains.

She cleared her throat and frowned at him. "I've been wondering. . . . What made you suspicious of Berianov, Yurimengri, and Ogust when you debriefed them?"

He thought back. "I guess it was just a gut feeling at first. They seemed legitimate, I have to admit that. God knows they gave us good intelligence. But they were never all that worried the way most defectors are. You have to understand, defectors spend a lot of time looking over their shoulders. There are those in Russian intelligence who might want one or more of their skins even today. Plus the KGB has always hated traitors, and their institutional memory is long. Then you add in the fact that there are private contract killers who still travel here chasing émigrés to settle old scores. For all those reasons and more, a lot of defectors took on assumed names and identities because they were afraid of retaliation."

"So our three didn't seem worried. What else?"

"There was the issue of timing. Do you know much about the coup attempt in ninety-one?"

"Just what I read in the newspaper."

He nodded, his gaze surveying the traffic. "As I told you, Berianov was chief of the FCD, the KGB's elite foreign espionage arm. Around him, everything was crumbling—the KGB's sword-and-shield empire, authority throughout the country, and very visibly the state itself. Meanwhile, the leader back then, Mikhail Gorbachev, seemed to be just letting the Soviet Union fall apart. Berianov knew he had to make changes in the FCD because his officers were being recruited away by the West. So he tried to improve morale. He told his people they were no longer fighting just for Marxism-Leninism, but for Mother Russia—"

"He was instilling patriotism."

"Exactly. But things kept getting worse. Finally a group of Communist hardliners, including Vladimir Kryuchkov, who headed the entire KGB, contacted Berianov. Geography came into play at this point. See, FCD was headquartered on the outskirts of Moscow in a little town called Yasenevo. Kryuchkov and his cronies secretly asked Berianov to put his FCD forces at their disposal near the Kremlin to help with the military coup they were planning to take back the country."

"Did Berianov agree?"

"Yes, enthusiastically. He sent his agents into Moscow to spy, and he reported their findings to Kryuchkov. He also ordered the FCD's paramilitary unit to go to the KGB's club in Moscow and hold themselves ready to act. He expected to use them to crush the reformers who were rallying around a new political force—Boris Yeltsin. When the hardliners captured Gorbachev, the coup began, and Berianov was excited. He waited. And waited. But Kryuchkov stopped calling. No directions ever came. Finally, Berianov made a tough decision—he told his people to stand down, because he figured the coup was collapsing."

She asked, "Why? How did it fall apart?"

"He said the committee—even Kryuchkov—lacked will. They had no strong sense of direction. There was no single figure who had the guts or vision to shoulder responsibility and use the force of his personality to make events happen. The chilling part is, Berianov openly admitted to us that if the orders for aggressive action had come, he would've obeyed. If the coup's committee had used the levers of power at their disposal, they would've succeeded. The result would've been to hurl the Soviet Union back into Communist rule, and the Cold War would've resumed in a big way."

"Wow. Thank God that didn't happen. So Berianov's a real patriot of the old Soviet Union."

"Right. And then there was the swift success of all three men afterwards in the United States."

She nodded. "It does seem as if they must've had some kind of organization in place here."

"Or in Moscow. Maybe both places. But Berianov threw the FBI and the CIA off the scent by a remarkable revelation that would've hurt him if he'd been planning a comeback."

"And that was?"

"Aldrich Ames. He told us Rick Ames was a deeply buried double agent who'd seriously compromised American intelligence."

"But I thought—"

"Yes, I know. No one knows the tip came from a defector. No one in the Bureau or the Company wanted that particular embarrassment aired. Much better John Q. Public believed we discovered him on our own. Of course, Berianov was happy to keep the whole thing quiet, because with that single revelation, he bought freedom for himself and his two pals. I've waited a decade to find out what they were really up to. Now I may be getting close. What I didn't figure on was you."

She shrugged. "My specialty—throwing monkey wrenches into other people's plans. Do you know any of their associates here? Surely someone must've been close to them."

"If they were grooming any successors, I don't know who they are. And if we're right that Berianov was responsible for both Ogust's and Yurimengri's deaths, then that tells me he eliminated them because he was taking over completely, for whatever it was he was planning. I'm hoping we're going to find some clue to that at the dairy farm in Pennsylvania." He hesitated. "That reminds me of Caleb Bates. I keep wondering what that's all about. Why would Bates's bills for his hunt club in little Stone Point, West Virginia, be hidden in Berianov's Washington house?"

"Doesn't make a lot of sense, unless Berianov paid the bills. After all, you said he'd become a legitimate businessman." She stopped. "Oh, my God! This might be relevant. It seems like a decade ago, but this happened recently: I received a message from a friend about HanTech Industries." She described the contract Michelle wanted so much, which HanTech had wrested from her company. "According to my friend, Caleb Bates is one of HanTech's new secret owners. In fact, he owns the largest interest. All the rest have Russian names, and one is the son of the director of Minatom. Others also have close ties to Minatom."

"The Russian Ministry of Atomic Energy?" He whistled. "Nuclear weapons. That's huge."

She nodded. "My friend says HanTech has been secretly buying up weapons-grade uranium from Third World countries and returning it to Russia." She felt a chill. "I wondered at the time why Russia wanted back that kind of uranium while at the same time it was selling the same grade to us, supposedly to make certain it was never used for war. But now I'm beginning to rethink it all. If Berianov had some kind of plot in mind . . . maybe it had to do with the terrorist act your boss told you about."

"Go on." His voice was tense.

"Caleb Bates has effective controlling interest in HanTech. So he's calling the shots over a group of Russians who have a lot of shares, too. Maybe that's the missing organization you've been looking for."

"Do you remember the names?"

"Some of them." She reeled off six then added the ones she knew to be connected to Minatom and Uridium.

He blanched. "I recognize four. Two are related to oligarchs, one's the brother of General Kripinski, and the fourth's father-in-law is in charge of what's left of the Russian navy."

She was silent. "But Bates is an American name. Or British. Why would a Yank or a Brit head a Russian-owned business? Unless . . . maybe Caleb Bates is a Soviet defector, too, but he decided he'd better take on a fake identity to protect himself from the past. Ergo, 'Caleb Bates,' an American with serious interests in Russia."

"It's possible." His stomach was suddenly tight as he remembered. . . . "Decades ago, the KGB set up a clandestine training camp in the Ural Mountains outside Moscow. That's where it sent its most talented espionage recruits. Apparently, it looked like a typical American city—a tree-line main street, library, courthouse, and everything else— new and used cars, the latest food, clothes, music, and movies. Newspapers like *The New York Times,* the *Los Angeles Times,* and *The Washington Post* delivered weekly but handed out one day at a time, just as if everyone was really living in the United States. The only language was a Midwestern-accented English. The students were steeped in everything from our table habits to how to shop in a super market. There were other training sites for spies who were going to be assigned to France and Britain, too. Sometimes students would live in these fake towns for a year or more, as long as it took, until they could pass as a native in every way."

"Good heavens, I'd never heard that."

"You weren't supposed to. Remember, it was the Cold War, so we didn't want what was going on to get out and create panic. People would've started looking at their neighbors, their kid's teacher, even the town mayor and wonder . . . Is he a red? Is she?"

She grimaced. "You're right. A big 'red scare.' That easily could've happened. Did we have secret camps like that, too, to train people to spy in the Soviet Union?"

"You bet. And to spy in Poland, Czechoslovakia, and other Iron Curtain countries as well. Our agents were effective, and they delivered a lot of first-rate intelligence."

She shivered. "All part of the Cold War, I suppose."

"Right."

He pulled the Ferrari off onto the shoulder and turned to face her. He inhaled, disgusted with himself. He should have seen the linkages earlier, and now that he did, he was alternately furious with himself and afraid for what it meant.

"There's more." His voice was hard. "Point one: When I was in that West Virginia town asking around for Berianov, I described him as having a Russian accent. All three—Berianov, Yurimengri, and Ogust—had thick accents when we debriefed them. Afterwards, when I interviewed them for the *Post,* they spoke better English, but still with noticeable Russian inflections. I always assumed it was because their English was improving from living here. That was probably true of Yurimengri and

Ogust, but not necessarily of Berianov. Now that I really think about it, I recall other defectors had told us he'd worked undercover here. Which seems to me to indicate he must've trained in the American camp the Soviets built."

"Meaning he was fooling you. He may have had no Russian accent at all. Okay, that makes sense. What's point two?"

"The box of makeup we found in the station wagon. Point two is that the sniper who was trying to kill you was obviously an expert at disguise. Point three takes me back to your idea, which started my mind to working on all this—that Caleb Bates may be a nervous Russian defector who's gone undercover. Point four is what I'd told you about the photo for Caleb Bates that I'd seen in the Stone Point weekly—remember, there seemed to be something familiar about him, something I couldn't quite put my finger on."

"I remember." She frowned. "What are you getting at?"

His broad features coalesced into chiseled granite as he stared over her shoulder. "Point five: We have no concrete evidence Alexei Berianov is dead. It's just a report. None of our people saw his corpse—"

The deviousness of it took her breath away. "No Russian accent. Access to and probably very good training in disguise. Knows our culture inside out. Berianov may be alive—"

He nodded grimly. "The way money greases palms in Moscow, it would've been easy to fake his death. If so, Berianov could be not only alive but here. And if his body and face were padded up, I think he'd look exactly like the photo I saw of Caleb Bates in the Stone Point newspaper."

"You think Berianov *is* Bates?"

"Yes. It'd explain why I haven't been able to locate him for weeks at a time. He's been underground as some kind of wealthy owner of a hunt club." He shook his shoulders under his jacket, trying to relieve tension. "Which leads me to point six: We're being hunted by a well-organized, vicious group, several of whom speak English with Russian accents. And to point seven: Stone Point was where I was set up for murder. My going to Stone Point could've been the final blow to Berianov's patience with me. I was getting much too close. He had to take me out of action."

"So the group that's after you . . . and me . . . seems to be Berianov's. Which is enough to scare the skin off most people, me included. Logically, it makes sense that they're up to something that they think we're close to discovering, or maybe we've already stumbled onto it."

"Yes, the terrorist event my boss asked me to look into." He grimaced with worry. "But what is it? And when and where?"

PART THREE

33

There were days when a deep and brooding shadow seemed to fall over the office of FBI director Thomas Earle Horn. A parade of all the hard, twisted, and empty people from his long career came to weigh heavily on him at the end of a long day of murders and rapes, terrorists and hate crimes, corruption and spies. Horn had been a policeman, a U.S. attorney, and a federal judge in Denver before being appointed to the appellate bench for the Tenth Circuit and eventually tapped for the FBI directorship. He had seen every kind of violence one human could inflict upon another. Yet as the faces flashed through his mind, they were, to him, all—criminal and victim alike—sad and lost souls.

Today he was having one of those moments. He was sitting contemplatively in his semidark office, a big, thick-necked shadow himself, when National Security Adviser Cabot Lowell entered unannounced through his private door and headed straight for an armchair. For an instant, it seemed to Tom Horn that Cabot Lowell, staring at him as he sat down, wrapped in all his ancestry and power, was no more than another lost soul.

Then his sense of who he was kicked in, and he said coldly, "It's customary to call before you appear in my office, Cabot."

Lowell said, "Do you have an undercover agent placed close to the community of Soviet defectors? A man who supposedly resigned from the Bureau under a cloud some ten years ago but who has actually been working for you ever since?"

Surprised, almost stunned, Tom Horn snapped, "You know I can't, and won't, answer that, Cabot. If it were true, it'd be part of an ongoing investigation." He leaned across his desk toward the national security adviser. "And I have to say, I'm more than a little annoyed you'd even ask such a question."

"That's unfortunate, Tom. Still, I require an answer. "

Horn studied Lowell's solemn face and cold blue eyes behind the rimless glasses, the mouth thinner than a razor and with no trace of humor. "Really? And when did the daily operation of this agency come under your authority?"

"The day the president assigned the attorney general and me to find the deep mole in the Bureau. Or determine there was none."

All the shadows and lost souls of his melancholy were swept from the director's mind, replaced by a white anger he could barely keep from exploding. "The president did *what?*"

Lowell brushed a thin strand of his wispy gray hair from his eyes. "He ordered an outside investigation of the Bureau." The national security adviser made his voice a shade softer. "This mole business has been going on too long, Tom. You know that, and long before your watch, I might add. It's high time we found out once and for all if the loss of information and the ruined operations really were being caused by a mole operating so deeply that he's escaped detection—for God-knows-how-many years."

"I see," Horn said through gritted teeth. "And exactly what does a possible undercover agent of ours have to do with the mole?"

"We think the agent *is* the mole."

He hesitated. "You'd better have a hell of a lot of evidence. Who exactly is 'we'?"

"Millicent Taurino, Don Chen, and me."

"So? Doing your own investigations now?"

Lowell didn't answer.

"No, you'd need some real investigators, wouldn't you. Within the Bureau." The two men locked eyes in the curtained twilight of the director's office. Horn said, "I should resign, you know. No director can function under such conditions."

"But you won't. You want to find the mole as much as we do." Lowell's ruthless mouth gave a wry smile. "You—and the Bureau—will get the credit, of course."

Horn thought that one over. The offer had considerable attraction. "Only fair, considering it seems some of our own people did the actual digging. Sooner or later I'll find out who they are, too, you know."

"Perhaps." Lowell shrugged. The fate of Eli Kirkhart was of no concern to him or the attorney general. The president would never know, even if he were still in office.

"How did they come to this stunning conclusion about my undercover man?"

"Think about it." Lowell inclined his short frame an inch, his pale eyes as bright and ruthless as a Grand Inquisitor searching for sinners. "He has direct access to you, correct? And to all those under you who know about him. That would be most, if not all, of the top brass of the Bureau, correct?"

"More or less, yes."

"He can come and go under your protection, without having to account for his presence to anyone else. For those not in the know, he has a cover job that explains his presence in the building. If worst comes to worst, and he's actually detained by agents not in the know, you'll do everything you can to make certain he's taken care of. He's probably got a code signal to alert his handler. He'll either be quietly released, or cleared and then released."

"It's far more complex than that. But say all of it might be possible. Suppose such a nameless undercover agent existed. . . . What proof do you have he's the mole?"

Lowell leaned back. "Let's stop being coy, Tom. We're talking about Jeffrey Hammond, former special agent and now foreign news analyst and investigative reporter for the *Post*. A man who has connections to almost every KGB defector in the country and is probably responsible for the exposure of many double agents the Bureau's caught. A man supposedly under a cloud with the Bureau, but actually completely trusted by you and a small cadre. What better cover for a mole? A fixture rarely visible, always there, and accountable, in the final analysis, only to you."

Horn was silent. Each word of Lowell's analysis of Hammond as the mole had hit him like a hammer blow. It made complete sense, would account for the type of intelligence lost, and explain the invincibility and longevity of the mole. But not Jeffrey Hammond. No, he didn't believe that. Lowell and his investigators were on the right trail, he was suddenly sure of that . . . but they were chasing the wrong fox.

The answer Horn saw in his mind was far more shocking, but it gave him a grim satisfaction, even celebration, which he took care not to show. Lowell's erroneous guesses about Jeffrey Hammond had revealed the situation to Horn in a new way, and now, suddenly, he knew who the mole had to be. The mole's placement was simple, cunning in its cleverness. But he would not tell Lowell. He would give none of them, including the president, the satisfaction. The Bureau—*his* Bureau—would deal with its own problems. It always had, and it always would. He would not betray that trust.

He made his expression solemn and concerned. "I think you may be right, Cabot. Yes, it makes sense now that I give it some thought. Still, we must be certain. This is a serious matter. We need a smoking gun. Have your people continue to investigate Hammond, while I alert mine to make certain he does no more damage."

Cabot Lowell nodded and stood. "Smoking gun or not, we need to put an end to his activities quickly."

"We will. You can assure the president the mole has nowhere left to hide."

"He'll be pleased."

As the private door closed, and Cabot Lowell's soft steps disappeared, Tom Horn came to another conclusion: He would deal with this one personally. Make the arrest himself, just as J. Edgar Hoover used to do in the old days before World War II when the FBI was becoming a legend. He owed something to the past, to all the Bureau men and women who had sacrificed to keep America free. He had an obligation to serve his country, and this was his chance. He would honor that, and he knew exactly how.

As the sun dropped low in the sky, and a narcotic warmth spread across the highway, Beth and Jeff continued to discuss the worldwide threat of a terrorist act by Alexei Berianov in America. He told her the warning had come from some secret informer named Perez. Frustrated and worried, they watched other cars for signs they had been recognized, but as the Ferrari followed the trail of vehicles that snaked up into the forested Catoctin Mountains, they saw no one and nothing suspicious.

Jeff pulled the Ferrari into a gas station and mini-grocery north of Thurmont, Maryland, that served a pricey area of young, upwardly mobile Washingtonians who had laid out big bucks for weekend retreats in the country. Gray, eerie shadows cast by leafing sugar maples surrounded the station buildings as he pumped gas and Beth ran in to buy supplies.

Immediately she noted the television set hanging on the wall above the cash register, and that it was tuned to *CNN Headline News*. As she casually monitored the TV screen, she quickly chose cheese, a baguette, fruit, and raw carrots. Then in a gourmet refrigerated case, she saw small jars of a lesser caviar—sevruga, not her favorite, which was beluga, but without a doubt, this was what she needed. *Caviar.* Without another thought, she grabbed a jar and hurried to pay.

But as she stood with her arms filled with groceries, a photo of Jeff appeared on the TV screen. Her knees went weak. But she flashed a brilliant smile to the young man behind the register. "Hi." She set the food on the counter and reached across for a paper sack.

His face was speckled with acne. As he rang up her items, he asked, "You from around here?" He almost licked his lips as his eyes glinted at her.

She smiled more, hoping to distract him from the news. "Just moved to Thurmont. You work here regularly?" She handed him cash and bagged her groceries.

"Sure do." As he extended his hand with her change, the news story shifted. Now her photo was on the screen, too. "*. . . lawyer who was recently fired from her job at a prominent Washington, D.C., law firm. A witness allegedly saw her shoot and kill a man in Georgetown. According to the victim's driver's license, he was a tourist from Miami. No weapon has been recovered. Convey is believed to be in the company of fugitive Jeffrey Hammond, driving a yellow 1987 Plymouth station wagon. Conflicting accounts . . .*"

The youth's palm stopped midair, her change still in it. His eyes rounded with astonishment, and he turned to her. "Is that you?"

"Don't be silly." She grabbed the change and her groceries and rushed out the door. Her heart pounded so hard it seemed to thump against her ribs. Would this never end? Would she and Jeff be hunted the rest of their lives?

As soon as she jumped into the Ferrari, Jeff peeled away into traffic. The sun was lower in the sky, spreading a fiery glow across the mountaintops. They ate as he drove, and she told him about the newscast. She was growing so accustomed to watching for danger that it seemed automatic. Which made her less than happy. The feeling of being hounded and hunted was oppressive. Claustrophobic.

"You bought caviar?" Jeff finally asked, repressing a smile. "That's a little rich for fugitives, isn't it?"

"You bet. I know it seems outrageous, but I wanted it. Actually, I had an incredible urge to have it." She explained lamely, "I'm not usually an impulse shopper."

"Well, thanks for sharing. It was good."

"Thank Mikhail Ogust." She smiled. "At least he had good taste in some things."

Jeff watched her swallow pills. "You have to take them at regular intervals, don't you? Seems like a lot."

"Not so much. It could be worse."

It was a fact of her life. Suddenly she wanted to tell him about it, but she felt shy. How he reacted would say a lot.

She explained, "This blue-and-brown capsule is CellCept. It's to reduce the chances my body will reject a 'foreign' object. In this case, my new heart. I also take Cytovene. That's this green capsule. It helps to prevent disease. These others are prednisone, an anti-inflammatory, and Prograf, an immunosuppressant. I also take coenzyme, flaxseed oil, vitamin E, and alpha lipoic acid. Not so much."

Until medicine made more advances, she would be on all these or similar strong drugs the rest of her life. But it no longer mattered. She savored the rhythmic pulse of her heart and wondered about Mikhail Ogust. Wondered how much he had really impacted her, and whether she would ever find peace with it all. But she also said silent words of thanks to him and his family. They had given her life.

Jeff was direct: "Do the transplant and drugs make you afraid for your future?"

"If you're asking whether I can have a normal life, I guess what we're doing now is hardly normal. At least for me. And I seem to be coping."

"Coping exceptionally well," he corrected. "But these drugs have dangerous side effects, especially over a long period of time."

"What you're implying is if my heart doesn't kill me, one of the side effects could. And you're right. Kidney damage, hypertension, diabetes, anemia." She shrugged a bit too casually. "Risk defines life. I'm just going to do everything I can to keep myself healthy and expect no side effects. Meanwhile, I figure science will come up with even more long-term answers for transplant recipients while I wait." He was making her uncomfortable, asking questions she tried to avoid asking herself.

"Good attitude. I'd do the same, or try to." He saw her uneasiness and wondered whether she would live long—that is, if she survived their current trouble.

She said, "Does it bother you, the uncertainty of my health? It's not something I think about much. But it's always there. I'd understand if it did. If the tables were turned, I'd probably be asking the same questions you are."

Her features had turned neutral, her beauty buried behind an impersonal mask. He had a sense she had just put on her cross-examination face. Or maybe the poker face she wore into a boardroom where she was meeting the opposition for the first time. She had raised a defensive bulwark, and she had done it quickly and automatically. He was glad. Relieved. He wanted distance. Fantasies were one thing. Real life another.

He said, "Must've been pretty hard for you back there, waiting for a heart."

"You could say that. I think the worst part is realizing that to survive, someone else has to die. That does something to the spirit. To benefit from another's death when one is so close to death oneself seems . . . impossible. Unconscionable. And yet, the drive to survive is so strong. Incredible."

He did not know what to say. They continued north another five miles until she insisted he turn over the wheel. "You're tired, Jeff. I can see it in your face. We don't know what we're facing ahead. Do us both a favor and get some sleep."

She was right, and he did not fight her. He pulled off the highway, and they traded seats. As she drove off, watching for patrol cars, he fell into a troubled slumber.

Northeast of Washington, a wiry man in his early thirties paced a Silver Spring, Maryland, hotel room, puzzled and worried, fighting off simmering rage. He returned to the portable computer on the bedside desk and logged onto the Internet again. He e-mailed the Kremlin in code and disconnected.

Smoking furiously, he marched around the room, waiting. Finally he pulled a bottle of Miller Lite from the mini-bar. He twisted off the cap and drank deeply. He liked the light American beers. They lacked bite, but by drinking them he felt he came closer to comprehending the culture. Yes, there was something curious about a nation willing to forgo taste to cut back on calories. Too much food was available here. A good famine would wipe out such shallow priorities.

He fell into his desk chair, put out his Camel, and lighted another. He glanced down at his watch, which he wore on his right wrist above a small white scar. It was a very useful watch, waterproof, with a radiant digital dial, a stop watch, and a timer. When he was working, he could slide it up under the sleeve of his tight-knit black turtleneck where he had access but it could not be seen unless he exposed it.

Time was growing short. Agitated, he stared at the stack of printouts on his desk. They held background on Caleb Bates, Alexei Berianov, Anatoli Yurimengri, Mikhail Ogust, Beth Convey, and Jeff Hammond. He checked his e-mail again. This time there was an answer. Instantly he responded, slammed his fist down onto the desk, rose, and hurried out.

* * *

As she turned west off onto another Pennsylvania highway, Beth studied Gettysburg, which had escaped the urban commercialism of Philadelphia and Pittsburgh. Out of the way, still a center of farming, the countryside remained similar to what it had looked like in 1863 when the North and South had fought the bloodiest battle ever on American soil. Now bathed in the violet light of dusk, the neat orchards, small stands of woods, and old farmhouses were interspersed with fields of rich, dark Piedmont earth. Stone walls outlined many of the roads, while rolling ridges towered in the distance. Fireflies flickered off and on along the roadside and out into the fields and woods.

Finally Beth woke Jeff. "We're almost there." Following the directions she had memorized from the advertisement, she turned the Ferrari south onto Emmetsburg Road. They passed President Dwight D. Eisenhower's farm, now a national historic site, and continued south through more farmlands.

He asked, "Anything happen while I was asleep?"

"It's been quiet. I've been wondering what we'll find. Maybe this has all been just our wild speculation. Maybe some nice elderly couple from Buffalo bought the place and live there with their grandchildren and a bunch of milk cows."

"I've been thinking something like that, too. Either way, we'll know soon."

"On the other hand—" Numbered posts marked driveways. As she read them, she said, "I once had a client tell me, 'You Americans are like lapdogs. We Russians are like street dogs.' In a way, he was right. They had to learn to survive by their wits."

Jeff nodded. "Brezhnev made everything worse. After the nineteen-seventies, criminals started to organize, and the government sanctioned it by looking the other way. That solidified a perception that if you could get away with it, it wasn't really a crime. Now people wonder why we've got the Russian mafia."

"Still, the Soviet Union educated its people. From what I saw in my practice, they could figure out any system. And they didn't get hung up on race, religion, or ethnicity. What mattered was making money. They'd do business with anyone. A sort of profit-based tolerance."

"But sometimes it's been taken too far—doing business with criminals, for instance. And it's partly our fault. We ignored a critical weakness by expecting the Russian state to be a vehicle for orderly change when it was really just a fat bureaucracy stuck in graft, incompetence, and political infighting."

"You're right. After seventy-four years of communism, they couldn't have produced an Alan Greenspan or a Robert Rubin or anyone close to mastering market economics."

"I remember when our fiscal specialists were flying over there for three weeks at a time to advise," he said. "We were so naïve, so excited and hopeful, that we thought intensive bursts of good old American know-how would compensate for three generations of institutionalized ignorance. If the IMF and World Bank hadn't hurled Russia into the free market, sink or swim, we might have been able to help them lay solid groundwork, just as we did Germany after World War Two. But there wasn't time, and it still hasn't happened."

"That reminds me of one of my clients last year. He started two health clubs in Moscow that were hugely successful. Then all of a sudden, he was desperate for new members. Why? Because so many of the old ones had been murdered in mob hits."

"I've got another shocker," Jeff said worriedly. "Some of our intelligence analysts believe Russia's returned to its usual cycle of disintegration and fragmentation, and this time it'll stop only when some leader—probably from the military—reassembles the country by force. Of course, that makes me think of Berianov."

"Good point. He's not strictly military, but he was part of the KGB leadership, which means he'd have had plenty of military contacts in both defense and security." She stopped, her gaze caught by the address on a white post. "This is it." She nodded at the post, which stood on the highway outside a chain-link fence with rolled concertina wire on top. Beyond the fence and up on the slopes of a hill stood a red barn, other outbuildings, white-fenced pastures, and a three-story white colonial mansion with columns. "That's the house I saw in the advertisement."

His head swiveled. "They've got good security."

The fence fronted the country road and extended back on either side of the farm. Inside the property, pine trees dotted the fence line. White posts framed the driveway and connected the fence to a pair of heavy wrought-iron gates. Although decorative, the gates would be difficult to breach, and the fence with its sharp wire posed even more difficulties.

As they drove past, two men in jeans, denim jackets, and work boots slipped out the gate and walked away down the road in the moonlight. She cruised onward another half-mile in the deepening twilight, turned around, and retraced the route. Now the two men were standing at a bus stop. Fireflies danced around them. She continued along the road until they passed the dairy farm a second time and were heading uphill.

He said, "Let's park on the other side of this rise and walk back to watch."

She drove over the crest so they were beyond the farm's view. As she parked off the road, he pulled out night-vision binoculars from the sniper's box of surveillance equipment. It was dark now, and stars were just beginning to twinkle across the vast sky. The temperature was dropping, and the air was ripe with the scent of raw soil.

He asked, "Just how comfortable are you with that gun? I know you said your father took you to target practice. Obviously you know how to shoot."

"Yes, but I'm not well trained. I can aim and fire, and I've got common sense. If you're worried I'm going to try to tell you what to do, forget it. I know my limits."

He nodded. "Good."

They padded through the dark night. For a moment she allowed herself to enjoy moving alongside him, as if they had more in common than survival. He had a long, graceful stride, a man who enjoyed his body and what it could do. But he had changed toward her. Loneliness, an emotion she knew intimately, overcame her, leaving her chilled. Ever since she had told him about her medication and they had talked about what it meant to her future to have had a heart transplant, he had been withdrawn, as if he were far away in a land to which she was not invited. It hurt her. Was this what she would have to deal with the rest of her life? Fear of her heart transplant, of the unknown? Pity and distance?

He indicated a spot behind a large boulder that shielded them from the road. She crouched there, and he settled beside her. She watched as he studied the farm through the binoculars. It seemed to her he was particularly male as he focused utterly on the task at hand. In the cooling air, the heat of his body in the tight jeans and herringbone jacket was almost tactile

"No activity," he muttered. "The dairy herd's been taken into the barn or someplace else. No light there or in any of the other outbuildings. But someone's in the big house. There's light upstairs in two of the central windows and downstairs to the right of the front door." He handed her the binoculars.

She studied the farm's immaculate grounds, wondering whether danger lurked.

"See anything?" he asked.

She described the various buildings, the light, the absence of cows and vehicles. Everything was just as he had said.

"Check out the farm's entrance again."

She moved the binoculars to scrutinize the ornate wrought-iron gates, the posts, and the chain-link fence. "Looks sturdy. What did you see?"

"Look at the pine trees on either side of the gates."

She moved the binoculars slowly, scanning the needles of one of the young trees. "A camera!" She moved the binoculars again. "There's a second one. The entrance is under surveillance!"

"Yeah. No way to know for sure about motion sensors, but my guess is the fence and gate are equipped with them, too. Whoever's in there has major security concerns. That's all it tells us, but it's sure enough to keep me interested."

"Wait a minute. I see a pickup. It's coming out of a building at the base of the hills. Probably a garage." She studied the structure's opening—more than wide enough for two cars and unusually tall for a simple garage. As soon as the pickup cleared, the door began to lower.

He said, "All I can see is headlights moving onto the drive."

"There's something in there. People. Equipment. Hard to make it out."

"Let me."

She handed him the binoculars.

He quickly adjusted them as his gaze sought the building. "Damn. They've sure dropped that door fast. Can't see—" He stopped. "Notice something?" he asked softly.

She continued to stare in the direction of the structure's light. And then she knew what he meant. "The light's gone. Suddenly. All of it at once. You can't tell me all those people turned out every single bulb at the very same instant. Or that someone threw a master switch when there were people inside. It's illogical."

He nodded. His voice was still soft, and she had the sense of a cobra waiting to strike. "I'll bet the light's still burning in that building."

"How could it? Light seeps out around windows and doors, through cracks. It'd show somewhere. They'd have to have blackout curtains."

"Exactly. Somehow they've made the place light-proof. I want to know why." He handed her the binoculars so she could look again.

She glared at him through the night. In the rising moon, his light brown hair had a bright sheen. She warned, "You're not going in without me."

He looked startled, then gave a sardonic grin. "Figures. I'm resigned to my fate."

Tension grew as they watched and analyzed. Every half-hour or so, people left the garage. Sometimes it was just one on a motorcycle or a bicycle. Other times it was two or three on foot, in a car, or in a pickup.

"No one's going in at all," he said grimly. "It's an exodus. But where in hell are all of them headed?"

"And where inside the farm are they coming from?" Restlessness gripped her. It was that same relentless energy she had felt after her transplant. Silently she told Mikhail Ogust to go away. *It's my heart now.* "Next time some of them come out on foot, let's try to grab them. We've got to find out what's going on in there."

34

Beth and Jeff lay in a black shadow beside the fence, far enough from the dairy farm's entrance to be outside the cameras' view. Baby frogs chirped and serenaded. The night air was full of the sweet scent of new grass. But there was no way Beth could enjoy the pastoral atmosphere. Her blood raced, waiting. When eventually another two men left the farm's double-wide gates on foot, Jeff touched her shoulder and mouthed the words "Not yet." She nodded, irritated he would think she would move too soon.

The men headed down the country highway toward the bus stop, talking quietly. As soon as they passed, Jeff touched her shoulder again. In unison, they jumped up and ran on the grass beside the highway, hiding the sounds of their footfalls. As soon as he was close enough, Jeff crashed the barrel of his Beretta down onto the spot where the shoulder met the neck of the man on the right. At the same time, Beth slammed a foot straight between the shoulder blades of the one on the left. He flew forward and landed hard. Since the first man had been knocked unconscious, Jeff turned and pressed his Beretta into the second man's ear.

Beth patted him down and lifted his jacket. "He's got a gun." It was holstered in the small of his back. She pulled it out.

"Get up," Jeff told him. "Do it carefully."

"Who are you?" he demanded. "What do you want?"

The fellow's voice was strained. But Beth heard repressed excitement in it, too. He was worked up, ready for something. He rose slowly to his feet. He had a long face, clean-shaved, with close-set dark eyes barely visible in the night. He looked down at his companion, who was starting to move and would soon be conscious.

"We're just a couple of folks with a real big problem," Jeff told him. "And that's you and your friend. Who are *you*? And what's going on at that farm?"

Beth was already searching the fallen man for a weapon. "He's armed, too." She pulled a pistol from beneath his windbreaker, located just where it had been on his companion.

"What are you anyway—police?" the man demanded. "ATF?"

Jeff ignored the question. "Tell us about Caleb Bates and Alexei Berianov. *Vi gavaréetye pa-rússky?*" Do you speak Russian?

"Don't know who you're talking about," the man said with a sneer. "What kind of sick language is *that?*" But he had flinched at Caleb Bates's name and looked terrified at the sound of the Russian words. He bent to his fallen companion. "Wake up, Chet. Dammit, man. Wake up! They've caught us. You understand, man? We're caught. The Feds."

"We're a lot worse than the Feds," Jeff told him.

"Fuck you!" the standing man said.

The prone man rolled over, his face white, and in an exchange so fleeting that neither Beth nor Jeff had time to react, the two men looked into each other's eyes. A silent message seemed to pass between them, and they moved their jaws.

"No!" Jeff bellowed.

The standing man collapsed, his limbs thrashing, and Jeff tried to pry open his mouth as the second man also went into convulsions. Froth appeared at the corners' of the men's mouths, and their bodies arched, writhed, and shook. Their faces were twisted in awful pain.

"What's happening?" Beth said. "Tell me what to do!"

Jeff groaned and sat back on his heels. "Too late."

"My God. What was it?" She stared at the pair, who were ominously motionless. "It was so fast. What did they do?"

He leaned down and sniffed above the face of the first man, then the second. "I can smell bitter almonds. On both of them. Which means they had cyanide capsules hidden somewhere in their teeth. Maybe in place of teeth. All I know is they had to have been huge doses to kill so quickly."

She fell to her knees beside Jeff and stared in shock from one man to the other. "They committed suicide," she said numbly. "I've been fighting to stay alive for more than a year, and, just like that . . . they kill themselves." She paused, trying to understand. Finally, she recited in a whisper, " 'The secret of human life, the universal secret, the root secret from which all other secrets spring, is the longing for more life. The furious and insatiable desire to be everything else without ever ceasing to be ourselves.' " She lifted her gaze to stare across the two corpses at Jeff.

"Who said that?"

"Miguel de Unamuno, the Spanish philosopher, wrote it. This is unbelievable. Horrible. What could possibly be so bad that they'd *choose* to die? All we wanted to do was talk to them."

"I guess they couldn't take the chance they'd reveal something they shouldn't. It's a tragedy, all right." He looked through the pockets of the first man. "We can't stay out here beside the highway long. We don't want to be discovered by some passing motorist."

She searched the pockets of the second. "Imagine the power of a group so blindly dedicated that they're willing to kill themselves rather than put some goal at risk. Whatever's happening in that farm, it's made complete believers of them."

"We're getting close to finding out what it is. That's for sure. And I don't like any of it. Fanatics are the worst kind of danger. When they're this far gone, they're almost impossible to stop except by killing them dead in their tracks. And that's not something our government's willing to do, at least I hope it's not. And I'm sure as hell not, either. The question is, what's so important that they're willing to die for it?"

"I'll bet it's not going to improve society."

"Yeah, the word *bloodbath* comes to mind. We need to find out everything we can." He pulled the windbreaker off the bigger man and put it on over his herringbone jacket. It was short in the sleeves. "It'll do."

"They didn't have Russian accents." She tried on the other man's jacket. It fit almost perfectly.

"It would've been a lot simpler if they'd had. What it means is we still don't know for sure who or what we're dealing with."

They dragged the bodies across the dark road and into a small woods. As they returned to scoop up the men's things, dread filled her. Whoever was behind all this had so little regard for human life—not even valuing his own people's—that he had sent them out with what was essentially an order to die if they so much as sensed failure. The leader—Alexei Berianov, Caleb Bates, or whoever—was not just a murderer, he was a monster, and if these were his methods, he would stop at nothing to succeed.

*　　*　　*

Moving urgently through the farm's mansion, Alexei Berianov locked the door to his bedroom and went into his private bath. He stopped before the full-length mirror to study his heavy body and face. There was a solidness to Caleb Bates that promised stability and authority. From his squarish face to his thick torso, he was a success in all ways. Now he would die, like the male black widow spider, his job done. Berianov smiled, bidding Bates farewell.

With relief he pulled out his rubber mouth inserts. His cheek contours collapsed, altering the proportions of all his facial features. No longer did his nose and eyes appear small. Instead he once again had even features—straight nose, blue-brown eyes set handsomely apart, and a wide mouth. Very northern European. His face had a mobile strength he always controlled. He greeted himself in Russian and studied himself. Soon all of this would be over. It was worth it, he promised.

Berianov stripped off Bates's padded clothing as he returned to his bedroom. From his closet he took old jeans, a flannel shirt, and a faded denim jacket. He put them on. They fit perfectly.

He returned to the bathroom and leaned toward the mirror. He frowned. He smiled. He studied the lines that resulted on his face. He took out a mascara pencil and deepened the lines. He brushed ash color beneath his eyes and into the hollows of his cheeks. As he worked, Berianov's face grew older . . . sixties . . . seventies. And stopped. He painted brown age spots on the backs of his hands, and, as a final touch, he returned to his closet for the thrashed, dirty Stetson he had hidden there.

He put it on in front of the full-length mirror and laughed aloud with pleasure. He looked like an old cowhand or farmer, someone ravaged by the elements but still spry enough to get around and be useful. Perfect.

Using the Ferrari's two small map lights, Jeff and Beth examined the items they had taken from the two dead men.

Discouraged, she said, "Nothing."

"Nothing I can see," he admitted.

There was the usual assortment—a couple of pocketknives, billfolds with cash, credit cards, Arizona driver's licenses that could easily be fake, a Snickers bar, two men's combs, a Bic lighter, and a crush-proof package of Camels that Jeff had emptied and found contained only cigarettes. There was nothing indicating where the men had been going or what they had planned. There were not even matches from a local diner.

Beth still ached, but continuing to move relieved a lot of her misery. Earlier they had used presoaked tissues from the sniper's makeup box to wash their faces of blood and clean their scratches and other small wounds. After that, they had applied dark foundation powder to reduce the reflection from moonlight on their faces.

He decided, "I can't wear a baseball cap onto the farm. None of the people we saw wore hats. I'll stand out with one on, or if I have long hair."

"You want me to cut your hair?"

"That's the idea."

She fished in the makeup box and pulled out scissors. "Just call me Delilah." When she turned to face him, he had taken off his cap. In the small confines of the Ferrari, she was suddenly struck again by his maleness. By the density of his body and the appealing length from his wide shoulders to his narrow waist and hips. She liked the power in his face, with its square jaw and large, intelligent eyes.

But since she had told him about her medicine and what it meant, he had been removed. He seldom looked at her directly. His body remained beside her, but little else. She felt bereft, as if the warmth had gone out of a fire. She repressed a sigh. Her condition was going to frighten away all men, and there was nothing she could do to change that. A hard, lonely knot seemed to tighten around her heart.

He turned away. Scissors in hand, she silently reached up and smoothed the back of his long hair. It was bristly, as strong and quirky as he. She hated to shorten it. She bit her lower lip. Then she made the first cut. A hank of rich brown hair fell into her lap.

She sighed. "If we're going to do this, we might as well go all the way. To get a different look, I'll have to make it really short."

"I know. Do it."

She hesitated then went to work. She clipped quickly. No point in dragging it out. She sheared the top of his head, then around his ears, and finally the back of his head. In the map light, it was far from a perfect job, but it was short. All of a sudden he looked like a boxer or marine.

"I'll even it out later," she decided. "Better yet, get someone who knows what they're doing to fix it up." Good advice, if they survived.

He turned to her. "Thanks." He smiled.

For a moment it seemed as if they had gone back in time to when they had first discovered they had liked each other. It seemed long ago. Then his expression changed. He was again cold, distant, very businesslike.

He dropped the strap of the night-vision binoculars around his neck and opened his door. "Make sure you've got your Walther and flashlight."

She slipped her gun into her waistband. Carrying flashlights, they climbed out of the car and trotted down the hill toward the farm's entrance.

"Look," she said. "The mansion's lights are going off now, too. The second floor is completely dark. And the first floor's going dark, too."

He gazed through the chain-link fence and nodded. "Don't take any stupid chances," he warned. "Follow my lead."

"Aye, aye, Captain." She forced a light tone to her voice, which she did not feel. Nervousness swept through her. She watched his big frame move easily with the darkness, almost as if it were his friend. Then he dropped to the grass and weeds, and she followed. They slithered on their bellies. Twigs and rocks bit her flesh as they approached the gate. In position, they looked up at the farm, ghostly and deserted in the moonlight. Time stretched. She could almost hear the beating of her heart.

"Here comes one." Jeff's voice was low in her ear.

The headlights were high off the ground. As the vehicle rounded a shallow curve and headed down toward the gate, she saw it was a pickup.

"We'll use the lights of the car for a distraction in case someone's monitoring the surveillance cameras," he warned. "Get ready to move."

The heavy wrought-iron gates inched opened. The headlamps were brilliant, dazzling. She closed her eyes then opened them to slits, keeping watch. Heat from the pickup's motor warmed the air. The exhaust stung her nose.

"Now." His voice was hidden by the growl of the engine.

The gates were wide open. The night was aglow with the vehicle's light. Her heart pounding, she followed Jeff as he crouched and slipped low to the ground past the gates and the pickup. They were inside. Unspeaking, they rolled off to the side into the dark, jumped up, and sprinted away from the cameras.

On the first floor of the farm's mansion, the old man resisted looking in any of the mirrors. He was having the strange sense again of not knowing who he was. He hated the queasy feeling, and he longed to be simply, and always, himself. But then he thought about the tragedy of his people—the increasing suicide rates across Russia, the starvation, and the homeless children who wandered ragged and begging. There were thousands of dying villages as the collective farms disbanded. That was not his country. It was a travesty. A sick joke. It infuriated and mortified him. In the world's eyes, even in the eyes of her people, Russia was a reeling giant, sick and impotent.

With an effort, he shrugged it all away and resumed his march through the dark mansion, planting plastic explosives with electronic detonators that could be triggered from a distance. The big house seemed ready for its fate, milk-white moonlight streaming in through the windows and ink-black shadows behind the furniture. There was no color anywhere. Upstairs a board creaked as it adjusted to the cooling temperatures of night.

Once the explosives were arranged, the old man strode outdoors to stand in his battered denim jacket and jeans on the front portico to survey Caleb Bates's land. It was quiet, too. As usual, he was the last to leave.

The moon had risen, and it was full—a good omen. He headed down the steps and out into the cool night to make his rounds. A sense of anticipation began to overtake him. Much had been done, but there was still much to do. And of course there was the lingering issue of Beth Convey and Jeff Hammond. The quiet grounds beckoned like a tomb.

35

Moving at a steady lope, Jeff led Beth off the drive and onto the grass. They held their pistols lightly at their sides, kept their flashlights dark, and skirted the fences and hugged the trees for cover. The grounds seemed deserted, glowing in the moonlight with nothing moving anywhere, only them. Whoever operated the farm seemed to rely on the high fence and the monitored front gate for protection, dispensing with guards. Or perhaps everyone had gone.

Jeff said nothing to Beth. Guilt fueled him, and he could hardly look at her. She was foolishly brave, which had made him afraid to tell her she could not go with him. If he had left her in the car, he knew she would simply have waited until he was out of sight and then tried to break into the farm on her own.

With his peripheral vision he kept anxious watch over her. They stopped at the first building—the dark barn. Using hand signals, he gestured her to wait at the corner. At least she did what he wanted when they were in action. But not this time. This time she continued around to the window, which was where he had intended to go. She flattened back against the wall, her pistol up in both hands, and peered around inside. He stopped next to her.

"I don't see anyone," she whispered. "Just chickens and cows."

"When I tell you to do something, do it!" His voice was low and outraged. "I don't want you to get killed!"

"Why not? I'm going to die soon anyway. That's what you think, isn't it?"

"I—"

She jogged back around to the front of the barn. He was on her heels.

She stopped at the door. "Cover me. I'll open it."

"Beth, stop. We're not going in. There's no reason to. We're looking for evidence, not trouble. Let's get to that garage. It's off to the side, and it's where everyone was coming from. If we find nothing there, we'll try the mansion."

Her long eyelashes lowered and raised. "You're right."

They ran again, finding cover where they could. At last they arrived at what appeared to be a large garage. It was the width of nearly three, with a second story. The opening was just as it had appeared in the binoculars—double wide and two levels high.

"Some garage," she muttered. "It's big enough for tanks."

They scouted around and found no windows. There was one other door, at a rear corner near the hill. She turned on her flashlight briefly to scan the area. When she saw nothing useful, he pressed his ear against the door, listening.

"Anything?"

"Not a sound." And they had seen no light as they had circled the structure. He felt the door. It was metal. "Nothing ventured, etcetera." He tried the handle. "Locked, dammit."

Suddenly a man's voice sounded behind them, old and quavery. "Maybe I can help you folks? Thought everyone was gone. You two are real late, ain't you?"

Beth and Jeff spun around. He wore a cowboy hat tipped low over his brow. His lined face looked almost skull-like in the moonlight. He had turned on a flashlight, and it was trained on them. He reached over and, with an age-spotted hand, flipped a switch on the wall.

Instantly an overhead floodlight burned on, illuminating the back of the concrete structure and the three of them as they stood gathered tensely at the door.

"Now, I'm just the idiot caretaker," he said drily, "but seems to me you were supposed to be gone by now." He glanced at their pistols but said nothing.

Jeff's face was immobile. Quickly he took in the old man and the fact that he was neither surprised nor afraid they were armed. He relaxed a fraction. "You're right. We're late. Hope we're not going to catch hell for it. We don't have our assignments. Do you know where we're supposed to meet everyone?"

The stranger's eyes narrowed suspiciously. "I don't get to have that kind of information. You know that. You lose your assignment, my guess is you're in deep shit. Excuse me, miss." He glanced at Beth apologetically. "I wouldn't want to be you. You know how the colonel can be."

Beth said, "We didn't explain well. We just got back, and that's why we're late. Tell us about the colonel? How's he been?"

The old man backed off. "How do I know? He don't talk to me."

Now they knew with certainty Bates—Berianov—was part of the picture here.

"Well," the old caretaker continued, "you two should go on in. Somebody's probably waiting to send you on your way." He glanced up. White moths were gathering by the floodlight, diving at it out of the dark from all directions.

"The door's locked," Jeff said. "How about opening it?"

The old man cackled with laughter. "Talk about dumb. That's me." He pulled out a clanking key chain and unlocked the deadbolt. "When you leave, close up after yourselves, okay?"

"Will do." Jeff headed inside.

As Beth followed, she glanced back and saw one old hand reach up and close so swiftly on a moth she almost missed it. As the caretaker looked down at his cupped hand, his shoulders tightened under his jeans jacket, and she heard a soft *crunch.* He had killed the moth, squeezed it to death. He switched off the floodlight, plunging them into darkness, and turned away. The last vision Beth had was of him stepping away into black night, his bright, sharp eyes, slowly vanishing like the grin on the Cheshire cat. Eyes that had not looked old at all. Shuddering, she felt an unsettling sense of having seen those eyes before.

"Let's go." It was a whisper. Jeff had opened the garage door.

Putting her hand on his shoulder, she let him lead her into utter blackness. She closed the door behind them.

Jeff's foot hit a hard surface, and he reached out and felt a wall until he realized it was a door. A second door. He inched it open. Intense light spilled toward them through the narrow opening. He listened again and peered around through the door's crack. Then he opened the door wider and looked again.

He turned to say into her ear, "Deserted."

They exchanged a look. Using hand signals, he gestured to her to stay close behind. His chest tight, he raised his pistol, clamped his flashlight against the binoculars to pin them against his chest, and slid around the corner into a big central area. His back to the wall, he scanned the gun across the two-story room, looking for trouble. She followed immediately, her pistol ready.

They stared. Then slowly lowered their weapons. From the walls hung no tools, no empty gas cans, no old tires or rusted car parts. The building was simply an empty shell. Not only was it no garage, it was something they had come nowhere near guessing. Surprised, they studied the concrete floor. In the center was the mouth of an over-wide driveway that descended at about a five-percent slope and disappeared.

She said, "What in heaven's name is this?"

"We'd better find out."

They listened for the sound of vehicles or voices. Silence. They moved down the tunnel, their weapons ready. That was when they heard the hum of a ventilation system. Above them, exposed pipes, conduits, ventilation and heating shafts, support beams, and fluorescent lights were fastened to the rock ceiling. Nothing was painted. It was all raw concrete, plastic, metal, and stone.

She said, "The building was set against the hill. That may explain it. What we're in now could be part of a natural cave system. There are quite a few in Pennsylvania."

The tunnel flattened out, and they stepped into a paved area as wide as a football field where white painted lines indicated slots for motorcycles, cars, and trucks. It was empty now, a deserted underground parking garage, probably the source of all the vehicles that had been leaving the farm. The low hum was getting on her nerves. There was a sense of oppressive grayness everywhere.

As they continued on, watching, she studied the walls for an opening. "There's a door." It was in a dark nook where the wall angled in and out. She was amazed she had noticed it. It was painted gray, difficult to distinguish from the rock around it.

She tried the knob. "Locked." She stared at it, thinking there was something familiar about it.

Jeff called, "It's probably just a utility closet with gauges and switches for pipes and ventilation. Come here, Beth. I've found something else. Another ramp."

But she was still considering the locked door: No, not a closet. Something else. She tried to focus. Metal construction. Shelves? A storage room?

"Beth? There's another tunnel here. Let's go."

She abandoned her reverie. Jeff was standing where another tunnel sloped down toward the rear. This one was as wide as the first but had a steeper grade, perhaps ten degrees. Beth forgot the door. She ran to follow him down. They passed between more rough-hewn rock walls. Soon they heard the sound of rushing water. The air grew dank. The temperature dropped. The noisy water turned into a roar. Almost in unison they stopped their rapid descent.

"Look at that!" Jeff said.

She echoed his astonishment. "Who would have thought?"

Below them extended a massive, arched cavern. The walls were at least four stories high. To the left, a wide waterfall crashed down into a pond so black that it looked bottomless. Green and brown moss covered the cavern wall above it. But to the right extended the majority of the cave, and there was the more compelling sight—

"My God, it's the Oval Office!" Jeff stared. Alarms went off in his brain. "The windows, the colonnades, the patio furniture overlooking the Rose Garden. A lot of the West Wing."

"But nothing's finished," she said, wondering. "It looks as if it's just been tacked together and paint slapped on."

The Oval Office reproduction stood out like a glaring warning. They trotted down the damp ramp, their footsteps echoing. The rest of the replica of the two-story West Wing of the White House was cut away, with walls and floors ending midair. Still, someone had taken the time to fill out much of the Rose Garden, from the broad lawn flanked by flower beds to the "limestone" steps on which stood a podium. But this time, the limestone was unpainted particle board.

"It's all fake. Even the grass." She shivered.

He pulled open a French door that had never held glass and strode into the president's sham office. "So's the furniture." Particle board was the material of choice here, too, from the big desk to the chairs on either side of the fake fireplace.

She turned in terrified wonder, studying the third-rate rendition. "What is this? What does it mean?"

"Maybe this is what the terrorist plot is all about. The presidency. The Oval Office. What you're looking at is the kind of replica an army or a secret service builds to train troops, guerrillas, undercover agents, anyone who needs to attack, defend, or infiltrate. Remember when I told you about the simulated American city the KGB built as a training ground for spies in the Ural Mountains? That's what this reminds me of."

Above ground in the security building, Alexei Berianov sat before a wall of monitors, watching their progress. As soon as Ivan Vok had reported he had tracked the station wagon to where it had been abandoned in the parking lot of the Philmalee Group, Berianov knew he was in danger. Beth Convey and Jeff Hammond were no longer traceable, and he was vulnerable here. He had kept close watch for them. When they had invaded his farm, his needle-nose security cameras recorded all their moves. The tiny cameras were hidden in trees and in eaves, and they surveilled inside and outside buildings. Small and nearly invisible, they were very different from the clunky ones at the gates that he had ordered to satisfy the Keepers.

Once the pair had stumbled onto his farm, it had been inevitable they would fall into his trap. The deduction was simply an extension of what he knew: Both were driven to succeed. Now they had seen the prize . . . the simulated White House grounds he had built for Sergeant Austin and his guerrillas to practice on.

It was obvious Convey and Hammond were not only worried but excited. It was at this peak—just as they thought they had solved the puzzle, just as they felt a heavy duty to their country—that he would destroy them. There was little glory in taking out the weak. But the strong . . . that was intriguing. That was worthwhile.

While they had been exploring deeper into the cavern, he had been laying plastic explosives in the garage and down the ramp into the parking lot. He wanted no one to know about the caves or the mansion and the evidence they contained. At the same time, the blasts would eliminate Convey and Hammond. He smiled. He liked the neatness of it, the efficiency.

He reached to the console and pushed the first button. There was an ear-assaulting explosion, and the ground shook.

36

In Washington, the two FBI cars left the hurtling stream of bumper-to-bumper traffic on the I-495 Beltway at exit 13 and sped along Route 193. Alone in the rear seat of the lead vehicle—his personal Bureau limousine—Director Tom Horn was acutely aware of the weight of the 10mm Smith & Wesson semiautomatic under his left arm. There was an excitement to feeling that weight and knowing what it was. It had been thirty years since he had regularly carried a weapon, not since he was a Denver detective. He had occasionally carried when he was a U.S. attorney, but that was twenty years ago now. The gun gave a strange lift to his spirits. He was in action again.

He needed that boost, anything to relieve the gloominess of the last few hours and take his mind off what he both feared and hoped he was going to have to do. Ever since Cabot Lowell left his office that afternoon, he had been vaguely depressed as well as excited by the sudden prospect of capturing the elusive, long-hidden mole. More than anything, it was the identity of the man he suspected of being the mole that depressed him. He was the one man whose crimes could easily pass for those of Jeff Hammond. And yet, the unmasking excited him, too. Of course, it did. Thank God the Bureau at last would be rid of this scourge.

The headlights of oncoming vehicles alternately illuminated the face of the director and plunged him back into darkness as he sat in the backseat, mulling over the situation. His phone call to his suspect to arrange this clandestine meeting had not been all that unusual. Anytime he wished to discuss a subject without creating curiosity inside the Bureau, he would meet the members of his top staff outside the building, occasionally at tonight's location. He had no idea how his predecessors had handled such matters, although he suspected they had done much the same, but he far preferred external meetings to closed-door, in-the-office sessions. In the paranoid, back-stabbing, power-brokering, intrigue-ridden world inside the Beltway, the conspiracies were too often real and the paranoia too often justified.

"We're here, sir," his agent driver announced quietly.

Tom Horn looked out at the darkened entrance to Great Falls Park. Here were eight hundred wooded acres alongside the rapids and waterfalls of the Potomac. Less than twenty minutes from the District, it was ideal. Closed after dark, there would be no one to see, hear, or interfere with what he had to do. One way or another, right or wrong, this was the way it must be: Only he and his suspect to know what had happened should he be wrong, and only he and his agents to claim the credit if he were right.

As he reached for the door handle, apprehension knotted his stomach, a sensation so unfamiliar he did not recognize it for a few seconds. He had not felt such unease since his first few months as a rookie patrolman long ago in Denver. The bull of the Colorado Buffalos was never afraid or even nervous, so he brushed the useless emotion aside, stepped out into the night, and allowed himself to enjoy the thrill and once-familiar adrenaline of physical action.

"What do you want me to do, Director?" the driver asked, walking around the car to check the flimsy barrier that blocked the entry into the park. "I can remove this if you want me to take you on in."

The second car had come to a gliding stop directly behind the director's limo, and agents Graham and Thoma joined the director and his driver.

Graham asked, "What's the plan, sir? Can you fill us in now?" As always, Graham looked as if he had stepped from a store window, so pressed and immaculate were his dark suit, white shirt, and wing-tip shoes.

"I'm meeting someone in the park near the falls," Horn said in a low voice. "It's an extremely delicate matter, and I have to handle it alone. That's all I can tell you. Your job is to be my backup. I anticipate no trouble, but there's always the chance. I don't need to tell you that."

"No, sir," Graham agreed.

Thoma nodded vigorously, so eager to serve the director he would have been wagging his tail if he had one. Thoma had his voracious ambition and simmering violence under close control right now, and the director knew it. But then, tonight's rendezvous was just the sort of assignment for which a man like Thoma was especially useful.

"How close do you want us?" Graham continued.

"As close as you can get without being detected. You don't have to worry about witnessing the meeting. In fact, I order you not to. And I don't want you eavesdropping either. This is a very sensitive, very confidential matter. Only if I raise my voice do I want you to be in earshot."

"Yes, sir."

"Understand, Thoma?" Horn was concerned, Thoma could be a stupid hothead.

"Yes, Director. Out of sight, out of earshot. But we've got to be able to hear if you call us. Not a problem."

"I didn't think it would be." The director checked his Smith 10, reholstered it under his arm, and gave an affectionate pat to the faint bulge in his suit jacket. He nodded to his men and stepped over the barrier to enter the park. As he disappeared into the trees and the darkness and the nighttime odors of pine needles and the cooling forest, he felt that faint uneasiness once more. He had seen no other car. Was his suspect even here?

Tom Horn moved awkwardly but steadily ahead on the dark, tourist-beaten path. The moon and stars cast sooty shadows, but Horn's eyes had adjusted and the path was wide enough that he usually could see where to place his feet. The ancient songs of rapids and small waterfalls filled the night long before he came in sight of the river. In Colorado, his mountain state, the music of flowing water had soothed him for as long as he could remember. Tonight it would serve a different purpose—to cover the words that would be said in this meeting, hide them from Graham and Thoma or anyone else, in case he was wrong.

As he reached the broad, silver-black Potomac, he saw movement in a grove of oaks and maples to his left, isolated by a meadow and close to the edge of the water. His old detective instincts kicked in. It was exactly the spot he would have chosen had he wanted to be sure the other fellow was alone, and it told him the suspect knew the reason for his boss's summons, or at least he was prepared for the possibility.

It gave Horn a surge of confidence. The man had come to cut a deal, and he wanted no one to hear what that deal was. Encouraged, he marched straight toward the grove of trees. There was no sign of Graham or Thoma. Graham knew his work and how to do it, and he would monitor Thoma. As Horn reached the periphery of the circle of shadows cast by the trees, reflected light from the river glinted on the light-colored eyes and white skin of the man waiting in the umbra.

Without hesitation, Horn strode into the woods and straight up to the waiting man and said, "Hello, Bobby."

"Director." In the darkness beneath the trees, the assistant director inclined his head toward his boss.

Tom Horn sensed rather than saw the polite gesture. He took it as a sign of guilt and regret, and softened his voice. "Why, Bobby?"

"Why what, Director? What did you want to talk about out here in the middle of nowhere?"

Horn tried to see Kelsey's eyes, the set of his face, his body language, but there were only brief glimpses like reflections in a window lighted by blinking neon. "You can't guess?"

"Guess? No, sir, I can't. Is it Hammond? I assure you he didn't kill those two kids, and with all three of his Soviet defectors dead, I've got him working on that rumored terrorism our informant told us about. He'll—"

Horn said, "It's not about Hammond. Well, maybe indirectly."

"Indirectly?"

Horn moved his shoulder to feel the weight of the Smith under the arm of his unbuttoned suit jacket. He took a slow breath. "The attorney general and Cabot Lowell have been running a covert investigation in the Bureau to find our mole. They think they have him now. They say all the evidence points to Hammond. But it's not Hammond, is it? It's you."

Bobby Kelsey lived in a world of grays. It was no conscious philosophy he had developed over the years; it was simply the result of life. Born on a hardscrabble farm in the panhandle of Texas where the heat and cold were fierce and strong opinions the backbone of everyday events, he had learned early a beating was something you took without ever showing you cared. His father knew all the answers, he had repeatedly told Bobby, and Bobby had too much Irish in him for his own good. So take your licking and learn.

With his carrot-top head and smiling blue eyes, young Kelsey understood quickly that charm was a potent tool for survival. When he left the farm at age sixteen, it was to go on scholarship to the University of Texas. His father was opposed, which had increased the lure of an education. Ruthless in the pursuit of grades and a good time, he graduated at the top of his undergraduate and law school classes. Which made him a hot recruitment target for the wheeling-spieling law firms of Dallas and Houston. Instead, he had joined the FBI, because it wielded a stick bigger than his father or any law firm ever fantasized. That stick was national government, armed with a badge, a gun, and secrecy. All that he lacked was the big income. He figured that would come eventually.

Ten years later, after he was transferred out of the field to his first management job at the Hoover building in Washington, Kelsey sold out to the Communists. The Cold War was whimpering to a close, and they were desperate and generous. The dollars rolled in. He was not a jerk like Rick Ames, who threw it around like a flasher with his cash-bought houses and Jaguars. Kelsey banked his offshore, kept his Irish smile and wry sense of humor, and played the game he had learned so well.

His last Cold War handler had been the notorious Alexei Berianov, head of Yasenevo. When Berianov defected, Kelsey had taken him on as a sideline client; Berianov's private retainer was far too handsome to ignore. Of course, he still performed the occasional job for the Kremlin.

To earn his release from questioning, Berianov had revealed that Rick Ames had been spying for the Soviets since the mid 1980s. It was the smart thing to do: Ames's carelessness with his espionage income was going to be his undoing soon anyway, and it took the heat off the FBI's pursuit of its own traitor, Bobby Kelsey. But now it appeared Bobby's luck had run out. He knew what he had to do. Maybe the old Irish charm would still work.

Bobby Kelsey smiled, his teeth glossy white in reflected light. "Why, for money, of course, Tom."

Taken aback by the matter-of-fact, almost cheerful, reason, Horn blurted, "You *admit* it?"

"Why not? That's the nature of a mole. Once they put a spotlight on you, the illusion is broken, and it's over. You'll find the evidence now."

"And for money? Nothing else?"

"What would you like better?"

"Conviction, maybe. Idealism. I might respect those. But *money?* Sell out your own people, your friends, your family and loved ones, the history of this country, what this country stands for today . . . the *flag,* for God's sakes! For nothing more than *money?* Shit, Bobby."

"That's all there is, Tom. Don't be ridiculous. Everything else is a waste of time. You can't eat religion. Ideals won't keep you warm and dry in an ice storm. Try making your money by digging the rocks that pass for dirt in Texas, and you'll learn what's important and what isn't."

"Excuses? That's more despicable than the money. We were at war, Bobby! Against an enemy so powerful it could destroy us in an instant.

Today it's not all that much better. They still have tens of thousands of nuclear warheads. We're *still* at war, it's just that nobody will admit it!"

"Bullshit, Tom. We were never in any real danger from the Soviets. It was all a con job to keep the defense contracts rolling in, keep the good citizens from asking too many questions about how things are run and for whom." Kelsey laughed. "Come off it, you know that as well as I do. It was a shell game, still is. Dwight Eisenhower even warned us about it in the fifties, but nobody listened. 'The military-industrial establishment,' remember? For the past half-century all those people have been getting more than their share, so why shouldn't I get mine now, too?" He laughed again. "Ideals? You're too ingenuous to be believed!"

Rage shook Tom Horn. The bald gall of this man he had counted among his friends and most valuable associates in the Bureau was beyond all belief. He snarled, "You don't do this because when the game's over, and the money's gone, you'll have nothing, you understand? Nothing. Not even your self-respect to keep you warm."

"Why should the game ever end? It won't, you know. It's too damn much fun. We all enjoy it. Even you, Tom. Don't pretend you don't. Look at you, out here in the dead of night, in a clandestine meeting that could just as well have been held at a Harvey's. The only idiots who don't like the games and the lethal toys and the secrets—oh, so many secrets—aren't running things. They're farming. Campaigning for city council. Figuring out how to squirrel pennies away so they can afford an RV for retirement. So we're the ones in charge, aren't we, old friend? It's our game after all." He grinned.

The sound of the falls seemed louder in the director's ear. It started to drown out his thoughts, but then he steeled himself. He needed to stay alert. He despised Bobby Kelsey and everything he stood for. For the damage he had done to America. But Horn was the director of the FBI, he had to think of the future good of his country, too. What had been done, had been done.

"Let's talk about a deal, Kelsey."

"Why not? I could work for the Bureau, for the CIA, for NSA. I'd feed my current employers false information and pass on to you the shopping lists they gave me so you could pinpoint their concerns and their weaknesses."

"If we could trust you."

"Trust doesn't enter into it, you know that. Just pay me as well as they do—more would be better—and you'll know soon enough if I'm playing it double."

"We can talk about it, but now I'm taking you in."

"Just you?" Kelsey laughed again. "That's good. Like J. Edgar and Al Karpis."

"Something like that, Bobby. The Bureau does its own job."

Kelsey's voice dropped almost to a whisper. "So do I, Tom."

The director saw only what seemed like a part of the darkness under the trees move, and at first felt no pain as the knife entered between his ribs and angled upward. Only when it entered his heart, and the pain exploded, and he was already falling, did he feel another human beside him, feel hands propping him up. By the time Bobby Kelsey lowered him to the ground under the trees, Thomas Horn felt nothing at all.

Alert and wary, Kelsey moved deeper into the impenetrable shadow under the trees and listened. The director had made no sound at all, Kelsey's reward for knowing what to do with one's weapons. There would be backup close by, but not too close. Which was why he had picked the grove in which to wait. Kelsey had counted on the director's silly fantasies to make him foolish. They all wanted to be J. Edgar.

The instant he had received the phone call and heard what the director wanted him to do, he had guessed what was up. He had guessed, too, from years of experience in counterintelligence, that the director was still not positive he was the mole, which meant the director would come alone, and he would tell no one of his suspicions. What Kelsey had said was true: Once a mole came under any suspicion, he was through. He could not allow himself to be arrested or the director to reveal his suspicions to anyone else.

Bobby Kelsey listened in the darkness. When he was satisfied no one had seen or heard Tom Horn die, he took a small, flat, air-tight metal box from his pocket, opened it, and removed a specially treated surgical glove. He slipped it carefully onto his right hand, knelt beside the body, and gripped the smooth handle of the knife still in Horn's ribs. He stood again and dropped a swizzle stick from the bar in Stone Point where Jeff Hammond had asked so many questions. Then he turned and padded soundlessly away into the night.

From inside the edge of the woods, Chuck Graham stared across the meadow in the hazy moonlight toward the grove of trees through which the director had entered. From where he was, he could see nothing in the grove, and he could hear nothing over the rush of the falls.

"Anything?" Thoma asked nervously.

The moon had poked above the trees less than ten minutes ago. "Not a damn thing." Graham continued to study the silent grove.

"How long's it been?"

"Nearly an hour."

As he spoke, the moon rose higher and its light angled into the shadowed woods. The two agents could see individual trees emerge by rows until the heart of the grove became visible.

"I don't see anything. Where are they?" Thoma worried.

Graham peered. Then he was on his feet. "Come on! Keep low."

The two agents ran in crouches across the meadow. At the trees, Thoma looked around and said, "There's no one in there."

"Yes, there is."

Graham parted bushes and walked slowly until he stood over the body of FBI director Thomas Earle Horn. Thoma joined him. They looked at each other and back down at the man whom they were supposed to have protected but who had made it impossible for them to do their job.

"Christ," Thoma whispered.

Graham bent down. "Knife. It's still in him. Bag it."

While Thoma used his handkerchief to remove the murder weapon, Chuck Graham searched the leaves and grass inch by inch. When he found the swizzle stick—red with gold flecks, half covered with dirt, but the name of the bar still visible—he balanced it on his pocketknife and stood up.

He extended it toward Thoma. Graham's voice carried a world of hate. "Hammond!"

At the first shaking of the ground, Jeff pulled Beth down beside an upright support in the tunnel. They crouched together, his arm around her
shoulders. Her heart pounded, and her throat tightened. Rock dust
rained down, coating them. They sneezed and fought to breathe.

Before the earth stopped shuddering, Jeff seized her arm and yanked
her to her feet. "We've got to get out of here." They holstered their guns
and tore up the ramp, heading for the parking area.

"What was it?" she asked. "An earthquake? Are there earthquakes
in Pennsylvania?"

As they breeched the top and ran onto the flat parking area, he said,
"No earthquake. Felt more like a bomb or some other kind of explosive. I could hear it through the ground like thunder."

"You think there'll be more?"

Just then the earth quaked and rolled again. This time they dropped
down together, arms over heads. She had heard a dull *thunk* arrive
from somewhere far away. The sound of the blast, she decided. As the
ground quieted, there were low groaning noises, as rock fought rock.

"Let's go!" He had her on her feet again, and they were running before she could understand.

And then she knew: "Someone's dynamiting the farm."

"That's my take, too."

"If it's Berianov . . . and he knows we're down here . . . he's dynamiting these caves to kill us."

"I call that solid deductive thinking."

Suddenly the cavern rocked. They lost their balances and toppled. They sneezed and coughed. The detonation seemed almost as if it were directly on top of them. Rock sheered off the ceiling and walls and crashed down. A gray-and-brown dust cloud blasted toward them from the ramp on the far side of the parking area, which led up into the building.

"Look." He wiped dust from his eyes and pointed ahead. The rolling cloud was spreading out and thinning. "Check out that gray lump on the wall. Looks like Playdoh—that's plastic explosive. And there's another and another. Someone must've laid them out after we passed. Otherwise, I would've noticed. They could go off any second. There are too many for me to disarm in time."

"We've got to get out of here." She looked wildly around, feeling trapped but not wanting to admit it.

"But not the way we came in. From the size of that dust storm, there's got to be tons of rock blocking the entrance now."

Another explosion shook the cavern. Flung against the wall, she was momentarily dazed. How could they escape this stone tomb? Suddenly as if from a distant part of her mind, a memory came. From her nightmare. *From her heart?* It swept over her, and she was back in it, living it—

She pounded down a tunnel with rough rock walls. At last she saw a gray metal door. She yanked it open. Inside was a shaft just large enough for one person. She slammed the door and climbed the ladder, escaping. . . .

"That door I found!" She ran. " Come on!"

"It's probably just a utility closet."

"No! I saw it in my nightmares. Mikhail Ogust must've known about these caverns. If I'm right, it's a shaft with a ladder. It's a way out!"

Jeff rushed to catch up. "Maybe you're right. Berianov wouldn't build anything like this without a secret way to save his skin."

Abruptly another massive convulsion shook the cavern. It tossed them down as if they were puppets. Beth landed on her back, the wind knocked out of her. There was a thunderous roar, and rocks and boulders smashed down. Beth and Jeff rolled together, their arms protecting each other's heads. All the lights between them and the entrance died, and rock dust turned the remaining flourescent light into gray dusk. The air stank of mold and rock.

"Beth! Are you all right?" He pulled her close. His heart pounded with fear for both of them.

She coughed. "Fine . . . I'm fine."

"Then let's go. We might not survive the next one. And there's still plastic on the wall. There's going to be at least one more blast."

They limped toward the hidden door, skirting mounds of debris. Rocks still fell, shattering into piles. The other side of the cavern, where they had entered, had disappeared behind a monstrous rock slide.

"The door's locked." She swore.

"Not a problem." With his pistol, he fired into the keyhole, turned the knob, and yanked it open to reveal the shaft she remembered from her post-op dreams. It was narrow, and a pipe ladder was screwed into the rock face. It rose straight up what looked like a hundred feet or more. It was such a straight, towering distance that it made her queasy. In the past, she had been afraid of heights. Far away, as if she were at the bottom of a well, she could see a round piece of the night sky, glittering with stars. Despite her fear, she had never seen a finer sight. *Thank you, heart.*

"You first," he insisted.

"But, Jeff—"

"Go! I'll be right behind!"

She scrambled up the ladder into the starlit tunnel, Jeff following. She could not have an attack of vertigo, because if she fell, she would take Jeff with her. So she looked neither up nor down but straight ahead at the rock wall. She made herself breathe evenly. She climbed slowly, building a steady rhythm, one foot after another, each hand after the other, trying not to think about where she was or what she was doing.

Another blowout detonated, and the shaft shook and reeled.

They gripped the ladder. Her flashlight dropped, missing Jeff by inches. She closed her eyes, fighting dizziness. Stones and dust exploded around them. For a few harrowing seconds it seemed as if the ladder were peeling away from the wall. Beneath them, the door burst open with a terrible screech of ripping metal. She opened her eyes long enough to see rocks and debris shoot in and force their way up the base of the shaft past the doorway, blocking it. They were trapped. The only exit was up.

She shook her head, trying to regain her equilibrium. She would not lose control, she told herself. She must not. Not here.

Abruptly the shaft thundered with new noise. It sounded as if part of the cavern had collapsed. Dust and detritus again shot up the shaft in a reverse rain of lung-scarring proportions. They coughed and struggled to breathe.

And then there was a muffled, deadly silence. An occasional pebble *pinged* past them, stinging their faces and hands. The ladder wobbled against the wall. It was loose.

"There's no going back," Jeff called from below. "Let's get the hell out of here!"

Coughing, she lifted her foot. The ladder swayed. She broke out in a sweat and swore.

"We've got to move at odds with each other," Jeff told her. "If we both lift the same foot at the same time, we'll get the ladder to swinging like a snake, and it'll go down and take us with it."

He released his flashlight so he could use both hands. It hit the rocks below with a metallic shatter. To his count, they alternated feet and hands, placing each gently—her left, his right—and in unison they progressed up the ladder.

"One more blast, and this ladder will collapse like Pickup Stix," she muttered.

"Keep moving!"

The ladder's looseness grew more evident the more they climbed. Sweat drenched her, and her stomach knotted. When she reached the top, she reached her hand out over the lip and touched grass. Hot tears of relief ran down her cheeks. She crawled out into a small area ringed with boulders then collapsed and threw back her head, staring at the starry sky. She breathed deeply and said emotional words of thanks.

Then she wiped away her tears and reached a hand down. "Can I help you, Jeff?"

He looked up, and for a few seconds he thought he was looking at an angel. Moonlight glowed around her. Dirt streaked her face and clotted her short hair, and her jacket and jeans were filthy, but to him she could not have looked more beautiful.

"No, thanks," he said gruffly. "I can do it." He hauled himself up.

She was sitting beside the shaft's entrance, which was concealed by a tight circle of high boulders. There was not room for both, so they climbed over and out.

"You've been crying," he said from behind.

"Only a little."

They fell onto the grassy hillside, exhausted and almost giddy with relief. Jeff ached. His back and legs throbbed from the blows of rocks. Higher on the hill, a Holstein cow mooed, and the bucolic call echoed across the hills. He looked back and saw a herd. He inhaled, amazed they were still alive.

Just down the slope stood Berianov's farm, plus two huge smoking craters. One of the big holes was where the mansion had been, and the other the fake garage.

She said, "You figure it was that old man who set the plastic?"

"Maybe. I'd like to get my hands on him. I thought he was harmless. One way or another, you can bet he knows something."

"The police will come, or whatever local authorities they have here. Those blasts must've scared everyone for miles."

"Speak of the devil." He nodded and lifted the night-vision binoculars to his eyes.

A vehicle was driving into the property from the road. The headlights were luminous cones in the rising ground fog. He focused on the vehicle.

"What is it?" she demanded.

"Dark green van. Not a cop car. Oh, man. You're not going to believe this. Actually, you will. It's our garrulous pal, the too-friendly caretaker. He's walking over to meet it."

She remembered his vanishing eyes, so bright—and so very much *not* old. And the advertisement for this farm that she had found hidden in Berianov's office. "I'll bet that's Berianov! In disguise again. The *caretaker*. We both missed it!"

"You're right. It could be him. He was always a master of . . . Wait!" He stared through the night binoculars. "There's someone else. See? Behind the van!"

The man was dressed in his work clothes, completely in black—turtleneck, jacket, ski mask, gloves, trousers, socks, and shoes. Equipment, including a pistol, hung from a black web belt at his waist. He melted along the edge of the pines and then up the side of the road, low to the ground, a spectral shade against the white fence. Gray fog caught at his ankles.

As he approached the van, which had now pulled to a stop, he took out his pistol and studied the old man who was moving away from the smoking remains of what must have been a large building. This was the farm that had been in the advertisement he had taken from Beth Convey at Alexei Berianov's house, but nowhere was the mansion visible. Which made him believe the ruins had once been that building.

He was puzzled. The e-mail from his bosses in the Kremlin had told him their sources reported that a Colonel Caleb Bates had bought this property. But that was the extent of the information. That and it had been important enough to Beth Convey for her to want to confiscate the advertisement.

He studied the wizened fellow in his jeans and cowboy hat as he climbed into the van. He did not recognize him. But then he saw Ivan Vok behind the wheel. A jubilant thrill hit his chest. Ivan Vok—the notorious KGB assassin . . . in the United States . . . at this mysterious Caleb Bates's farm. Excited, his pistol firmly in hand, he closed in on the big vehicle.

As soon as Alexei Berianov slid open the door and jumped in, Ivan Vok hit the accelerator and circled the big vehicle around the drive that fronted the smoldering remains of the farm's main house. He nodded at Berianov, putting a cool smile of greeting on his Mongolian features that only hinted at his allegiance and his pride at what he, Vok, was creating with his long-time leader.

He asked the general, *"Kak vi pazhiváyitye?"* How did things go?

Berianov was equally unemotional. They were KGB. There was no better training ground to learn the value of understatement. Besides, he knew Ivan Vok's attachment ran deep. He pulled off his Stetson, settled into the front passenger seat, and offered the customary response in Russian: *"Kharashóh. A vi?"* Good. And with you?

"A long night, Alexei," Vok continued in Russian. "Convey and Hammond escaped me. They switched vehicles before I could arrive."

Berianov smiled. "They didn't escape me."

"So?"

As Vok turned the van down the driveway toward the highway, Berianov explained the explosions and the deaths of Hammond and the Convey woman. "They'll be no more bother."

Vok laughed, both amused and relieved.

Berianov said suddenly, "What's that?"

A shadow darted off to the left in front of white fencing. It crouched, gun lifted. Vok saw it, too. Before they could react, a bullet exploded through the driver's door of the moving van and blasted out inches from Berianov's chest.

Vok wrenched the wheel and hit the accelerator again. Without a word, Berianov reached up and grabbed the handle above the door for balance as the big vehicle roared across the driveway straight at the dark figure.

The man stood and fired into the van, but it was accelerating so fast he could get off only the single shot, and it seemed to have no effect. He turned and sprinted.

Vok let out a low growl of pleasure as he hurtled the van onward across the lawn, struck the man with its fender, and crashed through the fencing and into a pasture. The van lurched over the grass, and Vok spun the wheel again, aiming it back in a loop toward the drive.

Berianov asked, "Who do you think he was?"

Vok shrugged. "Doesn't matter, Alexei. If he's not dead, he's injured bad enough to knock him out." He turned the van back onto the driveway and drove it downhill again toward the front gate, which stood open and waiting between the pines.

Over the engine's purr, a siren sounded in the distance. Berianov smiled. With the deaths of Convey and Hammond, his plans were back on track. The local authorities would arrive soon, but they would find little more than empty holes in the ground—and, now, an injured or dead man. It would puzzle them. They would look into the ownership of the farm and discover an ultraright-wing nationalist named Colonel Caleb Bates had taken it over, and they would wonder about that, too. Then they would find Caleb Bates had disappeared. Eventually, they would know about the Keepers of the Truth, and the puzzle would fit its pieces together for them in the way he wanted: A web of fabrications that seemed solid as truth.

He heard Ivan Vok swear. "Bad news, Alexei. There, in back of us."

Berianov turned to look. Two dusty figures had run down the hillside and reached the road behind them. Rage spiked through his entrails. It was Beth Convey and Jeff Hammond. *Impossible.* He stared, shocked, as they found the man Ivan had hit with the van. At the same time, from the corners of his eyes he could see a ruddy glow rise from the south. Police beacons. The sirens were growing louder. They would be here soon.

"How did they escape?" He swore. "No time to deal with them now. They'd be too alert to an attack, in any case."

"The police will be here before we can kill them," Vok agreed. "That's too dangerous for us."

Berianov thought quickly. "They must have parked their car somewhere near. Do you have a tracking device with you?"

"Yes, but no reader." Vok allowed himself a smile. "I will make a call. Get help." He slammed the gas pedal, and the van rocketed out onto the country highway. They had to find Convey and Hammond's car, plant the device, and contact one of their men with a reader to follow.

As the scream of the sirens grew in intensity, Beth and Jeff crouched beside the unconscious, crumpled form in black. While Jeff felt for his carotid artery, Beth pulled off the knit stocking cap.

"Do you know him?" Beth asked.

He was about her age, she guessed—early thirties. He had a strong, triangular face with smooth skin and thin eyebrows. The chin itself was flat and square. There was something turbulent about his features even in unconsciousness, as if whatever forces drove him seldom rested. He was striking, she decided. Attractive in a predatory sort of way.

"Never seen him before. But at least he's alive." Jeff ran his hands over the man's body looking for obvious broken bones. "He appears okay, but we won't know anything for sure until he can tell us. He must've glanced off the fender. We're taking him with us. I'm tired of leaving good information sources behind."

She was watching the lights of the patrol cars speed toward Berianov's farm. "We've got to hurry. They're going to be here in a couple of minutes."

Jeff picked up the man's feet, while Beth stripped off his gloves, stuck them into her windbreaker's pockets, and grabbed his hands. Hurrying sideways, they carried him over the crushed white fence and downhill toward the pines that rimmed the road on this side of the tall security fence.

As the patrol cars rushed up the drive, their beacons flashing, Beth and Jeff lay the man down on pine needles and crouched to wait, hidden in the trees. The rotating lights winked across them, and she lowered her gaze. That was when she saw it: She had put the man's hands on his chest, crossed. There was a scar on his right wrist.

"Jeff! It's him." She pointed to the small white scar. "He's the man I told you about. The one who attacked me and tied me up in Berianov's house!"

He repressed a powerful urge to beat the crap out of the injured guy. He made his voice noncommittal: "He should have some interesting things to tell us."

The man twitched. He was waking up. Jeff searched his equipment belt and confiscated a pistol and two knives. They picked him up and carried him alongside the fence line again, hidden among the pines, until they reached the open gates. They set him down again and warily surveyed back up to the end of the long drive where officers were pouring out of their patrol cars. The beacons still revolved and glinted. Voices shouted orders. Soon the farm would be locked, everything sealed off with yellow crime tape. The arson experts were probably already on their way, prepared to pick through ashes, to sift, and to analyze.

But right now, the wrought-iron gates remained wide open. Beth and Jeff scanned all around. Carrying the unconscious man, they slipped out between the gates and hurried up the hill on the grassy space between the quiet road and the fence. The pines would help protect them from being seen by anyone in the farm, and the highway was lightly traveled. With luck, they would reach the Ferrari before another car passed.

Beth sweated and panted. The distance stretched. Her arms grew numb. The intruder was her height, but he had to weigh one-sixty at least. She kept reminding herself this was a good idea. Finally, on the far side of the hill's crown and out of sight of the farm, they let him drop to the grass. He landed a little harder than they had intended.

Jeff took a ragged breath and straightened. His broad, tanned face glistened with sweat. Beth remembered the first time she saw him, as he was crossing the lobby at the *Post,* with his gold earring and long ponytail. She had liked his cockiness. Had found his self-confidence hypnotically attractive. And was drawn by his off-beat handsomeness.

He rested his hands on his hips and shook his head as if to clear it. "I'll get the Ferrari." He trotted away.

The unconscious man carried no identification, and they had seen no other cars parked alongside the country road. So who was he, and how did he get to the farm? Working quickly while Beth kept watch, Jeff tied his ankles, tied his hands, and stuffed him into what passed for the Ferrari's backseat.

Beth took the wheel, while Jeff sat at an angle in the passenger seat, his Beretta easy in his hand, waiting for the man to come to.

"Patience isn't my strong suit," Jeff muttered.

"Oh? I never would've guessed." She smiled, feeling for a moment a sense of triumph because they had survived. Then everything came rushing back over her, and suddenly the future looked bleak .

Jeff watched as she drove the car back the way they had come to avoid passing the farm. The worst thing about her was that he liked her. After you have just escaped death with someone, and they have held up their end through it all, your opinion can do some radical shifts. No, that was not it. Too simple an explanation. Some inner battle was raging on the terrain of his heart.

The injured man in back moaned.

Jerked back to the present, Jeff watched the stranger's eyes flicker as he moaned again. Abruptly the man bit off what could have been a curse, and his eyes snapped open. He tried to sit erect, but his head smashed into the ceiling above the small backseat. He fell back, staring at the ropes that tied his wrists. Finally he raised his gaze to Jeff, and in those eyes for just a moment Jeff saw rage and cunning. And then it was erased. The man's eyes—his entire face—turned neutral.

"Here's the score," Jeff told him in an impersonal tone. "I've got your weapons. It's obvious you're a pro, but you're going nowhere, because I know what I'm doing, too. Right now, you're hurting. You're wondering who in the hell I am and whether you can outwit or bullshit me. But because I'm a nice guy, I'm going to give you a break. I'm going to tell you the truth. Without us, the cops would have you. Since you busted into the farm dressed like a second-story man, I've got to think you'd prefer our company to theirs. Since you also took down my friend here last night—"

Jeff watched the man's pale blue gaze shift to the back of Beth's head. There was something about the move. . . . The man was interested in Beth. Sexually interested. Attracted to her.

She turned and gave a little wave of her fingertips. "Good to see you under these improved circumstances."

Jeff's chest contracted. But he showed nothing on his face. "She holds no grudge. I, however, do. But we'll discuss that later. As I was saying . . . since you also took down my friend, we're aware you searched Alexei Berianov's house and . . . fortunately for you . . . that you let my friend go unharmed. We appreciate that. In fact, it leads us to guess that perhaps we might have a few things in common."

Jeff studied him—the triangular face, the deep-set, almost colorless blue eyes. The man's uninvolved expression had remained unchanged except when he had briefly acknowledged Beth. It gave Jeff an idea.

He said, "Perhaps you'd like to know what we found that you didn't."

He waited. The man was a rock. He remembered Beth saying he had not uttered a single word the entire time he searched Berianov's house. The one advantage Jeff had was he had nothing to lose. So he leaned back against the door, kept his Beretta ready and in plain sight so the prisoner would not forget which one of them was armed, and he whistled "The Internationale," the song that had emerged after the Paris Commune and had become the Communist anthem.

That apparently did it. The voice was soft, very Russian-sounding: "Okay. Tell me who you are. Maybe we talk."

Beth laughed. "Come on, no one believes that accent."

The man's face clouded. His eyes narrowed. He seemed to come to a decision. "Very well. You're obviously Jeff Hammond and Beth Convey. You can credit the thoroughness of the American press for plastering your photos everywhere. I'd appreciate your telling me what you found that I didn't." He raised his bound hands. "No. Don't say it, Hammond. I can see it in your face. In return, I'll reveal what I've learned. We can, as you say in this country, make a deal."

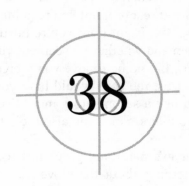

38

Beth and Jeff exchanged a long look. She glanced over her shoulder, saw something in the man's face that told her he was hurt worse than he wanted them to know. Despite that, she also saw a cool intelligence analyzing them in return. She would never forget the image of the black-clad, menacing intruder who had come upon her in Berianov's office and how easily he had overpowered her.

She fell back upon her profession. This was a simple negotiation, she told herself. Sometimes the cleverest tactic was to throw a bone onto the table. All her senses told her that was where they were now. Which meant it was time to gamble.

Her gaze focused on the dark road as she drove the Ferrari onward. Off to the side, trees whipped in a rising night wind. Cars passed occasionally in the other lane. In the distance, lights shone from houses set back from the rural highway.

She threw out: "Did you know Caleb Bates and Alexei Berianov are the same man?"

There was shocked silence in the backseat. Then a slow exhalation of breath, and he swore in Russian. "That explains a lot. I knew they were linked, but . . . I should've guessed."

Jeff asked, "Had you heard Berianov died recently in Moscow?"

"No. You were told that?"

Jeff nodded. "He must've planted it for our benefit, not yours. Which means he may not realize you're investigating him."

"That's good. Since you've given me that, I'll return the favor. Beri-

anov, Anatoli Yurimengri, and Mikhail Ogust stole a significant amount
of money when they left the Soviet Union. And recently they stole even
more from old KGB funds here."

"That's what I'd figured, too. That's how they bankrolled their businesses, and the slush funds financed expansions and maybe something
else." Jeff cast a shrewd look at the man in the backseat. "Since you
know all that, you must be MVD." He looked at Beth and explained,
"The MVD is the Russian national police. They've been sending their
people here on the trail of vanished rubles."

Again there was silence in the back. Instead of admitting it, the man
said, "When President Yeltsin was in office, he hired Kroll Associates
to track state property that had been vanishing from our treasuries
since the early nineteen-eighties." Kroll Associates was an international
corporate investigation firm. "From nineteen eighty-nine to ninety-one
alone, our Communist officials used secret Central Committee decrees
to steal eight metric tons of platinum, sixty metric tons of gold, stores
of diamonds, and—in your dollars—between fifteen and fifty billion in
cash. All transferred into unknown hands."

Beth was astonished. "That's more than most countries' annual
budgets."

The voice behind her agreed. "It's a national outrage and shame.
And it wasn't just the Communists. Our new government officials and
businessmen have been raiding the country since, even though we're
desperate for money to finance our recovery. Everything was in chaos
back in ninety-one when Berianov and his friends took advantage during the coup against Gorbachev. They skimmed fifty million dollars the
KGB was laundering through Swiss banks for our people—"

Jeff interrupted, "No doubt to agents, provocateurs, and front organizations."

"Ah, yes. You understand how it works. Your CIA uses similar
channels. We uncovered Berianov's thefts only last year. Kroll
tracked the money to a private Swiss bank, which had invested it on
Wall Street. We all know what happened to anyone who invested
wisely in the nineties, and the Swiss are particularly savvy at it. From
what Kroll discovered, Berianov, Yurimengri, and Ogust withdrew
money off and on to finance their enterprises. Then three years ago
they took out all of it." He paused. "It'd grown to nearly a billion of
your dollars."

Beth inhaled, surprised. "That's a tremendous amount for any nation
to lose."

The MVD man nodded. "Two weeks ago, Kroll hit a dead end. They could track the money no farther, so my superiors sent me." He paused. "You're still with the FBI, aren't you, Hammond? But undercover now."

Jeff's expression remained unchanged. "I left the Bureau a long time ago."

The younger man gave a chuckle. "I have my sources. Do you know a man named Evans Olsen?"

Beth said promptly, "He's a White House aide. I've met him at some embassy parties, although I haven't seen him for a while."

Jeff turned to her. "I've never heard of him," he admitted.

"Caleb Bates has been calling him on his cell phone," the MVD man continued. "The calls were encrypted, so we couldn't understand what they were saying, but we could track the signal. The very fact they were talking at all is curious."

Jeff saw the connection: "You're the one who leaked the information to the Bureau that an underground group was planning a terrorist act. You meant Caleb Bates's people. You've got to be 'Perez.' "

The MVD man was motionless. He did not acknowledge he was Perez, but he did not deny it either. "They call themselves the Keepers of the Truth," he continued. "Or simply the Keepers. That's everything I know that's useful. Now I have work to do, and I must make a report. I'd appreciate your driving me back. I hid my motorcycle two kilometers from the farm. The police shouldn't notice us."

Beth shook her head. "You're hurt. I've been watching you in the rearview mirror. Every time you move, you wince."

"Just cracked ribs." He smiled into the mirror.

Jeff saw the smile. With effort he pushed down a wave of jealousy.

Beth advised, "You need to see a doctor. You can't take care of your ribs by yourself."

"Sure I can. Done it before. Now it's your turn. I've given you good information. Drive me back, and tell me what you know."

Beth slowed the Ferrari, circled into a driveway, and reversed course. For a moment she thought she saw a car behind them delay and drop back, but the headlights disappeared off onto a side road.

Together she and Jeff related highlights from the last three days— Meteor Express, Stone Point, the killer who had tracked Beth, and the suicides by cyanide of the two Keepers outside Bates's farm. They explained about Michelle Philmalee and the HanTech list, then about the old caretaker, whom they had last seen climbing into the van that had run down Perez.

Perez had been looking relaxed, almost convivial. Now his blue eyes hardened. "So that's who was in the van. I recognized only the driver— Ivan Vok."

"Ivan Vok!" Jeff shook his head. "I don't like the sound of any of this." He described the mockup of the Oval Office buried deep under the hillside.

Perez's eyebrows rose in astonishment. "The Oval Office. Then they're planning to assassinate President Stevens, just as I suspected. And it must be soon, since you say all the Keepers are gone from the farm now."

"That's what we think, too," Beth said. "Your president arrived in Washington today. Maybe that has something to do with the timing. What do you think Bates—or Berianov—expects to gain by assassinating our president?"

"Nothing from our viewpoint," Perez said. "From his perspective, perhaps a lot. My sources say Berianov, Yurimengri, and Ogust never gave up hoping the Communists would return to power and reunite the old Soviet Union."

"They're not the only ones," Jeff muttered.

Perez nodded. "Nine years ago, that would've been impossible. In fact, our parliament talked about outlawing the Party altogether. But it's still a power in the Duma, and it's still the only political movement with a nationwide network capable of calling out hundreds of thousands of protesters into the streets. The Party's been a big critic of the new free-market approach—shock therapy—which it blames for our economy's shrinking to the size of the Netherlands, and of the almost total disintegration of our military. And, of course, since then the ruble collapsed, the stock market dropped into a black hole, and we defaulted on our big international loans. Everything's fucked up. The *Kursk* submarine disaster. The Ostankino TV tower fire. Terrorists in Moscow. And, of course, there's always the pain of Chechnya."

Beth said, "The Communists wouldn't have a hope of regaining control in a stable Russia. They certainly know that."

Perez agreed. "This may be their last chance. Many Russians still remember Communist rule with pride for its defeat of fascism. The international loans we defaulted on were no more than the value of one of your new Internet companies. Still, foreign governments and the IMF condemned my country as if we were the irresponsible bad boy of the world, and that strengthened the Communists' position. Their platform's simple and appealing: We're still the second-biggest nuclear power, our land crosses three continents, our natural resources are rich and vast, and we have a veto on the UN Security Council."

"You're implying Berianov may figure by assassinating President Stevens he can destabilize Russia enough for the Communists to take over," Jeff decided. "If that's true, he'd have laid the groundwork over there already."

For the first time Perez looked nervous. "We know they were forming alliances and buying into Russian utilities, factories, and politicians. Besides the die-hard Communists, they could've connected with the disaffected military commanders, the ultra-nationalists, and the old-guard apparatchiks. I'll tell my superiors. They'll check your HanTech list and uncover their penetration."

"But why kill President Stevens *now?*" Beth wondered.

"In my experience, nothing happens in a vacuum," Jeff said. "Back in the early nineteen-seventies when Henry Kissinger was secretary of state, he dropped out of sight for a few days while he was overseas. Reporters wanted to know what was going on. His spokesman said he was sick. Had the flu, as I recall. So the media picked it up and reported Kissinger had fallen ill while traveling on official business. Only later did we learn he'd really been in hiding, setting up a secret agreement with what was called Red China in those days, to open it to the West for the first time in twenty years. Maybe that's what this assassination is all about. President Stevens and President Putin could be meeting for a much bigger reason than the usual state ceremonies . . . maybe to announce some accord that will finally stabilize Russia, block the Communists, and anchor the country firmly in democracy. If that's the case, Berianov might figure that if he murders our president, the deal collapses."

Beth said, "Or at least he buys himself enough time to finish whatever he's set in motion in Russia."

Tense silence filled the sports car as it continued on through the starry night. At last Perez directed Beth to stop. They were back near Gettysburg, but on a lightly traveled stretch of road. There were no lights from houses anywhere in sight. One lone pickup sped past and disappeared as Beth pulled the Ferrari onto the shoulder.

She turned off the motor, and Jeff untied Perez and helped him out of the car.

His arms clutching his chest, Perez indicated thick ironwood bushes. Jeff found a path, disappeared inside, and returned, rolling a big BMW motorcycle. On the other side of the narrow, two-lane road, woods rustled with night sounds. Overhead, dusty clouds had appeared, a filter against the moon.

Perez limped to the big bike and, with pain, swung his leg over the seat. "My weapons, please." As Jeff handed them over, Perez said, "I'll give you one more piece of information that could be useful." He described the politics of Caleb Bates's right-wing zealots. "Now that I know Berianov is Bates, a lot of what I learned about Bates and the Keepers makes sense. It looks to me as if Berianov has set everything up in such a way that the Keepers will go down for the assassination, while he walks away free and clear."

"What makes you think that?" Beth demanded.

"I followed one of Bates's top staff people. He ordered a lot of belt buckles with tracking chips, enough for the whole group. Most probably the Keepers have no idea there's anything different about the belts. For the ones who need to know, Bates could've explained them easily as a way to keep track of everyone during the operation. And now that we know Berianov is in disguise again, this time as an old man, it makes me think he's not planning to be part of it. He's getting ready to disappear."

Beth understood. "After the assassination, he'll make an anonymous phone tip to the Secret Service about the Keepers and tell them about the belts. All they have to do is capture or kill one Keeper, and they'll be able to track all of them. If Berianov doesn't wear a belt, and we all know he won't, he's free."

"That's how I see it," Perez agreed.

"We can check that out." Beth exchanged a look with Jeff, remembering the two men who had committed suicide. They—and their belts—should still be in the trees. To Perez she said, "Where will you go next?"

Perez smiled at Beth, and in that instant he looked youthful and carefree. "No, I think we don't tell each other that. But we should stay in touch. How do I contact you?"

"You don't," Jeff said curtly. "Unless you have a number you want to give us."

Perez smiled, shook his head. Moonlight emerged from between the clouds to bathe the three in cool light. Perez put on his motorcycle helmet. His voice was muffled as he spoke directly to Beth, "I saw your medicine at Berianov's house. You've been very ill, but now you're strong. If this one doesn't work out"—he nodded at Jeff—"I'll know, and I'll find you. Then we'll see whether we enjoy the same music and . . . other entertainment." He touched his fingers to his helmet's black glass in a salute to Beth. "Until we meet again."

A curious thrill raced along Beth's spine. She remembered her pill bottles when she had located them in Berianov's office behind her chair—they had been lined up like soldiers, as if someone had examined them. He knew all about her, and *he* was still interested.

Perez stomped the starter. The engine thundered awake, and he peeled off onto the highway, speeding south through silver moonlight toward Washington. Jeff and Beth watched his taillight grow smaller.

"It's funny how time can change everything," she said. "Perez is simply trying to protect his country's interests, but in the old days, we would've been enemies."

"Yes. The Free World versus the Evil Empire."

"He seemed courageous. Determined to help his people. Russia needs more like him. What do you think?"

Jeff frowned. "I suppose you're right—" And then stopped. In the distance, the headlights of a car appeared, heading south, too, in the same direction as Perez. Driving fast. As Perez disappeared from sight, the new vehicle's headlights grew larger and more menacing.

Jeff grabbed Beth's arm. "Come on!"

As they ran, he pulled out his pistol. She yanked open the Ferrari's front door. The approaching car, a sedan, screeched to a halt twenty-five feet away on the shoulder, facing them. The headlights were blinding.

"Get in the car!" Jeff bellowed. He scrambled over to the driver's seat and turned on the ignition.

Beth jumped into the passenger seat, her pulse hammering, and slammed the door. Two bursts of gunfire shot out the Ferrari's front tires. The front end dropped, and two men leaped out of the sedan. Weapons firing, they dashed toward the Ferrari.

39

"Ferrari claims these things are nearly indestructible," Jeff growled. "Let's find out." He threw the car into gear and tromped the gas pedal. Lumbering on its front rims, the powerful sports car rushed forward on the shoulder. The two attackers were almost impossible to see, black shadows against the glare. They dove to either side—left, onto the road, and right, into the bushes. It appeared that one carried a rifle, the other a pistol.

Jeff's chin jutted. He gripped the steering wheel and bore the Ferrari straight at the sedan.

"You're crazy!" Beth took a deep breath and held on.

If he had learned anything, Jeff told himself grimly, it was never to do the expected when your life was on the line. He had watched Ivan Vok give Perez enough time to dodge the worst of the van's onslaught. Jeff would not make the same mistake.

The attackers froze, indecisive, not sure whether the Ferrari had become a two-thousand-pound suicide torpedo and was about to fulfill their assignment for them.

At the last second, Jeff spun the steering wheel, and the low-slung Ferrari arced ninety degrees and roared straight at the attacker frozen on the road. The move had been so swift the thug had no time to run. The car slammed into him. His eyes and mouth opened wide in a terrified scream that never left his throat. The impact flung him high onto the Ferrari's hood. Still reflexively gripping his rifle, he skidded toward them face down. The crown of his crew cut crashed into the windshield inches from their faces, spraying blood across the glass. He was no longer a problem.

From the side of the highway, the second man fired his pistol. A bullet smashed through Beth's window and out through the windshield. The glass shattered onto the prone attacker. The shards coated him and sparkled like ice in the glare of the sedan's headlights.

Beth had watched it all, tense but noting each detail vividly, almost as if time had stood still: The sedan to the right . . . the man now sliding off the Ferrari's sloping hood like a limp punching bag . . . the remaining attacker with his pistol raised to fire again.

Another bullet blasted through the Ferrari, this time nicking Jeff's knuckles. He swore, jammed the gearshift into reverse, and hit the gas pedal. The car roared backwards, rear tires squealing.

Before the second attacker could shoot again, Beth leaned out the window, aimed, and fired. He went down with a loud curse. She had hit only his thigh, but her 9mm bullet packed enough force to knock him off his feet. Still, he had managed to hold on to his gun.

Jeff yanked up the emergency brake and vaulted out of the car just in time for the fellow to be up on one knee, aiming his weapon. The man's finger closed on the trigger. The weapon was pointed at Jeff—

Beth and Jeff fired simultaneously. The bullets exploded the attacker's chest. He pitched back against the ironwood brush, arms flung open. Black-red stains erupted on his jacket as he was caught suspended in the stiff, woody claws.

Beth gulped for air. Was suddenly exhilarated. She had shot so fast to save Jeff that she'd had no time to think, to figure out the repercussions, to weigh the morality of the act. To censor or to consciously free herself. Nevertheless, this time she had not continued to squeeze the trigger. She looked down at her hands as they held the Walther. She was trembling. But the terrible drive to empty her gun . . . keep killing . . . had not taken her over.

When she finally stopped shaking and looked up, Jeff was bent over the man they had shot. "He's dead."

She ran to the other one. "This one is, too."

Jeff was searching the attackers' Buick. "This explains a lot—an electronic reader. I'll bet there's a tracking device on the Ferrari, and that's how they found us. But I don't see how they could've planted it."

"Berianov or Vok must've spotted us as we were going down the hill after they tried to run over Perez. At least, that's what makes sense. That way they would've known we'd survived."

Jeff nodded. "You're right. And if they had a tracking device with them, all they had to do was look around for our car."

She turned from the Buick to study the once-sleek red Ferrari. It was lying on the shoulder with its nose so close to the ground it looked as if it were a dog asleep on a carpet. Its front tires had shredded off, and the rims were dented. The windshield was gone. Bullet holes riddled the expensive body.

She said, "No way is that Ferrari going anywhere now." She felt a stab of guilt. The Ferrari was Michelle's most joyful toy. But Michelle would not complain—not if Beth went back to her. In any case, Michelle was insured to her waxed eyebrows, and she would just buy another. "Can we take their car?"

"It's not a good idea. There could be a tracking device on it, too, and I don't have the equipment to sweep for one." He shook his head, disgusted.

Then she remembered. "I think we passed a phone a quarter-mile back. I'll go look for it if you want to finish checking their sedan and searching these guy's pockets. Should I call your boss? Maybe it's time we asked for some help."

"No. But there's an old family friend you can call." He gave her the number and instructions.

Beth nodded, memorized the information, and trotted away along the highway. She was exhausted, but she pushed herself on. Her mind was heavy with the events of the past few days, and her eyes were tired of constantly searching for danger. As she slogged onward, watching all around, she worried about the president. They had to stop Berianov's plot against him.

When at last she found the roadside telephone, she was panting. She grabbed it and . . . stopped. There was no dial tone. Then she saw the telephone wire was cut. Someone had deliberately clipped it, a nice, smooth slice. Berianov's crazies? To discourage anyone from loitering too close to the farm? She shook her head, frustrated.

She reversed course and resumed her tired run. Gray clouds scudded across the night sky, hiding stars and the moon. She was dripping with sweat. Minutes later, she neared the place where she had left Jeff and the two damaged cars. She could see the dark shapes of the vehicles, and as the cloud floated out of the way overhead, moonlight illuminated the silhouettes of two men. Her chest contracted, and she felt a wave of nauseating fear. She crouched low to watch. Down the road, between the Buick and the Ferrari, a man held a gun aimed straight at Jeff.

*   *   *

Jeff had heard the sound an instant too late. He had been gathering up various items of disguise and other tools of the assassin's trade from the black boxes in the Ferrari's trunk and had packed what he wanted—plus Beth's purse—into the smallest black box. As he worked, he had heard a soft rustling in the bushes, but with no car in sight, he had ascribed it to a rabbit or a squirrel. Only when he heard a twig snap close behind did he spin around, reaching for his Beretta.

"That's quite far enough, Jeff." Eli Kirkhart stood behind him with his Smith 10 pointed. "I'll take the Beretta, thank you. Carefully. Butt first, if you please."

"What the hell is this, Eli?'

"I'm afraid I'm taking you in." Kirkhart motioned impatiently with the Smith. "The Beretta. *Now!*"

Jeff completed his turn and handed it over. "How the hell did you find me?"

"Give me some credit, old man. You've given me the slip all year. Fortune was bound to change eventually and shine down her beatific smile on me."

"All year? You've been trying to tail me a whole year?'

"Off and on. What do you think happened after I agreed to meet you in the shopping center?"

Jeff stared. "Since when is the Bureau interested in a reporter with an obsession that got him kicked out of the sacred bosom?"

"What utter hogwash. Start walking. That way, if you please." Kirkhart motioned with his gun toward the trees and bushes on the west side of the road.

Jeff walked. "What does that mean—*hogwash?* And who sent you after me?"

"I'm not working for the Bureau on this, not exactly. And 'hogwash' means I know your name's still secretly on the roster, and that you've been undercover the entire decade, using your job and your 'obsession' to stay close to the defector community."

Jeff said nothing. Kirkhart had startled him. How many others, inside or outside the Bureau, knew? Did Berianov? It would explain how Berianov seemed always a step ahead of him. But how? Kirkhart had said he was not working for the Bureau on this, but he was clearly still in the Bureau. So who was in charge of the inquiry?

"All right," Jeff said, "I'll bite. So who *are* you working for, and how *did* you find me?"

"It's really the same question, Jeff. I spotted you when you were talk-ing with that Convey woman at the paper and tailed you to that miserable little hamlet in West Virginia where I saw Graham and Thoma pick you up. After that, of course, was the safe house where you took a bunk. That was the real tip-off. It was obvious you had an ally in a high place, and that your escape had been prearranged. Ergo, you were still in the Bureau on undercover duty. Then I picked you up during that fracas at Convey's picturesque Victorian, lost you again, but recalled Convey worked with the Philmalee Group. I went there, and lo, there you and the lady were. And, now, here I am."

"Okay, I'm still on the job. Then you know I didn't kill those two kids, so—"

"This has nothing to do with them. Although you could've killed them, I suppose, considering all the rest."

Now Jeff was totally confused. "Given what 'all the rest'?"

But Kirkhart said, "Ah, here we are. If you'll just step into the car, we can be off." He took handcuffs from his pocket. "Sorry, but you know the drill."

They had emerged onto a dirt road that seemed to lead to a distant farmhouse, lights still on in its first-floor windows. A sturdy gray Volvo—hardly the traditional Bureau car—was parked at the side of the road. Eli opened a rear door.

Jeff made no move to get in. "I asked you a question, Eli. What is this 'all the rest' you're talking about. As far as I know, what I've admitted is everything there is. I'm undercover, have been—"

"Oh, you're undercover, right enough. But it's not just for the Bureau, is it?"

"What the hell are you talking about? Has your brain turned to cottage cheese?"

"Hardly," Kirkhart snapped, his smooth voice suddenly cold, his bulldog face and muscular shoulders belligerent. "You asked who I'm working for? For the last two years I've been on special assignment for the president and the office of the attorney general." He related the names of his three most direct bosses—Millicent Taurino and Donald Chen at Justice, and National Security Adviser Cabot Lowell. "I've been searching for the mole burrowed inside the Bureau, old pal. And now I've found him."

Jeff was stunned. "The mole?" There had been rumors that a mole might be at work inside the Bureau, but he had given them little credence. Over the years, he had heard them repeated, but with the arrest of Aldrich Ames over at Langley, and Pitts in the Bureau, he figured the issue was put to rest.

Kirkhart said impatiently, "Why else would you be so interested in

Beth Convey, right? The Philmalee Group, HanTech, Uridium, and, of course, Minatom. I imagine you've been having a field day sniffing out tidbits to pass on to Minatom about all that rather lucrative but danger-ous business. Potentially globe-shaking, isn't it? Which reminds me . . . where *is* our Ms. Convey? Have you—?"

Beth's voice came from the night. "Right behind you. My gun's aimed at the middle of your back. Your spine, to be specific. I'm not a terrific shot, so I go after . . ."

Kirkhart whirled, and without hesitation Beth slashed the barrel of her Walther down on his wrist, sending his Smith flying. At the same time, Jeff chopped a fist into Kirkhart's half-turned jaw. Eli Kirkhart collapsed sideways. He lay unmoving.

Jeff inhaled. "Nice timing. Thanks."

"A little melodramatic, but I had to be careful he didn't hear me."

"You saw him grab me?"

She nodded and explained about the cut telephone line. "So I was hurrying back to tell you the latest lousy news. After that, it wasn't hard to follow you here. He's a grandstander, isn't he? Likes the sound of his own voice. I caught on pretty fast he was FBI and he knew you. What was all that about a mole?"

"Damned if I know. There was a suggestion every year or so that a deep mole might be responsible for a lot of our intelligence failures. But I never heard a word about an outside investigation, and I sure as hell have no clue why Eli picked me. A secret outside probe into the Bureau is unheard of. At least, I never heard of one."

"You have now." She nodded at the fallen Kirkhart. "What do we do with him?"

"Leave him." He picked up the handcuffs from where Kirkhart had dropped them and found the key in the agent's pocket. He hauled the inert figure up and dragged him to a young oak. "I'll hold his arms around the tree. You cuff him."

She snapped the cuffs onto Kirkhart's wrists, Jeff retrieved the keys to the Volvo from Kirkhart's pants pocket, and they left him locked to the tree and beginning to groan. He was in sight of the dirt road and would be found in the morning.

"By then we'll be in D.C., and we can get rid of the Volvo," Jeff told her. "Luckily, Eli wouldn't use a company car on this job because he'd be worried I'd spot him. It's probably a rental. Let's go."

She took the wheel, and Jeff climbed into the passenger seat. As she drove back onto the highway, he checked the glove compartment and found the papers that confirmed the Volvo was indeed a rental. She paused the car where the Ferrari still rested nose down on the side of the road, the Buick facing it from the shoulder.

He jumped out, retrieved the sniper's black box, and dropped it into the backseat. As he climbed back inside, he told her, "Your handbag's in here, along with all the makeup and spy tools I thought we might need."

"Good. Let's go get those belts." She pressed the accelerator and sped them off toward the place where they had left the two corpses. "We'll have to watch for cops."

"Right. Assuming we can get the belts, we'll take them to my old family friend. I have an idea, but the problem is, it's not going to be easy to talk him into helping us."

"Why?"

"Because he thinks I'm a murderer."

"Him and everyone else. Nothing new there."

He grinned at her. "No one ever said this was going to be easy, counselor."

"No," she smiled, but her chest was twisted into a knot. Was life ever going to make sense again? As if to answer her silent question, a harsh, intermittent buzzing filled the car. A cell phone.

"Where the hell is it?" Jeff looked through the dark as the maddening buzz continued. At last he found the phone clipped under the driver's seat.

She told him, "They'll expect a man to answer. Pretend you're Kirkhart."

He searched rapidly through his memory of Eli and the sound of his voice answering a phone. "Yes, hello. Kirkhart here."

"What the hell took you so long?" An angry male voice swore. "Never mind. Get back to the Bureau. *Now!*"

"Can't. I'm on a vital—"

"Yes you can. Listen up! We just learned from the attorney general's office that an outside investigation has closed in on the Bureau mole, and the director was informed of the identity this afternoon. The director said he'd take care of it, and then, a few hours later, he went off on a deep-cover meeting. Since nothing else was on his docket, and the two agents he took for protection said it looked like unusually serious business, we think the director was 'taking care of it' right then and there. Only the mole killed the director instead. Stabbed him to death, and the prints on the knife belonged to Jeffrey Hammond. Same name as we had for the mole. You remember him—your old partner. Well, Hammond's the fucking mole. As of now, everyone's on this operation, including you. Where the hell are you?"

Shocked, Jeff made himself think fast. "Among the haystacks, I'm afraid. Iowa."

"Be here tomorrow!"

The line went dead. Jeff handed it to Beth, his face blanched of color. "I'm wanted for the murder of FBI director Thomas Horn. It's not just Kirkhart . . . the entire Bureau thinks I'm the mole."

"Wonderful. The whole country will be looking for you."

"The whole world."

A tense silence descended on the Volvo. It appeared the answer to Beth's question—was life ever going to make sense again?—was definitely no. She said, "Don't you think it's time you went in? You could call the man who handles you, couldn't you? We need help, Jeff. It's not smart for us to go on alone. The stakes are too high now. This is the president's *life* we're talking about."

"Damn!" Jeff slammed the dashboard with the palm of his hand. "I wish I could! I wish I bloody well could phone Bobby! But now not only does the Bureau think I'm the mole, they think I killed the director. There's a chance even Bobby would believe that. So say I phone him. . . . If no trigger-happy agent picks me off and I survive the first five minutes, they're still not going to listen to anything I say that remotely smacks of distraction or excuse. Not now that they've got my prints on the weapon that killed the director. They'll think I concocted an assassinate-the-president story to throw them off. By the time I convince someone to listen, the president could be dead." He scowled with frustration. "The only way it can work is for me to go in with solid information, no suppositions or guesses. *Where, when, how.* Everything. They'll listen to specifics, so we've got to stick to our plan. It's just going to be harder. A lot harder."

40

It was the early hours of the morning in Moscow, and word had reached the glittery Russian Roulette nightclub of a tragic accident in which a big Mercedes 600 carrying famous publisher Oleg Dudash, two security men, and a driver had been sideswiped by one of the city's anonymous cowboy taxis. The big luxury sedan had been going so fast that it had blasted through the guardrails of the Tver Street bridge and plunged into the Moscow River, shattered an ice floe, and sunk, drowning everyone in the frigid water long before the car could be hooked and hauled to shore.

The entrepreneur who brought the news of the accident had been on his way home from the nightclub when his driver had heard all about it on his police scanner. Stunned that he had been enjoying the same elite watering hole with the honored newspaperman just a few hours before, the man had immediately ordered the driver to return him to the club.

He had entered shakily, ordered a stiff drink, and related the tragic events. The music stopped, voices rose, and glasses were filled and re-filled as he was required to tell the story over and over, to which he did not object. He also was able to describe his new line of pocket comput-ers and hand out his business card. The tiny computers were knockoffs that he sold at full price, but no one needed to know that. As the alco-hol flowed, the gloom lifted. The music and dancing resumed, and Pro-fessor Georgi Malko left after sadly accepting everyone's condolences for the death of his long-time friend.

His driver took Malko straight home to his restored nineteenth-century mansion near the Cathedral of Christ the Savior. The butler helped Malko off with his coat, and Malko went directly upstairs to his bedroom. His bed was turned down, displaying freshly ironed satin sheets. A pot of hot chocolate waited at his bedside, covered in a needlepoint cozy. The large room was filled with the inviting scent of burning pine from the fire that crackled in the fireplace.

Malko loosened his tie and peeled off his suit coat as he gazed above the fireplace to an oil painting of Peter the Great, empire-creator, modernizer, and tyrant. "Well, Peter," he announced familiarly, "we're back in the game. It's cold outside, but less than twenty-four hours from now, things are going to sizzle in the Kremlin." He chuckled as he considered how silly and idealistic Oleg Dudash had always been. Stubborn, stupid, and now dead as yesterday's news.

Before he headed into the bathroom, still chortling to himself, he turned on his television set to the national station, ORT, the only one that reached all corners of the country. As of today, he and Alexei Berianov owned the largest private share of it, which meant it was now their personal media tool.

For a moment, he remembered how much he disliked Berianov's presumptuous ways, his high-handedness. Then he shrugged. There was no way around it: Professor Georgi Malko was unelectable, just as Oleg had charged. Which was why he needed Alexei Berianov as much as Berianov needed him. Berianov was not only untainted by scandal, he was a legitimate, highly successful international merchant who could promise new avenues of commerce with the United States. Plus, he was handsome, educated, and charming. In the eyes of the public, he would be the perfect replacement for Putin.

As he prepared for bed, the second TV rerun of the day appeared of the strangely hypnotic Roman Tyrret, who six months ago had first appeared on ORT with his own brand of populist humor and transfixed the country: "I've got a joke for you tonight, folks, straight from one of those ritzy private clubs where they won't let in the likes of me or"—he paused for dramatic effect—"*you*. But on the other hand, we can't afford to go there anyway, right? Remember, you heard it here first: So . . . one oligarch says to the other, 'I just bought the most fab-u-lous wristwatch in Geneva. It cost twenty thousand rubles.' 'Oh, really,' says the other proudly. 'I just bought the same one for *thirty* thousand!' "

Tyrret threw back his head and howled. His freckled face with the infectious grin was irresistible. He was thirty-six years old, energetic, and radiated charisma. "Oh, the arrogance of it," he said, wiping his eyes. "They don't even know they've just conned each other. But we know it, folks, don't we. So why aren't *we* rich?"

The reality was, Roman Tyrret was wealthy, the most highly paid TV celebrity in the history of the country, with the most widely watched show. He had risen from announcing local TV news in St. Petersburg to the Olympian heights of his own personal national television show that shouted the gospel of equality, shared values, and returning Russia to her rightful place in the firmament.

Yet as soon as he was able to afford to live better than an Everyman, he did. Now he collected expensive women, was chauffeured around in his own armor-plated limousine, and—as if he were in a bad movie— counted among his closest acquaintances the very people he lambasted for a living. Which all went to prove, Malko decided, that everything was a game, even the truth when it was in the hands of someone with an audience of millions.

Chuckling and shaking his head, the media star continued his soothing rant, voicing the public's resentment, confusion, and jealousy, kindling for today's politics: "Our churchgoing mafia runs car-theft gangs, protection rings, and import-export rackets. Our respected briefcase barons bribe Kremlin officials and members of the parliament for contracts, licenses, and jewels from the great privatization scam. And then, their buttons busting, all of them tell us their success comes because they're such astute *biznesmeni*. While the rest of us are dying like mosquitoes in a bug-zapper because they're stealing food from our mouths, they have the gall to tell us it's our fault because we're not hardworking enough, not clever enough, not *biznesmeni!*" He smacked his forehead and rolled his eyes. "They're criminals, my friends! Gangsters! Oligarchs! I think it's time we told them that, don't you?"

Before he could cock his head and dramatically cup one hand behind an ear to listen, cheers of agreement erupted in the studio. Station hands were typically jaded, hearing every kind of spiel and con story possible, but five days a week, even the most cynical at ORT shouted for and applauded Roman Tyrret. And truth be told, Malko liked him, too. And now he owned him, just as he would—sooner rather than later—the Kremlin.

As the van carrying Ivan Vok and Alexei Berianov rode on through the Pennsylvania night, Berianov found himself lost in reverie. The traffic signs, the trees, the distinctive North American architecture blended and blurred as the van swept past, and suddenly the vegetation was different, the architecture was different, the signs, geography, cars . . . everything was different, and he was back home in Moscow.

It was the 1970s, and hope infused the air. Excited Kremlin planners expected Moscow to be a model urban community by the year 2000. There were new flats, new factories, and so many jobs that there was a shortage of workers. A new trade center was going up on the Moscow River. A French company was planning deluxe hotels. But despite all the growth, the Kremlin was wisely preserving the center of Moscow with its classic beauty and long history for future generations.

He had a baby son, his first child. He was in love with his wife with her satin skin that turned into freckles as soon as the last of the snows melted. She was a mechanical engineer. Together they went off to work each morning, making their contribution to the nation's dream of a workers' paradise. They left the baby in a nursery where the nannies cooed over him. In those days, children were fed, bundled, educated, and prized.

Disappointment is an elusive quality. It starts with tiny moments of despair, lingers in the shadows of the mind, and grows to take over one's life. Five years later, he had risen in Department Eight. He was good at his work and believed he was making a real contribution. He planned events, as they were called, in which his forces cut down enemy leaders and trained and fought alongside guerrillas to free their homelands so they could enter the exciting Communist fold.

But in his apartment, his wife had grown sad and fat. She developed acne. They had another child, a daughter. His wife started quarrels with him all the time. He stayed late at the office and drank.

His new secretary had obsidian hair that was as black and mysterious as an arctic night. So he divorced his wife and married his secretary. They moved in with her parents, who had a government apartment high above the Moscow River. He would stand at the window and look down at the river's wide expanse, an artery of trade since the Middle Ages. Now there were modern barges and boats with diesel engines. As always, there were swimmers, too. Even in winter a few hearty souls paddled amid the ice floes. Everyone called them walruses, real Muscovites, who understood the joys of a challenging climate.

He and his new wife had two children, too, another boy and girl. Her parents spoiled the children, but gradually he had less time for them, anyway. In the summer, everyone but him went off to her parents' dacha on the Black Sea, while he traveled on assignment or stayed in Moscow to work at his desk. In the beginning, his wife sent him many letters. But there were fewer each summer until finally there were none. She did not like the way Alexei treated her, she complained—his rages and long absences. She hated the guns he kept in the apartment. Besides, she had fallen in love with a lumberman. She stayed with her lumberman and the two children in the dacha on the Black Sea and divorced Alexei.

All that winter he wandered among Moscow's yellow-plastered buildings and shaded courtyards. Iron railings rimmed the steep roofs to protect the men who shoveled snow from tumbling off. On the coldest days, the sky was translucent blue, but when it was warm, snow fell in large, hushed flakes.

He was taking a walk in Gorky Park when a troika nearly ran him down. He dove into a snowbank and rolled over onto his back to look up as a slim-faced woman with a shiny red nose and eyes that glinted in the winter sun passed by, driving high above on the troika. The bells on the traditional Russian sleigh jingled, and there was great appeal in the three horses with their flared nostrils and whipping manes. She turned the charging animals around in a wide arc and returned with apologies to see whether he needed help. He married the driver with the fierce Cossack soul and flaming red hair, and they moved to a flat all their own. He was a quickly rising KGB official by then, and his superiors had their eyes on him. Her name was Tamara.

When the cell phone inside his jacket vibrated against his ribs, Berianov jerked himself back to the present. The van was quiet. Ivan Vok was concentrating on his driving as they approached the secret apartment near Washington. The assassin's face was severe. He was unhappy with the erratic traffic, which he blamed on congenital American sloppiness.

Berianov answered the phone in a neutral voice, unsure which of his two groups—Bates's Keepers or Berianov's operatives—was calling.

"Colonel?"

Instantly Berianov's voice changed to the low, gravelly rasp of Caleb Bates. "Yes, Sergeant. Make your report." Now that they were in the final stage, he had turned over direct command to the sergeant, who would lead the assassination team.

Eager pride filled the sergeant's brisk voice. "Right on track, sir. Almost everyone's arrived at the depots. They're resting. At 0700 sharp I'll begin dispatching them to their assignments. We could do it sooner, but it might attract attention."

Most of the Keepers would be stationed along the escape route, enabling the assassination team to get out of the White House and through Washington with car changes along circuitous routes. The roving van would track everyone to make certain they arrived back at the West Virginia hunt club, where the federal authorities could be counted upon to trap them. With luck, all would bite into their cyanide capsules. The only one who would not be tracked or trapped was Caleb Bates, who did not wear the belt and who would never again willingly be within ten miles of a Keeper.

"Morale is excellent," the sergeant continued. "But there's an odd situation—two of our men didn't show up. They were supposed to take the bus, and it's possible they're lost. They'd been assigned to lookout duties tomorrow."

"Give them a few hours," Bates decided. "You can always make adjustments to cover their responsibilities. The absence of two men so easily lost isn't enough to disrupt our plan, is it, Sergeant?"

"No, sir! It sure isn't."

"What about the invitations? They're far more important."

"As you ordered, I'll pick them up at 0700 sharp at the mailbox near the Mall."

"Good. At that early hour, you'll be able to slip in and out easily. Now I have a final order. This is very important. *Crucial.* Make certain you carry your cell phone tomorrow so you can call me five minutes before you go into the White House. There's going to be a slight change in your assignment. It won't alter any of our other plans. I can count on you to make this one vital call, can't I, Sergeant?"

"Yes, sir." Austin's voice was reproving. He knew his job and his cause.

"Of course, my error," Berianov smiled. There was nothing else as reliable as a well-trained, committed soldier. As long as he was breathing, Austin would phone. "Anything else, Sergeant?"

"No, sir."

"Then I'll wait to hear from you." He paused, thoroughly adjusted to Caleb Bates's way of thinking. "I'm proud of you, Aaron." He had never been so familiar, but he knew it was the right moment to solidify the military man's allegiance by calling him by his first name.

There was almost a gasp of pleasure on the other end. "Thank you, sir. You won't regret the trust you've put in me, Colonel. You know that, don't you?"

"Absolutely, Aaron. I'll be waiting at the hunt club, and as soon as you get back we'll have a drink of that fine sour mash I've been saving. Shall we make that a date?"

"Yes, sir!"

Berianov laughed aloud as he ended the connection. He felt jovial.
The event was as good as carried out. All the years of waiting and planning . . . the sacrifice of living in this foreign land . . . were going to pay
off in ways Yurimengri and Ogust with their small ideas could never
have envisioned or carried out.

He settled back into his seat, unconsciously resuming the more polished demeanor of top KGB official Alexei Berianov.

"Alexei!" Vok had turned on the radio, on which an agitated voice
was reporting the murder of FBI director Thomas Earle Horn by an
enemy mole within the Bureau who used the name Jeffrey Hammond.
"Do you hear that, Alexei?"

Berianov smiled. "I hear." He felt a surge of confidence. The murderer of the FBI director . . . now that was something. Hammond was
as good as dead. Berianov had no idea what had happened, but he suspected his man inside the Bureau had had a hand in it. He slid out his
cell phone again.

Vok glanced at him, his heavy face mirroring Berianov's relief.
"Things are going our way now. What about the Keepers? Anything
new there?"

"They are in place, Ivan Ivanovich, and they'll begin tomorrow at
seven A.M. as planned. It couldn't be better."

Before he could dial his call, the phone vibrated again. Once more
he spoke cautiously in a neutral voice. "Yes?"

It was one of Vok's people, Sergei, and he sounded breathless and
unsure as he babbled in Russian: "I don't know how it could've happened, but Hammond and Convey killed our two people. Our car was
there, of course, as was the Ferrari." He described the scene in detail.
"We planted fake identification on our two men. It'll look like a drug
sale gone bad. The authorities won't be able to connect any of it to us."

"At least that's good." Berianov's chest was tight with urgency. With
an act of will, he forced himself to relax. "Very well, Convey and Hammond will have to surface somewhere. Break up your pairs. One person
alone to each surveillance post so we can spread out and cover more
possibilities. I'll get back to you with locations." He ended the connection.

Vok was glowering. "They escaped, Alexei?"

Berianov filled him in. "Nothing must stop the Keepers. We need
less than twelve more hours to protect them and keep them on track."
Berianov's eyes snapped, and adrenaline surged through him. He
thought for a moment, then dialed.

Vok shook his head. "Hammond and Convey have turned out to be a much bigger problem than we ever thought." As usual, his words were an understatement. His eyes told the truth: They radiated violence.

Berianov listened as the telephone's ring ended. No voice answered. Instead, there was a long squeal that to someone else's ear would sound as if the line were dedicated to faxes. But after about sixty seconds the noise ended abruptly.

Berianov ordered into the silence: "Call me immediately." He hung up. Within two minutes, his phone pulsed. He punched it on and spoke in English. "What happened to the Bureau director?"

Bobby Kelsey's low voice answered. "Somehow the son of a bitch got the idea I was the mole, and he was going to expose me. Luckily, he wasn't one-hundred-percent sure he was right, so he didn't tell anyone, and he met me alone. He had delusions of making the grand gesture and arresting me himself. Of course, what he ended up doing was giving me time to prepare for our meeting."

Berianov smiled. "And so you planted evidence against Hammond."

"Never miss an opportunity, I say."

"Excellent," Berianov approved. "But we have another problem. Unfortunately, Hammond and Convey have learned—or guessed—too much, and they're still on the loose. I need every piece of information you have on them. Every possible contact they might make. Forget risk. . . . There's no more time to worry about that."

"I understand. How shall I get it to you?"

"Coded e-mail. The usual address." Berianov snapped off the connection, shoved the phone into his pocket, and crossed his arms, scowling ahead at the highway as if he were looking for the end to it.

41

It was midnight near Dupont Circle, ten minutes from the White House and five minutes from elegant Embassy Row. Beth and Jeff left the Volvo and walked five blocks to Senator Ty Crocker's house, which was on a street lined with historic homes and tall, branching trees. The place was silent and dark, and Jeff led Beth into the side yard, past a magnolia tree, and into an enclosed rear garden of shadowy rose bushes and herbs. He rang the back doorbell.

Rousted from his bed, the seventy-eight-year-old senator tried to slam the door the moment he opened it and saw Jeff on his doorstep. Jeff jammed the door open with his foot, and then, both hands on the edge of the door, he forced it open against the angry resistance of the older man.

"Ty—"

"Not a word! You hear me! Are you here to murder me, too?" Crocker was enraged. He stood in the doorway in pinstriped pajamas, a Chinese silk robe, and leather slippers. "To think I . . . I—" So furious he could only sputter, the senator stopped trying, and for a long ten seconds the two men glared at each other.

His voice thick with emotion, Jeff finally shook his head. "I'm sorry, Ty. It never occurred to me you'd still think I'd killed those kids. Not after Tom Horn's murder. You had to know his murder, piled onto the first two, was too much. Too unbelievable that I'd do all three. You really think I could've killed the director, Ty? Of all people, I had expected *you* to see the truth." He hesitated. "Did I expect too much from you?"

Ty Crocker flinched. He finally found his voice. "You could easily have murdered them if you're a mole for the Russians."

Jeff looked around at the nighttime backyard. He could see no one, and the houses on either side of Ty's were distant. Still, he lowered his voice. "You honestly think I've been a mole all these years? You've known me my entire life. Your observations and judgment are *that* bad?"

Ty's voice dropped, too. "Then what? *Why?* Quitting the Bureau . . . those kids . . . that safe house . . . the *director,* for God's sakes! Tom Horn was a good man!"

"Quitting the Bureau and escaping from the safe house are the same thing—I've been working undercover ten years. That was a *new* safe house, dammit. You know that. I was never in it. I would've had to have help to get out."

Ty Crocker frowned and nodded. "Yes, it was new."

"As for those kids and the director . . . I told you at the safe house I'd been framed. Someone wants me out of the way badly."

"But why?"

"Because we're close to uncovering a plot to assassinate President Stevens."

As the senator cocked his head in disbelief, Beth insisted, "It's the truth. They've tried to stop me, too."

Ty Crocker looked from one to the other. He sighed. "Come in. We'll talk."

Inside, Jeff lay the belts out on the kitchen table, and he and Beth recapitulated everything as Ty Crocker made a pot of Earl Gray tea. Beth stood beside the door, watching the backyard for signs they had been followed, until at last the tea was ready. Sighing, she sat with the senator at the table with their cups. Jeff paced.

The senator sipped the hot tea, his halo of white hair smoothed back but the lines on his face deep and uncertain. He seemed weary; the shocks of the last few days had taken a toll. On his lap, his short-haired, black-and-white cat, Flubby, purred. "You say these belts have tracking devices?" Crocker nodded at the two leather belts with heavy buckles curled atop the varnished wood table. "So these Keepers you've told me about can be tracked and caught?"

"Everything we've told you is the truth, Ty." Jeff's rugged features were knit in an impatient scowl. "Everything."

Beth added, "We think Berianov wants them caught, expects they'll kill themselves, and he'll be free and clear."

Jeff resumed stalking the parquet floor in his lizard-skin cowboy boots. He was a study in motion—larger than life from his big head to his square shoulders and broad feet. He stopped at an antique cupboard and turned to face them again. His hands were dug into his windbreaker pockets.

The senator growled, "Russians. Ultra-right-wing American nationalists. Caves near Gettysburg. A fake Oval Office. Alexei Berianov. And now the mysterious mole within the Bureau who keeps cropping up whenever something happens that no one can explain. There's an expression I've heard my grandchildren use that seems to cover every word you both have uttered tonight: Give me a break!"

"Okay," Jeff said. "Let's assume what we've told you is a big lie. What would I gain? What would Beth gain? Explain to me why we've both risked our lives." He shook his head. "Ty, I'm asking for your help. I've never asked for anything from you, but now I need you to believe us. For my parents' sake. For the time my father helped you. Think of it as a way to pay off an old debt from your family to mine."

Beth looked from the senator to the intense expression on Jeff's face. There was an odd nostalgia there, too, as if the past had suddenly crashed hard into the present.

Ty Crocker gazed away. Absentmindedly he petted Flubby. "That was a long time ago. But you're right. If Henry hadn't stepped in . . ." He glanced back at Beth. "It was during the McCarthy hearings. My career was on the block. I was a young diplomat, and my first wife had been a member of the Communist party back when she was a teenager in the thirties and socialism was a good way to help people out. I could've divorced and denounced Denise to get out of the guilt-by-association that McCarthy liked to tar everyone with, but she was dying of cancer . . . and I loved her—" His voice broke. "But if I'd gone before that panel, my career would've been over."

Jeff's tone was somber. "Dad wanted to help, Ty. He felt honored to." He looked down at Beth, where she sat wearily at the table, and explained, "Dad found out something on McCarthy through his work at the CIA. Whatever it was, it was enough to make McCarthy cancel the hearing he'd called to accuse Ty of being a pinko-Commie, as they said in those days. A month later, it was all over. McCarthy had gotten so extreme in his accusations on television that he showed he was a madman on a witch hunt. That was the end of his power."

What he did not add was that Ty's wife died that month, too. It had all happened a decade before Jeff was born, but it was a story Ty had told occasionally when the two families gathered. A story of one man's helping another when he was under a dark cloud of suspicion. Now Jeff was under a similar cloud.

Silence filled the old-fashioned kitchen. Ty heaved a sigh. "All right, Jeff. I'm sorry I doubted you. You're right, I should've been a better friend than that. Sometimes being a senator, a public watchdog, makes a man forget to be human, forget his heart. At least, until he knows the truth for certain. I'd like to find out myself whether there are tracking chips in those belts. I'd better make a phone call. If there are, and if it turns out they're part of the equipment of a gang of militant terrorists, I guess even this old senator will know the whole story is true, right?" Ty smiled, patted Flubby on the head, and set him on the floor. Flubby yawned and licked a front paw. His steps deliberate, the senator headed toward the door. "I'm going upstairs to my den. You stay here and wait where it's safe."

"Can't do it, Ty. Sorry." Jeff tapped his foot impatiently.

Beth explained, "If we're right, Berianov isn't wearing a belt. We'll have to stop him some other way."

"We're not going to tell you where we're going," Jeff added. "You're involved enough. I don't see how anyone could've followed us, but so many people have died that we have to face the possibility you could be in danger, too. The only way we're going to survive and stop Berianov is to never go anywhere they might look for us."

"Right. I'll take precautions. But *you* must, too. Use my car." Ty Crocker took keys from a hook near the stove and handed them to Jeff with instructions. Then he stopped in the doorway and turned, his naked legs thin and white above his slippers. "I'd better bypass the Bureau under the circumstances. Since this involves the president, it's got to go to the Secret Service anyway. After all, if the chair of the Senate Intelligence Committee can't get something like this taken care of immediately, who can? As for President Stevens, he's a stubborn man. He won't stay out of the Oval Office just because a cadre of lunatics may be out to get him, but we can increase protection and maybe track down these killers before they do any harm."

Beth said, "The president may change his mind if you can confirm the existence of the tracking clips in the belts."

"True. Before I do anything else though, I've got to calm down Anna. I know she's lying upstairs fuming because I'm not getting a good night's sleep. Call me later, and I'll let you know what I've found. Be sure to turn out the lights and lock up. And be damn careful yourselves." He turned and padded down the hall, thinking fondly of his second wife. Then his mind turned anxiously to what Jeff and Beth had told him.

Concerned and out-of-sorts, Ty Crocker sat in the funnel of light made by his desk lamp in the dark den. Books lined the walls. The cool air was touched by the faint odor of well-oiled leather furniture. He punched in the home phone number of Secret Service director Dean Jennings. After introducing himself, the senator spoke for five minutes. "That's as much of the story as I'm going to tell you," he said firmly.

"But your source—?"

"No. If the belts pan out, then I'll tell you who gave them and all the other information to me. Meanwhile, consider it an imminent threat against President Stevens. You'll want to find everyone who's wearing them."

There was a long silence. Finally Jennings said, "I'll have one of my people there in five minutes to pick up the belts. We'll analyze the buckles and go from there."

Evans Olsen lived at a good address in Foggy Bottom. Beth knew this because she had once driven him home from a party after he had drunk so much he could no longer remember where he had left his car. Now she and Jeff parked the senator's car a block away and hurried to the upscale apartment house, keeping close to the buildings and moving from shadow to shadow. They saw no one who looked suspicious and nothing threatening. Their luck was holding for now. In the lobby, Beth ran her finger along the names on the mailboxes.

"That's odd." She frowned. "He's not here. I know this was where I brought him that night. Let's try the manager."

The building's manager was an older man with a sleepy face who was less than pleased to be rousted from his bed. He was instantly wary when Beth asked for Evans Olsen. "Are you from his office?"

"No, just an old friend who needs to find him," Beth told him. "Has he moved?"

"We had to ask him to leave, I'm afraid. Too bad, I rather liked the boy."

Beth guessed, "His drinking?"

The man nodded and became less wary. "The owners insisted."

"I'm sorry. He can really get out of control. Do you know where he went?"

He studied her a moment, then nodded again. "It's in the Northeast. I'll see if I can find the address. Perhaps you can help him."

Olsen's new address proved to be a run-down stuccoed cottage in a derelict neighborhood. Trash stuck to curbs. The odors of marijuana and stale beer were in the air. Thrift-store toys lay out in dark yards that were more dirt than grass. After leaving Ty's Mercedes a block away,

Beth and Jeff ran through the cold air to stand across the street from the unlighted cottage. They studied it.

"You didn't date this joker, too, did you?" Jeff sounded irritated.

"Didn't have to. One look at his alcohol habits told me everything I needed to know. I prefer my excess in more exciting situations than drunken stupors."

He gave a brief smile.

"Shall I ring the doorbell? Let me amend that. Shall I *try* the door-bell to see if it works?"

"Not yet. Wait here. I'll be right back. If anyone so much as winks, yell." He took off at a trot, his long body subtly adjusting. He grew lean and fluid, melting through the shadows. He pushed aside broken slats on a wood fence and disappeared into the cottage's side yard.

Beth continued to watch the house, but there was nothing to see— no light inside, not even the gray flickers of a TV screen reflecting on the window. She was getting cold. But more than anything, she wanted to lose this omnipresent sense of danger that haunted her. It was early Saturday now. Four days since she had phoned Meteor Express and the Russian—some still-unidentified Russian—had answered.

Full of nervous energy, she stood on one foot then the other. Finally she dashed across the dingy street and ran up the brick steps to the cot-tage. She listened. Nothing. She crept across the wood porch. When a floorboard creaked, she stopped for a long time. At last she reached the front door. She stretched out her hand.

Abruptly light glared inside. She stepped back, startled. Turned to run.

"Beth!" The door swung open, and Jeff stood there. "I told you to wait."

"I waited. Now I'm not waiting. I didn't agree to any time limit. In fact, I never even agreed to wait."

"Come in. You're shivering."

She hurried through the doorway. "Where's Olsen?"

Jeff dropped the shade at the window beside the door. "He was out back in his car, drunk, keys still in his hand. He was too oblivious to even stumble from his car. The way he looks and smells, he's been on a real bender. I dumped him in the kitchen."

She followed him back through a narrow hallway that ran the length of the cottage. The wallpaper was faded in squares and rectangles that told her at one time there had been photographs hanging along here. She imagined family faces, children from infancy through high school graduation. Wedding photos. She shook her head. What had happened to the world—to *her* world—that such a simple idea as a record of family life held such poignancy and seemed such a remote dream? Automatically she clutched her shoulder bag with its life-saving drugs.

"Watch him, will you?" Jeff said. "I'm going to close the curtains and see what kind of security there is, if any. This is going to take longer than we thought." He left, his footsteps quiet as he roamed the small one-story structure.

She stared at what once had been an attractive, dynamic man. In his late thirties, Evans Olsen had a mop of curly black hair prematurely salted with gray. He lay in a fetal position on the painted wood table of a breakfast nook. His hands were balled up in fists and shoved up under his unshaved chin. His eyes were closed tightly, the corners wrinkled, as if the act of shutting off the light would shut off the world. He wore a black trenchcoat that stank of vomit, high-top sneakers crossed at the ankles, and Dockers slacks that were mottled with grime and God knew what else.

"Evans!" She dropped to her haunches so her face was on a level with his. She shouted, "Evans, wake up!"

He did not flinch. Not even the sound of his name being bellowed was enough to shake him.

She sighed. "Evans, you're disgusting. Come on. We've got to sober you up."

Still no response. She took off her windbreaker and grabbed his hand. It was sticky. This was not going to be one of her all-time favorite jobs. She stripped off one of his trenchcoat sleeves, peeled the coat off his back, then rolled him enough to pull off the other sleeve. She held her breath, trying not to smell the wretched stink, and carried the trenchcoat out to the back porch where she dropped it. Once more inside, she locked the door and turned.

Jeff had set Evans upright on the bench in the breakfast nook, his head propped up in the corner. Evans's mouth hung open. He was snoring.

Beth said, "He's so out of it that I'm worried if we try to pour coffee down him, he'll choke. It could start him to vomiting, and if he aspirates vomit, we could be in real trouble. He could die."

Jeff frowned. "You're saying we'd better let him sleep it off."

"I don't think we have a choice. He's even peed himself. In a few hours, he'll start to come out of it. Then we can try the coffee routine. It's not like we have to wait for him to get a good eight hours." She sighed. "What's the security like?"

He shrugged unhappily. "Nonexistent. The doors and windows have locks, but that's all. Anyone who really wants in is going to find no challenge."

They stared across the scarred kitchen tiles. With most of Washington and points east, west, north, and south looking for them, they were stuck with a drunk who could not talk, in a house that was not secure. Stuck . . . with each other.

Jeff shook his head. "You're right. We'll just have to wait it out. God, how long could he have been like this? I mean, the Secret Service finds out how far down he's sunk, they'll bounce him out of the White House in ten seconds."

"I've never seen him this bad. He's got to be in some kind of deep trouble. That's what a drunk does, he hides from trouble." Beth glanced around the shabby kitchen. "We'd better search the place. There's got to be some reason Berianov was calling him. We just have to figure out what the reason was."

"Yeah, and they haven't killed him, even though he's probably easy to find. Considering Berianov's track record, that's significant. It must mean they still need him for some reason."

Beth helped Jeff carry Olsen into the bathroom. Jeff stayed to strip him and put him in the shower, while Beth did a quick survey of the cottage—two bedrooms, one bath, living room, small dining room, and kitchen. Everything smelled of dust, cheap liquor, and cigarette butts. There was a full basement with an ancient Maytag washer that looked as if it had not been used in years. She searched past an old workbench with a few dusty tools, and on into a corner where discarded tires and hubcaps had been tossed. The detritus of years lay in haphazard piles everywhere. Nothing current.

She returned upstairs to the living room, where a desk stood in the corner. The top was littered with candy packages, bills, junk mail, and catalogues. She sat to open and read—illegal, but at this point she had committed so many crimes she had given up worrying.

She discovered Olsen had moved here a few months before from Foggy Bottom and was renting. The bill included a note warning his security deposit was subject to forfeit if the owners found he had not taken care of their property. She shook her head, doubting it could have been in significantly better shape when he rented it. There were old bills from creditors demanding payment instantly, and credit-card notices saying he was over his borrowing limit. Automatic deposit records told her Evans Olsen was still employed by the White House, and bank records showed his money rushed out much quicker than it flowed in. He was on the way down, and descending at a fast clip.

Jeff's voice sounded behind her. "He's clean and tucked into bed.

Never so much as opened his eyes. It was like taking a corpse into that shower."

She turned to summarize how bad Olsen's financial situation was. But as she talked, her words slowed and faltered. She found herself breathing harder and harder. "What could Berianov want from him?"

"Whatever it is, we'll find out." Jeff was standing in the doorway, dressing.

His skin glowed from the shower, golden and tempting. He had arrived in briefs, a tiny strip of underwear that hid none of his assets. He leaned over to step into his jeans. The muscles across his shoulders kneaded and pulsed as he pulled up the denim pants, buttoned the fly, and stopped at the waist. There was a red crease across the top of one shoulder where a bullet had seared a path. The pants hung from his flat belly and narrow hips as if they had been tailored. Tiny tufts of golden-brown hair showed beneath his naval. He reached for his shirt, which was hanging on the doorknob. Light glowed in his eyes, something dangerous and alluring. He had changed. Whatever questions he'd had about her had somehow been resolved.

"Aren't you going to button your waist?" Her voice was husky.

"In a minute. Are those M&M's?" He strode toward her.

His short hair was mussed. He reached up and ran long fingers through it as he approached. The knuckles of his right hand were red where another bullet had scored him. He had cut his nails flat across. She could see that even from a distance. He smelled of soap and intent.

She found herself pushing away from the desk and out of his path. The desk chair's old rollers creaked on the thin carpet. The noise was sharp and loud in the quiet house. She forced herself to breathe.

He ignored her and walked past to the desk, and she felt a pang of regret. He snapped up the M&M's package that she had shoved off to the side with the other candy when she had sorted through Olsen's papers.

He grinned at her. Again there was that light in his eyes, glowing like coals. "Come on. I have something you should try."

She could spend the rest of her life—no matter how short or how long—looking at his naked back. He had muscles even along his spine. They bunched and stretched temptingly out toward his tapered sides. There was a little gap in his jeans at the top of his tailbone where the loose waistband hung open. And then there was the back of his handsome head, the short brown hairs still damp and glistening.

She followed, not asking herself whether she should go.

42

"Aha. I thought I remembered a microwave." Jeff opened cupboard doors until he found a microwavable bowl. He ripped open the M&M's package, dumped the contents into the ceramic bowl, and slid it into the microwave. He set the timer for sixty-five seconds. "You nuke them on HIGH for a minute and five seconds. No more, because they'll burn. Too little . . . and you'll see. Now we wait. So tell me what else you found on Olsen's desk."

Her lips were dry. She resisted licking them. She made herself give a recital of her findings.

He listened carefully, his gaze entirely on her. There was nothing small about him anywhere. He bristled with energy and intelligence and good looks, and he knew it. For some reason, that made him even more attractive. There were small cuts on his cheeks and chin, probably from splinters and cement chips that had exploded from bullets that had landed near. They showed clearly now that his skin was clean. From his wide-set dark eyes to his aristocratic nose and full lips, he was male. Testosterone at its tactile best. And it was all complicated in her mind because she liked him. Actually liked him too much.

As the microwave's timer went off, he said, "Olsen's in such bad shape financially, he's prime bait for blackmail. He worked at the White House, and we think Berianov plans to kill the president. So it seems to me that the big attraction for Berianov is just what we thought— Olsen's job. Could be he needed Olsen to find out something for him or do something for him."

He opened the door, and the tempting scent of warm chocolate filled the kitchen.

She forced herself to think. "Or he needed something from Olsen."

"Right." He turned, smiling. He had even white teeth that would be worth a fortune in advertising to a major toothpaste maker. He held out the cheap ceramic bowl. Inside lay the candies in a multitude of bright colors.

"Go ahead. Try one."

Gingerly she chose a red one. It was hot. The edge had cracked, and dark brown chocolate oozed out. She dropped it into her mouth. The sugar coating was crisp, and the chocolate was warm and melting inside. The delicious taste coated her tongue.

"Like it?" he asked.

She nodded.

"Here. Have another." He chose a brown one. "Open wide."

Obediently, she parted her lips. She looked up. Their eyes locked. He slipped the chocolate into her mouth and, without looking into the bowl, picked up another and slipped it between his lips. They chewed and smiled.

"I'm practically a virgin." Her voice was thick. "It's been a long time. A *real* long time. I don't think this is a good idea. I don't believe in casual sex anymore. Besides, you have all these issues about how long I'm going to live. *I* have issues about how long I'm going to live."

"Wasn't Phil Stageman casual sex?"

"More like impetuous and stupid. At the time, I hadn't made a commitment against casualness. I'm still working on impetuous and stupid. Besides, that relationship—if you could call it that—was over long before my heart transplant. Remember, my heart's from a man. Maybe I won't know how to do it as a woman anymore."

"I'll take the chance." He chuckled. "Try another one." His black eyes were mysterious and inviting. Hypnotic.

Whatever aches and pains she had felt disappeared. He never took his gaze from hers as he reached into the bowl for a chocolate.

She gripped his hand, stopping its progress toward her mouth. "I could have cardiac arrest while we're making love and die. You'd feel guilty."

"You'd be dead a half-dozen times over the last two days from the stress and physical demands if that were true. Besides, what did the doctor say about sex?"

"He said that six weeks after surgery I could drive and have sex."

"At the same time?"

"That's what *I* asked him. He laughed." She loved his short, spiky black lashes. Heat radiated from him, pulling her toward him.

"You're not laughing."

"I seem to be distracted." She released his hand, and he fed her another M&M's. She chewed. "You knew we were going to have sex?"

"Thought about it," he admitted. "Does that bother you?"

"I thought about it, too. Here, my turn." She moved closer, reached into the bowl, and lifted an M&M's to his mouth.

He leaned over, and his lips took the candy and her fingers. His lips were hot and moist. Electricity jolted her.

"Oh, my." She swayed into him.

He caught her with one arm and set the bowl down with his free hand. She was still looking up into that broad face, now just an inch above her own. His breath was spicy and delicious. He wrapped his other arm around her. Naked chest. Two naked arms. So very male.

She gasped. "Now's your chance to back out. It's still not too late."

His voice dropped what seemed an octave. "Don't think that's a good idea. I have this thing about gorgeous women with brains and guts. You might say I'm a sucker for them. But I will admit to a lousy track record, so you're going to have to help me along with this . . . this—"

"Relationship?"

"That's not such a bad word, is it?" His lips brushed hers and then were gone.

She said, "Sometimes it's hard to say. I've been wanting to kiss you for a long time. You have dimples on your cheeks. I'm going to touch them. Okay?"

He swallowed. "Okay."

She slid her fingers up and pressed them against the dimples, pulling down on his face. Their lips touched. Fire swept through her. Whatever control she had retained was gone. He yanked her close and kissed her. She felt herself crawling up his body, sinking into it. She pressed closer and closer, her heart racing. He kissed her throat, her eyes, her nose, her ears. She shuddered with desire.

He slid his hands up through her short hair, cradled her head, and pulled her away so he could see her. "There's a bed in the other bedroom." His voice was hoarse. His eyes lidded. "I stripped it. Threw on a blanket that looked clean. There's a lock on the door."

She nodded mutely, unable to talk. So she broke free and ran. He followed. Their feet thundered into the small spare bedroom. A bedside lamp was alight.

He grabbed her hand and spun her around. "I'm going to undress you. Slowly. You'll like it."

She was panting. "I admire a man with opinions."

Suddenly his hands were gone. He stepped back and just stared.

She watched his gaze, the hunger in it, and felt renewed heat whip through her.

And then his hands were back. "I've changed my mind. Fast is better right now."

He pulled up her turtleneck. His fingers brushed down her scar. "Beautiful. It saved your life."

"Thank you," she whispered.

He kissed the top of it and then back up to her neck while he unzipped her jeans. He locked his thumbs into her waist band and pushed the jeans down. She wriggled to help him. As his hands traveled lower, so did his face, his breath humid and puffing against her chest, her belly, her crotch, her thighs.

"Sit," he rasped.

She sat on the floor, and he pulled off her athletic shoes, her socks, and finally her jeans. He stood back up, towering over her. She looked up from the floor and felt giddy. He was gloriously handsome, rising above her like a mountain in his tight-fitting jeans and golden muscles. A woman's sexual fantasy.

He extended his hands. She let him pull her up.

"You're so pretty," he murmured as he drank in the sight of her in her black lace bra and black thong brief. He touched her nipples through the silk. He was riveted by the long length of her body, the flowing curves, and the paleness of her skin. Her breasts were small and high, and her belly flat. Muscles gave her a sculpted look. He inhaled sharply. His breathing was ragged.

"My turn." She fumbled with the buttons on his jeans, finally unhooking the top one, then the next, until all were open, and his pants parted. She ran a finger down the vertical line of curly light-brown hair that began just below his navel. "Talk about pretty—" Breathing erratically, she slid her hands inside the front of his jeans.

He groaned. She pulled out her hands and yanked the jeans down, kissing the insides of his thighs.

His heart hammered. He reminded himself to breathe, to slow down . . . before he exploded. She skinned down his underwear, and he dropped free. And she was kissing him. Making greedy, happy sounds and kissing him.

Blood shot to his head. He was losing control—

He grabbed her under her arms, lifted her up, kept lifting until her feet were off the carpet. He felt his muscles ache with the strain, a good distraction. He pressed his lips into her belly and tasted her, savory as buttermilk.

He carried her around to the bed, his face burrowing, his lips kissing and tasting. Above him, she moaned. When he set her feet down on the floor, their eyes met, and for a moment they were caught in each other's hot gazes. Acknowledgment and a strange kind of excited comprehension passed between them.

He reached around and unsnapped her bra. Her small breasts swung loose. He kissed one nipple then the other and peeled her thong down her legs. Panting, she kicked it off. As he rose, she wrapped herself around him, arms over his shoulders and neck, a leg around his thigh, her breasts pressed into his chest, and fell back, drawing him down with her onto the bed. If she were going to die during sex, this was as good a time as any. They kissed, touched, and moved together, skin sliding and sweating.

In the back of her mind, the fear was still there. That climaxing would mean death, and yet she could not stop. She wanted him more than she had ever wanted a man. And it was not just the sex. It was everything else, too. She had told him that risk defined life, and this was perhaps her biggest one, not that she could die but that she would live.

Still, she raised her knees and opened her legs. He leaned forward, pulled her legs up around his neck, and entered her. All her senses were ablaze. Her nails scratched down his back. He thrust, and she quickly caught his rhythm. They moved together. Stared into each other's eyes. Mesmerized by sensation and desire and each other.

Caught in that other world where one is never enough. In and out, pulsing, until she knew she was going to come. He made a guttural sound deep in his throat. His lids were half-lowered, and he stared with feral eyes. She stared back, and the first roll of her explosion began. It shook her just as he shouted with his orgasm. They rocked together, breathing, arching. Hearts pounding, alive.

Two states north, Eli Kirkhart sat with his cheek against the rough bark of a tree, swearing in the dark night at Jeff Hammond and Beth Convey and everything else in the perverse universe conspiring to get in his way. The handcuffs were biting into his wrists, and his shoulders ached from sitting with his arms lashed in front of him. He was so angry at Jeff Hammond and the dirty tricks that life had played on him that he was unaware of the pickup truck approaching along the dirt road.

Then he saw it. "Hey! Help! Stop! Help!"

Raising a cloud of dust that was only slightly lighter than the night's shadows, the pickup drew abreast of Kirkhart. All he could see was a shadowed head in the driver's seat looking straight ahead.

"Hello! Help! Over here! Stop! I need help!"

Trailing a dust cloud that floated like a towering wraith in the night, the truck passed on.

"Bloody hell and damn!" he bellowed.

In a screech of brakes, the pickup stopped up the road. It sat motionless as the dust cloud settled back down to the road's deep ruts. At last it backed up until it was next to Kirkhart. The passenger window rolled down, and a pasty face peered out.

Eli rattled the handcuffs and shouted, "FBI! I've been kidnaped. You hear? *Federal Bureau of Investigation!* I need help."

The face peered for another long minute, and then the motor turned off, the driver's door opened, and the man walked around the rear of the pickup, a shotgun in his hands. Squinting to see through the night, he approached warily.

"FBI," Kirkhart repeated. "I'm cuffed to this stupid tree, and—"

"What the hell you doin' sittin' out here?"

Kirkhart took a calming breath. "I'm a special agent of the FBI," he said patiently. "If you look in my jacket pocket, you'll find my badge and credentials. I was arresting a murderer, when . . ."

But the man had stopped listening, was circling around to look at the other side of the tree. "My wallet's in my pocket," Kirkhart suggested.

He felt his jacket being lifted, and then his wallet was neatly slid out. The man grunted with surprise. "Well, I'll be damned." He returned to face Eli, the shotgun resting on his shoulder, a big grin on his weather-seamed face. "Now how the hell'd you get into such a fix—you, one of America's finest?"

Kirkhart sighed. He explained again what had happened, feeling about as foolish as the man seemed to think he was. "Can you get me out of these cuffs?"

"Guess so. " He checked the credentials in the wallet one more time. "Special Agent Kirkhart. Now don't you go nowhere." Chortling, the man returned to his pickup, dug around in back, and returned to Eli, a large wire-cutter dangling from his hand. Without another word, he snapped apart the cuffs. After Eli Kirkhart was on his feet and had swung and stamped his circulation back, they walked to the truck.

The man said, "Lucky for you I was in town late. That's my place up ahead, and ain't no other on this here road."

The farmer took a hacksaw to the two bracelet parts of the cuffs and carefully sawed through. That was more difficult and took longer, but eventually they came off. Meanwhile, Eli had convinced the fellow to drive him into Gettysburg.

"So you're a G-man," the farmer chuckled as they sped away in the truck. "Must be a pretty damn exciting job. Guess you guys've got your hands full now. Your director gettin' killed and all."

Kirkhart stared. "Our director? You mean Thomas Horn?"

"That's him, all right. Stabbed, what I heard. Some kind of spy did it."

Kirkhart felt a sudden sinking in his stomach. "When was this?"

"Tonight earlier, I guess."

"You have a radio in the truck? A news station?"

The farmer reached down and turned it on, pressed a button, and a voice appeared, droning the local news. Eli waited impatiently, his fingers drumming on the door's armrest.

And then he heard it. "This bulletin just in: A massive manhunt is on for Jeffrey Hammond, the alleged assassin of FBI director Thomas Horn, who was stabbed to death at about nine o'clock tonight as he sought to arrest Hammond, who is suspected of being a mole within the Bureau. All evidence points to Hammond as both the killer and the mole, according to FBI sources. The president has . . ."

Eli Kirkhart barely heard the rest as he battled confusion and anger, battled the knowledge he had wasted his time—wasted everyone's time—trying to prove his suspicions that Hammond was the long-sought mole. What had been wrong with him? Pain flashed through his mind, and a deep loneliness that seemed to come from everywhere enveloped him. *Aida.* Oh, God, he still missed her. He was hollow without her, and he had done nothing to fill the void. Even the weeks grieving beside her bed as she faded toward death had been better than the emptiness he felt after her frail body had finally stopped breathing, an emptiness he still felt.

Now as he listened to the news report finish, he had a sickening feeling he had been too eager to bring down Jeff, who had once been almost as close to him as Aida. That since Aida had died, he had become something a little less than human, yet dangerously armed with a gun and a badge. *Persecution . . . not prosecution.* Was that how he had tried to block out the pain and make himself feel whole again? By making other people hurt instead?

The unpleasant truth was the Bureau was wrong now, as he had been even more wrong up until now. Obviously, Jeff Hammond was here in Pennsylvania when the director was killed. And if Hammond did not kill Director Horn, but the real mole did—

Worry flooded him. He pushed his sense of guilt aside and thought quickly. He had a lot to make up for. His mind flipped through names of the top people in the Bureau as if they were printed on flash cards. Which one could be the mole? He stopped and considered this one, then that one. Who was it? *Who in hell was it?*

43

An hour later in Evans Olsen's shabby cottage, the air still smelled of sex, and the bedroom was dim in the light of the small lamp. On the bed, Beth yawned and stretched. "I'm never going to think about M&M's in the same way."

"I was inspired."

"Well, if you want to ignore the old one: 'Want a piece of candy, little girl?' "

Jeff laughed, "I'd forgotten that." He slapped her naked thigh, smiling.

"That's my thigh, sir."

He was immediately contrite. "I'm sorry, darling. I'll kiss it." He untangled himself, pulled her around, and licked the red skin. "Mmm. Delicious."

"That's not kissing."

"You didn't mind before. Do you mind now? Do you want me to bite you instead? I'm multitalented."

She chuckled. "Indeed. I'd testify to that in court. So now do you have a higher opinion of lawyers?"

"Higher *and* lower. Inside and out. Yup. You're just about the best."

"I have a joke for you. It covers all my obvious talents—dumb blond and avaricious lawyer."

"Fascinating. Let's hear it."

She sat up, her breasts naked and pink. She grinned unselfconsciously. "A male lawyer and a blond woman are sitting next to each other on an airplane. He invites her to play a game. He says, 'I'll ask a question, and if you don't know the answer, you pay me five dollars. You ask me a question, and if I don't know the answer, I'll pay *you* fifty dollars.' He figures since she's a blond, he'll clean up. She agrees. So the lawyer asks, 'What's the distance from the earth to the moon?' The blond doesn't say a word. She reaches into her purse and hands him a five-dollar bill. Now, it's her turn. She says, 'What goes up a hill with three legs and comes down with four?' The lawyer thinks and thinks and can't figure it out. Finally he gives her fifty dollars and says, 'So what *is* the answer?' Without a word, she hands him five dollars."

She howled. She doubled over and held her sides. She laughed and laughed.

"That's good. Got to admit. Very good." He chuckled.

Still laughing, she wiped her eyes. "Oh, my. You didn't think it was funny?"

"Hilarious."

"But you didn't laugh."

"Yes, I did. But it was more fun watching you. You enjoy life so much. It's precious to you. I'd forgotten about that. Maybe I never knew." He kissed her, and his heart was full of emotion. It felt strange, yet . . . good. "You're teaching me to live again."

"No. You're teaching *me.*"

They smiled at each other. She rested her head on his shoulder and yawned. He pulled her close. They lay in the lamplight, talking quietly, trying to shut off the danger that waited somewhere out in the city.

"You need to sleep," he told her at last. "You've got to take care of yourself. I'll help you. I want you to live."

The old loneliness and fear seemed to crush her. "And what if I die?"

"We're all going to die sometime. That's the cliché, isn't it? But let's you and me make a pact. Whichever one of us goes first, the other will be right there, too. I'll hold your hand. Will you hold mine?"

She felt tears burn her eyelids. "Of course."

Senator Ty Crocker was on his fourth cup of hot tea in the upstairs office of his house near Dupont Circle, surrounded by his books and the quiet creaks of the old house. Flubby the cat lay curled around his slippered feet, snoring and twitching, chasing some elusive dream mouse.

Still in his pajamas and robe, the senator waited impatiently for the phone to ring. Worries about pending Senate bills and the biopsy on his prostate—the results were due next week—receded from his mind.

Instead, he felt a deep, nagging anxiety, and it kept him chained to his desk. He had to admit he still had some doubts about Jeff Hammond. He was ashamed, but he could not stop his suspicions. He had been in public service too long, a watchdog for the good of the country. His hand lay in a bony clutch next to the phone. He glared at the instrument, willing it to ring. He wanted Dean Jennings from the Secret Service to tell him there were tracking bugs in the two belt buckles, which would mean Jeff Hammond had not gone mad and was no killer. At the same time, he feared what the information meant. That President James Emmet Stevens was in mortal danger.

In his long life, the senator had learned seldom did anyone's character change overnight. Something he had, for the last few days, forgotten in his zeal to protect the nation. He had known Jeff since infancy, watched him grow into an athletic and intelligent young man, and seen his pride when he joined the Bureau. Seen the pride in his parents and older sister, too. None had understood why Jeff had left the Bureau, and the fact that he had gone to work at the *Post* had been little compensation. After Jeff's parents died, the senator had made it a point to have lunch with him every two months or so. It was the least he could do for Henry Hammond's son. At no time during those long, ranging conversations had he seen any erosion in Jeff's character.

In fact, Jeff had thrown himself into his work at the newspaper. He had quickly become the *Post*'s Russian and Eastern European expert, winning several awards for his coverage and essays. It had been hard for the senator to believe he was the murderer police in two states and the District claimed, despite the seemingly overwhelming evidence. But he had believed it. To his shame, he had believed them and not Jeff.

He was still struggling with all that, when his phone finally rang. He grabbed it.

Dean Jennings was agitated. "You're right, Ty. There are small tracking devices in both belts. State-of-the-art. Transmit-only, with preset frequencies. Easily followed within a fifty-mile radius, and we can display their positions on geo-referenced digital maps as we go." As director of the Secret Service, his primary goal was to stop all threats against the president, and now it looked as if he had just felt the first rumble of a national cataclysm.

"I was afraid of that," the senator said soberly, while inwardly he wanted to shout for joy. Jeff was telling the truth. "What can I do?"

"I need every piece of information you have. And I need it now. I'm sorry to drag you out at this hour . . . what time is it? Hell! It's already four A.M. Sorry, Ty. But you understand. Can you drive over here so we can tape your debriefing? I'm assembling a team right now. We'll start with the identity of that secret source of yours."

"I've got to dress. Give me a half-hour. Less, if I can slip out without my wife catching me."

"Thanks, Senator. Thank you very much. Meanwhile, we're going to start throwing out our nets and see what bottom-feeders we snare."

In the brightly lit conference room in the dark Federal Triangle, Dean Jennings slammed back in the desk chair, his unshaved chin bristly black in the harsh overhead light, the wrinkles around his gray eyes deep with uneasiness.

"Senator Crocker will be here shortly," he told the top men and women he had assembled from the Secret Service, the U.S. Marshal's office, and the FBI. "According to his source, there are around fifty people believed to be wearing these belts. He claims he has no idea where they are, only that they're ultra-nationalists who've targeted the president sometime today. I want everyone in position to move as soon as we debrief the senator. We're going to surprise the whole lot. Take all of them simultaneously, if possible. I don't want even a short-peckered crow to escape. Questions?"

Drinking black coffee, the twenty specialists and heads of departments shot questions back and forth, examined what few facts they had, and speculated, all in preparation for whatever problems and disasters lay ahead.

When the discussion at last slowed, one man excused himself to go to the bathroom. It was FBI man Bobby Kelsey. As soon as the conference room door closed, he raced down the shadowy hall, trying doors until one opened. It was a storage room. He slipped in, locked the door, and took out his cell phone.

Soon after Alexei Berianov arrived at his secret headquarters in Bethesda, on the outskirts of Washington, he washed off his old-man's makeup and changed into casual trousers and an open-necked Egyptian cotton shirt. He put on his shoulder holster, slid in his pistol, and took a seat before the wall of windows that looked out over the sea of lights that was the nighttime metropolis.

But his mind was once again in the past, back in Moscow, reveling in his third wife, Tamara, and her glorious flaming hair, her angular face, her green Cossack eyes, and intense presence. As far as Berianov was concerned, the poet Aleksandr Pushkin had captured the Cossacks best: "Eternally on horseback, eternally ready to fight, eternally on guard." That was Tamara.

She had been born in Novocherkassk near the legendary River Don in southern Russia. As she grew, she had tended walnut trees and chickens, sprinkled herbs on the family's clay floors for aroma, and helped raise ten younger brothers and sisters. In the usual way, her father had strapped a saber onto the leg of each of her brothers as soon as he turned forty days old. When she was ten years old, she finally strapped on her own saber. Horses were in her blood, and her blood was as hot as any of her brothers.

Which was why she had escaped to Moscow. In sex, she was wild and exciting. Her eyes would be back-lighted, and her skin would smell pungent, like ripe olives. Although he begged her, she would never let him see her completely naked. And even when they had twin daughters, she refused to give up driving her troika, hired by laughing Muscovites and adventurous tourists who never realized she had no interest in them, only in her horses.

As soon as the girls were old enough, she took them with her. She wore her flat-topped military hat Cossack style, jaunty on the back of her red hair, and she carried in her tall boot the traditional four-foot-long *nagaika*, her cavalry whip.

In those days, he was gone a lot—in Afghanistan because the bitter war was dragging on, in the United States because of President Reagan's technological threats, and in East Germany because of rising political tensions. The Soviet Union was losing the Cold War, outspent and outlasted by the Americans, but only the most elite in the government knew how bad the situation was.

Once the center of his universe, his work now made his gut ache. Low pay, plunging morale, and increasingly repressive measures were draining his agents and the state. He scrambled to make his job and his country strong again.

The Kremlin rewarded him by giving him three promotions three spectacular years in a row until at last he headed the FCD—the KGB's foreign espionage arm—in Yasenevo. There were more whispered promises: First the Politburo, then Gorbachev's job. Yes, Berianov was that good. Loyal, smart, a natural leader. He could be counted upon to deliver, whatever the cost.

Still, one political crisis after another made government, down to the smallest Soviet, quake as if it were built on quicksand. His agents grumbled, something they never would have dared before. Some simply disappeared, and through the Gavrilov channel—an ultra-secret communication network he had set up with the CIA—he learned they had defected to the West. Surely, it could get no worse.

Then that spring he discovered Tamara was having an affair with a friend of her brothers', another Cossack. Jealous and crazed, Berianov stormed out of the apartment, his daughters clinging to his pant legs. He peeled off their little fingers and drove recklessly down to Red Square. During that ride, nothing made sense: The Lenin Hills were green with leafing birches. Colorful tourist boats rode the river. Families picnicked in the sun while children played. How could the world be so normal when his country and his marriage were falling apart?

Bitterness filled him as he watched preparations for the annual May Day parade. One banner wrenched him with longing for the dreams he had once held so dear: LONG LIVE THE WORKING CLASS OF THE COUNTRY, THE LIVING FORCE IN THE BODY OF COMMUNISM!

That was when the weight of the years forced on him a choice that had directed every decision since. He had to choose. How much did he still honor his sick country? How could he continue to honor his lying wife? That was when he knew what to do.

He drove to his office in the suburbs, summoned his favorite assassin, Ivan Vok, and gave him orders. Just as Peter the Great had carried the head of the famed independence leader Kondrati Bulavin to Cherkassk—now Starocherkassk—to subdue its Cossacks, Ivan Vok appeared at Tamara's door with a pine box lined in plastic.

He opened the lid for her, displaying her lover's bloody head, which Vok had severed under Berianov's orders. As she stood frozen with horror, Vok spelled out Berianov's terms: She could not divorce him. She could have no more lovers. She must raise his daughters to be loyal Communists. He would not kill her as long as she did this.

Later, Vok reported that she had screamed and cried. That the girls had hidden as she ran to get her long whip. But in the end, she had deferred, and Berianov had conquered his Cossack. He never saw her again. He could not. He was bent on a new future with a far greater commitment than either could have given the other, far greater than he had ever had with anyone. In the end, he gave himself to his country.

In their Bethesda hideout, Ivan Vok had spread plates of food before him on the glass-topped dining room table—cold sturgeon, dark bread, sour cream, and fresh cucumbers. The subtle scent of the good fish made Vok yearn for Moscow. He sprinkled rock salt onto the cucumbers. In between talking with Alexei, he ate with gusto—shoving bread between his thick lips, then a huge piece of sturgeon slathered with sour cream, followed by a slice of crisp cucumber.

Their discussion had been wide-ranging, but now it had narrowed to preparing Russia to be receptive to their plans. Vok decided, "Soviets should have their history returned. No one should be without history."

From his easy chair in front of the tall windows, Berianov nodded agreement. "Whiners and the timid don't populate the history books."

Berianov's people were in position to take over Russia's seven storage sites for blister and nerve gases. They would easily control the nearly one hundred nuclear warhead depots, the four thousand tactical warheads for battlefield use, and all the fissile material on Soviet soil. The deal he had finessed between HanTech and Minatom would assure the nuclear program remained strong. Plus, of course, there was the *pièce de résistance*—the intercontinental ballistic missile bases.

Berianov said thoughtfully, "A couple of years ago, there was an opinion poll in Novgorod. They asked, 'Who are the enemies of the people today?' There were three choices—gangsters, businessmen, or the government. Fifteen percent said gangsters. Fifteen percent said businessmen." He paused for effect. "Seventy percent said government. A compelling majority. From the tsars to Brezhnev, we have always needed our autocratic leaders."

Vok chewed and nodded. "That's what we know. Always give the bear the honey he prefers."

"Our comrades miss our old Soviet-style medicine—nationalism. They need a leader who will take care of them and make sure everyone has bread, work, and an education. But at the same time, they also want our country raised back up to its rightful place in the world." From his dark hair to his blue-brown eyes and apparently relaxed mouth, he exuded the kind of confidence that could lead a people. A nation. His medium height and build were attractive but nothing more. It was his presence that turned heads.

With conviction, Ivan Vok said, "You're right, Alexei. You're always right. You're the one we need. A leader like you rises from the tundra with a sword in one hand and a loaf of bread in the other. No more stealing from the people. The others don't love our country, but we do."

Berianov nodded and turned back to gaze out the windows at the foreign metropolis in which he had lived a decade. Lights blinked off across the panorama of Bethesda and into Washington. As morning approached, the great city had fallen from restless lethargy into slumber, while here in this apartment violent resentment simmered. He was so wearied by this country. He longed to go home, where he would hear his good, strong language every day and he could work with people who understood what really mattered.

Vok pushed away from the table, the plates clean. He stretched, his short, massive body lengthening then returning to its usual compact, vigorous form.

Berianov waved a hand. "Ivan, bring vodka. It's a good night for vodka, eh?" As he spoke, his cell phone vibrated.

He pressed it against his ear and listened to the whispered voice of Bobby Kelsey speaking rapidly in English. Berianov's chest clamped as if caught in a monster's grip. "And you did nothing? How could you have let it go so far!"

Kelsey swore, "Damn it, Alexei, don't try to blame this on me. The senator sent the belts directly to Dean Jennings at the Secret Service. Out of my jurisdiction. I didn't know a thing about it until a few minutes ago. If anyone let this get out of hand, it was your own people. The only way I can figure those belts got to Crocker is through Jeff Hammond. They're old family friends."

A tidal wave of anger engulfed Berianov. Hammond again. He snapped, "You've got to stop them from going after the Keepers."

"There's no way. Not only the Secret Service and the Bureau are involved, so are local police and the marshals. The belts are already being tracked. Your Keepers aren't going to be in any position to go through with the assassination. You have to abort. Walk away while you can."

"*Nyet!*" The word was an explosion from his entrails. His blood raced. An enraged flush rose up his neck. He would find a way. Too much was at stake for his people. "You've got to locate Hammond and Convey before they do any more damage. Once you know where they are, I'll send in my people. I'll keep looking, but this is your problem, too."

"You think I don't know that?" Kelsey's voice was grim. "I killed the director of the FBI, for God's sake. You've got to abort. There'll be another day."

"No! *This* is the day. This is *my country's* day! You hear me? And if you think your big worry is having your identity exposed, you're naïve. If you try to turn back now, I'll send Vok to *kill* you."

There was a shocked pause. "Alexei, you're mad."

"And you're a small-time thinker, Kelsey. I've never been more sane in my life. Find Hammond and Convey, and *wipe them out.*"

He punched his cell phone's OFF button. He sensed Ivan Vok's presence before he saw him in his peripheral vision. "Go away, Vok. God-*dammit*, go away!"

Suddenly gunfire erupted. A man with a Russian accent was shouting, insisting she go to the address in Chevy Chase again. It was crucial. "Yes, I've taken you there many time, but it's different now. You must go!"

She grabbed her AK-47 and ran until she spotted Berianov's estate, bathed in filmy moonlight. With a chill, she saw the garage door rise just as before. An engine roared, and a motorcycle appeared in the opening. She was transfixed, horrified. She stepped back. She would not kill Mikhail Ogust again. Absolutely not.

But she was saved: Someone else was getting on. Astonished, she saw it was Berianov himself. He straddled the powerful machine, his shoulders square, his head particularly erect. He gave a little lift to his shoulders and tilted his head back as he pulled a helmet with a metallic visor down over his face. Immediately he gunned the motor and hurtled the bike at her. She wanted to escape. She wanted to fire the assault rifle. But she could not move.

Panicked, she watched helplessly as the motorcycle plowed into her and hurled her up into the silvery air. She caught sight of her reflection on Berianov's visor—but it was not her. It was Ogust, his gray hair flying, his face wrenched in pain. Her skull cracked open, and she screamed. . . .

She jolted upright, sweaty and shaking.

"Beth. Beth." Jeff crooned her name. He tugged her back down into his arms in the warm bed in the small room in Evans Olsen's house. "You had a nightmare. That's all. Don't worry. Just a nightmare."

She pressed into him. Burrowed like an animal seeking refuge. "Berianov killed Ogust. I'm sure now." As she described the dream, she knew there was something she had missed. Something important.

Jeff's calm voice comforted her. "You're safe here. Darling Beth. You're safe."

"Stephanie said other cellular memory recipients reported their dreams and ideas changed as time passed, too." Ever since she had stopped herself from shooting the Russian woman at the Watergate, rage and restlessness had plagued her less. She relaxed into him. His skin was smooth, but with the appealing, slightly rougher texture of a man's. The bristles of his unshaved chin tickled her ear. She wanted to stay here. Never leave. Safe forever.

Senator Ty Crocker emerged from his house and looked up at the stars, a distant dusting of diamonds sparkling across the black morning sky. He felt an excited buzz. His arteries might be hardening, but his blood could still rush. He was on his way to tell everything he knew to the Secret Service.

But he was late. Anna had awakened, and he'd had to stay and placate her. Eventually she had let him leave. Now he eagerly anticipated meeting with Dean Jennings. Not only would they put a stop to whatever insane plot had been hatched against the president, he would be able to clear Jeff's name.

He walked past peony and iris beds, leaving behind the house where he had lived nearly forty years. He liked the white Doric pillars, the brick facing, and the three tall stories. Up on the top floor had been the children's playroom. A light wind whispered through the big magnolia tree that sheltered much of the rear and side gardens. Behind him he heard his cat yawn loudly from the front porch.

Smiling, he pulled open the side door to the garage and stepped into the dark interior. Before he could react, hands grabbed his shoulders. A thin cord was around his neck, tightening, digging into his flesh. He struggled. He gasped for breath. There was no air. The garage spun in violent circles, flashing green and red and black. . . . Blurry faces. No light. Black shadows. Images of Anna, their two daughters, and his grandchildren flashed through his mind. Thoughts about next week's doctor's appointment, the stalemate with the speaker of the house, the new transportation bill. So much left undone—so much—

An hour later in Evans Olsen's cottage in Northeast Washington, Jeff rolled away from Beth, suddenly uneasy. She'd had a restless night, but she was asleep again at last. He had been up and down the last three hours, checking Olsen and listening to the house, worrying about intruders.

His Beretta was on the floor next to the bed. He picked it up and gazed down at Beth with a helpless feeling in his stomach. A line of moonlight crossed her face, illuminating her features as she lay gently in sleep. Her lips were parted, and her lashes cast shadows onto her cheeks. Her fair hair lay around her face like a halo. She looked so vulnerable. He remembered the sex. Thinking about it made him hard again. He flexed his shoulders, shaking away anger and the desire to kiss her. He had work to do.

He pulled on his briefs and jeans and padded into Olsen's bedroom. Olsen was still snoring. Every time he had checked, Olsen seemed more twitchy, so he had hopes he could awaken him now. He closed the door, flicked on the light, and went to stare at the sleeping man. Olsen exhaled, and a blast of alcohol steamed the cool air. Jeff pulled him up by the shoulders and propped him against the wall, because there was no headboard. The White House aide's skin was sallow, and his features were swollen from too much drink. His black beard had sprouted at least a quarter inch and made his chin purple. He was wearing only the pajama bottoms Jeff had found on the bathroom floor.

"Evans! Wake up!" He slapped one cheek then the other.

Olsen groaned.

"Evans Olsen! Open your eyes!"

The man's eyelids fluttered.

Jeff slapped him again and shouted his name.

"Who . . . who are you?" Olsen's words were slurred. He was still drunk. Fear radiated from his red-rimmed eyes. He raised a shaky hand, feeling his cheek.

Jeff was relieved. At last the man was talking. He boomed, "I'm Satan himself, asshole. You're a dead man unless you tell me what you and Alexei Berianov are doing!" He raised his Beretta in front of Olsen's face.

Olsen's puffy eyes grew large. He swallowed. "I'm going to be sick—" He bolted for the bathroom.

Jeff sighed as he listened to the man vomit. After a while the toilet flushed. Then there were more vomiting sounds. At last the toilet flushed again.

Beth appeared, dressed in her jeans and turtleneck. "He's awake?"

"I guess no one could've slept through that. Sorry I was so loud."

She smiled, crossed to him, and slipped an arm around his shoulders. "Miss me?" She kissed him.

He grabbed her and held her close. "Like you wouldn't believe."

"Ohhh." The groan was from the doorway. Then in a shocked voice: "Beth? What are *you* doing here?" Too feeble to stand, he slid down the doorjamb to the floor.

She said, "Hi, Evans. Every time we meet lately you seem to be falling down."

Jeff picked him up and helped him into the kitchen. While Jeff made coffee, Beth turned on the television news in the living room. In the kitchen, Jeff put Olsen back into the breakfast nook. Weak and disoriented, Olsen leaned forward until his cheek rested on the table. He sighed and closed his eyes.

"Don't get too comfortable," Jeff warned.

As the aroma of percolating coffee filled the small kitchen, Jeff used the wall phone to dial Ty Crocker's house. When Anna answered in a sleepy voice, he hung up. No point worrying her. If Ty were still there, he would have answered himself. Ty must be meeting with the Secret Service by now.

Jeff tried to shake off tension as he poured coffee and carried it to Olsen. "Time to get sober, Olsen. Drink this. We've got to talk."

Olsen moaned.

"Coffee. Drink. Or do you want me to pour it down you?"

"Jeff!" It was Beth's voice from the living room. "Come and listen to this!"

He trotted into the small room that fronted the street. The dusty blinds were closed, and the old furniture was draped in shadows from the light of two weak lamps.

Beth was sitting on the faded sofa. She pressed a finger to her lips and nodded at the TV screen, where Washington's *Up to the Minute* news program was airing on WUSA, the local CBS affiliate.

Jeff stopped in the doorway where he could see the TV set and still quickly turn his head to keep watch on the hallway that led into the kitchen and out the back door.

The junior senator from Mississippi was speaking: ". . . our president borders on perfidy for his liberal views on international relations. We have the perfect example right now. The Russian president is spending tonight in the Russian Embassy, but tomorrow night, this . . . *Communist* will be sleeping in the Lincoln Bedroom. Who knows what else these two like-thinking leaders have in mind to turn our fine nation away from the democracy we've fought so long and hard to preserve. . . ."

"Maybe we were right," Beth said over the senator's voice. "Maybe

Berianov plans to kill President Stevens because there's some secret pact between the two presidents that they're going to sign and announce during the visit."

"Not that I know of." Evans Olsen's thin voice carried down the hall.

Jeff and Beth rushed back into the kitchen. He was sitting up. His bloated face was pasty, but his gaze was clearer. He had drunk the coffee and shoved the empty cup across to the edge of the table. He leaned back and sighed.

"Go on," Beth said impatiently. "Tell us why you think there's no secret deal between the presidents."

He seemed to rally. "Because I would've heard something. The White House is a sieve. President Stevens is grandstanding. That's all it is. They're going to address the American and Russian peoples live on TV and radio at the press conference, and then tonight Putin's going to sleep in the White House. It's a good-neighbor gesture to show how much more alike the two peoples are than dissimilar. Nothing subversive. But it sure has caused a lot of controversy here and in Russia. Some people in either place just don't want the Cold War to be over, I guess."

Beth studied him. Mustering an intelligent response had exhausted him. He drooped low over the table. Looking at him in his stupid state, she could not believe he was part of the inner circle of any diabolical plot. "You're being used," she guessed. "Is that why you're drinking so much? What does Berianov want you to do?"

He said huffily, "I've taken a small vacation. I'm entitled to drink if I like. And I don't know any Berianov."

"Alexei Berianov, former KGB general," Jeff told him as he poured more coffee. "He defected back in nineteen-ninety-one."

"Don't know him," Olsen repeated. He looked warily around, seemed to listen to the TV in the other room, then settled on Jeff. "Are the doors locked? And who the hell are you?"

Jeff's expression was severe. "The doors are locked. And the windows. What's made you so afraid?"

Olsen's lips thinned. Terror compressed his features. He looked at his wrist for his watch, but Jeff had taken it off before showering him. "I can't be late! He'll *kill* me!" It was a scream of horror. Frantically his gaze found the wall clock. "Oh! Thank God, it's only five-thirty. There's time—"

Jeff grabbed him. "Settle down, Olsen. Tell me exactly who's going to kill you."

"I . . . I . . ." He gulped air, too frightened to speak.

"We'll help you," Jeff promised. "I'm FBI. Tell us what you know about the president's assassination."

Surprised, Olsen wrenched away and fell back into the breakfast nook. "They're going to *assassinate* him? Oh, no!" He wiped a hand across his face as if trying to erase a lifetime of misdeeds. "Some guy named Yakel's been working me. It started when he offered me money, but then when I realized he didn't just want souvenirs from the White House, I tried to get rid of him. But it was too late. He had deposited a hundred thousand dollars into an account in Mexico for me. He said he wanted invitations for himself and three vet buddies for the ten A.M. press conference in the Rose Garden so they could see the president. That's all. Innocent, you know?"

"The Rose Garden!" Beth looked at Jeff. "We were wrong."

He nodded, remembering the mock-up of the Oval Office and the Rose Garden in the big underground cavern. "I should've guessed. They did a much more detailed job recreating the garden than they did the Oval Office."

Beth said, "Anytime the American and Russian presidents get together, it's historic, and the Rose Garden isn't all that large. The press conference will be a hot-ticket item." She had heard about it during the newscaster's recapitulation of the day's schedule.

"What did this guy, Yakel, look like?" Jeff said.

"We met only once, in a bar. The rest of the time we talked by phone. He was old. Not very tall, but he gave the impression he owned the world. A cowboy in battered jeans and a Stetson."

Beth and Jeff exchanged a look. "The 'old caretaker,' " Beth said.

"Well, if he was a caretaker, he wasn't the usual run-of-the-mill," Olsen said. "This guy knew a lot. I mean, he read books, he was on top of events, and—worst—he knew things about me and my family he couldn't have found out easily. He'd been snooping in my past, or someone had. When I wanted out, he threatened to kill me. I believed him. He said he had ways I couldn't imagine to make me suffer."

"Did you see the car he arrived in?" Jeff asked. "Maybe a license plate number? Or did he give you some way to get in touch with him?"

Olsen shook his head. "No, he was careful. I never saw his car, and he was the one who did the calling. One time I tried to trace back his phone number, but it was blocked. Some kind of electronic door, according to a hacker friend of mine."

Beth frowned. "So tell us about the invitations."

"Oh, God," he moaned. "I'm supposed to tape them under a mail box near the Mall by seven o'clock. If they're not there, I know they'll come looking for me. As soon as I delivered them, I was going to fly to Rio and hide. I won't be safe here. Once they have what they want, they'll try to kill me anyway. It's the only logical thing."

"We'll help you," Jeff assured him. "We'll stow you away in a secure safe house. Where are the invitations?"

"In my trench coat. I hid them in an IRS envelope. Nobody ever looks inside anything from the IRS, if they can avoid it. I figured it was the best place."

"Oh, damn!" Beth raced to the back door. "I threw that smelly coat onto the back porch. Anyone could've walked off with it!" She spun open the dead bolt and yanked. Cool morning air gusted in.

"Wait a minute!" Jeff strode past her and stared around outside. He grabbed up the trench coat and carried it in. The IRS envelope was in an inner pocket. He threw the reeking coat back toward the door and tore open the taped envelope. Inside were four white envelopes, and inside each was a handsome engraved invitation on heavy paper. Each contained an etching of the White House and the invitee's name written in calligraphy. Tasteful, restrained, and the fulfillment of Berianov's plan.

Olsen explained, "I marked off that I'd received an RSVP from each of them, and since part of my duties is to oversee background checks, I got Yakel's friends okayed for fake Social Security numbers and dates of birth."

"Then what happens?" Beth asked.

Olsen looked miserable. "There's a list at the White House gate. When a guest gets there, he has to say his name and show the invitation and some kind of photo ID. After that, guests have to walk through a machine like airports use, a metal detector. Plus there's an X-ray machine to check purses and bags. Yakel said he'd take care of getting identification for his four friends."

"We're going to stop him before it gets to that point," Jeff said.

Beth nodded. "Yes. The mailbox. Someone will go there to pick up the invitations—" She paused to listen. "Did you hear that?" She ran back into the living room where the television was still on.

". . . Senator Ty Crocker, one of America's most beloved and eminent Republican leaders, was found strangled to death in his garage early this morning. His wife discovered his body when . . ."

Jeff's face went ashen as he gazed at the screen. His body seemed to shudder as if struck by a blow. Beth watched Jeff a moment, then took his hand.

"Jeff—"

"They killed him. It's all my fault." His voice was hoarse, as if the words were stuck deep in his throat, impossible to squeeze out.

"You warned him. He knew he was taking a risk. You can't save everybody."

He turned his face away from the news. "Ty was special. Honest. Decent. After Mom and Dad died . . . he'd call me up at the paper every couple of months, and we'd have lunch at the country club. Play a round of golf. He'd talk about his grandkids and that cat of his. Tell me what Anna was up to. You know. The usual stuff that we all live with but doesn't add up to much . . . until it's taken away." There were tears in his voice.

"I'm sorry, Jeff. It's terrible. Really terrible."

He nodded. "And of course, it puts all of us in a worse position. Especially President Stevens."

"You're right!" Fear shot through her. "There's no way for us to know whether Ty actually got those belt buckles to the Secret Service."

"Or if he did, whether he told them about the significance to the president's life."

"Or that we're the ones who delivered them to him," she added. "We may still have no credibility. Which means we could be right back where we started."

In Olsen's bedroom, a telephone rang. Olsen jumped as if a firecracker had exploded beneath him. He stared around wildly, terrified.

"It's him," he whimpered. "It's got to be him!"

His face ravaged with grief and rage, Jeff picked up Olsen under a shoulder and hauled him into the bedroom. A cell phone lay on a table beside Olsen's rumpled bed. It rang again.

Jeff ordered, "Answer it. If it's him, tell him you're on your way. Don't screw this up, Olsen. I'm warning you!"

His lower lip trembling, Olsen picked up the phone. "Hello?"

As his insides ached, Jeff watched and listened. He was still trying to comprehend that Ty was dead. But even though his emotions roiled, his mind had a diamond-like clarity. Now he had one more reason to stop Berianov: He felt as if a vital organ had been torn out. He wanted Ty back.

And he wanted his own life back. In one savage stroke, Ty had become the symbol of all he had lost. He wanted to go back to when everything made sense and he was young and could afford to take huge risks. Chasing Berianov had been the greatest gamble of his life. As he stood there glaring at Olsen, he saw he had taken the risk thoughtlessly, without concern not only for how he would pay, but more importantly for how it would hurt the people he loved. How it had cost one of them his life. Ty's life. Being right was not always compensation.

"I'm not drunk, Yakel," Olsen said in a high, frightened voice into the cell phone. "Maybe a little hung over." He listened, his bloated face tense. "I'm sorry, but I'm running a bit behind schedule—"

Olsen held the phone away from his ear, and an enraged voice bellowed, "You candy-assed twerp, I don't care about your problems! Deliver those invitations!"

"I'm leaving right now." Olsen clicked the OFF button. Sweat dripped from his forehead. "He's given me a different drop-off place—at the foot of the statue in the Jefferson Memorial." He described it in greater detail.

Now Jeff knew everything he needed—the time and place of the assassination, and a way to find Berianov. He spun on his heel and headed for the kitchen. "I've got to call my boss."

"Bobby Kelsey?" Beth followed. "You're going to warn him about the Rose Garden and the invitations?"

"Yes. Now we know place and approximate time," Jeff said grimly. "I'm going to handle the invitations myself. Whoever picks them up will lead me to Berianov. I'll drop them off, and then I'll get Berianov. He's *mine.*"

"No. He's mine, too. Ours. I'm part of this, too, dammit!"

He hardly heard her. He wanted to keep Olsen's cell phone free, in case Berianov called again. So he snatched the telephone receiver off the kitchen wall and dialed his boss's secret number. He waited for the fake fax squeal to end and left Olsen's phone number and the agreed-upon message: *The sky is coming down in flames.* It was a risk to stay here and wait, because if anyone had put a tracer on Bobby Kelsey's line, they would know by now the phone number from which he had dialed and the address where the phone was located. The dangerous scenario he had described earlier to Beth about why he had not wanted to go in yet still held true, but now he had firm information, and he had to take the risk. The president's life was at stake.

He looked at Beth and sighed, thinking about Ty. "Sorry."

"It's okay, Jeff. I know how hard it is to lose people you love."

She wrapped her arms around his chest, and he let her hold him. But his mind was on Bobby Kelsey. He wanted the phone to ring.

45

The abandoned ruins of what had once been an elegant townhouse was just one more of a hundred other old, crumbling brick buildings in Southeast Washington. Litter marred the dark street, and graffiti scarred the blackened walls. Most of the street lights had been shot out. That night as they did every night, drug dealers and pimps plied their ancient trades openly. But in the derelict townhouse, none of that mattered. The group of men and women who were working in the various rooms had more important matters on their minds.

Sergeant Aaron Austin had roused the Keepers from fitful sleeps less than a half-hour before. As the bulk of the zealots prepared their weapons and gear, Austin conferred on final plans with the three other members of his personal team. Together, the four-man unit would enter the White House grounds using the invitations secured from Evans Olsen. It was Sergeant Austin himself who would have the privilege of assassinating America's traitorous president, James Emmet Stevens.

Austin was once more going over each phase of the operation in detail, completely focused, when all the townhouse's doors and windows burst open with thunderous crashes, feet pounded upstairs and through hallways, and ear-splitting commands boomed from bullhorns.

"Drop your weapons! This is the FBI!"

"Secret Service! Stand where you are! Raise your hands! Now!"

"You're surrounded. Put down your weapons and come out single file!"

Whatever their assigned tasks, the stunned Keepers stopped, paralyzed, their scared, angry eyes focused on each other. In the living room, where he had been consulting with his men, Sergeant Austin never hesitated. He gave a sharp nod, and his bellow sounded so loudly that he could be heard throughout the entire building: *"Do it!"* His jaw moved, and he collapsed. From one floor to the next, room after room, in dying testament to their fanaticism and brainwashed discipline, the other Keepers obediently followed his—and Colonel Bates's—orders.

Max Bitsche stepped out of his headquarters trailer at the rear of the large mobile-home park just off the parkway that joined Washington to Dulles International Airport. His company of support troops who would supply and transport the assassination team and its security guards to West Virginia were leaving their trailers to fall in before him. Pallid and hunched in the dawn, Bitsche had never felt more alive. In his detail-obsessed existence, he had never dared to dream he would stand before a company of hard men as their leader, ready to take them on a great and sacred mission.

He made his voice commanding, "Fall in, soldiers!"

The Keepers were still dressing their ranks when the police cars and military vehicles roared into the trailer camp, beacons flashing, and SWAT teams and soldiers poured out to surround the startled fanatics.

The bullhorns boomed, "Freeze! You're all under arrest."

Terrified, Max Bitsche wavered.

A voice trembled from the ranks. "Oh, God, we're caught!"

Max Bitsche closed his eyes, his skinny body shaking. He summoned his nerve, focused on his dreams for a better world, and screamed, *"Do it!"* He bit down. He never saw the others writhing in the dirt as the police and soldiers, their weapons slowly lowering, stared in stunned horror.

The warehouse was the third in a row of warehouses behind the buildings of a light industrial park in Arlington, Virginia. When the cars carrying the Virginia police and the FBI, all in SWAT gear, screeched to a stop in front, two men burst out of the south side of the warehouse, carrying weapons. Their eyes and body language said it all: They intended to escape.

"They're wearing the belts!" the officer in charge of the tracking unit shouted.

Four FBI men raced after them, finally cornering the pair in a cul-de-sac against the high wall of a railroad embankment. Otis Odet and a man later identified as Jesse Crabtree, a parolee from the Texas state prison at Huntsville, tried to shoot it out. They lost.

In the otherwise empty warehouse, the Virginia police and FBI found sleeping bags, weapons, and twenty-four people who had died painfully from what looked like self-administered cyanide. Oddly, despite the contorted features, there was a look of peace in many of the open, staring eyes.

Bobby Kelsey watched the teams of special agents and Secret Service carry the bodies of the Keepers out of the crumbling building in Southeast Washington, shaking his head in admiration. Damn, but Berianov was good. The general really knew how to pick his people and train and motivate them. The reports from the other teams showed that only two of the zealots had tried to escape, and even they went down in a shootout rather than surrender. Hell, that crazy throwback general might pull this off yet, take over Russia, and give Kelsey an even sweeter life than he already had.

He turned to follow the last of his agents out when his cell phone sounded. "Yes?"

It was the office. "You have an urgent message, sir. On the secure line."

"What is it?"

" 'The sky is coming down in flames.' "

Bobby Kelsey gave a tight smile. That was Jeffrey Hammond's code, and it had come in on the highly secure, clandestine line with rotating numbers assigned to undercover agents and those on top-secret missions. "You have the location?"

"Yes, sir. The caller is dialing from a private residence in the Northeast section." She recited the telephone number and address.

He said neutrally, "Got it."

Bobby Kelsey severed the connection. There could be only one reason Hammond had contacted him—he wanted to meet. Which told him everything he needed to know. He slipped his cell phone back into its case and barked orders.

In Evans Olsen's cottage, Beth poured a cup of coffee. "Here, drink this, Jeff. And for God's sake, sit down. Try to relax. You look as if you're going to detonate."

From his broad face with the heavy cheekbones to his naked chest and tight jeans, Jeff radiated outrage and menace. He shook his short-cropped head as if to clear it. He grabbed the steaming cup and stalked across the old linoleum and returned. He had work to do, and Bobby

Kelsey was taking a long time to return his phone call. He was frustrated and angry.

He stopped in front of Olsen. "How tall are you? Six feet?"

"Six-two," Olsen said indignantly.

Jeff nodded, assessing him. "You don't stand up straight. You're bigger around the middle than I am. I'm going to take one of your jackets."

"Now, just a minute—"

But Jeff was already heading away. In the bedroom he and Beth had shared, he put on his blue work shirt and tucked it into his jeans. He left behind his herringbone jacket and the windbreaker he had taken off the dead Keeper in Pennsylvania and went into Olsen's bedroom, where he found a flannel shirt. As he shoved his arms into the sleeves, he heard Beth shout from the living room.

"Jeff, come here!"

"Oh, God," Olsen was moaning. "This is so terrible. All those poor people."

Jeff hurried into the living room, where Beth and Olsen were staring riveted at the television set. The network newscaster was reporting that police agencies led by the FBI and the Secret Service had made a series of raids on a fringe group called the Keepers of the Truth en masse earlier this morning. The clandestine band had apparently been planning some kind of terrorist act, but authorities would say at this time only that they were investigating. All the Keepers had killed themselves. Coming on the heels of the murders of Senator Ty Crocker and FBI director Thomas Earle Horn, it was one more shocking incident that reaffirmed the capital's violent underbelly.

As the nation watched appalled, images of sixty-two dead bodies, stashes of arms, military-style clothing, and state-of-the-art communications equipment were displayed. A spokesman conjectured that if the group had planned to commit an act of violence, the members must have memorized their roles . . . or perhaps there was a master blueprint somewhere yet to be found.

The meetings of presidents Stevens and Putin today at the White House dropped in prominence from the headlines, now something of an afterthought following the morning's tragedy. No one mentioned President Putin's invitation to sleep in the Lincoln Bedroom, but live coverage of the press conference in the Rose Garden was still scheduled.

"Unbelievable," Beth said. She had a sick feeling in her stomach. "Those poor people. Berianov took advantage of them. Maybe they wouldn't have turned to violence if he hadn't led them."

"He's got a lot to answer for." Jeff nodded somberly. "But so does our society and its perverted frontier mentality. The only good thing is the Keepers have been stopped. But we've still got to get Berianov."

"You don't think it's over now that his followers are dead?" Beth asked.

"Not if I know Berianov." He glanced at his watch. "Damm it, we're losing time. What's taking Bobby so long to call back?"

Eli Kirkhart parked his rented Chrysler on the litter-strewn, graffiti-marked street in Southeast Washington. Ambulances were lined up in front of the derelict townhouse, and teams of agents were carrying out corpses in body bags. He had heard the shocking news the moment he stepped into the lobby of the Hoover building and had immediately found out to which site Bobby Kelsey and his team had been sent.

All the way down from Pennsylvania, driving fast in the dark, predawn hours, he had pondered the evidence that had pointed to Jeff Hammond. Because of it, he had originally been convinced Jeff was the mole. Where had he gone wrong? How? Finally, as the sun rose in a golden shower over the Potomac, the answer came to him. So simple that it made him groan aloud. What a fool he had been. . . . What if instead of the director himself, Jeff's FBI handler had been the chief of the last division for which he had worked—Bobby Kelsey?

Kirkhart drummed his fingers on the steering wheel with excitement. All the evidence that pointed to Jeff could also point to Bobby Kelsey. Had the director realized that, too? Kirkhart thought it likely. He could see where the director might not have been utterly convinced he was right about Bobby Kelsey, but at the same time he would have wanted the Bureau to uncover its own traitor. He would have told himself it was a matter of institutional pride, while in truth it was nothing but personal vanity. Which meant the director might have been arrogant enough to confront Bobby alone. With backup, of course, but probably too far away to see or hear a knife attack.

Yes, it was logical that Bobby Kelsey was the mole. But this time Kirkhart had to be sure, because he had been wrong about Jeff, and he was determined to not be wrong again. Besides, one did not lightly accuse FBI assistant directors of being double agents. Since Aida had died, the Bureau had been the core of Kirkhart's life, really all he had left, and just thinking about jeopardizing his career any more than he already had made his stomach weak. No, he would do nothing until he could conclusively prove Bobby Kelsey was the mole.

Kirkhart climbed out of his car and ducked under the yellow plastic

Crime Scene tape. He could not find Bobby and figured he must still be in the townhouse. As he headed for the entrance, he spotted off to his left, just inside an alley, Bobby's graying red hair. Bobby Kelsey was talking and gesturing to a group of five agents. Kirkhart recognized two from the Bureau's criminal division plus Chuck Graham and Steve Thoma from Bobby's own national-security division. The fifth man he did not know.

As Kirkhart watched, Bobby drew his Smith 10, checked the clip, and reholstered it. Graham and one of the criminal division agents carried M-16 assault rifles.

Kirkhart studied them. It almost seemed as if Bobby were organizing a team for some operation. The six men split into two groups and headed for separate FBI cars. Thoma came Kirkhart's way. He appeared fired up .

Kirkhart said, "Steve, old buddy. What's up?"

"It's Hammond! Bobby knows where the bastard asshole is hiding. We're going to pick him up."

"So? Interesting. I'd like to be in on that."

"Sure. Ask Bobby."

Kirkhart thought quickly. If he were right that Bobby Kelsey was Jeff's handler, then Bobby could know exactly where Jeff was if Jeff had called to report in or to ask for help. He had serious doubts Bobby intended simply to arrest Jeff.

He approached Bobby. "Sir, I missed the operation here with the Keepers. I'd appreciate being able to at least help you out with Hammond."

"You're Kirkhart, right? You used to be pretty close to Hammond, right?"

"Yessir," Kirkhart said and grimaced. "Too damned close."

Bobby nodded. Kirkhart could be useful if they had to talk Jeff out into the open. "Okay, sure. Grab a rifle. You can ride with Thoma."

Bobby Kelsey watched Eli Kirkhart hurry after Thoma. As the two agents conferred, Kelsey smiled and trotted to his own car. His heart was beating fast, and he had a feeling of exaggerated importance, as if the whole world rested upon what he did now. He knew that was untrue, but it was a reflection of his sense of destiny. What happened to him mattered, and he was not going to go down just because that freak Jeff Hammond had a burr on his butt about the defectors that he had been unable to pick off since 1991. The hot summers and cold winters of Texas flashed into his mind. He saw his father's mean, narrow face, his mother's constant fear, and the desolation of his hometown, so small and poor it dotted no map. It seemed just yesterday he had escaped, and he was not going back. Not to that place or anywhere like it on earth.

Once again, his goals were clear. Jeff Hammond and Beth Convey were in his way. A danger to General Berianov and to him. They must not be taken alive.

46

Jeff Hammond paced Evans Olsen's bungalow, angry and disturbed. Every few minutes he peeled back the dusty drapes a fraction of an inch to study the street. Beth tried to sit calmly, but she was worried, and Evans Olsen was distraught. Trembling, Evans leaned against the hall-way arch, alcohol pouring from him in rivers of sweat. He alternately stared at the clock on the kitchen wall and then gazed back at them. Time was becoming critical, and if Beth and Jeff could not reach the Jefferson Memorial soon, they would be unable to leave the invitations for Berianov to find. Which meant Berianov's killers would be at Olsen's door minutes later.

Beth jumped up to join Jeff at the windows. That's when they heard a noise from the kitchen. Evans squealed and fell back away from the doorway and into the hall. She spun instantly, her Walther leveled. Jeff was already crouching low, his Beretta aimed.

At that moment, Special Agent Eli Kirkhart walked into the archway that led to the kitchen, his hands high above his head, his bulldog face somber. "I was wrong. Sorry, old man." He stared gravely at Jeff.

"Really?" Jeff came smoothly up out of his crouch and stepped toward Kirkhart, his pistol still pointed. He had thought he knew Eli, but the events of the past few days had taught him he had not even known himself, so how could he claim to have understood anyone else, especially from that long-ago era in the Bureau when they had been so young and idealistic? Just a short time ago he would have thrown his shoulder into a man who had done to him what Eli had done, knocked him flat, disarmed him, and not bothered to listen to a word. Now he was more cautious. "Fill me in. I'm all ears. Don't leave anything out."

Eli nodded. "I owe you an apology. You were in Pennsylvania when the director was murdered. I know that, of course, because of the little contretemps between you and me. Which means, of course, there's no way you can be the mole, not if the mole killed the director, and that is exactly what the evidence points to. The real mole could've planted the evidence to frame you. Since that evidence was your fingerprints again, just as it was in Stone Point, I suspect the same device was used to set you up in both places, and it backs up the evidence that the mole was behind both pieces of dirty work. Besides, Jeff, you're too damn smart to leave behind such a clear clue at two crime scenes. You may be many things, but you're no amateur."

Jeff snorted but said nothing.

"So now we have a problem," Eli went on. "We *both* have a problem. . . . He's out in the front, getting set up and quite prepared to kill you and Convey, and I'm exceedingly unhappy about that. But we don't have a lot of time to fix things, alas."

"Jesus." Jeff spun back to the windows, flattened against the wall, and peeled back the drape just enough to peer out. "There are four out there. I see Bobby Kelsey. Damn! Are you saying Bobby's the mole? Not *Bobby!*"

"Yes, Jeff. It's him. He has the kind of access required, and he knew everything you knew. If it's not you, it's got to be him."

As Jeff digested that, Beth asked, "How did you get in here?"

"Back door. The lock's a bleeding farce. Would you mind if I lowered my arms now? I'm not as young as I used to be, and they're going to sleep."

"Sure. Go ahead," Beth told him.

Eli Kirkhart rubbed his arms. "Ah, yes. Assistant Director Bobby Kelsey. You've been reporting to the mole all these years without knowing it, Jeff. You didn't tumble, and neither did I. But then, no one else did either. Now the bugger's out there with a fully weaponized team to 'arrest' you."

Jeff shook his head, disgusted. "Some arrest. He can't afford to let me live, not if he hopes to get away with blaming me for what he's done." He fought back the queasy sensation of being betrayed. He had liked Bobby, had admired the way Bobby had braced the director of a decade ago and insisted he be allowed to go underground for the Bureau. But it had all been a sham. Bobby and he had not been on the same team. No, all the while Bobby had been disloyal to the country, to the Bureau, and to Jeff. He had used and betrayed all of them.

Beth asked, "How many are there?"

"Six, including me. I convinced Kelsey to send me and Thoma to cover the alley and the rear of the house. Thoma's napping, thanks to a little encouragement from me. And shazam, here I am. I'd appreciate it if you two would take a bunk out the back and let me deal with our busy mole."

There was a knock on the front door. Not loud, but firm, and the raised voice was unmistakable: "Jeff, it's Bobby. I got your phone call. Let me in. I'm here to help."

Inside the bungalow, all four silently looked at one another. Jeff checked through the slit between the drape and the window and saw Kelsey on the front porch, looking innocent. His three men were no longer beside him. One was hiding behind the large tree in the front yard, his elbow and the muzzle of his rifle intermittently showing. Another hunched next to the porch, also carrying a rifle, while the third was out of sight somewhere. Bobby, however, appeared unarmed, but Jeff had no doubt his pistol was in his jacket.

"It's clear out back," Kirkhart said in a low voice. "I'll delay Kelsey and his pals until you're safely away. Remember, they don't want me or the gentleman on the floor. Actually, you'll be doing us both a favor. As long as you're around, we're in danger."

Beth looked at Jeff and spoke rapidly. "He's right. Plus we've got to reach the Jefferson Memorial before seven A.M. with the invitations. We're going to be late if we don't leave now."

Evans Olsen had been listening to everything. "Take my car," he urged.

Kirkhart nodded. "Once you're away, we'll surrender. I'll tell Kelsey I came in the back, and you were both already gone. Without you, Kelsey won't take the risk of shooting us. Will you kindly get the hell out of here?"

Beth decided. "We're going. Give me your keys, Evans." She took the thrown keys and touched Jeff's arm. "We've got to stop Berianov. You said yourself that he's not going to give up. He'll have another plan. Come on, Jeff. We need to get to the Jefferson Memorial before we lose this opportunity to stop Berianov once and for all."

From the front porch, Bobby Kelsey's voice was louder this time: "Jeff? We've got to talk. I need your report about what you found out, and I want to know what you've been up to. They think you're the mole. Did you know that? I'm here to help. Let me in, Jeff!" He rattled the doorknob.

"Will you go?" Kirkhart demanded impatiently "Bobby's going to figure out soon that there's something wrong with the troops at the rear of the house. The sooner you're gone, the sooner we can give up."

Jeff holstered his Beretta and grabbed Beth's hand. "I hate to leave you . . . but thanks, Eli."

They ran through the kitchen, out the back door, and across the tiny yard in the chilly dawn. Thoma was motionless, lying face up in tangled weeds, his jaw red from a blow. The sun was rising, sending pastel yellows and pinks across the horizon. Olsen's blue Oldsmobile Cutlass was parked behind the house at the side of a ramshackle garage. Beth slid behind the wheel, and Jeff jumped into the front passenger seat. The car stank of old liquor and cigarettes, but to them it was a king's carriage. As Beth accelerated away, Jeff, full of misgivings, stared back over his shoulder.

It was 6:35 A.M., and traffic was light. Much of the bustling city still slept, enjoying the arrival of the weekend. As Beth drove them into more middle-class neighborhoods where jobs and careers played a large role in life, a few people were already picking up newspapers from their yards and climbing into cars with coffee mugs in their hands. Both automatically watched for trouble.

As they drove on through Washington, he had the disorienting sense that the firm foundation on which he had based his most critical decisions over the past decade was disintegrating into ash. For a moment, his head swam. His stomach knotted.

Then: "I've been a damned fool." His voice crackled with bitter anger. "How did my fingerprints show up in Stone Point at the murder scene of those teenagers? Besides, how would anyone even know I was going to Stone Point? But Berianov could've known if he were already checking up on me. And he would've been, since I was the one who saved you after you stumbled onto Yuri's body. His goons probably recognized me, and that would've made Berianov feel I was getting too close."

"You think Bobby Kelsey got your fingerprints to Berianov, and then Berianov killed the teenagers and planted the prints to incriminate you?"

He gave a furious nod. "Bobby had access to the Bureau's technology. They know how to not only steal fingerprints but plant them. God knows, he could've taken mine dozens of times." He hesitated. "It was his idea I go undercover. Now that I think about it, it was a good way to get rid of me and all my questions about the defectors without raising any red flags, which is exactly what would've happened if I'd had some fatal 'accident.' "

Beth tried to focus on her driving. "What that man could've passed on to the Kremlin. And if he's working with Berianov—" She stopped.

Her insides were shaking at the enormity of it all . . . a spy that high and trusted inside the FBI for God-knew-how-many years.

He nodded again. "He had access to so many secrets I don't even want to think about it. The names and addresses of our agents. Their assignments. Operations we were planning." In his lap, his hands involuntarily flexed as if they gripped Kelsey's throat. "It explains a lot of the 'unfortunate incidents' we saw happening at the Bureau when suddenly a vital source just disappeared or some bizarre development brought a crucial mission to a screeching halt. And now there's Ty. . . . The only way Berianov could've known he was taking the belts to the Secret Service was if Kelsey knew and told him. Bobby Kelsey, the mole. He's the one who really murdered Ty." He mourned Ty and all the lost years. Regret made him ache. Regret for everything.

The atmosphere in the Oldsmobile was tense and silent. As Beth drove, they passed through downtown Washington with its neoclassical architecture and magnificent statues set back among great lawns and spring flower beds. Traffic was picking up, but compared to a weekday, the capital city was quiet. The morning sun cast cool, gray shadows from structures and trees onto the streets. At this hour, there was an oddly peaceful atmosphere, as if nothing bad could ever touch the city.

Beth looked at Jeff. "Bobby Kelsey has probably already alerted Berianov that we found Evans. My guess is, he's gotten the whole story of the invitations from him. Berianov will figure the invitations are either destroyed or we have them. His whole plan's blown, and he won't be at the Jefferson Memorial or the Rose Garden. He'll have to come up with a new plan. Or he'll give up."

Jeff shook his head. "I wonder. Today was supposed to be the culmination, the high point of his life. It's cost him years and a fortune. He's murdered two of his oldest comrades and taken enormous risks that would've destroyed most men." He paused, thinking. "He may think we'll show up at the memorial to catch him, but still, all his history says one thing to me: He won't give up. So on the chance the invitations will be delivered, he'll have to send someone to pick them up. Which means we have to get there first, leave them, and tail the courier back to Berianov."

"He'll assume we'll try that, Jeff," Beth reasoned.

"And his courier will work to lose us. I agree. We'll just have to make sure that doesn't happen."

Beth frowned. "I doubt Berianov would send anyone. My guess is he'll come himself, probably with that KGB assassin we saw with him in Pennsylvania."

"Ivan Vok."

"Yes. That way they can get the invitations *and* eliminate us. He may decide to arrive before we do in hopes of trapping us."

He said, "We'll have to play it by ear. Outwit the bastard."

"Maybe not. What if we get there *late*, after the memorial has opened? We'll have a better chance that there'll be guards, park rangers, tourists. He'll try to scare us and get the invitations, but he'll be a lot less likely to kill us and risk exposing himself to capture."

"But we won't care about any ruckus. He'll be vulnerable to us."

"I could be wrong," she said. "He could decide not to wait when we don't show up. Or maybe he has some entirely different plan."

"If he leaves, he won't get the invitations, and we'll be no worse off."

She nodded. "This whole thing has got me to thinking. We like to believe an evil person is one-dimensional—a monster who commits monstrous acts, an aberration. That's a comfortable target, because the monster isn't at all like us, right? But the truth is, the bigger threat comes from regular people like you and me. We can become so trapped in our fears and hopes that outside ideas, outside questions, anything or anyone different from us . . . feels like an assault. Fanaticism is simply attachment taken to an extreme. But uncritical devotion allows zealots to rise up on scales large and small. That's when leaders who seem so very human to followers at the time—like a dog-loving Hitler, or a sincere revolutionary like Stalin, or a patriot like Berianov—can take hold."

"Yes, and threaten the very foundations of our world," he agreed. "Alexei Berianov's absolutely committed to his vision of a restored Soviet Union. He's such an ideological Communist that even in the nineteen-ninety-one coup, he was prepared to sacrifice his life. He never hid his feelings from us about that, but at the same time he never argued against the consensus during his debriefing that he was simply an aging tiger with little bite. Plus, of course, he seemed eager to sell out and become a 'Capitalist pig' like the rest of us. What none of us realized—not even me—was he was planning to bankroll and organize some long-range political plan."

"But you sensed it. You knew he was up to something."

"I don't get a lot of satisfaction from that." He shrugged. "When fanatics triumph, it's because their dreams and promises have caught others in their snare. Somehow Berianov did that in his role as Caleb Bates. Look how he manipulated and used the Keepers. But on the other hand, it sounds as if they ran willingly into his arms, too, fueled by their own bigoted visions."

She checked her watch. "We've got only a half-hour." She pressed the accelerator, weaving among the traffic and speeding through yellow lights.

As she rounded a corner, the tires gripping the pavement, Jeff said, "If I ever rob a bank, I know who I want as my getaway driver."

She glanced at him and gave a small smile. "Mikhail Ogust might've had something to do with it, too."

As they continued south, the nearly two thousand blooming cherry trees that rimmed the Tidal Basin came into view. It was almost the end of the flowers' peak, but still they formed a radiant pink wreath around the mirror-like lake. The sight of them in glorious flush reminded Beth of the promises she had made herself as she lay dying in the transplant center, hoping for a new heart. She had told herself if she survived she would earn partnership in the firm, fall in love again and make it work, and take time to enjoy life—like walking again among the cherry blossoms. The first was a definite failure, but she had a chance to succeed at the other two.

Then she saw the Jefferson Memorial. As she studied it, an idea occurred to her. She glanced at Jeff. "Before we get there, I have a thought. It's a ruse. Maybe . . . just maybe, it will help."

Ten minutes later, trying to shake off a sudden sense of impending catastrophe, Jeff walked toward the white marble Thomas Jefferson Memorial, whose dome towered above the Tidal Basin. This Saturday morning, the circular, colonnaded memorial had barely opened. Joggers and bicyclists passed by on the path around the basin, an older couple stood on the bank fishing, and a park ranger picked up trash with a long stick beside the monument's steps. Few cars were parked in the lot, and Jeff saw no one among the shadows of the great memorial. He studied the cars, but none looked familiar or suspicious.

Disappointed, he decided Berianov might have sent someone else to collect the invitations after all. Or maybe Berianov was hidden somewhere and waiting for Jeff to appear. As he strode toward the steps, a bicyclist shot past, leaning low over his handlebars. Jeff stopped to study him, but the man rode on out of sight.

He climbed the marble steps and entered the hushed quiet of the tall, open rotunda. The floor was pink marble, and in the center stood a six-foot-high, black-granite pedestal topped by a spectacular bronze statue of President Jefferson. From between the marble columns he could see a panoramic view across the Tidal Basin to the Washington Monument and the White House beyond.

As he moved through shadows toward the pedestal on which he was to leave the four invitations, an uneasy feeling settled in the pit of his stomach. It was nothing to which he could point directly—no sound, no odor, simply the accumulation of the years. More from instinct than anything else, he pulled out his pistol and whirled.

He stared at the figure behind him. It was the park ranger, who had been picking up trash outside. But instead of the litter bag and stick, he held an Uzi submachine gun aimed straight at Jeff. The gun must have been hidden in the burlap litter bag. The man wore an official ranger hat and large reflecting sunglasses. But now that he was erect and looking directly at Jeff, there was no mistaking him. Jeff's head suddenly ached, and he trembled with anger. He desperately tried to control the rage and anguish that welled up inside him.

"Berianov!" he snarled.

47

Dressed in his park ranger disguise, General Alexei Berianov, former head of the FCD at Yasenevo, future chief of state of a new Soviet Union, gave a cool smile of satisfaction and stepped into the shadows with Jeffrey Hammond, his cocked Uzi steady on the enemy. "Good morning, Mr. Hammond. A fine morning, wouldn't you say? Yes, a very fine morning indeed. But where is the lady? The persistent Ms. Convey?" Not a trace of an accent. The man sounded as American as jazz and bubble gum.

Berianov appeared relaxed, the Uzi steady in his grip, but inside he was livid. Bobby Kelsey had phoned not long ago to report he had gone to kill Hammond and Convey at Evans Olsen's bungalow but found neither there. Instead, Eli Kirkhart had tried to persuade him the pair had tired of waiting and left. But Kelsey had not believed it. No, Hammond would have stayed put until his phone call was answered. Which meant one thing—Eli Kirkhart, the mole hunter, must have figured out everything and warned Hammond. When Kelsey realized that, an altercation errupted, and Evans Olsen was killed. "There was a trail of blood leading out the back door," Kelsey had reported, "but then it disappeared in the weeds. We didn't see any cars moving. My men are still searching for Kirkhart. They'll find him."

Because Berianov had kept much of his plan secret, never trusting Kelsey enough to fill him in completely, Kelsey was unaware keeping Evans Olsen alive was vital. At this point in the conversation, Berianov coldly hung up and ordered Ivan Vok to park on Ohio Drive where he could think.

Soon he calmed himself. All was not lost. In fact, that weakling Evans Olsen was sure to have told Convey and Hammond about the Rose Garden invitations. Which meant the invitations would have been either destroyed or lost by now, or else Convey and Hammond had taken them in order to trap him. Fortunately, he had already planned to arrive early in disguise in case anything went wrong and because he had never intended to let the White House aide live beyond delivering the invitations.

Dressed in the park ranger uniform, Berianov had watched Hammond arrive. But now he was concerned. He scanned the shadowy memorial. Where was Convey?

Jeff laughed. "You didn't seriously think I'd bring her here? We expected you to try something. If I don't return in a half-hour, she'll go to the police, the Bureau, the Secret Service, the marshals . . . to everyone. You'll never escape Washington."

Berianov scowled at the tall American, who looked like some menacing rural gangster in his flannel shirt and jeans. He decided Hammond was probably lying: Beth Convey was in no position to run to the authorities. She was a wanted felon, and by the time anyone listened to her, it would be too late. Hammond would know that.

"No, she'll go to no authorities," Berianov assured him. "But I'll ignore the insult to my intelligence of that specious bit of reasoning as long as you've brought the invitations. Where are they?"

Jeff shook his head. "Not so fast. First you've got to tell me exactly what you're planning."

"Really, Mr. Hammond? Are we back at that remote safe house for defectors where you kept us jailed for your interrogations?"

When Jeff and Beth had seen the mock-up of the Rose Garden and Oval Office, they were certain it was part of a plan to assassinate President Stevens. But now Jeff wondered, and he had to know. So he ignored Berianov's attempt to provoke him. "Who's your target?" he demanded. "My president . . . or yours?"

The two men were motionless, glaring, weapons pointed at each other, the tension between them electric, while out on Ohio Drive traffic sounds were increasing as Saturday workers and visitors streamed into the nation's capital. On the paths below the shadowy rotunda, strollers and joggers continued their constitutionals, still unheeding of the two combatants, who each desperately wanted something from the other. It was only a matter of time until sunlight illuminated the pair, or some venturesome soul decided to climb the steps.

"Okay," Jeff said, making his tones even when all he wanted to do was empty his gun into Berianov and watch him die in an ocean of blood. He spoke quickly. "You can see the invitations if you answer my question. Who's your target?"

Berianov scowled, swiftly considering. Then he nodded. "Your President Stevens. He's got the World Bank, the IMF, and every industrialized country aligned to keep driving Putin deeper and deeper into capitalism. Stevens is destroying Russia. But when he's assassinated in front of the cameras of the world, Putin, his security team, and all Russia will be shamed. It's the kind of rough politics we Russians respond to. Vladimir Putin will be finished at home."

"But the Keepers—your trained killers—are dead. You outsmarted yourself there. Are you planning to kill him yourself?"

Berianov gave a wolfish grin that said nothing and everything. "The invitations, Hammond. Now!"

He shrugged and locked eyes with Berianov as he eased a hand into his flannel shirt. He moved slowly, and then he began to talk in a low, rapid voice, hoping to provoke Berianov into making a mistake so he could take him down. "You think you're going to save Russia this way? Bring back the revolution? You're wrong. All you're doing is repeating Stalin's horrors. He began like you with a few 'necessary' deaths. First his so-called friends, like Ogust and Yurimengri. Then anyone in his way, like Ty Crocker and Stephanie Smith." With the tips of his fingers, he pulled out the four white envelopes and concluded, "Finally he sent masses of the expendable, like the Keepers, to their deaths. You're doing exactly the same thing, Berianov. You're no better than any murderer." He held the envelopes vertically in front of him.

Berianov acknowledged the envelopes with a flicker of his eyes, but his expression was unreadable. "This isn't for me. It's for Russia. If you knew the death of one person would save millions, wouldn't you kill that person? If you'd had the chance, wouldn't you have killed Hitler? Of course you would!"

"President Stevens is hardly Hitler. He's *helping* Russia."

"You're a fool, Hammond. In Moscow, the morning weatherman reports conditions for today only. At night, he forecasts for tomorrow, never the day after. Do you know why?" His eyes flashed with anger, and he did not wait for an answer. "My country feels perishable, as if we've got an expiration date. That's not the way it used to be. We had real power when we were Communists. We had ideas, vision, commitment, *endurance*. All of us were pulling together. We could do anything in those days. We had a future!"

Jeff studied Berianov's outraged face beneath the park ranger's cap. He saw longing there, too, and a wistfulness that made him even more uneasy than the anger. There was a thin line between honest aspiration and cynical justification, and Berianov was walking it too easily, as if he had done it so long that he was impervious to reason. "It won't work, Berianov. Even your own people want what we have."

"Streets paved with gold?" He snorted with disgust. "That's enough talk. Hand over the invitations. *Now.*"

"In case you haven't noticed, General," Jeff said icily, "you're not the only one with a weapon. My gun is pointed at you, and I won't miss."

From where she had been listening behind a pillar at the left side of the monument, Beth peered out at the two men, each armed, each unyielding in their post-Cold War game of chicken. She had a keen sense of déjà vu, as if she had witnessed scenes like this many times before. But as she continued to focus on Berianov, really study him for the first time, her stomach felt hollow and pain seemed to split the top of her skull. She leaned against the column, feeling weak. Was she imagining her physical reactions? Was she such a suggestible fool that the nightmares about landing on her head were coming back to haunt her now? She could not decide, her mind assaulted by images and thoughts, a cyclone of sensations. And pain at the crown of her head.

Still, she forced herself to keep her gaze on Berianov. She searched back through her nightmares and saw him sitting at the campfire . . . running beside her with their weapons in their arms . . . lifting his head to shout a warning. She remembered him jumping up onto the motorcycle. . . . *His shoulders square, his head particularly erect. He gave a little lift to his shoulders and tilted back his head as he pulled a helmet with a metallic visor down over his face.* . . . She would not forget him. Could not.

She glanced at Jeff and remembered three days before when she had feared he was a killer. Right now, watching him, she believed he could be, even though he was the same man she had slept with and whom she knew to be kind and gentle. For him, neither was an act. Not only would Berianov shoot to kill Jeff, but Jeff would shoot to kill Berianov. It was all she could do to remain hidden. To not go to Jeff's aid. Every fiber strained to step out with her Walther and take Berianov by surprise. The sight of him enraged her. Kill him. Kill him. *Stop it, Mikhail. Do you hear me? I don't need you. Leave me alone!* She must wait. Wait for whatever trick Berianov had planned.

She did not have long. Berianov's low voice echoed a command in the cavernous memorial. *"Ivan."*

"I am here, Alexei Petrovich." The guttural words sounded from behind the imposing six-foot granite pedestal.

Again she had that queasy feeling of memory. She studied the squat, massive figure of Ivan Vok as he appeared at the cube's side, silenced pistol in hand. With the conditioned reflex of a trained agent, Jeff half turned in the shadows, his gun moving between the two targets. Beth returned her gaze to Vok. He was familiar. Like Alexei Berianov, he seemed like a haunting ghost from her past.

Berianov smiled. "What will you do now, Special Agent Hammond? You can't fire at Ivan or at me before he kills you." He shrugged. "But you're right. We don't want to cause a furor here. So hand me the envelopes, and we'll let you live."

Jeff stared from one to the other. He sighed and conceded, "I guess I don't have a choice." He lowered his pistol.

As she watched, Beth made herself breathe slowly, evenly, willing her mind to stay free to react. This was the critical moment. Berianov would not let Jeff live; everyone knew that. Her pistol was steady in both hands as Jeff carefully extended the envelopes toward Berianov.

But just as Berianov reached out, Jeff let them slip from his fingers and fall to the marble floor in front of his cowboy boots. "Come and get them."

Berianov scowled. "Step back," he ordered.

Jeff moved back, his tall frame looming toward the short, powerful Ivan Vok, but Vok held his ground, his weapon firmly aimed. There was no way Jeff could move on Vok without being shot and killed.

Berianov stepped warily toward the envelopes and bent to pick them up. In that instant, as Berianov was looking down and Ivan Vok was focused on Jeff, a comforting certainty descended over Beth. It was almost as if she had spent her life preparing for this moment, even though she knew that was impossible. She raised her gun and stepped out from her hiding place.

She said coolly, "Don't move an inch, Vok!" Her gun was aimed at him.

There was a shocked moment in the shadowy rotunda with its big open spaces and crisp morning air. The two killers were motionless, Berianov in a crouch. But when Jeff started to move his pistol back up toward Berianov, the general suddenly flung himself forward into Jeff's legs.

Ivan Vok reacted quickly. Protecting his boss, he swung his pistol onto Beth and, with no time to aim, fired. At the same moment, Beth squeezed her trigger.

Vok took Beth's bullet through the collar of his white shirt, severing his carotid artery. Blood and red flesh erupted through the thin cloth and sprayed the air. The veteran assassin saw it and was astonished. *Pizduk.* Bastard. They were all bastards. Pain exploded in his head, and he landed at the base of the pedestal, slammed up against it as if he were litter blown against a curb. A shroud of black enveloped him, and he collapsed into death.

At the same time, Vok's 9mm bullet ripped along Beth's side just above her waist. The impact was searing, and she felt a lurch of nausea. She spun away, her shoulder bag flying, frantic to keep her balance, but she hit her head against the marble pillar that had sheltered her. The pain was like a knife through her brain, and she fell.

Within a second of the two shots, Russia's would-be leader, Alexei Berianov, was already up and moving. On the hard floor, bleeding and dizzy, Beth looked around in time to see him tear down the steps, the four white envelopes locked in his fist, as Jeff raised up on his elbows and squeezed off a shot.

The bullet bit into the grass, never touching Berianov, and Jeff jumped up to pursue. His rugged face was a mask of determination. Then he saw Beth bleeding on the floor. "Beth!"

She must have passed out. When she awoke, a park ranger—a real one this time—was using a cell phone to call for help, and Jeff was kneeling over her, rubbing her wrists and talking. "Beth, wake up. It's okay. It's only a small wound, and the ambulance is coming. You'll be fine. Beth?"

"Easy for you to say. I'm the one with the wound."

He smiled. "That's better. I'm more worried about your head. That was a rough fall."

"Marble appears to be harder than bone." She gave a half-smile. Then she remembered. Where was Berianov? She sat up abruptly, but her head spun, and she had to lie down again. She asked anxiously, "Berianov?"

"He got away, but at least he didn't get the invitations." At her suggestion, the sealed envelopes had held only cardboard pieces torn from the covers of an old AAA tour book of Washington they had found in Evans Olsen's glove compartment.

"Thank God." Her side burned and throbbed. She saw Ivan Vok lying sprawled in blood, his pistol nearby. "Vok?"

"Dead. That was some shot."

She had killed another man. Thinking about it made her feel ill.

Once more, she'd had no choice, but she would never get used to it. She took a deep breath and sat up again. This time her head did not spin.

"What are you doing?" His voice rose. "Lie down!"

She ignored him. Her side was bloody. She pulled up her sweater and looked at the wound. It was a purple slice just beneath her ribcage, still oozing red. "All I need is aspirin, an antibiotic cream, and a bandage."

"Beth, you're nuts! You passed out!"

Some indomitable spirit possessed her. She had to go on. Logically it made sense that Jeff could use her help, but this was no rational drive that pushed her to continue. "So I fainted." She rose to her feet. This time the dizziness was small and soon passed. She tried to smile at him. "You didn't really think you were going after Berianov alone, did you?"

"You've got to have that wound looked at. With your transplant, you're susceptible to infection!"

"Big deal. That's why I take all my meds on time, in case a little thing like a bullet happens to shake things up. Look, women used to have nine-pound babies and then go back into the field to plow. I think I can handle a scratch. Men can be such wusses. Where's my bag? I've got antibiotic wipes in it."

Jeff was thunderstruck. Then he was angry. But there was no stopping her. Already she had waved good-bye to the ranger, picked up her shoulder bag, and was limping off across the rotunda.

The park ranger stared at her as if puzzled. Then he checked out Jeff, and there was a strange expression on his face. "Don't I know you two? I swear—"

Jeff turned away. They had to get out of there fast. "Maybe. We come here a lot. We're just tourists at heart. Well, I'd better get my wife home." He rushed after Beth. Somewhere an ambulance siren sounded, heading their way.

"Hey!" The park ranger trotted after them and snared Jeff's shoulder. "You've got to stick around. There's a dead man here. The police will want to talk to you!"

"Sorry, friend." Jeff turned, grabbed the man's arm, and flipped him over his back. The ranger landed hard, air gusting from his lungs. Jeff took off running down the steps after Beth.

She was already sitting in the passenger seat of the Olds. As he got in behind the steering wheel, she said, "I hope you don't mind driving." She had found her moist antibiotic tissues and was wiping her side.

"Hell, at least there's *something* you won't do!" He turned on the engine, circled the car around the lot, and accelerated toward the street.

She leaned back tiredly. She felt dizzy again, but she was not going to tell Jeff. "Something weird . . . I've quit talking to my heart. When I was waiting behind the pillar, I actually started talking to Mikhail Ogust directly. I think it was because I saw Berianov. Maybe I'm losing my mind."

He shook his head. "Just as long as it's not your life that you're losing."

"Where are we going?"

"You're one enormous pain in the butt, you know that?"

She gave a little smile. "But I'm adorable, too. Come on, Jeff. You're not going to get rid of me. I have to see this through to the end. It's not just for me, it's for Stephanie and Ty and Mikhail Ogust. I owe all of them."

"You don't owe Ogust a damn thing for getting you into this mess."

"I've thought about that." She rolled her head to the side so she could study his intense profile. "Maybe not, but I think he wants me to stop Berianov for him." As they entered traffic on Ohio Drive, an ambulance rushed past toward the Jefferson Memorial. "But how are we going to find Berianov now? We don't have anywhere else we know to look. His whole plan is destroyed—he doesn't even have the invitations. If he gives up now, we'll never catch him without a countrywide, probably worldwide, search."

"Once the Keepers were all dead, most people would've dropped the assassination. Aborted it." Jeff watched the ambulance for a moment, thinking. "But not Berianov. Everything we know about him says he won't give up. That he's unable to." He nodded as if agreeing with some decision he had just made. "Here's what we're going to do. First, I'm going to pull off and find a phone booth so I can make an anonymous tip to the Secret Service. Since the warning won't be tarnished by any connection to me, they'll at least heighten security. Plus they'll make an effort to convince the president to bow out of the ceremonies. "

"I hope they succeed," she said fervently. "What else do you have in mind?"

"All four of these invitations are in men's names, but one of them, for a Mercer Somebody, could be a woman's. I know an artist who can make us good fake ID. If you really think you're up to it, we'll use two of the invitations to get into the reception and press conference in the Rose Garden. That way, if Berianov tries to kill President Stevens, maybe we can stop him."

As Bobby Kelsey sat alone in his darkened office in the Hoover building, he felt his rage build. He had lost all trace of Jeffrey Hammond and Beth Convey, and in the process he had probably destroyed his one chance for the final big score—helping Alexei Berianov to become the dictator of a reborn Soviet Union. It would have meant millions of dollars to him. Kelsey knew Berianov had other sources in the U.S. government, particularly one each in State and Commerce, but he was Berianov's prime contact in the American intelligence community. Berianov had paid and would continue to pay handsomely for that.

Kelsey had no illusions. When he had reported the disaster about Hammond and Convey to Berianov, the general had sounded reasonable, not overly angry, but Kelsey heard behind the measured tones a depth of distrust that might never be bridged. Berianov could kill him and decide about replacing him later.

Worried, he turned his executive chair around so he could check his personal e-mail. It was a long shot, but still—

What he saw at first made his spirits soar. And then dread filled him. There was a new encrypted message from Berianov in his code name, but no clue in the subject line whether it was good news or bad. Instantly he opened it. With relief, he transcribed Berianov's message: "I need you, Kelsey. I'm not finished yet. I'll make this worth your while." Instructions followed to meet at Berianov's secret lair north of Washington.

Nervous and suspicious, Bobby checked the message's posting time to make certain Berianov had sent it after he had received the bad news about Hammond and Convey. Yes, just ten minutes ago. Kelsey allowed himself a smile. Berianov still needed him.

Activity in the Justice Department was picking up as workers arrived, computers flashed on, and the aroma of morning coffee floated through the halls. In Deputy Attorney General Millicent Taurino's corner office, she was already at work, glowering first at National Security Adviser Cabot Lowell and then at Assistant Attorney General Donald Chen. The three of them were sitting in a triangle, she behind her utilitarian desk and the two men in the armchairs facing her.

"We blew it," Millicent said glumly, chin resting on a fist. "We didn't bring Hammond in fast enough. So now he's killed the director. Besides all the usual police stuff, what are we doing about locating him before he does any more damage, Donald?"

"Millicent, if I weren't deeply in love with my wife, I'd beg you to marry me. You're so supportive." Donald Chen's Buddha face was just as gloomy as hers. "I refuse to let the buck stop with me on this. What I want to know is where's Eli Kirkhart? He was our point man. *He's* the one who's fallen down on the job."

Cabot Lowell's sleek head rotated from one to the other, his eyelids lowering and then rising. His lips were thinner than usual, scalpel sharp. "You've missed the point, both of you," the older man said. "We now have enough evidence to satisfy most people that Jeffrey Hammond is the mole. It would be gratifying to bring him in alive so he could tell us exactly what he's passed on to the Soviets and then to the Russians over the years, but it's not essential. In fact, for the good of the nation, it may be best that he *not* come in alive. It would save a lot of messiness, not to mention the expense of a trial."

"Really, Cabot, you're outrageous, not to mention pitiless." Millicent Taurino glared at him.

"But realistic," Cabot Lowell reminded her.

"We're going to have to answer a lot of questions when he's arrested," Donald Chen agreed unhappily. "I don't like to think about the press inquiries. We're not going to look good. In fact, we're going to look plain incompetent."

"If the shoe fits and all that." Millicent pressed her palms down on her desk top and arose, a small woman who exuded a towering sense of power. She growled, "Maybe we screwed up by not moving faster on Hammond, but it's too late to bring Director Horn back to life. If you think we look bad now, imagine what the public would say if word ever leaked out that you two had considered authorizing a hit on Hammond? Forget it, you ghouls. Not while I'm on the job."

Cabot Lowell rose, too. "Now, Millicent, you know none of us ever said that. That certainly wasn't part of this conversation, was it, Donald?"

As he stood and gazed at Lowell, Chen frowned, puzzled. Then he realized that the NSA director was covering all their asses with his disclaimer. "You're right. Absolutely. We're all lawful here. Murder is against the law."

Millicent studied first one then the other. "Good. Then we're in agreement. If either of you comes up with any serious ideas about how to bring in Hammond more quickly, I'd like to hear them. Now is a good time."

But Cabot Lowell shook his head. "Sorry. Nothing occurs to me."

Chen added, "I'll give you a call if I think of something."

As the two men left and the door closed, Millicent Taurino sank worriedly into her chair. She picked up her phone to ask for the latest reports on Hammond and on the group of loonies who had apparently, at least according to Ty Crocker's mysterious informant, planned to assassinate the president. The public did not know about the assassination allegation, and the few in government who had been told were not at liberty to talk about it. But it all made her wonder whether the two events—the mole's murder of Director Horn and the patriot group's alleged plot—were connected.

She listened to her assistant's report, which was full of gory details about the terrorist group's painful end. Her assistant excused herself and was back instantly. "The Secret Service received a tip early this morning that some defector guy . . . wait a minute, I've got his name here." She spelled it: "B-e-r-i-a-n-o-v. That this Berianov guy is going to try to assassinate President Stevens in the Rose Garden this morning."

"Oh, no. This we do not need. General Alexei Berianov! I'll be damned. What's the Secret Service doing about it?"

"The Secret Service says it's stepping up security measures. You know, the usual increase in sharpshooters on the roof. Detailed inspections of employees and guests and their IDs when they enter the grounds—"

Millicent cut her off. "I know the drill. Is there anything else about Berianov and who might be with him?"

"No, ma'am. That's all I've got here."

"Thanks." Millicent Taurino hung up and leaned back in her chair. She stared up at the portrait of Chief Justice John Marshall, thinking. At last she snatched up the phone again and dialed Dean Jennings. "I hear you boys have a hot alert about an attempt on the president's life during that reception for Putin in the Rose Garden."

"You know I can't comment."

"Okay, I've got another tip for you: I think our mole's involved somehow. We believe he was working for Alexei Berianov, and one of them is your potential shooter today. That being the case, you'd better watch out for both of them. Yes, that's right. Jeffrey Hammond and General Alexei Berianov. You have photos of both? Good. Plaster them everywhere. Oh, and Dean, put me on the staff list for this shindig. I'll be there. Yes, honey, with my war paint on!"

In Moscow, Professor Georgi Malko had arisen at noon, completely recovered from his long but fruitful duty at his Russian Roulette club the night before. The morning papers and newscasts were full of the tragic death of Oleg Dudash and the rumor that he had sold *True or False* the very night he had perished. All morning long, the phone rang and the door knocker sounded at Malko's mansion, but the butler deflected all press inquiries until Malko could breakfast, shower, shave, and dress in one of his proper banker's suits, this one a dark-blue blend of silk and wool.

Looking admirably dependable and prosperous, Malko then met the suspicious media in his office high above the city center, where he displayed the signed contract and expressed his sorrow for the great publisher's passing. He had no idea whether they believed him. In any case, it did not matter. The completed sales agreement spoke the loudest.

Now it was night again, and as he strolled along Tverskaya Street near the Kremlin, he decided his day had been satisfying. Yes, quite enjoyable. He liked being on the way up again. Skirting the curb, he clasped his hands behind him and moved smartly along with the other pedestrians hurrying through the starry night. Above them, neon signs glowed raucously, advertising Volvo, New Balance, and designer clothes and jewelry. Yes, there was a splendid future here in Russia, for those who knew how to take advantage of it.

As he was thinking that, a long black Zhiguli sedan pulled alongside him and slowed. The back window rolled down. Feigning surprise,

Malko leaned over and said in a low voice, "General Kripinski. What a surprise."

"Get in, Malko," the general growled. "No one's staring yet. But they will."

Without another word, General Igor Kripinski slid across the seat, and Malko climbed in, smiling coolly. He rolled up the window, the driver pressed the gas pedal, and the sedan slid into the thick traffic.

"We've got twice as many cars now," the general grumbled as he stared at the congestion, "but half the amount of wheat. Explain the wisdom in that, Mr. Oligarch."

"There's nothing to explain. It's a free market. People would rather spend their money on cars. It's that simple."

The general shook his head. "It's not simple. It's stupid. We've let all this free-market shit get out of hand. Keep your billions, Malko. That's over with, and I don't care. But enough's enough. We've got to get this country back on track. When I was a boy, we used to hunt down the rich and jail them. Now my soldiers moonlight guarding them. For money, because I don't have enough to pay them even the stinking little pittances Putin grudgingly promised. Look around at all the new buildings going up. They're awful. Our country's losing its traditions. Everything's pretentious, and the construction itself is nothing but cheap crap." He grimaced and asked hopefully, "What's the situation in Washington? Is Berianov going to pull off this thing?"

"I spoke to him yesterday, and the event's on schedule."

General Kripinski gave a satisfied grunt. "Good. I can't wait. We three are a strange troika, aren't we? Berianov, the unrepentant Communist. You, the free-wheeling entrepreneur. And me, the old war horse who wants nothing more than stability. But that's the way it's always been in our country, right? Byzantine, to be sure, but we understand that strength . . . real power . . . comes from a sword that's sharpened by many. And we do love our troikas. One of us will arise as the supreme leader eventually, as Lenin did over Stalin and Trotski, but until then, we will work together for the good of Russia."

He shot a cagey look at the oligarch, remembering that after Lenin died, Stalin took over and later arranged to have Trotski killed in Mexico. He wondered whether Malko was thinking the same thing. Or perhaps Malko was recalling Khrushchev, who had beaten out Molotov and Malenkov to run the country and then, to solidify his position, had exiled the ailing Molotov to Mongolia where he nearly died, and Malenkov to run a minor power station in Ust-Kamenogorsk, after which he was never officially heard of again.

But the former math professor said nothing, his gaze on the teeming street.

General Kripinski studied his short, oxlike face, which looked as innocent as a baby's. Finally he shrugged. "You expect to take over eventually, don't you, Malko? The supreme leader. Let me assure you, you're not electable, neither by the people nor by an old-fashioned Politburo. You've burned too many bridges. No one loves a man who loves only money, especially not here, not today. We've learned at least that much."

Malko gave a cold chuckle. "Unless, of course, *you're* the one with the bank accounts and investments. Or you hope someday it'll be you. There's always the chance that after Berianov's event and the change of leadership that you'll become rich, too. Then what will you think? Who will you be? What affluence does to the individual is not only an interesting question, but a critical one. In fact, one on which empires rise and fall. Certainly it's been true of Russia. After all, what is communism about if not money and the distribution of it? No wonder they were so easily corrupted."

"What a crock." The general launched into an outraged tirade against what he called the professor's cynicism, and they continued arguing about politics and the country's proper future as the driver rounded two more corners and slowed. The man walking along the sidewalk had just stopped to talk to two women. As the car pulled up next to him and stopped, he bent down and scribbled into one woman's small book and then into the other's.

"Must be a couple of fans," Georgi Malko explained to the general.

"That's Roman Tyrret? Doesn't look like much." Kripinski studied the man under the ermine-trimmed hat. In his late thirties, he was of medium height and gave off no sense of athleticism. His overcoat was expensive, his wing-tip shoes shined, and his profile clean-cut. To the general, he looked soft and spoiled.

Malko said, "You've got to watch his TV show."

"I hate all that populist bullshit. They prey on everyone's fears, and then they never offer any kind of real solution, except send me money, money, money."

Malko nodded. "You're learning, General." He rolled down his window. "Mr. Tyrret, could we have a word?"

They could hear Tyrret excuse himself. He turned and reached for the door handle. "Professor Malko? Is it really you?" There was something boyish and earnest in his freckled face. "I'm so honored, sir. May I get in?"

"Of course. That's why I called."

Georgi Malko turned to glare at the general, who grudgingly slid closer to the door. Malko followed him, and the television celebrity climbed into the luxury sedan. As soon as the door closed, the general grunted, and the driver returned the car into traffic.

The professor began the introductions: "This is—"

But Roman Tyrret interrupted. "—General Igor Kripinski. Our great scourge of Afghanistan and Chechnya. You're one of my heroes, sir. I'm very honored to meet you, too."

There was a rumble of disgust in Kripinski's throat that never quite got started as Tyrret's honeyed flattery affected even him. Instead, he listened and watched as Professor Malko asked Tyrret to tell them about himself and his goals. Roman Tyrret had charisma, there was no doubt about that. He was also a lot smarter than he wanted anyone to know, and more needy. Beneath his modest claims for wanting simply a bigger audience so he could help people, the general saw hunger for applause and personal influence. The general nodded to himself. Yes, perhaps Malko was right again. There could be all sorts of uses in a new Soviet Union for someone like Tyrret.

Harvey Grossman's apartment overlooked the Potomac River in the historic town of Alexandria just south of Washington. Mediocre abstract paintings hung on the walls and stood against every piece of furniture. The odor of oil paint permeated the rooms, a reminder that an artist—in more ways than one—lived and worked here.

Beth and Jeff were in Grossman's second bedroom. Jeff was searching through the closet, while Beth rested on the bed.

Her side still ached. "How do you know this man Grossman?"

As Jeff searched for the right clothes to disguise them, he told her, "Once when I was consulting with Treasury on a counterfeiting case, Harvey was one of the suspects. We never could get enough evidence to charge him, which was unfortunate then."

"But useful now."

"Harvey needs the money so he can afford to paint his masterpieces."

"I hope he's a better forger and counterfeiter than he is a painter."

She was tense, even though they had plenty of time to reach the White House by 9:00 A.M., which they must do in order to have time enough to pass through the security checks with the other invited guests. She felt a little sick, but she got up to help Jeff look through the clothes. At the back of the closet she found a few women's things, faintly scented with perfume. She pulled out a long, tailored coat, white microfiber pants, and a sun-colored silk blouse. "These look as if they'll work. I'll go dye my hair now."

"Good. A shower will make you feel better. Be careful of that wound." A variety of hair colorings were among the items Jeff had taken from the black box in the assassin's station wagon.

As she grabbed one of the dye packets and disappeared into the bathroom, he continued to pull out and try on clothes. He went into the studio, told Grossman to hurry up, and returned to the bedroom. When Beth emerged from the bath with brown hair, her torso wrapped in a towel, he stared. The dark hair altered her appearance more than he had expected. It made her skin and eyes paler. The eyes were sea blue, startling in their light color as they contrasted with the dark-brown hair.

She picked up sunglasses from the bedside table and put them on. "I bandaged my side. The wound's sore, but it looks clean and uninfected. And I do feel better now. What do you think?" She had dried her hair and teased it, so that instead of its lying against her head in a sleek corn-silk cap it was fluffy and curly brown. With the sunglasses hiding much of her face, no one would easily recognize her.

"Good. In fact, excellent. I particularly like that towel. A nice touch."

She grinned and opened it. Her slender body was damp and luminous from the shower. A gauze bandage was taped to her side. He was gripped by her sensuous curves, the pink nipples, and the triangle of blond fur. The long scar down her chest seemed normal to him now. It took every ounce of his self-control not to rip away the towel and take her to bed again.

He checked his watch and shook his head ruefully. "*Now* she decides to seduce me. Four hours ago I could've done something about it—"

Careless of her side, this time she ran to him, wrapped the towel around him, too, and pressed her naked breasts against his shirt. She could not resist him. She nipped and kissed his neck.

He growled, "Your timing stinks. But what the hell." He kissed her long and deep.

She wriggled from his arms, her face flushed, her eyes beginning to shimmer as she fought for restraint. "You wouldn't. There's no time. You said so yourself."

He laughed. "Gave you some of your own medicine. I'll dye my hair now."

She pressed into him again and kissed him. "You're awful."

He kissed her back. "I know. You'll get used to me. But now I have to take care of my hair color."

She sighed. "Well, if you must." As she watched him disappear into the bathroom, she smiled and stretched gently, trying her side. It was tender, but that was all. No fresh blood had soaked through the bandage. She put on the new clothes and hurried out to have Grossman shoot her photo with her new brown hair. In the kitchen, she took her meds. By the time she returned to the bedroom, Jeff had finished his shower and dressed.

She stared. "You look different."

"That's the goal." No longer the cocky renegade, he wore a dark, pinstriped suit. The sleeves and trouser pants were a little short, but Grossman's wide girth compensated enough for Jeff's height that the suit was passable. What was more remarkable was the change in his face. With his hair colored black and his naturally golden skin, he took on a faintly Mediterranean look. He enhanced the shift with some kind of inserts in his cheeks that made his face rounder. With oval, wire-rimmed glasses, the transformation was striking.

"You look mainstream," Beth decided. "I don't think *I'd* recognize you." It gave her an odd sensation, and she smiled, aware there was still a lot more to him she could look forward to discovering. "We'd better go."

"Are you really sure you're up to it? You can back out. I won't think any the less of you." He studied her face. "I know your side hurts. Really, Beth. For both our sakes. I don't want to lose you."

She held his chin in both her hands. He had shaved, and his skin had the silky texture of a baby's. "Who would've thought I'd ever be with an undercover spy? I must be out of my mind."

He gave a dry chuckle. "We both are. Imagine me with another lawyer."

"What else could you expect in Washington? It's a lawyer's town. But what a way to go. God forbid we'd die in some boring fashion."

Jeff held her shoulders. "Don't say that. Don't even think it. We're going to make it."

His gaze was fierce, and she wanted to believe him. "You're right." She shook off her uncertainty. In last night's nightmare, it had been her heart donor whom Berianov murdered, not her. She had survived Ivan Vok's bullet just a few hours ago. They were going to be fine. Had to be fine.

In his large, sunny studio, Harvey Grossman leaned back from his drawing table, finished with both IDs. Brushes and paint cans stood on a paint-splattered worktable and in clumps on the floor. An easel displayed a half-finished canvas with disjointed slashes of red and yellow. Colorful koi swam in a large aquarium across the room. Grossman stood up, a tall, heavyset man with jowls and a pink face.

He waved two Virginia driver's licenses at them. "Ready, folks. That'll be one thousand dollars cash, the cheapest piece of art in the building."

"But among the best, no doubt," Beth said smoothly.

"Let's have a look." Jeff studied the driver's licenses Harvey had rebuilt from stolen ones. "Good job," he decided. "Now how about a couple of your hidden guns?"

"W-what?" Grossman seemed to shrink.

"Don't bullshit me, Harvey. We both know you're a gun dealer, too. The thing was, we couldn't find them last time. I don't have a badge now to keep me from doing something illegal. You don't want me to do anything illegal, do you, Harvey?" He took out his Beretta and aimed it casually at Grossman. "I really need those guns, Harvey. Something that will go through X-ray machines without being detected."

Grossman swallowed. He had a prominent Adam's apple that bobbed and seemed to catch midway. He swallowed again. "Right. But it'll cost you extra."

"I don't think so. A thousand dollars seems plenty, considering the circumstances." They did not have enough cash to pay more, but Grossman did not need to know that.

Grossman's gaze flickered to the gun. "Guess so."

He crossed the studio to the big aquarium, where sea grass waved, and the koi swam lazily. He pressed a panel at the back of the wood cabinet on which the tank sat. There was a quiet *whir*, and a three-inch-deep drawer slid out of the cabinet just beneath the tank. Grossman pulled it all the way out.

The drawer held three pistols with ceramic barrels and firing pins, metal springs, and the rest of the parts in hard, clear plastic. They could be disassembled and sent through an X-ray reader as camera or machine pieces. Plus there was a sturdy-looking cane, about three inches in diameter.

"What's in the cane?" Jeff demanded.

For a moment pride showed in Grossman's gaze. "A surprise." He twisted one of the brass decorative beads that lined the side then shoved the bead inside. Instantly the brass handle slid up a fraction of an inch. Grossman unscrewed the handle, tipped the hollow cane, and metal parts for two palm-sized pistols slid out, plus a miniature tool kit and four .22-caliber bullets wrapped in paper.

Jeff nodded appreciatively. "The cane's lined in lead?"

"You bet. No machine can see inside. The best." He could not resist adding, "One of my finest designs."

Beth said, "You're an artist, Harvey."

Jeff examined the parts. "Looks good. In fact, very good." He would have no trouble assembling the small, one-shot pistols. "Are they reliable guns?"

"Like I said, for their size, they're the best." Grossman sounded proud.

Jeff was unhappy going into a confrontation with Berianov with just a single .22-caliber bullet for Beth and him, but getting even that past White House security would be a triumph. "The metal spring on those full-size plastic weapons would never get through the White House scanners unless they were disguised inside something with metal on it. You have anything that would do the job?"

"Nope. The customer always handles that part. I just buy and sell the guns."

"Then it'll have to be the cane," Jeff decided.

"Does that do it?" Beth asked. Part of her was already out the door.

"I'm satisfied." Jeff slid the gun parts back into the cane. "Sort of. It's not much firepower, but with luck it's all we'll need. Pay the man."

Beth pulled from her shoulder bag the thousand dollars in cash she had taken from her desk drawer Thursday night after Stephanie Smith was killed. For a moment she was transported back to Stephanie's terrible death in the fiery car crash.

She looked down at her hand as she passed the money to Harvey. Her hand was steady. And in that instant she saw how much stronger she had become. She was the same person, but different. All the new restlessness and rage had settled into an odd kind of confidence that allowed her to feel a range of emotions she had never attained. She glanced up at Jeff.

Jeff handed one of the IDs to Beth. "This one's yours. Your name's Mercer Bell, and I'm Thomas Koster. We have the Social Security numbers from Olsen, and now we have the photo ID. We're ready."

Grossman was counting his money. "Groove on, folks. My painting calls."

Jeff said, "Not yet, Harvey."

Grossman looked back at the Beretta in Jeff's hand. His eyebrows raised, and his jowls quivered. "Come on, Jeff. You're not going to kill me for a thousand bucks, are you? That's shitty." His face was tight with fear.

"Not as long as you do what I say. Go into the living room."

"I don't think this is a good idea—" Grossman froze as he saw Beth pull out a pistol, too.

She said, "Come on, Harvey. Hurry it up. *Move!*"

Without another word, the artist scuttled into the living room, Beth and Jeff close behind. As Jeff tied him to a spindle chair, Beth gagged him, then hurried out the door.

Jeff grabbed the cane. "If all goes well, we'll be back in a couple of hours to untie you. Keep that thought, Harvey. And say a little prayer we make it—and so does the president."

The gray morning sky had turned flinty blue. A few smoky clouds hung low above the Beltway as Jeff sped the car past Reagan airport, heading toward downtown Washington. He and Beth were talking about everything that had happened since she found the dying Colonel Yurimengri at Meteor Express.

"Have you noticed how so many people think we won the Cold War?" she was saying. "Boy, are they wrong. We *bought* victory, paid for it fair and square. Of course, the Soviets helped by underproducing us and pillaging their own government's treasury. An odd collusion."

"What I think's interesting is Americans' believing we're the only su-perpower left, when all anyone has to do is look at the mammoth inter-national corporations like Microsoft and Enron, with budgets larger than most nations and profits bigger than any. Global market leaders are today's real superpowers, and individual countries are an indul-gence they keep around like favorite aunts."

She nodded. "In my practice, it's clear nothing fundamental has really changed despite all the talk about the technology revolution and our new information-based economies. Just as Machiavelli and the Medicis would've been right at home jawboning with Carnegie, Ford, and Rockefeller, all of them would come to a quick meeting of the minds today with Bill Gates and his kingly pals. It's still nothing but power and profits at those rarified heights, just as it's always been."

As they rode on, she worried about what would happen at the Rose Garden. What it would mean if Berianov were to succeed in killing the president.

Finally she asked, "Do you have any idea what Berianov's going to look like?"

"I've been asking myself the same question. I've seen the FBI and CIA produce masks with skin so lifelike you'd think it sweats, blushes, and has to be watched for acne. We can thank university labs and the space program for that. Considering how well-equipped Berianov has been so far, I've got no reason to believe he doesn't have all the same tools and compounds." He paused and added with disgust, "I thought I knew him well. After all, I'd spent weeks debriefing him after he defected, and then I stayed in touch with him over the years. But in the end, I didn't have a clue he was the old man or Caleb Bates. He disguised not only his face, but his voice and his posture. I *believed* he was that dairy farm's caretaker, and so did he."

"Me, too." She sighed worriedly. "The president could be in serious trouble."

49

It was 9:25 A.M., and the Rose Garden bustled with activity as TV and radio people checked mikes, feeds, and cables. White House press aides circulated among the crews, answering questions and setting up postconference interviews, while stern-faced American and Russian security teams conferred in low, urgent voices by walkie-talkie.

The Secret Service had instructed the staff to be doubly alert, that there had been a threat against the president's life that sounded more legitimate than usual. As expected, the two presidents had refused to cancel or alter their schedules, so security was not only tight but tense.

Atop the limestone steps off the West Wing, with white pillars and the Cabinet Room's white French doors as a backdrop, twin podiums stood awaiting the beginning of the internationally televised media event.

Neat rows of white chairs were arranged on the Rose Garden's thick green lawn, facing the podiums. Divided into thirds, the central group of chairs would seat more than a hundred reporters from around the globe. On either side of the reporters' section, separated by aisles, were rows for special guests. Already many of the chairs were occupied. Overlooking the animated scene from the distant end of the garden was a temporary platform on which camera crews and still photographers with long telephoto lenses busily prepared their equipment.

Keeping watch from the rooftops were Secret Service sharpshooters. Meanwhile, inside the White House, white-uniformed waiters padded silently in and out of the elegant state dining room with its gilded chandelier and sconces. They were setting two dozen round tables with the White House's classic Vermeil flatware and the red-and-gold rimmed Reagan china. Aides would shepherd special guests in to dine with the Russian and American heads of state immediately after the press affair.

All this activity was situation normal for the White House, except for the intensified security. And on top of that was an added element—a subtle undercurrent of quiet frenzy due to the weighty nature of the occasion. A visit by the Russian president was a world-class event, now shadowed by potential danger.

In the Oval Office, the two men—the calm center of today's business—sat apparently relaxed in gold damask chairs on either side of the fireplace, interpreters behind and beside. They discussed the traditional items—the weather, crops in America's Midwest and Russia's neighboring Ukraine, and the problems of getting away for a vacation. No one mentioned the recent unpleasantness in Chechnya or Colombia, or Russia's continuing problems with the IMF, or America's embarrassing campaign-finance scandals. This was no working meeting. It was social, and both presidents seemed relieved to be responsible only for their media images.

Out on East Executive Avenue, the queue of invited guests moved ahead under budding trees. To their left was the wrought-iron fence and bushes that surrounded the White House grounds, while towering to their right was the gothic Treasury Building. Dressed in suits and springtime dresses, polished wing-tips and attractive low-heeled pumps, many were holding their envelopes and invitations while they chatted. It was a festive atmosphere, and Beth and Jeff in their disguises made every effort to fit right in.

Except that their sharp gazes watched everywhere. Was Berianov here in line with them? It made Beth's skin crawl. Would they be able to determine who Berianov was? Perhaps at this very instant he was figuring out who they were so he could monitor them.

They had been careful. They had parked six blocks away. Jeff had left the car first and was ahead of her in line by ten people. She and he made no eye contact. He was an elegant stranger in his pinstriped suit and cane. He limped slightly.

When the woman ahead turned to admire the cane, he gave a stalwart smile and said, "Old war wound. Desert Storm. Quite an action that was." Soon he was chatting away with the woman, Grace, and her husband, Duane, discussing America's wars, from the Big One—World War II—right through to the peacekeeping missions in Yugoslavia.

Beth struck up a conversation with a family that included a young boy of about twelve named Justin. He kept staring at her, licking dry lips, trying to think of topics to keep him the focus of her attention. His hormone-fueled adoration was sweet, and she would have enjoyed his company far more if she were not using him for cover.

Above them through the leafing branches, the clouds had thinned to a high haze, and the sun sent out a friendly warmth. Excitement rippled along the crowd as the line trickled past concrete-block posts toward wrought-iron gates. Everything felt wretchedly out of sync, Beth thought: A gorgeous day. A lovely setting. Good cheer and conviviality. Yet somewhere nearby death might lurk.

Was that man with horn-rimmed glasses Berianov? Perhaps the heavyset woman with the floppy hat?

A group of killers had to struggle to blend and disappear, but one assassin could be the proverbial straw in the haystack, impossible to single out. In the end, there was nothing more dangerous than a lone human with a fanatical mission and the training, intelligence, and financing of a Berianov. Beth's throat tightened. Unconsciously she put a hand over her wound.

On either side of the gated entrance, White House security in gold-trimmed black trousers, jackets, and caps stood sentry. They asked to see invitations, and as guests held them up, the guards politely instructed the visitors to continue on in. Beth made her smile casual and showed her invitation while keeping up an animated conversation with Justin. She looked up just in time to see Jeff disappear into a white building ahead.

As he stepped indoors, Jeff quickly scrutinized the scene. He had been through here many times as an FBI man and then as a reporter. Now it was important he look like an interested outsider. Plus he was studying faces and body types, searching constantly for Berianov.

The interior resembled the standard security check at an airlines terminal, but much more attractive—big glass windows and decorative ferns. If a guest felt insulted to be security-checked, at least this was no prison-like atmosphere. There were the usual metal detectors and conveyor belts with X-ray machines to examine packages, purses, and other items guests might be carrying. One of the guards divided the line in half to speed passage. Still the security people were thorough, and their trained gazes missed little.

Jeff kept his face and voice cheerful, although he was brittle with tension. "Of course, that's the UN's job, Grace," he was saying to the woman who had first asked him about the cane.

She had turned out to be the perfect distraction—an interesting and vivacious conversationalist. Apparently at ease, he laid the cane with its sinister contents on the moving conveyor belt and stepped through the metal detector. He did not glance back at the cane, although every nerve cell was raw with worry. When no flashing lights or alarms went off, he suppressed a sigh of relief, trying to keep out of his mind the two small guns in the lead-lined cane.

"Your Social Security number and photo identification, sir." Guards were waiting on the other side to speak to each guest.

Jeff repeated the memorized number and dug out the fake Virginia driver's license. "Sure. How are you today?" Jeff handed over the license.

"Just fine. Is this your cane, sir?" The guard held on to the driver's license and picked the cane up at the end of the conveyor belt. "Heavy, isn't it?"

Jeff frowned. "I'm a big man," he said smoothly. "A lot of weight to put on a stick, even a metal stick."

"Had it specially made, did you?" The guard nodded to a second one, who joined him.

Jeff assumed a puzzled expression. He peered through his oval glasses at the guard. "I don't know whether it's one of a kind, if that's what you're asking. A friend gave it to me."

The guards studied the cane. The second one took it, turned it around, glanced up quizzically at Jeff, then ran a hand up and down it, his fingers probing and feeling.

Behind them, Beth watched, holding her breath. The guards were detaining Jeff, while letting everyone else go on. She did not understand it. Anxiously she strained to hear the conversation as she put her own bag onto the conveyor belt.

Jeff continued, "It was a coming-home gift after Desert Storm, if you know what I mean. I've always liked that cane."

"You were injured?"

Sweat was beginning to collect under Jeff's suit. He limped back a step as if unsure. It was good they thought him modest; he was less threatening that way. "Took some shrapnel in my leg." He chuckled. "No big deal."

The two guards exchanged a glance. Neither had found anything obviously wrong with the cane, but there was still something bothering them. Jeff did not recognize either man, but maybe they had a sense they had seen him somewhere before.

Then a woman's voice called, "Tom, how great to see you!" Beth waved as she came out through the metal detector. She picked up her straw bag with one hand, while with the other she took the hand of her new young friend, Justin. "Justin, come meet Tom Koster. He was in Desert Storm. Justin has a collection of to-scale tanks. Weren't you in a tank in Desert Storm, Tom?"

At first he was furious she had risked exposure by connecting herself with him. But from the corners of his eyes he could see both guards were caught by her charms—the dark sunglasses, the dark, wind-blown hair, the beautiful red lips, the lean figure, the throaty voice.

If it worked, he would use it. "Mercer, my God, how long's it been?" He pumped Beth's hand enthusiastically then leaned down and took the boy's hand. "Glad to meet you, Justin. Yes, I was in an armored battalion. Lot of sand over there. More sand than I ever want to see again."

"What battalion?" Justin asked eagerly.

"The two-seventy. Second Brigade, First Armored. Rode an M-1 Abrams. A real dirt-eater. Great machine."

The boy beamed. He had probably memorized every unit in Desert Storm. Meanwhile, Beth had handed over her fake ID and repeated her phony Social Security number. "Can we go on in?" she gazed around with awe. "This is my first time at the White House, and I can't wait to get wherever we're going."

The two guards looked at one another. The other guests were surging impatiently.

Beth asked innocently, "Is something wrong with my ID?" Of course, she was not the reason the two guards were holding them up, but she wanted them to be pressured into making a quicker decision than they wanted. She pointed. "Oh, Justin! There are your folks!"

"Come along, Justin!" his father called.

"Want to go in with us, Tom?" Beth suggested. She smiled at Jeff then at the guards.

"How about it?" Jeff prodded. "Unless, of course, you've found something wrong—?"

That did it. He had put them on the spot. They had to decide. This was a happy occasion, one to celebrate the ongoing relationship between the Russian and American democracies, and the guards had no real reason to hold Jeff, only a faint suspicion, and faint suspicions without facts would not play well if Mr. Koster, Desert Storm veteran, decided to raise a fuss, despite the unusually high security.

"Sure, sorry. Enjoy yourselves," the first guard decided. He handed Jeff the cane and driver's license.

"Move right along," said the second.

Without exchanging a glance, Beth and Jeff followed Justin and his parents on a walkway bordered by tulips and shrubbery and up steps toward the White House's ground-floor entrance.

"Jesus," Jeff breathed. "That was close."

"I had no idea security would be so difficult," Beth whispered.

"Yeah. They're doing a good job. Hell, I remember when Lesley Stahl was writing her autobiography. Her publisher wanted to reproduce her White House press pass on the book jacket, but the Secret Service had a fit. Said it'd endanger White House security. That's how careful they can get here."

They stepped indoors, moving with the crowd along the burnt-orange carpet on the ground-floor corridor. They raised their voices to normal and inquired about each other's imaginary relatives as if they were two old friends who had not seen one another in years. They passed the library and diplomatic reception room and gazed inside, just like several of the other guests. At last they reached the glassy corridor that led to the West Wing, where the president and his closest staff worked. From there, guards pointed everyone outdoors to the Rose Garden.

It was a dramatic sight. Rimmed with blooming tulips and boxwood shrubs, the postcard-perfect lawn was filling rapidly with well-dressed guests. Aides and reporters bustled about. In the distance spread a panoramic view of the Ellipse.

White House staff were handing out earphones so whoever wished could hear simultaneous translations of the two presidents and their questioners. "Channel one is Russian," explained one smiling aide. "Channel two is English."

Jeff muttered, "I'll go into the men's bathroom and assemble the pistols."

Beth nodded as she anxiously examined faces. How was she going to know Berianov? She strolled toward a side buffet where waiters were serving punch and cookies on napkins decorated with an etching of the White House. She nodded and smiled pleasantly at everyone who made eye contact. Justin caught her attention, and they exchanged a wave.

She paused to survey the festivities and suddenly realized she was seeing with different eyes, and she had been for several days. In the past, her gaze would pick out an arresting facial feature here, an interesting shirt there, and then move on, forgetting and discarding, not really registering any of it or the people themselves.

But now, right at this moment, as her gaze roamed over the throng, she recognized most of those who had stood in the entry line on the outside sidewalk with her—perhaps ten people in front, and another ten in back. She *remembered* them. An entire twenty people, and she even recalled snatches of conversations and the first and last names she had overheard.

As she continued to scan the crowd, she found herself analyzing and easily remembering postures, gestures, strides, complexions, faces, hairstyles and colors . . . but perhaps strangest of all, she was noting and recording in her mind the angles of each person's neck, and the relative positions of shoulders and heads. For an odd instant, it seemed as if some internal knowing told her they could be a signature as distinct as a fingerprint or DNA. No two people's shoulder-neck-head postures and shapes were identical, and although they could be disguised, they could not be completely erased. *Is that your idea, Mikhail Ogust? Part of your training perhaps?*

As she thought about Alexei Berianov and what he had looked like at the Jefferson Memorial, she made herself move on. She held his lean, muscled frame in her mind as she continued to look around. She recognized some of the guests: The secretaries of State, Justice, and Defense. The mayor of Washington. Plus there was a sprinkling of movie, sports, and business celebrities. Then she spotted Zach Housley from her old law firm. Her throat constricted. Despite her changed appearance, there was always the chance he might place her. She turned away.

That was when she noticed a man with graying red hair. He was standing at the top of the steps in front of the West Wing. Her attention was riveted. He wore dark sunglasses and had a medium build. Most importantly, he wore an FBI lapel pin. From behind a flowering crab-apple tree, she studied him as his alert eyes surveyed the crowd like a predatory hawk peering down from its lair. She studied him and his attitude.

He looked familiar. All her senses screamed that she knew him somehow. She frantically searched back through her memory, trying to reassemble images from her old life, when she had paid so little attention . . . and then she knew that was wrong. He was not from the distant past at all; he was recent. In fact, he looked exactly as Jeff had described Bobby Kelsey. Graying red hair, medium build, the traditional FBI sunglasses, the upturned Irish nose, the cocky attitude. Alarm rushed through her. He was the mole. The traitor. If Kelsey were here, then Alexei Berianov surely was, too. But where?

50

In a stall inside the men's bathroom, Jeff assembled the hand-crafted pistols. They were precision made, each small piece sliding into the other and tightening silently with the miniature tools that were also in the cane. As he worked, he pictured the Rose Garden. He isolated sections of it. Analyzed the geography and activity. Considered where Berianov—if he were here—would most likely take up position to kill President Stevens.

Someone banged on the stall's door.

He flinched. He was too jumpy. "Be right out."

"What in hell are you doing in there? Setting up camp?"

"I said I'd be right out." The pistols were finished. He dropped them into his suit jacket pockets, one on each side, and quickly snapped the cane together. The one good thing about White House security was once you were past the initial check, none of the guards would bother you again . . . unless you tried to wander where you did not belong or made some kind of threatening move. He pulled open the stall's door. A red-faced man with resolve in his gaze was about to pound on it again.

Jeff put on an innocent smile even as he studied the man carefully. "Nice day, isn't it?"

The stranger appeared momentarily taken aback by Jeff's good cheer. He looked at Jeff and at the cane. Was he looking too long at the cane? Had he been alerted by the gate guards?

Then the man snorted and pushed angrily past into the stall, slamming the door and muttering, "Foreigners!"

Jeff breathed easier and headed back to the Rose Garden.

Beth was circling the white folding chairs. She had picked up a glass of punch at one of the white-skirted tables and made her way between the back row of chairs and the high platform on which TV camera crews worked. She was now returning up the far side, facing again the podiums where the presidents would talk. Ahead was Zach Housley. She bent her knees to make herself shorter and looked straight ahead. He was talking with two other men, both expensively dressed. Zach wore his traditional misshapen suit.

He seemed to be staring at her. She pouted her lips, which was something she never did. She hoped it would alter her face enough that with the different hair color and big round sunglasses she would trigger no memories of the old Beth Convey he was accustomed to using. Then she almost laughed. She had not taken into account Zach's self-absorption. He was not looking at her or anyone else. He was gazing off into the distance with that all-knowing expression that announced he was holding forth, oblivious to everyone but himself. As she passed, she could hear him instructing his audience of two on the latest squabble among the American Bar Association board.

With every step, she studied people and their myriad characteristics, particularly the way they held their upper bodies. It had quickly become easy, as if she had been trained for it, just as she had felt when she discovered what a fast driver she could be. Still, she was beginning to feel claustrophobic, near panic. *Which one was Berianov?* As she reached the front of the Rose Garden again, Jeff appeared. He gave a slight inclination of his head, a signal the pistols were ready.

Aides were moving through the throng, urging guests and the press to sit down.

"I'd like one," she told one of the harried staff members who was handing out head sets.

"Sure. Channel one is Russian, and channel two is English."

"Thanks." Beth took the head phones and tried them on as she strolled past the steps above which the podiums stood. Bobby Kelsey had disappeared.

"Excuse me!" Jeff bumped into her.

She felt her purse abruptly grow heavier. He had dropped the pistol inside.

She took off the headphones and said brightly, "Oh, I'm sorry. I wasn't looking where I was going. My fault."

"No problem," he said. Then quietly: "Anything?"

"I think I saw Bobby Kelsey up on the walkway," she whispered. "Be careful."

"Just what we need." His gaze swept the crowds. People were choosing chairs and sitting. It was almost ten o'clock. "You stay on the left, I'll stay on the right."

"There's Kelsey," she breathed.

Jeff followed her gaze up to the colonnaded walkway to where the podiums waited.

Bobby Kelsey was feeling good. His face itched, but that was a minor concern. From his handsome suit to his FBI identification and the pistol in his armpit holster, he was in his element. He enjoyed the bustle of activity, the freedom to move through it, and the power that came with his position on the inside of government. He had a small detail of agents with him, and he had placed them from here all the way to his car, which was parked in the lot between the White House and the Old Executive Office Building. They would help him leave, since he had warned them he had an important meeting and would have to exit unobtrusively and quickly, shortly after the press conference got under way.

Now he stood again at his self-assigned post near the doors to the Cabinet Room. He surveyed the merry crush in the garden below and watched the guests find chairs. The confusion was settling into order. In minutes, the two heads of state would emerge through the French doors and stride to the podiums. Already TV cameras were turned on, and CNN and other networks were airing prespeech coverage. The eyes of the world were watching.

Then he had a nasty jolt. A large man with a cane was walking to the sidelines, apparently looking for a seat. Bobby studied him, alarmed. There was something he recognized about him. . . . Six-foot-five in cowboy boots. No one could hide that height. And he was no thin rail either, but a man of muscle and substance. The hair color was different, and so was the shape of the face. But his activity was revealing: He was covertly watching all around.

Bobby Kelsey was not absolutely positive, but he had been told when he entered the grounds that there was concern Jeffrey Hammond might show up. The security guard had insisted he look at a photo, even though he had told the man he had worked with Jeff until 1991. He spun on his heel and hurried to the nearest Secret Service agent. He talked urgently. Persuasively.

"Mr. President, I don't advise this." It was President Stevens' chief of staff, Linda Patton. "We should call off the press conference at least. You can have the luncheon still, and you both can make your remarks there. The press pool will cover it. It'll have almost the same impact with the public but with far fewer risks."

President Stevens was dignified in a conservative gray suit and muted red tie. Still, he had the kind of appealingly handsome face that attracted voters and had gotten him into more trouble with women than he cared to think about. But now he was happily married and the father of an infant daughter, and he had every intention of winning reelection.

He said calmly, "Take it easy, Linda. This is a big event. How would I look if I cowered every time there was a threat?" He nodded to President Putin, who understood English, although he preferred to use translators at official functions. "What do you think, Mr. President?" Vladimir Putin was not the best leader he could imagine for New Russia, but right now he was the best available.

"We should brave the bear, Mr. President," Putin said without hesitation. "In my country, it is wise to not appear the coward, especially in these uncertain times."

Putin was smaller than Stevens, with a bland, weary-looking face notable only for the eyes, which were sharp, intelligent, and missed nothing. President Stevens thought about this little, nondescript man and the country he led, the teetering giant that was Russia. Stevens had never liked his predecessor, Boris Yeltsin. In fact, he had considered him scheming and selfish, a blustery type who could jump up on a tank and wave his fist but would not discipline himself to see the long-term costs of the cruel decisions he was making. Worse yet, perhaps Yeltsin had simply not cared.

Putin, however, was a thinker. If Putin could finally wrest himself from the mire of Russia's ubiquitous corruption and violence . . . if he could develop a clear vision of a Russia with a Western sensibility of democracy . . . and if he could stand more firmly against those who shamelessly raped Russia's resources and economy . . . he could be the leader Russia needed. In Stevens's opinion, Vladimir Putin showed signs of all this, and Stevens's plan was simple: Ignore all the naysayers and the chronic dyspeptics, and do everything he could to propel Putin forward on the path.

He thought about all this as they stood in the Cabinet Room, their wives nearby as well as a dozen aides. Above the long oval table, busts of George Washington and Benjamin Franklin looked down. The room was hushed, uncertain.

"That does it," President Stevens announced. "President Putin and I are agreed. We're going out there."

"Sir! We've identified an intruder—"

As soon as he saw Bobby Kelsey talking with one of the Secret Service agents, Jeff knew he was in trouble. He turned and moved away through the thinning crowd to put as much distance as possible between him and Kelsey as well as between him and Beth. But it did no good. The Secret Service came at him from every side. There was nothing he could do short of shooting one of them.

"Mr. Hammond, please don't move." The agent had a crew cut. His pistol was pressed into Jeff's side. His voice was deceptively polite.

Jeff said tensely, "Look, this isn't what it seems at all. Bobby Kelsey's the—"

"We'll talk about it inside."

There were six agents, and atop the West Wing two sharpshooters aimed their sniping rifles down at him. Near him, people froze, terrified. Television and still cameras moved in. From the corner of his eye he could see Beth about twenty feet away. Fortunately, none of the agents showed any interest in her.

His voice low, he started talking. He let them usher him around the West Wing to a side entrance. They barred the media from following. And the whole time he described as convincingly as he could what had happened over the past few days. But the agents said nothing. Their faces were stern, immobile. Impervious. As soon as they had him out of sight of the Rose Garden, they slammed him up against a stone post and frisked him. They were not gentle.

One of them said excitedly, "He's armed!"

If they had heard a word he had said, it was all meaningless now. To them, his concealed weapon proved their assumptions.

He said desperately, "I've been undercover for ten years! I've been waiting for this moment. I always knew Alexei Berianov was up to something. He's *here,* I tell you! You've got to find him and *stop him!*"

The agent with the crew cut snorted. "Right, sports fan. And this little toy in your pocket's a grape-flavored lollipop. We're going to lock you up and lose the key!"

Just then they heard a woman's voice behind them. "Let me through, dammit. Here's my identification. Millicent Taurino, deputy AG. *Jus-*

tice, for God's sakes. Don't look at me like that. I *know* Dean Jennings told you to cooperate with me."

Before Jeff could speak, the agents yanked him from the stone post, turned him, and pushed him toward a door that would lead to a swept room where they would interrogate him.

"Ms. Taurino," he tried. "They've got this all wrong. The president's in mortal danger—"

"Not from you, buddy. Not any longer. You say he had a gun?" She wore an expensive knit suit open at the throat, a pony tail, and a blue butterfly tattoo that peeked out near her collarbone. "Well, Special Agent Hammond, you've done one hell of a job pissing on your badge. Get him inside, men. I'm not here to chitchat. Let's find out what this Benedict Arnold knows."

"You say there's an intruder?" President Stevens frowned. "You've caught him?"

He was speaking to the head of today's Secret Service team, Bill Hughes. Hughes's somber face was flushed and sweating. "Yes, sir. But I'm afraid we weren't able to do it as quietly as we'd like. The press got film. It's Jeffrey Hammond, that former FBI man who's wanted for several murders, including Director Horn's. We were tipped off by Assistant Director Kelsey, head of the National Security Division at the Bureau."

The president swore. "How in hell did this Hammond get in?"

"This is not good." President Putin shook his head. "But perhaps this means the problem is taken care of?"

"Yes, I'm sure it does," President Stevens said heartily. He rubbed his hands. "Shall we go talk to the world, Vladimir?"

"By all means, Jim. Let us show the disbelievers we are two countries united against violence and tyranny."

"But, sir—" The security leader tried.

"Put a stopper on it," President Stevens decided. "You've done your job superbly. Now let us do ours."

He and the Russian president strode toward the French doors. Beyond the glass they could see the twin podiums and the mass of people eagerly waiting.

Outwardly calm, smiling expectantly, Beth found a seat on the right aisle, near the front. She had seen agents take Jeff away, and now Bobby Kelsey had returned to stand again on the West Wing walkway above the crowd, where the presidents would speak. There was a satisfied smile on his face. For an instant she had a strong desire to smash her fists into it.

Worried about Jeff, she desperately scanned guests, reporters, and staff, looking for something to identify Berianov. Where was he? What did he look like? *Mikhail, where's General Berianov? Where's the man who killed you?* Her gaze moved again to the smug Kelsey, who looked as if he were waiting, too. His presence gave her a feeling of hopelessness, almost as if she were back in the transplant hospital, dying. She could not take her gaze from him. What was that all about?

Suddenly the crowd quieted. An excited tremor swept through the seated guests. Reporters took out notebooks and turned on tape recorders. And those who had not yet donned their headphones put them on as the two presidents of the former enemy nations strode out proudly side by side from the Cabinet Room. Applause exploded. The presidents beamed and waved. They took their places behind the podiums.

"Ladies and gentlemen. Guests and members of the press," President Stevens began. "It is my honor to stand before you today with a fellow citizen of the world and a friend for peace. . . ."

She glanced at Bobby Kelsey, whose self-satisfied features were rapt with attention. He stood to the side, among the American and Russian security force. All the agents exhibited the usual appearance of casual alertness. But it was a lie. Just as the brilliantly colored tulips and monarch butterflies in flight gave the scene a charming innocence, the agents' informality masked deadly skills.

Engrossed in his mission, Bobby Kelsey did not notice the tall brunette sitting on the aisle who was staring up at him. As a monarch butterfly sailed past, he absentmindedly reached up and snared it. In an expert motion, he crushed it and let it fall. And then he slid his hand inside his suit jacket and grasped the handle of the Bureau pistol. He was shielded on all sides by the Russian and American agents.

Beth's heart seemed to stop as Kelsey's motions replayed in her mind. The angle of his neck and head. The movement of his shoulders. The idiosyncratic fluidity of it all. She remembered Berianov from earlier this morning at the Jefferson Memorial, how he had stood, the shoulders so square, the head so erect, just like Kelsey now. She remembered her recent nightmare: *He straddled the powerful machine, his shoulders square, his head particularly erect. He gave a little lift to his shoulders and tilted back his head as he pulled a helmet with a metallic visor down over his face.* She replayed how Kelsey had just now given a little lift to his shoulders and tilted his head back as he had reached for the butterfly. . . .

And then she knew. With a clarity that rocked her, she *knew*. The old caretaker had reached up and grabbed a moth and crushed it just before she had followed Jeff into the dark garage. Berianov had been that old man. Now Berianov was Bobby Kelsey. She did not understand how that could be, but she believed it.

She stood up slowly, planting an interested smile on her face. Her new confidence—*thank you, Mikhail*—settled firmly inside her, preparing her for whatever she must do. She slipped her hand into her purse and gripped the pistol as she moved toward the front of the garden. Other people were on their feet, too. But they were media people, working and talking quietly on the sidelines. Her throat was dry with fear as she wove among them, closing in on "Bobby Kelsey."

51

Millicent Taurino stood over Jeffrey Hammond, who sat at the only table in the small, gray Secret Service room, his fingers laced together on the tabletop, his chin jutting angrily.

"Bullshit, Hammond," she announced, fists on hips. "You can't expect us to believe that your supposedly phoning in a tip to watch for Alexei Berianov to try to assassinate President Stevens today corroborates the rest of your story. You're not only a killer, you're stupid!"

Another Secret Service man entered. "President Stevens is concluding his welcome, and everyone's quieted down." His gaze swept the five people sitting and standing around the secure room and finally settled on Bill Hughes, the head of today's Secret Service detail. "It looks normal, Bill. Putin's getting ready to start. I think they've pretty much forgotten the trouble with Hammond."

"Good," Hughes told him. "Get back out there. Let us know when Putin's finished." He looked at Deputy AG Taurino. "Let's move Hammond out of here now, before the party breaks up. I'd like to get him away with the least amount of fanfare."

Millicent Taurino nodded. "Sounds good."

One of the FBI agents announced, "He's ours. He goes to the Hoover building. It's not just that he's gone after the president today, he's our mole. We've got to find out what he knows and what he's passed on. No press. No visitors. No phone calls—"

Abruptly, Jeff slammed the palms of his hands down on the table. Everyone jumped and reached for their weapons, but Hammond made no other threatening move. Instead, eyes blazing, he bellowed around the room, "Are you people *insane?* I thought your job was to protect the president! Goddammit, *listen* to me! I didn't kill Tom Horn. I was in Pennsylvania, going head-to-head with Eli Kirkhart when Tom died. And if I remember correctly, you, Ms. Taurino, are part of the secret team that Eli's been reporting to. If I know that, then the person who most likely revealed that closely held information to me had to be Eli himself. *Right?"*

Millicent Taurino leaned her elbows on the table, resting her small chin on one fist, only a foot from Hammond's face. Her voice was low and dangerous. "You have said nothing . . . I repeat, *nothing* . . . to convince me you didn't kill Tom Horn or the young couple in West Virginia. In fact, your behavior now sucks, and I'm even more certain you're nothing but an overgrown gasbag traitor. You're guilty as hell. Tom could've easily told you about me before you murdered him, and it's damn fortunate we grabbed you before you put a bullet into President Stevens and made me *really* mad!"

Jeff Hammond glared back into Millicent Taurino's angry eyes. "Get as mad as you like, lady. But find Eli. He'll tell you everything I've said is the God's truth. And you've still got a powder keg just waiting to explode in the Rose Garden."

"Right. And I've got *cajones* instead of boobs, and you're the first baseman for the Red Sox. No way, buddy. You're in deep shit, and the president's alive, no thanks to you."

Just then the door cracked open again, and a weary voice asked in a faintly English accent, "Jeff, old boy, what's going on? They told me you're being held—" Eli Kirkhart stopped, amazed. He was gripping his right arm. The hand and sleeve of his suit jacket were dark with dried blood. More blood had hardened on the right side of his face.

As she approached the raised walkway where the two presidents stood above the Rose Garden, Beth thought she knew the truth about Alexei Berianov and Bobby Kelsey. Gripping her hidden pistol, she studied Kelsey. Around him, the well-trained security men and women formed an intimidating barricade of suits, uniforms, and grave, watchful faces.

Beth ignored them, concentrating on Kelsey. *Was* he Berianov? Maybe she was wrong. It was disorienting. Impossible, and yet . . . he was taking out his hand from inside his suit jacket.

"Stop him!" she yelled. With one hand she shoved aside a reporter and sprinted. "He's got a gun!" She pulled out her little palm pistol as everyone on the West Wing's colonnaded walkway seemed to turn in slow motion to stare at her.

The Secret Service paid no attention to Bobby Kelsey. Naturally he would have a weapon; he was FBI and one of their own. The lady, however, was not. For a single long beat, they stared down at her and reached for their weapons. At the same time, she saw the open path that existed between Bobby Kelsey and the podiums. From Kelsey's perspective, it seemed to her that he had only one clear shot, and it was not at President Stevens. No, he was in position to assassinate only the Russian president.

Her head briefly rang with confusion, and then the answer came to her clearly: It had been a ruse; Berianov had lied. He must have planned all along to assassinate Putin, and he had expected the ultra-nationalist Keepers to be held responsible. A sitting Russian president assassinated on American soil by fanatic Americans would outrage and ignite the Russian nation, make it an easy takeover target for the much-decorated General Berianov and his vision of a reunited, rearmed, morally righteous Soviet Union.

Before Beth could follow the logic any farther, agents hurled themselves off the walkway and over the bushes toward her. Others rushed to protect the presidents. The audience reacted with screams and shouts. Some jumped up to see what was happening.

But in those few seconds before any of the agents arrived at their destinations . . . before the crowd had time to run away in terror . . . and before Beth could reach him . . . General Alexei Berianov—master of disguise, genius of the covert action—aimed Bobby Kelsey's big Smith 10. Berianov was smiling. He was lost in his dream, a captive of the magnificent vision for which he had sacrificed everything. He could hear the ringing words of the great Soviet leader Lenin: "History will not forgive revolutionaries for procrastinating when they can be victorious."

As the American and Russian agents raced away from him to do their jobs, he stood exposed, his pistol in full view. But in his mind, he was unworried, savoring the moment. Already he was back in the Kremlin where he belonged, sitting at the head of the historic Politburo table and calling the regular Thursday meeting to order. There was much to be done. Wrongs to be righted. A corrupt private economy of gangsters to return to the ownership of the whole people. The greatest mission of his life would be achieved: He would see the Soviet Union rise again, a great Phoenix from the ashes of capitalism, more magnificent than ever.

As the Secret Service agents converged on her, Beth's hand sweated on her little palm pistol. The faces of the two men she had killed threatened to overwhelm her: The burly KGB assassin, Ivan Vok. And the nameless Russian who had attacked them from the station wagon. She did not want to kill again . . . but she saw Bobby Kelsey's finger on his trigger—

She jerked herself out of her trance. *This is for your people and mine.* Inwardly she nodded quick agreement. As the sun's rays pounded down, and a rumble of panic rolled through the crowd, she fired at the man she suspected of being Alexei Berianov, not because he might be Berianov, but because she knew he was trying to assassinate the Russian leader. At nearly the same time, the assassin fired at Vladimir Putin. The noise of the two almost simultaneous explosions seemed to shatter the sky as if it were a windowpane. The audience screamed.

Blood burst from Berianov's chest, and he fell back. Dizziness swept over him, and then anger as he realized he had been shot. He craned to see who could have done such a thing. . . . It was a tall woman with wind-blown brown hair . . . no, flaming red hair. It was his Cossack, the beautiful Tamara, the love of his life. A shoulder crashed into him, and he fell hard. Someone yanked away his weapon. Bastard. His fingers went numb, and his blood poured out smelly and hot against his skin. Somewhere inside he realized the bullet must have pierced his heart. Pain detonated a final time, and darkness swept over him.

Russia's president, Vladimir Putin, lay under a pile of bodies. The scent of American aftershave overwhelmed him. He groaned, the weight on him oppressive. "What was it?" he demanded, reverting in the heat of the moment to his native language. "What's happened?"

"Someone shot at you, sir. The bullet missed. Stay down, sir!"

One of his own agents repeated the message in Russian, and Putin forced himself to be patient.

President Stevens was also buried beneath protective agents. His ribs ached, and he craned to see. But more than anything, he worried that he had an explosive international incident on his hands. If an American had attempted to assassinate the Russian leader . . . he did not want to think about how bad it could get.

"Is he all right?" he demanded. "Who tried to kill him? Was it one of ours?"

On the other side of the walkway beside the bushes from where Beth had shot the would-be assassin, rough hands tore away her gun and dragged her toward the steps. Another agent ripped away her purse. It broke open, and her pills spilled across the grass, jewels on a bed of green.

Then she heard Jeff's powerful voice, "No! Leave her alone! Don't hurt her!"

She felt odd. No longer herself. She had shot the assassin purposefully, and now her emotions raged. Disgust. Outrage. Relief. And at the same time, she felt peaceful. She felt as if a year-long, painful burden had been lifted. The man who had killed her heart donor and had tried to kill her and Jeff was—

She looked up and saw Jeff. His tall figure. He was tossing people out of the way as he rushed to reach her. "How's Putin?" she asked him. "Did he survive?"

"He's fine. Are you all right?" he demanded. "Let her go. *Dammit!* Let her go!"

Secret Service team leader Hughes was right behind Jeff. "He's right," he ordered the agents. "Do what he says. Release her."

Freed, Beth fell into Jeff's arms.

The Rose Garden was controlled chaos. The Secret Service and White House aides ordered everyone back into their chairs. A few chattered nervously. Many were still in shock. Word spread like burning oil that a top FBI man had tried to assassinate the Russian president. Or had it been the American president? Some wept. Under the bright-blue sky of a perfect April day, in the protective setting of the White House's lovely Rose Garden, they shook their heads and asked each other exactly what could have happened.

Beth and Jeff moved aside. She stood away so she could see him. The padding was gone from his cheeks, and he looked again like her Jeff. She drank in the sight of his aquiline nose, his dark, handsome eyes, and his high-planed face. There was something about him that was both aristocratic and rugged, an irresistible combination that right now was also comforting. He pulled her close.

As he held her, Beth said, "Is Kelsey dead?"

"Yes." He shook his head, mystified. "I never thought he'd go so wrong. He must've tried to kill Putin for Berianov. We'll probably never find Berianov now."

"Can I see Kelsey, Jeff?"

"Why?"

"Call it a hunch . . ."

He led her up the steps to the colonnaded passageway outside the Cabinet Room, which was teeming with agents. Jeff pushed through, she at his heels. Every time agents tried to stop them, Bill Hughes ordered them to back off.

By the time they reached the corpse, agents were making notes, taking Polaroids, talking on cell phones, and examining the pockets. The dead man lay on his side, his face turned up as if he were surprised. Bobby Kelsey's characteristic gray-red hair was in a shadow, but his face and body were spotlighted by the sun. His right hand lay close to his side, open as if he were waiting for someone to return his gun.

"Here he is," Jeff said.

Beth knelt beside the dead man and probed around his face. The skin felt rubbery and a little stiff, not quite normal. She ran her fingers under the chin and around the throat. There was something there . . . this time she was certain she was touching a layer of thin rubber. She pried at it.

"Hey! What's she doing!" an FBI agent demanded above her. "Get her out of here!"

Concentrating, she said nothing. Starting with the chin, she peeled the rubber mask up over the mouth. Above her, she heard a gasp. She used both hands, still rolling up the mask until, at last, a smooth oval face with Northern European features appeared.

"What in hell?" Hughes wondered.

"Who is he?" one of his agents wanted to know.

Jeff said grimly, "It's Alexei Berianov. General Alexei Berianov, formerly of the KGB. I'll be damned. He was right in front of us the whole time. Close enough to the two presidents to have whispered in their ears."

In life, Berianov had been a handsome chameleon. In death, deep-seated fury had twisted his lower lip back in an ugly grimace, and his body looked small, almost shrunken. Whatever power had fueled his maniacal drive had also been the source of his larger size, his attractiveness, and his charismatic charm. Death had taken with it the indefinable qualities that had brought him close to being a giant.

As the agents talked and took more photographs, Jeff pulled Beth away from the crowd. He stopped on the steps, took her shoulders in his hands, and looked down into her face. The horrors and betrayals of the last few days were a heavy weight between them. "How did you know it was Berianov?"

"A combination of things. Maybe even cellular memory." She told him about the nightmare in which Berianov had put the motorcycle helmet on his head, and then about the old caretaker catching the moth at the Pennsylvania dairy farm. She described how Berianov's movements when he had caught the butterfly had alerted her. "I'm just relieved I was right." She sighed and rested her cheek against his shoulder. "When they took you away, I worried the next time we met you'd be behind bars or on a slab at the morgue. That was awful. How did you get them to release you?"

"Thank Eli here."

Beth looked around and saw a bloody, bandaged Eli Kirkhart approaching, smiling down at her. His right arm was in a sling, and heavy white gauze dressed the right side of his face. Behind him was a small, slender woman in a ponytail, wearing a tailored knit suit.

"Pleasant to see you again, Ms. Convey," Eli said. "Especially under these improved circumstances." He introduced Millicent Taurino. "My boss . . . actually my *former* boss, now that I'm out of the mole-hunting business. Glad I could help Jeff out."

"We're both glad." Millicent heaved a sigh. "We almost screwed up bigtime. Would've been one big pile of shit to clean up later. Not to mention a presidential corpse and one hellish international incident."

Eli turned his bulldog face to look at Millicent. As he considered her, he seemed to fight back a smile. "You know something, Ms. Taurino. You've got a foul mouth. I've been meaning to mention that."

Millicent blinked, surprised. "Get out the popcorn. Thank you, Special Agent Kirkhart. You're a smart fellow, although a bit sexist. We can discuss that later." She cocked her head to study him a moment.

Beth looked from one to the other and then back at Jeff. He raised his eyebrows and grinned. She turned to Eli and asked, "Where's Evans? Did he ever get sobered up?"

Eli shook his head. "Sorry. Bobby Kelsey killed poor Olsen, but his death saved me. Everyone outside the cottage finally had started shooting, and Olsen panicked, ran out, and tried to surrender. I'd given him an M-16, but he was so scared he forgot he was still carrying it, so of course the Bureau gunned him down." He sighed. "But in the melee, I managed to escape out the back, bloody but unbowed. I crawled into some thick bushes, and they missed me. They searched for hours. As soon as I could, I hitched a ride here."

"Lucky for me," Jeff said.

Kirkhart gave a grim smile. "My pleasure."

Millicent said, "You might be interested in what Mr. Kirkhart and I just learned. Our people found the real Bobby Kelsey in his car in the east parking lot. You could see him only if you walked directly up and stared down. He was lying on the front seat, a wound the size of the

Treasury Building in his cranium, and a scribbled suicide note on the floor."

"A note?" Beth was beginning to understand.

Eli nodded. "It said the Keepers were right—if Putin were allowed to sleep in the Lincoln Bedroom, it'd be not only a sacrilege but conclusive evidence that our country had permanently lost its way. As a good American citizen, Kelsey had to make some kind of grand gesture to stop the decline, but he was torn. After all, he was a member of the FBI. So in the end, he knew it'd been necessary to assassinate Putin, but the only honorable resolution was to sacrifice himself as well."

"What nonsense," Jeff snorted. "Who would believe that?"

"I'm afraid a lot of people would. Worst of all, some would've empathized." Beth frowned. "Berianov must've had a damn good escape route planned."

"Right you are," Millicent Taurino said. "The fake Kelsey had ordered his team of agents stationed between the West Wing and the east parking lot. He'd told them he couldn't stay on in the Rose Garden too long because he had an important meeting to attend. Their job was to get him away smoothly, without putting the Russian delegation's noses out of joint. We think he planned then to send them away as soon as he reached the car. Once they were out of sight, he would've propped Kelsey up behind the wheel, put the assassination weapon in his hand, and slipped away, heading back to Moscow."

"It had to be something like that." Beth shook her head. "Now it all makes sense. With the Keepers wiped out, he needed another American to blame for the assassination. Kelsey was perfect. I can see the headlines around the world: FBI Assistant Director Assassinates Russian Leader at White House."

Jeff nodded. "In Russia, all hell would've broken loose. Berianov and his allies would've taken over the Kremlin, and the world would've been hurled back into the Cold War. It'd be the old nuclear Balance of Terror all over again."

Shaken, the four of them stood silently amidst the chattering reporters, the spokespersons, and the last of the departing guests. The world had nearly turned upside down. They looked at one another, realizing what they had almost lost.

Jeff looked at Beth. He smiled with relief. "Let's get out of here."

Beth's face brightened. "Now that's an idea." She took his hand, and they left together.

EPILOGUE

It was October, six months since the near catastrophe in the Rose Garden, and Beth and Jeff had spent most of the past week at the cottage they had bought together on Chesapeake Bay. Here in the heart of this rich tidal basin it was said no one lived more than a few minutes from a stream. Their board-and-batten cottage rested just above the reeds, where they could dock their new boat at an old wooden pier they had repaired together. From their windows and the deck, they could bask in the million-dollar view of shining waters, great flying herons, and jumping bass. This peacefulness mattered to them.

For weeks the world's media had covered the assassination attempt on Vladimir Putin that had come so frighteningly close to succeeding. In Russia, the list of HanTech names triggered an investigation across the highest echelons of government to the most decorated of military men. And then there was silence. Inquiries were "continuing." There would be charges "when all evidence was gathered."

At the same time in Washington, Jeff and Beth spent weeks testifying behind closed doors at joint sessions of the House and Senate Intelligence Committees. Both felt jaded, exhausted, and weary of the fish bowl. They bought the cottage, and, in the nature of things, other crises captured the headlines, and the Rose Garden incident began its inevitable journey toward eclipse from the public's memory.

A new FBI director was appointed. A woman this time, perhaps on the theory that a woman would not feel she had to be J. Edgar. She offered Jeff his real job back with a pay increase, but Jeff politely said no. He had been right about Berianov, and it had cost him greatly. But he no longer regretted the sacrifices and felt only sorrow for what he had lost in family and friends. At the same time, despite his and Beth's being lauded as heroes, *The Washington Post* had not wanted him back at all. He understood. The paper had been tricked into serving as Jeff's cover, an unethical position. *Time,* however, jumped at his availability. After assuring them he was out of the spy business for good, they had given him a weekly column in which he could continue analyzing the explosive changes in Eastern Europe and Russia, but now for a wider audience. Plus, at last he would be able to satisfy an old desire: After the first of the year, he would begin teaching international relations part-time at the Georgetown School of Diplomacy.

As promised, Beth walked away from Edwards & Bonnett after writing a formal resignation letter that had left Zach Housley apoplectic. Michelle was as good as her word, and Beth set up her own practice with the Philmalee Group as her first client. Soon other clients approached her, and when four senior associates disgusted with Edwards & Bonnett asked to join her, they formed a partnership and rented offices at 601 Thirteenth Street Northwest, the same building as White & Case, an international law firm she admired. She was a partner at last, but her way. At the same time, she wanted to give back to the community, so in the last month she had begun doing weekly pro bono work for refugees and emigrants who could never afford the standard $500 hourly fee of the District's attorneys. Having her self-respect again was priceless.

At the cottage, twilight spread, and the bay was radiant, almost purple. The crests of waves glistened silver and gold, reflecting the lights from docks, houses, and passing boats, and the humid air was warm and sweet, a lingering gift of summer. It had been a good day. They had invited over a few friends for grilled crabs and barbequed ribs, and now they stood waving farewell as their guests drove off, returning to busy Washington.

"Eli looked well," Beth decided. "I had no idea he could be so funny. Millicent must be good for him."

Jeff nodded. "He'd become such an uptight stick, it's a wonder Taurino was willing to take him on. He got lucky, like me."

"I'm the lucky one, darling." She kissed his cheek. "Mmm . . . delicious. Just a soupçon of barbecue sauce. Exactly the way I like my men." She brushed his brown hair back from his forehead. She was content for the first time that she could recall.

He chuckled. "I aim to please. I think Amy had a good time today,

don't you?" Amy was his sister. As soon as she had heard the news report about the near assassination, she had left a worried message on his
answering machine at home. He returned her call, and in time he apologized for his years of being so difficult. They were friends again, their
parents' deaths no longer a wall dividing them. She, her husband, Tony,
and their two children had spent the past week vacationing with them
here on the bay.

"Amy had a great time," she assured him. "And so did Tony and the
kids."

"I think we should invite all of them to our wedding. Amy, Tony, the
girls, Eli, Millicent, Michelle . . . even Michelle's new boy toy." He
paused, watching her. When she said nothing, he continued, "I'm serious, Beth. I want us to get married."

She turned away, her mouth dry with fear. She moved across the
deck and leaned out over the railing, inhaling the fertile scent of the
bay's waters. "I can't, Jeff. You know that. Don't ask me to."

He hesitated, steeling himself. He knew he had to do it. Take the
risk. "If you don't, then what's the point? I might as well move out.
We're adults, not kids. I don't want a roommate. I'll love you for a long
time, but I'll go on alone, if I have to."

She stiffened. "I love you, Jeff. Really I do. But I've already explained
that I can't marry you. I can't marry anyone."

"What I remember is you also said that risk defines life. Okay, so
take the risk that you and I won't have a marriage like your parents.
That we'll hang out a lot with our kids. That we won't have drinking
problems, and that we'll love each other forever." He paused and said
the words that he knew would terrify her. "And that one of us won't die
tomorrow, or accidently cause the death of the other."

Emotion welled up in her chest. "You think I won't marry you because of what happened to my parents."

"Considering everything else . . . the fact that you ran through as
many men as I did women trying to avoid marriage . . . and then that
you had the heart attack and actually died . . . it makes sense to me."

Trembling, she inhaled. "Yes." He was partly right. But she had also
learned to face death, lived with it for weeks while she waited for a
transplant, and then there were those intense, frightening days when
she and Jeff had been on the run, hunted while looking for Berianov.
Thinking about it all, marriage began to seem doable. "Will you hold
me?"

They met in the middle of the deck, and he brushed the tears from
her eyes and held her tightly. She could feel his heart beating against

her, reassuring. Then she listened to her own heart and began to smile because as long as she could hear and feel it, she knew she was breathing, still alive.

"What are you thinking?" he asked.

She hesitated. "I guess about life in general. I think we get mesmerized by circumstances, and that's what happened to me. We get trapped in the cracks of life by choices and accidents and things we never could've imagined. Like what happened with my parents' deaths, and my ambition to make partner in the firm, and then even the cellular memory. After a while, we get so caught up in all of it that we're on some kind of automatic pilot, and we can't see or do or even think there's a better way to be."

"You're right. I'd say that's true of countries as well." He waited as she seemed to burrow into him. He was smiling. "Go on. Say it."

She squeezed him and gave a little laugh. "I'll marry you, darling. Thank you for waiting."

An hour or so before dawn, Beth woke up to see Jeff standing by the bed, holding his Beretta. He pressed his fingers to her lips. "Shhh."

She nodded and got silently to her feet.

He pulled on his shorts. He was sweating. "Someone's in the living room," he whispered. "There's light under the door."

She nodded again and threw on a robe. On his signal, she jerked open the door.

He jumped through with the Beretta up. "Perez!" he exploded.

The Russian was sitting on the living room sofa, wearing his usual black turtleneck, trousers, and high-tops, but he had pulled off his ski mask. A single table lamp cast a weak circle of light, leaving the rest of the large room in dark shadow.

"I don't have much time," he said quietly. "I'll be flying out tomorrow, returning home to Moscow."

Jeff shook his head, disgusted. "Just saying good-bye, are you?"

But Beth was studying him. "You want to tell us something?"

Perez nodded. "President Putin's position is weaker. Most of Berianov's coconspirators are in jail, but remember the men behind our ninety-one coup? One fool committed suicide while the rest went to jail for a short time. A very short time. That's all that happened to them."

"In our country," Beth said, "if an armed group attacked the White House or Congress, you can bet the ones who survived would still be behind bars."

"Exactly, where criminals—terrorists—belong," Perez agreed. "But these terrorists were politicians, businessmen, and military officials, and after an uproar of a few months, that's what they returned to being, as if nothing had ever happened."

"You're saying," Jeff said carefully, "Berianov's backers will get no worse."

"Yes, just a few slaps on the wrist." He shook his head worriedly. "I've been digging, and I've come up with a list of men and a few women I know, or suspect, were players in Alexei Berianov's coup attempt. Many of their names were also on the HanTech list, but not all. I've reported all of this to my superiors, and they tell me they've sent the information upstairs to those in charge of the investigation."

Beth said, "You don't trust them."

Jeff added, "You think Berianov's plan is still alive?"

Perez leaned forward, his face intense. "Someone outside Russia should know."

"Aren't you concerned about yourself?" Beth asked. "Your survival?"

Perez gazed out the front windows, east toward the bay. The first pale rays of dawn were rising on the eastern horizon. He stood. "I've got to go. I enjoyed seeing you again." There was a wistful expression on his face, then he shrugged and took a plain white envelope from inside his clothes. "If anything happens to Russia . . ."

Jeff took the envelope.

After Perez disappeared, they sat in the cool house and listened to the sounds of morning. At last they stood up to go into the kitchen to make coffee and breakfast. As they passed the dining room table, Beth saw a stack of mail. "Perez must've brought it in. We forgot it yesterday. The party and all."

Jeff smiled, and then he pulled out a brown padded envelope addressed to Beth. "What's this? It's from Moscow." It had been forwarded from her office.

She grabbed it and stared at the return address. Right after the Rose Garden episode, she had sent a note to the coordinator at the transplant hospital, asking her to forward a letter to the family of her heart donor. By going through the facility, Beth had not broken the confidentiality agreement she had signed, and she hoped the coordinator would read her letter, find it simply an expression of her gratitude for the family's gift, and feel comfortable mailing it to Mikhail Ogust's widow.

Jeff squeezed her shoulder. "Come into the kitchen, darling. You can read it there. I'll start the coffee."

"Good idea." As he turned on the radio, and music filled the room, she sat at the table in the morning sunshine and opened the padded envelope. Inside was a note and a tissue-wrapped parcel. She read the note, translating the Russian aloud:

Moscow

Dear Ms. Convey,

I apologize for not answering your kind letter more quickly, but I've just returned from several months with my children at our dacha in the Crimea. We had a relaxing time. It seemed this year the fruits and vegetables were especially large and fresh. Every night we sat on the porch and drank cold tea and remembered the old days. It was lovely.

I don't understand about voices from the dead talking to the living, but I must say Mikhail had a strong personality. He believed it was important to care about something, to give oneself over to something bigger—a religion, an idea, a love, or perhaps one's country.

He used to say he was an atheist, so religion was out, and he had so many ideas that he could never settle on just one. His deep love was for our family, and he always said he loved us enough to want to provide a country in which everyone would be safe to grow and thrive. When we lost the Soviet Union, he . . . all of us . . . lost our way for a while.

Sometime near the end, he quarreled with Alexei Berianov. Mikhail was furious with him, and he tried to convince him to change his mind about some business they were in together. What more happened between them I never knew.

I'm still brokenhearted to have lost my Mikhail, and I grieve for him every day. Then came your letter. To think you felt influenced by him, that you wanted to know about him, that you cared about who he was and what he thought touches me deeply. It helps me to go on, knowing that a part of him lives on in you.

I hope you'll accept the enclosed gift. It's only a small memento from his boyhood, but wherever we lived, he hung it in our bedroom. He said it explained the Russian character perfectly, the dark and the light. I think you'll understand it. I hope you'll enjoy it, too.

I am most sincerely yours,
Tatiana Ogust

Jeff was already unwrapping the tissue from the parcel. Soon a polished wood plaque emerged from the thin paper. He handed it to her, and her fingers trembled as she held it up. On it was a poem, hand-painted in Cyrillic lettering:

> If you love, then love without reason.
> If you threaten, don't threaten in play.
> If you storm, to full fury give way.
> If you punish, let punishment tell.
> If you feast, then be sure you eat well.
>
> —Tolstoi

"The answer to where my mystery lines came from." She laughed as they studied the poem together. "It's so very Russian, isn't it? Work hard. Play hard. And make sure you eat well, too."

"Of course, I don't believe any of it," he dead-panned as he pulled her close. "Cellular memory's a scam. Everything that happened to you was pure coincidence, starting with that impulsive phone call of yours to Meteor Express."

"Absolutely," she said equally solemnly. Then she grinned, relieved. "I'm so glad to know where those lines were from. So it was Tolstoi. It's as if the poem's the last piece I needed to complete the puzzle."

"Tell me the truth. Seriously." He paused. "Do you believe it all really happened? That you were getting messages from Ogust?"

Beth turned in his arms, and he released her. She held up the plaque and read it again, this time in Russian. At last she pressed it to her chest. For a moment it almost seemed as if she could feel the vital beat of a heart. "It's embarrassing to admit. After all, I *am* still a lawyer. But yes, I believe."

"Good. Me, too." He smiled.

February arrived in Washington with a cold, bitter storm that swept the bustling streets of pedestrians and traffic. By Saturday, everyone was relieved to stay home. That afternoon, Beth and Jeff met in their den for coffee. That's when they heard the news on the radio—

". . . in Russia. Prime Minister Nechayev's limousine was sideswiped by one of the city's so-called gypsy taxis and plunged off a bridge into the ice-covered Moscow River. By the time the limo was pulled out, all the occupants, including the prime minister, his wife, and three security agents from the MVD, were dead. The accident occurred at night, and no witnesses could be found to conclusively identify the driver or cab that had caused it. President Vladimir Putin moved quickly to replace the popular reform-minded prime minister with Roman Tyrret, a recently elected member of the Duma who is also the number-one TV personality in the nation. Congratulations on the appointment flooded the Kremlin. Leading oligarch Georgi Malko called Tyrret 'my dear old friend' and offered the support of the business community. Renowned general Igor Kripinski issued a press release suggesting that Tyrret would make a fine successor for Putin. . . ."

Jeff stared at Beth. "Under the Russian constitution, the prime minister assumes the presidency if the president's incapacitated. The prime minister is required to call for an election in three months, but he'd have the advantage of incumbency. If anything were to happen to Vladimir Putin . . ."

"Yes, Roman Tyrret would take over." She shook her head worriedly. "Both Georgi Malko and General Kripinski were on Perez's list of Berianov's coconspirators. Now they're supporting this fellow Tyrret. The security agents who died?—"

"Yes. They were MVD, the national Russian police. Perez is MVD." He paused and grimaced. "Perez could be dead."

A chill wind seemed to cut through the warm, comfortable room. They stared at each other.

She said what they were both thinking: "It's not over yet."

AUTHOR'S NOTE

The ancient Greek philosopher Aristotle believed the mind originated in the heart. Just as in today's scientific community, experts more than two thousand years ago had their disagreements. The Greek physician Hippocrates had earlier taken the opposite stand—that the mind was where all thought and emotion began.

Which fits tidily into two adages: The more things change, the more they remain the same; and controversy stimulates knowledge.

When I was a little girl growing up in Council Bluffs, Iowa, my mother came in to breakfast one morning, her face ashen. A neighbor had just dropped dead while shoveling snow. We were shaken, since this young family man had given every appearance of being not only healthy but robust. But that sort of event happened in those days. People mysteriously dropped dead of heart attacks. A lot of people.

According to the *Journal of the American Medical Association*, that has not changed. Heart disease is the number-one killer in developed countries. Fortunately, care and early diagnosis are greatly improved, and for those on whom the death sentence of end-stage heart disease is leveled, which was true of Beth Convey in this novel, there is hope—a heart transplant. When one considers how many surgeries offer a patient only a fifty-percent chance of survival, it is amazing that doctors can take a heart from one person and put it into another and know they can expect a ninety-percent survival rate.

What was science fiction forty years ago is now reality. People are walking around with other people's hearts, and some claim to have received characteristics, tastes, and even memories from their donors. Was Aristotle at least partly right? Is there a relationship between a heart and a brain that goes beyond simple wiring?

Only fifty years ago neuroscientists believed all brain matter did basically the same thing. Not until 1995 did we learn many different brain systems were needed to retrieve something as apparently simple as words. For instance, nouns and verbs are stored in separate areas of the brain, an unknown concept just a few years before.

So now it is the year 2001, and our knowledge of the mind-body complex is still in its infancy. Meanwhile, heart recipients are coming forward in the hundreds from self-imposed silence to describe experiences that make sense only in the light of the identities of their heart donors. These anecdotal testimonies seem to attack the foundations of our current scientific, psychological, and spiritual communities. Some consider them offensive. Even heretical. But on the other hand . . . what an opportunity to explore and learn.

If you would like to read more on the subject of cellular memory, I recommend these books:

A *Change of Heart: A Memoir,* by Claire Sylvia with William Novak. Heart-transplant recipient Sylvia describes her journey from heart failure through her new life with the heart of a young man who died in a motorcycle crash.

The HeartMath Solution, by Doc Childre and Howard Martin with Donna Beech. Childre is the founder of the Institute of HeartMath, to which medical doctors and psychologists refer patients for treatment of such ailments as hypertension and arrhythmia of the heart.

The Heart's Code, by Paul Pearsall, Ph.D., psychoneuroimmunologist and author. Here you can read about new cellular-memory findings and their role in the mind/body/spirit connection. Pearsall worked with several heart-transplant recipients.

Molecules of Emotion: Why You Feel the Way You Feel, by Candace B. Pert, Ph.D., former chief of brain chemistry at the National Institutes of Health and now a research professor at Georgetown Medical Center in Washington. She discusses her theory that neuropeptides and their receptors are the biochemicals of emotions, carrying information in a vast network linking the material world of molecules with the nonmaterial world of the psyche.

The Touchstone of Life: Molecular Information, Cell Communication, and the Foundations of Life, by Werner R. Loewenstein, former professor of physiology and director of the Cell Physics Laboratory at Columbia University and currently director of the Laboratory of Cell Communication at the Marine Biological Laboratory, Woods Hole, Massachusetts.

Because of the tremendous need for organ donations, please consider filling out a donor card for yourself—call (800) 355-SHARE. You can learn more about organ donations by phoning the United Network for Organ Sharing at (800) 933-0440.